# John Grisham

# John Grisham

The Client

The Firm

This edition first published by Cresset Editions in 1994
an imprint of the Random House Group
20 Vauxhall Bridge Road
London SW1V 2SA

ISBN 0 09 178610 X

Typeset in Baskerville 10.5/12 by
SX Composing Limited, Rayleigh, Essex
Printed and bound in Great Britain by
Mackays of Chatham PLC, Chatham, Kent

# CONTENTS

# The Client

*For Ty and Shea*

# CHAPTER ONE

Mark was eleven and had been smoking off and on for two years, never trying to quit but being careful not to get hooked. He preferred Kools, his ex-father's brand, but his mother smoked Virginia Slims at the rate of two packs a day, and he could in an average week pilfer ten or twelve from her. She was a busy woman with many problems, perhaps a little naive when it came to her boys, and she never dreamed her eldest would be smoking at the age of eleven.

Occasionally Kevin, the delinquent two streets over, would sell Mark a pack of stolen Marlboros for a dollar. But for the most part he had to rely on his mother's skinny cigarettes.

He had four of them in his pocket this afternoon as he led his brother Ricky, age eight, down the path into the woods behind their trailer park. Ricky was nervous about this, his first smoke. He had caught Mark hiding the cigarettes in a shoe box under his bed yesterday, and threatened to tell all if his big brother didn't show him how to do it. They sneaked along the wooded trail, headed for one of Mark's secret spots where he'd spent many solitary hours trying to inhale and blow smoke rings.

Most of the other kids in the neighborhood were into beer and pot, two vices Mark was determined to avoid. Their ex-father was an alcoholic who'd beaten both boys and their mother, and the beatings always followed his nasty bouts with beer. Mark had seen and felt the effects of alcohol. He was also afraid of drugs.

'Are you lost?' Ricky asked, just like a little brother, as they left the trail and waded through chest-high weeds.

'Just shut up,' Mark said without slowing. The only time their father had spent at home was to drink and sleep and abuse them. He was gone now, thank heavens. For five years Mark had been in charge of Ricky. He felt like an eleven-year-old father. He'd taught him how to throw a football and ride a bike. He'd explained what he knew about sex. He'd warned him about drugs, and protected him from bullies. And he felt terrible about this introduction to vice. But it was just a cigarette. It could be much worse.

The weeds stopped and they were under a large tree with a rope hanging from a thick branch. A row of bushes yielded to a small clearing, and beyond it an overgrown dirt road disappeared over a hill. A highway could be heard in the distance.

Mark stopped and pointed to a log near the rope. 'Sit there,' he instructed, and Ricky obediently backed onto the log and glanced around anxiously as if the police might be watching. Mark eyed him like a drill sergeant while picking a cigarette from his shirt pocket. He held it with his right thumb and index finger, and tried to be casual about it.

'You know the rules,' he said, looking down at Ricky. There were only two rules, and they had discussed them a dozen times during the day, and Ricky was frustrated at being treated like a child. He rolled his eyes away and said, 'Yeah, if I tell anyone, you'll beat me up.'

'That's right.'

Ricky folded his arms. 'And I can smoke only one a day.'

'That's right. If I catch you smoking more than that, then you're in trouble. And if I find out you're drinking beer or messing with drugs, then – '

'I know, I know. You'll beat me up again.'

'Right.'

'How many do you smoke a day?'

'Only one,' Mark lied. Some days, only one. Some days, three or four, depending on supply. He stuck the filter between his lips like a gangster.

'Will one a day kill me?' Ricky asked.

Mark removed the cigarette from his lips. 'Not anytime soon. One a day is pretty safe. More than that, and you could be in trouble.'

'How many does Mom smoke a day?'

'Two packs.'

'How many is that?'

'Forty.'

'Wow. Then she's in big trouble.'

'Mom's got all kinds of troubles. I don't think she's worried about cigarettes.'

'How many does Dad smoke a day?'

'Four or five packs. A hundred a day.'

Ricky grinned slightly. 'Then he's gonna die soon, right?'

'I hope so. Between staying drunk and chain-smoking, he'll be dead in a few years.'

'What's chain-smoking?'

'It's when you light the new one with the old one. I wish he'd smoke ten packs a day.'

'Me too.' Ricky glanced toward the small clearing and the dirt road. It was shady and cool under the tree, but beyond the limbs the sun was bright. Mark pinched the filter with his thumb and index finger and sort of waved it before his mouth. 'Are you scared?' he sneered as only big brothers can.

'No.'

'I think you are. Look, hold it like this, okay?' He waved it closer, then with great drama withdrew it and stuck it between his lips. Ricky watched intently.

Mark lit the cigarette, puffed a tiny cloud of smoke, then held it and admired it. 'Don't try to swallow the smoke. You're not ready for that yet. Just suck a little then blow the smoke out. Are you ready?'

'Will it make me sick?'

'It will if you swallow the smoke.' He took two quick drags and puffed for effect. 'See. It's really easy. I'll teach you how to inhale later.'

'Okay.' Ricky nervously reached out with his thumb and index finger, and Mark placed the cigarette carefully between them. 'Go ahead.'

Ricky eased the wet filter to his lips. His hand shook and he took a short drag and blew smoke. Another short drag. The smoke never got past his front teeth. Another drag. Mark watched carefully, hoping he would choke and cough and turn blue, then get sick and never smoke again.

'It's easy,' Ricky said proudly as he held the cigarette and admired it. His hand was shaking.

'It's no big deal.'

'Tastes kind of funny.'

'Yeah, yeah.' Mark sat next to him on the log and picked another one from his pocket. Ricky puffed rapidly. Mark lit his, and they sat in silence under the tree enjoying a quiet smoke.

'This is fun,' Ricky said, nibbling at the filter.

'Great. Then why are your hands shaking?'

'They're not.'

'Sure.'

Ricky ignored this. He leaned forward with his elbows on his knees, took a longer drag, then spat in the dirt like he'd seen Kevin and the big boys do behind the trailer park. This was easy.

Mark opened his mouth into a perfect circle and attempted a smoke ring. He thought this would really impress his little brother, but the ring failed to form and the gray smoke dissipated.

'I think you're too young to smoke,' he said.

Ricky was busy puffing and spitting, and thoroughly enjoying this giant step toward manhood. 'How old were you when you started?' he asked.

'Nine. But I was more mature than you.'

'You always say that.'

'That's because it's always true.'

They sat next to each other on the log under the tree, smoking quietly and staring at the grassy clearing beyond the shade. Mark *was* in fact more mature than Ricky at the age of eight. He was more mature than any kid his age. He'd always been mature. He had hit his father with a baseball bat when he was seven. The aftermath had not been pretty, but the drunken idiot had stopped beating their mother. There had been many fights and many beatings, and Dianne Sway had sought refuge and advice from her eldest son. They had consoled each other and conspired to survive. They had cried together after the beatings. They had plotted ways to protect Ricky. When he was nine, Mark convinced her to file for divorce. He had called the cops when his father showed up drunk after being served with divorce papers. He had testified in court about the abuse and neglect and beatings. He was very mature.

Ricky heard the car first. There was a low, rushing sound coming from the dirt road. Then Mark heard it, and they stopped smoking. 'Just sit still,' Mark said softly. They did not move.

A long, black, shiny Lincoln appeared over the slight hill and eased toward them. The weeds in the road were as high as the front bumper. Mark dropped his cigarette to the ground and covered it with his shoe. Ricky did the same.

The car slowed almost to a stop as it neared the clearing, then circled around, touching the tree limbs as it moved slowly. It stopped and faced the road. The boys were directly behind it, and hidden from view. Mark slid off the log, and crawled through the weeds to a row of brush at the edge of the clearing. Ricky followed. The rear of the Lincoln was thirty feet away. They watched it carefully. It had Louisiana license plates.

'What's he doing?' Ricky whispered.

Mark peeked through the weeds. 'Shhhhh!' He had heard stories around the trailer park of teenagers using these woods to meet girls and smoke pot, but this car did not belong to a teenager. The engine quit, and the car just sat there in the weeds for a minute. Then the door opened, and the driver stepped into the weeds and looked around. He was a chubby man in a black suit. His head was fat and round and without hair except for neat rows above the ears and a black-and-gray beard. He stumbled to the rear of the car, fumbled with the keys, and finally opened the trunk. He removed a water hose, stuck one end into the exhaust pipe, and ran the other end through a crack in the left rear window. He closed the trunk, looked around again as if he were expecting to be watched, then disappeared into the car.

The engine started.

'Wow,' Mark said softly, staring blankly at the car.

'What's he doing?' Ricky asked.

'He's trying to kill himself.'

Ricky raised his head a few inches for a better view. 'I don't understand, Mark.'

'Keep down. You see the hose, right? The fumes from the tail pipe go into the car, and it kills him.'

'You mean suicide?'

'Right. I saw a guy do it like this in a movie once.'

They leaned closer to the weeds and stared at the hose running from the pipe to the window. The engine idled smoothly.

'Why does he want to kill himself?' Ricky asked.

'How am I supposed to know? But we gotta do something.'

'Yeah, let's get the hell outta here.'

'No. Just be still a minute.'

'I'm leaving, Mark. You can watch him die if you want to, but I'm gone.'

Mark grabbed his brother's shoulder and forced him lower. Ricky's breathing was heavy and they were both sweating. The sun hid behind a cloud.

'How long does it take?' Ricky asked, his voice quivering.

'Not very long.' Mark released his brother and eased onto all fours. 'You stay here, okay. If you move, I'll kick your tail.'

'What're you doing, Mark?'

'Just stay here. I mean it.' Mark lowered his thin body almost to the ground and crawled on elbows and knees through the weeds toward the car. The grass was dry and at least two feet tall. He knew the man couldn't hear him, but he worried about the movement of the weeds. He stayed directly behind the car and slid snakelike on his belly until he was in the shadow of the trunk. He reached and carefully eased the hose from the tail pipe, and dropped it to the ground. He retraced his trail with a bit more speed, and seconds later was crouched next to Ricky, watching and waiting in the heavier grass and brush under the outermost limbs of the tree. He knew that if they were spotted, they could dart past the tree and down their trail and be gone before the chubby man could catch them.

They waited. Five minutes passed, though it seemed like an hour.

'You think he's dead?' Ricky whispered, his voice dry and weak.

'I don't know.'

Suddenly, the door opened, and the man stepped out. He was crying and mumbling, and he staggered to the rear of the car where he saw the hose in the grass, and cursed it as he shoved it back into the tail pipe. He held a bottle of whiskey and looked around wildly at the trees, then stumbled back into the car. He mumbled to himself as he slammed the door.

The boys watched in horror.

'He's crazy as hell,' Mark said faintly.

'Let's get out of here,' Ricky said.

'We can't! If he kills himself, and we saw it or knew about it, then we could get in all kinds of trouble.'

Ricky raised his head as if to retreat. 'Then we won't tell anybody. Come on, Mark!'

Mark grabbed his shoulder again and forced him to the ground. 'Just stay down! We're not leaving until I say we're leaving!'

Ricky closed his eyes tightly and started crying. Mark shook his head in disgust but didn't take his eyes off the car. Little brothers were more trouble than they were worth. 'Stop it,' he growled through clenched teeth.

'I'm scared.'

'Fine. Just don't move, okay. Do you hear me? Don't move. And stop the crying.' Mark was back on his elbows, deep in the weeds and preparing to ease through the tall grass once more.

'Just let him die, Mark,' Ricky whispered between sobs.

Mark glared at him over his shoulder and eased toward the car, which was still running. He crawled along his same trail of lightly trampled grass so slowly and carefully that even Ricky, with dry eyes now, could barely see him. Ricky watched the driver's door, waiting for it to fly open and the crazy man to lunge out and kill Mark. He perched on his toes in a sprinter's stance for a quick getaway through the woods. He saw Mark emerge under the rear bumper, place a hand for balance on the tail-light, and slowly ease the hose from the tail pipe. The grass crackled softly and the weeds shook a little and Mark was next to him again, panting and sweating and, oddly, smiling to himself.

They sat on their legs like two insects under the brush, and watched the car.

'What if he comes out again?' Ricky asked. 'What if he sees us?'

'He can't see us. But if he starts this way, just follow me. We'll be gone before he can take a step.'

'Why don't we go now?'

Mark stared at him fiercely. 'I'm trying to save his life, okay? Maybe, just maybe, he'll see that this is not working, and maybe he'll decide he should wait or something. Why is that so hard to understand?'

'Because he's crazy. If he'll kill himself, then he'll kill us. Why is that so hard to understand?'

Mark shook his head in frustration, and suddenly the door opened again. The man rolled out of the car growling and talking to himself, and stomped through the grass to the rear. He grabbed the end of the hose, stared at it as if it just wouldn't behave, and looked slowly around the small clearing. He was breathing heavily and perspiring. He looked at the trees, and the boys eased to the ground. He looked down, and froze as if he suddenly understood. The grass was slightly trampled around the rear of the car and he knelt as if to inspect it, but then crammed the hose back into the tail pipe instead and hurried back to his door. If someone was watching from the trees, he seemed not to care. He just wanted to hurry up and die.

The two heads rose together above the brush, but just a few inches. They peeked through the weeds for a long minute. Ricky was ready to run, but Mark was thinking.

'Mark, please, let's go,' Ricky pleaded. 'He almost saw us. What if he's got a gun or something?'

'If he had a gun he'd use it on himself.'

Ricky bit his lip and his eyes watered again. He had never won an argument with his brother, and he would not win this one.

Another minute passed, and Mark began to fidget. 'I'll try one more time, okay. And if he doesn't give up, then we'll get outta here. I promise, okay?'

Ricky nodded reluctantly. His brother stretched on his stomach and inched his way through the weeds into the tall grass. Ricky wiped the tears from his cheek with his dirty fingers.

The lawyer's nostrils flared as he inhaled mightily. He exhaled slowly and stared through the windshield while trying to determine if any of the precious, deadly gas had entered his blood and begun its work. A loaded pistol was on the seat next to him. A half-empty fifth of Jack Daniels was in his hand. He took a sip, screwed the cap on it, and placed it on the seat. He inhaled slowly and closed his eyes to savor the gas. Would he simply drift away? Would it hurt or burn or make him sick before it finished him off? The note was on the dash above the steering wheel, next to a bottle of pills.

He cried and talked to himself as he waited for the gas to hurry, dammit!, before he'd give up and use the gun. He was a coward, but a very determined one, and he much preferred this sniffing and float-ing away to sticking a gun in his mouth.

He sipped the whiskey, and hissed as it burned on its descent. Yes, it was finally working. Soon, it would be all over, and he smiled at himself in the mirror because it was working and he was dying and he was not a coward after all. It took guts to do this.

He cried and muttered as he removed the cap of the whiskey bottle for one last swallow. He gulped, and it ran from his lips and trickled into his beard.

He would not be missed. And although this thought should have been painful, the lawyer was calmed by the knowledge that no one would grieve. His mother was the only person in the world who loved him, and she'd been dead four years so this would not hurt her. There was a child from the first disastrous marriage, a daughter he'd not seen in eleven years, but he'd been told she had joined a cult and was as crazy as her mother.

It would be a small funeral. A few lawyer buddies and perhaps a judge or two would be there all dressed up in dark suits and whisper-ing importantly as the piped-in organ music drifted around the near-empty chapel. No tears. The lawyers would sit and glance at their watches while the minister, a stranger, sped through the standard comments used for dear departed ones who never went to church.

It would be a ten-minute job with no frills. The note on the dash required the body to be cremated.

'Wow,' he said softly as he took another sip. He turned the bottle up, and while gulping glanced in the rearview mirror and saw the weeds move behind the car.

Ricky saw the door open before Mark heard it. It flew open, as if kicked, and suddenly the large, heavy man with the red face was run-ning through the weeds, holding onto the car and growling. Ricky stood, in shock and fear, and wet his pants.

Mark had just touched the bumper when he heard the door. He froze for a second, gave a quick thought to crawling under the car, and the hesitation nailed him. His foot slipped as he tried to stand and run, and the man grabbed him. 'You! You little bastard!' he screamed as he grabbed Mark's hair and flung him onto the trunk of the car. 'You little bastard!' Mark kicked and squirmed, and a fat hand slapped him in the face. He kicked once more, not as violently, and he got slapped again.

Mark stared at the wild, glowing face just inches away. The eyes were red and wet. Fluids dripped from the nose and chin. 'You little bastard,' he growled through clenched, dirty teeth.

When he had him pinned and still and subdued, the lawyer stuck the hose back into the exhaust pipe, then yanked Mark off the trunk by his collar and dragged him through the weeds to the driver's door, which was open. He threw the kid through the door and shoved him across the black leather seat.

Mark was grabbing at the door handle and searching for the door lock switch when the man fell behind the steering wheel. He slammed the door behind him, pointed at the door handle, and screamed, 'Don't touch that!' Then he backhanded Mark in the left eye with a vicious slap.

Mark shrieked in pain, grabbed his eyes and bent over, stunned, crying now. His nose hurt like hell and his mouth hurt worse. He was dizzy. He tasted blood. He could hear the man crying and growling. He could smell the whiskey and see the knees of his dirty blue jeans with his right eye. The left was beginning to swell. Things were blurred.

The fat lawyer gulped his whiskey and stared at Mark, who was all bent over and shaking at every joint. 'Stop crying,' he snarled.

Mark licked his lips and swallowed blood. He rubbed the knot above his eye and tried to breathe deeply, still staring at his jeans. Again, the man said, 'Stop crying,' so he tried to stop.

The engine was running. It was a big, heavy, quiet car, but Mark could hear the engine humming very softly somewhere far away. He turned slowly and glanced at the hose winding through the rear window behind the driver like an angry snake sneaking toward them for the kill. The fat man laughed.

'I think we should die together,' he announced, all of a sudden very composed.

Mark's left eye was swelling fast. He turned his shoulders and looked squarely at the man, who was even larger now. His face was chubby, the beard was bushy, the eyes were still red and glowed at him like a demon in the dark. Mark was crying. 'Please let me out of here,' he said, lip quivering, voice cracking.

The driver stuck the whiskey bottle in his mouth and turned it up. He grimaced and smacked his lips. 'Sorry, kid. You had to be a cute ass, had to stick your dirty little nose into my business, didn't you? So I think we should die together. Okay? Just you and me, pal. Off to La La Land. Off to see the wizard. Sweet dreams, kid.'

Mark sniffed the air, then noticed the pistol lying between them. He glanced away, then stared at it when the man took another drink from the bottle.

'You want the gun?' the man asked.

'No sir.'

'So why are you looking at it?'

'I wasn't.'

'Don't lie to me, kid, because if you do, I'll kill you. I'm crazy as hell, okay, and I'll kill you.' Though tears flowed freely from his eyes, his voice was very calm. He breathed deeply as he spoke. 'And besides, kid, if we're gonna be pals, you've got to be honest with me. Honesty's very important, you know? Now, do you want the gun?'

'No sir.'

'Would you like to pick up the gun and shoot me with it?'

'No sir.'

'I'm not afraid of dying, kid, you understand?'

'Yes sir, but I don't want to die. I take care of my mother and my little brother.'

'Aw, ain't that sweet. A real man of the house.'

He screwed the cap onto the whiskey bottle, then suddenly grabbed the pistol, stuck it deep into his mouth, curled his lips around it, and looked at Mark, who watched every move, hoping he would pull the trigger and hoping he wouldn't. Slowly, he withdrew the barrel from his mouth, kissed the end of it, then pointed it at Mark.

'I've never shot this thing, you know,' he said, almost in a whisper. 'Just bought it an hour ago at a pawnshop in Memphis. Do you think it'll work?'

'Please let me out of here.'

'You have a choice, kid,' he said, inhaling the invisible fumes. 'I'll blow your brains out, and it's over now, or the gas'll get you. Your choice.'

Mark did not look at the pistol. He sniffed the air and thought for an instant that maybe he smelled something. The gun was close to his head. 'Why are you doing this?' he asked.

'None of your damned business, okay, kid. I'm nuts, okay. Over the edge. I planned a nice little private suicide, you know, just me and my hose and maybe a few pills and some whiskey. Nobody looking for me. But, no, you have to get cute. You little bastard!' He lowered the pistol and carefully placed it on the seat. Mark rubbed the knot on his forehead and bit his lip. His hands were shaking and he pressed them between his legs.

'We'll be dead in five minutes,' he announced officially as he raised the bottle to his lips. 'Just you and me, pal, off to see the wizard.'

Ricky finally moved. His teeth chattered and his jeans were wet, but he was thinking now, moving from his crouch onto his hands and knees and sinking into the grass. He crawled toward the car, crying and gritting his teeth as he slid on his stomach. The door was about to fly open. The crazy man, who was large but quick, would leap from nowhere and grab him by the neck, just like Mark, and they'd all die in the long, black car. Slowly, inch by inch, he pushed his way through the weeds.

Mark slowly lifted the pistol with both hands. It was as heavy as a brick. It shook as he raised it and pointed it at the fat man, who leaned toward it until the barrel was an inch from his nose.

'Now, pull the trigger, kid,' he said with a smile, his wet face glowing and dancing with delightful anticipation.' Pull the trigger, and I'll be dead and you go free.' Mark curled a finger around the trigger. The man nodded, then leaned even closer and bit the tip of the barrel with flashing teeth. 'Pull the trigger!' he shouted.

Mark closed his eyes and pressed the handle of the gun with the palms of his hands. He held his breath, and was about to squeeze the trigger when the man jerked it from him. He waved it wildly in front of Mark's face, and pulled the trigger. Mark screamed as the window behind his head cracked into a thousand pieces but did not shatter. 'It works! It works!' he yelled as Mark ducked and covered his ears.

Ricky buried his face in the grass when he heard the shot. He was ten feet from the car when something popped and Mark yelled. The fat man was yelling, and Ricky peed on himself again. He closed his eyes and clutched the weeds. His stomach cramped and his heart pounded, and for a minute after the gunshot he did not move. He cried for his brother, who was dead now, shot by a crazy man.

'Stop crying, dammit! I'm sick of your crying!'

Mark clutched his knees and tried to stop crying. His head pounded and his mouth was dry. He stuck his hands between his knees and bent over. He had to stop crying and think of something. On a television show once some nut was about to jump off a building, and this cool cop just kept talking to him and talking to him, and finally the nut started talking back and of course did not jump. Mark quickly smelled for gas, and asked, 'Why are you doing this?'

'Because I want to die,' the man said calmly.

'Why?' he asked again, glancing at the neat, little round hole in his window.

'Why do kids ask so many questions?'

11

'Because we're kids. Why do you want to die?' He could barely hear his own words.

'Look, kid, we'll be dead in five minutes, okay? Just you and me, pal, off to see the wizard.' He took a long drink from the bottle, now almost empty. 'I feel the gas, kid. Do you feel it? Finally.'

In the side mirror, through the cracks in the window, Mark saw the weeds move and caught a glimpse of Ricky as he slithered through the weeds and ducked into the bushes near the tree. He closed his eyes and said a prayer.

'I gotta tell you, kid, it's nice having you here. No one wants to die alone. What's your name?'

'Mark.'

'Mark who?'

'Mark Sway.' Keep talking, and maybe the nut won't jump. 'What's your name?'

'Jerome. But you can call me Romey. That's what my friends call me, and since you and I are pretty tight now you can call me Romey. No more questions, okay, kid?'

'Why do you want to die, Romey?'

'I said no more questions. Do you feel the gas, Mark?'

'I don't know.'

'You will soon enough. Better say your prayers.' Romey sank low into the seat with his beefy head straight back and eyes closed, completely at ease. 'We've got about five minutes, Mark, any last words?' The whiskey bottle was in his right hand, the gun in his left.

'Yeah, why are you doing this?' Mark asked, glancing at the mirror for another sign of his brother. He took short, quick breaths through the nose, and neither smelled nor felt anything. Surely Ricky had removed the hose.

'Because I'm crazy, just another crazy lawyer, right. I've been driven crazy, Mark, and how old are you?'

'Eleven.'

'Ever tasted whiskey?'

'No,' Mark answered truthfully.

Suddenly, the whiskey bottle was in his face, and he took it.

'Take a shot,' Romey said without opening his eyes.

Mark tried to read the label, but his left eye was virtually closed and his ears were ringing from the gunshot, and he couldn't concentrate. He sat the bottle on the seat where Romey took it without a word.

'We're dying, Mark,' he said almost to himself. 'I guess that's tough at age eleven, but so be it. Nothing I can do about it. Any last words, big boy?'

Mark told himself that Ricky had done the trick, that the hose was now harmless, that his new friend Romey here was drunk and crazy, and that if he survived he would have to do so by thinking and talking. The air was clean. He breathed deeply and told himself that he could make it. 'What made you crazy?'

Romey thought for a second and decided this was humorous. He snorted and actually chuckled a little. 'Oh, this is great. Perfect. For weeks now, I've known something no one else in the entire world knows, except my client, who's a real piece of scum, by the way. You see, Mark, lawyers hear all sorts of private stuff that we can never repeat. Strictly confidential, you understand. No way we can ever tell what happened to the money or who's sleeping with who or where the body's buried, you follow?' He inhaled mightily, and exhaled with enormous pleasure. He sank lower in the seat, eyes still closed. 'Sorry I had to slap you.' He curled his finger around the trigger.

Mark closed his eyes and felt nothing.

'How old are you, Mark?'

'Eleven.'

'You told me that. Eleven. And I'm forty-four. We're both too young to die, aren't we, Mark?'

'Yes sir.'

'But it's happening, pal. Do you feel it?'

'Yes sir.'

'My client killed a man and hid the body, and now my client wants to kill me. That's the whole story. They've made me crazy. Ha! Ha! This is great, Mark. This is wonderful. I, the trusted lawyer, can now tell you, literally seconds before we float away, where the body is. The body, Mark, the most notorious undiscovered corpse of our time. Unbelievable. I can finally tell!' His eyes were open and glowing down at Mark. 'This is funny as hell, Mark!'

Mark missed the humor. He glanced at the mirror, then at the door lock switch a foot away. The handle was even closer.

Romey relaxed again and closed his eyes as if trying desperately to take a nap. 'I'm sorry about this, kid, really sorry, but, like I said, it's nice to have you here.' He slowly placed the bottle on the dash next to the note and moved the pistol from his left hand to his right, caressing it softly and stroking the trigger with his index finger. Mark tried not to look. 'I'm really sorry about this, kid. How old are you?'

'Eleven. You've asked me three times.'

'Shut up! I feel the gas now, don't you? Quit sniffing, dammit! It's odorless, you little dumbass. You can't smell it. I'd be dead now and you'd be off playing GI Joe if you hadn't been so cute. You're pretty stupid, you know.'

Not as stupid as you, thought Mark. 'Who did your client kill?'

Romey grinned but did not open his eyes. 'A United States Senator. I'm telling. I'm telling. I'm spilling my guts. Do you read newspapers?'

'No.'

'I'm not surprised. Senator Boyette from New Orleans. That's where I'm from.'

'Why did you come to Memphis?'

'Dammit, kid! Full of questions, aren't you?'

'Yeah. Why'd your client kill Senator Boyette?'

'Why, why, why, who, who, who. You're a real pain in the ass, Mark.'

'I know. Why don't you just let me go?' Mark glanced at the mirror, then at the hose running into the backseat.

'I might just shoot you in the head if you don't shut up.' His bearded chin dropped and almost touched his chest. 'My client has killed a lot of people. That's how he makes money, by killing people. He's a member of the Mafia in New Orleans, and now he's trying to kill me. Too bad, ain't it, kid. We beat him to it. Joke's on him.'

Romey took a long drink from the bottle and stared at Mark.

'Just think about it, kid, right now, Barry, or Barry The Blade as he's known, these Mafia guys all have cute nicknames, you know, is waiting for me in a dirty restaurant in New Orleans. He's probably got a couple of his pals nearby, and after a quiet dinner he'll want me to get in the car and take a little drive, talk about his case and all, and then he'll pull out a knife, that's why they call him The Blade, and I'm history. They'll dispose of my chubby little body somewhere, just like they did Senator Boyette, and, bam!, just like that, New Orleans has another unsolved murder. But we showed them, didn't we, kid? We showed them.'

His speech was slower and his tongue thicker. He moved the pistol up and down on his thigh when he talked. The finger stayed on the trigger.

Keep him talking. 'Why does this Barry guy want to kill you?'

'Another question. I'm floating. Are you floating?'

'Yeah. It feels good.'

'Buncha reasons. Close your eyes, kid. Say your prayers.' Mark watched the pistol and glanced at the door lock. He slowly touched each fingertip to each thumb, like counting in kindergarten, and the coordination was perfect.

'So where's the body?'

Romey snorted and his head nodded. The voice was almost a

whisper. 'The body of Boyd Boyette. What a question. First U.S. Senator murdered in office, did you know that? Murdered by my dear client Barry The Blade Muldanno, who shot him in the head four times, then hid the body. No body, no case. Do you understand, kid?'

'Not really.'

'Why aren't you crying, kid? You were crying a few minutes ago. Aren't you scared?'

'Yes, I'm scared. And I'd like to leave. I'm sorry you want to die and all, but I have to take care of my mother.'

'Touching, real touching. Now, shut up. You see, kid, the Feds have to have a body to prove there was a murder. Barry is their suspect, their only suspect, because he really did it, you see, in fact they know he did it. But they need the body.'

'Where is it?'

A dark cloud moved in front of the sun and the clearing was suddenly darker. Romey moved the gun gently along his leg as if to warn Mark against any sudden moves. 'The Blade is not the smartest thug I've ever met, you know. Thinks he's a genius, but he's really quite stupid.'

You're the stupid one, Mark thought again. Sitting in a car with a hose running from the exhaust. He waited as still as could be.

'The body's under my boat.'

'Your boat?'

'Yes, my boat. He was in a hurry. I was out of town, so my beloved client took the body to my house and buried it in fresh concrete under my garage. It's still there, can you believe it? The FBI has dug up half of New Orleans trying to find it, but they've never thought about my house. Maybe Barry ain't so stupid after all.'

'When did he tell you this?'

'I'm sick of your questions, kid.'

'I'd really like to leave now.'

'Shut up. The gas is working. We're gone, kid. Gone.' He dropped the pistol on the seat.

The engine hummed quietly. Mark glanced at the bullet hole in the window, at the millions of tiny crooked cracks running from it, then at the red face and heavy eyelids. A quick snort, almost a snore, and the head nodded downward.

He was passing out! Mark stared at him and watched his thick chest move. He'd seen his ex-father do this a hundred times.

Mark breathed deeply. The door lock would make noise. The gun was too close to Romey's hand. Mark's stomach cramped and his feet were numb.

The red face emitted a loud, sluggish noise, and Mark knew there would be no more chances. Slowly, ever so slowly, he inched his shaking finger to the door lock switch.

Ricky's eyes were almost as dry as his mouth, but his jeans were soaked. He was under the tree, in the darkness, away from the bushes and the tall grass and the car. Five minutes had passed since he had removed the hose. Five minutes since the gunshot. But he knew his brother was alive because he had darted behind trees for fifty feet until he caught a glimpse of the blond head sitting low and moving about in the huge car. So he stopped crying, and started praying.

He made his way back to the log, and as he crouched low and stared at the car and ached for his brother, the passenger door suddenly flew open, and there was Mark.

Romey's chin dropped onto his chest, and just as he began his next snore Mark slapped the pistol onto the floor with his left hand while unlocking the door with his right. He yanked the handle and rammed his shoulder into the door, and the last thing he heard as he rolled out was another deep snore from the lawyer.

He landed on his knees and grabbed at the weeds as he scratched and clawed his way from the car. He raced low through the grass and within seconds made it to the tree where Ricky watched in muted horror. He stopped at the stump and turned, expecting to see the lawyer lumbering after him with the gun. But the car appeared harmless. The passenger door was open. The engine was running. The exhaust pipe was free of devices. He breathed for the first time in a minute, then slowly looked at Ricky.

'I pulled the hose out,' Ricky said in a shrill voice between rapid breaths. Mark nodded but said nothing. He was suddenly much calmer. The car was fifty feet away, and if Romey emerged, they could disappear through the woods in an instant. And hidden by the tree and the cover of the brush, they would never be seen by Romey if he decided to jump out and start blasting away with the gun.

'I'm scared, Mark. Let's go,' Ricky said, his voice still shrill, his hands shaking.

'Just a minute.' Mark studied the car intently.

'Come on, Mark. Let's go.'

'I said just a minute.'

Ricky watched the car. 'Is he dead?'

'I don't think so.'

So the man was alive, and had the gun, and it was becoming

obvious that his big brother was no longer scared and was thinking of something. Ricky took a step backward. 'I'm leaving,' he mumbled. 'I want to go home.'

Mark did not move. He exhaled calmly and studied the car. 'Just a second,' he said without looking at Ricky. The voice had authority again.

Ricky grew still and leaned forward, placing both hands on both wet knees. He watched his brother, and shook his head slowly as Mark carefully picked a cigarette from his shirt pocket while staring at the car. He lit it, took a long draw, and blew smoke upward to the branches. It was at this point that Ricky first noticed the swelling.

'What happened to your eye?'

Mark suddenly remembered. He rubbed it gently, then rubbed the knot on his forehead. 'He slapped me a couple of times.'

'It looks bad.'

'It's okay. You know what I'm gonna do?' he said without expecting an answer. 'I'm gonna sneak back up there and stick the hose into the exhaust pipe. I'm gonna plug it in for him, the bastard.'

'You're crazier than he is. You're kidding, right, Mark?'

Mark puffed deliberately. Suddenly, the driver's door swung open, and Romey stumbled out with the pistol. He mumbled loudly as he faltered to the rear of the car, and once again found the garden hose lying harmlessly in the grass. He screamed obscenities at the sky.

Mark crouched low and held Ricky with him. Romey spun around and surveyed the trees around the clearing. He cursed more, and started crying loudly. Sweat dripped from his hair, and his black jacket was soaked and glued to him. He stomped around the rear of the car, sobbing and talking, screaming at the trees.

He stopped suddenly, wrestled his ponderous bulk onto the top of the trunk, then squirmed and slid backward like a drugged elephant until he hit the rear window. His stumpy legs stretched before him. One shoe was missing. He took the gun, neither slowly nor quickly, almost routinely, and stuck it deep in his mouth. His wild red eyes flashed around, and for a second paused at the trunk of the tree above the boys.

He opened his lips and bit the barrel with his big, dirty teeth. He closed his eyes, and pulled the trigger with his right thumb.

# CHAPTER TWO

The shoes were shark, and the vanilla silks ran all the way to the kneecaps where they finally stopped and caressed the rather hairy calves of Barry Muldanno, or Barry The Blade, or simply The Blade, as he liked to be called. The dark green suit had a shine to it and appeared at first glance to be lizard or iguana or some other slimy reptile, but upon closer look it was not animal at all but polyester. Double-breasted with buttons all over the front. It hung handsomely on his well-built frame. And it rippled nicely as he strutted to the pay phone in the rear of the restaurant. The suit was not gaudy, just flashy. He could pass for a well-dressed drug importer or perhaps a hot Vegas bookie, and that was fine because he was The Blade and he expected people to notice, and when they looked at him they were supposed to see success. They were supposed to gawk in fear and get out of his way.

The hair was black and full, colored to hide a bit of gray, slicked down, laden with gel, pulled back fiercely and gathered into a perfect little ponytail that arched downward and touched precisely at the top of the dark green polyester jacket. Hours were spent on the hair. The obligatory diamond earring sparkled from the proper left lobe. A tasteful gold bracelet clung to the left wrist just below the diamond Rolex, and on his right wrist another tasteful gold chain rattled softly as he strutted.

The swagger stopped in front of the pay phone, which was near the rest rooms in a narrow hallway in the back of the restaurant. He stood in front of the phone, and cut his eyes in all directions. To the average person, the sight of Barry The Blade's eyes cutting and darting and searching for violence would loosen the bowels. The eyes were very dark brown, and so close together that if one could stand to look directly into them for more than two seconds, one would swear Barry was cross-eyed. But he wasn't. A neat row of black hair ran from temple to temple without the slightest break for the furrow above the rather long and pointed nose. Solid brow. Puffy brown skin half-circled the eyes from below and said without a doubt that this man enjoyed booze and the fast life. The shady eyes confessed many hangovers, among other things. The Blade loved his eyes. They were legendary.

He punched the number of his lawyer's office, and said rapidly

18

without waiting for a reply, 'Yeah, this is Barry! Where's Jerome? He's late. Supposed to meet me here forty minutes ago. Where is he? Have you seen him?'

The Blade's voice was not pleasant either. It had the menacing resonance of a successful New Orleans street thug who had broken many arms and would gladly break one more if you lingered too long in his path or weren't quick enough with your answers. The voice was rude, arrogant, and intimidating, and the poor secretary on the other end had heard it many times and she'd seen the eyes and the slick suits and the ponytail. She swallowed hard, caught her breath, thanked heavens he was on the phone and not in the office standing before her desk cracking his knuckles, and informed Mr. Muldanno that Mr. Clifford had left the office around 9 A.M. and had not been heard from since.

The Blade slammed the phone down and stormed through the hallway, then caught himself and began the strut as he neared the tables and the faces. The restaurant was beginning to fill. It was almost five.

He just wanted a few drinks and then a nice dinner with his lawyer so they could talk about his mess. Just drinks and dinner, that's all. The Feds were watching, and listening. Jerome was paranoid and just last week told Barry he thought they had wired his law office. So they would meet here and have a nice meal without worrying about eavesdroppers and bugging devices.

They needed to talk. Jerome Clifford had been defending prominent New Orleans thugs for fifteen years – gangsters, pushers, politicians – and his record was impressive. He was cunning and corrupt, completely willing to buy people who could be bought. He drank with the judges and slept with their girlfriends. He bribed the cops and threatened the jurors. He schmoozed with the politicians and contributed when asked. Jerome knew what made the system tick, and when a sleazy defendant with money needed help in New Orleans he invariably found his way to the law offices of W. Jerome Clifford, Attorney and Counselor-at-Law. And in that office he found a friend who thrived on the dirt and was loyal to the end.

Barry's case, however, was something different. It was huge, and growing by the moment. The trial was a month away and loomed like an execution. It would be his second murder trial. His first had come at the tender age of eighteen when a local prosecutor attempted to prove, with only one most unreliable witness, that Barry had cut the fingers off a rival thug and slit his throat. Barry's uncle, a well-respected and seasoned mobster, dropped some money here and there, and young Barry's jury could not agree on a verdict and thus simply hung itself.

Barry later served two years in a pleasant federal joint on racketeering charges. His uncle could've saved him again, but he was twenty-five at the time and ready for a brief imprisonment. It looked good on his résumé. The family was proud of him. Jerome Clifford had handled the plea bargain, and they'd been friends ever since.

A fresh club soda with lime awaited Barry as he swaggered to the bar and assumed his position. The alcohol could wait a few hours. He needed steady hands.

He squeezed the lime and watched himself in the mirror. He caught a few stares; after all, at this moment he was perhaps the most famous murder defendant in the country. Four weeks from trial, and people were looking. His face was all over the papers.

This trial was much different. The victim was a Senator, the first ever to be murdered, they alleged, while in office. *United States of America versus Barry Muldanno*. Of course, there was no body, and this presented tremendous problems for the United States of America. No corpse, no pathology reports, no ballistics, no bloody photographs to wave around the courtroom and display for the jury.

But Jerome Clifford was cracking up. He was acting strange – disappearing like this, staying away from the office, not returning calls, always late for court, always mumbling under his breath and drinking too much. He'd always been mean and tenacious, but now he was detached and people were talking. Frankly, Barry wanted a new lawyer.

Just four short weeks, and Barry needed time. A delay, a continuance, something. Why does justice move so quickly when you don't want it to? His life had been lived on the fringes of the law, and he'd seen cases drag on for years. His uncle had once been indicted, but after three years of exhaustive warfare the government finally quit. Barry had been indicted six months ago, and bam!, here's the trial. It wasn't fair. Romey wasn't working. He had to be replaced.

Of course, the Feds had a hole or two in their case. No one saw the killing. There would be a decent circumstantial case against him, with motive, perhaps. But no one actually saw him do it. There was an informant who was unstable and unreliable and expected to be chewed up on cross-examination, if he indeed made it to trial. The Feds were hiding him. And, Barry had his one marvelous advantage – the body, the diminutive, wiry corpse of Boyd Boyette rotting slowly away in concrete. Without it, Reverend Roy could not get a conviction. This made Barry smile, and he winked at two peroxide blondes at a table near the door. Women had been plentiful since the indictment. He was famous.

Reverend Roy's case was weak all right, but it hadn't slowed his nightly sermons in front of the cameras, or his pompous predictions of swift justice, or his blustering interviews with any journalist bored enough to quiz him. He was an oily-voiced, leather-lunged, pious U.S. Attorney with obnoxious political aspirations and a thunderous opinion about everything. He had his very own press agent, a most overworked soul charged with the task of keeping the Reverend in the spotlight so that one day very soon the public would insist he serve them in the United States Senate. From there, only the Reverend knew where God might lead him.

The Blade crunched his ice at the repulsive thought of Roy Foltrigg waving his indictment before the cameras and bellowing all sorts of forecasts of good triumphing over evil. But six months had passed since the indictment, and neither Reverend Roy nor his confederates, the FBI, had found the body of Boyd Boyette. They followed Barry night and day – in fact, they were probably waiting outside right now, as if he were stupid enough to have dinner, then go look at the body just for the hell of it. They had bribed every wino and street bum who claimed to be an informant. They had drained ponds and lakes; they had dragged rivers. They had obtained search warrants for dozens of buildings and sites in the city. They had spent a small fortune on backhoes and bulldozers.

But Barry had it. The body of Boyd Boyette. He would like to move it, but he couldn't. The Reverend and his host of angels were watching.

Clifford was an hour late now. Barry paid for two rounds of club soda, winked at the peroxides in their leather skirts, and left the place cursing lawyers in general and his in particular.

He needed a new lawyer, one who would return his phone calls and meet him for drinks and find some jurors who could be bought. A real lawyer!

He needed a new lawyer, and he needed a continuance or a postponement or a delay, hell, anything to slow this thing down so he could think.

He lit a cigarette and walked casually along Magazine between Canal and Poydras. The air was thick. Clifford's office was four blocks away. His lawyer wanted a quick trial! What an idiot! No one wanted a quick trial in this system, but here was W. Jerome Clifford pushing for one. Clifford had explained not three weeks ago that they should push hard for a trial because there was no corpse, thus no case, et cetera, et cetera. And if they waited, the body might be found, and since Barry was such a lovely suspect and it was a sensational killing with a ton of pressure behind its prosecution, and since Barry had actually performed the killing, was in fact guilty as hell, then they should go to trial immediately. This had shocked Barry. They had argued viciously in Romey's office, and things had not been the same since.

At one point in the discussion, three weeks ago, things got quiet and Barry boasted to his lawyer that the body would never be found. He'd disposed of lots of them, and he knew how to hide them. Boyette had been hidden rather quickly, and though Barry wanted to move the little fella, he was nonetheless secure and resting peacefully without the threat of disturbance from Roy and the Fibbies.

Barry chuckled to himself as he strolled along Poydras.

'So where's the body?' Clifford had asked.

'You don't want to know,' Barry had replied.

'Sure I want to know. The whole world wants to know. Come on, tell me if you've got the guts.'

'You don't want to know.'

'Come on. Tell me.'

'You're not gonna like it.'

'Tell me.'

Barry flicked his cigarette on the sidewalk, and almost laughed out loud. He shouldn't have told Jerome Clifford. It was a childish thing to do, but harmless. The man could be trusted with secrets, attorney-client privilege and all, and he had been wounded when Barry hadn't come clean initially with all the gory details. Jerome Clifford was as crooked and sleazy as his clients, and if they got blood on them he wanted to see it.

'You remember what day Boyette disappeared?' Barry had asked.

'Sure. January 16.'

'Remember where you were January 16?'

At this point, Romey had walked to the wall behind his desk and studied his badly scrawled monthly planners. 'Colorado, skiing.'

'And I borrowed your house?'

'Yeah, you were meeting some doctor's wife.'

'That's right. Except she couldn't make it, so I took the Senator to your house.'

Romey froze at this point, and glared at his client, mouth open, eyes lowered.

Barry had continued. 'He arrived in the trunk, and I left him at your place.'

'Where?' Romey had asked in disbelief.

'In the garage.'

'You're lying.'

'Under the boat that hasn't been moved in ten years.'

'You're lying.'

The front door of Clifford's office was locked. Barry rattled it and cursed through the window. He lit another cigarette and searched the usual parking places for the black Lincoln. He'd find the fat bastard if it took all night.

Barry had a friend in Miami who was once indicted for an assortment of drug charges. His lawyer was quite good, and had managed to stall and delay for two and a half years until finally the judge lost patience and ordered a trial. The day before jury selection, his friend killed his very fine lawyer, and the judge was forced to grant another continuance. The trial never happened.

If Romey died suddenly, it would be months, maybe years, before the trial.

# CHAPTER THREE

Ricky backed away from the tree until he was in the weeds, then found the narrow trail and started to run. 'Ricky,' Mark called, 'Hey, Ricky, wait,' but it didn't work. He stared once more at the man on the car with the gun still in his mouth. The eyes were half-open and the feet twitched at the heels.

Mark had seen enough. 'Ricky,' he called again as he jogged toward the trail. His brother was ahead, running slowly in an odd way with both arms stiff and straight down by his legs. He leaned forward at the waist. Weeds hit him in the face. He tripped but didn't fall. Mark grabbed him by the shoulders and spun him around. 'Ricky, listen! It's okay.' Ricky was zombie-like, with pale skin and glazed eyes. He breathed hard and rapidly, and emitted a dull, aching moan. He couldn't talk. He jerked away and resumed his trot, still moaning as the weeds slapped him in the face. Mark followed close behind as they crossed a dry creek bed and headed for home.

The trees thinned just before the crumbling board fence that encircled most of the trailer park. Two small children were throwing rocks at a row of cans lined neatly along the hood of a wrecked car. Ricky ran faster and crawled through a broken section of the fence. He jumped a ditch, darted between two trailers, and ran into the street. Mark was two steps behind. The steady groan grew louder as Ricky breathed even harder.

The Sway mobile home was twelve feet wide and sixty feet long, and parked on a narrow strip on East Street with forty others. Tucker Wheel Estates also included North, South, and West streets, and all four curved and crossed each other several times from all directions. It was a decent trailer park with reasonably clean streets, a few trees, plenty of bicycles, and few abandoned cars. Speed bumps slowed traffic. Loud music or noise brought the police as soon as it was reported to Mr. Tucker. His family owned all the land and most of the trailers, including Number 17 on East Street, which Dianne Sway rented for two hundred and eighty dollars a month.

Ricky ran through the unlocked door and fell onto the couch in the den. He seemed to be crying, but there were no tears. He curled his knees to his stomach as if he were cold, then, very slowly, placed his right thumb in his mouth. Mark watched this intently. 'Ricky, talk to me,' he said, gently shaking his shoulder. 'You gotta talk to me, man, okay, Ricky. It's okay.'

He sucked harder on the thumb. He closed his eyes and his body shook.

Mark looked around the den and kitchen, and realized things were exactly as they had left them an hour ago. An hour ago! It seemed like days. The sunlight was fading and the rooms were a bit darker. Their books and backpacks from school were piled, as always, on the kitchen table. The daily note from Mom was on the counter next to the phone. He walked to the sink and ran water in a clean coffee cup. He had a terrible thirst. He sipped the cool water and stared through the window at the trailer next door. Then he heard smacking noises, and looked at his brother. The thumb. He'd seen a show on television where some kids in California sucked their thumbs after an earthquake. All kinds of doctors were involved. A year after it hit the poor kids were still sucking away.

The cup touched a tender spot on his lip, and he remembered the blood. He ran to the bathroom and studied his face in the mirror. Just below the hairline there was a small, barely noticeable knot. His left eye was puffy and looked awful. He ran water in the sink and washed a spot of blood from his lower lip. It was not swollen, but suddenly began throbbing. He'd looked worse after fights at school. He was tough.

He took an ice cube from the refrigerator and held it firmly under his eye. He walked to the sofa and studied his brother, paying particular attention to the thumb. Ricky was asleep. It was almost five-thirty, time for their mother to arrive home after nine long hours at the lamp factory. His ears still rang from the gunshots and the blows he took from his late friend Mr. Romey, but he was beginning to think. He sat next to Ricky's feet and slowly rubbed around his eye with the ice.

If he didn't call 911, it could be days before anyone found the body. The fatal shot had been severely muffled, and Mark was certain no one heard it but them. He'd been to the clearing many times, but suddenly realized he had never seen another person there. It was secluded. Why had Romey chosen the place? He was from New Orleans, right?

Mark watched all kinds of rescue shows on television, and knew for certain that every 911 call was recorded. He did not want to be recorded. He would never tell anyone, not even his mother, what he had just lived through, and he really needed, at this crucial moment, to discuss the matter with his little brother so they could get their lies straight. 'Ricky,' he said, shaking his brother's leg. Ricky groaned but did not open his eyes. He pulled himself tighter into a knot. 'Ricky, wake up!'

There was no response to this, except a sudden shudder as if he were freezing. Mark found a quilt in a closet and covered his brother, then wrapped a handful of ice cubes in a dish towel and placed the pack gingerly over his own left eye. He didn't feel like answering questions about his face.

He stared at the phone and thought of cowboy and Indian movies with bodies lying around and buzzards circling above and everyone concerned about burying the dead before the damned vultures got them. It would be dark in an hour or so. Do buzzards strike at night? Never saw that in a movie.

The thought of the fat lawyer lying out there with the gun in his mouth, one shoe off, probably still bleeding, was horrible enough, but throw in the buzzards ripping and tearing, and Mark picked up the phone. He punched 911 and cleared his throat.

'Yeah, there's a dead man, in the woods, and, well, someone needs to come get him.' He spoke in the deepest voice possible, and knew from the first syllable that it was a pitiful attempt at disguise. He breathed hard and the knot on his forehead pounded.

'Who's calling please?' It was a female voice, almost like a robot's.

'Uh, I really don't want to say, okay.'

'We need your name, son.' Great, she knew he was a kid. He hoped he could at least sound like a young teenager.

'Do you want to know about the body or not?' Mark asked.

'Where is the body?'

This is just great, he thought, already telling someone about it. And not someone to be trusted, but someone who wore a uniform and worked with the police, and he could just hear this taped conversation as it would be repeatedly played before the jury, just like on television. They would do all those voice tests and everyone would know it was Mark Sway on the phone telling about the body when no one else in the world knew about it. He tried to make his voice even deeper.

'It's near Tucker Wheel Estates, and – '

'That's on Whipple Road.'

'Yes, that's right. It's in the woods between Tucker Wheel Estates and Highway 17.'

'The body is in the woods?'

'Sort of. The body is actually lying on a car in the woods.'

'And the body's dead?'

'The guy's been shot, okay. With a gun, in the mouth, and I'm sure the man's dead.'

'Have you seen the body?' The woman's voice was losing its professional restraint. It had an edge to it now.

What kind of stupid question is that, Mark thought. Have I seen it? She was stalling, trying to keep him on the line so she could trace it.

'Son, have you seen the body?' she asked again.

'Of course I've seen it.'

'I need your name, son.'

'Look, there's a small dirt road off Highway 17 that leads to a small clearing in the woods. The car is big and black, and the dead man is lying on it. If you can't find it, well, tough luck. Bye.'

He hung up and stared at the phone. The trailer was perfectly still. He walked to the door and peered through the dirty curtains, half-expecting squad cars to come flying in from all directions – loud-speakers, SWAT teams, bulletproof vests.

Get a grip. He shook Ricky again, and, touching his arm, noticed how clammy it was. But Ricky was still sleeping and sucking his thumb. Mark gently grabbed him around the waist and dragged him across the floor, down the narrow hallway to their bedroom where he shoveled him into bed. Ricky mumbled and wiggled a bit along the way, but quickly curled into a ball. Mark covered him with a blanket and closed the door.

Mark wrote a note to his mother, told her Ricky felt bad and was sleeping so please be quiet, and he'd be home in an hour or so. The boys were not required to be home when she arrived, but if they weren't, there'd better be a note.

The distant beat of a helicopter went unnoticed by Mark.

He lit a cigarette along the trail. Two years ago, a new bike had disappeared from a house in the suburbs, not far from the trailer park. It was rumored to have been seen behind one of the mobile homes, and the same rumor held that it was being stripped and repainted by a couple of trailer park kids. The suburb kids enjoyed classifying their lesser neighbors as trailer park kids, the implications being obvious. They attended the same school, and there were daily fights between the two societies. All crime and mischief in the suburbs were automatically blamed on the trailer people.

Kevin, the delinquent on North Street, had the new bike and had shown it to a few of his buddies before it was repainted. Mark had seen it. The rumors flew and the cops poked around, and one night there was a knock at the door. Mark's name had been mentioned in the investigation, and the policeman had a few questions. He sat at the kitchen table and glared down at Mark for an hour. It was very unlike television where the defendant keeps his cool and sneers at the cop.

Mark admitted nothing, didn't sleep for three nights, and vowed to live a clean life and stay away from trouble.

But this was trouble. Real trouble, much worse than a stolen bike. A dead man who told secrets before he died. Was he telling the truth? He was drunk and crazy as hell, talking about the wizard and all. But why would he lie?

Mark knew Romey had a gun, and even held and touched the trigger. And the gun killed the man. It had to be a crime to watch someone commit suicide and not stop it.

He would never tell a soul! Romey had stopped talking. Ricky would have to be dealt with. Mark had kept silent about the bike, and he could do it again. No one would ever know he had been in the car.

There was a siren in the distance, then the steady thump of a helicopter. Mark eased under a tree as the chopper swept close by. He crept through the trees and brush, staying low and in no hurry, until he heard voices.

Lights flashed everywhere. Blue for the cops and red for the ambulance. The white Memphis Police cars were parked around the black Lincoln. The orange-and-white ambulance was arriving on the scene as Mark peeked through the woods. No one seemed anxious or worried.

Romey had not been moved. One cop took pictures while the others laughed. Radios squawked, just like on television. Blood ran from under the body and down across the red-and-white tail-lights. The pistol was still in his right hand, on top of his bulging stomach. His head slumped to the right, his eyes closed now. The paramedics walked up and looked him over, then made bad jokes and the cops laughed. All four doors were open and the car was being carefully inspected. There was no effort to remove the body. The helicopter made a final pass then flew away.

Mark was deep in the brush, maybe thirty feet from the tree and the log where they had lit the first smokes. He had a perfect view of the clearing, and of the fat lawyer lying up there on the car like a dead cow in the middle of the road. Another cop car arrived, then another ambulance. People in uniform were bumping into each other. Small white bags with unseen things in them were removed with great caution from the car. Two policemen with rubber gloves rolled up the hose. The photographer squatted in each door and flashed away. Occasionally, someone would stop and stare at Romey, but most of them drank coffee from Styrofoam cups and chatted away. A cop laid Romey's shoe on the trunk next to the body, then placed it in a white bag and wrote something on it. Another cop knelt by the license plates and waited with his radio for a report to come back.

Finally, a stretcher emerged from the first ambulance and was carried to the rear bumper and laid in the weeds. Two paramedics grabbed Romey's feet and gently pulled him until two other paramedics could grab his arms. The cops watched and joked about how fat Mr. Clifford was because they knew his name now. They asked if more paramedics were needed to carry his big ass, if the stretcher was reinforced or something, if he would fit in the ambulance. Lots of laughter as they strained to lower him.

A cop put the pistol in a bag. The stretcher was heaved into the ambulance, but the doors were not closed. A wrecker with yellow lights arrived and backed itself to the front bumper of the Lincoln.

Mark thought of Ricky and the thumb-sucking. What if he needed help? Mom would be home soon. What if she tried to wake him and got scared? He would leave in just a minute, and smoke the last cigarette on the way home.

He heard something behind him, but thought nothing of it. Just the snap of a twig, then, suddenly, a strong hand grabbed his neck and a voice said, 'What's up, kid?'

Mark jerked around and looked into the face of a cop. He froze and couldn't breathe.

'What're you doing, kid?' the cop asked as he lifted Mark up by the neck. The grip didn't hurt, but the cop meant to be obeyed. 'Stand up, kid, okay. Don't be afraid.'

Mark stood and the cop released him. The cops in the clearing had heard and were staring.

'What're you doing here?'

'Just watching,' Mark said.

The cop pointed with his flashlight to the clearing. The sun was down and it would be dark in twenty minutes. 'Let's walk over there,' he said.

'I need to go home,' Mark said.

The cop placed his arm around Mark's shoulders and led him through the weeds. 'What's your name?'

'Mark.'

'Last name?'

'Sway. What's yours?'

'Hardy. Mark Sway, huh?' the cop repeated thoughtfully. 'You live in Tucker Wheel Estates, don't you?'

He couldn't deny this, but he hesitated for some reason. 'Yes sir.'

They joined the circle of policemen who were now quiet and waiting to see the kid.

'Hey, fellas, this is Mark Sway, the kid who made the call,' Hardy announced. 'You did make the call, didn't you, Mark?'

He wanted to lie, but at the moment he doubted a lie would work. 'Uh, yes sir.'

'How'd you find the body?'

'My brother and I were playing.'

'Playing where?'

'Around here. We live over there,' he said, pointing beyond the trees.

'Were you guys smoking dope?'

'No sir.'

'Are you sure?'

'Yes sir.'

'Stay away from drugs, kid.' There were at least six policemen in the circle, and the questions were coming from all directions.

'How'd you find the car?'

'Well, we just sort of walked up on it.'

'What time was it?'

'I don't remember, really. We were just walking through the woods. We do it all the time.'

'What's your brother's name?'

'Ricky.'

'Same last name?'

'Yes sir.'

'Where were you and Ricky when you first saw the car?'

Mark pointed to the tree behind him. 'Under that tree.'

A paramedic approached the group and announced they were leaving and taking the body to the morgue. The wrecker was tugging at the Lincoln.

'Where is Ricky now?'

'At home.'

'What happened to your face?' Hardy asked.

Mark instinctively reached for his eye. 'Oh, nothing. Just got in a fight at school.'

'Why were you hiding in the bushes over there?'

'I don't know.'

'Come on, Mark, you were hiding for a reason.'

'I don't know. It's sort of scary, you know. Seeing a dead man and all.'

'You've never seen a dead man before?'

'On television.'

One cop actually smiled at this.

'Did you see this man before he killed himself?'

'No sir.'

'So you just found him like this?'

'Yes sir. We walked up under that tree and saw the car, then, we, uh, we saw the man.'

'Where were you when you heard the gunshot?'

He started to point to the tree again, but caught himself. 'I'm not sure I understand.'

'We know you heard the gunshot. Where were you when you heard it?'

'I didn't hear the gunshot.'

'You sure?'

'I'm sure. We walked up and found him right here, and we took off home and I called 911.'

'Why didn't you give your name to 911?'

'I don't know.'

'Come on, Mark, there must be a reason.'

'I don't know. Scared, I guess.'

The cops exchanged looks as if this were a game. Mark tried to breathe normally and act pitiful. He was just a kid.

'I really need to go home. My mom's probably looking for me.'

'Okay. One last question,' Hardy said. 'Was the engine running when you first saw the car?'

Mark thought hard, but couldn't remember if Romey had turned it off before he shot himself. He answered very slowly. 'I'm not sure, but I think it was running.'

Hardy pointed to a police car. 'Get in. I'll drive you home.'

'That's okay. I'll just walk.'

'No, it's too dark. I'll give you a ride. Come on.' He took his arm, and walked him to the car.

# CHAPTER FOUR

Dianne Sway had called the children's clinic and was sitting on the edge of Ricky's bed, biting her nails and waiting for a doctor to call. The nurse said it would be less than ten minutes. The nurse also said there was a very contagious virus in the schools and they had treated dozens of children that week. He had the symptoms, so don't worry. Dianne checked his forehead for a fever. She shook him gently again, but there was no response. He was still curled tightly, breathing normally and sucking his thumb. She heard a car door slam and went back to the living room.

Mark burst through the door. 'Hi, Mom.'

'Where have you been?' she snapped. 'What's wrong with Ricky?'

Sergeant Hardy appeared in the door, and she froze.

'Good evening, ma'am,' he said.

She glared at Mark. 'What have you done?'

'Nothing.'

Hardy stepped inside. 'Nothing serious, ma'am.'

'Then why are you here?'

'I can explain, Mom. It's sort of a long story.'

Hardy closed the door behind him, and they stood in the small room looking awkwardly at one another.

'I'm listening.'

'Well, me and Ricky were back in the woods playing this afternoon, and we saw this big black car parked in a clearing with the motor running, and when we got closer there was this man lying across the trunk with a gun in his mouth. He was dead.'

'Dead!'

'Suicide, ma'am,' Hardy offered.

'And we ran home as fast as we could and I called 911.'

Dianne covered her mouth with her fingers.

'The man's name is Jerome Clifford, male white,' Hardy reported officially. 'He's from New Orleans, and we have no idea why he came here. Been dead for about two hours now, we think, not very long. He left a suicide note.'

'What did Ricky do?' Dianne asked.

'Well, we ran home, and he fell on the couch and started sucking his thumb and wouldn't talk. I took him to his bed and covered him.'

'How old is he?' Hardy asked with a frown.

'Eight.'

'May I see him?'

'Why?' Dianne asked.

'I'm concerned. He witnessed something awful, and he might be in shock.'

'Shock?'

'Yes ma'am.'

Dianne walked quickly through the kitchen and down the hall with Hardy behind her and Mark following, shaking his head and clenching his teeth.

Hardy pulled the covers off Ricky's shoulders and touched his arm. The thumb was in the mouth. He shook him, called his name, and the eyes opened for a second. Ricky mumbled something.

'His skin is cold and damp. Has he been ill?' Hardy asked.

'No.'

The phone rang, and Dianne raced for it. From the bedroom, Hardy and Mark listened as she told the doctor about the symptoms and the dead body the boys had found.

'Did he say anything when you guys saw the body?' Hardy asked quietly.

'I don't think so. It happened pretty fast. We, uh, we just took off running once we saw it. He just moaned and grunted all the way, ran sort of funny with his arms straight down. I never saw him run like that, and then as soon as we got home he curled up and hasn't spoken since.'

'We need to get him to a hospital,' Hardy said.

Mark's knees went weak and he leaned on the wall. Dianne hung up and Hardy met her in the kitchen. 'The doctor wants him at the hospital,' she said in panic.

'I'll call an ambulance,' Hardy said, heading for his car. 'Pack a few of his clothes.' He disappeared and left the door open.

'Are you telling the truth?' she asked.

'Yes ma'am. We saw the dead body, and Ricky freaked out I guess, and we just ran home.' It would take hours to tell the truth at this point. Once they were alone, he might reconsider and tell the rest of the story, but the cop was here now and it would get too complicated. He was not afraid of his mother, and generally came clean when she pressed. She was only thirty, younger than any of his friends' moms, and they had been through a lot together. Their brutal ordeals fighting off his father had forged a bond much deeper than any ordinary mother–son relationship. It hurt to hide this from her. She was scared and desperate, but the things Romey told him had nothing to do with

Ricky's condition. A sharp pain hit him in the stomach and the room spun slowly.

'What happened to your eye?'

'I got in a fight in school. It wasn't my fault.'

'It never is. Are you okay?'

'I think so.'

Hardy lumbered through the door. 'The ambulance'll be here in five minutes. Which hospital?'

'The doctor said to go to St. Peter's.'

'Who's your doctor?'

'Shelby Pediatric Group. They said they would call in a children's psychiatrist to meet us at the hospital.' She nervously lit a cigarette. 'Do you think he's okay?'

'He needs to be looked at, maybe hospitalized, ma'am. I've seen this before with kids who witness shootings and stabbings. It's very traumatic, and it could take time for him to get over it. Had a kid last year who watched his mother get shot by a crack dealer, in one of the projects, and the poor little fella is still in the hospital.'

'How old was he?'

'Eight, now he's nine. Won't talk. Won't eat. Sucks his thumb and plays with dolls. Really sad.'

Dianne had heard enough. 'I'll pack some clothes.'

'You'd better pack clothes for yourself too, ma'am. You might have to stay with him.'

'What about Mark?' she asked.

'What time does your husband get home?'

'I don't have one.'

'Then pack clothes for Mark too. They might want to keep you overnight.'

Dianne stood in the kitchen with her cigarette inches from her lips, and tried to think. She was scared and uncertain. 'I don't have health insurance,' she mumbled to the window.

'St. Peter's will take indigent cases. You need to get packed.'

A crowd gathered around the ambulance as soon as it stopped at Number 17 East Street. They waited and watched, whispering and pointing as the paramedics went inside.

Hardy laid Ricky on the stretcher, and they strapped him down under a blanket. Ricky tried to curl, but the heavy Velcro bands kept him straight. He moaned twice, but never opened his eyes. Dianne gently freed his right arm and made the thumb available. Her eyes were watery, but she refused to cry.

The crowd backed away from the rear of the ambulance as the paramedics approached with the stretcher. They loaded Ricky, and Dianne stepped in behind. A few neighbors called out their concerns, but the driver slammed the door before she could answer. Mark sat in the front seat of the police car with Hardy, who hit a switch and suddenly blue lights were fluttering and bouncing off the nearby trailers. The crowd inched away, and Hardy gunned the engine. The ambulance followed.

Mark was too worried and scared to be interested in the radios and mikes and guns and gadgets. He sat still and kept his mouth shut.

'Are you telling the truth, son?' Hardy, suddenly the cop again, asked from nowhere.'

'Yes sir. About what?'

'About what you saw?'

'Yes sir. You don't believe me?'

'I didn't say that. It's just a little strange, that's all.'

Mark waited a few seconds, and when it was obvious Hardy was waiting for him, he asked, 'What's strange?'

'Several things. First, you made the call, but wouldn't give your name. Why not? If you and Ricky just stumbled upon the dead man, why not give your name? Second, why did you sneak back to the scene and hide in the woods. People who hide are afraid. Why didn't you simply return to the scene and tell us what you saw? Third, if you and Ricky saw the same thing, why has he freaked out and you're in pretty good shape, know what I mean?'

Mark thought for a while, and realized he could think of nothing to say. So he said nothing. They were on the interstate headed for downtown. It was neat to watch the other cars get out of the way. The red ambulance lights were close behind.

'You didn't answer my question,' Hardy finally said.

'Which question?'

'Why didn't you give your name when you made the call?'

'I was scared, okay. That's the first dead body I ever saw, and it scared me. I'm still scared.'

'Then why did you sneak back to the scene? Why were you trying to hide from us?'

'I was scared, you know, but I just wanted to see what was going on. That's not a crime, is it?'

'Maybe not.'

They left the expressway, and were now darting through traffic. The tall buildings of downtown Memphis were in sight.

'I just hope you're telling the truth,' Hardy said.

'Don't you believe me?'

'I've got my doubts.'

Mark swallowed hard and looked in the side mirror. 'Why do you have doubts?'

'I'll tell you what I think, kid. You want to hear it?'

'Sure,' Mark said slowly.

'Well, I think you kids were in the woods smoking. I found some fresh cigarette butts under that tree with the rope. I figure you were under there having a little smoke and you saw the whole thing.'

Mark's heart stopped and his blood ran cold, but he knew the importance of trying to appear calm. Just shrug it off. Hardy wasn't there. He didn't see anything. He caught his hands shaking, so he sat on them. Hardy watched him.

'Do you arrest kids for smoking cigarettes?' Mark asked, his voice a shade weaker.

'No. But kids who lie to cops get in all sorts of trouble.'

'I'm not lying, okay. I've smoked cigarettes there before, but not today. We were just walking through the woods, thinking about maybe having a smoke, and we walked up on the car and Romey.'

Hardy hesitated slightly, then asked, 'Who's Romey?'

Mark braced himself and breathed deeply. In a flash, he knew it was over. He'd blown it. Said too much. Lied too much. He'd lasted less than an hour with his story. Keep thinking, he told himself.

'That's the guy's name, isn't it?'

'Romey?'

'Yeah. Isn't that what you called him?'

'No. I told your mother his name was Jerome Clifford, from New Orleans.'

'I thought you said it was Romey Clifford, from New Orleans.'

'Who ever heard of the name Romey?'

'Beats me.'

The car turned right, and Mark looked straight ahead. 'Is this St. Peter's?'

'That's what the sign says.'

Hardy parked to the side, and they watched the ambulance back up to the emergency dock.

# CHAPTER FIVE

The honorable J. Roy Foltrigg, United States Attorney for the Southern District of Louisiana at New Orleans, and a Republican, sipped
properly from a can of tomato juice and stretched his legs in the rear
of his customized Chevrolet van as it raced smoothly along the expressway. Memphis was five hours to the north, straight up
Interstate 55, and he could've caught a plane, but there were two
reasons why he hadn't. First, the paperwork. He could claim it was
official business related to the Boyd Boyette case, and he could
stretch things here and there and make it work. But it would take
months to get reimbursed and there would be eighteen different
forms. Second, and much more important, he didn't like to fly. He
could've waited three hours in New Orleans for a flight that would
last for an hour and place him in Memphis around 11 P.M., but they
would make it by midnight in the van. He didn't confess this fear of
flying, and he knew he would one day be forced to see a shrink to
overcome it. For the meantime, he had purchased this fancy van with
his own money and loaded it down with appliances and gadgets,
two phones, a television, even a fax machine. He buzzed around
the Southern District of Louisiana in it, always with Wally Boxx
behind the wheel. It was much nicer and more comfortable than any
limousine.

He slowly kicked off his loafers and watched the night fly by as
Special Agent Trumann listened to the telephone stuck in his ear. On
the other end of the heavily padded back bench sat Assistant U.S.
Attorney Thomas Fink, a loyal Foltrigg subordinate who'd worked
on the Boyette case eighty hours a week and would handle most of
the trial, especially the nonglamorous grunt work, saving of course
the easy and high-profile parts for his boss. Fink was reading a document, as always, and trying to listen to the mumblings of Agent
Trumann, who was seated across from him in a heavy swivel seat.
Trumann had Memphis FBI on the phone.

Next to Trumann, in an identical swivel recliner, was Special
Agent Skipper Scherff, a rookie who'd worked little on the case but
happened to be available for this joyride to Memphis. He scribbled
on a legal pad, and would do so for the next five hours because in this
tight circle of power he had absolutely nothing to say and no one
wanted to hear him. He would obediently stare at his legal pad and

record orders from his supervisor, Larry Trumann, and, of course, from the general himself, Reverend Roy. Scherff stared intently at his scribbling, avoiding with great diligence even the slightest eye contact with Foltrigg, and tried in vain to discern what Memphis was telling Trumann. The news of Clifford's death had electrified their office only an hour earlier, and Scherff was still uncertain why and how he was sitting in Roy's van speeding along the expressway. Trumann had told him to run home, pack a change of clothes, and go immediately to Foltrigg's office. And this is what he'd done. And here he was, scribbling and listening.

The chauffeur, Wally Boxx, actually had a license to practice law, though he didn't know how to use it. Officially, he was an Assistant United States Attorney, same as Fink, but in reality he was a fetch-and-catch boy for Foltrigg. He drove his van, carried his briefcase, wrote his speeches, and handled the media, which took fifty percent of his time because his boss was gravely concerned with his public image. Boxx was not stupid. He was deft at political maneuvering, quick to the defense of his boss, and thoroughly loyal to the man and his mission. Foltrigg had a great future, and Boxx knew he would be there one day whispering importantly with the great man as only the two of them strolled around Capitol Hill.

Boxx knew the importance of Boyette. It would be the biggest trial of Foltrigg's illustrious career, the trial he'd been dreaming of, the trial to thrust him into the national spotlight. He knew Foltrigg was losing sleep over Barry The Blade Muldanno.

Larry Trumann finished the conversation and replaced the phone. He was a veteran agent, early forties, with ten years to go before retirement. Foltrigg waited for him to speak.

'They're trying to convince Memphis PD to release the car so we can go over it. It'll probably take an hour or so. They're having a hard time explaining Clifford and Boyette and all this to Memphis, but they're making progress. Head of our Memphis office is a guy named Jason McThune, very tough and persuasive, and he's meeting with the Memphis chief right now. McThune's called Washington and Washington's called Memphis, and we should have the car within a couple of hours. Single gunshot wound to the head, obviously self-inflicted. Apparently he tried to do it first with a garden hose in the tail pipe, but for some reason it didn't work. He was taking Dalmane and codeine, and washing it all down with Jack Daniels. No record on the gun, but it's too early. Memphis is checking it. A cheap .38. Thought he could swallow a bullet.'

'No doubt it's suicide?' Foltrigg asked.

'No doubt.'

'Where did he do it?'

'Somewhere in north Memphis. Drove into the woods in his big black Lincoln, and took care of himself.'

'I don't suppose anyone saw it?'

'Evidently not. A couple of kids found the body in a remote area.'

'How long had he been dead?'

'Not long. They'll do an autopsy in a few hours, and determine the time of death.'

'Why Memphis?'

'Not sure. If there's a reason, we don't know it yet.'

Foltrigg pondered these things and sipped his tomato juice. Fink took notes. Scherff scribbled furiously. Wally Boxx hung on every word.

'What about the note?' Foltrigg asked, looking out the window.

'Well, it could be interesting. Our guys in Memphis have a copy of it, not a very good copy, and they'll try and fax it to us in a few minutes. Apparently the note was handwritten in black ink, and the writing is fairly legible. It's a few paragraphs of instructions to his secretary about the funeral – he wants to be cremated – and what to do with his office furniture. The note tells the secretary where to find his will. Nothing about Boyette, of course. Nothing about Muldanno. Then, he apparently tried to add something to the note with a blue Bic pen, but it ran out of ink after he started his message. It's badly scrawled, and hard to read.'

'What is it?'

'We don't know. The Memphis Police still have possession of the note, the gun, the pills, all the physical evidence removed from the car. McThune is trying to get it now. They found a Bic pen, no ink, in the car, and it appears to be the same pen he tried to use to add something to the note.'

'They'll have it when we arrive, won't they?' Foltrigg asked in a tone that left no doubt he expected to have it all as soon as he got to Memphis.

'They're working on it,' Trumann answered. Foltrigg was not his boss, technically, but this case was a prosecution now, not an investigation, and the Reverend was in control.

'So Jerome Clifford drives to Memphis and blows his brains out,' Foltrigg said to the window. 'Four weeks before trial. Man oh man. What else can go crazy with this case?'

No answer was expected. They rode in silence waiting for Roy to speak again.

'Where's Muldanno?' he finally asked.

'New Orleans. We're watching him.'

'He'll have a new lawyer by midnight, and by noon tomorrow he'll file a dozen motions for continuances claiming the tragic death of Jerome Clifford seriously undermines his constitutional right to a fair trial with assistance of counsel. We'll oppose it of course, and the judge will order a hearing for next week, and we'll have the hearing, and we'll lose, and it'll be six months before this case goes to trial. Six months! Can you believe it?'

Trumann shook his head in disgust. 'At least it'll give us more time to find the body.'

It certainly would, and of course Roy had thought of this. He needed more time, really, he just couldn't admit it because he was the prosecutor, the people's lawyer, the government fighting crime and corruption. He was right, justice was on his side, and he had to be ready to attack evil at any moment, any time, any place. He had pushed hard for a speedy trial, because he was right, and he would get a conviction. The United States of America would win! And Roy Foltrigg would deliver the victory. He could see the headlines. He could smell the ink.

He also needed to find the damned body of Boyd Boyette, or else there might be no conviction, no front page pictures, no interviews on CNN, no speedy ascent to Capitol Hill. He had convinced those around him that a guilty verdict was possible with no corpse, and this was true. But he didn't want to chance it. He wanted the body.

Fink looked at Agent Trumann. 'We think Clifford knew where the body is. Did you know that?'

It was obvious Trumann did not know this. 'What makes you think so?'

Fink placed his reading material on the seat. 'Romey and I go way back. We were in law school together twenty years ago at Tulane. He was a little crazy back then, but very smart. About a week ago, he called me at home and said he wanted to talk about the Muldanno case. He was drunk, thick-tongued, out of his head, and kept saying he couldn't go through with the trial, which was surprising given how much he loves these big cases. We talked for an hour. He rambled and stuttered – '

'He even cried,' Foltrigg interrupted.

'Yeah, cried like a child. I was surprised by all this at first, but then nothing Jerome Clifford did really surprised me anymore, you know. Not even suicide. He finally hung up. He called me at the office at nine the next morning scared to death he'd let something slip the night before. He was in a panic, kept hinting he might know where the body is and fishing to see whether he'd dropped off any clues during his drunken chitchat. Well, I played along, and thanked him for the information he gave me the night before, which was nothing. I thanked him twice, then three times, and I could feel Romey sweating on the other end of the phone. He called twice more that day, at the office, then called me at home that night, drunk again. It was almost comical, but I thought I could string him along and maybe he'd let something slip. I told him I had to tell Roy, and that Roy had told the FBI, and that the FBI was now trailing him around the clock.'

'This really freaked him out,' Foltrigg added helpfully.

'Yeah, he cussed me out pretty good, but called the next day at the office. We had lunch, and the guy was a nervous wreck. He was too scared to come right out and ask if we knew about the body, and I played it cool. I told him we were certain we'd have the body in plenty of time for the trial, and I thanked him again. He was cracking up before my eyes. He hadn't slept or bathed. His eyes were puffy and red. He got drunk over lunch, and started accusing me of trickery and all sorts of sleazy, unethical behavior. It was an ugly scene. I paid the check and left, and he called me at home that night, remarkably sober. He apologized. I said no problem. I explained to him that Roy was seriously considering an indictment against him for obstruction of justice, and this set him off. He said we couldn't prove it. I said maybe not, but he'd be indicted, arrested, and put on trial, and there would be no way he could represent Barry Muldanno. He screamed and cussed for fifteen minutes, then hung up. I never heard from him again.'

'He knows, or he knew, where Muldanno put the body,' Foltrigg added with certainty.

'Why weren't we informed?' Trumann asked.

'We were about to tell you. In fact, Thomas and I discussed it this afternoon, just a short time before we got the call.' Foltrigg said this with an air of indifference, as if Trumann should not question him about such things. Trumann glanced at Scherff, who was glued to his legal pad, drawing pictures of handguns.

Foltrigg finished his tomato juice and tossed the can in the garbage. He crossed his feet. 'You guys need to track Clifford's movements from New Orleans to Memphis. Which route did he take? Are there friends along the way? Where did he stop? Who did he see in Memphis? Surely he must've talked to someone from the time he left New Orleans until he shot himself. Don't you think so?'

Trumann nodded. 'It's a long drive. I'm sure he had to stop along the way.'

'He knew where the body is, and he obviously planned to commit suicide. There's an outside chance he told someone, don't you think?'

'Maybe.'

'Think about it, Larry. Let's say you're the lawyer, heaven forbid. And you represent a killer who's murdered a United States Senator. Let's say that the killer tells you, his lawyer, where he hid the body. So, two, and only two, people in the entire world know this secret. And you, the lawyer, go off the deep end and decide to kill yourself. And you plan it. You know you're gonna die, right? You get pills and whiskey and a gun and a water hose, and you drive five hours from home, and you kill yourself. Now, would you share your little secret with anyone?'

'Perhaps. I don't know.'

'There's a chance, right?'

'Slight chance.'

'Good. If we have a slight chance, then we must investigate it thoroughly. I'd start with his office personnel. Find out when he left New Orleans. Check his credit cards. Where did he buy gas? Where did he eat? Where did he get the gun and the pills and the booze? Does he have family between here and there? Old lawyer friends along the way? There are a thousand things to check.'

Trumann handed the phone to Scherff. 'Call our office. Get Hightower on the phone.'

Foltrigg was pleased to see the FBI jump when he barked. He grinned smugly at Fink. Between them on the floor was a storage box crammed with files and exhibits and documents all related to *U.S.A. versus Barry Muldanno*. Four more boxes were at the office. Fink had their contents memorized, but Roy did not. He pulled out a file and flipped through it. It was a thick motion filed by Jerome Clifford two months earlier that still had not been ruled upon. He laid it down, and stared through the window at the dark Mississippi landscape passing in the night. The Bogue Chitto exit was just ahead. Where do they get these names?

This would be a quick trip. He needed to confirm that Clifford was in fact dead, and had in fact died by his own hand. He had to know if any clues were dropped along the way, confessions to friends or loose talk to strangers, perhaps notes with last words that might be of help. Longshots at best. But there had been many dead ends in the search for Boyd Boyette and his killer, and this would not be the last.

# CHAPTER SIX

A doctor in a yellow jogging suit ran through the swinging doors at the end of the emergency hallway and said something to the receptionist sitting behind the dirty sliding windows. She pointed, and he approached Dianne and Mark and Hardy as they stood by a Coke machine in one corner of the Admissions lobby of St. Peter's Charity Hospital. He introduced himself to Dianne as Dr. Simon Greenway and ignored the cop and Mark. He was a psychiatrist, he said, and had been called moments earlier by Dr. Sage, the family's pediatrician. She needed to come with him. Hardy said he would stay with Mark.

They hurried away, down the narrow hallway, dodging nurses and orderlies, darting around gurneys and parked beds, and disappeared through the swinging doors. The Admissions lobby was crowded with dozens of sick and struggling patients-to-be. There were no empty chairs. Family members filled out forms. No one was in a hurry. A hidden intercom rattled nonstop somewhere above, paging a hundred doctors a minute.

It was a few minutes after seven. 'Are you hungry, Mark?' Hardy asked.

He wasn't, but he wanted to leave this place. 'Maybe a little.'

'Let's go to the cafeteria. I'll buy you a cheeseburger.'

They walked through a busy hallway, down a flight of stairs to the basement where a mass of anxious people roamed the corridor. Another hall led to a large open area, and suddenly they were in a cafeteria, louder and more crowded than the lunchroom at school. Hardy pointed to the only empty table in view, and Mark waited there.

Of particular concern to Mark at this moment was, of course, his little brother. He was worried about Ricky's physical condition, although Hardy had explained that he was in no danger of dying. He said that some doctors would talk to him and try to bring him round. But it could take time. He said that it was terribly important for the doctors to know exactly what happened, the truth and nothing but the truth, and that if the doctors were not told the truth then it could be severely damaging to Ricky and his mental condition. Hardy said Ricky might be locked up in some institution for months, maybe years, if the doctors weren't told the truth about what the boys witnessed.

43

Hardy was okay, not too bright, and he was making the mistake of talking to Mark as if he were five years old instead of eleven. He described the padded walls, and rolled his eyes around with great exaggeration. He told of patients being chained to beds as if spinning some horror story around the campfire. Mark was tired of it.

Mark could think of little except Ricky and whether he would remove his thumb and start talking. He desperately wanted this to happen, but he wanted to have first crack at Ricky when the shock ended. They had things to discuss.

What if the doctors or, heaven forbid, the cops got to him first, and Ricky told the whole story and they all knew Mark was lying? What would they do to him if they caught him lying? Maybe they wouldn't believe Ricky. Since he'd blanked out and left the world for a while, maybe they would tend to believe Mark instead. This conflict in stories was too awful to think about.

It's amazing how lies grow. You start with a small one that seems easy to cover, then you get boxed in and tell another one. Then another. People believe you at first, and they act upon your lies, and you catch yourself wishing you'd simply told the truth. He could have told the truth to the cops and to his mother. He could have explained in great detail everything that Ricky saw. And the secret would still be safe because Ricky didn't know.

Things were happening so fast he couldn't plan. He wanted to get his mother in a room with the door locked and unload all this, just stop it now before it got worse. If he didn't do something, he might go to jail and Ricky might go to the nuthouse for kids.

Hardy appeared with a tray covered with french fries and cheeseburgers, two for him and one for Mark. He arranged the food neatly and returned the tray.

Mark nibbled on a french fry. Hardy launched into a burger.

'So what happened to your face?' Hardy asked, chomping away.

Mark rubbed the knot and remembered he had been wounded in a the fray. 'Oh nothing. Just got in a fight in school.'

'Who's the other kid?'

Dammit! Cops are relentless. Tell one lie to cover another. He was sick of lying. 'You don't know him,' he answered, then bit into his cheeseburger.

'I might want to talk to him.'

'Why?'

'Did you get in trouble for this fight? I mean, did your teacher take you to the principal's office, or anything like that?'

'No. It happened when school was out.'

'I thought you said you got in a fight at school.'

'Well, it sort of started at school, okay. Me and this guy got into it at lunch, and agreed to meet when school was out.'

Hardy drew mightily on the tiny straw in his milk shake. He swallowed hard, cleared his mouth, and said, 'What's the other kid's name?'

'Why do you want to know?'

This angered Hardy and he stopped chewing. Mark refused to look into his eyes, and he bent low over his food and stared at the ketchup.

'I'm a cop, kid. It's my job to ask questions.'

'Do I have to answer them?'

'Of course you do. Unless, of course, you're hiding something and afraid to answer. At that point, I'll have to get with your mother and perhaps take the both of you down to the station for more questioning.'

'Questioning about what? What exactly do you want to know?'

'Who is the kid you had a fight with today?'

Mark nibbled forever on the end of a long fry. Hardy picked up the second cheeseburger. A spot of mayonnaise hung from the corner of his mouth.

'I don't want to get him in trouble,' Mark said.

'He won't get in trouble.'

'Then why do you want to know his name?'

'I just want to know. It's my job, okay?'

'You think I'm lying, don't you?' Mark asked, looking pitifully into the bulging face.

The chomping stopped. 'I don't know, kid. Your story is full of holes.'

Mark looked even more pitiful. 'I can't remember everything. It happened so fast. You expect me to give every little detail, and I can't remember it that way.'

Hardy stuck a wad of fries in his mouth. 'Eat your food. We'd better get back.'

'Thanks for the dinner.'

Ricky was in a private room on the ninth floor. A large sign by the elevator labeled it as the PSYCHIATRIC WING, and it was much quieter. The lights were dimmer, the voices softer, the traffic much slower. The nurses' station was near the elevator, and those stepping off were scrutinized. A security guard whispered with the nurses and watched the hallways. Down from the elevators, away from the rooms, was a small, dark sitting area with a television, soft drink machines, magazines, and Gideon Bibles.

Mark and Hardy were alone in the waiting area. Mark sipped a Sprite, his third, and watched a rerun of 'Hill Street Blues' on cable while Hardy dozed fitfully on the terribly undersized couch. It was almost nine, and half an hour had passed since Dianne had walked him down the hall to Ricky's room for a quick peek. He looked small under the sheets. The IV, Dianne had explained, was to feed him because he wouldn't eat. She assured him Ricky would be all right, but Mark studied her eyes and knew she was worried. Dr. Greenway would return in a bit, and wanted to talk to Mark.

'Has he said anything?' Mark had asked as he studied the IV.

'No. Not a word.'

She took his hand and they walked through the dim hallway to the sitting area. At least five times, Mark had almost blurted something out. They had passed an empty room not far from Ricky's and he thought of dragging her inside for a confession. But he didn't. Later, he kept telling himself, I'll tell her later.

Hardy had stopped asking questions. His shift ended at ten, and it was obvious he was tired of Mark and Ricky and the hospital. He wanted to return to the streets.

A pretty nurse in a short skirt walked past the elevators and motioned for Mark to follow her. He eased from his chair, holding his Sprite. She took his hand, and there was something exciting about this. Her fingernails were long and red. Her skin was smooth and tanned. She had blond hair and a perfect smile, and she was young. Her name was Karen, and she squeezed his hand a bit tighter than necessary. His heart skipped a beat.

'Dr. Greenway wants to talk to you,' she said, leaning down as she walked. Her perfume lingered, and it was the most wonderful fragrance Mark could remember.

She walked him to Ricky's room, Number 943, and released his hand. The door was closed, so she knocked slightly and opened it. Mark entered slowly, and Karen patted him on the shoulder. He watched her leave through the half-open door.

Dr. Greenway now wore a shirt and tie with a white lab jacket over it. An ID tag hung from the left front pocket. He was a skinny man with round glasses and a black beard, and seemed too young to be doing this.

'Come in, Mark,' he said after Mark was already in the room and standing at the foot of Ricky's bed. 'Sit here.' He pointed to a plastic chair next to a foldaway bed under the window. His voice was low, almost a whisper. Dianne sat with her feet curled under her on the bed. Her shoes were on the floor. She wore blue jeans and a sweater, and stared at Ricky under the sheets with a tube in his arm. A lamp on a table near the bathroom door provided the only light. The blinds were shut tight.

Mark eased into the plastic chair, and Dr. Greenway sat on the edge of the foldaway, not two feet away. He squinted and frowned, and projected such somberness that Mark thought for a second they were all about to die.

'I need to talk to you about what happened,' he said. He was not whispering now. It was obvious Ricky was in another world and they were unafraid of waking him. Dianne was behind Greenway, still staring blankly at the bed. Mark wanted her alone so he could talk and work out of this mess, but she was back there in the darkness, behind the doctor, ignoring him.

'Has he said anything?' Mark asked first. The past three hours with Hardy had been nothing but quick questions, and the habit was hard to break.

'No.'

'How sick is he?'

'Very sick,' Greenway answered, his tiny, dark eyes glowing at Mark. 'What did he see this afternoon?'

'Is this in secret?'

'Yes. Anything you tell me is strictly confidential.'

'What if the cops want to know what I tell you?'

'I can't tell them. I promise. This is all very secret and confidential. Just you and me and your mother. We're all trying to help Ricky, and I've got to know what happened.'

Maybe a good dose of the truth would help everyone, especially Ricky. Mark looked at the small, blond head with hair sticking in all directions on the pillow. Why oh why didn't they just run when the black car pulled up and parked? He was suddenly hit with guilt, and it terrified him. All of this was his fault. He should have known better than to mess with a crazy man.

His lip quivered and his eyes watered. He was cold. It was time to tell all. He was running out of lies and Ricky needed help. Greenway watched every move.

And then Hardy walked slowly by the door. He paused for a second in the hall and locked eyes with Mark, then disappeared. Mark knew he wasn't far away. Greenway had not seen him.

Mark started with the cigarettes. His mother looked at him hard, but if she was angry she didn't convey it. She shook her head once or twice, but never said a word. He spoke in a low voice, his eyes alternating quickly between Greenway and the door, and described the tree with the rope and the woods and the clearing. Then the car. He left out a good chunk of the story, but did admit to Greenway, in a soft voice and in extreme confidence, that he once crawled to the car and removed the hose. And when he did so, Ricky cried and peed in his pants. Ricky begged him not to do it. He could tell Greenway liked this part. Dianne listened without expression.

Hardy walked by again, but Mark pretended not to see him. He paused in his story for a few seconds, then told how the man stormed out of the car, saw the garden hose lying harmlessly in the weeds, and crawled on the trunk and shot himself.

'How far away was Ricky?' Greenway asked.

Mark looked around the room. 'You see that door across the hall?' he asked, pointing. 'From here to there.'

Greenway looked and rubbed his beard. 'About forty feet. That's not very far.'

'It was very close.'

'What exactly did Ricky do when the shot was fired?'

Dianne was listening now. It apparently had just occurred to her that this was a different version from the earlier one. She wrinkled her forehead and looked hard at her eldest.

'I'm sorry, Mom. I was too scared to think. Don't be angry with me.'

'You actually saw the man shoot himself?' she asked in disbelief.

'Yes.'

She looked at Ricky. 'No wonder.'

'What did Ricky do when the shot was fired?'

'I wasn't looking at Ricky. I was watching the man with the gun.'

'Poor baby,' Dianne mumbled in the background. Greenway held up a hand to cut her off.

'Was Ricky close to you?'

Mark glanced at the door, and explained faintly how Ricky had frozen, then started away in an awkward jog, arms straight down, a dull moaning sound coming from his mouth. He told it all with dead accuracy from the point of the shooting to the point of the ambulance, and he left out nothing. He closed his eyes and relived each step, each movement. It felt wonderful to be so truthful.

'Why didn't you tell me you watched the man kill himself?' Dianne asked.

This irritated Greenway. 'Please, Ms. Sway, you can discuss it with him later,' he said without taking his eyes off Mark.

'What was the last word Ricky said?' Greenway asked.

He thought and watched the door. The hall was empty 'I really can't remember.'

Sergeant Hardy huddled with his lieutenant and Special Agent Jason McThune of the FBI. They chatted in the sitting area next to the soft drink machines. Another FBI agent loitered suspiciously near the elevator. The hospital security guard glared at him.

The lieutenant explained hurriedly to Hardy that it was now an FBI matter, that the dead man's car and all other physical evidence had been turned over by Memphis PD, that print experts had finished dusting the car and found lots of fingerprints too small for an adult, and they needed to know if Mark had dropped any clues or changed his story.

'No, but I'm not convinced he's telling the truth,' Hardy said.

'Has he touched anything we can take?' McThune asked quickly, unconcerned about Hardy's theories or convictions.

'What do you mean?'

'We have a strong suspicion the kid was in the car at some point before Clifford died. We need to lift the kid's prints from something and see if they match.'

'What makes you think he was in the car?' Hardy asked with great anticipation.'

'I'll explain later,' his lieutenant said.

Hardy looked around the sitting area, and suddenly pointed to a trash basket by the chair Mark had sat in. 'There. The Sprite can. He drank a Sprite while sitting right there.' McThune looked up and down the hall, and carefully wrapped a handkerchief around the Sprite can. He placed it in the pocket of his coat.

'It's definitely his,' Hardy said. 'This is the only trash basket, and that's the only Sprite can.'

'I'll run this to our fingerprint men,' McThune said. 'Is the kid, Mark, staying here tonight?'

'I think so,' Hardy said. 'They've moved a portable bed into his brother's room. Looks like they'll all sleep in there. Why is the FBI concerned with Clifford?'

'I'll explain later,' said his lieutenant. 'Stay here for another hour.'

'I'm supposed to be off in ten minutes.'

'You need the overtime.'

Dr. Greenway sat in the plastic chair near the bed and studied his notes. 'I'm gonna leave in a minute, but I'll be back early in the morning. He's stable, and I expect little change through the night. The nurses will check in every so often. Call them if he wakes up.' He flipped a page of notes and read the chicken scratch, then looked at Dianne. 'It's a severe case of acute post-traumatic stress disorder.'

'What does that mean?' Mark asked. Dianne rubbed her temples and kept her eyes closed.

'Sometime a person sees a terrible event and cannot cope with it. Ricky was badly scared when you removed the garden hose from the tail pipe, and when he saw the man shoot himself he was suddenly exposed to a terrifying experience that he couldn't handle. It triggered a response in him. He sort of snapped. It shocked his mind and body. He was able to run home, which is quite remarkable because normally a person traumatized like Ricky would immediately become numb and paralyzed.' He paused and placed his notes on the bed. 'There's not a lot we can do right now. I expect him to come around tomorrow, or the next day at the latest, and we'll start talking about things. It may take some time. He'll have nightmares of the shooting, and flashbacks. He'll deny it happened, then he'll blame himself for it. He'll feel isolated, betrayed, bewildered, maybe even depressed. You just never know.'

'How will you treat him?' Dianne asked.

'We have to make him feel safe. You must stay here at all times. Now, you said the father is of no use.'

'Keep him away from Ricky,' Mark said sternly. Dianne nodded.

'Fine. And there are no grandparents or relatives nearby.'

'No.'

'Very well. It's imperative that both of you stay in this room as much as possible for the next several days. Ricky must feel safe and secure. He'll need emotional and physical support from you. He and I will talk several times a day. It will be important for Mark and Ricky to talk about the shooting. They need to share and compare their reactions.'

'When do you think we might go home?' Dianne asked.

'I don't know, but as soon as possible. He needs the safety and familiarity of his bedroom and surroundings. Maybe a week. Maybe two. Depends on how quickly he responds.'

Dianne pulled her feet under her. 'I, uh, I have a job. I don't know what to do.'

'I'll have my office contact your employer first thing in the morning.'

'My employer runs a sweatshop. It is not a nice, clean corporation with benefits and sympathy. They will not send flowers. I'm afraid they won't understand.'

'I'll do the best I can.'

'What about school?' Mark asked.

'Your mother has given me the name of the principal. I'll call first thing in the morning and talk to your teachers.'

Dianne was rubbing her temples again. A nurse, not the pretty one, knocked while entering. She handed Dianne two pills and a cup of water.

'It's Dalmane,' Greenway said. 'It should help you rest. If not, call the nurses' station and they'll bring something stronger.'

The nurse left and Greenway stood and felt Ricky's forehead. 'See you guys in the morning. Get some sleep.' He smiled for the first time, then closed the door behind him.

They were alone, the tiny Sway family, or what was left of it. Mark moved closer to his mother, and leaned on her shoulder. They looked at the small head on the large pillow less than five feet away.

She patted his arm. 'It'll be all right, Mark. We've been through worse.' She held him tight and he closed his eyes.

'I'm sorry, Mom.' His eyes watered, and he was ready for a cry. 'I'm so sorry about all this.' She squeezed him, and held him tight for a long minute. He sobbed quietly with his face buried in her shirt.

She gently lay down with Mark still in her arms, and they curled together on the cheap foam mattress. Ricky's bed was two feet higher. The window was above them. The lights were low. Mark stopped the crying. It was something he was lousy at anyway.

The Dalmane was working, and she was exhausted. Nine hours of packing plastic lamps into cardboard boxes, five hours of a full-blown crisis, and now the Dalmane. She was ready for a deep sleep.

'Will you get fired, Mom?' Mark asked. He worried about the family finances as much as she did.

'I don't think so. We'll worry about it tomorrow.'

'We need to talk, Mom.'

'I know we do. But let's do it in the morning.'

'Why can't we talk now?'

She relaxed her grip and breathed deeply, eyes already closed. 'I'm very tired and sleepy, Mark. I promise we'll have a long talk first thing in the morning. You have some questions to answer, don't you? Now go brush your teeth and let's try and sleep.'

Mark was suddenly tired too. The hard line of a metal brace protruded through the cheap mattress, and he crept closer to the wall and pulled the lone sheet over him. His mother rubbed his arm. He stared at the wall, six inches away, and decided he could not sleep like this for a week.

Her breathing was much heavier and she was completely still. He thought of Romey. Where was he now? Where was the chubby little body with the bald head? He remembered the sweat and how it poured from his shiny scalp and ran down in all directions, some dripping from his eyebrows and some soaking his collar. Even his ears were wet. Who would get his car? Who would clean it up and wash the blood off? Who would get the gun? Mark realized for the first time that his ears were no longer ringing from the gunfire in the car. Was Hardy still out there in the sitting room trying to sleep? Would the cops return tomorrow with more questions? What if they asked about the garden hose? What if they asked a thousand questions?

He was wide awake now, staring at the wall. Lights from the outside trickled through the blinds. The Dalmane worked well because his mother was breathing very slow and heavy. Ricky had not moved. He stared at the dim light above the table, and thought of Hardy and the police. Were they watching him? Was he under surveillance, like on television? Surely not.

He watched them sleep for twenty minutes, and got bored with it. It was time to explore. When he was a first-grader, his father came home drunk late one night, and started raising hell with Dianne. They fought and the trailer shook, and Mark eased open the shoddy window in his room and slid to the ground. He went for a long walk around the neighborhood, then through the woods. It was a hot, sticky night with plenty of stars, and he rested on a hill overlooking the trailer park. He prayed for the safety of his mother. He asked God for a family in which everyone could sleep without fear of abuse. Why couldn't they just be normal? He rambled for two hours. All was quiet when he returned home, and thus began a habit of night-time excursions that had brought him much pleasure and peace.

Mark was a thinker, a worrier, and when sleep came and went or wouldn't come at all, he went for long secret walks. He learned much. He wore dark clothing and moved like a thief through the shadows of Tucker Wheel Estates. He witnessed petty crimes of theft and vandalism, but he never told. He saw lovers sneak from windows. He loved to sit on the hill above the park on clear nights and enjoy a quiet smoke. The fear of getting caught by his mother had vanished years ago. She worked hard and slept sound.

He was not afraid of strange places. He pulled the sheet over his mother's shoulder, did the same for Ricky, and quietly closed the door behind him. The hall was dark and empty. Karen the gorgeous was busy at the nurses' desk. She smiled beautifully at him and stopped her writing. He wanted to go for some orange juice in the cafeteria, he said, and he knew how to get there. He'd be back in a minute. Karen grinned at him as he walked away, and Mark was in love.

Hardy was gone. The sitting room was empty but the television was on. 'Hogan's Heroes.' He took the empty elevator to the basement.

The cafeteria was deserted. A man with casts on both legs sat stiffly in a wheelchair at one table. The casts were shiny and clean. An arm was in a sling. A band of thick gauze covered the top of his head and it looked as though the hair had been shaven. He was terribly uncomfortable.

Mark paid for a pint of juice, and sat at a table near the man. He grimaced in pain, and shoved his soup away in frustration. He sipped juice through a straw, and noticed Mark.

'What's up?' Mark asked with a smile. He could talk to anyone and felt sorry for the guy.

The man glared at him, then looked away. He grimaced again and tried to adjust his legs. Mark tried not to stare.

A man with a white shirt and tie appeared from nowhere with a tray of food and coffee, and sat at a table on the other side of the injured guy. He didn't appear to notice Mark. 'Bad injury,' he said with a large smile. 'What happened?'

'Car wreck,' came the somewhat anguished reply. 'Got hit by an Exxon truck. Nut ran a stop sign.'

The smile grew even larger and the food and coffee were ignored. 'When did it happen?'

'Three days ago.'

'Did you say Exxon truck?' The man was standing and moving quickly to the guy's table, pulling something out of his pocket. He took a chair and was suddenly sitting within inches of the casts.

'Yeah,' the guy said warily.

The man handed him a white card. 'My name's Gill Teal. I'm a lawyer, and I specialize in auto accidents, especially cases involving large trucks.' Gill Teal said this very rapidly, as if he'd hooked a large fish and had to work quickly or it might get away. 'That's my specialty. Big-truck cases. Eighteen wheelers. Dump trucks. Tankers. You name it, and I go after them.' He thrust his hand across the table. 'Name's Gill Teal.'

Luckily for the guy, his good arm was his right one, and he lamely slung it over the table to shake hands with this hustler. 'Joe Farris.'

Gill pumped it furiously, and eagerly moved in for the kill. 'What you got – two broke legs, concussion, coupla puncture wounds?'

'And broken collarbone.'

'Great. Then we're looking at permanent disability. What type work you do?' Gill asked, rubbing his chin in careful analysis. The card was lying on the table, untouched by Joe. They were unaware of Mark.

'Crane operator.'

'Union?'

'Yeah.'

'Wow. And the Exxon truck ran a stop sign. No doubt about who's at fault here?'

Joe frowned and shifted again, and even Mark could tell he was rapidly tiring of Gill and this intrusion. He shook his head no.

Gill made frantic notes on a napkin, then smiled at Joe and announced, 'I can get you at least six hundred thousand. I take only a third, and you walk away with four hundred thousand. Minimum. Four hundred grand, tax free, of course. We'll file suit tomorrow.'

Joe took this as if he'd heard it before. Gill hung in mid-air with his mouth open, proud of himself, full of confidence.

'I've talked to some other lawyers,' Joe said.

'I can get you more than anybody. I do this for a living, nothing but truck cases. I've sued Exxon before, know all their lawyers and corporate people locally, and they're terrified of me because I go for the jugular. It's warfare, Joe, and I'm the best in town. I know how to play their dirty games. Just settled a truck case for almost half a million. They threw money at my client once he hired me. Not bragging, Joe, but I'm the best in town when it comes to these cases.'

'A lawyer called me this morning and said he could get me a million.'

'He's lying. What was his name? McFay? Ragland? Snodgrass? I know these guys. I kick their asses all the time, Joe, and anyway I said six hundred thousand is a minimum. Could be much more. Hell, Joe, if they push us to trial, who knows how much a jury might give us. I'm in trial every day, Joe, kicking ass all over Memphis. Six hundred is a minimum. Have you hired anybody yet? Signed a contract?'

Joe shook his head 'No, not yet?'

'Wonderful. Look, Joe, you've got a wife and kids, right?'

'Ex-wife, three kids.'

'So you've got child support, man, now listen to me. How much child support?'

'Five hundred a month.'

'That's low. And you've got bills. Here's what I'll do. I'll advance you a thousand bucks a month to be applied against your settlement. If we settle in three months, I withhold three thousand. If it takes two years, and it won't, but if it does I'll withhold twenty-four thousand. Or whatever. You follow me, Joe? Cash now on the spot.'

Joe shifted again and stared at the table. 'This other lawyer came by my room yesterday and said he'd advance two thousand now and float me two thousand a month.'

'Who was it? Scottie Moss? Rob LaMoke? I know these guys, Joe, and they're trash. Can't find their way to the courthouse. You can't trust them. They're incompetent. I'll match it – two thousand now, and two thousand a month.'

'This other guy with some big firm offered ten thousand up front and a line of credit for whatever I needed.'

Gill was crushed, and it was at least ten seconds before he could speak. 'Listen to me, Joe. It's not a matter of advance cash, okay. It's a matter of how much money I can get for you from Exxon. And nobody, I repeat, nobody will get more than me. Nobody. Look. I'll advance five thousand now, and allow you to draw what you need to pay bills. Fair enough?'

'I'll think about it.'

'Time is critical, Joe. We must move fast. Evidence disappears. Memories fade. Big corporations move slow.'

'I said I'll think about it.'

'Can I call you tomorrow?'

'No.'

'Why not?'

'Hell, I can't sleep now for all the damned lawyers calling. I can't eat a meal without you guys bargin' in. There are more lawyers around this damned place than doctors.'

Gill was unmoved. 'There are a lot of sharks out here, Joe. A lot of really lousy lawyers who'll screw up your case. Sad but true. The profession is overcrowded, so lawyers are everywhere trying to find business. But don't make a mistake, Joe. Check me out. Look in the yellow pages. There's a full-page, three-color ad for me, Joe. Look up Gill Teal, and you'll see who's for real.'

'I'll think about it.'

Gill came forth with another card and handed it to Joe. He said good-bye and left, never touching the food or coffee on his tray.

Joe was suffering. He grabbed the wheel with his right arm, and slowly rolled himself away. Mark wanted to help, but thought better of asking. Both of Gill's cards were on the table. He finished his juice, glanced around, and picked up one of the cards.

Mark told Karen, his sweetheart, that he couldn't sleep and would be watching television if anyone needed him. He sat on the couch in the waiting area and flipped through the phone book while watching

'Cheers' reruns. He sipped another Sprite. Hardy, bless his heart, had given him eight quarters after dinner.

Karen brought him a blanket and tucked it around his legs. She patted his arm with her long, thin hands, and glided away. He watched every step.

Mr. Gill Teal did indeed have a full-page ad in the Attorneys section of the Memphis yellow pages, along with a dozen other lawyers. There was a nice picture of him standing casually outside a courthouse with his jacket off and sleeves rolled up. 'I FIGHT FOR YOUR RIGHTS!' it said under the photo. In bold red letters across the top, the question 'HAVE YOU BEEN INJURED?' cried out. Thick green print answered just below, 'IF SO, CALL GILL TEAL – HE'S FOR REAL.' Farther down, in blue print, Gill listed all the types of cases he handled, and there were hundreds. Lawnmowers, electrical shock, deformed babies, car wrecks, exploding water heaters. Eighteen years' experience in all courts. A small map in the corner of the ad directed the world to his office, which was just across the street from the courthouse.

Mark heard a familiar voice, and suddenly there he was, Gill Teal himself, on television standing beside a hospital emergency entrance talking about injured loved ones and crooked insurance companies. Red lights flashed in the background. Paramedics ran behind him. But Gill had the situation under control, and he would take your case for nothing down. No fee unless he recovered.

Small world! In the past two hours, Mark had seen him in person, picked up one of his business cards, was literally looking at his face in the yellow pages, and now, here he was speaking to him from the television.

He closed the phone book and laid it on the cluttered coffee table. He pulled the blanket over him and decided to go to sleep.

Tomorrow he might call Gill Teal.

# CHAPTER SEVEN

Foltrigg liked to be escorted. He especially enjoyed those priceless moments when the cameras were rolling and waiting for him, and at just the right moment he would stroll majestically through the hall or down the courthouse steps with Wally Boxx in front like a pit bull and Thomas Fink or another assistant by his side brushing off idiotic questions. He spent many quiet moments watching videos of himself darting in and out of courthouses with a small entourage. His timing was usually perfect. He had the walk perfected. He held his hands up patiently as if he would love to answer questions but, being a man of great importance, he just didn't have the time. Soon thereafter, Wally would call the reporters in for an orchestrated press conference in which Roy himself would break from his brutal work schedule and spend a few moments in the lights. A small library in the U.S. Attorney's suite had been converted to a press room, complete with floodlights and a sound system. Roy kept make-up in a locked cabinet.

As he entered the Federal Building on Main Street in Memphis, a few minutes after midnight, he had an escort of sorts with Wally and Fink and agents Trumann and Scherff, but there were no anxious reporters. In fact, not a soul waited for him until he entered the offices of the FBI where Jason McThune sipped stale coffee with two other weary agents. So much for grand entrances.

Introductions were handled quickly as they walked to McThune's cramped office. Foltrigg took the only available seat. McThune was a twenty-year man who'd been shipped to Memphis four years earlier against his wishes and was counting the months until he could leave for the Pacific Northwest. He was tired and irritated because it was late. He'd heard of Foltrigg, but never met him. The rumors described him as a pompous ass.

An agent who was unidentified and unintroduced closed the door, and McThune fell into his seat behind the desk. He covered the basics: the finding of the car, the contents of it, the gun, the wound, the time of death, and on and on. 'Kid's name is Mark Sway. He told Memphis PD he and his younger brother happened upon the body and ran to call the authorities. They live about a half a mile away in a trailer park. The younger kid is in the hospital now and suffering from what appears to be traumatic shock. Mark Sway and his mother, Dianne, divorced, are also at the hospital. The father lives here in the city, and has a record of petty stuff. DUIs, fights, and the like. Sophisticated criminal. Low-class white people. Anyway, the kid's lying.'

'I couldn't read the note,' Foltrigg interrupted, dying to say something. 'The fax was bad.' He said this as if McThune and the Memphis FBI were inept because he, Roy Foltrigg, had received a bad fax in his van.

McThune glanced at Larry Trumann and Skipper Scherff standing against the wall, and continued. 'I'll get to that in a minute. We know the kid's lying because he says they arrived on the scene after Clifford shot himself. Looks doubtful. First, the kid's fingerprints are all over the car, inside and out. On the dash, on the door, on the whiskey bottle, on the gun, everywhere. We lifted a print from him about two hours ago, and we've had our people all over the car. They'll finish up tomorrow, but it's obvious the kid was inside. Doing what, well, we're not yet certain. We've also found prints all around the rear tail-lights just above the exhaust pipe. And there were also three fresh cigarette butts under a tree near the car. Virginia Slims, the same brand used by Dianne Sway. We figure the kids were being kids, took the cigarettes from their mother, and went for a smoke. They were minding their own business when Clifford appears from nowhere. They hide and watch him – it's a dense area and hiding is no problem. Maybe they sneak around and pull out the hose, we're not sure and the kids aren't telling. The little boy can't talk right now, and Mark evidently is lying. Anyway, it's obvious the hose didn't work. We're trying to match prints on it, but it's tedious work. May be impossible. I'll have photos in the morning to show the location of the hose when Memphis PD arrived.'

McThune lifted a yellow notepad from the wreckage on his desk. He spoke to it, not to Foltrigg. 'Clifford fired at least one shot from inside the car. The bullet exited through the center, almost exactly, of the front passenger window, which cracked but did not shatter. No idea why he did this, and no idea when it was done. The autopsy was finished an hour ago, and Clifford was full of Dalmane, codeine, and Percodan. Plus his blood alcohol content was point two-two, so he was drunk as a skunk, as these people say down here. My point being, not only was he off his rocker enough to kill himself, but he was also drunk and stoned, so there's no way to figure out a lot of this. We're not tracking a rational mind.'

'I understand that.' Roy nodded impatiently. Wally Boxx hovered behind him like a well-trained terrier.

McThune ignored him. 'The gun's a cheap .38 he purchased illegally at a pawnshop here in Memphis. We've questioned the owner, but he won't talk without his lawyer present, so we'll do that in the morning, or this morning I should say. A Texaco receipt shows a purchase of gasoline in Vaiden, Mississippi, about an hour and a half from here. The clerk is a kid who says she thinks he stopped around 1 P.M. No other evidence of any stops. His secretary says he left the office around 9 A.M., said he had an errand to run and she didn't hear a word until we called. Frankly, she was not very upset at the news. It looks as though he left New Orleans shortly after nine, drove to Memphis in five or six hours, stopped once for gas, stopped to buy the gun, and drove off and shot himself. Maybe he stopped for lunch, maybe to buy whiskey, maybe a lot of things. We're digging.'

'Why Memphis?' Wally Boxx asked. Foltrigg nodded, obviously approving the question.

'Because he was born here,' McThune said solemnly while staring at Foltrigg, as if everyone prefers to die in the place of their birth. It was a humorous response delivered by a serious face, and Foltrigg missed it all. McThune had heard he was not too bright.

'Evidently, the family moved away when he was a child,' he explained after a pause. 'He went to college at Rice and law school at Tulane.'

'We were in law school together,' Fink said proudly.

'That's great. The note was handwritten and dated today, or yesterday I should say. Handwritten with a black felt tip pen of some sort – the pen wasn't found on him or in the car.' McThune picked up a sheet of paper and leaned across the desk. 'Here. This is the original. Be careful with it.'

Wally Boxx leaped at it and handed it to Foltrigg, who studied it. McThune rubbed his eyes and continued. 'Just funeral arrangements and directions to his secretary. Look at the bottom. It looks as though he tried to add something with a blue ballpoint pen, but the pen was out of ink.'

Foltrigg's nose got closer to the note. 'It says "Mark, Mark where are," and I can't make out the rest of it.'

'Right. The handwriting is awful and the pen ran out of ink, but our expert says the same thing. "Mark, Mark where are." He also thinks that Clifford was drunk or stoned or something when he tried to write this. We found the pen in the car. Cheap Bic. No doubt it's the pen. He has no children, nephews, brothers, uncles, or cousins by the name of Mark. We're checking his close friends – his secretary said he had none – but as of now we haven't found a Mark.'

'So what does it mean?'

'There's one other thing. A few hours ago, Mark Sway rode to the hospital with a Memphis cop by the name of Hardy. Along the way, he let it slip that Romey said or did something. Romey. Short for Jerome, according to Mr. Clifford's secretary. In fact, she said more people called him Romey than Jerome. How would the kid know the nickname unless Mr. Clifford himself told him?'

Foltrigg listened with his mouth open. 'What do you think?' he asked.

'Well, my theory is that the kid was in the car before Clifford shot himself, and that he was there for some time because of all the prints, and that he and Clifford talked about something. Then, at some point, the kid leaves the car, Clifford tries to add something to his note, and shoots himself. The kid is scared. His little brother goes into shock, and here we are.'

'Why would the kid lie?'

'One, he's scared. Two, he's a kid. Three, maybe Clifford told him something he doesn't need to know.'

McThune's delivery was perfect, and the dramatic punch line left a heavy silence in the room. Foltrigg was frozen. Boxx and Fink stared blankly at the desk with open mouths.

Because his boss was temporarily at a loss, Wally Boxx moved in defensively and asked a stupid question. 'Why do you think this?'

McThune's patience with U.S. Attorneys and their little flunkies had been exhausted about twenty years ago. He'd seen them come and go. He'd learned to play their games and manipulate their egos. He knew the best way to handle their banalities was simply to respond. 'Because of the note, the prints, and the lies. The poor kid doesn't know what to do.'

Foltrigg placed the note on the desk, and cleared his throat. 'Have you talked to the kid?'

'No. I went to the hospital two hours ago, but did not see him. Sergeant Hardy of Memphis PD talked to him.'

'Do you plan to?'

'Yes, in a few hours. Trumann and I will go to the hospital around nine or so and talk to the kid and maybe his mother. I'd also like to talk to the little brother, but it'll depend on his doctor.'

'I'd like to be there,' Foltrigg said. Everyone knew it was coming.

McThune shook his head. 'Not a good idea. We'll handle it.' He was abrupt and left no doubt that he was in charge. This was Memphis, not New Orleans.

'What about the kid's doctor? Have you talked to him?'

'No, not yet. We'll try this morning. I doubt if he'll say much.'

'Do you think these kids would tell the doctor?' Fink asked innocently.

McThune rolled his eyes at Trumann as if to say, 'What kind of dumbasses have you brought me?' 'I can't answer that, sir. I don't know what the kids know. I don't know the doctor's name. I don't know if he's talked to the kids. I don't know if the kids will tell him anything.'

Foltrigg frowned at Fink, who shrank with embarrassment. McThune glanced at his watch and stood. 'Gentlemen, it's late. Our people will finish with the car by noon, and I suggest we meet then.'

'We must know everything Mark Sway knows,' Roy said without moving. 'He was in that car, and Clifford talked to him.'

'I know that.'

'Yes, Mr. McThune, but there are some things you don't know. Clifford knew the location of the body, and he was talking about it.'

'There are a lot of things I don't know, Mr. Foltrigg, because this is a New Orleans case, and I work Memphis, you understand. I don't want to know any more about poor Mr. Boyette and poor Mr. Clifford. I'm up to my ass in dead bodies here. It's almost 1 A.M., and I'm sitting here in my office working on a case that's not mine, talking to you fellas and answering your questions. And I'll work on the case until noon tomorrow, then my pal Larry Trumann here can have it. I'll be finished.'

'Unless, of course, you get a call from Washington.'

'Yes, unless of course I get a call from Washington, then I'll do whatever Mr. Voyles tells me.'

'I talk to Mr. Voyles every week.'

'Congratulations.'

'The Boyette case is the FBI's top priority at this moment, according to him.'

'So I've heard.'

'And I'm sure Mr. Voyles will appreciate your efforts.'

'I doubt it.'

Roy stood slowly and stared at McThune. 'It is imperative that we know everything Mark Sway knows. Do you understand?'

McThune returned the stare and said nothing.

# CHAPTER EIGHT

Karen checked on Mark throughout the night, and brought him orange juice around eight. He was alone in the small waiting room. She woke him gently.

In spite of his many problems at the moment, he was falling hopelessly in love with this beautiful nurse. He sipped the juice and looked into her sparkling brown eyes. She patted the blanket covering his legs.

'How old are you?' he asked.

She smiled even wider. 'Twenty-four. Thirteen years older than you. Why do you ask?'

'Just a habit. Are you married?'

'No.' She gently removed the blanket and began folding it. 'How was the sofa?'

Mark stood, stretched, and watched her. 'Better than that bed Mom had to sleep on. Did you work all night?'

'From eight to eight. We're doing twelve-hour shifts, four days a week. Come with me. Dr. Greenway is in the room and wants to see you.' She took his hand, which helped immensely, and they walked to Ricky's room. Karen left and closed the door behind her.

Dianne looked tired. She stood at the foot of Ricky's bed with an unlit cigarette in her trembling hand. Mark stood next to her, and she put her arm on his shoulder. They watched as Greenway rubbed Ricky's forehead and spoke to him. His eyes were closed and he was not responding.

'He doesn't hear you, Doctor,' Dianne said finally. It was difficult to listen to Greenway chat away in baby talk. He ignored her. She wiped a tear from her cheek. Mark smelled fresh soap and noticed her hair was wet. She had changed clothes. But there was no make-up and her face was different.

Greenway stood straight. 'A most severe case,' he said properly, almost to himself while staring at the closed eyes.

'What's next?' she asked.

'We wait. His vital signs are stable, so there's no physical danger. He'll come around, and when he does, it's imperative that you be in this room.' Greenway was looking at them now, rubbing his beard, deep in thought. 'He must see his mother when he opens his eyes, do you understand this?'

'I'm not leaving.'

'You, Mark, can come and go a bit, but it's best if you stay here as much as possible too.'

Mark nodded his head. The thought of spending another minute in the room was painful.

'The first moments can be crucial. He'll be frightened when he looks around. He needs to see and feel his mother. Hold him and re-assure him. Call the nurse immediately. I'll leave instructions. He'll be very hungry, so we'll try and get some food in him. The nurse'll re-move the IV, so he can walk around the room. But the important thing is to hold him.'

'When do you – '

'I don't know. Probably today or tomorrow. There's no way to pre-dict.'

'Have you seen cases like this before?'

Greenway looked at Ricky, and decided to go for the truth. He shook his head. 'Not quite this bad. He's almost comatose, which is a bit unusual. Normally, after a period of good rest, they'll be awake and eating.' He almost managed a smile. 'But, I'm not concerned. Ricky will be all right. It'll just take some time.'

Ricky seemed to hear this. He grunted and stretched, but did not open his eyes. They watched intently, hoping for a mumble or word. Though Mark preferred that he remain silent about the shooting until they discussed it alone, he desperately wanted his little brother to wake up and start talking about other matters. He was tired of looking at him curled up on the pillow, sucking that damned thumb.

Greenway reached into his bag and produced a newspaper. It was the *Memphis Press*, the morning paper. He laid it on the bed, and handed Dianne a card. 'My office is in the building next door. Here's the phone number, just in case. Remember, the moment he wakes up, call the nurses' station, and they'll call me immediately. Okay?'

Dianne took the card and nodded. Greenway unfolded the news-paper on Ricky's bed in front of them. 'Have you seen this?'

'No,' she answered.

At the bottom of the front page was a headline about Romey. 'NEW ORLEANS LAWYER COMMITS SUICIDE IN NORTH MEMPHIS.' Under the headline to the right was a big photo of W. Jerome Clifford, and to the left was the smaller headline – 'FLAMBOYANT CRIMINAL LAWYER WITH SUSPECTED MOB TIES.' The word 'Mob' jumped at Mark. He stared at Romey's face, and suddenly needed to vomit.

Greenway leaned forward and lowered his voice. 'It seems as though Mr. Clifford was a rather well-known lawyer in New Orleans.

He was involved in the Senator Boyette case. Apparently, he was the attorney for the man charged with the murder. Have you kept up with it?'

Dianne actually put the unlit cigarette in her mouth. She shook her head no.

'Well, it's a big case. The first U.S. Senator to be murdered in office. You can read this after I leave. There are police and FBI downstairs. They were waiting when I arrived an hour ago.' Mark grabbed the railing on the foot of the bed. 'They want to talk to Mark, and of course they want you present.'

'Why?' she asked.

Greenway looked at his watch. 'The Boyette case is complicated. I think you'll understand more after you read the story here. I told them you and Mark could not speak with them until I say so. Is this all right?'

'Yes,' Mark blurted. 'I don't want to talk to them.' Dianne and Greenway looked at him. 'I may end up like Ricky if these cops keep bugging me.' For some reason, Mark knew the police would return with a lot of questions. They were not finished with him. But the photo on the front page of the paper and the mention of the FBI suddenly sent chills over him, and he needed to sit down.

'Keep them away for now,' Dianne said to Greenway.

'They asked if they could see you at nine, and I said no. But they won't go away.' He looked at his watch again. 'I'll be here at noon. Perhaps we should talk to them then.'

'Whatever you think,' she said.

'Very well. I'll put them off until twelve. My office has called your employer and the school. Try not to worry about that. Just stay by this bed until I return.' He almost smiled as he closed the door behind him.

Dianne ran to the bathroom and lit her cigarette. Mark punched the remote control by Ricky's bed until the television was on and he found the local news. Nothing but weather and sports.

Dianne finished the story about Mr. Clifford and placed the paper on the floor under the foldaway bed. Mark watched anxiously.

'His client killed a United States Senator,' she said in awe.

No kidding. There were about to be some tough questions, and Mark was suddenly hungry. It was past nine. Ricky hadn't moved. The nurses had forgotten about them. Greenway seemed like ancient history. The FBI was waiting somewhere in the darkness. The room was growing smaller by the minute, and the cheap cot on which he was sitting was ruining his back.

'I wonder why he did that,' he said because he could think of nothing else to say.

'It says Jerome Clifford had ties with the New Orleans mob, and that his client is widely thought to be a member.'

He'd seen *The Godfather* on cable. In fact, he'd even seen the first sequel to *The Godfather*, and he knew all about the mob. Scenes from the movies flashed before his eyes, and the pains in his stomach grew sharper. His heart pounded. 'I'm hungry, Mom. Are you hungry?'

'Why didn't you tell me the truth, Mark?'

'Because the cop was in the trailer, and it wasn't a good time to talk. I'm sorry, Mom. I promise I'm sorry. I planned to tell you as soon as we were alone, I promise.'

She rubbed her temples and looked so sad. 'You never lie to me, Mark.'

Never say never. 'Can we talk about this later, Mom? I'm really hungry. Give me a couple of bucks and I'll run down to the cafeteria and get some doughnuts. I'd love a doughnut. I'll get you some coffee.' He was on his feet waiting for the money.

Fortunately, she was not in the mood for a serious talk about truthfulness and such. The Dalmane lingered and her thoughts were slow. Her head pounded. She opened her purse and gave him a five-dollar bill. 'Where's the cafeteria?'

'Basement. Madison Wing. I've been there twice.'

'Why am I not surprised? I suppose you've been all over this place.'

He took the money and crammed it in the pocket of his jeans. 'Yes ma'am. We're on the quietest floor. The babies are in the basement and it's a circus down there.'

'Be careful.'

He closed the door behind him. She waited, then took the bottle of Valium from her purse. Greenway had sent it.

Mark ate four doughnuts during 'Donahue' and watched his mother try to nap on the bed. He kissed her on the forehead, and told her he needed to roam around a bit. She told him not to leave the hospital.

He used the stairs again because he figured Hardy and the FBI and the rest of the gang might be hanging around somewhere downstairs waiting for him to happen by.

Like most big-city charity hospitals, St. Peter's had been built over time whenever funds could be squeezed, with little thought of architectural symmetry. It was a sprawling and bewildering configuration of additions and wings, with a maze of hallways and corridors and mezzanines trying desperately to connect everything. Elevators and escalators had been added wherever they would fit. At some point in history, someone had realized the difficulty of moving from one point to another without getting hopelessly lost, and a dazzling array of color-coded signs had been implemented for the orderly flow of traffic. Then more wings were added. The signs became obsolete, but the hospital failed to remove them. Now they only added to the confusion.

Mark darted through now familiar territory and exited the hospital through a small lobby on Monroe Avenue. He'd studied a map of downtown in the front of the phone book, and he knew Gill Teal's office was within easy walking distance. It was on the third floor of a building four blocks away. He moved quickly. It was Tuesday, a school day, and he wanted to avoid truant officers. He was the only kid on the street, and he knew he was out of place.

A new strategy was developing. What was wrong, he asked himself as he stared at the sidewalk and avoided eye contact with the pedestrians passing by, with making an anonymous phone call to the cops or FBI and telling them exactly where the body was? The secret would no longer belong only to him. If Romey wasn't lying, then the body would be found and the killer would go to jail.

There were risks. His phone call to 911 yesterday had been a disaster. Anybody on the other end of the phone would know he was just a kid. The FBI would record him and analyze his voice. The Mafia wasn't stupid.

Maybe it wasn't such a good idea.

He turned on Third Street, and darted into the Sterick Building. It was old and very tall. The lobby was tile and marble. He entered the elevator with a crowd of others, and punched the button for the third floor. Four other buttons were pushed by people wearing nice clothes and carrying briefcases. They chatted quietly, in the normal hushed tones of elevator talk.

His stop was first. He stepped into a small lobby with hallways running left, right, and straight ahead. He went left, and roamed about innocently, trying to appear calm, as if lawyer-shopping were a chore he'd done many times. There were plenty of lawyers in the building. Their names were etched on distinguished bronze plates screwed into the doors, and some doors were covered with rather long and intimidating names with lots of initials followed by periods. J. Winston Buckner. F. MacDonald Durston. I. Hempstead Crawford. The more names Mark read, the more he longed for plain old Gill Teal.

He found Mr. Teal's door at the end of the hall, and there was no bronze plate. The words 'GILL TEAL – THE PEOPLE'S LAWYER' were painted in bold black letters from the top of the door to the bottom. Three people waited in the hall beside it.

Mark swallowed, and entered the office. It was packed. The small waiting room was filled with sad people suffering from all sorts of injuries and wounds. Crutches were everywhere. Two people sat in wheelchairs. There were no empty seats, and one poor man in a neck brace sat on the cluttered coffee table, his head wobbling around like a newborn's. A lady with a dirty cast on her foot cried softly. A small girl with a horribly burned face clung to her mother. War could not have been more pitiful. It was worse than the emergency room at St. Peter's.

Mr. Teal certainly had been busy rounding up clients. Mark decided to leave, when someone called out rudely, 'What do you want?'

It was a large lady behind the receptionist's window. 'You, kid, you want something?' Her voice boomed around the room, but no one noticed. The suffering continued unabated. He stepped to the window and looked at the scowling, ugly face.

'I'd like to see Mr. Teal,' he said softly, looking around.

'Oh you would. Do you have an appointment?' She picked a clipboard and studied it.

'No ma'am.'

'What's your name?'

'Uh, Mark Sway. It's a very private matter.'

'I'm sure it is.' She glared at him from head to toe. 'What type of injury is it?'

He thought about the Exxon truck and how it had excited Mr. Teal, but he knew he couldn't pull it off. 'I, uh, I don't have an injury.'

'Well, you're in the wrong place. Why do you need a lawyer?'

'It's a long story.'

'Look, kid, you see these people? They've all got appointments to see Mr. Teal. He's a very busy man, and he only takes cases involving death or injuries.'

'Okay.' Mark was already retreating and thinking about the mine field of canes and crutches behind him.

'Now please go bother someone else.'

'Sure. And if I get hit by a truck or something, I'll come back to see you.' He walked through the carnage, and made a quick exit.

He took the stairs down and explored the second floor. More

lawyers. On one door he counted twenty-two bronze names. Lawyers on top of lawyers. Surely one of these guys could help him. He passed a few of them in the hall. They were too busy to notice.

A security guard suddenly appeared and walked slowly toward him. Mark glanced at the next door. The words 'REGGIE LOVE – LAWYER' were painted on it in small letters, and he casually turned the knob and stepped inside. The small reception area was quiet and empty. Not a single client was waiting. Two chairs and a sofa sat around a glass table. The magazines were arranged neatly. Soft music came from above. A pretty rug covered the hardwood floor. A young man with a tie but no coat stood from his desk behind some potted trees, and walked a few steps forward. 'May I help you?' he asked, quite pleasantly.

'Yes. I need to see a lawyer.'

'You're a bit young to need a lawyer, aren't you?'

'Yes, but I'm having some problems. Are you Reggie Love?'

'No. Reggie's in the back. I'm her secretary. What's your name?'

He was her secretary. Reggie was a she. The secretary was a he. 'Uh, Mark Sway. You're a secretary?'

'And a paralegal, among other things. Why aren't you in school?' A nameplate on the desk identified him as Clint Van Hooser.

'So you're not a lawyer?'

'No. Reggie's the lawyer.'

'Then I need to speak with Reggie.'

'She's busy right now. You can have a seat.' He waved at the sofa.

'How long will it be?' Mark asked.

'I don't know.' The young man was amused by this kid needing a lawyer. 'I'll tell her you're here. Maybe she can see you for a minute.'

'It's very important.'

The kid was nervous and sincere. His eyes glanced at the door as if someone had followed him here. 'Are you in trouble, Mark?' Clint asked.

'Yes.'

'What type of trouble? You need to tell me a little about it, or Reggie won't talk to you.'

'I'm supposed to talk to the FBI at noon, and I think I need a lawyer.'

This was good enough. 'Have a seat. It'll be a minute.'

Mark eased into a chair, and as soon as Clint disappeared he opened a yellow phone book and flipped through the pages until he found the attorneys. There was Gill Teal again in his full-page spread. Pages and pages of huge ads, all crying out for injured people. Photos of busy and important men and women holding thick law books or sitting behind wide desks or listening intently to the telephones stuck in their ears. Then half-page ones, then quarter. Reggie Love was not there. What kind of lawyer was she?

Reggie Love was one of thousands in the Memphis yellow pages. She couldn't be much of a lawyer if the yellow pages thought so little of her, and the thought of racing from the office crossed his mind. But then there was Gill Teal, the one for real, the people's lawyer, the star of the yellow pages who also had enough fame to get himself on television, and just look at his office down the hall. No, he quickly decided, he'd take his chances with Reggie Love. Maybe she needed clients. Maybe she had more time to help him. The idea of a woman lawyer suddenly appealed to him because he'd seen one on 'L.A. Law' once and she had ripped up some cops pretty good. He closed the book and returned it carefully to the magazine rack beside the chair. The office was cool and pretty. There were no voices.

Clint closed the door behind him and eased across the Persian rug to her desk. Reggie Love was on the phone, listening more than talking. Clint placed three phone messages before her, and gave the standard hand signal to indicate someone was waiting in the reception area. He sat on the corner of the desk, straightening a paper clip and watching her.

There was no leather in the office. The walls were papered with light floral shades of rose and pink. A spotless desk of glass and chrome covered one corner of the rug. The chairs were sleek and upholstered with a burgundy fabric. This, without a doubt, was the office of a woman. A very neat woman.

Reggie Love was fifty-two years old, and had been practicing law for less than five years. She was of medium build with very short, very gray hair that fell in bangs almost to the top of her perfectly round, black-framed glasses. The eyes were green, and they glowed at Clint as if something funny had been said. Then she rolled them and shook her head. 'Good-bye, Sam,' she finally said, and hung up.

'Got a new client for you,' Clint said with a smile.

'I don't need new clients, Clint. I need clients who can pay. What's his name?'

'Mark Sway. He's just a kid, ten may be twelve years old. And he says he's supposed to meet with the FBI at noon. Says he needs a lawyer.'

'He's alone?'

'Yeah.'

'How'd he find us?'

'I have no idea. I'm just the secretary, remember. You'll have to ask some questions yourself.'

Reggie stood and walked around the desk. 'Show him in. And rescue me in fifteen minutes, okay. I've got a busy morning.'

'Follow me, Mark,' Clint said, and Mark followed him through a narrow door and down a hallway. Her office door was covered with stained glass, and a small brass plate again said 'REGGIE LOVE – LAWYER.' Clint opened the door, and motioned for Mark to enter.

The first thing he noticed about her was her hair. It was gray and shorter than his; very short above the ears and in the back, a bit thicker on top with bangs halfway down. He'd never seen a woman with gray hair worn so short. She wasn't old and she wasn't young.

She smiled appropriately as they met at the door. 'Mark, I'm Reggie Love.' She offered her hand, he took it reluctantly, and she squeezed hard and shook firm. Shaking hands with women was not something he did often. She was neither tall nor short, thin nor heavy. Her dress was straight and black and she wore black and gold bracelets on both wrists. They rattled.

'Nice to meet you,' he said weakly as they shook hands. She was already leading him to a corner of the office where two soft chairs faced a table with picture books on it.

'Have a seat,' she said. 'I only have a minute.'

Mark sat on the edge of his seat, and was suddenly terrified. He'd lied to his mother. He'd lied to the police. He'd lied to Dr. Greenway. He was about to lie to the FBI. Romey had been dead less than a day, and he was lying right and left to everyone who asked. Tomorrow he would certainly lie to the next person. Maybe it was time to come clean for a change. Sometimes it was frightening to tell the truth, but he usually felt better afterward. But the thought of unloading all this baggage on a stranger made his blood run cold.

'Would you like something to drink?'

'No ma'am.'

She crossed her legs. 'Mark Sway, right? Please do not call me ma'am, all right? My name is not Ms. Love or any of that, my name is Reggie. I'm old enough to be your grandmother, but you call me Reggie, okay?'

'Okay.'

'How old are you, Mark? Tell me a little about yourself.'

'I'm eleven. I'm in the fifth grade at Willow Road.'

'Why aren't you in school this morning?'

'It's a long story.'

'I see. And you're here because of this long story?'

'Yes.'

'Do you want to tell me this long story?'

'I think so.'

'Clint said you're supposed to meet with the FBI at noon. Is this true?'

'Yes. They want to ask me some questions at the hospital.'

She picked up a legal pad from the table and wrote something on it. 'The hospital?'

'It's part of the long story. Can I ask you something, Reggie?' It was strange calling this lady by a baseball name. He'd watched a cheap TV movie about the life of Reggie Jackson, and remembered the crowd chanting Reggie! Reggie! in perfect unison. Then there was the Reggie candy bar.

'Sure.' She grinned a lot, and it was obvious she enjoyed this scene with the kid who needed a lawyer. Mark knew the smiles would disappear if he made it through the story. She had pretty eyes, and they sparkled at him.

'If I tell you something, will you ever repeat it?' he asked.

'Of course not. It's privileged, confidential.'

'What does that mean?'

'It means simply that I can never repeat anything you tell me, unless you tell me I can repeat it.'

'Never?'

'Never. It's like talking to your doctor or minister. The conversations are secret and held in trust. Do you understand?'

'I think so. Under no circumstances – '

'Never. Under no circumstances can I tell anyone what you tell me.'

'What if I told you something that no one else knows?'

'I can't repeat it.'

'Something the police really want to know?'

'I can't repeat it.' She at first was amused by these questions, but his determination made her wonder.

'Something that could get you in a lot of trouble.'

'I can't repeat it.'

Mark looked at her without blinking for a long minute, and convinced himself she could be trusted. Her face was warm and her eyes were comforting. She was relaxed and easy to talk to.

'Any more questions?' she asked.

'Yeah. Where'd you get the name Reggie?'

'I changed my name several years ago. It was Regina, and I was married to a doctor, and then all sorts of bad things happened so I changed my name to Reggie.'

'You're divorced?'

'Yes.'

'My parents are divorced.'

'I'm sorry.'

'Don't be sorry. My brother and I were really happy when they got a divorce. My father drank a lot and beat us. Beat Mom too. Me and Ricky always hated him.'

'Ricky's your brother?'

'Yes. He's the one in the hospital.'

'What's the matter with him?'

'It's part of the long story.'

'When would you like to tell me this story?'

Mark hesitated a few seconds and thought about a few things. He wasn't quite ready to tell all. 'How much do you charge?'

'I don't know. What kind of case is it?'

'What kind of cases do you take?'

'Mostly cases involving abused or neglected children. Some abandoned children. Lots of adoptions. A few medical malpractice cases involving infants. But mainly abuse cases. I get some pretty bad cases.'

'Good, because this is a really bad one. One person is dead. One is in the hopsital. The police and FBI want to talk to me.'

'Look, Mark, I assume you don't have a lot of money to hire me, do you?'

'No.'

'Technically, you're supposed to pay me something as a retainer, and once this is done I'm your lawyer and we'll go from there. Do you have a dollar?'

'Yes.'

'Then why don't you give it to me as a retainer.'

Mark pulled a one-dollar bill from his pocket and handed it to her. 'This is all I've got.'

Reggie didn't want the kid's dollar, but she took it because ethics were ethics and because it would probably be his last payment. And he was proud of himself for hiring a lawyer. She would somehow return it to him.

She laid the bill on the table, and said, 'Okay, now I'm the lawyer and you're the client. Let's hear the story.'

He reached into his pocket again and pulled out the folded clipping from the newspaper Greenway had given them. He handed it to her. 'Have you seen this?' he asked. 'It's in this morning's paper.' His hand was trembling and the paper shook.

'Are you scared, Mark?'

'Sort of.'

'Try to relax, okay.'

'Okay. I'll try. Have you seen this?'

'No, I haven't seen the paper yet.' She took the clipping and read it. Mark watched her eyes closely.

'Okay,' she said when she finished.

'It mentions the body was found by two boys. Well, that's me and Ricky.'

'Well, I'm sure that must've been awful, but it's no crime to find a dead body.'

'Good. Because there's much more to the story.'

Her smile had disappeared. The pen was ready. 'I want to hear it now.'

Mark breathed deeply and rapidly. The four doughnuts churned away in his stomach. He was scared, but he also knew he would feel much better when it was over. He settled deep in the chair, took a long breath, and looked at the floor.

He started with his career as a smoker, and Ricky catching him, and going to the woods. Then the car, the water hose, the fat man who turned out to be Jerome Clifford. He spoke slowly because he wanted to remember it all, and because he wanted his new lawyer to write it all down.

Clint attempted to interrupt after fifteen minutes, but Reggie frowned at him. He quickly closed the door and disappeared.

The first account took twenty minutes with few interruptions from Reggie. There were gaps and holes, none the fault of Mark, just soft spots that she picked through during the second pass, which took another twenty minutes. They broke for coffee and ice water, all fetched by Clint, and Reggie moved the conversation to her desk where she spread out her notes and prepared for the third run-through of this remarkable story. She filled one legal pad, and started another. The smiles were long gone. The friendly, patronizing chitchat from the grandmother to her grandchild had been replaced with pointed questions picking for details.

The only details Mark withheld were the ones describing the exact location of the body of Senator Boyd Boyette, or rather Romey's story about the body. As the secret and confidential conversation unfolded, it became obvious to Reggie that Mark knew where the body was allegedly buried, and she skillfully and fearfully danced around this information. Maybe she would ask, maybe she wouldn't. But it would be the last thing discussed.

An hour after they started, she took a break and read the newspaper story twice. Then again. It seemed to fit. He knew too many details to be lying. This was not a story a hyperactive mind could fabricate. And the poor kid was scared to death.

Clint interrupted again at eleven-thirty to inform Reggie her next appointment had been waiting for an hour. Cancel it, Reggie said without looking from her notes, and Clint was gone. Mark walked around her office as she read. He stood in her window and watched the traffic on Third Street below. Then he returned to his seat and waited.

His lawyer was deeply troubled, and he almost felt sorry for her. All those names and faces in the yellow pages, and he had to drop this bomb on Reggie Love.

'What are you afraid of, Mark?' she asked, rubbing her eyes.

'Lots of things. I've lied to the police about this, and I think they know I'm lying. And that scares me. My little brother's in a coma because of me. It's all my fault. I lied to his doctor. And all that scares me. I don't know what to do, and I guess that's why I'm here. What should I do?'

'Have you told me everything?'

'No, but almost.'

'Have you lied to me?'

'No.'

'Do you know where the body is buried?'

'I think so. I know what Jerome Clifford told me.'

For a split second, Reggie was terrified he would blurt it out. But he didn't, and they stared at each other for a long time.

'Do you want to tell me where it is?' she finally asked.

'Do you want me to?'

'I'm not sure. What keeps you from telling me?'

'I'm scared. I don't want anybody to know that I know, because Romey told me his client had killed many people and was planning on killing Romey too. If he's killed lots of people, and if he thinks I know this secret, he'll come after me. And if I tell this stuff to the cops then he'll come after me for sure. He's in the Mafia, and that really scares me. Wouldn't it scare you?'

'I think so.'

'And the cops have threatened me if I don't tell the truth, and they think I'm lying anyway, and I just don't know what to do. Do you think I should tell the police and the FBI?'

Reggie stood and walked slowly to the window. She had no wonderful advice at this point. If she suggested that her newest client spill his guts to the FBI, and he followed her advice, his life could indeed be in danger. There was no law requiring him to tell. Obstruction of justice, maybe, but he was just a kid. They didn't know for certain what he knew, and if they couldn't prove it, he was safe.

'Let's do this, Mark. Don't tell me where the body is, okay? For now anyway. Maybe later, but not now. And let's meet with the FBI and listen to them. You won't have to say a word. I'll do the talking, and we'll both do the listening. And when it's over, you and I will decide what to do next.'

'Sounds good to me.'

'Does your mother know you're here?'

'No. I need to call her.'

Reggie found the number in the phone book and dialed the hospital. Mark explained to Dianne that he had gone for a walk and would be there in a minute. He was a smooth liar, Reggie noticed. He listened for a while and looked disturbed. 'How is he?' he asked. 'I'll be there in a minute.'

He hung up and looked at Reggie. 'Mom's upset. Ricky's coming out of the coma and she can't find Dr. Greenway.'

'I'll walk with you to the hospital.'

'That would be nice.'

'Where does the FBI want to meet?'

'I think at the hospital.'

She checked her watch and threw two fresh legal pads into her briefcase. She was suddenly nervous. Mark waited by the door.

# CHAPTER NINE

The second lawyer hired by Barry The Blade Muldanno to defend him on these obnoxious murder charges was another angry hatchet man by the name of Willis Upchurch, a rising star among the gang of boisterous mouthpieces trotting across the country performing for crooks and cameras. Upchurch had offices in Chicago and Washington, and any other city where he could hook a famous case and rent space. As soon as he talked with Muldanno after breakfast, he was on a plane to New Orleans to, first, organize a press conference, and, second, meet with his famous new client and plot a noisy defense. He had become somewhat rich and noted in Chicago for his passionate defense of mob assassins and drug traffickers, and in the past decade or so had been called in by mob brass around the country for all sorts of representation. His record was average, but it was not his won/lost ratio that attracted clients. It was his angry face and bushy hair and thunderous voice. Upchurch was a lawyer who wanted to be seen and heard in magazine articles, news stories, advice columns, quickie books, and gossip shows. He had opinions. He was unafraid of predictions. He was radical and would say anything, and this made him a favorite of the loony daytime TV talk shows.

He took only sensational cases with lots of headlines and cameras. Nothing was too repulsive for him. He preferred rich clients who could pay, but if a serial killer needed help, Upchurch would be there with a contract giving himself exclusive book and movie rights.

Though he enjoyed his notoriety immensely, and received some praise from the far left for his vigorous defense of indigent murderers, Upchurch was little more than a Mafia lawyer. He was owned by the mob, yanked around by their strings, and paid whenever they decided. He was allowed to roam a bit and spout at the mouth, but if they called, he came running.

And when Johnny Sulari, Barry's uncle, called at four in the morning, Willis Upchurch came running. The uncle explained the scarce facts about the untimely death of Jerome Clifford. Upchurch drooled into the receiver as Sulari asked him to fly immediately to New Orleans. He skipped to the bathroom at the thought of defending Barry The Blade Muldanno in front of all those cameras. He whistled in the shower when he thought of all the ink the case had already generated, and how he would now be the star. He grinned at himself in the mirror as he tied his ninety-dollar tie and thought of spending the next six months in New Orleans with the press at his beck and call.

This was why he went to law school!

The scene was frightening at first. The IV had been removed because Dianne was in the bed clutching Ricky and rubbing his head. She hugged him fiercely and wrapped her legs around his. He was moaning and grunting, twisting and jerking. His eyes were open, then shut. Dianne pressed her head to his and spoke softly through her tears. 'It's okay, baby. It's okay. Mommy's here. Mommy's here.'

Greenway stood close by, arms folded, rubbing his beard. He appeared puzzled, as if he hadn't seen this before. A nurse held the other side of the bed.

Mark entered the room slowly and no one noticed. Reggie had stopped at the nurses' station. It was almost noon, time for the FBI and all, but Mark knew immediately that no one in the room was remotely concerned with the cops and their questions.

'It's okay, baby. It's okay. Mommy's here.'

Mark inched to the foot of the bed for a closer look. Dianne managed a quick, uncomfortable smile, then closed her eyes and kept whispering to Ricky.

After a few long minutes of this, Ricky opened his eyes, seemed to notice and recognize his mother, and grew still. She kissed him a dozen times on the forehead. The nurse smiled and patted his shoulder and cooed something at him.

Greenway looked at Mark and nodded at the door. Mark followed him outside, into the quiet hallway. They walked slowly toward the end of it, away from the nurses' station.

'He woke up about two hours ago,' the doctor explained. 'It looks like he's coming out of it slowly.'

'Has he said anything yet?'

'Like what?'

'Well, you know, like about what happened yesterday.'

'No. He's mumbled a lot, which is a good sign, but he hasn't made any words yet.'

This was comforting, in a sense. Mark would have to stick close to the room just in case. 'So he's gonna be okay?'

'I didn't say that.' The lunch cart stopped in the middle of the hall and they walked around it. 'I think he'll be okay, but it could take time.' There was a long pause in which Mark worried if Greenway expected him to say something.

'How strong is your mother?'

'Pretty strong, I guess. We've been through a lot.'

'Where's the family? She'll need plenty of help.'

'There's no family. She has a sister in Texas, but they don't get along. And her sister has problems too.'

'Your grandparents?'

'No. My ex-father was an orphan. I figure his parents probably dumped him somewhere when they got to know him. My mother's father is dead, and her mother lives in Texas too. She's sick all the time.'

'I'm sorry.'

They stopped at the end of the hall and looked through a dirty window at downtown Memphis. The Sterick Building stood tall.

'The FBI is bugging me,' Greenway said.

Join the club, Mark thought. 'Where are they?'

'Room 28. It's a small conference room on the second floor that's seldom used. They said they'd be expecting me, you, and your mother at exactly noon, and they sounded very serious.' Greenway glanced at his watch, and started to walk back to the room. 'They are quite anxious.'

'I'm ready for them,' Mark said in a weak effort at boldness.

Greenway frowned at him. 'How's that?'

'I've hired us a lawyer,' he said proudly.

'When?'

'This morning. She's here now, down the hall.'

Greenway looked ahead but the nurses' station was around a bend in the corridor. 'The lawyer's here?' he asked in disbelief.

'Yep.'

'How'd you find a lawyer?'

'It's a long story. But I paid her myself.'

Greenway pondered this as he shuffled along. 'Well, your mother cannot leave Ricky right now, under any circumstances. And I certainly need to stay close.'

'No problem. Me and the lawyer will handle it.'

They stopped at Ricky's door, and Greenway hesitated before pushing it open. 'I can put them off until tomorrow. In fact, I can order them out of the hospital.' He was attempting to sound tough, but Mark knew better.

'No, thanks. They won't go away. You take care of Ricky and Mom, and me and the lawyer'll take care of the FBI.'

Reggie had found an empty room on the eighth floor, and they hurried down the stairs to use it. They were ten minutes late. She closed the door quickly, and said, 'Pull up your shirt.'

He froze, and stared at her.

'Pull up your shirt!' she insisted, and he began pulling at his bulky Memphis State Tigers sweatshirt. She opened her briefcase and removed a small, black recorder and a strip of plastic and Velcro. She checked the micro-cassette tape, then punched the buttons. Mark watched every move. She'd used this device many times before, he could tell. She pressed it to his stomach, and said, 'Hold it right here.' Then she threaded the plastic strap through a clip on the recorder, wrapped it around his mid-section and back, and fastened it snugly with the Velcro ends. 'Breathe deeply,' she said, and he did.

He tucked the sweatshirt into his jeans. Reggie took a step back and stared at his stomach. 'Perfect,' she said.

'What if they frisk me?'

'They won't. Let's go.'

She grabbed her briefcase, and they were out the door.

'How do you know they won't frisk me?' he asked again, very anxious. He walked fast to keep up with her. A nurse looked at them suspiciously.

'Because they're here to talk, not to arrest. Just trust me.'

'I trust you, but I'm really scared.'

'You'll do fine, Mark. Just remember what I told you.'

'Are you sure they can't see this thing?'

'I'm positive.' She pushed hard through a door and they were back in the stairwell, descending quickly on green concrete steps. Mark was one step behind. 'What if the beeper goes off or something and they freak out and pull guns? What then?'

'No beeper.' She took his hand, squeezed it hard, and zigzagged downward to the second floor. 'And they don't shoot kids.'

'They did in a movie once.'

The second floor of St. Peter's had been built many years before the ninth. It was gray and dirty, and the narrow corridors were swarming with the usual anxious traffic of nurses, doctors, technicians, and orderlies pushing stretchers, and patients rolling along in wheelchairs, and dazed families walking to nowhere in particular and trying to stay awake. Corridors met from all directions in chaotic little junctions, then branched out again in a hopeless labyrinth. Reggie asked three nurses about the location of Room 28, and the third pointed and talked but never stopped walking. They found a neglected hallway with ancient carpet and bad lighting, and six doors down to the right was their room. The door was cheap wood with no window.

'I'm scared, Reggie,' Mark said, staring at the door.

She held his hand firmly. If she was nervous, it was not apparent. Her face was calm. Her voice was warm and reassuring. 'Just do as I told you, Mark. I know what I'm doing.'

They retreated a step or two, and Reggie opened an identical door to Room 24. It was an abandoned coffee room now used for haphazard storage. 'I'll wait in here. Now, go knock on the door.'

'I'm scared, Reggie.'

She carefully felt the recorder, and worked her fingers around it until she pushed the button. 'Now go,' she instructed and pointed down the hall.

Mark took a deep breath and knocked on the door. He could hear chairs move inside. 'Come in,' someone said, and the voice was not friendly. He opened the door slowly, stepped inside, and closed it behind him. The room was narrow and long, just like the table in the center of it. No windows. No smiles from the two men who stood on each side of the table near the end. They could pass for twins – white button-down shirts, red-and-blue ties, dark pants, short hair.

'You must be Mark,' one said as the other stared at the door.

Mark nodded, but could not speak.

'Where's your mother?'

'Uh, who are you?' Mark managed to get it out.

The one on the right said, 'I'm Jason McThune, FBI, Memphis.' He stuck out his hand and Mark shook it limply. 'Nice to meet you, Mark.'

'Yeah, my pleasure.'

'And I'm Larry Trumann,' said the other. 'FBI, New Orleans.' Mark allowed Trumann the same feeble handshake. The agents exchanged nervous looks, and for an awkward second neither knew what to say.

Trumann finally pointed to the chair at the end of the table. 'Have a seat, Mark.' McThune nodded his agreement and almost smiled. Mark carefully sat down, terrified the Velcro would break away and the damned thing would somehow fall off. They'd handcuff his little butt so fast and throw him in the car and he'd never see his mother again. What would Reggie do then? They moved toward him in their rolling chairs. They slid their notepads on the table to within inches of him.

They were breathing on him, and Mark figured it was part of the game. Then he almost smiled. If they wanted to sit this close, fine. But the black recorder would get it all. No fading voices.

'We, uh, we really expected your mother and Dr. Greenway to be here,' Trumann said, glancing at McThune.

'They're with my brother.'

'How is he?' McThune asked gravely.

'Not too good. Mom can't leave his room right now.'

'We thought she'd be here,' Trumann said again and looked at McThune as if uncertain how to proceed.

'Well, we can wait a day or two until she's available,' Mark offered.

'No, Mark, we really need to talk now.'

'Maybe I can go get her.'

Trumann took his pen from his shirt pocket, and smiled at Mark. 'No, let's talk a few minutes, Mark. Just the three of us. Are you nervous?'

'A little. What do you want?' He was stiff with fear but breathing better. The recorder hadn't beeped or shocked him.

'Well, we want to ask you some questions about yesterday.'

'Do I need a lawyer?'

They looked at each other with perfectly symmetrical open mouths, and at least five seconds passed before McThune cocked his head at Mark and said, 'Of course not.'

'Why not?'

'Well, we just, you know, want to ask you a few questions. That's all. If you decide you want your mother, then we'll go get her. Or something. But you don't need a lawyer. Just a few questions, that's all.'

'I've already talked to the cops once. In fact, I talked to the cops for a long time last night.'

'We're not cops. We're FBI agents.'

'That's what scares me. I think maybe I need a lawyer to, you know, protect my rights and all.'

'You've been watching too much TV, kid.'

'The name's Mark, okay? Can you at least call me Mark?'

'Sure. Sorry. But you don't need a lawyer.'

'Yeah,' Trumann chimed in. 'Lawyers just get in the way. You have to pay them money, and they object to everything.'

'Don't you think we should wait until my mother can be here?'

They exchanged matching little smiles, and McThune said, 'Not really, Mark. I mean, we can wait if you want to, but you're a smart kid and we're really in a hurry here, and we just have a few quick questions for you.'

'Okay. I guess. If I have to.'

Trumann looked at his notepad, and went first. 'Good. You told the Memphis Police that Jerome Clifford was already dead when you

81

and Ricky found the car yesterday. Now, Mark, is this really the truth?' He sort of sneered toward the end of the question as if he knew damned well it wasn't the truth.

Mark fidgeted and looked straight ahead. 'Do I have to answer the question?'

'Sure you do.'

'Why?'

'Because we need to know the truth, Mark. We're the FBI, and we're investigating this thing, and we must know the truth.'

'What happens if I don't answer?'

'Oh, lots of things. We might be forced to take you down to our office, in the backseat of the car of course, no handcuffs, and ask some really tough questions. May have to bring along your mother too.'

'What will happen to my mother? Can she get in trouble?'

'Maybe.'

'What kind of trouble?'

They paused for a second and exchanged nervous looks. They had started on shaky ground, and things were getting shakier by the minute. Children are not to be interviewed without first talking to the parents.

But what the hell. His mother didn't show. He had no father. He was a poor kid, and here he was all alone. It was perfect, really. They couldn't ask for a better situation. Just a couple of quick questions.

McThune cleared his throat and went into a deep frown. 'Mark, have you ever heard of obstruction of justice?'

'I don't think so.'

'Well, it's a crime, okay. A federal offense. A person who knows something about a crime, and withholds this information from the FBI or the police, might be found guilty of obstruction.'

'What happens then?'

'Well, if found guilty, such a person might be punished. You know, sent to jail or something like that.'

'So, if I don't answer your questions, me and Mom might go to jail?'

McThune retreated a bit and looked at Trumann. The ice was getting thinner. 'Why don't you want to answer the question, Mark?' Trumann asked. 'Are you hiding something?'

'I'm just scared. And it doesn't seem fair since I'm just eleven years old and you're the FBI, and my mom's not here. I don't know what to do, really.'

'Can't you just answer the questions, Mark, without your mother? You saw something yesterday, and your mother was not around. She can't help you answer the questions. We just want to know what you saw.'

'If you were in my place, would you want a lawyer?'

'Hell no,' McThune said. 'I would never want a lawyer. Pardon my language, son, but they're just a pain in the ass. A real pain. If you have nothing to hide, you don't need a lawyer. Just answer our questions truthfully, and everything will be fine.' He was becoming angry, and this did not surprise Mark. One of them had to be angry. It was the good guy–bad guy routine Mark had seen a thousand times on television. McThune would get ugly, and Trumann would smile a lot and sometimes even frown at his partner for Mark's benefit, and this would somehow endear Trumann to Mark. McThune would then get disgusted and leave the room, and Mark would then be expected to spill his guts all over the table.

Trumann leaned to him with a drippy smile. 'Mark, was Jerome Clifford already dead when you and Ricky found him?'

'I take the Fifth Amendment.'

The drippy smile vanished. McThune's face reddened, and he shook his head in absolute frustration. There was a long pause as the agents stared at each other. Mark watched an ant crawl across the table and disappear under a notepad.

Trumann, the good guy, finally spoke. 'Mark, I'm afraid you've been watching too much television.'

'You mean, I can't take the Fifth Amendment?'

'Lemme guess,' McThune snarled. 'You watch "L.A. Law", right?'

'Every week.'

'Figures. Are you gonna answer any questions, Mark? Because if you're not, then we have to do other things.'

'Like what?'

'Go to court. Talk to the judge. Convince him to require you to talk to us. It's pretty nasty, really.'

'I need to go to the rest room,' Mark said as he slid his chair away from the table and stood.

'Uh, sure, Mark,' Trumann said, suddenly afraid they'd made him sick. 'I think it's just down the hall.' Mark was at the door.

'Take five minutes, Mark, we'll wait. No hurry.'

He left the room and closed the door behind him.

For seventeen minutes, the agents made small talk and played with their pens. They weren't worried. They were experienced agents with many tricks. They'd been here before. He would talk.

A knock, and McThune said, 'Come in.' The door opened, and an attractive lady of fifty or so walked in and closed the door as if this were her office. They scrambled to their feet just as she said, 'Keep your seats.'

'We're in a meeting,' Trumann said officially.

'You're in the wrong room,' McThune said rudely.

She placed her briefcase on the table and handed each agent a white card. 'I don't think so,' she said. 'My name is Reggie Love. I'm an attorney, and I represent Mark Sway.'

They took it well. McThune inspected the card while Trumann just stood there, arms dangling by his legs, trying to say something.

'When did he hire you?' McThune said, looking wildly at Trumann.

'That's really none of your business, is it now? I'm not hired. I'm retained. Sit down.'

She eased gracefully into her seat and rolled it to the table. They backed awkwardly into theirs, and kept their distance.

'Where's, uh, where's Mark?' Trumann asked.

'He's off somewhere taking the Fifth. Can I see your ID, please?'

They instantly reached for their jackets, fished around desperately, and simultaneously produced their badges. She held both, studied them carefully, then wrote something on a legal pad.

When she finished, she slid them across the table and asked, 'Did you in fact attempt to interrogate this child outside the presence of his mother?'

'No,' said Trumann.

'Of course not,' said McThune, shocked at this suggestion.

'He tells me you did.'

'He's confused,' said McThune. 'We initially approached Dr. Greenway, and he agreed to this meeting, which was supposed to include Mark, Dianne Sway, and the doctor.'

'But the kid showed up alone,' Trumann added quickly, very anxious to explain things. 'And we asked where his mother was, and he said she couldn't make it right now, and we sort of thought she was on her way or something, so we were just chitchatting with the kid.'

'Yeah, while we waited for Ms. Sway and the doctor,' McThune chimed in helpfully. 'Where were you during this?'

'Don't ask questions that are irrelevant. Did you advise Mark to talk to a lawyer?'

The agents locked eyes and searched each other for help. 'It wasn't mentioned,' Trumann said, shrugging innocently.

It was easier to lie because the kid wasn't there. And he was just a scared little kid who'd gotten things confused, and they were, after all, FBI agents, so she'd eventually believe them.

McThune cleared his throat and said, 'Uh, yeah, once, Larry remember Mark said something, or maybe I said something about "L.A. Law", and then Mark said he might need a lawyer, but he was sort of kidding and we, or at least I, took it as a joke. Remember, Larry?'

Larry now remembered. 'Oh, sure, yeah, something about "L.A. Law", Just a joke though.'

'Are you sure?' Reggie asked.

'Of course I'm sure,' Trumann protested. McThune frowned and nodded along with his partner.

'He didn't ask you guys if he needed a lawyer?'

They shook their heads and tried hopelessly to remember. 'I don't remember it that way. He's just a kid, and very scared, and I think he's confused,' McThune said.

'Did you advise him of his Miranda rights?'

Trumann smiled at this and was suddenly more confident. 'Of course not. He's not a suspect. He's just a kid. We need to ask him a few questions.'

'And you did not attempt to interrogate him without his mother's presence or consent?'

'No.'

'Of course not.'

'And you did not tell him to avoid lawyers after he asked your advice?'

'No ma'am.'

'No way. The kid's lying if he told you otherwise.'

Reggie slowly opened her briefcase and lifted out the black recorder and the micro-cassette tape. She sat them in front of her, and placed the briefcase on the floor. Special Agents McThune and Trumann stared at the devices and seemed to shrink a bit in their seats.

Reggie rewarded each with a bitchy smile, and said, 'I think we know who's lying.'

McThune slid two fingers down the bridge of his nose. Trumann rubbed his eyes. She let them suffer for a moment. The room was silent.

'It's all right here on tape, fellas. You boys attempted to interrogate a child outside the presence of his mother and without her consent. He specifically asked you if you shouldn't wait until she was available and you said no. You attempted to coerce the child with the threat of criminal prosecution not only for the child but also for his mother. He told you he was scared, and twice he specifically asked you if he needed a lawyer. You advised him not to get a lawyer, giving as one of your reasons the opinion that lawyers are a pain in the ass. Gentlemen, the pain is here.'

They sunk lower. McThune pressed four fingers against his forehead and gently rubbed. Trumann stared in disbelief at the tape, but was careful not to look at this woman. He thought of grabbing it, and ripping it to shreds, and stomping on it because it could be his career, but for some reason he believed with all his troubled heart that this woman had made a copy of it.

Getting slapped with a lie was bad enough, but their problems ran much deeper. There could be serious disciplinary proceedings. Reprimands. Transfers. Crap in the record. And at this moment, Trumann also believed that this woman knew all there was to know about the disciplining of wayward FBI agents.

'You wired the kid,' Trumann said meekly to no one in particular.

'Why not? No crime. You're the FBI, remember. You boys run more wire than AT&T.'

What a smartass! But then, she was a lawyer, wasn't she? McThune leaned forward, cracked his knuckles, and decided to offer some resistance. 'Look, Ms. Love, we – '

'It's Reggie.'

'Okay, okay. Reggie, uh, look, we're sorry. We, uh, got a little carried away, and, well, we apologize.'

'A little carried away? I could have your jobs for this.'

They were not about to argue with her. She was probably right, and even if there was room for debate they simply were not up to it.

'Are you taping this?' Trumann asked.

'No.'

'Okay, we were out of line. 'We're sorry.' He could not look at her.

Reggie slowly placed the tape in her coat pocket. 'Look at me, fellas.' They slowly lifted their eyes to hers, but it was painful. 'You've already proven to me that you'll lie, and that you'll lie quickly. Why should I trust you?'

Trumann suddenly slapped the table, hissed, and made a noisy show of standing and pacing to the end of the table. He threw up his hands. 'This is incredible. We came here with just a few questions for the kid, just doing our jobs, and now we're fighting with you. The kid didn't tell us he had a lawyer. If he'd told us, then we would have backed off. Why'd you do this? Why'd you deliberately pick this fight? It's senseless.'

'What do you want from the kid?'

'The truth. He's lying about what he saw yesterday. We know he's lying. We know he talked to Jerome Clifford before Clifford killed himself. We know the kid was in the car. Maybe I don't blame him for lying. He's just a kid. He's scared. But dammit, we need to know what he saw and heard.'

'What do you suspect he saw and heard?'

The nightmare of explaining this to Foltrigg suddenly hit Trumann, and he leaned against the wall. This is exactly why he hated lawyers – Foltrigg, Reggie, the next one he met. They made life so complicated.

'Has he told you everything?' McThune asked.

'Our conversations are extremely private.'

'I know that. But do you realize who Clifford was, and Muldanno and Boyd Boyette? Do you know the story?'

'I read the paper this morning. I've kept up with the case in New Orleans. You boys need the body, don't you?'

'You could say that,' Trumann said from the end of the table. 'But at this moment we really need to talk to your client.'

'I'll think about it.'

'When might you reach a decision?'

'I don't know. Are you boys busy this afternoon?'

'Why?'

'I need to talk to my client some more. Let's say we'll meet in my office at 3 P.M.' She took her briefcase and placed the recorder in it. It was obvious this meeting was over. 'I'll keep the tape to myself. It'll just be our little secret, okay?'

McThune nodded his agreement, but knew there was more.

'If I need something from you boys, like the truth or a straight answer, I expect to get it. If I catch you lying again, I'll use the tape.'

'That's blackmail,' said Trumann.

'That's exactly what it is. Indict me.' She stood and grabbed the doorknob. 'See you boys at three.'

McThune followed her. 'Uh, listen, Reggie, there's this guy who'll probably want to be at the meeting. His name is Roy Foltrigg, and he's – '

'Mr. Foltrigg is in town?'

'Yes. He arrived last night, and he'll insist on attending this meeting at your office.'

'Well, well. I'm honored. Please invite him.'

# CHAPTER TEN

The front page story in the *Memphis Press* about Clifford's death was written top to bottom by Slick Moeller, a veteran police reporter who had been covering crime and cops in Memphis for thirty years. His real name was Alfred, but no one knew it. His mother called him Slick, but not even she could remember the nickname's origins. Three wives and a hundred girlfriends had called him Slick. He did not dress exceptionally well, did not finish high school, did not have money, was blessed with average looks and build, drove a Mustang, could not keep a woman, and so no one knew why he was called Slick.

Crime was his life. He knew the drug dealers and pimps. He drank beer at the topless bars and gossiped with the bouncers. He kept charts on the who's who of motorcycle gangs that supplied the city with drugs and strippers. He could move deftly through the toughest projects of Memphis without a scratch. He knew the rank and file of the street gangs. He had busted no less than a dozen stolen car rings by tipping the police. He knew the ex-cons, especially the ones who returned to crime. He could spot a fencing operation simply by watching the pawnshops. His cluttered downtown apartment was most unremarkable except for an entire wall of emergency scanners and police radios. His Mustang had more junk than a police cruiser, except for a radar gun, and he didn't want one.

Slick Moeller lived and moved in the dark shadows of Memphis. He was often on the crime scene before the cops. He moved freely about the morgues and hospitals and black funeral parlors. He had nurtured thousands of contacts and sources, and they talked to Slick because he could be trusted. If it was off the record, then it was off the record. Background was background. An informant would never be compromised. Tips were guarded zealously. Slick was a man of his word, and even the street gang leaders knew it.

He was also on a first-name basis with virtually every cop in the city, many of whom referred to him with great admiration as the Mole. Mole Moeller did this. Mole Moeller said that. Since Slick had become his real name, the added nickname did not bother him. Nothing bothered Slick much. He drank coffee with cops in a hundred all-night diners around town. He watched them play softball, knew when their wives filed for divorce, knew when they got themselves reprimanded. He was at Central Headquarters at least twenty hours a day, it seemed, and it was not uncommon for cops to stop him and ask what was going on. Who got shot? Where was the holdup? Was the driver drunk? How many were killed? Slick told them as much as he could. He helped them whenever possible. His name was often mentioned in classes at the Memphis Police Academy.

And so it was no surprise to anyone that Slick spent the entire morning fishing around Central. He'd made his calls to New Orleans and knew the basics. He knew Roy Foltrigg and New Orleans FBI were in town, and that everything had been turned over to them. This intrigued him. It was not just a simple suicide; there were too many blank faces and 'no comments'. There was a note of some sort, and all questions about it were met with sudden denials. He could read the faces of some of these cops, been doing it for years. He knew about the boys and that the younger one was in bad shape. There were some fingerprints, some cigarette butts.

He left the elevator on the ninth floor and walked away from the nurses' station. He knew the number of Ricky's room, but this was the psychiatric ward and he was not about to go barging in with his questions. He didn't want to scare anyone, especially an eight-year-old kid who was in shock. He stuck two quarters in the soft drink machine and sipped on a diet Coke as if he'd been there all night walking the floors. An orderly in a light blue jacket pushed a cart of cleaning supplies to the elevator. He was a male, about twenty-five, long hair, and certainly bored with his menial job.

Slick stepped to the elevators, and when the door opened he followed the orderly onto it. The name Fred was sewn into the jacket above the pocket. They were alone.

'You work the ninth floor?' Slick asked, bored but with a smile.

'Yeah.' Fred did not look at him.

'I'm Slick Moeller with the *Memphis Press*, working on a story about Ricky Sway in Room 943. You know, the shooting and all.' He'd learned early in his career that it was best to tell them up front who and what.

Fred was suddenly interested. He stood erect and looked at Slick as if to say 'Yeah, I know plenty, but you're not getting it from me.' The cart between them was filled with Ajax, Comet, and twenty bottles of generic hospital supplies. A bucket of dirty rags and sponges covered the bottom tray. Fred was a toilet scrubber, but in a flash, he became a man with the inside scoop. 'Yeah,' he said calmly.

'Have you seen the kid?' Slick asked nonchalantly while watching the numbers light up above the door.

'Yeah, just left there.'

'I hear it's severe traumatic shock.'

'Don't know,' Fred said smugly as if his secrets were crucial. But he wanted to talk, and this never ceased to amaze Slick. Take an average person, tell him you're a reporter, and nine times out of ten he'll feel obligated to talk. Hell, he'll want to talk. He'll tell you his deepest secrets.

'Poor kid,' Slick mumbled to the floor as if Ricky were terminal. He said nothing else for a few seconds, and this was too much for Fred. What kind of a reporter was he? Where were the questions? He, Fred, knew the kid, had just left his room, had talked to his mother. He, Fred, was a player in this game.

'Yeah, he's in bad shape,' Fred said, also to the floor.

'Still in a coma?'

'In and out. May take a long time.'

'Yeah. That's what I heard.'

The elevator stopped on the fifth floor, but Fred's cart blocked the door and no one entered. The door closed.

'There's not much you can do for a kid like that,' Slick explained. 'I see it all the time. Kid sees something horrible in a split second, goes into shock, and it takes months to drag him out. All kinds of shrinks and stuff. Really sad. This Sway kid ain't that bad, is he?'

'I doubt it. Dr. Greenway thinks he'll snap out in a day or two. It'll take some therapy, but he'll be fine. I see it all the time. Thinking about med school myself.'

'Have the cops been snooping around?'

Fred cut his eyes around as if the elevator were bugged. 'Yeah, FBI was here all day. The family has already hired a lawyer.'

'You don't say.'

'Yeah, cops are real interested in this case, and they're talking to the kid's brother. Somehow a lawyer's got in the middle of it.'

The elevator stopped on the second floor, and Fred grabbed the handles on his cart.

'Who's the lawyer?' Slick asked.

The door opened and Fred pushed forward. 'Reggie somebody. I haven't seen him yet.'

'Thanks,' Slick said as Fred disappeared and the elevator filled. He rode it to the ninth floor to search for another fish.

By noon, the Reverend Roy Foltrigg and his sidekicks, Wally Boxx and Thomas Fink, had become a collective nuisance around the offices of the United States Attorney for the Western District of Tennessee. George Ord had held the office for seven years, and he did not care for Roy Foltrigg. He had not invited him to Memphis. Ord had met Foltrigg before at numerous conferences and seminars where the various U.S. Attorneys gather and plot ways to protect the government. Foltrigg usually spoke at these forums, always anxious to share his opinions and strategies and great victories with anyone who would listen.

After McThune and Trumann returned from the hospital and broke the frustrating news about Mark and his new lawyer, Foltrigg, along with Boxx and Fink, had once again situated himself in Ord's office to analyze the latest. Ord sat in his heavy leather chair behind his massive desk, and listened as Foltrigg interrogated the agents and occasionally barked orders to Boxx.

'What do you know about this lawyer?' he asked Ord.

'Never heard of her.'

'Surely someone in your office has dealt with her?' Foltrigg asked. The question was nothing short of a challenge for Ord to find someone with the scoop on Reggie Love. He left his office and consulted with an assistant. The search began.

Trumann and McThune sat very quietly in one corner of Ord's office. They had decided to tell no one of the tape, at least for the moment. Maybe later. Maybe, they hoped, never.

A secretary brought sandwiches, and lunch was eaten amid aimless speculation and chatter. Foltrigg was anxious to return to New Orleans, but more anxious to hear from Mark Sway. The fact that the kid had somehow obtained the services of an attorney was most troublesome. He was afraid to talk. Foltrigg was convinced Clifford had told him something, and as the day wore on he became more convinced the kid knew about the body. He was never one to hesitate before drawing conclusions. By the time the sandwiches were finished, he had persuaded himself and everyone in the room that Mark Sway knew precisely where Boyette was buried.

David Sharpinski, one of Ord's many assistants, presented himself at the office and explained he'd gone to law school at Memphis State with Reggie Love. He sat next to Foltrigg, in Wally's seat, and answered questions. He was busy and would rather have been working on a case.

'We finished law school together four years ago,' Sharpinski said.

'So she's only practiced for four years,' Foltrigg surmised quickly. 'What kind of work does she do? Criminal law? How much criminal law? Does she knew the ropes?'

McThune glanced at Trumann. They'd been nailed by a four-year lawyer.

'A little criminal stuff,' Sharpinski replied. 'We're pretty good friends. I see her around from time to time. Most of her work is with abused children. She's, well, she's had a pretty rough time of it.'

'What do you mean by that?'

'It's a long story, Mr. Foltrigg. She's a very complex person. This is her second life.'

'You know her well, don't you?'

'I do. We were in law school together for three years, off and on.'

'What do you mean, off and on?'

'Well, she had to drop out, let's say, emotional problems. In her first life, she was the wife of a prominent doctor, an ob-gyn. They were rich and successful, all over the society pages, charities, country clubs, you name it. Big house in Germantown. His and her Jaguars. She was on the board of every garden club and social organization in Memphis. She had worked as a schoolteacher to put him through med school, and after fifteen years of marriage he decided to trade her in for a new model. He started chasing women, and became involved with a younger nurse, who eventually became wife number two. Reggie's name back then was Regina Cardoni. She took it hard, filed for divorce, and things got nasty. Dr. Cardoni played hardball, and she slowly cracked up. He tormented her. The divorce dragged along. She felt publicly humiliated. Her friends were all doctors' wives, country club types, and they ran for cover. She even attempted suicide. It's all in the divorce papers in the clerk's office. He had a truckload of lawyers, and they pulled strings and had her committed to an institution. Then he cleaned her out.'

'Children?'

'Two, a boy and a girl. They were young teenagers, and of course he got custody. He gave them their freedom and enough money to finance it, and they turned their backs on their mother. He and his lawyers kept her in and out of mental institutions for two years, and by then it was all over. He got the house, kids, the trophy wife, everything.'

Describing this tragic history of a friend troubled Sharpinski, and he was obviously uncomfortable telling it all to Mr. Foltrigg. But most of it was public record.

'So how'd she become a lawyer?'

'It wasn't easy. The court order prohibited visitation with the children. She lived with her mother, who, I think, probably saved her life. I'm not sure, but I've heard that her mother mortgaged her home to finance some pretty heavy therapy. It took years, but she slowly pieced her life back together. She pulled out of it. The kids grew up and left Memphis. The boy went to prison for selling drugs. The daughter lives in California.'

'What kind of law student was she?'

'At times, very astute. She was determined to prove to herself she could succeed as a lawyer. But she continued to battle depression. She struggled with booze and pills, and finally dropped out halfway through. Then she came back, clean and dry, and finished with a vengeance.'

As usual, Fink and Boxx scribbled furiously on legal pads, trying importantly to take down every word as if Foltrigg would later quiz them on their notes. Ord listened but was more concerned with the pile of past due work on his desk. With each minute, he resented Foltrigg and this intrusion more and more. He was just as busy and important as Foltrigg.

'What kind of lawyer is she?' Roy asked.

Mean as hell, thought McThune. Shrewd as the devil, thought Trumann. Quite talented with electronics.

'She works hard, doesn't make much money, but then I don't think money is important to Reggie.'

'Where in the world did she get a name like Reggie?' Foltrigg asked, thoroughly baffled by it. Perhaps it comes from Regina, Ord thought to himself.

Sharpinski started to speak, then thought for a second. 'It would take hours to tell what I know about her, and I really don't want to. It's not important, is it?'

'Maybe,' Boxx snapped.

Sharpinski glared at him, then looked at Foltrigg. 'When she started law school, she tried to erase most of her past, especially the painful years. She took back her maiden name of Love. I guess she got Reggie from Regina, but I've never asked. But she did it legally, court orders and all, and there's no trace of the old Regina Cardoni, at least not on paper. She didn't talk about her past in law school, but she was the topic of a lot of conversation. Not that she gives a damn.'

'Is she still sober?'

Foltrigg wanted the dirt, and this irritated Sharpinski. To McThune and Trumann she appeared remarkably sober.

'You'll have to ask her, Mr. Foltrigg.'

'How often do you see her?'

'Once a month, maybe twice. We talk on the phone occasionally.'

'How old is she?' Foltrigg asked the question with a great deal of suspicion, as if perhaps Sharpinski and Reggie had a little thing going on the side.

'You'll have to ask her that too. Early fifties, I'd guess.'

'Why don't you call her now, ask her what's going on, just friendly small talk, you know. See if she mentions Mark Sway.'

Sharpinski gave Foltrigg a look that would sour butter. Then he looked at Ord, his boss, as if to say 'Can you believe this nut?' Ord rolled his eyes and began refilling a stapler.

'Because she's not stupid, Mr. Foltrigg. In fact, she's quite smart, and if I call she'll immediately know the reason why.'

'Perhaps you're right.'

'I am.'

'I would like for you to go with us at three to her office, if you can work it in.'

Sharpinski looked at Ord for guidance. Ord was deeply involved with the stapler. 'I can't do it. I'm very busy. Anything else?'

'No. You can go now,' Ord suddenly said. 'Thanks, David.' Sharpinski left the office.

'I really need him to go with me,' Foltrigg said to Ord.

'He said he was busy, Roy. My boys work,' he said, looking at Boxx and Fink, A secretary knocked and entered. She brought a two-page fax to Foltrigg, who read it with Boxx. 'It's from my office,' he explained to Ord as if he and he alone had such technology at his fingertips. They read on, and Foltrigg finally finished. 'Ever hear of Willis Upchurch?'

'Yes. He's a big shot defense lawyer from Chicago, lot of mob work. What's he done?'

'It says he just finished a press conference before a lot of cameras in New Orleans, and that he's been hired by Muldanno, that the case will be postponed, his client will be found not guilty, etc., etc.'

'That sounds like Willis Upchurch. I can't believe you haven't heard of him.'

'He's never been to New Orleans,' Foltrigg said with authority, as if he remembered every lawyer who dared to step on his turf.

'Your case just became a nightmare.'

'Wonderful. Just wonderful.'

# CHAPTER ELEVEN

The room was dark because the shades were pulled. Dianne was curled along the end of Ricky's bed, napping. After a morning of mumbling and thrashing and getting everyone's hopes aroused, he had drifted away again after lunch and had returned to the now familiar position of knees pulled to his chest, IV in the arm, thumb in the mouth. Greenway assured her repeatedly that he was not in pain. But after squeezing and kissing him for four hours, she was convinced her son was hurting. She was exhausted.

Mark sat on the foldaway bed with his back against the wall under the window, and stared at his brother and his mother in the bed. He, too, was exhausted, but sleep was not possible. Events where whirling around his overworked brain, and he tried to keep thinking. What was the next move? Could Reggie be trusted? He'd seen all those lawyer shows and movies on TV, and it seemed as if half the lawyers could be trusted and the other half were snakes. When should he tell Dianne and Dr. Greenway? If he told them everything, would it help Ricky? He thought about this for a long time. He sat on the bed listening to the quiet voices in the hallway as the nurses went about their work, and debated with himself about how much to tell.

The digital clock next to the bed gave the time as two thirty-two. It was impossible to believe that all this crap had happened in less than twenty-four hours. He scratched his knees and made the decision to tell Greenway everything that Ricky could have seen and heard. He stared at the blond hair sticking out from under the sheet, and he felt better. He would come clean, stop the lying, and do all he could to help Ricky. The things Romey told him in the car were not heard by anyone else, and, for the moment, and subject to advice from his lawyer, he would hold them private for a while.

But not for long. These burdens were getting heavy. This was not a game of hide-and-seek played by trailer park kids in the woods and ravines around Tucker Wheel Estates. This was not a sly little escape from his bedroom for a moonlit walk through the neighborhood. Romey stuck a real gun in his mouth. These were real FBI agents with real badges, just like the true crime stories on television. He had hired a real lawyer who'd stuck a real tape recorder to his stomach so she could outfox the FBI. The man who killed the Senator was a professional killer who'd murdered many others, according to Romey, and was a member of the Mafia, and those people would think nothing of rubbing out an eleven-year-old kid.

This was just too much for him to handle alone. He should be at school right now, fifth period, doing math which he hated but suddenly missed. He'd have a long talk with Reggie. She'd arrange a meeting with the FBI, and he'd tell them every stinking detail Romey had unloaded on him. Then they would protect him. Maybe they would send in bodyguards until the killer went to jail, or maybe they would arrest him immediately and all would be safe. Maybe.

Then he remembered a movie about a guy who squealed on the Mafia and thought the FBI would protect him, but suddenly he was on the run with bullets flying over his head and bombs going off. The FBI wouldn't return his phone calls because the guy didn't say something right in the courtroom. At last twenty times during the movie someone said, 'The mob never forgets.' In the final scene, this guy's car was blown to bits just as he turned the key, and he landed a half a mile away with no legs. As he took his final breath, a dark figure stood over him and said, 'The mob never forgets.' It wasn't much of a movie, but its message was suddenly clear to Mark.

He needed a Sprite. His mother's purse was on the floor under the bed, and he slowly unzipped it. There were three bottles of pills. There were two packs of cigarettes and for a split second he was tempted. He found the quarters and left the room.

A nurse whispered to an old man in the waiting area. Mark opened his Sprite and walked to the elevators. Greenway had asked him to stay in the room as much as possible, but he was tired of the room and tired of Greenway, and there seemed little chance of Ricky waking anytime soon. He entered the elevator and pushed the button to the basement. He would check out the cafeteria, and see what the lawyers were doing.

A man entered just before the doors closed, and seemed to look at him a bit too long. 'Are you Mark Sway?' he asked.

This was getting odd. Starting with Romey, he'd met enough strangers in the past twenty-four hours to last for months.

He was certain he'd never seen this guy before. 'Who are you?' he asked cautiously.

'Slick Moeller, with the *Memphis Press*, you know, the newspaper. You're Mark Sway, aren't you?'

'How'd you know?'

'I'm a reporter. I'm supposed to know these things. How's your brother?'

'He's doing great. Why do you want to know?'

'Working on a story about the suicide and all, and your name keeps coming up. Cops say you know more than you're telling.'

'When's it gonna be in the paper?'

'I don't know. Tomorrow maybe.'

Mark felt weak again, and stopped looking at him. 'I'm not answering any questions.'

'That's fine.' The elevator door suddenly opened and a swarm of people entered. Mark could no longer see the reporter. Seconds later it stopped on the fifth floor, and Mark darted out between two doctors. He hit the stairs and walked quickly to the sixth floor.

He'd lost the reporter. He sat on the steps in the empty stairwell, and began to cry.

Foltrigg, McThune, and Trumann arrived in the small but tasteful reception area of Reggie Love, Attorney-at-Law, at exactly 3 P.M., the appointed hour. They were met by Clint, who asked them to be seated, then offered coffee or tea, all of which they stiffly declined. Foltrigg informed Clint right properly that he was the United States Attorney for the Southern District of Louisiana, New Orleans, and that he was now present in this office and did not expect to wait. It was a mistake.

He waited for forty-five minutes. While the agents flipped through magazines on the sofa, Foltrigg paced the floor, glanced at his watch, fumed, scowled at Clint, even barked at him twice and each time was informed Reggie was on the phone with an important matter. As if Foltrigg was there for an unimportant matter. He wanted to leave so badly. But he couldn't. For one of the rare times in his life he had to absorb a subtle ass-kicking without a fight.

Finally, Clint asked them to follow him to a small conference room lined with shelves of heavy law books. Clint instructed them to be seated, and explained that Reggie would be right with them.

'She's forty-five minutes late,' Foltrigg protested.

'That's quite early for Reggie, sir,' Clint said with a smile as he closed the door. Foltrigg sat at one end of the table with an agent close to each side. They waited.

'Look, Roy,' Trumann said with hesitation, 'you need to be careful with this gal. She might be taping this.'

'What makes you think so?'

'Well, uh, you just never – '

'These Memphis lawyers do a lot of taping,' McThune added helpfully. 'I don't know about New Orleans, but it's pretty bad up here.'

'She has to tell us up front if she's taping, doesn't she?' Foltrigg asked, obviously without a clue.

'Don't bet on it,' said Trumann. 'Just be careful, okay.'

The door opened and Reggie entered, forty-eight minutes late. 'Keep your seats,' she said as Clint closed the door behind her. She offered a hand to Foltrigg, who was half-standing. 'Reggie Love, you must be Roy Foltrigg.'

'I am. Nice to meet you.'

'Please be seated.' She smiled at McThune and Trumann, and for a brief second all three of them thought about the tape. 'Sorry I'm late,' she said as she sat alone at her end of the conference table. They were eight feet away, huddled together like wet ducks.

'No problem,' Foltrigg said loudly as if it was very much a problem.

She pulled a large tape recorder from a hidden drawer in the table and sat it in front of her. 'Mind if I tape this little conference?' she asked as she plugged in the microphone. The little conference would be taped whether they liked it or not. 'I'll be happy to provide you with a copy of the tape.'

'Fine with me,' Foltrigg said, pretending he had a choice.

McThune and Trumann stared at the tape recorder. How nice of her to ask! She smiled at the two of them as they smiled at her, then all three smiled at the recorder. She was as subtle as a rock through a window. The damnable micro-cassette could not be far away.

She pushed a button. 'Now, what's up?'

'Where's your client?' Foltrigg asked. He leaned forward and it was clear he would do all the talking.

'At the hospital. The doctor wants him to stay in the room near his brother.'

'When can we talk to him?'

'You're assuming that you will in fact talk to him.' She looked at Foltrigg with very confident eyes. Her hair was gray and cut like a boy's. The face was quite colorful. The eyebrows were dark. The lips were soft red and meticulously painted. The skin was smooth and free of heavy make-up. It was a pretty face, with bangs, and eyes that glowed with a calm steadiness. Foltrigg looked at her, and thought of all the misery and suffering she'd seen. She covered it well.

McThune opened a file and flipped through it. In the past two hours they had assembled a two-inch-thick dossier on Reggie Love, aka Regina L. Cardoni. They had copied the divorce papers and commitment proceedings from the clerk's office in the county court-house. The mortgage papers and land records on her mother's home were in the folder. Two Memphis agents were attempting to obtain her law school transcripts.

Foltrigg loved the trash. Whatever the case and whoever the opponent, Foltrigg always wanted the dirt. McThune read the sordid legal history of the divorce with its allegations of adultery and alcohol and dope and unfitness and, ultimately, the attempted suicide. He read it carefully, though, without being seen. He did not, under any circumstances, want to make this woman angry.

'We need to talk to your client, Ms. Love.'

'It's Reggie. Okay, Roy?'

'Whatever. We think he knows something, plain and simple.'

'Such as?'

'Well, we're convinced little Mark was in the car with Jerome Clifford prior to his death. We think he spent more than a few seconds with him. Clifford was obviously planning to kill himself, and we have reason to believe he wanted to tell someone where his client, Mr. Muldanno, had disposed of the body of Senator Boyette.'

'What makes you think he wanted to tell?'

'It's a long story, but he had contacted an assistant in my office on two occasions and hinted that he might be willing to cut some deal and get out. He was scared. And he was drinking a lot. Very erratic behavior. He was sliding off the deep end, and wanted to talk.'

'Why do you think he talked to my client?'

'There's just a chance, okay. And we must look under every stone. Surely you understand.'

'I sense a bit of desperation.'

'A lot of desperation, Reggie. I'm leveling with you. We know who killed the Senator, but, frankly, I'm not ready for trial without a corpse.' He paused and smiled warmly at her. Despite his many obnoxious flaws, Roy had spent hours before juries and he knew how and when to act sincere.

And she'd spent many hours in therapy, and she could spot a fake. 'I'm not telling you that you cannot talk to Mark Sway. You cannot talk to him today, but maybe tomorrow. Maybe the next day. Things are moving fast. Mr. Clifford's body is still warm. Let's slow down a bit, and take it one step at a time. Okay?'

'Okay.'

'Now, convince me Mark Sway was in the car with Jerome Clifford prior to the shooting.'

No problem. Foltrigg looked at a notepad, and reeled off the many places where fingerprints were matched. Rear tail-lights, trunk, front passenger door handle and lock switch, dash, gun, bottle of Jack Daniels. There was a tentative match on the hose, but it was not definite. They were working on it. Foltrigg was the prosecutor now, building a case with indisputable evidence . . .

Reggie took pages of notes. She knew Mark had been in the car, but she had no idea he'd left such a wide trail.

'The whiskey bottle?' she asked.

Foltrigg flipped a page for the details. 'Yes, three definite prints. No question about it.'

Mark had told her about the gun, but not about the bottle. 'Seems a bit strange, doesn't it?'

'It's all strange at this point. The police officers who talked to him do not recall smelling alcohol, so I don't think he drank any of it. I'm sure he could explain it, you know, if only we could talk to him.'

'I'll ask him.'

'So he didn't tell you about the bottle?'

'No.'

'Did he explain the gun?'

'I cannot divulge what my client has explained to me.'

Foltrigg waited desperately for a hint, and this really angered him. Trumann likewise waited breathlessly. McThune stopped reading the report of a court-appointed psychiatrist.

'So he hasn't told you everything?' Foltrigg asked.

'He's told me a lot. It's possible he missed some of the details.'

'These details could be crucial.'

'I'll determine what's crucial and what's not. What else do you have?'

'Hand her the note,' Foltrigg instructed Trumann, who produced it from a file and handed it to her. She read it slowly, then read it again. Mark had not mentioned the note.

'Obviously two different pens,' Foltrigg explained. 'We found the blue one in the car, a cheap Bic, out of ink. Just speculating, it looks as though Clifford tried to add something after Mark left the car. The word 'where' seems to indicate the boy was gone. It's obvious they talked, exchanged names, and that the kid was in the car long enough to touch everything.'

'No prints on this?' she asked, waving the note.

'None. We've checked it thoroughly. The kid did not touch it.'

She calmly placed it next to her legal pad and folded her hands together. 'Well, Roy, I think the big question is, how did you guys match his fingerprints? How did you obtain one of his to match with the ones in the car?' She asked this with the same confident sneer Trumann and McThune had seen when she produced the tape less than four hours ago.

'Very simple. We lifted one off a soft drink can at the hospital last night.'

'Did you ask either Mark Sway or his mother before doing so?'
'No.'
'So you invaded the privacy of an eleven-year-old child.'
'No. We are trying to obtain evidence.'
'Evidence? Evidence for what? Not for a crime, I dare say. The crime has been committed and the body has been disposed of. You just can't find it. What other crime do we have here? Suicide? Watching a suicide?'
'Did he watch the suicide?'
'I can't tell you what he did or saw because he has confided in me as his lawyer. Our talks are privileged, you know that, Roy. What else have you taken from this child?'
'Nothing.'
She snorted as if she didn't believe this. 'What else do you have?'
'This is not enough?'
'I want it all.'
Foltrigg flipped pages back and forth and did a slow burn. 'You've seen the puffy left eye and the knot on his forehead. The police said there was a trace of blood on his lip when they found him at the scene. Clifford's autopsy revealed a spot of blood on the back of his right hand, and it's not his type.'
'Let me guess. It's Mark's.'
'Probably so. Same blood type.'
'How do you know his blood type?'
Foltrigg dropped the legal pad and rubbed his face. The most effective defense lawyers are those who keep the fighting away from the issues. They bitch and throw rocks over the tiny subplots of a case and hope the prosecution and the jury are diverted away from the obvious guilt of their clients. If there's something to hide, then scream at the other guy for violating technicalities. Right now they should be nailing down the facts of what, if anything, Clifford said to Mark. It should be so simple. But now the kid had a lawyer, and here they were trying to explain how they obtained certain crucial information. There was nothing wrong with lifting prints from a can without asking. Good police work. But from the mouth of a defense lawyer, it's suddenly a vicious invasion of privacy. Next she would threaten a lawsuit. And now, the blood.
She was good. He found it difficult to believe she'd been practicing only four years.
'From his brother's hospital admission records.'
'And how did you obtain the hospital records?'
'We have ways.'

Trumann braced for a reprimand. McThune hid behind the file. They had been burned by this temper. She'd made them stutter and stammer and sweat blood, and now it was time for old Roy to take a few punches. It was almost funny.

But she kept her cool. She slowly extended a skinny finger with white nail polish and pointed it at Roy. 'If you get near my client again and attempt to obtain anything from him without my permission, I'll sue you and the FBI. I'll file an ethics complaint with the state bar in Louisiana and Tennessee, and I'll haul your ass into Juvenile Court here and ask the judge to lock you up.' The words were spoken in an even voice, no emotion, but so matter-of-factly that everyone in the room, including Roy Foltrigg, knew that she would do exactly as she promised.

He smiled and nodded. 'Fine. Sorry if we've gotten a bit out of line. But we're anxious, and we must talk to your client.'

'Have you told me everything you know about Mark?'

Foltrigg and Trumann checked their notes. 'Yes, I think so.'

'What's that?' she insisted, pointing to the file McThune was lost in. He was reading about her suicide attempt, by pills, and it was alleged in the pleadings, sworn under oath, that she'd been in a coma for four days before pulling out. Evidently, her ex-husband, Dr. Cardoni, a real piece of scum according to the pleadings, was a nasty sort with all the money and lawyers, and as soon as Regina/Reggie here took the pills he ran to court with a pile of motions to get the kids. Looking at the dates stamped on the papers, it was obvious the good doctor was filing requests and asking for hearings while she was lost in a coma and fighting for her life.

McThune didn't panic. He looked at her innocently and said, 'Just some of our internal stuff.' It was not a lie, because he was afraid to lie to her. She had the tape, and had sworn them to truthfulness.

'About my client?'

'Oh no.'

She studied her legal pad. 'Let's meet again tomorrow,' she said. It was not a suggestion, but a directive.

'We're really in a hurry, Reggie,' Foltrigg pleaded.

'Well I'm not. And I guess I'm calling the shots, aren't I?'

'I guess you are.'

'I need time to digest this and talk with my client.'

This was not what they wanted, but it was painfully clear this was all they would get. Foltrigg dramatically screwed the top onto his pen and slid his notes into his briefcase. Trumann and McThune followed his lead and for a minute the table shook as they shuffled paper and files and restuffed everything.

'What time tomorrow?' Foltrigg asked, slamming his briefcase and pushing away from the table.

'Ten. In this office.'

'Will Mark Sway be here?'

'I don't know.'

They stood and filed out of the room.

# CHAPTER TWELVE

Wally Boxx called the office in New Orleans at least four times every hour. Foltrigg had forty-seven Assistant U.S. Attorneys fighting all sorts of crime and protecting the interests of the government, and Wally was in charge of relaying orders from the boss in Memphis. In addition to Thomas Fink, three other attorneys were working on the Muldanno case, and Wally felt the need to call them every fifteen minutes with instructions, and the latest on Clifford. By noon, the entire office knew of Mark Sway and his little brother. The place buzzed with gossip and speculation. How much did the kid know? Would he lead them to the body? Initially, these questions were pondered in hushed whispers by the three Muldanno prosecutors, but by mid-afternoon the secretaries in the coffee room were exchanging wild theories about the suicide note and what was told to the kid before Clifford ate his bullet. All other work virtually stopped as Foltrigg's office waited for Wally's next call.

Foltrigg had been burned by leaks before. He'd fired people he suspected of talking too much. He'd required polygraphs for all lawyers, paralegals, investigators, and secretaries who worked for him. He kept sensitive information under lock and key for fear of leakage by his own people. He lectured and threatened.

But Roy Foltrigg was not the sort of person to inspire intense loyalty. He was not appreciated by many of the assistants. He played the political game. He used cases for his own raw ambition. He hogged the spotlight and took credit for all the good work, and blamed his subordinates for all the bad. He sought marginal indictments against elected officials for a few cheap headlines. He investigated his enemies and dragged their names through the press. He was a political whore whose only talent with the law was in the courtroom where he preached to juries and quoted scripture. He was a Reagan appointee with one year left, and most of the assistant attorneys were counting the days. They encouraged him to run for office. Any office.

The reporters in New Orleans began calling at 8 A.M. They wanted an official comment about Clifford from Foltrigg's office. They did not get one. Then Willis Upchurch performed at two o'clock, with Muldanno glowering at his side, and more reporters came snooping around the office. There were hundreds of phone calls to Memphis and back.

People talked.

They stood before the dirty window at the end of the hall on the ninth floor, and watched the rush-hour traffic of downtown. Dianne nervously lit a Virginia Slim, and blew a heavy cloud of smoke. 'Who is this lawyer?'

'Her name is Reggie Love.'

'How'd you find her?'

He pointed to the Sterick Building four blocks away. 'I went to her office in that building right there, and I talked to her.'

'Why, Mark?'

'These cops scare me, Mom. The police and FBI are crawling all over this place. And reporters. I had one catch me in the elevator this afternoon. I think we need some legal advice.'

'Lawyers don't work for free, Mark. You know we can't afford a lawyer.'

'I've already paid her,' he said like a tycoon.

'What? How can you pay a lawyer?'

'She wanted a small retainer, and she got one. I gave her a dollar from that five that went for doughnuts this morning.

'She's working for a dollar? She must be a great lawyer.'

'She's pretty good. I've been impressed so far.'

Dianne shook her head in amazement. During her nasty divorce, Mark, then age nine, had constantly criticized her lawyer. He watched hours of reruns of 'Perry Mason' and never missd 'L.A. Law.' It had been years since she'd won an argument with him.

'What has she done so far?' Dianne asked, as if she were emerging from a dark cave and seeing sunlight for the first time in a month.

'At noon, she met with some FBI agents, and ripped them up pretty good. And later, she met with them again in her office. I haven't talked with her since then.'

'What time is she coming here?'

'Around six. She wants to meet you and talk to Dr. Greenway. You'll really like her, Mom.'

Dianne filled her lungs with smoke, and exhaled. 'But why do we need her, Mark? I don't understand why she's entered the picture. You've done nothing wrong. You and Ricky saw the car, you tried to help the man, but he shot himself anyway. And you guys saw it. Why do you need a lawyer?'

'Well, I did lie to the cops at first, and that scares me. And I was afraid we might get in trouble because we didn't stop the man from shooting himself. It's all pretty scary, Mom.'

She watched him intently as he explained this, and he avoided her eyes. There was a long pause. 'Have you told me everything?' She asked this very slowly, as if she knew.

At first he'd lied to her at the trailer while they waited on the ambulance, with Hardy lingering nearby, all ears. Then last night, in Ricky's room, under cross-examination by Greenway, he had told the first version of the truth. He remembered how sad she had been when she heard this revised story, and later how she'd said, 'You never lie to me, Mark.'

They'd been through so much together, and here he was dancing around the truth, dodging questions, telling Reggie more than he'd told his mother. It made him sick.

'Mom, it all happened so fast yesterday. It was all a blur in my mind last night, but I've been thinking about it today. Thinking hard. I've gone through each step, minute by minute, and I'm remembering things now.'

'Such as?'

'Well, you know how this has affected Ricky. I think it shocked me sort of like that. Not as bad, but I'm remembering things now that I should have remembered last night when I talked to Dr. Greenway. Does this make sense?'

Actually, it did make sense. Dianne was suddenly concerned. Two boys see the same event. One goes into shock. It's reasonable to believe the other would be affected. She hadn't thought of this. She leaned down next to him. 'Mark, are you all right?'

He knew he had her. 'I think so,' he said with a frown, as if a migraine were upon him.

'What have you remembered?' she asked cautiously.

He took a deep breath. 'Well, I remember – '

Greenway cleared his throat and appeared from nowhere. Mark whirled around. 'I need to be going,' Greenway said, almost as an apology. 'I'll check back in a couple of hours.'

Dianne nodded but said nothing.

Mark decided to get it over with. 'Look, Doctor, I was just telling Mom that I'm remembering things now for the first time.'

'About the suicide?'

'Yes sir. All day long I've been seeing flashes and recalling details. I think some of it might be important.'

Greenway looked at Dianne. 'Let's go back to the room and talk,' he said.

They walked to the room, closed the door behind them, and listened as Mark tried to fill in the gaps. It was a relief to unload this baggage, though he did most of the talking in the direction of the floor. It was an act, this painful pulling of scenes from a shocked and badly scarred mind and he carried it off with finesse. He paused quite often, long pauses in which he searched for words to describe what was already firmly etched in his memory. He glanced at Greenway occasionally, and the doctor's expression never changed. He glanced at his mother from time to time, and she didn't appear to be disappointed. She maintained a look of motherly concern.

But when he got to the part about Clifford grabbing him, he could see them fidget. He kept his troubled eyes on the floor. Dianne sighed when he talked about the gun. Greenway shook his head when he told of the gunshot through the window. At times, he thought they were about to yell at him for lying last night, but he plowed ahead, obviously disturbed and deep in thought.

He carefully replayed every single event that Ricky could have seen and heard. The only details he kept to himself were Clifford's confessions. He vividly recalled the crazy stuff: La La Land and floating off to see the wizard.

When he finished, Dianne was sitting on the foldaway bed rubbing her head, talking about Valium. Greenway sat in a chair, hanging on every word. 'Is this all of it, Mark?'

'I don't know. It's all I can remember right now,' he mumbled, as if he had a toothache.

'You were actually in the car?' Dianne said without opening her eyes.

He pointed to his slightly swollen left eye. 'You see this. This is where he slapped me when I tried to get out of the car. I was dizzy for a long time. Maybe I was unconscious, I don't know.'

'You told me you were in a fight at school.'

'I don't remember telling you that, Mom, and if I did, well, maybe I was in shock or something.' Dammit. Trapped by another lie.

Greenway stroked his beard. 'Ricky saw you get grabbed, thrown in the car, the gunshot. Wow.'

'Yeah. It's coming back to me, real clear. I'm sorry I didn't remember it sooner, but my mind just went blank. Sort of like Ricky here.'

Another long pause.

'Frankly, Mark, I find it hard to believe you couldn't remember some of this last night,' Greenway said.

'Gimme a break, would you? Look at Ricky here. He saw what happened to me, and it drove him to the ozone. Did we talk last night?'

'Come on, Mark,' Dianne said.

'Of course we talked,' Greenway said with at least four new wrinkles across his forehead.

'Yeah, I guess we did. Don't remember much of it though.'

Greenway frowned at Dianne and their eyes locked. Mark walked into the bathroom and drank water out of a paper cup.

'It's okay,' Dianne said. 'Have you told the police this?'

'No. I just remembered it. Remember?'

Dianne nodded slowly and managed a very slight grin at Mark. Her eyes were narrow, and his suddenly found the floor. She believed all of his story about the suicide, but this sudden surge of clear memory did not fool her. She would deal with him later.

Greenway had his doubts too, but he was more concerned with treating his patient than reprimanding Mark. He gently stroked his beard and studied the wall. There was a long pause.

'I'm hungry,' Mark finally said.

Reggie arrived an hour late with apologies. Greenway had left for the day. Mark stumbled through the introductions. She smiled warmly at Dianne as they shook hands, then sat beside her on the bed. She asked her a dozen questions about Ricky. She was an immediate friend of the family, anxious and properly concerned about everything. What about her job? School? Money? Clothes?

Dianne was tired and vulnerable, and it was nice to talk to a woman. She opened up, and they went on for a while about Greenway saying this and that, about everything unrelated to Mark and his story and the FBI, the only reason for Reggie's being there.

Reggie had a sack of deli sandwiches and chips, and Mark spread them on a crowded table by Ricky's bed. He left the room to get drinks. They hardly noticed.

He bought two Dr Peppers in the waiting area and returned to the room without being stopped by cops, reporters, or Mafia gunmen. The women were deep into a conversation about McThune and Trumann trying to interrogate Mark. Reggie was telling the story in such a manner that Dianne had no choice but to mistrust the FBI. They were both shocked. Dianne was alive and animated for the first time in many hours.

Jack Nance and Associates was a quiet firm that advertised itself as security specialists, but was in fact nothing more than a couple of private investigators. Its ad in the yellow pages was one of the smallest in town. It did not want the run-of-the-mill divorce cases in which one spouse was sleeping around and the other wanted photos. It did not own a polygraph. It did not snatch children. It did not track down thieving employees.

Jack Nance himself was an ex-con with an impressive record who'd managed to avoid trouble for ten years. His associate was Cal Sisson, also a convicted felon who'd run a terrific scam with a bogus roofing company. Together they scratched out a nice living doing dirty work for rich people. They had once broken both hands of the teenaged boyfriend of a rich client's daughter after the kid slapped her. They had once deprogrammed a couple of Moonies, the children of another rich client. They were not afraid of violence. More than once, they had beaten a business rival who'd taken money from a client. They had once burned the downtown love nest of a client's wife and her lover.

There was a market for their brand of investigative work, and they were known in small circles as two very nasty and efficient men who would take your cash, do your dirty work, and leave no trail. They achieved amazing results. Every client came by referral.

Jack Nance was in his cluttered office after dark when someone knocked on the door. The secretary had left for the day. Cal Sisson was stalking a crack dealer who'd hooked the son of a client. Nance was around forty, not a big man, but compact and extremely agile. He walked through the secretary's office and opened the front door. The face was a strange one.

'Looking for Jack Nance,' the man said.

'That's me.'

The man stretched out his hand, and they shook. 'My name's Paul Gronke. Can I come in?'

Nance opened the door wider and motioned for Gronke to enter. They stood in front of the secretary's desk. Gronke looked around the cramped and messy room.

'It's late,' Nance said. 'What do you want?'

'I need some fast work.'

'Who referred you?'

'I've heard of you. Word gets around.'

'Give me a name.'

'Okay. J. L. Grainger. I think you helped him on a business deal. He also mentioned a Mr. Schwartz who was also quite pleased with your work.'

Nance thought about this for a second as he studied Gronke. He was a burly man with a thick chest, late thirties, badly dressed but didn't know it. Because of his clipped drawl, Nance immediately

knew he was from New Orleans. 'I got a two-thousand-dollar retainer up front, nonrefundable, all in cash, before I lift a finger.'
Gronke pulled a roll of bills from his left front pocket and peeled off
twenty big ones. Nance relaxed. It was his fastest retainer in ten
years. 'Sit down,' he said, taking the money and waving at a sofa.
'I'm listening.'

Gronke took a folded newspaper clipping from his jacket and
handed it to Nance. 'Did you see this in today's paper?'

Nance looked at it. 'Yeah. I read it. How are you involved?'

'I'm from New Orleans. In fact, Mr. Muldanno is an old pal, and
he's very disturbed to see his name suddenly show up here in the
Memphis paper. It says he has Mafia ties and all. Can't believe a
word in the newspapers, The press is going to ruin this country.'

'Was Clifford his lawyer?'

'Yeah. But now he has a new one. That's not important, though.
Lemme tell you what's worrying him. He has a good source telling
him these two boys know something.'

'Where are the boys?'

'One's in the hospital, a coma or something. He freaked out when
Clifford shot himself. His brother was actually in the car with Clifford prior to the shooting, and we're afraid this kid might know
something. He's already hired a lawyer, and is refusing to talk to the
FBI. Looks real suspicious.'

'Where do I fit in?'

'We need someone with Memphis connections. We need to see the
kid. We need to know where he is at all times.'

'What's his name?'

'Mark Sway. He's at the hospital, we think, with his mother. Last
night they stayed in the room with the younger brother, a kid named
Ricky Sway. Ninth floor at St. Peter's. Room 943. We want you to
find the kid, determine his location as of now, and then watch him.'

'Easy enough.'

'Maybe not. There are cops and probably FBI agents watching
too. The kid's attracting a crowd.'

'I get a hundred bucks an hour, cash.'

'I know that.'

She called herself Amber, which along with Alexis happened to be
the two most popular acquired names among strippers and whores in
the French Quarter. She answered the phone, then carried it a few
feet to the tiny bathroom where Barry Muldanno was brushing his
teeth. 'It's Gronke,' she said, handing it to him. He took it, turned off

the water, and admired her naked body as she crawled under the sheets. He stepped into the doorway. 'Yeah,' he said into the phone.

A minute later, he placed the phone on the table next to the bed, and quickly dried himself off. He dressed in a hurry. Amber was somewhere under the covers.

'What time are you going to work?' he asked, tying his tie.

'Ten. What time is it?' Her head appeared between the pillows.

'Almost nine. I gotta run an errand. I'll be back.'

'Why? You got what you wanted.'

'I might want some more. I pay the rent here, sweetheart.'

'Some rent. Why don't you move me outta this dump? Get me a nice place?'

He tugged his sleeves from under his jacket, and admired himself in the mirror. Perfect, just perfect. He smiled at Amber. 'I like it here.'

'It's a dump. If you treated me right, you'd get me a nice place.'

'Yeah, yeah. See you later, sweetheart.' He slammed the door. Strippers. Get them a job, then an apartment, buy some clothes, feed them nice dinners, and then they get culture and start making demands. They were an expensive habit, but one he could not break.

He bounced down the steps in his alligator loafers, and opened the door onto Dumaine. He looked right and left, certain that someone was watching, and took off around the corner onto Bourbon. He moved in shadows, crossing and recrossing the street, then turned corners and retraced some of his steps. He zigzagged for eight blocks, then disappeared into Randy's Oysters on Decatur. If they stuck to him, they were supermen.

Randy's was a sanctuary. It was an old-fashioned New Orleans eatery, long and narrow, dark and crowded, off-limits for tourists, owned and operated by the family. He ran up the cramped staircase to the second floor where reserved seating was required and only a select few could get reservations. He nodded to a waiter, grinned at a beefy thug, and entered a private room with four tables. Three were empty, and at the fourth a solitary figure sat in virtual darkness reading by the light of a real candle. Barry approached, stopped, and waited to be invited. The man saw him and waved at a chair. Barry obediently took a seat.

Johnny Sulari was the brother of Barry's mother, and the undisputed head of the family. He owned Randy's, along with a hundred other assorted ventures. As usual, he was working tonight, reading financial statements by candlelight and waiting for dinner. This was Tuesday, just another night at the office. On Friday, Johnny would be here with an Amber or an Alexis or a Sabrina, and on Saturday he would be here with his wife.

He did not appreciate the interruption. 'What is it?' he asked.

Barry leaned forward, well aware that he was not wanted here at this moment. 'Just talked to Gronke in Memphis. Kid's hired a lawyer, and is refusing to talk to the FBI.'

'I can't believe you're so stupid, Barry, you know that?'

'We've had this conversation, okay?'

'I know. And we'll have it again. You're a dumbass, and I just want you to know that I think you're a real dumbass.'

'Okay. I'm a dumbass. But we need to make a move.'

'What?'

'We need to send Bono and someone else, maybe Pirini, maybe the Bull, I don't care, but we need a couple of men in Memphis. And we need them now.'

'You want to hit the kid?'

'Maybe. We'll see. We need to find out what he knows, okay? If he knows too much, then maybe we'll take him out.'

'I'm embarrassed we're related by blood, Barry. You're a complete fool, you know that?'

'Okay. But we need to move fast.'

Johnny picked up a stack of papers, and began reading. 'Send Bono and Pirini, but no more stupid moves. Okay? You're an idiot, Barry, an imbecile, and I don't want anything done up there until I say so. Understand?'

'Yes sir.'

'Leave now.' Johnny waved his hand, and Barry jumped to his feet.

# CHAPTER THIRTEEN

By Tuesday evening, George Ord and his staff had managed to confine the activities of Foltrigg, Boxx, and Fink to the expansive library in the center of the offices. Here they'd set up camp. They had two phones. Ord loaned them a secretary and an intern. All other assistant attorneys were ordered to stay out of the library. Foltrigg kept the doors closed and spread his papers and mess over the sixteen-foot conference table in the middle of the room. Trumann was allowed to come and go. The secretary fetched coffee and sandwiches whenever the Reverend ordered.

Foltrigg had been a mediocre student of the law, and had managed to avoid the drudgery of legal research for the past fifteen years. He had learned to hate libraries in law school. Research was to be done by egghead scholars; that was his theory. Law could be practiced only by real lawyers who could stand before juries and preach.

But out of sheer boredom, here he was in George Ord's library with Boxx and Fink, nothing to do but wait at the beck and call of one Reggie Love, and so he, the great Roy Foltrigg, lawyer extraordinaire, had his nose stuck in a thick law book with a dozen more stacked around him on the table. Fink, the egghead scholar, was on the floor between two shelves of books with his shoes off and research materials littered about. Boxx, also a lightweight legal intellect, went through the motions at the other end of Foltrigg's table. Boxx had not opened a law book in years, but for the moment there was simply nothing else to do. He wore his only clean pair of boxer shorts and hoped like hell they left Memphis tomorrow.

At issue, at the heart of their research, was the question of how Mark Sway could be made to divulge information if he didn't want to. If someone possesses information crucial to a criminal prosecution, and that person chooses not to talk, then how can the information be obtained? For issue number two, Foltrigg wanted to know if Reggie Love could be made to divulge whatever Mark Sway had told her. The attorney–client privilege is almost sacred, but Roy wanted it researched anyway.

The debate over whether or not Mark Sway knew anything had

ended hours ago with Foltrigg clearly victorious. The kid had been in the car. Clifford was crazy and wanted to talk. The kid had lied to the cops. And now the kid had a lawyer because the kid knew something and was afraid to talk. Why didn't Mark Sway simply come clean and tell all? Why? Because he was afraid of the killer of Boyd Boyette. Plain and simple.

Fink still had doubts, but was tired of arguing. His boss was not bright and was very stubborn, and when he closed his mind it remained closed forever. And there was a lot of merit to Foltrigg's arguments. The kid was making strange moves, especially for a kid.

Boxx, of course, stood firm behind his boss and believed everything he said. If Roy said the kid knew where the body was, then it was the gospel. Pursuant to one of his many phone calls, a half dozen Assistant U.S. Attorneys were doing identical research in New Orleans.

Larry Trumann knocked and entered the library around ten Tuesday night. He'd been in McThune's office for most of the evening. Following Foltrigg's orders, they had begun the process of obtaining approval to offer Mark Sway safety under the Federal Witness Protection Program. They had made a dozen phone calls to Washington, twice speaking with the Director of the FBI, F. Denton Voyles. If Mark Sway didn't give Foltrigg the answers he wanted in the morning, they would be ready with a most attractive offer.

Foltrigg said it would be an easy deal. The kid had nothing to lose. They would offer his mother a good job in a new city, one of her choosing. She would earn more than the six lousy bucks an hour she got at the lamp factory. The family would live in a house with a foundation, not a cheap trailer. There would be a cash incentive, maybe a new car.

Mark sat in the darkness on the thin mattress, and stared at his mother lying above him next to Ricky. He was sick of this room and this hospital. The foldaway bed was ruining his back. Tragically, Karen the beautiful was not at the nurses' station. The hallways were empty. No one waited for the elevators.

A solitary man occupied the waiting area. He flipped through a magazine and ignored the 'M*A*S*H' reruns on the television. He was on the sofa, which happened to be the spot Mark had planned to sleep. Mark stuck two quarters in the machine, and pulled out a Sprite. He sat in a chair and stared at the TV. The man was about forty, and looked tired and worried. Ten minutes passed, and 'M\*A\*S\*H' went away. Suddenly, there was Gill Teal, the people's lawyer, standing calmly at the scene of a car wreck talking about defending rights and fighting insurance companies. Gill Teal, he's for real.

Jack Nance closed the magazine and picked up another. He glanced at Mark for the first time, and smiled. 'Hi there,' he said warmly, then looked at a *Redbook*.

Mark nodded. The last thing he needed in his life was another stranger. He sipped his drink, and prayed for silence.

'What're you doing here?' the man asked.

'Watching television,' Mark answered, barely audible.

The man stopped smiling and began reading an article. The midnight news came on, and there was a huge story about a typhoon in Pakistan. There were live pictures of dead people and dead animals piled along the shore like driftwood. It was the kind of footage one had to watch.

'That's awful, isn't it,' Jack Nance said to the TV as a helicopter hovered over a pile of human debris.

'It's gross,' Mark said, careful not to get friendly. Who knows – this guy could be just another hungry lawyer waiting to pounce on wounded prey.

'Really gross,' the man said, shaking his head at the suffering. 'I guess we have much to be thankful for. But it's hard to be thankful in a hospital, know what I mean?' He was suddenly sad again. He looked painfully at Mark.

'What's the matter?' Mark couldn't help but ask.

'It's my son. He's in real bad shape.' The man threw the magazine on the table and rubbed his eyes.

'What happened?' Mark asked. He felt sorry for this guy.

'Car wreck. Drunk driver. My boy was thrown out of the car.'

'Where is he?'

'ICU, first floor. I had to leave and get away. It's a zoo down there, people screaming and crying all the time.'

'I'm very sorry.'

'He's only eight years old.' He appeared to be crying, but Mark couldn't tell.

'My little brother's eight. He's in a room around the corner.'

'What's wrong with him?' the man asked without looking.

'He's in shock.'

'What happened?'

'It's a long story. And getting longer. He'll make it, though. I sure hope your kid pulls through.'

Jack Nance looked at his watch and suddenly stood. 'Me too. I need to go check on him. Good luck to you, uh, what's your name?'

'Mark Sway.'

'Good luck, Mark. I gotta run.' He walked to the elevators and disappeared.

Mark took his place on the couch, and within minutes was asleep.

# CHAPTER FOURTEEN

The photos on the front page of Wednesday's edition of the *Memphis Press* had been lifted from the yearbook at Willow Road Elementary School. They were a year old – Mark was in the fourth grade and Ricky the first. They were next to each other on the bottom third of the page, and under the cute, smiling faces were the names. Mark Sway. Ricky Sway. To the left was a story about Jerome Clifford's suicide and the bizarre aftermath in which the boys were involved. It was written by Slick Moeller, and he had pieced together a suspicious little story. The FBI was involved; Ricky was in shock; Mark had called 911 but hadn't given his name; the police had tried to interrogate Mark but he hadn't talked yet; the family had hired a lawyer, one Reggie Love (female); Mark's fingerprints were all over the inside of the car, including the gun. The story made Mark look like a cold-blooded killer.

Karen brought it to him around six as he sat in an empty semi-private room directly across the hall from Ricky's. Mark was watching cartoons and trying to nap. Greenway wanted everyone out of the room except Ricky and Dianne. An hour earlier, Ricky had opened his eyes and asked to use the bathroom. He was back in the bed now, mumbling about nightmares and eating ice cream.

'You've hit the big time,' Karen said as she handed him the front section and put his orange juice on the table.

'What is it?' he asked, suddenly staring at his face in black and white. 'Damn!'

'Just a little story. I'd like your autograph when you have time.'

Very funny. She left the room and he read it slowly. Reggie had told him about the fingerprints and the note. He'd dreamed about the gun, but through a legitimate lapse in memory had forgotten about touching the whiskey bottle.

There was something unfair here. He was just a kid who'd been minding his own business, and now suddenly his picture was on the front page and fingers were pointed at him. How can a newspaper dig up old yearbook photos and run them whenever it chooses? Wasn't he entitled to a little privacy?

He threw the paper to the floor and walked to the window. It was dawn, drizzling outside, and downtown Memphis was slowly coming to life. Standing in the window of the empty room, looking at the blocks of tall buildings, he felt completely alone. Within an hour, a half million people would be awake, reading about Mark and Ricky Sway while sipping their coffee and eating their toast. The dark buildings would soon be filled with busy people gathering around desks and coffeepots, and they would gossip and speculate wildly about him and what happened with the dead lawyer. Surely the kid was in the car. There are fingerprints everywhere! How did the kid get in the car? How did he get out? They would read Slick Moeller's story as if every word were true, as if Slick had the inside dope.

It was not fair for a kid to read about himself on the front page and not have parents to hide behind. Any kid in this mess needed the protection of a father and the sole affection of a mother. He needed a shield against cops and FBI agents and reporters, and god forbid, the mob. Here he was, eleven years old, alone, lying, then telling the truth, then lying some more, never certain what to do next. The truth can get you killed – he'd seen that in a movie one time, and always remembered it when he felt the urge to lie to someone in authority. How could he get out of this mess?

He retrieved the paper from the floor and entered the hall. Greenway had stuck a note on Ricky's door forbidding anyone from entering, including nurses. Dianne was having back pains from sitting in his bed and rocking, and Greenway had ordered another round of pills for her discomfort.

Mark stopped at the nurses' station, and handed the paper to Karen. 'Nice story, huh,' she said with a smile. The romance was gone. She was still beautiful but now playing hard to get, and he just didn't have the energy.

'I'm going to get a doughnut,' he said. 'You want one?'

'No thanks.'

He walked to the elevators, and pushed the call button. The middle door opened and he stepped in.

At that precise second, Jack Nance turned in the darkness of the waiting room and whispered into his radio.

The elevator was empty. It was just a few minutes past six, a good half an hour before the rush hit. The elevator stopped at floor number eight. The door opened, and one man stepped in. He wore a white lab jacket, jeans, sneakers, and a baseball cap. Mark did not look at his face. He was tired of meeting new people.

The door closed, and suddenly the man grabbed Mark and pinned him in a corner. He clenched his fingers around Mark's throat. The man fell to one knee and pulled something from a pocket. His face was inches from Mark's, and it was a horrible face. He was breathing heavy. 'Listen to me, Mark Sway,' he growled. Something clicked in his right hand, and suddenly a shiny switch-blade entered the picture. A very long switchblade. 'I don't know what Jerome Clifford told you,' he said urgently. The elevator was moving. 'But if you repeat a single word of it to anyone, including your lawyer, I'll kill you. And I'll kill your mother and your little brother. Okay? He's in Room 943. I've seen the trailer where you live. Okay? I've seen your school at Willow Road.' His breath was warm and had the smell of creamed coffee, and he aimed it directly at Mark's eyes. 'Do you understand me?' he sneered with a nasty smile.

The elevator stopped, and the man was on his feet by the door with the switchblade hidden by his leg. Although Mark was paralyzed, he was able to hope and pray that someone would get on the damned elevator with him. It was obvious he was not getting off at this point. They waited ten seconds at the sixth floor, and nobody entered. The doors closed, and they were moving again.

The man lunged at him again, this time with the switchblade an inch or two from Mark's nose. He pinned him in the corner with a heavy forearm, and suddenly jabbed the shiny blade at Mark's waist. Quickly and efficiently, he cut a belt loop. Then a second one. He'd already delivered his message, without interruption, and now it was time for a little reinforcement.

'I'll slice your guts out, do you understand me?' he demanded, and then released Mark.

Mark nodded. A lump the size of a golf ball clogged his dry throat, and suddenly his eyes were wet. He nodded yes, yes, yes.

'I'll kill you. Do you believe me?'

Mark stared at the knife, and nodded some more. 'And if you tell anyone about me, I'll get you. Understand?' Mark kept nodding, only faster now.

The man slid the knife into a pocket and pulled a folded eight by ten color photograph from under the lab jacket. He stuck it in Mark's face. 'You seen this before?' he asked, smiling now.

It was a department store portrait taken when Mark was in the second grade, and for years now it had hung in the den above the television. Mark stared at it.

'Recognize it?' the man barked at him.

Mark nodded. There was only one such photograph in the world.

The elevator stopped on the fifth floor, and the man moved quickly, again by the door. At the last second, two nurses stepped in, and Mark finally breathed. He stayed in the corner, holding the railings, praying for a miracle. The switchblade had come closer with each assault, and he simply could not take another one. On the third floor, three more people entered and stood between Mark and the man with the knife. In an instant, Mark's assailant was gone; through the door as it was closing.

'Are you okay?' A nurse was staring at him, frowning and very concerned. The elevator kicked and started down. She touched his forehead and felt a layer of sweat between her fingers. His eyes were wet. 'You look pale,' she said.

'I'm okay,' he mumbled weakly, holding the railings for support.

Another nurse looked down at him in the corner. They studied his face with much concern. 'Are you sure?'

He nodded, and the elevator door suddenly opened on the second floor. He darted through bodies and was in a narrow corridor dodging gurneys and wheelchairs. His well-worn Nike hightops squeaked on the clean linoleum as he ran to a door with an EXIT sign over it. He pushed through the door, and was in the stairwell. He grabbed the rails and started up, two steps at a time, churning and churning. The pain hit his thighs at the sixth floor, but he ran harder. He passed a doctor on the eighth floor, but never slowed. He ran, climbing the mountain at a record pace until the stairwell stopped on the fifteenth floor. He collapsed on a landing under a fire hose, and sat in the semi-darkness until the sun filtered through a tiny painted window above him.

Pursuant to his agreement with Reggie, Clint opened the office at exactly eight, and after turning on the lights, made the coffee. It was Wednesday, southern pecan day. He looked through the countless one-pound bags of coffee beans in the refrigerator until he found southern pecan, and measured four perfect scoops into the grinder. She would know in an instant if he'd missed the measurement by half a teaspoon. She would take the first sip like a wine connoisseur, smack her lips like a rabbit, then pass judgment on the coffee. He added the precise quantity of water, flipped the switch, and waited for the first black drops to hit the canister. The aroma was delicious.

Clint enjoyed the coffee almost as much as his boss, and the meticulous routine of making it was only half-serious. They began each morning with a quiet cup as they planned the day and talked about the mail. They had met in a detox center eleven years ago when she was forty-one and he was seventeen. They had started law school at the same time, but he flunked out after a nasty round with coke. He'd been perfectly clean for five years, she for six. They had leaned on each other many times.

He sorted the mail and placed it carefully on her clean desk. He poured his first cup of coffee in the kitchen, and read with great interest the front page story about her newest client. As usual, Slick had his facts. And, as usual, the facts were stretched with a good dose of innuendo thrown in. The boys favored each other, but Ricky's hair was a shade lighter. He smiled with several teeth missing.

Clint placed the front page in the center of Reggie's desk.

Unless she was expected in court, Reggie seldom made it to the office before 9 A.M. She was a slow starter who usually hit her stride around four in the afternoon and preferred to work late.

Her mission as a lawyer was to protect abused and neglected children, and she did this with great skill and passion. The juvenile courts routinely called her for indigent work representing kids who needed lawyers but didn't know it. She was a zealous advocate for small clients who could not say thanks. She had sued fathers for molesting daughters. She had sued uncles for raping their nieces. She had sued mothers for abusing their babies. She had investigated parents for exposing their children to drugs. She served as legal guardian for more than twenty children. And she worked the Juvenile Court as appointed counsel for kids in trouble with the law. She performed pro bono work for children in need of commitment to mental facilities. The money was adequate, but not important. She had money once, lots of it, and it had brought nothing but misery.

She sipped the southern pecan, pronounced it good, and planned the day with Clint. It was a ritual adhered to whenever possible.

As she picked up the newspaper, the buzzer rang as the door opened. Clint jumped to answer it. He found Mark Sway standing in the reception room, wet from the drizzle and out of breath.

'Good morning, Mark. You're all wet.'

'I need to see Reggie.' His bangs stuck to his forehead and water dripped from his nose. He was in a daze.

'Sure.' Clint backed away from him, and returned with a hand towel from the rest room. He wiped Mark's face, and said, 'Follow me.'

Reggie was waiting in the center of her office. Clint closed the door and left them alone.

'What's the matter?' she asked.

'I think we need to talk.' She pointed, and he sat in a wingback chair and she sat on the sofa.

'What's going on, Mark?' His eyes were red and tired. He stared at the flowers on the coffee table.

121

'Ricky snapped out of it early this morning.'

'That's great. What time?'

'A couple of hours ago.'

'You look tired. Would you like some hot cocoa?'

'No. Did you see the paper this morning?'

'Yeah, I saw it. Does it scare you?'

'Of course it scares me.' Clint knocked on the door, then opened it and brought hot cocoa anyway. Mark thanked him and held it with both hands. He was cold and the warm cup helped. Clint closed the door and was gone.

'When do we meet with the FBI?' he asked.

'In an hour. Why?'

He sipped the cocoa and it burned his tongue. 'I'm not sure I want to talk to them.'

'Okay. You don't have to, you know. I've explained all this.'

'I know. Can I ask you something?'

'Of course, Mark. You look scared.'

'It's been a rough morning.' He took another tiny sip, then another. 'What would happen to me if I never told anyone what I know?'

'You've told me.'

'Yeah, but you can't tell. And I haven't told you everything, right?'

'That's right.'

'I've told you that I know where the body is, but I haven't told – '

'I know, Mark. I don't know where it is. There's a big difference, and I certainly understand it.'

'Do you want to know?'

'Do you want to tell me?'

'Not really. Not now.'

She was relieved but didn't show it. 'Okay, then I don't want to know.'

'So what happens to me if I never tell?'

She'd thought about this for hours, and still had no answer. But she'd met Foltrigg, had watched him under pressure, and was convinced he would try all legal means to extract the information from her client. As much as she wanted to, she could not advise him to lie.

A lie would work just fine. One simple lie, and Mark Sway could live the rest of his life without regard to what happened in New Orleans. And why should he worry about Muldanno and Foltrigg and the late Boyd Boyette? He was just a kid, guilty of neither crime nor major sin.

'I think that an effort will be made to force you to talk.'

'How does it work?'

'I'm not sure. It's very rare, but I believe steps can be taken in court to force you to testify about what you know. Clint and I have been researching it.'

'I know what Clifford told me, but I don't know if it's the truth.'

'But you think it's the truth, don't you, Mark?'

'I think so, I guess. I don't know what to do.' He was mumbling softly, at times barely audible, unwilling to look at her. 'Can they make me talk?' he asked.

She answered carefully. 'It could happen. I mean, a lot of things could happen. But, yes, a judge in a courtroom one day soon could order you to talk.'

'And if I refused?'

'Good question, Mark. It's a gray area. If an adult refuses a court order, he's in contempt of court and runs the risk of being locked up. I don't know what they'd do with a child. I've never heard of it before.'

'What about a polygraph?'

'What do you mean?'

'Well, let's say they drag me into court, and the judge tells me to spill my guts, and I tell the story but leave out the most important part. And they think I'm lying. What then? Can they strap me in the chair and start asking questions? I saw it in a movie one time.'

'You saw a child take a polygraph?'

'No. It was some cop who got caught lying. But, I mean, can they do it to me?'

'I doubt it. I've never heard of it, and I'd be fighting like crazy to stop it.'

'But it could happen.'

'I'm not sure. I doubt it.' These were hard questions coming at her like gunfire, and she had to be careful. Clients often heard what they wanted to hear, and missed the rest. 'But I must warn you, Mark, if you lie in court you could be in big trouble.'

He thought about this for a second, and said, 'If I tell the truth I'm in bigger trouble.'

'Why?'

She waited a long time for a response. Every twenty seconds or so, he would take a sip of the cocoa, but he was not at all interested in answering this question. The silence did not bother him. He stared at the table, but his mind whirled away somewhere else.

'Mark, last night you indicated you were ready to talk to the FBI and tell them your story. Now, it's obvious you've changed your mind. Why? What's happened?'

Without a word, he gently placed the cup on the table and covered his eyes with his fists. His chin dropped to his chest, and he started crying.

The door opened into the reception area and a Federal Express lady ran in with a box three inches thick. All smiles and perfect efficiency, she handed it to Clint and showed him where to sign. She thanked him, wished him a nice day, and vanished.

The package was expected. It was from Print Research, an amazing little outfit in D.C. that did nothing but scan two hundred daily newspapers nationwide and catalogue the stories. The news was clipped, copied, computerized, and readily available within twenty-four hours for those willing to pay. Reggie didn't want to pay, but she needed quick background on Boyette et al. Clint had placed the order yesterday, as soon as Mark left and Reggie had herself a new client. The search was limited to the New Orleans and Washington papers.

He removed the contents, a neat stack of eight and a half by eleven Xerox copies of newspaper stories, headlines, and photos, all arranged in perfect chronological order, all copied with the columns straight and the photos clean.

Boyette was an old Democrat from New Orleans, and he'd served several terms as an undistinguished rank and file member of the U.S. House, when one day Senator Dauvin, an antebellum relic from the Civil War, suddenly died in office at the age of ninety-one. Boyette pulled strings and twisted arms, and in keeping with the great tradition of Louisiana politics rounded up some cash and found a home for it. He was appointed by the Governor to fill the unexpired portion of Dauvin's term. The theory was simple: if a man had enough sense to accumulate a bunch of cash, then he would certainly make a worthy U.S. Senator.

Boyette became a member of the world's most exclusive club, and with time proved himself quite capable. Over the years he narrowly missed a few indictments, and evidently learned his lessons. He survived two close reelections, and finally reached a point attained by most southern senators where he was simply left alone. When this happened, Boyette slowly mellowed, and changed from a hell-raising segregationist to a rather liberal and open-minded statesman. He lost favor with three straight governors in Louisiana, and in doing so became an outcast with the petroleum and chemical companies that had ruined the ecology of the state.

So Boyd Boyette became a radical environmentalist, something unheard of among southern politicians. He railed against the oil and gas industry, and it vowed to defeat him. He held hearings in small bayou towns devastated by the oil boom and bust, and made enemies in the tall buildings in New Orleans. Senator Boyette embraced the crumbling ecology of his beloved state, and studied it with a passion.

Six years ago, someone in New Orleans had floated out a proposal to build a toxic waste dump in Lafourche Parish, about eighty miles southwest of New Orleans. It was quickly killed for the first time by local authorities. As is true with most ideas created by rich, corporate minds, it didn't go away, but rather came back a year later with a different name, a different set of consultants, new promises of local jobs, and a new mouthpiece doing the presenting. It was voted down by the locals for the second time, but the vote was much closer. A year passed, some money changed hands, cosmetic changes were made to the plans, and it was suddenly back on the agenda. The folks who lived around the site were hysterical. Rumors were rampant, especially a persistent one that the New Orleans mob was behind the dump and would not stop until it was a reality. Of course, millions were at stake.

The New Orleans papers did a credible job of linking the mob to the toxic waste site. A dozen corporations were involved, and names and addresses led to several known and undisputed crime figures.

The stage was set, the deal was done, the dump was to be approved, then Senator Boyd Boyette came crashing in with an army of federal regulators. He threatened investigations by a dozen agencies. He held weekly press conferences. He made speeches all over southern Louisiana. The advocates of the waste site ran for cover. The corporations issued terse statements of no comment. Boyette had them on the ropes, and he was enjoying himself immensely.

On the night of his disappearance, the Senator had attended an angry meeting of local citizens at a packed high school gymnasium in Houma. He left late, and alone, as was his custom, for the hour drive to his home near New Orleans. Years earlier, Boyette had grown weary of the constant small talk and incessant ass kissing of aides, and he preferred to drive by himself whenever possible. He was studying Russian, his fourth language, and he cherished the solitude of his Cadillac and the language tapes.

By noon the next day, it was determined the Senator was missing. The splashy headlines from New Orleans told the story. Bold headlines in the *Washington Post* suspected foul play. Days went by and the news was scarce. No body was found. A hundred old photos of the

Senator were dug up and used by the newspapers. The story was becoming old when, suddenly, the name of Barry Muldanno was linked to the disappearance and this set off a frenzy of Mafia dirt and trash. A rather frightening mug shot of a young Muldanno ran on page one in New Orleans. The paper rehashed its earlier stories about the waste site and the mob. The Blade was a known hit man with a criminal record. And on and on.

Roy Foltrigg made a grand entrance into the story when he stepped in front of the cameras to announce the indictment of Barry Muldanno for the murder of Senator Boyd Boyette. He, too, got the front page in both New Orleans and Washington, and Clint remembered a similar photo in the Memphis paper. Big news, but no body. This, however, did not throttle Mr. Foltrigg. He ranted against organized crime. He predicted certain victory. He preached his carefully prepared remarks with the flair of a veteran stage actor, shouting at all the right moments, pointing his finger, waving the indictment. He had no comment about the absence of a corpse, but hinted that he knew something he couldn't tell and said he had no doubt the remains of the late Senator would be found.

There were pictures and stories when Barry Muldanno was arrested, or rather, turned himself in to the FBI. He spent three days in jail before bail was arranged, and there were photos of him leaving just as he had arrived. He wore a dark suit and smiled at the cameras. He was innocent, he proclaimed. It was a vendetta.

There were photos of bulldozers, taken from a distance, as the FBI trenched its way through the soggy soil of New Orleans searching for the body. More of Foltrigg performing for the press. More investigative reports of New Orleans's rich history of organized crime. The story seemed to lose steam as the search continued.

The Governor, a Democrat, appointed a crony to serve the remaining year and a half of Boyette's term. The New Orleans paper ran an analysis of the many politicians waiting anxiously to run for the Senate. Foltrigg was one of two Republicans rumored to be interested.

He sat next to her on the sofa, and wiped his eyes. He hated himself for crying, but it could not be helped. Her arm was around his shoulder, and she patted him gently.

'You don't have to say a word,' she repeated quietly.

'I really don't want to. Maybe later, if I have to, but not now. Okay?'

'Okay, Mark.'

There was a knock at the door. 'Come in,' Reggie said just loud enough to be heard. Clint appeared holding a stack of papers and looking at his watch.

'Sorry to interrupt. But it's almost ten, and Mr. Foltrigg will be here in a minute.' He placed the papers on the coffee table in front of her. 'You wanted to see these before the meeting.'

'Tell Mr. Foltrigg we have nothing to discuss,' Reggie said.

Clint frowned at her and looked at Mark. He sat close to her as if he needed protecting. 'You're not going to see him?'

'No. Tell him the meeting's been canceled because we have nothing to say,' she said, and nodded at Mark.

Clint glanced at his watch again and backed awkwardly to the door. 'Sure,' he said with a smile as if he suddenly enjoyed the idea of telling Foltrigg to take a hike. He closed the door behind him.

'Are you okay?' she asked.

'Not really.'

She leaned forward and began flipping through the copies of the clippings. Mark sat in a daze, tired and drained, still frightened after talking things over with his lawyer. She scanned the pages, reading the headlines and captions and pulling the photographs closer to her. About a third of the way through, she suddenly stopped and leaned back on the sofa. She handed Mark a close-up of Barry Muldanno as he smiled at the camera. It was from the New Orleans paper. 'Is this the man?'

Mark looked without touching it. 'No. Who is it?'

'It's Barry Muldanno.'

'That's not the man who grabbed me. I guess he's got a lot of friends.'

She placed the copy in the stack on the coffee table, and patted him on the leg.

'What're you gonna do?' he asked.

'Make a few calls. I'll talk to the administrator of the hospital and arrange security around Ricky's room.'

'You can't tell him about this guy, Reggie. They'll kill us. We can't tell anybody.'

'I won't. I'll explain to the hospital that there have been some threats. It's routine in criminal cases. They'll place a few guards on the ninth floor around the room.'

'I don't want to tell Mom either. She's stressed out with Ricky, and she's taking pills to sleep and pills to do this and that, and I just don't think she can handle this right now.'

'You're right.' He was a tough little kid, raised on the streets and wise beyond his years. She admired his courage.

'Do you think Mom and Ricky are safe?'

'Of course. These men are professionals, Mark. They won't do anything stupid. They'll lay low and listen. They may be bluffing.' She did not sound sincere.

'No, they're not bluffing. I saw the knife, Reggie. They're here in Memphis for one reason, and that's to scare the hell out of me. And it's working. I ain't talking.'

# CHAPTER FIFTEEN

Foltrigg yelled only once, then stormed from the office making threats and slamming the door. McThune and Trumann were frustrated, but also embarrassed at his antics. As they left, McThune rolled his eyes at Clint as if he wanted to apologize for this pompous loudmouth. Clint relished the moment, and when the dust settled he walked to Reggie's office.

Mark had pulled a chair to the window, and sat watching it rain on the street and sidewalk below. Reggie was on the phone with the hospital administrator discussing security on the ninth floor. She covered the phone, and Clint whispered that they were gone. He left to get more cocoa for Mark, who never moved.

Within minutes, Clint took a call from George Ord, and he buzzed Reggie on the intercom. She'd never met the U.S. Attorney from Memphis, but was not surprised that he was now on the phone. She allowed him to hold for one full minute, then picked up the phone. 'Hello.'

'Ms. Love, this is – '

'It's Reggie, okay. Just Reggie. And you're George, right?' She called everyone by their first name, even stuffy judges in their proper little courtrooms.

'Right, Reggie. This is George Ord. Roy Foltrigg is in my office, and – '

'What a coincidence. He just left mine.'

'Yeah, and that's why I'm calling. He didn't get a chance to talk to you and your client.'

'Give him my apologies. My client has nothing to say to him.' She was talking and looking at the back of Mark's head. If he were listening, she couldn't tell. He was frozen in the chair at the window.

'Reggie, I think it would be wise if you at least meet with Mr. Foltrigg again.'

'I have no desire to meet with Roy, nor does my client.' She could picture Ord speaking gravely into the phone with Foltrigg pacing around the office waving his arms.

'Well, this will not be the end of it, you know?'

'Is that a threat, George?'

'It's more of a promise.'

'Fine. You tell Roy and his boys that if anyone attempts to contact my client or his family I'll have their asses. Okay, George?'

'I'll relay the message.'

It was really sort of funny – it was not, after all, his case – but Ord could not laugh. He returned the receiver to its place, smiled to himself, and said, 'She says she ain't talking, the kid ain't talking, and if you or anyone else contacts the kid or his family she'll, uh, have your asses, as she put it.'

Foltrigg bit his lip and nodded at every word as if this was fine because he could play hardball with the best of them. He had regained his composure and was already implementing Plan B. He paced around the office as if in deep thought. McThune and Trumann stood by the door like sentries. Bored sentries.

'I want the kid followed, okay,' Foltrigg finally snapped at McThune. 'We're leaving for New Orleans, and I want you guys to tail him twenty-four hours a day. I want to know what he does, and, more importantly, he needs to be protected from Muldanno and his henchmen.'

McThune did not take orders from any U.S. Attorney, and at this moment he was sick of Roy Foltrigg. And the idea of using three or four overworked agents to follow an eleven-year-old kid was quite stupid. But, it was not worth the fight. Foltrigg had a hot line to Director Voyles in Washington, and Director Voyles wanted the body and he wanted a conviction almost as bad as Foltrigg.

'Okay,' he said. 'We'll get it done.'

'Paul Gronke's already here somewhere,' Foltrigg said as though he'd just heard fresh gossip. They knew the flight number and his time of arrival eleven hours ago. They had, however, managed to lose his trail once he left the Memphis airport. They had discussed it with Ord and Foltrigg and a dozen other FBI agents for two hours this morning. At this very moment, no less than eight agents were trying to find Gronke in Memphis.

'We'll find him,' McThune said. 'And we'll watch the kid. Why don't you get your ass back to New Orleans.'

'I'll get the van ready,' Trumann said officially as if the van was in fact *Air Force One*.

Foltrigg stopped pacing in front of Ord's desk. 'We're leaving, George. Sorry for the intrusion. I'll probably be back in a couple of days.'

What wonderful news, Ord thought. He stood, and they shook hands. 'Anytime,' he said. 'If we can help, just call.'

'I'll meet with Judge Lamond first thing in the morning. I'll let you know.'

Ord offered his hand again for one final shake. Foltrigg took it and headed for the door. 'Watch out for these thugs,' he advised McThune. 'I don't think he's dumb enough to touch the kid, but who knows.' McThune opened the door and waved him through. Ord followed.

'Muldanno's heard something,' Foltrigg continued, 'and they're just snooping around here.' He was in the outer office where Wally Boxx and Thomas Fink waited. 'But keep an eye on them, okay, George? These guys are really dangerous. And follow the kid, too, and watch his lawyer. And thanks a million. I'll call you tomorrow. Where's the van, Wally?'

After an hour of watching the sidewalks, sipping hot cocoa, and listening to his lawyer practice law, Mark was ready for a move. Reggie had called Dianne and explained that Mark was in her office killing time and helping with the paperwork. Ricky was much better, sleeping again. He'd consumed half a gallon of ice cream while Greenway asked him a hundred questions.

At eleven, Mark parked himself at Clint's desk and inspected the dictating equipment. Reggie had a client, a woman who desperately wanted a divorce, and they needed to plot strategy for an hour. Clint typed away on long paper and grabbed the phone every five minutes.

'How'd you become a secretary?' Mark asked, very bored with this candid view of the practice of law.

Clint turned and smiled at him. 'It was an accident.'

'Did you want to be a secretary when you were a kid?'

'No. I wanted to build swimming pools.'

'What happened?'

'I don't know. I got messed up on drugs, almost flunked out of high school, then went to college, then went to law school.'

'You have to go to law school to be a secretary in a law office?'

'No. I flunked out of law school, and Reggie gave me a job. It's fun, most of the time.'

'Where'd you meet Reggie?'

'It's a long story. We were friends in law school. We've been friends for a long time. She'll probably tell you about it when you meet Momma Love.'

'Momma who?'

'Momma Love. She hasn't told you about Momma Love?'

'No.'

'Momma Love is Reggie's mother. They live together, and she loves to cook for the kids Reggie represents. She fixes inside-out ravioli and spinach lasagna and all sorts of delicious Italian food. Everyone loves it.'

After two days of doughnuts and green Jell-O, the mention of thick, cheesy dishes cooked at someone's home was terribly inviting. 'When do you think I might meet Momma Love?'

'I don't know. Reggie takes most of her clients home, especially the younger ones.'

'Does she have any kids?'

'Two, but they're grown and live away.'

'Where does Momma Love live?'

'In midtown, not far from here. It's an old house she's owned for years. In fact, it's the house Reggie grew up in.'

The phone rang. Clint took the message and returned to his typewriter. Mark watched intently.

'How'd you learn to type so fast?'

The typing stopped, and he slowly turned and looked at Mark. He smiled, and said, 'In high school. I had this teacher who was like a drill sergeant. We hated her, but she made us learn. Can you type?'

'A little. I've had three years of computer at school.'

Clint pointed to his Apple next to the typewriter. 'We've got all sorts of computers around here.'

Mark glanced at it, but was not impressed. Everybody had computers. 'So how'd you get to be a secretary?'

'It wasn't planned. When Reggie finished law school, she didn't want to work for anybody, so she opened this office. It was about four years ago. She needed a secretary, and I volunteered. Have you seen a male secretary before?'

'No. Didn't know men could be secretaries. How's the money?'

Clint chuckled at this. 'It's okay. If Reggie has a good month, then I have a good month. We're sort of like partners.'

'Does she make a lot of money?'

'Not really. She doesn't want a lot of money. A few years ago she was married to a doctor, and they had a big house and lots of money. Everything went to hell, and she blames the money for most of it. She'll probably tell you about it. She's very honest about her life.'

'She's a lawyer and she doesn't want money?'

'Unusual, isn't it?'

'I'll say. I mean, I've seen a lot of lawyer shows on television, and all they do is talk about money. Sex and money.'

The phone rang. It was a judge, and Clint got real nice and chatted with him for five minutes. He hung up and returned to his typing. As he reached full speed, Mark asked, 'Who's that woman in there?'

Clint stopped, stared at the keys, and slowly turned around. His chair squeaked. He forced a quick smile. 'In there with Reggie?'

'Yeah.'

'Norma Thrash.'

'What's her problem?'

'She's got a bunch of them, really. She's in the middle of a nasty divorce. Husband's a real jerk.'

Mark was curious about how much Clint knew. 'Does he beat her up?'

'I don't think so,' he answered slowly.

'Do they have kids and all?'

'Two. I really can't say much about it. It's confidential, you know?'

'Yeah, I know. But you probably know everything, don't you? I mean, after all, you type it up.'

'I know most of what goes on. Sure. But Reggie doesn't tell me everything. For example, I have no idea what you've told her. I assume it's pretty serious, but she'll keep it to herself. I've read the newspaper. I've seen the FBI and Mr. Foltrigg, but I don't know the details.'

This was exactly what Mark wanted to hear. 'Do you know Robert Hackstraw? They call him Hack.'

'He's a lawyer, isn't he?'

'Yeah. He represented my mother in her divorce a couple of years ago. A real moron.'

'You weren't impressed with her lawyer?'

'I hated Hack. He treated us like dirt. We'd go to his office and wait for two hours. Then he'd talk to us for ten minutes, and tell us he was in a big hurry, had to get to court because he was so important. I tried to convince Mom to get another lawyer, but she was too stressed out.'

'Did it go to trial?'

'Yeah. My ex-father thought he should get one kid, didn't really care which one but he preferred Ricky 'cause he knew I hated him, so he hired a lawyer, and for two days my mother and my father trashed each other in court. They tried to prove each other was unfit. Hack was a complete fool in the courtroom, but my ex-father's lawyer was even worse. The judge hated both lawyers, and said he wasn't about to separate me and Ricky. I asked him if I could testify. He thought about it during lunch on the second day, and decided he wanted to hear what I had to say. I had asked Hack the same question, and he said something smart, like I was too young and dumb to testify.'

'But you testified.'

'Yeah, for three hours.'

'How'd it go?'

'I was pretty good, really. I just told about the beatings, the bruises, the stitches. I told him how much I hated my father. The judge almost cried.'

'And it worked?'

'Yeah. My father wanted some visitation rights, and I spent a lot of time explaining to the judge that I had no desire to ever see the man again once the trial was over. And, that Ricky was terrified of him. So the judge not only cut off all visitation, but also told my father to stay away from us.'

'Have you seen him since?'

'No. But I will one day. When I grow up, we'll catch him somewhere, me and Ricky, and we'll beat the living hell out of him. Bruise for bruise. Stitch for stitch. We talk about it all the time.'

Clint was no longer bored with this little conversation. He listened to every word. The kid was so casual about his plans for beating his father. 'You might go to jail.'

'He didn't go to jail when he beat us. He didn't go to jail when he stripped my mother naked and threw her in the street with blood all over her. That's when I hit him with the baseball bat.'

'You what?'

'He was drinking one night at home, and we could tell he was about to get out of hand. We could always tell. Then he left to buy more beer. I ran down the street and borrowed an aluminum tee ball bat from Michael Moss. I hid it under my bed, and I remember praying for a good car wreck so he wouldn't come home. But he did. Mom was in their bedroom, hoping he would just pass out, which he did all the time. Ricky and I stayed in our room, waiting for the explosion.'

The phone rang again, and Clint quickly took the message and returned to the story.

'About an hour later there was all this yelling and cussing. The trailer was shaking. We locked the door. Ricky was under the bed, crying. Then Mom started yelling for me. I was seven years old, and Mom wanted me to rescue her. He was just beating the hell out of her, throwing her around, kicking her, ripping her shirt off, calling her a whore and a slut. I didn't even know what those words meant. I walked to the kitchen. I guess I was too scared to move. He saw me and threw a beer can at me. She tried to run outside, but he caught her and tore her pants off. God, he was hitting her so hard. Then he ripped off her underwear. Her lip was busted and there was blood everywhere. He threw her outside, completely naked, and dragged her into the street where, of course, the neighbors were watching. Then he laughed at her, and left her lying there. It was horrible.'

Clint leaned forward and hung on every word. Mark was speaking in a monotone, showing absolutely no emotion.

'When he came back to the trailer, the door was of course open, and I was waiting. I had pulled a kitchen chair beside the door, and I damned near took his head off with the baseball bat. A perfect shot to his nose. I was crying and scared to death, but I'll always remember the sound of the bat crunching his face. He fell on the sofa, and I hit him once in the stomach. I was trying to land a good one in the crotch, because I figured that would hurt the most. Know what I mean? I was swinging like crazy. I hit him once more on the ear, and that was all she wrote.'

'What happened?' Clint snapped.

'He got up, slapped me in the face, knocked me down, cussed me, then started kicking me. I remember being so scared I couldn't fight. His face was a bloody mess. He smelled awful. He was growling and slapping and tearing my clothes off. I started kicking like crazy when he pulled at my underwear, but he got them off and threw me outside. Not a bit of clothing. I guess he wanted me in the street with my mother, but about that time she made it to the door and fell on me.'

He told it all so calmly, as if he'd done it a hundred times and the script was memorized. No emotion, just the facts in short clipped sentences. He would look at the desk, then stare at the door without missing a word.

'What happened?' Clint asked, almost out of breath.

'One of the neighbors had called the cops. I mean, you can hear everything in the next trailer, so our neighbors had suffered through this with us. And that was not the first fight, not by a long shot. I remember seeing blue lights in the street, and he disappeared somewhere inside the trailer. Me and Mom got up real quick and ran inside and got dressed. Some of the neighbors saw me naked, though. We tried to wash the blood off before the cops came in. My father had settled down quite a bit, and was suddenly real friendly with the cops. Me and Mom waited in the kitchen. His nose was the size of a football, and the cops were more concerned with his face than with me and Mom. He called one of the cops Frankie as if they were buddies. There were two cops, and they got everybody separated. Frankie took him to the bedroom to cool him off. The other cop sat with Mom at the kitchen table. This is what they always did. I went to our room, and got Ricky out from under the bed. Mom told me later that he got real chummy with the cops, said it as just a family fight, nothing serious, and that most of it was my fault because I, for no reason, had attacked him with a baseball bat. The cops referred to it as just another domestic disturbance, something they always said. No charges were filed. They took him to the hospital where he spent the night. Had to wear this ugly white mask for a while.'

'What'd he do to you?'

'He didn't drink for a long time after that. He apologized to us, promised it would never happen again. Sometimes he was okay when he wasn't drinking. But then he got worse. More beatings and all. Mom finally filed for divorce.'

'And he tried to get custody – '

'Yeah. He lied in court, and he was doing a pretty good job of it. He didn't know I was going to testify, so he denied a bunch of it and said Mom was lying about the rest. He was real cocky and cool in court, and our dumbass lawyer couldn't do anything with him. But, when I testified and told about the baseball bat and getting my clothes ripped off, that's when the judge had tears in his eyes. He got real mad at my ex-father, accused him of lying. Said he ought to throw his sorry ass in jail for lying. I told him I thought that's exactly what he should do.' He paused for a second.

The sentences were a bit slower, and Mark was losing steam. Clint was still mesmerized.

'Of course, Hack took full credit for another brilliant courtroom victory. Then he threatened to sue Mom if she didn't pay him. She had a bunch of bills, and he was calling twice a week wanting the rest of his fee, so she had to file for bankruptcy. Then she lost her job.'

'So you've been through a divorce, and then a bankruptcy?'

'Yeah. The bankruptcy lawyer was a real bozo too.'

'But you like Reggie?'

'Yeah. Reggie's cool.'

'That's good to hear.'

The phone rang, and Clint picked it up. A lawyer from Juvenile Court wanted some information on a client, and the conversation dragged on. Mark left to find the hot cocoa. He passed the conference room with pretty books covering the walls. He found the tiny kitchen next to the rest room.

There was a Sprite in the refrigerator, and he unscrewed the top. Clint was amazed by his story, he could tell. He had left out many of the details, but it was all true. He was proud of it, in a way, proud of defending his mother, and the story always amazed people.

Then the tough little kid with the baseball bat remembered the knife attack in the elevator, and the folded photograph of the poor, fatherless family. He thought of his mother at the hospital, all alone and unprotected. He was suddenly scared again.

He tried to open a package of saltines, but his hands shook and the plastic wouldn't open. The shaking got worse and he couldn't stop it. He slumped to the floor and spilled the Sprite.

# CHAPTER SIXTEEN

The light rain had stopped in time for the rush of secretaries who moved in hurried groups of three and four along the damp sidewalks in pursuit of lunch. The sky was gray and the streets were wet. Clouds of mist boiled and hissed behind each passing car along Third Street. Reggie and her client turned on Madison. Her briefcase was in her left hand, and with her right she held his hand and guided him through the crowd. She had places to go and walked quickly.

From a generic white Ford van parked almost directly in front of the Sterick Building, Jack Nance watched and radioed ahead. When they turned on Madison and were lost from sight, he listened. Within minutes, Cal Sisson, his partner, had them and was watching as they headed for the hospital, as expected. Five minutes later, they were in the hospital.

Nance locked the van and jaywalked across Third. He entered the Sterick Building, rode the elevator to the second floor, and gently turned the knob of the door with REGGIE LOVE – LAWYER on it. It was unlocked, which was a pleasant surprise. Eleven minutes had passed since noon. Virtually every lawyer with a nickel and dime solo practice in this city broke for lunch and locked the office. He opened the door and stepped inside as a hideous buzzer went off above his head and announced his arrival. Dammit! He'd hoped to enter through a locked door, something he was very proficient at, and dig through files without being interrupted. It was easy work. Most of these small outfits thought nothing of security. The big firms were a different story, although in the off-hours Nance could enter any one of a thousand law offices in Memphis and find whatever he wanted. He'd done it at least a dozen times. There were two things ham and egg lawyers did not have at their offices – cash and security devices. They locked their doors, and that was it.

A young man appeared from the back, and said, 'Yes. Can I help you?'

'Yeah,' Nance said without a smile. All business. Rough day. 'I'm with the *Times-Picayune*, you know the paper in New Orleans. Looking for Reggie Love.'

Clint stopped ten feet away. 'She's not here.'

'When might she return?'

'Don't know. You have any identification?'

Nance was headed for the door. 'You mean, like little white cards you lawyers throw on the sidewalks. No, pal, I don't carry business cards. I'm a reporter.'

'Fine. What's your name?'

'Arnie Carpentier. Tell her I'll catch her later.' He opened the door, the buzzer worked again, and he was gone. Not a productive visit, but he'd met Clint and seen the front room and reception area. The next visit would take longer.

The ride to the ninth floor was uneventful. Reggie held his hand, which normally would have irritated him but was rather comforting under the circumstances. He studied his feet as they ascended. He was afraid to look up, afraid of more strangers. He squeezed her hand.

They spilled into the lobby on the ninth floor and had taken no more than ten steps before three people rushed them from the direction of the waiting area. 'Ms. Love! Ms. Love,' one of them yelled. Reggie at first was startled, but gripped Mark's hand tighter and kept walking. One had a microphone, one a notepad, and one a camera. The one with the notepad said, 'Ms. Love, just a few quick questions.'

They walked faster toward the nurses' station. 'No comment.'

'Is it true your client is refusing to cooperate with the FBI and the police?'

'No comment,' she said, looking ahead. They followed like bloodhounds. She leaned quickly to Mark, and said, 'Don't look at them and don't say a word.'

'Is it true that the U.S. Attorney from New Orleans was in your office this morning?'

'No comment.'

Doctors, nurses, patients, everybody vacated the center of the hallway as Reggie and her famous client raced along followed by the yelping dogs.

'Did your client talk to Jerome Clifford before he died?'

She squeezed his hand harder and walked faster. 'No comment.'

As they neared the end of the hall, the clown with the camera suddenly dashed in front of them, knelt low as he backpedaled, and managed to get a shot before he landed on his ass. The nurses laughed. A security guard stepped forward at the nurses' station and raised his hands at the yelpers. They had met him before.

As Reggie and Mark rounded a bend in the hall, one called out, 'Is it true your client knows where Boyette is buried?'

There was a slight hesitation in her step. The shoulders jumped and the back arched, then she was over it and she and her client were gone.

Two overweight security guards in uniform sat in folding chairs by Ricky's door. They had pistols on their hips, and Mark noticed the pistols before anything else. One had a newspaper, which he promptly lowered as they approached. The other stood to greet them. 'Can I help you?' he asked Reggie.

'Yes. I'm the attorney for the family, and this is Mark Sway, the patient's brother.' She spoke in a professional whisper as if she had a right to be there and they didn't, so be quick with the questions because she had things to do. 'Dr. Greenway is expecting us,' she said as she walked to the door and knocked. Mark stood behind her, staring at the pistol, which was remarkably similar to the one poor Romey had used.

The security guard returned to his seat and his partner returned to his paper. Greenway opened the door and stepped outside, followed by Dianne, who had been crying. She hugged Mark and placed her arm on his shoulder.

'He's asleep,' Greenway said quietly to Reggie and Mark. 'Doing much better, but very tired.'

'He was asking about you,' Dianne whispered to Mark.

He looked at the moist eyes and asked, 'What's the matter, Mom?'

'Nothing. We'll talk about it later.'

'What's happened?'

Dianne looked at Greenway, then at Reggie, then at Mark. 'It's nothing,' she said.

'Your mother was fired this morning, Mark,' Greenway said. He looked at Reggie. 'These people sent a letter by courier informing her she'd been fired. Can you believe it? Had it delivered to the nurses here on the ninth floor, and one of them delivered it about an hour ago.'

'Let me see the letter,' Reggie said. Dianne pulled it from a pocket. Reggie unfolded it and read slowly. Dianne hugged Mark, and said, 'It'll be all right, Mark. We've managed before. I'll find another job.'

Mark bit his lip and wanted to cry.

'Can I keep this?'' Reggie said as she stuffed it in her briefcase. Dianne nodded yes.

Greenway studied his watch as if he couldn't determine the correct time. 'I'm gonna grab a quick sandwich, and I'll be back here in twenty minutes. I want to spend a couple of hours with Ricky and Mark, alone.'

Reggie glanced at her watch. 'I'll be back around four. There are reporters here, and I want you to ignore them.' She was talking to all three of them.

'Yeah, just say no comment, no comment,' Mark added helpfully. 'It's really fun.'

Dianne missed the fun. 'What do they want?'

'Everything. They've seen the newspaper. The rumors are rampant. They smell a story, and they'll do anything to get information. I saw a television van on the street, and I suspect they're somewhere close by. I think it's best if you stay here with Mark.'

'Okay,' Dianne said.

'Where's a telephone?' Reggie asked.

Greenway pointed in the direction of the nurses' station. 'Come on. I'll show you.'

'I'll see you guys at four, okay?' she said to Dianne and Mark. 'Remember, not a word to anyone. And stay close to this room.'

She and Greenway disappeared around the bend. The security guards were half-asleep. Mark and his mother entered the dark room and sat on the bed. A stale doughnut caught his attention, and he devoured it in four bites.

Reggie called her office, and Clint answered. 'You remember that lawsuit we filed last year on behalf of Penny Patoula?' she asked softly, looking around for the bloodhounds. 'It was sex discrimination, wrongful discharge, harassment, the works. I think we thew in everything. Circuit Court. Yeah, that's it. Pull the file. Change the name from Penny Patoula to Dianne Sway. The defendant will be Ark-Lon Fixtures. I want you to name the president individually. His name is Chester Tanfill. Yeah, make him a defendant too, and sue for wrongful discharge, labor violations, sexual harassment, throw in an equal rights charge, and ask for a million or two in damages. Do it now, and quickly. Prepare a summons, and a check for the filing fee. Run over to the courthouse and file it. I'll be there in about thirty minutes to pick it up, so hurry. I'll personally deliver it to Mr. Tanfill.'

She hung up and thanked the nearest nurse. The reporters were loitering near the soft drink machine, but she was through the door to the stairwell before they saw her.

Ark-Lon Fixtures was a series of metal connected buildings on a street of such structures in a minimum wage industrial park near the airport. The front building was a faded orange in color, and expansion had taken place in every direction except toward the street.

The newer additions were of the same general architecture but with different shades of orange. Trucks waited near a loading dock in the rear. An enclosed chain-link fence protected rolls of steel and aluminum.

Reggie parked near the front in a space reserved for visitors. She held her briefcase, and opened the door. A chesty woman with black hair and a long cigarette ignored her and listened to the phone stuck in her ear. Reggie stood before her, waiting impatiently. The room was dusty, dirty, and clouded with blue cigarette smoke. Matted pictures of beagles adorned the walls. Half the fluorescent lights were out.

'May I help you?' the receptionist asked as she lowered the phone.

'I need to see Chester Tanfill.'

'He's in a meeting.'

'I know. He's a very busy man, but I have something for him.'

The receptionist placed the phone on the desk. 'I see. And what might that be?'

'It's really none of your business. I need to see Chester Tanfill. It's urgent.'

This really pissed her off. The nameplate declared her to be Louise Chenault. 'I don't care how urgent it is, ma'am. You can't just barge in here and demand to see the president of this company.'

'This company is a sweatshop, and I've just sued it for two million bucks. And I've also sued Chester boy for a couple of million, and I'm telling you to find his sorry ass and get him out here immediately.'

Louise jumped to her feet, and backed away from the desk. 'Are you some kind of lawyer?'

Reggie pulled the lawsuit and the summons from the briefcase. She looked at it, ignored Louise, and said, 'I am indeed a lawyer. And I need to serve these papers on Chester. Now find him. If he's not here in five minutes, I'll amend it and ask for five million in damages.'

Louise bolted from the room and ran through a set of double doors. Reggie waited a second, then followed. She walked through a room filled with tacky, cramped cubicles. Cigarette smoke seemed to ooze from every opening. The carpet was ancient shag and badly worn. She caught a glimpse of Louise's round rump darting into a door on the right, and she followed.

Chester Tanfill was in the process of standing behind his desk when Reggie barged in. Louise was speechless. 'You can leave now,' Reggie said rudely. 'I'm Reggie Love, Attorney-at-Law,' she said, glaring at Chester.

'Chester Tanfill,' he said without offering a hand. She wouldn't have taken it. 'This is a bit rude, Ms. Love.'

'The name is Reggie, okay, Chester? Tell Louise to leave.'

He nodded and Louise gladly left, closing the door behind her.

'What do you want?' he snapped. He was wiry and gaunt, around fifty, with a spotted face and puffy eyes partially hidden behind wire-rimmed glasses. A drinking problem, she thought. The clothes were Sears or Penney's. His neck was turning dark red.

She threw the lawsuit and the summons on his desk. 'I'm serving you with this lawsuit.'

He smirked at it, a man unafraid of lawyers and their games. 'For what?'

'I represent Dianne Sway. You fired her this morning, and we're suing you this afternoon. How's that for swift justice?'

Chester's eyes narrowed and he looked at the lawsuit again. 'You're kidding.'

'You're a fool if you think I'm kidding. It's all right there, Chester. Wrongful discharge, sexual harassment, the works. A couple of million in damages. I file these things all the time. I must say, however, that this is one of the best I've seen. This poor woman has been at the hospital for two days with her son. Her doctor says she cannot leave his bedside. In fact, he's called here and explained her situation, but no, you assholes fire her for missing work. I can't wait to explain this to a jury.'

It sometimes took Chester's lawyer two days to return a phone call, and this woman, Dianne Sway, files a full-blown lawsuit within hours of being terminated. He slowly picked up the papers and studied the front page. 'I'm named personally?' he asked as if his feelings were hurt.

'You fired her, Chester. Don't worry though, when the jury returns a verdict against you individually, you can simply file for bankruptcy.'

Chester pulled his chair under him and carefully sat down. 'Please, sit,' he said, waving at a chair.

'No thanks. Who's your attorney?'

'Ugh, geez, uh, Findley and Baker. But just wait a minute. Let me think about this.' He flipped the page and scanned the pleadings. 'Sexual harassment?'

'Yeah, that's a fertile field these days. Seems as though one of your supervisors has put the move on my client. Always suggesting things they might do in the rest room during lunch. Always telling dirty jokes. Lots of crude talk. It'll all come out at trial. Who should I call at Findley and Baker?'

'Just wait a minute.' He flipped the pages, then laid them on the desk. She stood next to his desk, glaring down. He rubbed his temples. 'I don't need this.'

'Neither did my client.'

'What does she want?'

'A little dignity. You run a sweatshop here. You prey on single working mothers who can barely feed their children on what you pay. They cannot afford to complain.'

He was rubbing his eyes now. 'Skip the lecture, okay. I just don't need this. There could, well, there might be some trouble at the top.'

'I couldn't care less about you and your troubles, Chester. A copy of this lawsuit will be hand-delivered to the *Memphis Press* this afternoon, and I'm sure it'll run tomorrow. The Sways are getting more than their share of ink these days.'

'What does she want?' he asked again.

'Are you trying to bargain?'

'Maybe. I don't think you can win this case, Ms. Love, but I don't need the headache.'

'It'll be more than a headache, I promise. She makes nine hundred dollars a month, and takes home around six-fifty. That's eleven thousand bucks a year, and I promise your legal costs on this lawsuit will run five times that much. I'll obtain access to your personnel records. I'll take the depositions of other female employees. I'll open up your financial books. I'll subpoena all your records. And if I see anything the least bit improper, I'll notify the Equal Employment Opportunity Commission, the National Labor Relations Board, the IRS, OSHA, and anybody else who might be interested. I'll make you lose sleep, Chester. You'll wish a thousand times you hadn't fired my client.'

He slapped the table with both palms. 'What does she want, dammit!'

Reggie picked up her briefcase, and walked to the door. 'She wants her job. A raise would be nice, say from six bucks an hour to nine, if you can spare it. And if you can't, then do it anyway. Transfer her to another section, away from the dirty supervisor.'

Chester listened carefully. This was not too bad.

'She'll be in the hospital for a few weeks. She has bills, so I want the payroll checks to keep coming. In fact, Chester, I want the payroll checks delivered to the hospital, just like you clowns delivered her termination letter this morning. Every Friday, I want the check delivered. Okay?'

He slowly nodded yes.

'You have thirty days to answer the lawsuit. If you behave and do as I say, I'll dismiss it on the thirtieth day. You have my word. You don't have to tell your lawyers about it. Is it a deal?'

'Deal.'

Reggie opened the door. 'Oh, and send some flowers. Room 943. A card would be nice. In fact, send some fresh flowers every week. Okay, Chester?'

He was still nodding.

She slammed the door and left the grungy corporate offices of Ark-Lon Fixtures.

Mark and Ricky sat on the end of the foldaway bed and looked up into the bearded and intense face of Dr. Greenway less than two feet away. Ricky wore a pair of Mark's hand-me-down pajamas with a blanket draped over his shoulders. He was cold, as usual, and scared, and uncertain about this first venture out of his bed, even though it was inches away. And he preferred his mother to be present, but the doctor had gently insisted on talking to the boys by themselves. Greenway had spent almost twelve hours now trying to win Ricky's confidence. He sat close to his big brother, who was bored with this little chat before it started.

The shades were pulled, the lights were dim, the room was dark except for a small lamp on a table by the bathroom. Greenway leaned forward with his elbows on his knees.

'Now, Ricky, I would like to talk about the other day when you and Mark went to the woods for a smoke. Okay?'

This frightened Ricky. How did Greenway know they were smoking? Mark leaned over an inch or two and said, 'It's okay, Ricky. I've already told them about it. Mom's not mad at us.'

'Do you remember going for a smoke?' Greenway asked.

Slowly, he nodded his head. 'Yes sir.'

'Why don't you tell me what you remember about you and Mark in the woods smoking a cigarette.'

He pulled the blanket tighter around him and knotted it with his hands at his stomach. 'I'm really cold,' he muttered, his teeth chattering.

'Ricky, the temperature is almost seventy-eight degrees in here. And you've got the blanket and wool pajamas. Try and think about being warm, okay?'

He tried but it didn't help. Mark gently placed his arm around Ricky's shoulder, and this seemed to help.

'Do you remember smoking a cigarette?'

'I think so. Uh-huh.'

Mark glanced up at Greenway, then at Ricky.

'Okay. Do you remember seeing the big black car when it pulled up in the grass?'

Ricky suddenly stopped shaking and stared at the floor. He mumbled the word 'Yes,' and that would be his last word for twenty-four hours.

'And what did the big black car do when you first saw it?'

The mention of the cigarette had scared him, but the image of the black car and the fear it brought were simply too much. He bent over at the waist and placed his head on Mark's knee. His eyes were shut tightly, and he began sobbing, but with no tears.

Mark rubbed his hair, and repeated, 'It's okay, Ricky. It's okay. We need to talk about it.'

Greenway was unmoved. He crossed his bony legs and scratched his beard. He had expected this, and had warned Mark and Dianne that this first little session would not be productive. But it was very important.

'Ricky, listen to me,' he said in a childlike voice. 'Ricky, it's okay. I just want to talk to you. Okay, Ricky.'

But Ricky had had enough therapy for one day. He began to curl under the blanket, and Mark knew the thumb could not be far behind. Greenway nodded at him as if all was well. He stood, carefully lifted Ricky, and placed him in the bed.

# CHAPTER SEVENTEEN

Wally Boxx stopped the van in heavy traffic on Camp Street, and ignored the horns and fingers as his boss and Fink and the FBI agents made a quick exit onto the sidewalk in front of the Federal Building. Foltrigg walked importantly up the steps with his entourage behind. In the lobby, a couple of bored reporters recognized him and began asking questions, but he was all business and had nothing but smiles and no comments.

He entered the offices of the United States Attorney for the Southern District of Louisiana, and the secretaries sprang to life. His assigned space in the building was a vast suite of small offices connected by hallways, and large open areas where the clerical staff performed, and smaller rooms where cubicles allowed some privacy for law clerks and paralegals. In all, forty-seven Assistant U.S. Attorneys labored here under the commands of Reverend Roy. Another thirty-eight underlings plowed through the drudgery and paperwork and boring research and tedious attention to mindless details, all in an effort to protect the legal interests of Roy's client, the United States of America.

The largest office of course belonged to Foltrigg, and it was richly decorated with heavy wood and deep leather. Whereas most lawyers allow themselves only one Ego Wall with pictures and plaques and awards and certificates for Rotary Club membership, Roy had covered no less than three of his with framed photographs and yellow fill-in-the-blank attendance diplomas from a hundred judicial conferences. He threw his jacket on the burgundy leather sofa, and headed directly for the main library where a meeting awaited him.

He had called six times during the five-hour trip from Memphis. There had been three faxes. Six assistants were waiting around a thirty-foot oak conference table covered with open law books and countless legal pads. All jackets were off and all sleeves rolled up.

He said hello to the group and took a chair at the center of the table. They each had a copy of a summarization of the FBI's findings in Memphis. The note, the fingerprints, the gun, everything. There was nothing new Foltrigg or Fink could tell them except that Gronke was in Memphis, and this was irrelevant to this group.

'What do you have, Bobby?' Foltrigg asked dramatically, as if the future of the American legal system rested upon Bobby and whatever he had uncovered in his research. Bobby was the dean of the assistants, a thirty-two-year veteran who hated courtrooms but loved libraries. In times of crisis when answers were needed for complex questions, they all turned to Bobby.

He rubbed his thick, gray hair and adjusted his black-rimmed glasses. Six months until retirement, when he would be through with the likes of Roy Foltrigg. He'd seen a dozen of them come and go, most never heard from again. 'Well, I think we've narrowed it down,' he said, and most of them smiled. He began every report with the same line. To Bobby, legal research was a game of clearing away the piles of debris heaped upon even the simplest of issues, and narrowing the focus to that which is quickly grasped by judges and juries. Everything got narrowed down when Bobby handled the research.

'There are two avenues, neither very attractive but one or both might work. First, I suggest the Juvenile Court approach in Memphis. Under the Tennessee Youth Code, a petition can be filed with the Juvenile Court alleging certain misconduct by the child. There are various categories of wrongdoing, and the petition must classify the child as either a delinquent or a child in need of supervision. A hearing is held, the Juvenile Court judge hears the proof and makes a determination as to what happens to the child. The same can be done for abused or neglected children. Same procedure, same court.'

'Who can file the petition?' Foltrigg asked.

'Well, the statute is very broad, and I think it's a terrible flaw in the law. But it plainly says that a petition can be filed by, and I quote, "any interested party". End of quote.'

'Can that be us?'

'Maybe. It depends on what we allege in our petition. And here's the sticky part – we must allege the kid has done, or is doing, something wrong, violating the law in some way. And the only violation even remotely touching this kid's behavior is, of course, obstruction of justice. So we must allege things we're not sure of, such as the kid's knowledge of where the body is. This could be tricky, since we're not certain.'

'The kid knows where the body is,' Foltrigg said flatly. Fink studied some notes and pretended not to hear, but the other six repeated the words to themselves. Did Foltrigg know things he hadn't yet told them? There was a pause as this apparent statement of fact settled in around the table.

'Have you told us everything?' Bobby asked, glancing at his cohorts.

'Yes,' Foltrigg replied. 'But I'm telling you the kid knows. It's my gut feeling.'

Typical Foltrigg. Creating facts with his guts, and expecting those under him to follow on faith.

Bobby continued. 'A Juvenile court summons is served on the child's mother, and a hearing is held within seven days. The child must have a lawyer, and I understand one has already been obtained. The child has a right to be at the hearing and may testify if he so chooses.' Bobby wrote something on his legal pad. 'Frankly, this is the quickest way to get the kid to talk.'

'What if he refuses to talk on the witness stand?'

'Very good question,' Bobby said like a professor pandering to a first-year law student. 'It is completely discretionary with the judge. If we put on a good case and convince the judge the kid knows something, he has the authority to order the kid to talk. If the kid refuses, he may be in contempt of court.'

'Let's say he's in contempt. What happens then?'

'Difficult to say at this point. He's only eleven years old, but the judge could, as a last resort, incarcerate the child in a youth court facility until he purges himself of contempt.'

'In other words, until he talks.'

It was so easy to spoon-feed Foltrigg. 'That is correct. Mind you, this would be the most drastic course the judge could take. We have yet to find any precedent for the incarceration of an eleven-year-old child for contempt of court. We haven't checked all fifty states, but we've covered most of them.'

'It won't go that far,' Foltrigg predicted calmly. 'If we file a petition as an interested party, serve the kid's mother with papers, drag his little butt into court with his lawyer in tow, then I think he'll be so scared he'll tell what he knows. What about you, Thomas?'

'Yeah, I think it'll work. And what if it doesn't? What's the downside?'

'There's little risk,' Bobby explained. 'All Juvenile Court proceedings are closed. We can even ask that the petition be kept under lock and key. If it's dismissed initially for lack of standing or whatever, no one will know it. If we proceed to the hearing and A, the kid talks but doesn't know anything, or B, the judge refuses to make him talk, then we haven't lost anything. And C, if the kid talks out of fear or under threat of contempt, then we've gotten what we wanted. Assuming the kid knows about Boyette.'

'He knows,' Foltrigg said.

'The plan would not be so attractive if the proceedings were made public. We would look weak and desperate if we lost. It could, in my opinion, seriously undermine our chances at trial here in New Orleans if we try this and fail, and if it's in some way publicized.'

The door opened and Wally Boxx, fresh from having successfully parked the van, entered and seemed irritated that they had proceeded without him. He sat next to Foltrigg.

'But you're certain it can be done in private?' Fink asked.

'That's what the law says. I don't know how they apply it in Memphis, but the confidentiality is explicit in the code sections. There are even penalties for disclosure.'

'We'll need local counsel, someone in Ord's office,' Foltrigg said to Fink as if the decision had already been made. Then he turned to the group. 'I like the sound of this. Right now the kid and his lawyer are probably thinking it's all over. This will be a wake-up call. They'll know we're serious. They'll know they're headed for court. We'll make it plain to his lawyer that we'll not rest until we have the truth from the kid. I like this. Little downside risk. It'll take place three hundred miles from here, away from these morons with cameras we have around here. If we try it and fail, no big deal. No one will know. I like the idea of no cameras and no reporters.' He paused as if deep in thought, the field marshal surveying the plains, deciding where to send his tanks.

To everyone except Boxx and Foltrigg, the humor in this was delicious. The idea of the Reverend plotting strategies that did not include cameras was unheard of. He, of course, did not realize it. He bit his lip and nodded his head. Yes, yes, this was the best course. This would work.

Bobby cleared his throat. 'There is one other possible approach, and I don't like it but it's worth mentioning. A real longshot. If you assume the kid knows – '

'He knows.'

'Thank you. Assuming this, and assuming he has confided in his lawyer, there is the possibility of a federal indictment against her for obstruction of justice. I don't have to tell you the difficulty in piercing the attorney–client privilege; it's virtually impossible. The indictment would, of course, be used to sort of scare her into cutting some deal. I don't know. As I said, a real longshot.'

Foltrigg chewed on this for a second, but his mind was still churning over the first plan and it simply couldn't digest the second.

'A conviction might be difficult,' Fink said.

'Yep,' Bobby agreed. 'But a conviction would not be the goal. She would be indicted here, a long way from home, and I think it would be quite intimidating. Lots of bad press. Couldn't keep this one quiet, you know. She'd be forced to hire a lawyer. We could string it out for months, you know, the works. You might even consider obtaining the indictment, keeping it sealed, breaking the news to her, and offering some deal in return for its dismissal. Just a thought.'

'I like it,' Foltrigg said to no one's surprise. It had the stench of the government's jackboot, and these strategies always appealed to him. 'And we can always dismiss the indictment anytime we want.'

Ah yes! The Roy Foltrigg Special. Get the indictment, hold the press conference, beat the defendant to the ground with all sorts of threats, cut the deal, then quietly dismiss the indictment a year later. He'd done it a hundred times in seven years. He'd also eaten a few of his Specials when the defendant and/or his lawyer refused to deal and insisted on a trial. When this happened Foltrigg was always too busy with more important prosecutions, and the file was thrown at one of the younger assistants who invariably got his ass kicked. Invariably, Foltrigg placed the blame squarely on the assistant. He'd even fired one for losing the trial brought about by a Roy Foltrigg Special.

'That's Plan B, okay, on hold for right now,' he said, very much in control. 'Plan A is to file a petition in Juvenile Court first thing tomorrow morning. How long will it take to prepare it?'

'An hour,' answered Tank Mozingo, a burly assistant with the ponderous name of Thurston Alomar Mozingo, thus known simply as Tank. 'The petition is set out in the code. We simply add the allegations and fill in the blanks.'

'Get it done.' He turned to Fink. 'Thomas, you'll handle this. Get on the phone to Ord and ask him to help us. Fly to Memphis tonight. I want the petition filed first thing in the morning, after you talk to the judge. Tell him how urgent this is.' Papers shuffled around the table as the research group began cleaning its mess. Their work was over. Fink took notes as Boxx darted for a legal pad. Foltrigg spewed forth instructions like King Solomon dictating to his scribes. 'Ask the judge for an expedited hearing. Explain how much pressure is behind this. Ask for complete confidentiality, including the closing of the petition and all other pleadings. Stress this, you understand. I'll be sitting by the phone in case I'm needed.'

Bobby was buttoning his cuffs. 'Look, Roy, there's something else we need to mention.'

'What is it?'

'We're playing hardball with this kid. Let's not forget the danger he's in. Muldanno is desperate. There are reporters everywhere. A leak here and a leak there, and the mob could silence the kid before he talks. There's a lot at stake.'

Roy flashed a confident smile. 'I know that, Bobby. In fact, Muldanno's already sent his boys to Memphis. The FBI up there is tracking them, and they're also watching the boy. Personally, I don't think Muldanno's stupid enough to try something, but we're not taking chances.' Roy stood and smiled around the room. 'Good work, men. I appreciate it.'

They mumbled their thank-yous and left the library.

On the fourth floor of the Radisson Hotel in downtown Memphis, two blocks from the Sterick Building and five blocks from St. Peter's, Paul Gronke played a monotonous game of gin rummy with Mack Bono, a Muldanno grunt from New Orleans. A heavily marked score sheet was on the floor under the table, abandoned. They had been playing for a dollar a game, but now no one cared. Gronke's shoes were on the bed. His shirt was unbuttoned. Heavy cigarette smoke clung to the ceiling. They were drinking bottled water because it was not yet five, but almost, and when the magic hour hit they'd call room service. Gronke checked his watch. He looked through the window at the buildings across Union Avenue. He played a card.

Gronke was a childhood friend of Muldanno's, a most trusted partner in many of his dealings. He owned a few bars and a tourist tee shirt shop in the Quarter. He'd broken his share of legs and had helped The Blade do the same. He did not know where Boyd Boyette was buried, and he wasn't about to ask, but if he pressed hard his friend would probably tell him. They were very close.

Gronke was in Memphis because The Blade had called him. And he was bored as hell sitting in this hotel room playing cards with his shoes off, drinking water and eating sandwiches, smoking Camels and waiting on the next move by an eleven-year-old kid.

Across the double beds, an open door led to the next room. It too had two beds and a cloud of smoke whirling around the ceiling vents. Jack Nance stood in the window watching the rush-hour traffic leave downtown. A radio and a cellular phone stood ready on a nearby table. Any minute Cal Sisson would call from the hospital with the latest about Mark Sway. A thick briefcase was open on one bed, and Nance in his boredom had spent most of the afternoon playing with his bugging devices.

He had a plan to drop a bug in Room 943. He had seen the lawyer's office, absent of special locks on the door, absent of cameras overhead, absent of any security devices. Typical lawyer. Wiring it would be easy. Cal Sisson had visited the doctor's office and found pretty much the same. A receptionist at a front desk. Sofas and chairs for the patients to wait for their shrink. A couple of drab offices down a hall. No special security. The client, this clown who liked to be called The Blade, had approved the wiring of the telephones in both the doctor's and lawyer's office. He also wanted files copied. Easy work. He also wanted a bug planted in Ricky's room. Easy work too, but the difficult part was receiving the transmission once the bug was in place. Nance was working on this.

As far as Nance was concerned, it was simply a surveillance job, nothing more or less. The client was paying top dollar in cash. If he wanted a child followed, it was easy. If he wanted to eavesdrop, no problem as long as he was paying.

But Nance had read the newspapers. And he had heard the whispers in the room next door. There was more here than simple surveillance. Broken legs and arms were not being discussed over gin rummy. These guys were deadly, and Gronke had already mentioned calling New Orleans for more help.

Cal Sisson was ready to bolt. He was fresh off probation, and another conviction would send him back for decades. A conviction for conspiracy to commit murder would send him away for life. Nance had convinced him to hold tight for one more day.

The cellular phone rang. It was Sisson. The lawyer just arrived at the hospital. Mark Sway's in Room 943 with his mother and lawyer.'

Nance placed the phone on the table, and walked into the other room.

'Who was it?' Gronke asked with a Camel in his mouth.

'Cal. Kid's still at the hospital, now with his mother and his lawyer.'

'Where's the doctor?'

'He left an hour ago.' Nance walked to the dresser and poured a glass of water.

'Any sign of the Feds?' Gronke grunted.

'Yeah. Same two are hanging around the hospital. Doing the same thing we are, I guess. The hospital's keeping two security guards by the door, and another one close by.'

'You think the kid told them about meeting me this morning?' Gronke asked for the hundredth time of the day.

'He told someone. Why else would they suddenly surround his room with security guards?'

'Yeah, but the security guards are not Fibbies, are they? If he'd told the Fibbies, then they'd be sitting in the hall, don't you think?'

'Yeah.' This conversation had been repeated throughout the day. Who did the kid tell? Why were there suddenly guards by the door? And on and on. Gronke couldn't get enough of it.

Despite his arrogance and street punk posture, he seemed to be a man of patience. Nance figured it went with the territory. Killers had to be cold-blooded and patient.

# CHAPTER EIGHTEEN

They left the hospital in her Mazda RX-7, his first ride in a sports car. The seats were leather but the floor was dirty. The car was not new, but it was cool, with a stick shift that she worked like a veteran race car driver. She said she liked to drive fast, which was fine with Mark. They darted through traffic as they left downtown and headed east. It was almost dark. The radio was on but barely audible, some FM station specializing in easy listening.

Ricky was awake when they left. He was staring at cartoons but saying little. A sad little tray of hospital food sat on the table, untouched by either Ricky or Dianne. Mark had not seen his mother eat three bites in two days. He felt sorry for her sitting there on the bed, staring at Ricky, worrying herself to death. The news from Reggie about the job and the raise had made her smile. Then it made her cry.

Mark was sick of the crying and the cold peas and the dark, cramped room, and he felt guilty for leaving but was delighted to be here in this sports car headed, he hoped, for a plate of hot, heavy food with warm bread. Clint had mentioned inside-out ravioli and spinach lasagne, and for some reason visions of these rich, meaty dishes had stuck in his mind. Maybe there would be a cake and some cookies. But if Momma Love served green Jell-O, he might throw it at her.

He thought of these things as Reggie thought of being trailed. Her eyes went from the traffic to the mirror, and back again. She drove much too fast, zipping between cars and changing lanes, which didn't bother Mark one bit.

'You think Mom and Ricky are safe?' he asked, watching the cars in front.

'Yes. Don't worry about them. The hospital promised to keep guards at the door.' She had talked to George Ord, her new pal, and explained her concern about the safety of the Sway family. She did not mention any specific threats, though Ord had asked. The family was getting unwanted attention, she had explained. Lots of rumors and gossip, most of it generated by a frustrated media. Ord had talked to McThune, then called her back and said the FBI would stay close to the room, but out of sight. She thanked him.

Ord and McThune were amused by it. The FBI already had people in the hospital. Now they had been invited.

She suddenly turned to the right at an intersection, and the tires squealed. Mark chuckled, and she laughed as though it was all fun but her stomach was flipping. They were on a smaller street with old homes and large oaks.

'This is my neighborhood,' she said. It was certainly nicer than his. They turned again, to another narrower street where the houses were smaller but still two and three stories tall with deep lawns and manicured hedgerows.

'Why do you take your clients home?' he asked.

'I don't know. Most of my clients are children who come from awful homes. I feel sorry for them, I guess. I get attached to them.'

'Do you feel sorry for me?'

'A little. But you're lucky, Mark, very lucky. You have a mother who's a good woman and who loves you very much.'

'Yeah, I guess so. What time is it?'

'Almost six. Why?'

Mark thought a second and counted the hours. 'Forty-nine hours ago Jerome Clifford shot himself. I wish we'd simply run away when we saw his car.'

'Why didn't you?'

'I don't know. It was like I just had to do something once I realized what was going on. I couldn't run away. He was about to die, and I just couldn't ignore it. Something kept pulling me to his car. Ricky was crying and begging me to stop, but I just couldn't. This is all my fault.'

'Maybe, but you can't change it, Mark. It's done.' She glanced at her mirror and saw nothing.

'Do you think we're gonna be okay? I mean, Ricky and me and Mom? When this is all over, will things be like they were?'

She slowed and turned into a narrow driveway lined with thick, untrimmed hedges. 'Ricky will be fine. It might take time, but he'll be all right. Kids are tough, Mark. I see it every day.'

'What about me?'

'Everything will work out, Mark. Just trust me.' The Mazda stopped beside a large two-story house with a porch around the front of it. Shrubs and flowers grew to the windows. Ivy covered one end of the porch.

'Is this your house?' he asked, almost in awe.

'My parents bought it fifty-three years ago, the year before I was born. This is where I grew up. My daddy died when I was fifteen, but Momma Love, bless her heart, is still here.'

'You call her Momma Love?'

'Everyone calls her Momma Love. She's almost eighty, and in better shape than me.' She pointed to a garage straight ahead, behind the house. 'You see those three windows above the garage? That's where I live.'

Like the house, the garage needed a good coat of paint on the trim. Both were old and handsome, but there were weeds in the flower beds and grass growing in the cracks of the driveway.

They entered through a side door, and the aroma from the kitchen hit Mark hard. He was suddenly starving. A small woman with gray hair in a tight ponytail and dark eyes met them and hugged Reggie.

'Momma Love, meet Mark Sway,' Reggie said, waving at him. He and Momma Love were exactly the same height, and she gently hugged him and pecked him on the cheek. He stood stiff, uncertain how to greet a strange eighty-year-old woman.

'Nice to meet you, Mark,' she said in his face. Her voice was strong and sounded much like Reggie's. She took his arm and led him to the kitchen table. 'Have a seat right here, and I'll get you something to drink.'

Reggie grinned at him as if to say 'Just do as she says because you have no choice.' She hung her umbrella on a rack behind the door and laid her briefcase on the floor.

The kitchen was small and cluttered with cabinets and shelves along three walls. Steam rose from the gas stove. A wooden table with four chairs sat squarely in the center of the room with pots and pans hanging from a beam above it. The kitchen was warm and created instant hunger.

Mark took the nearest chair and watched Momma Love scoot around, grabbing a glass from the cabinet, opening the refrigerator, filling the glass with ice, pouring tea from a pitcher.

Reggie kicked off her shoes and was stirring something in a pot on the stove. She and Momma Love chatted back and forth, the usual routine of how the day went and who'd called. A cat stopped at Mark's chair and examined him.

'That's Axle,' Momma Love said as she served the ice tea with a cloth napkin. 'She's seventeen years old, and very gentle.'

Mark drank the tea and left Axle alone. He was not fond of cats.

'How's your little brother?' Momma Love asked.

'He's doing much better,' he said, and suddenly wondered how much Reggie had told her mother. Then he relaxed. If Clint knew very little, Momma Love probably knew even less. He took another sip. She waited for a longer answer. 'He started talking today.'

'That's wonderful!' she exclaimed with a huge smile and patted him on the shoulder.

Reggie poured her tea from a different pitcher, and doctored it with sweetener and lemon. She sat across from Mark at the table, and Axle jumped into her lap. She sipped tea, rubbed the cat, and began slowly removing her jewelry. She was tired.

'Are you hungry?' Momma Love asked, suddenly darting around the kitchen, opening the oven, stirring the pot, closing a drawer.

'Yes ma'am.'

'It's so nice to hear a young man with manners,' she said as she stopped for a second and smiled at him. 'Most of Reggie's kids have no manners. I haven't heard a "yes ma'am" in this house in years.' Then she was off again, wiping out a pan and placing it in the sink.

Reggie winked at him. 'Mark's been eating hospital food for three days, Momma Love, so he wants to know what you're cooking.'

'It's a surprise,' she said, opening the oven and releasing a thick aroma of meat and cheese and tomatoes. 'But I think you'll like it, Mark.'

He was certain he would like it. Reggie winked at him again as she twisted her head and removed a set of small diamond earrings. The pile of jewelry in front of her now included half a dozen bracelets, two rings, a necklace, a watch, and the earrings. Axle was watching it too. Momma Love was suddenly hacking away with a large knife on a cutting board. She whirled around and laid a basket of bread, hot and buttery, in front of him. 'I bake bread every Wednesday,' she said, patting his shoulder again, then off to the stove.

Mark grabbed the biggest slice and took a bite. It was soft and warm, unlike any bread he'd eaten. The butter and garlic melted instantly on his tongue.

'Momma Love is full-blooded Italian,' Reggie said, stroking Axle. 'Both her parents were born in Italy and immigrated to this country in 1902. I'm half Italian.'

'Who was Mr. Love?' Mark asked, chomping away, butter on his lips and fingers.

'A Memphis boy. They were married when she was sixteen – '

'Seventeen,' Momma Love corrected without turning around.

Momma Love was now setting the table with plates and flatware. Reggie and her jewelry were in the way, so she gathered it all up and kicked and nudged Axle to the floor. 'When do we eat, Momma Love?' she asked.

'In a minute.'

'I'm going to run and change clothes,' she said. Axle sat on Mark's foot and rubbed the back of her head on his shin.

'I'm very sorry about your little brother,' Momma Love said, glancing at the door to make sure Reggie was indeed gone.

Mark swallowed a mouthful of bread, and wiped his mouth with the napkin. 'He'll be okay. We've got good doctors.'

'And you've got the best lawyer in the world,' she said sternly with no smile. She waited for verification.

'We sure do,' Mark said slowly.

She nodded her approval and started for the sink. 'What on earth did you boys see out there?'

Mark sipped his tea and stared at the gray ponytail. This could be a long night with plenty of questions. It would be best to stop it now. 'Reggie told me not to talk about it.' He bit into another piece of bread.

'Oh, Reggie always says that. But you can talk to me. All her kids do.'

In the last forty-nine hours, he'd learned much about interrogation. Keep the other guy on his heels. When the questions get odd, dish out a few of your own. 'How often does she bring a kid home?'

She slid the pot off the burner, and thought a second. 'Maybe twice a month. She wants them to eat good food, so she brings them to Momma Love's. Sometimes they spend the night. One little girl stayed a month. She was so pitiful. Name was Andrea. The court took her away from her parents because they were Satan worshipers, doing animal sacrifices and all that mess. She was so sad. She lived upstairs here in Reggie's old bedroom, and she cried when she had to leave. Broke my heart too. I told Reggie "No more kids," after that. But Reggie does what Reggie wants. She really likes you, you know.'

'What happened to Andrea?'

'Her parents got her back. I pray for her every day. Do you go to church?'

'Sometimes.'

'Are you a good Catholic?'

'No. It's a little, well, I'm not sure what kind of church it is. But it's not Catholic. Baptist, I think. We go every now and then.'

Momma Love listened to this with deep concern, terribly puzzled by the fact that he wasn't sure what kind of church he attended.

'Maybe I should take you to my church. St. Luke's. It's a beautiful church. Catholics know how to build beautiful churches, you know.'

He nodded but could think of nothing to say. In a flash, she'd forgotten about churches and was back to the stove, opening the oven door and studying the dish with the concentration of Dr. Greenway. She mumbled to herself and it was obvious she was pleased.

'Go wash your hands, Mark, right down the hall there. Kids nowadays don't wash their hands enough. Go along.' Mark crammed the last bite of bread into his mouth and followed Axle to the bathroom.

When he returned, Reggie was seated at the table, flipping through a stack of mail. The bread basket had been replenished. Momma Love opened the oven and pulled out a deep dish covered with aluminum foil. 'It's lasagne,' Reggie said to him with a trace of anticipation.

Momma Love launched into a brief history of the dish while she cut it into sections and dug out great hunks with a large spoon. Steam boiled from the pan. 'The recipe has been in my family for centuries,' she said, staring at Mark as if he cared about the lasagne's pedigree. He wanted it on his plate. 'Came over from the old country. I could bake it for my daddy when I was ten years old.' Reggie rolled her eyes a bit and winked at Mark. 'It has four layers, each with a different cheese.' She covered their plates with perfect squares of it. The four different cheeses ran together and oozed from the thick pasta.

The phone on the countertop rang, and Reggie answered. 'Go on and eat, Mark, if you want,' Momma Love said as she majestically set his plate in front of him. She nodded at Reggie's back. 'She might talk forever.' Reggie was listening and talking softly into the phone. It was obvious they were not supposed to hear.

Mark cut a huge bite with his fork, blew on it just enough to knock off the steam, and carefully raised it to his mouth. He chewed slowly, savoring the rich meat sauce, the cheeses, and who knew what else. Even the spinach was divine.

Momma Love watched and waited. She'd poured herself a second glass of wine, and held it halfway between the table and her lips as she waited for a response to her great-grandmother's secret recipe.

'It's great,' he said going for the second bite. 'Just great.' His only experience with lasagne had been a year or so earlier when his mother had pulled a plastic tray from the microwave and served it for dinner. Swanson's frozen, or something like that. He remembered a rubbery taste, nothing like this.

'You like it,' Momma Love said, taking a sip of her wine.

He nodded with a mouthful, and this pleased her. She took a small bite.

Reggie hung up and turned to the table. 'Gotta run downtown. The cops just picked up Ross Scott for shoplifting again. He's in jail crying for his mother, but they can't find her.'

'How long will you be gone?' Mark asked, his fork still.

'Couple of hours. You finish eating and visit with Momma Love. I'll take you to the hospital later.' She patted his shoulder, and then she was out the door.

Momma Love was silent until she heard Reggie's car start, then she said, 'What on earth did you boys see out there?'

Mark took a bite, chewed forever as she waited, then took a long drink of tea. 'Nothing. How do you make this stuff? It's great.'

'Well, it's an old recipe.'

She sipped the wine, and rattled on for ten minutes about the sauce. Then the cheeses.

Mark didn't hear a word.

He finished the peach cobbler and ice cream while she cleared the table and loaded the dishwasher. He thanked her again, said it was delicious for the tenth time, and stood with an aching stomach. He'd been sitting for an hour. Dinner at the trailer was usually a ten-minute affair. Most of the time they ate microwave meals on trays in front of the television. Dianne was too tired to cook.

Momma Love admired his empty bowl, and sent him to the den while she finished cleaning. The TV was color, but without remote control. No cable. A large family portrait hung above the sofa. He noticed it, then walked closer. It was an old photograph of the Love family, matted and framed by thick, curly wood. Mr. and Mrs. Love were on a small sofa in some studio with two boys in tight collars standing beside them. Momma Love had dark hair and a beautiful smile. Mr. Love was a foot taller, and sat rigid and unsmiling. The boys were stiff and awkward, obviously not happy to be dressed in starched shirts and ties. Reggie was between her parents, in the center of the portrait. She had a wonderful, smirky smile, and it was obvious she was the center of the family's attention and enjoyed this immensely. She was ten or eleven, about Mark's age, and the face of this pretty little girl caught his attention and took his breath. He stared at her face and she seemed to laugh at him. She was full of mischief.

'Beautiful children, huh?' It was Momma Love, easing beside him and admiring her family.

'When was this?' Mark asked, still staring.

'Forty years ago,' She said slowly, almost sadly. 'We were all so young and happy then.' She stood next to him, their arms touching, shoulder to shoulder.

'Where are the boys?'

'Joey, on the right there, is the oldest. He was a test pilot for the Air Force, and was killed in 1964 in a plane crash. He's a hero.'

'I'm very sorry,' Mark whispered.

'Bennie, on the left, is a year younger than Joey. He's a marine biologist in Vancouver. He never comes to see his mother. He was here about two years ago for Christmas, then off again. He's never married, but I think he's okay. No grandkids by him either. Reggie's got the only grandkids.' She was reaching for a framed five by seven next to a lamp on an end table. She handed it to Mark. Two graduation photos with blue caps and gowns. The girl was pretty. The boy had mangy hair, a teenager's beard, and a look of sheer hatred in his eyes.

'These are Reggie's kids,' Momma Love explained without the slightest trace of either love or pride. 'The boy was in prison last time we heard anything. Selling dope. He was a good boy when he was little, but then his father got him and just ruined him. This was after the divorce. The girl is out in California trying to be an actress or singer or something, or so she says, but she's had drug problems too and we don't hear much. She was a sweet child too. I haven't seen her in almost ten years. Can you believe it? My only granddaughter. It's so sad.'

Momma Love was now sipping her third glass of wine, and the tongue was loose. If she could talk about her family long enough, then maybe she'd get around to his. And once they'd covered the families, perhaps they might discuss exactly what on earth the boys saw out there.

'Why haven't you seen her in ten years?' Mark asked, but only because he needed to say something. It was really a dumb question because he knew the answer might take hours. His stomach ached from the feast and he wanted to simply lie on the couch and be left alone.

'Regina, I mean, Reggie, lost her when she was about thirteen. They were going through this nightmare of a divorce, he was chasing other women and had girlfriends all over town, they even caught him with a cute little nurse at the hospital, but the divorce was a horrible nightmare and Reggie got to where she couldn't handle it. Joe, her ex-husband, was a good boy when they got married, but then made a bunch of money and got the doctor's attitude, you know, and he changed. Money went to his head.' She paused and took a sip. 'Awful, just awful. I do miss them, though. They're my only grandbabies.'

They didn't look like grandbabies, especially the boy. He was nothing but a punk.

'What happened to him?' Mark asked after a few seconds of silence.

'Well.' She sighed as if she hated to tell, but would do it anyway. 'He was sixteen when his father got him, wild and rotten already, I mean, his father was an ob-gyn and never had time for the kids and a boy needs a father, don't you think; and the boy, Jeff is his name, was out of control early. Then his father, who had all the money and all the lawyers, got Regina sent away and took the kids, and when this happened Jeff was pretty much on his own. With his father's money, of course. He finished high school almost at gunpoint, and within six months got caught with a bunch of drugs.' She stopped suddenly, and Mark thought she was about to cry. She took a sip. 'The last time I hugged him was when he graduated from high school. I saw his picture in the newspaper when he got in trouble, but he never called or anything. It's been ten years, Mark. I know I'll die without ever seeing them again.' She quickly rubbed her eyes, and Mark looked for a hole to crawl in.

She took his arm. 'Come with me. Let's go sit on the porch.'

He followed through a narrow foyer, through the front door, and they sat in the swing on the front porch. It was dark and the air was cool. They rocked gently in silence. Momma Love sipped the wine.

She decided to continue the saga. 'You see, Mark, once Joe got the kids, he just ruined them. Gave them plenty of money. Kept his old sleazy girlfriends around the house. Flaunted it in front of the kids. Bought them cars. Amanda got pregnant in high school, and he arranged the abortion.'

'Why'd Reggie change her name?' he asked politely. Maybe when she answered, this saga would be finished.

'She spent several years in and out of institutions. This was after the divorce, and bless her heart, she was in bad shape, Mark. I cried myself to sleep every night worrying about my daughter. She lived with me most of the time. It took years, but she finally came through. Lots of therapy. Lots of money. Lots of love. And then she decided one day that the nightmare was over, that she would pick up the pieces and move on, and that she would create a new life. That's why she changed her name. She went to court and had it done legally. She fixed up the apartment over the garage. She gave me all these pictures, because she refuses to look at them. She went to law school. She became a new person with a new identity and a new name.'

'Is she bitter?'

'She fights it. She lost her children, and no mother can ever recover from that. But she tries not to think about them. They were brainwashed by their father, so they have no use for her. She hates him, of course, and I think it's probably healthy.'

'She's a very good lawyer,' he said as if he'd personally hired and fired many.

Momma Love moved closer, too close to suit Mark. She patted his knee and this irritated the hell out of him, but she was a sweet old woman and meant nothing by it. She'd buried a son and lost her only grandson, so he gave her a break. There was no moon. A soft wind gently rustled the leaves of the huge black oaks between the porch and the street. He was not anxious to return to the hospital, and so he decided this was pleasant after all. He smiled at Momma Love, but she was staring blankly into the darkness, lost in some deep thought. A heavy, folded quilt padded the swing.

He assumed she would work her way back to the shooting of Jerome Clifford, and this he wanted to avoid. 'Why does Reggie have so many kids for clients?'

She kept patting his knee. 'Because some kids need lawyers, though most of them don't know it. And most lawyers are too busy making money to worry about kids. She wants to help. She'll always blame herself for losing her kids, and she just wants to help others. She's very protective of her little clients.'

'I didn't pay her very much money.'

'Don't worry, Mark. Every month, Reggie takes at least two cases for free. They're called pro bono, which means the lawyer does the work without a fee. If she didn't want your case, she wouldn't have taken it.'

He knew about pro bono. Half the lawyers on television were laboring away on cases they wouldn't get paid for. The other half were sleeping with beautiful women and eating in fancy restaurants.

'Reggie has a soul, Mark, a conscience,' she continued, still patting gently. The wineglass was empty, but the words were clear and the mind was sharp. 'She'll work for no fee if she believes in the client. And some of her poor clients will break your heart, Mark. I cry all the time over some of these little fellas.'

'You're very proud of her, aren't you?'

'I am. Reggie almost died, Mark, a few years ago when the divorce was going on. I almost lost her. Then I almost went broke trying to get her back on her feet. But look at her now.'

'Will she ever get married again?'

'Maybe. She's dated a couple of men, but nothing serious. Romance is not at the top of her list. Her work comes first. Like tonight. It's almost eight o'clock, and she's at the city jail talking to a little troublemaker they picked up for shoplifting. Wonder what'll be in the newspaper in the morning.'

Sports, obituaries, the usual. Mark shifted uncomfortably and waited. It was obvious he was supposed to speak. 'Who knows.'

'What was it like having your picture on the front page of the paper?'

'I didn't like it.'

'Where'd they get those pictures?'

'They're school pictures.'

There was a long pause. The chains above them squeaked as the swing moved slowly back and forth. 'What was it like walking up on that dead man who'd just shot himself?'

'Pretty scary, but to be honest, my doctor told me not to discuss it because it stresses me out. Look at my little brother, you know. So, I'd better not say anything.'

She patted harder. 'Of course. Of course.'

Mark pressed with his toes, and the swing moved a bit faster. His stomach was still packed and he was suddenly sleepy. Momma Love was humming now. The breeze picked up, and he shivered.

Reggie found them on the dark porch, in the swing, rocking quietly back and forth. Momma Love sipped black coffee and patted him on the shoulder. Mark was curled in a knot beside her, his head resting in her lap, a quilt over his legs.

'How long has he been asleep?' she whispered.

'An hour or so. He got cold, then he got sleepy. He's a sweet child.'

'He sure is. I'll call his mother at the hospital, and see if he can stay here tonight.'

'He ate until he was stuffed. I'll fix him a good breakfast in the morning.'

# CHAPTER NINETEEN

The idea was Trumann's, and it was a wonderful idea, one that would work and thus would be snared immediately by Foltrigg and claimed as his own. Life with Reverend Roy was a series of stolen ideas and credits when things worked. And when things went to hell, Trumann and his office took the blame, along with Foltrigg's underlings, and the press, and the jurors, and the corrupt defense bar, everybody but the great man himself.

But Trumann had quietly massaged and manipulated the egos of prima donnas before, and he could certainly handle this idiot.

It was late, and as he picked at the lettuce in his shrimp rémoulade in the dark corner of a crowded oyster bar, the idea hit him. He called Foltrigg's private office number, no answer. He dialed the number in the library, and Wally Boxx answered. It was nine-thirty, and Wally explained he and his boss were still buried deep in the law books, just a couple of workaholics slaving over the details and enjoying it. All in a day's work. Trumann said he'd be there in ten minutes.

He left the noisy café and walked hurriedly through the crowds on Canal Street. September was just another hot, sticky summer month in New Orleans. After two blocks he removed his jacket and walked faster. Two more blocks, and his shirt was wet and clinging to his back and chest.

He darted through the crowds of tourists lumbering along Canal with their cameras and gaudy tee shirts, and wondered for the thousandth time why these people came to this city to spend hard-earned money on cheap entertainment and overpriced food. The average tourist on Canal Street wore black socks and white sneakers, was forty pounds overweight, and Trumann figured these people would return home and brag to their less fortunate friends about the delightful cuisine they had uniquely discovered and gorged themselves on in New Orleans. He bumped into a hefty woman with a small black box stuck in her face. She was actually standing near the curb and filming the front of a cheap souvenir store with suggestive street signs displayed for sale in the window. What sort of person would watch a video of a tacky souvenir shop in the French Quarter? Americans no longer experience vacations. They simply Sony them so they can ignore them for the rest of the year.

Trumann was in for a transfer. He was sick of tourists, traffic, humidity, crime, and he was sick of Roy Foltrigg. He turned by Rubinstein Brothers and headed for Poydras.

Foltrigg was not afraid of hard work. It came natural to him. He'd realized in law school that he was not a genius, and that to succeed he'd need to put in more hours. He studied his ass off, and finished somewhere in the middle of the pack. But he'd been elected president of the student body, and there was a certificate declaring this achievement framed in oak somewhere on one of his walls. His career as a political animal started at the moment when his law school classmates chose him as their president, a position most did not know existed and couldn't have cared less about. Job offers had been scarce for young Roy, and at the last minute he jumped at the chance to be an assistant city prosecutor in New Orleans. Fifteen thousand bucks a year in 1975. In two years he handled more cases than all the other city prosecutors combined. He worked. He put in long hours in a dead-end job because he was going places. He was a star but no one noticed.

He began dabbling in local Republican politics, a lonely hobby, and learned to play the game. He met people with money and clout, and landed a job with a law firm. He put in incredible hours and became a partner. He married a woman he didn't love because she had the right credentials and a wife brought respectability. Roy was on the move. There was a game plan.

He was still married to her but they slept in different rooms. The kids were now twelve and ten. A pretty family portrait.

He preferred the office to his home, which suited his wife just fine because she didn't like him but did enjoy his salary.

Roy's conference table was once again covered with law books and legal pads. Wally had shed his tie and jacket. Empty coffee cups littered the room. They were both tired.

The law was quite simple: every citizen owes to society the duty of giving testimony to aid in the enforcement of the law. And, a witness is not excused from testifying because of his fear of reprisal threatening his and/or his family's lives. It was black letter law, as they say, carved in stone over the years by hundreds of judges and justices. No exceptions. No exemptions. No loopholes for scared little boys. Roy and Wally had read dozens of cases. Many were copied and highlighted and thrown about on the table. The kid would have to talk. If the Juvenile Court approach in Memphis fell through, Foltrigg planned to issue a subpoena for Mark Sway to appear before the grand jury in New Orleans. It would scare the little punk to death, and loosen his tongue.

Trumann walked through the door and said, 'You guys are working late.'

Wally Boxx pushed away from the table and stretched his arms mightily above his head. 'Yeah, a lot of stuff to cover,' he said, exhausted, waving his hand proudly at the piles of books and notes.

'Have a seat,' Foltrigg said, pointing at a chair. 'We're finishing up.' He stretched too, then cracked his knuckles. He loved his reputation as a workaholic, a man of importance unafraid of painful hours, a family man whose calling went beyond wife and kids. The job meant everything. His client was the United States of America.

Trumann had heard this eighteen-hour-a-day crap for seven years now. It was Foltrigg's favorite subject – talking about himself and the hours at the office and the body that needed no sleep. Lawyers wear their loss of sleep like a badge of honor. Real macho machines grinding it out around the clock.

'I've got an idea,' Trumann said, sitting across the table. 'You told me earlier about the hearing in Memphis tomorrow. In Juvenile Court.'

'We're filing a petition,' Roy corrected. 'I don't know when the hearing will take place. But we'll ask for a quick one.'

'Yeah, well, what about this? Just before I left the office this afternoon, I talked to K. O. Lewis, Voyles's number-one deputy.'

'I know K.O.,' Foltrigg interrupted. Trumann knew this was coming. In fact, he paused just a split second so Foltrigg could interrupt and set him straight about how close he was to K.O., not Mr. Lewis, but simply K.O.

'Right. Well, he's in St. Louis attending a conference, and he asked about the Boyette case and Jerome Clifford and the kid. I told him what we knew. He said feel free to call if he could do anything. Said Mr. Voyles wants daily reports.'

'I know all this.'

'Right. Well, I was just thinking. St. Louis is an hour's flight from Memphis, right. What if Mr. Lewis presented himself to the Juvenile Court judge in Memphis first thing in the morning when the petition is filed, and what if Mr. Lewis has a little chat with the judge and leans on him? We're talking about the number-two man in the FBI. He tells the judge what we think this kid knows.'

Foltrigg began nodding his approval, and when Wally saw this he began nodding too, only faster.

Trumann continued. 'And there's something else. We know Gronke is in Memphis, and it's safe to assume he's not there to visit Elvis's grave. Right? He's been sent there by Muldanno. So I was thinking, what if we assume the kid is in danger, and Mr. Lewis explains to the Juvenile Court judge that it's in the best interests of the kid for us to take him into custody? You know, for his own protection?'

'I like this,' Foltrigg said softly. Wally liked it too.

'The kid'll crack under the pressure. First, he's taken into custody by order of the Juvenile Court, same as any other case, and that'll scare the hell out of him. Might also wake up his lawyer. Hopefully the judge orders the kid to talk. At that point, the kid'll crack, I believe. If not, he's in contempt, maybe. Don't you think?'

'Yeah, he's in contempt, but we can't predict what the judge will do at that point.'

'Right. So Mr. Lewis tells the judge about Gronke and his connections with the mob, and that we believe he's in Memphis to harm the kid. Either way, we get the kid in custody, away from his lawyer. The bitch.'

Foltrigg was wired now. He scribbled something on a legal pad. Wally stood and began pacing thoughtfully around the library, deep in thought as if things were conspiring to force him to make a significant decision.

Trumann could call her a bitch here in the privacy of an office in New Orleans. But he remembered the tape. And he would be happy to remain in New Orleans, far away from her. Let McThune deal with Reggie in Memphis.

'Can you get K.O. on the phone?' Foltrigg asked.

'I think so.' Trumann pulled a scrap of paper from a pocket and began punching numbers on the phone.

Foltrigg met Wally in the corner, away from the agent. 'It's a great idea,' Wally said. 'I'm sure this Juvenile Court judge is just some local yokel who'll listen to K.O. and do whatever he wants, don't you think?'

Trumann had Mr. Lewis on the phone. Foltrigg watched him while listening to Wally. 'Maybe, but regardless, we get the kid in court quickly and I think he'll fold. If not, he's in custody, under our control and away from his lawyer. I like it.'

They whispered for a while as Trumann talked to K. O. Lewis. Trumann nodded at them, gave the okay sign with a big smile, and hung up. 'He'll do it,' he said proudly. 'He'll catch an early morning flight to Memphis and meet with Fink. Then they'll get with George Ord and descend on the judge.' Trumann was walking toward them, very proud of himself. 'Think about it. The U.S. Attorney on one side, K. O. Lewis on the other, and Fink in the middle, first thing in the morning when the judge gets to the office. They'll have the kid talking in no time.'

Foltrigg flashed a wicked smile. He loved those moments when the power of the federal government shifted into high gear and landed hard on small, unsuspecting people. Just like that, with one phone call, the second in command of the FBI had entered the picture. 'It just might work,' he said to his boys. 'It just might work.'

In one corner of the small den above the garage, Reggie flipped through a thick book under a lamp. It was midnight, but she couldn't sleep, so she curled under a quilt and sipped tea while reading a book Clint had found titled *Reluctant Witnesses*. As far as law books go, it was quite thin. But the law was quite clear: every witness has a duty to come forth and assist those authorities investigating a crime. A witness cannot refuse to testify on the grounds that he or she feels threatened. The vast majority of the cases cited in the book dealt with organized crime. Seems the Mafia has historically frowned on its people schmoozing with the cops, and has often threatened wives and children. The Supreme Court has said more than once that wives and children be damned. A witness must talk.

At some point in the very near future, Mark would be forced to talk. Foltrigg could issue a subpoena and compel his attendance before a grand jury in New Orleans. She, of course, would be able to attend. If Mark refused to testify before the grand jury, a quick hearing would be held before the trial judge who would undoubtedly order him to answer Foltrigg's questions. If he refused, the wrath of the court would be severe. No judge tolerates being disobeyed, but federal judges can be especially nasty when their orders fall on deaf ears.

There are places to put eleven-year-old kids who find themselves in disfavor with the system. At the moment, she had no less than twenty clients scattered about in various training schools in Tennessee. The oldest was sixteen. All were secured behind fences with guards pacing about. They were called reform schools not long ago. Now they're training schools.

When ordered to talk, Mark would undoubtedly look to her. And this was why she couldn't sleep. To advise him to disclose the location of the Senator's body would be to jeopardize his safety. His mother and brother would be at risk. These were not people who could become instantly mobile. Ricky might be hospitalized for weeks. Any type of witness protection program would be postponed until he was healthy again. Dianne would be a sitting duck, if Muldanno were so inclined.

It would be proper and ethical and moral to advise him to co-operate, and that would be the easy way out. But what if he got hurt? He would point a finger at her. What if something happened to Ricky or Dianne? She, the lawyer, would be blamed.

Children make lousy clients. The lawyer becomes much more than a lawyer. With adults, you simply lay the pros and cons of each option on the table. You advise this way and that. You predict a little, but not much. Then you tell the adult it's time for a decision and you leave the room for a bit. When you return, you are handed a decision and you run with it. Not so with kids. They don't under-stand lawyerly advice. They want a hug and someone to make decisions. They're scared and looking for friends.

She'd held many small hands in courtrooms. She'd wiped many tears.

She imagined this scene: a huge, empty federal courtroom in New Orleans with the doors locked and two marshals guarding it; Mark on the witness stand; Foltrigg in all his glory strutting around on his home turf, prancing back and forth for the benefit of his little assist-ants and perhaps an FBI agent or two; the judge in a black robe. He was handling it delicately, and he probably disliked Foltrigg im-mensely because he was forced to see him all the time. He, the judge, asks Mark if he in fact refused to answer certain questions before the grand jury that very morning in a room just a short distance down the hall. Mark, looking upward at His Honor, answers yes. What was the first question? the judge asks Foltrigg, who's on his feet with a legal pad, strutting and prancing as if the room were filled with cameras. I asked him, Your Honor, if Jerome Clifford, prior to the suicide, said anything about the body of Senator Boyd Boyette. And he refused to answer, Your Honor. Then I asked him if Jerome Clif-ford in fact told him where the body is buried. And he refused to answer this question as well, Your Honor. And the judge leans down even closer to Mark. There is no smile. Mark stares at his lawyer. Why didn't you answer these questions? the judge asks. Because I don't want to, Mark answers, and it's almost funny. But there are no smiles. Well, the judge says, I am ordering you to answer these questions before the grand jury, do you undertand me, Mark? I'm ordering you to return to the grand jury room right now and answer all of Mr. Foltrigg's questions, do you understand this? Mark says nothing and doesn't move a muscle. He stares at his trusted lawyer, thirty feet away. What if I don't answer the questions? he finally asks, and this irritates the judge. You have no choice, young man. You must answer because I'm ordering it. And if I don't? Mark asks,

terrified. Well, then, I'll find you in contempt and I'll probably incarcerate you until you do as I say. For a very long time, the judge
growls.

Axle rubbed against the chair and startled her. The courtroom
scene was gone. She closed the book and walked to the window. The
best advice to Mark would be simply to lie. Tell a big one. At the
critical moment, just explain how the late Jerome Clifford said
nothing about Boyd Boyette. He was crazy and drunk and stoned,
and said nothing, really. Who in the world could ever know the difference?

Mark was a cool liar.

He awoke in a strange bed between a soft mattress and a heavy layer
of blankets. A dim lamp from the hallway cast a narrow light through
the slit in the doorway. His battered Nikes were in a chair by the
door, but the rest of his clothing was still on. He slid the blankets to
his knees and the bed squeaked. He stared at the ceiling and vaguely
remembered being escorted to this room by Reggie and Momma
Love. Then he remembered the swing on the porch and being very
tired.

Slowly, he swung his feet from the bed and sat on the edge of it. He
remembered being led and pushed up the stairs. Things were clearing up. He sat in the chair and laced his sneakers. The floor was
wooden and creaked softly as he walked to the door and opened it.
The hinges popped. The hallway was still. Three other doors opened
into it, and they were all closed. He eased to the stairway, and tiptoed
down, in no hurry.

A light from the kitchen caught his attention, and he walked faster.
The clock on the wall gave the time as two-twenty. He now remembered that Reggie didn't live here; she was above the garage.
Momma Love was probably sound asleep upstairs, so he stopped the
creeping along and crossed the foyer, unlocked the front door, and
found his spot in the swing. The air was cool and the front lawn was
pitch black.

For a moment, he was frustrated with himself for falling asleep and
being put to bed in this house. He belonged at the hospital with his
mother, sleeping on the same crippling bed, waiting for Ricky to snap
out of it so they could leave and go home. He assumed Reggie had
called Dianne, so his mother probably wasn't worried. In fact, she
was probably pleased that he was here at this moment, eating good
food and sleeping well. Mothers are like that.

He'd missed two days of school, according to his calculations.

Today would be Thursday. Yesterday, he'd been attacked by the man with the knife in the elevator. The man with the family portrait. And the day before that, Tuesday, he had hired Reggie. That, too, seemed like a month ago. And the day before that, Monday, he had awakened like any normal kid and gone off to school with no idea all this was about to happen. There must be a million kids in Memphis, and he would never understand how and why he was selected to meet Jerome Clifford just seconds before he put the gun in his mouth.

Smoking. That was the answer. Hazardous to your health. You could say that again. He was being punished by God for smoking and harming his body. Damn! What if he'd been caught with a beer.

A silhouette of a man appeared on the sidewalk, and stopped for a second in front of Momma Love's house. The orange glow of a cigarette flared in front of his face, then he walked very slowly out of sight. A little late for an evening stroll, Mark thought.

A minute passed, and he was back. Same man. Same slow walk. Same hesitation between the trees as he looked at the house. Mark held his breath. He was sitting in darkness and he knew he could not be seen. But this man was more than a nosy neighbor.

At exactly 4 A.M., a plain white Ford van with the license plates temporarily removed eased into Tucker Wheel Estates and turned onto East Street. The trailers were dark and quiet. The streets were deserted. The little village was peacefully asleep and would be for two more hours until dawn.

The van stopped in front of Number 17. The lights and engine were turned off. No one noticed it. After a minute, a man in a uniform opened the driver's door and stood in the street. The uniform resembled that of a Memphis cop – navy trousers, navy shirt, wide black belt with black holster, some type of gun on the hip, black boots, but no cap or hat. A decent imitation, especially at four in the morning when no one was watching. He held a rectangular cardboard container about the size of two shoe boxes. He glanced around, then carefully watched and listened to the trailer next door to Number 17. Not a sound. Not even the bark of a dog. He smiled to himself, and walked casually to the door of Number 17.

If he detected movement in a nearby trailer, he would simply knock slightly on the door and go through the routine of being a frustrated messenger looking for Ms. Sway. But it wasn't necessary. Not a peep from the neighbors. So he quickly sat the box against the door, got in the van, and drove away. He had come and gone without a trace, leaving behind his little warning.

Exactly thirty minutes later, the box exploded. It was a quiet explosion, carefully controlled. The ground didn't shake and the porch didn't shatter. The door was blown open, and the flames were directed at the interior of the trailer. Lots of red and yellow flames and black smoke rolling through the rooms. The matchbox construction of the walls and floors was nothing more than kindling for the fire.

By the time Rufus Bibbs next door could punch 911, the Sway trailer was engulfed and beyond help. Rufus hung up the phone, and ran to find his garden hose. His wife and kids were running wild, trying to dress and get out of the trailer. Screams and shouts echoed on the street as the neighbors ran to the fire in an amazing array of pajamas and robes. Dozens of them watched the fire as garden hoses came from all directions and water was applied to the trailers next door. The fire grew and the crowd grew, and windows popped in the Bibbs trailer. The domino effect. More screams as more windows popped. Then sirens and red lights.

The crowd moved back as the firemen laid lines and pumped water. The other trailers were saved, but the Sway home was nothing but rubble. The roof and most of the floor were gone. The rear wall stood with a solitary window still intact.

More people arrived as the firemen sprayed the ruins. Walter Deeble, a loudmouth from South Street, started babbling about how cheap these damned trailers were with aluminum wiring and all. Hell, we all live in firetraps, he said with the pitch of a street preacher, and what we ought to do is sue that sonofabitch Tucker and force him to provide safe housing. He just might see his lawyer about it. Personally, he had eight smoke and heat detectors in his trailer because of the cheap aluminum wiring and all, and he just might talk to his lawyer.

By the Bibbs trailer, a small crowd gathered and thanked God the fire didn't spread.

Those poor Sways. What else could happen to them?

# CHAPTER TWENTY

After a breakfast of cinnamon rolls and chocolate milk, they left the house and headed for the hospital. It was seven-thirty, much too early for Reggie but Dianne was waiting. Ricky was doing much better.

'What do you think'll happen today?' Mark asked.

For some reason this struck her as being funny. 'You poor child,' she said when she finished chuckling. 'You've been through a lot this week.'

'Yeah. I hate school, but it'd be nice to go back. I had this wild dream last night.'

'What happened?'

'Nothing. I dreamed everything was normal again, and I made it through a whole day with nothing happening to me. It was wonderful.'

'Well, Mark, I'm afraid I have some bad news.'

'I knew it. What is it?'

'Clint called a few minutes ago. You've made the front page again. It's a picture of both of us, evidently taken by one of those clowns at the hospital yesterday when we got off the elevator.'

'Great.'

'There's a reporter at the *Memphis Press* by the name of Slick Moeller. Everyone calls him the Mole. Mole Moeller. He covers the crime beat, sort of a legend around town. He's hot on this case.'

'He wrote the story yesterday.'

'That's right. He has a lot of contacts within the police department. It sounds as if the cops believe Mr. Clifford told you everything before he killed himself, and now you're refusing to cooperate.'

'Pretty accurate, wouldn't you say?'

She glanced at the rearview mirror. 'Yeah. It's spooky.'

'How does he know this stuff?'

'The cops talk to him, off the record of course, and he digs and digs until he puts the pieces together. And if the pieces don't fit perfectly, then Slick just sort of fills in the gaps. According to Clint, the story is based on unnamed sources within the Memphis Police department, and there's a great deal of suspicion about how much you know. The theory is that since you've hired me, you must be hiding something.'

'Let's stop and get a newspaper.'

'We'll get one at the hospital. We'll be there in a minute.'

'Do you think those reporters'll be waiting again?'

'Probably. I told Clint to find a back entrance somewhere, and to meet us in the parking lot.'

'I'm really sick of this. Just sick of it. All my buddies are in school today, having a good time, being normal, fighting with girls during recess, playing jokes on the teachers, you know, the usual stuff. And look at me. Running around town with my lawyer, reading about my adventures in the newspapers, looking at my face on the front page, hiding from reporters, dodging killers with switch-blades. It's like something out of a movie. A bad movie. I'm just sick of it. I don't know if I can take anymore. It's just too much.'

She watched him between glances at the street and traffic. His jaws were tight. He stared straight ahead, but saw nothing.

'I'm sorry, Mark.'

'Yeah, me too. So much for pleasant dreams, huh.'

'This could be a very long day.'

'What else is new? They were watching the house last night, did you know that?'

'I beg your pardon.'

'Yeah, somebody was watching the house. I was on the porch at two-thirty this morning, and I saw a guy walking along the sidewalk. He was real casual, you know, just smoking a cigarette and looking at the house.'

'Could be a neighbor.'

'Right. At two-thirty in the morning.'

'Maybe someone was out for a walk.'

'Then why did he walk by the house three times in fifteen minutes?'

She glanced at him again and hit her brakes to avoid a car in front of them.

'Do you trust me, Mark?' she asked.

He looked at her as if surprised by the question. 'Of course I trust you, Reggie.'

She smiled and patted his arm. 'Then stick with me.'

One advantage of an architectural horror like St. Peter's was the existence of lots of doors and exits few people knew about. With additions stuck here, and wings added over there as an afterthought, there had been created over the course of time little nooks and alleys seldom used and rarely discovered by lost security guards.

When they arrived, Clint had been hustling around the hospital for thirty minutes with no success. He'd managed to become lost himself three different times. He was sweating and apologizing as they met at the parking lot.

'Just follow me,' Mark said, and they darted across the street and entered through the emergency gate. They wove through heavy, rush-hour hall traffic and found an ancient escalator going down.

'I hope you know where you're going,' Reggie said, obviously in doubt and half-jogging in an effort to keep up with him. Clint was sweating even harder. 'No problem,' Mark said, and opened a door leading to the kitchen.

'We're in the kitchen, Mark,' Reggie said, looking around.

'Just be cool. Act like you're supposed to be here.'

He punched a button by a service elevator and the door opened instantly. He punched another button on the inside panel, and they lurched upward, headed for floor number ten. 'There are eighteen floors in the main section, but this elevator stops at number ten. It will not stop at nine. Figure it out.' He watched the numbers above the door and explained this like a bored tour guide.

'What happens on ten?' Clint asked between breaths.

'Just wait.'

The door opened on ten, and they stepped into a huge closet with rows of shelves filled with towels and bedsheets. Mark was off, darting between the aisles. He opened a heavy metal door and they were suddenly in the hallway with patient rooms right and left. He pointed to his left, kept walking, and stopped before an emergency exit door with red and yellow alarm warnings all over it. He grabbed the bar handle across the front of it, and Reggie and Clint stopped cold.

He pushed the door open, and nothing happened. 'Alarms don't work,' he said nonchalantly and bounded down the steps to the ninth floor. He opened another door, and suddenly they were in a quiet hallway with thick industrial carpet and no traffic. He pointed again, and they were off, past patient rooms, around a bend, and by the nurses' station where they glanced down another hall and saw the loiterers by the elevators.

'Good morning, Mark,' Karen the beautiful called out as they hurried by. But she said this without a smile.

'Hi, Karen,' he answered without slowing.

Dianne was sitting in a folding chair in the hall with a Memphis cop kneeling before her. She was crying, and had been for some time. The two security guards were standing together twenty feet away. Mark saw the cop and the tears and ran for his mother. She grabbed him and they hugged.

'What's the matter, Mom?' he asked, and she cried harder.

'Mark, your trailer burned last night,' the cop said. 'Just a few hours ago.'

Mark glared at him in disbelief, then squeezed his mother around the neck. She was wiping tears and trying to compose herself.

'How bad?' Mark asked.

'Real bad,' the cop said sadly as he stood and held his cap with both hands. 'Everything's gone.'

'What started the fire?' Reggie asked.

'Don't know right now. The fire inspector will be on the scene this morning. Could be electrical.'

'I need to talk to the fire inspector, okay,' Reggie insisted, and the cop looked her over.

'And who are you?' he asked.

'Reggie Love, attorney for the family.'

'Ah, yes. I saw the paper this morning.'

She handed him a card. 'Please ask the fire inspector to call me.'

'Sure, lady.' The cop carefully placed the hat on his head and looked down again at Dianne. He was sad again. 'Ms. Sway, I'm very sorry about this.'

'Thank you,' she said, wiping her face. He nodded at Reggie and Clint, backed away, and left in a hurry. A nurse appeared and stood by just in case.

Dianne suddenly had an audience. She stood and stopped crying, even managed a smile at Reggie.

'This is Clint Van Hooser. He works for me,' Reggie said.

Dianne smiled at Clint. 'I'm very sorry,' he said.

'Thank you,' Dianne said softly. A few seconds of awkward silence followed as she finished wiping her face. Her arm was around Mark, who was still dazed.

'Did he behave?' Dianne asked.

'He was wonderful. He ate enough for a small army.'

'That's good. Thanks for having him over.'

'How's Ricky?' Reggie asked.

'He had a good night. Dr. Greenway stopped by this morning, and Ricky was awake and talking. Looks much better.'

'Does he know about the fire?' Mark asked.

'No. And we're not telling him, okay?'

'Okay, Mom. Could we go inside and talk, just me and you?'

Dianne smiled at Reggie and Clint, and led Mark into the room. The door was closed, and the tiny Sway family was all alone with all its worldly possessions.

The Honorable Harry Roosevelt had presided over the Shelby County Juvenile Court for twenty-two years now, and despite the dismal and depressing nature of the court's business he had conducted its affairs with a great deal of dignity. He was the first black Juvenile Court judge in Tennessee, and when he'd been appointed by the Governor in the early seventies, his future was brilliant and there were glowing predictions of higher courts for him to conquer.

The higher courts were still there, and Harry Roosevelt was still here, in the deteriorating building known simply as Juvenile Court. There were much nicer courthouses in Memphis. On Main Street the Federal Building, always the newest in town, housed the elegant and stately courtrooms. The federal boys always had the best – rich carpet, thick leather chairs, heavy oak tables, plenty of lights, dependable air conditioning, lots of well-paid clerks and assistants. A few blocks away, the Shelby County Courthouse was a beehive of judicial activity as thousands of lawyers roamed its tiled and marbled corridors and worked their way through well-preserved and well-scrubbed courtrooms. It was an older building, but a beautiful one with paintings on the walls and a few statues scattered about. Harry could have had a courtroom over there, but he said no. And not far away was the Shelby County Justice Center with a maze of fancy new modern courtrooms with bright fluorescent lights and sound systems and padded seats. Harry could have had one of those too, but he turned it down.

He remained here, in the Juvenile Court Building, a converted high school blocks away from downtown with little parking and few janitors and more cases per judge than any other docket in the world. His court was the unwanted stepchild of the judicial system. Most lawyers shunned it. Most law students dreamed of plush offices in tall buildings and wealthy clients with thick wallets. Never did they dream of slugging their way through the roach-infested corridors of Juvenile Court.

Harry had turned down four appointments, all to courts where the heating systems worked in the winter. He had been considered for these appointments because he was smart and black, and he turned them down because he was poor and black. They paid him sixty thousand a year, lowest of any court in town, so he could feed his wife and four teenagers and live in a nice home. But he'd known hunger as a child, and those memories were vivid. He would always think of himself as a poor black kid.

And that's exactly the reason the once promising Harry Roosevelt remained a simple Juvenile Court judge. To him, it was the most important job in the world. By statute, he had exclusive jurisdiction over delinquent, unruly, dependent, and neglected children. He determined paternity of children born out of wedlock and enforced his own orders for their support and education, and in a county where half the babies were born to single mothers, this accounted for most of his docket. He terminated parental rights and placed abused children in new homes. Harry carried heavy burdens.

He weighed somewhere between three and four hundred pounds, and wore the same outfit every day – black suit, white cotton shirt, and a bow tie which he tied himself and did so poorly. No one knew if Harry owned one black suit or fifty. He always looked the same. He was an imposing figure on the bench, glaring down over his reading glasses at deadbeat fathers who refused to support their children. Deadbeat fathers, black and white alike, lived in fear of Judge Roosevelt. He would track them down and throw them in jail. He found their employers and tapped their paychecks. If you messed with Harry's subjects, or Harry's Kids, as they were known, you could find yourself handcuffed and standing pitifully before him with a bailiff on each side.

Harry Roosevelt was a legend in Memphis. The county fathers had seen fit to give him two more judges to help with the caseload, but he maintained a brutal work schedule. He usually arrived before seven and made his own coffee. He started court promptly at nine and god help the lawyer who was late for court. He'd thrown several of them in jail over the years.

At eight-thirty, his secretary hauled in a box of mail and informed Harry that there was a group of men waiting outside who desperately needed to speak with him.

'What else is new?' he asked, eating the last bite of an apple Danish.

'You might want to meet with these gentlemen.'

'Oh really. Who are they?'

'One is George Ord, our distinguished U.S. Attorney.'

'I taught George in law school.'

'Right. That's what he said, twice. There's also an Assistant U.S. Attorney from New Orleans, a Mr. Thomas Fink. And a Mr. K. O. Lewis, Deputy Director of the FBI. And a couple of FBI agents.'

Harry looked up from a file and thought about this. 'A rather distinguished group. What do they want?'

'They wouldn't say.'

'Well, show them in.'

She left, and seconds later Ord, Fink, Lewis, and McThune filed into the crowded and cluttered office and introduced themselves to

His Honor. Harry and the secretary moved files from the chairs and everyone looked for a seat. They exchanged brief pleasantries, and after a few minutes of this Harry looked at his watch and said, 'Gentlemen, I am scheduled to hear seventeen cases today. What can I do for you?'

Ord cleared his throat first. 'Well, Judge, I'm sure you've seen the papers the last two mornings, especially the front page stories about a boy by the name of Mark Sway.'

'Very intriguing.'

'Mr. Fink here is prosecuting the man accused of killing Senator Boyette, and the case is scheduled for trial in New Orleans in a few weeks.'

'I'm aware of this. I've read the stories.'

'We are almost certain that Mark Sway knows more than he is telling. He's lied to the Memphis Police on several occasions. We think he talked at length with Jerome Clifford before the suicide. We know without a doubt he was in the car. We've tried to talk to the kid, but he has been very uncooperative. Now he's hired a lawyer and she's stonewalling.'

'Reggie Love is a regular in my court. A very competent attorney. Sometimes a bit overprotective of her clients, but there's nothing wrong with that.'

'Yes sir. We're very suspicious of the boy, and we feel quite strongly that he is withholding valuable information.'

'Such as?'

'Such as the location of the Senator's body.'

'How can you assume this?'

'There's a lot to the story, Your Honor. And it would take a while to explain it.'

Harry played with his bow tie and gave Ord one of his patented scowls. He was thinking. 'So you want me to bring the kid in and ask him questions.'

'Sort of. Mr. Fink has brought with him a petition alleging the child to be a delinquent.'

This did not sit well with Harry. His shiny forehead was suddenly wrinkled. 'A rather serious allegation. What type of offense has the child committed?'

'Obstruction of justice.'

'You got any law?'

Fink had a file open, and he was on his feet handing a thin brief across the desk. Harry took it, and began reading slowly. The room was silent. K. O. Lewis had yet to say anything, and this bothered him because he was, after all, the number-two man at the FBI. And this judge seemed not to care.

Harry flipped a page and glanced at his watch. 'I'm listening,' he said in Fink's direction.

'It's our position, Your Honor, that through his misrepresentations Mark Sway has obstructed the investigation into this matter.'

'Which matter? The murder or the suicide?'

Excellent point, and as soon as he heard the question Fink knew Harry Roosevelt would not be a pushover. They were investigating a murder, not a suicide. There was no law against suicide, nor was there a law against witnessing one. 'Well, Your Honor, the suicide has some very direct links to the murder of Boyette, we think, and it's important for the kid to cooperate.'

'What if the kid knows nothing?'

'We can't be certain until we ask him. Right now he's impeding the investigation, and, as you well know, every citizen has a duty to assist law enforcement officials.'

'I'm well aware of that. It just seems a bit severe to allege the kid is a delinquent without any proof.'

'The proof will come, Your Honor, if we can get the kid on the witness stand, under oath, in a closed hearing and ask some questions. That's all we're trying to do.'

Harry tossed the brief into a pile of papers and removed his reading glasses. He chewed on a stem.

Ord leaned forward and spoke solemnly. 'Look, Judge, if we can take the kid into custody, then have an expedited hearing, we think this matter will be resolved. If he states under oath that he knows nothing about Boyd Boyette, then the petition is dismissed, the kid goes home, and the matter is over. It's routine. No proof, no finding of delinquency, no harm. But if he knows something relevant to the location of the body, then we have a right to know and we think the kid will tell us during the hearing.'

'There are two ways to make him talk, Your Honor,' Fink added. 'We can file this petition in your court and have a hearing, or we can subpoena the kid to face the grand jury in New Orleans. Staying here seems to be the quickest and best route, especially for the kid.'

'I do not want this kid subpoenaed before a grand jury,' Harry said sternly. 'Is that understood?'

They all nodded quickly, and they all knew full well that a federal grand jury could subpoena Mark Sway anytime it chose, regardless of the feelings of a local judge. This was typical of Harry. Immediately throwing his protective blanket around any child within reach of his jurisdiction.

'I'd much rather deal with it in my court,' he said, almost to himself.'

'We agree, Your Honor,' Fink said. They all agreed.

Harry picked up his daily calendar. As usual, it was filled with more misery than he could possibly handle in one day. He studied it. 'These allegations of obstruction are rather shaky, in my opinion. But I can't prevent you from filing the petition. I suggest we hear this matter at the earliest possible time. If the kid in fact knows nothing, and I suspect this to be the case, then I want it over and done with. Quickly.'

This suited everyone.

'Let's do it during lunch today. Where is the kid now?'

'At the hospital,' Ord said. 'His brother will be there for an unspecified period of time. The mother is confined to the room. Mark just sort of roams about. Last night he stayed with his lawyer.'

'That sounds like Reggie,' Harry said with affection. 'I see no need to take him into custody.'

Custody was very important to Fink and Foltrigg. They wanted the kid picked up, hauled away in a police car, placed in a cell of some sort, and in general frightened to the point of talking.

'Your Honor, if I may,' K.O. finally said. 'We think custody is urgent.'

'Oh you do? I'm listening.'

McThune handed Judge Roosevelt a glossy eight by ten. Lewis handled the narration. 'The man in the picture is Paul Gronke. He's a thug from New Orleans, and a close associate of Barry Muldanno. He's been in Memphis since Tuesday night. That photo was taken as he entered the airport in New Orleans. An hour later he was in Memphis, and unfortunately we lost him when he left the airport here.' McThune produced two smaller photos. 'The guy with the dark shades is Mack Bono, a convicted murderer with strong mob ties in New Orleans. The guy in the suit is Gary Pirini, another Mafia thug who works for the Sulari family. Bono and Pirini arrived in Memphis last night. They didn't come here to eat barbecued ribs.' He paused for dramatic effect. 'The kid's in serious danger, Your Honor. The family home is a house trailer in north Memphis, in a place called Tucker Wheel Estates.'

'I'm very familiar with the place,' Harry said, rubbing his eyes.

'About four hours ago, the trailer burned to the ground. The fire looks suspicious. We think it's intimidation. The kid has been roaming at will since Monday night. There's no father, and the mother cannot leave the younger son. It's very sad, and it's very dangerous.'

'So you've been watching him.'

'Yes sir. His lawyer asked the hospital to provide security guards outside the brother's room.'

'And she called me,' Ord added. 'She is very concerned about the kid's safety, and asked me to request FBI protection at the hospital.'

'And we complied,' added McThune. 'We've had at least two agents near the room for the past forty-eight hours. These guys are killers, Your Honor, and they're taking orders from Muldanno. And the kid's just roaming around oblivious to the danger.'

Harry listened to them carefully. It was a well-rehearsed full court press. By nature, he was suspicious of police and their kind, but this was not a routine case. 'Our laws certainly provide for the child to be taken into custody after the petition is filed,' he said to no one in particular. 'What happens to the kid if the hearing does not produce what you want, if the kid is in fact not obstructing justice?'

Lewis answered. 'We've thought about this, Your Honor, and we would never do anything to violate the secrecy of your hearings. But, we have ways of getting word to these thugs that the kid knows nothing. Frankly, if he comes clean and knows nothing, the matter is closed and Muldanno's boys will lose interest in him. Why should they threaten him if he knows nothing?'

'That makes sense,' Harry said. 'But what do you do if the kid tells you what you want to hear. He's a marked little boy at that point, don't you think? If these guys are as dangerous as you say, then our little pal could be in serious trouble.'

'We're making preliminary arrangements to place him in the witness protection program. All of them, Mark, his mother, and brother.'

'Have you discussed this with his attorney?'

'No sir,' Fink answered. 'The last time we were in her office she refused to meet with us. She's been difficult too.'

'Let me see your petition.'

Fink whipped it out and handed it to him. He carefully put on his reading glasses and studied it. When he finished, he handed it back to Fink.

'I don't like this, gentlemen. I just don't like the smell of it. I've seen a million cases, and never one involving a minor and a charge of obstructing justice. I have an uneasy feeling.'

'We're desperate, Your Honor,' Lewis confessed with a great deal of sincerity. 'We have to know what the kid knows, and we fear for his safety. This is all on the table. We're not hiding anything, and we're damned sure not trying to mislead you.'

'I certainly hope not.' Harry glared at them. He scribbled something on scratch paper. They waited and watched his every move. He glanced at his watch.

'I'll sign the order. I want the kid taken directly to the Juvenile Wing and placed in a cell by himself. He'll be scared to death, and I want him handled with velvet gloves. I'll personally call his lawyer later in the morning.'

They stood in unison and thanked him. He pointed to the door, and they left quickly without handshakes or farewells.

# CHAPTER TWENTY-ONE

Karen knocked lightly and entered the dark room with a basket of fruit. The card brought get-well messages from the congregation of Little Creek Baptist Church. The apples and bananas and grapes were wrapped in green cellophane, and looked pretty sitting next to a rather large and expensive arrangement of colorful flowers sent by the concerned friends at Ark-Lon Fixtures.

The shades were drawn, the television was off, and when Karen closed the door to leave none of the Sways had moved. Ricky had changed positions, and was now lying on his back with his feet on the pillows and his head on the blankets. He was awake, but for the last hour had been staring blankly at the ceiling without saying a word or moving an inch. This was something new. Mark and Dianne sat next to each other on the foldaway bed with their feet tucked under them and whispered about such things as clothing and toys and dishes. There was fire insurance, but Dianne didn't know the extent of the coverage.

They spoke in hushed voices. It would be days or weeks before Ricky knew of the fire.

At some point in the morning, about an hour after Reggie and Clint left, the shock of the news wore off and Mark started thinking. It was easy to think in this dark room because there was nothing else to do. The television could be used only when Ricky wanted it. The shades remained closed if there was a chance he was sleeping. The door was always shut.

Mark had been sitting in a chair under the television, eating a stale chocolate chip cookie, when it occurred to him that maybe the fire was not an accident. Earlier, the man with the knife had somehow entered the trailer and found the portrait. His intent had been to wave the knife and wave the portrait, and forever silence little Mark Sway. And he had been most successful. What if the fire was just another reminder from the man with the switchblade? Trailers were easy to burn. The neighborhood was usually quiet at four in the morning. He knew this from experience.

This thought had stuck like a thick knot in his throat, and his mouth was suddenly dry. Dianne didn't notice. She'd been sipping coffee and patting Ricky.

Mark had wrestled with it for a while, then had taken a short walk to the nurses' station where Karen showed him the morning paper.

The thought was so horrible it seared itself into his mind, and after two hours of thinking about it he was convinced the fire was intentional.

'What will the insurance cover?' he asked.

'I'll have to call the agent. There are two policies, if I remember correctly. One is paid by Mr. Tucker on the trailer, because he owns it, and the other is paid by us for the contents of the trailer. The monthly rent is supposed to include the premium for the insurance on the contents. I think that's how it works.'

This worried Mark immensely. There were many awful memories from the divorce, and he remembered his mother's inability to testify about any of the financial affairs of the family. She knew nothing. His ex-father paid the bills and kept the checkbook and filed the tax returns. Twice in the past two years the telephone had been cut off because Dianne had forgotten to pay the bills. Or so she said. He suspected each time that there was no money to pay the bills.

'But what will the insurance pay for?' he asked.

'Furniture, clothes, kitchen utensils, I guess. That's what it usually covers.'

There was a knock on the door, but it did not open. They waited, then another knock. Mark opened it slightly, and saw two new faces peering through the crack.

'Yes,' he said, expecting trouble because the nurses and security guards allowed no one to get this far. He opened the door a bit wider.

'Looking for Dianne Sway,' said the nearest face. There was volume to this, and Dianne started for the door.

'Who are you?' Mark asked, opening the door and walking into the hall. The two security guards were standing together to the right, and three nurses were standing together to the left, and all five appeared frozen as if witnessing a horrible event. Mark locked eyes with Karen, and knew instantly something was terribly wrong.

'Detective Nassar, Memphis PD. This is Detective Klickman.'

Nassar wore a coat and tie, and Klickman wore a black jogging suit with sparkling new Nike Air Jordans. They were both young, probably early thirties, and Mark immediately thought of the old 'Starsky and Hutch' reruns. Dianne opened the door and stood behind her son.

'Are you Dianne Sway?' Nassar asked.

'I am,' she answered quickly.

Nassar pulled papers from his coat pocket and handed them over Mark's head to his mother. 'These are from Juvenile Court, Ms. Sway. It's a summons for a hearing at noon today.'

Her hands shook wildly and the papers rattled as she tried hopelessly to make sense of this.

'Could I see your badges?' Mark asked, rather coolly under the circumstances. They both grabbed and reached and presented their identification under Mark's nose. He studied them carefully, and sneered at Nassar. 'Nice shoes,' he said to Klickman.

Nassar tried to smile. 'Ms. Sway, the summons requires us to take Mark Sway into custody at this time.'

There was a heavy pause of two or three seconds as the word 'custody' settled in.

'What!' Dianne yelled at Nassar. She dropped the papers. The 'What!' echoed down the hallway. There was more anger in her voice than fear.

'It's right here on the front page,' Nassar said, picking up the summons. 'Judge's orders.'

'You what!' she yelled again, and it shot through the air like the crack of a bullwhip. 'You can't take my son!' Dianne's face was red and her body, all hundred and fifteen pounds, was tense and coiled.

Great, thought Mark. Another ride in a patrol car. Then his mother yelled, 'You son of a bitch!' and Mark tried to calm her.

'Mom, don't yell. Ricky can hear you.'

'Over my dead body!' she yelled at Nassar, just inches away. Klickman backed away one step, as if to say this wild woman belonged to Nassar.

But Nassar was a pro. He'd arrested thousands. 'Look, Ms. Sway, I understand how you feel. But I have my orders.'

'Whose orders!'

'Mom, please don't yell,' Mark pleaded.

'Judge Harry Roosevelt signed the order about an hour ago. We're just doing our job, Ms. Sway. Nothing's gonna happen to Mark. We'll take care of him.'

'What's he done? Just tell me what's he done?' Dianne turned to the nurses. 'Can somebody help me here?' she pleaded and sounded so pitiful. 'Karen, do something, would you? Call Dr. Greenway. Don't just stand there.'

But Karen and the nurses just stood there. The cops had already warned them.

Nassar was still trying to smile. 'If you'll read these papers, Ms.

Sway, you'll see that a petition has been filed in Juvenile Court alleging Mark here to be a delinquent because he won't cooperate with the police and the FBI. And Judge Roosevelt wants to have a hearing at noon today. That's all.'

'That's all! You asshole! You show up here with your little papers and take away my son and you say "That's all"!'

'Not so loud, Mom,' Mark said. He hadn't heard such language from her since the divorce.

Nassar stopped trying to smile and pulled at the corners of his mustache. Klickman for some reason was glaring at Mark as if he were a serial killer they'd been tracking for years. There was a long pause. Dianne kept both hands on Mark's shoulders. 'You can't have him!'

Finally, Klickman said his first words. 'Look, Ms. Sway, we have no choice. We have to take your son.'

'Go to hell,' she snapped. 'If you take him, you whip me first.'

Klickman was a meathead with little finesse, and for a split second his shoulders flinched as if he would accept this challenge. Then he relaxed and smiled.

'It's okay, Mom. I'll go. Call Reggie and tell her to meet me at the jail. She'll probably sue these clowns by lunch and have them fired by tomorrow.'

The cops grinned at each other. Cute little kid.

Nassar then made the very sad mistake of reaching for Mark's arm. Dianne lunged and struck like a cobra. Whap! She slapped him on his left cheek and screamed, 'Don't touch him! Don't touch him!'

Nassar grabbed his face, and Klickman instantly grabbed her arm. She wanted to strike again, but was suddenly spun around, and somehow in the midst of this her feet and Mark's feet became tangled and they hit the floor. 'You son of a bitch!' she kept screaming. 'Don't touch him.'

Nassar reached down for some reason, and Dianne kicked him on the thigh. But she was barefoot and there was little damage. Klickman was reaching down, and Mark was scrambling to get up, and Dianne was kicking and swinging and yelling, 'Don't touch him!' The nurses rushed forward and the security guards joined in as Dianne got to her feet.

Mark was pulled from the fracas by Klickman. Dianne was held by the two security guards. She was twisting and crying. Nassar was rubbing his face. The nurses were soothing and consoling and trying to separate everyone.

The door opened, and Ricky stood in it holding a stuffed rabbit.

He stared at Mark, whose wrists were being held by Klickman. He stared at his mother, whose wrists were being held by the security guards. Everyone froze and stared at Ricky. His face was as white as the sheets. His hair stuck out in all directions. His mouth was open, but he said nothing.

Then he started the low, mournful groan that only Mark had heard before. Dianne yanked her wrists free and picked him up. The nurses followed her into the room and they tucked him in the bed. They patted his arms and legs, but the groaning continued. Then the thumb went in his mouth and he closed his eyes. Dianne lay beside him in the bed and began humming 'Winnie the Pooh' and patting his arm.

'Let's go, kid,' Klickman said.

'You gonna handcuff me?'

'No. This is not an arrest.'

'Then what the hell is it?'

'Watch your language, kid.'

'Kiss my ass, you big stupid jock.' Klickman stopped cold and glared down at Mark.

'Watch your mouth, kid,' Nassar warned.

'Look at your face, hotshot. I think it's turning blue. Mom cold-cocked you. Ha, Ha. I hope she broke your teeth.'

Klickman bent over and put his hands on his knees. He stared Mark directly in the eyes. 'Are you going with us, or shall we drag you out of here?'

Mark snorted and glared at him. 'You think I'm scared of you, don't you? Let me tell you something, meathead, I've got a lawyer who'll have me out in ten minutes. My lawyer is so good that by this afternoon you'll be looking for another job.'

'I'm scared to death. Now let's go.'

They started walking, a cop on each side of the defendant.

'Where are we going?'

'Juvenile Detention Center.'

'Is it sort of a jail?'

'It could be if you don't watch your smart mouth.'

'You knocked my mother down, you know that. She'll have your job for that.'

'She can have my job,' Klickman said. 'It's a rotten job because I have to deal with little punks like you.'

'Yeah, but you can't find another one, can you? There's no demand for idiots these days.'

They passed a small crowd of orderlies and nurses, and suddenly

189

Mark was a star. The center of attention. He was an innocent man being led away to the slaughter. He swaggered a bit. They turned the corner, and then he remembered the reporters.

And they remembered him. A flash went off as they got to the elevators, and two of the loiterers with pencils and pads were suddenly standing next to Klickman. They waited for the elevator.

'Are you a cop?' one of them asked, staring at the glow-in-the-dark Nikes.

'No comment.'

'Hey, Mark, where you going?' another asked from just a few feet behind. There was another flash.

'To jail,' he said loudly without turning around.

'Shut up, kid,' Nassar scolded. Klickman put a heavy arm on his shoulder. The photographer was beside them, almost to the elevator door. Nassar held up an arm to block his view. 'Get away,' he growled.

'Are you under arrest, Mark?' one of them yelled.

'No,' Klickman snapped just as the door opened. Nassar shoved Mark inside while Klickman blocked the door until it started to close.

They were alone in the elevator. 'That was a stupid thing to say, kid. Really stupid.' Klickman was shaking his head.

'Then arrest me.'

'Really stupid.'

'Is it against the law to talk to the press?'

'Just keep your mouth shut, okay?'

'Why don't you just beat the hell out of me, okay, meathead?'

'I'd love to.'

'Yeah, but you can't, right? Because I'm just a little kid, and you're a big stupid cop and if you touch me you'll get fired and sued and all that. You knocked my mother down, meathead, and you haven't heard the last of it.'

'Your mother slapped me,' Nassar said.

'Good for her. You clowns have no idea what she's been through. You show up to get me and act like it's no big deal, like just because you're cops and you've got this piece of paper then my mother is supposed to get happy and send me off with a kiss. A couple of morons. Just big, dumb, meatheaded cops.'

The elevator stopped, opened, and two doctors entered. They stopped talking and looked at Mark. The door closed behind them, and they continued down. 'Can you believe these clowns are arresting me?' he asked the doctors.

They frowned at Nassar and Klickman.

'Juvenile Court offender,' Nassar explained. Why couldn't the little punk just shut up?

Mark nodded at Klickman. 'This one here with the cute shoes knocked my mother down about five minutes ago. Can you believe it?'

Both doctors looked at the shoes.

'Just shut up, Mark,' Klickman said.

'Is your mother okay?' one of the doctors asked.

'Oh she's great. My little brother's in the psychiatric ward. Our trailer burned to the ground a few hours ago. And then these thugs show up and arrest me right in front of my mother. Bigfoot here knocks her to the floor. She's doing great.'

The doctors stared at the cops. Nassar watched his feet and Klickman closed his eyes. The elevator stopped and a small crowd boarded. Klickman stayed close to Mark.

When all was quiet and they were moving again, Mark said loudly, 'My lawyer'll sue you jerks, you know that, don't you? You'll be unemployed this time tomorrow.' Eight sets of eyes looked down in the corner, then up at the pained face of Detective Klickman. Silence.

'Just shut up, Mark.'

'And what if I don't? You gonna rough me up like you did my mother. Throw me down, kick me a few times. You're just another meathead cop, you know that, Klickman? Just another fat cop with a gun. Why don't you lose a few pounds?'

Neat rows of sweat broke out across Klickman's forehead. He caught the eyes darting at him from the crowd. The elevator was barely moving. He could have strangled Mark.

Nassar was pressed into the other rear corner, and his ears were now ringing from the slap to the head. He couldn't see Mark Sway, but he could certainly hear him.

'Is your mother all right?' a nurse asked. She was standing next to Mark, looking down and very concerned.

'Yeah, she's having a great day. She'd be a lot better, of course, if these cops would leave her alone. They're taking me to jail, you know that?'

'What for?'

'I don't know. They won't tell me. I was just minding my own business, trying to console my mother because our trailer burned to the ground this morning and we lost everything we own, when they showed up with no warning, and here I am on the way to jail.'

'How old are you?'

'Only eleven. But that's not important to these guys. They'd arrest a four-year-old.'

Nassar groaned softly. Klickman kept his eyes closed.

'This is awful,' the nurse said.

'You should've seen it when they had me and my mother on the floor. Happened just a few minutes ago on the Psychiatric Wing. It'll be on the news tonight. Watch the papers. These clowns will be fired tomorrow. Then the lawsuit.'

They stopped on the ground floor, and the elevator emptied.

He insisted on riding in the rear seat, like a real criminal. The car was an unmarked Chrysler but he spotted it a hundred yards away in the parking lot. Nassar and Klickman were afraid to speak to him. They rode in the front seat in complete silence, hoping he might do the same. They were not so lucky.

'You forgot to read me my rights,' he said as Nassar drove as fast as possible.

No response from the front seat.

'Hey, you clowns up there. You forgot to read me my rights.'

No response. Nassar drove faster.

'Do you know *how* to read me my rights?'

No response.

'Hey, meathead. Yeah, you with the shoes. Do you know how to read me my rights?'

Klickman's breathing was labored, but he was determined to ignore him. Oddly, Nassar had a crooked smile barely noticeable under the mustache. He stopped at a red light, looked both ways, then gunned the engine.

'Listen to me, meathead, okay. I'll do it to myself, okay. I have the right to remain silent. Did you catch that? And, if I say anything you clowns can use it against me in court. Get that, meathead? Of course, if I said anything you dumbasses would forget it. Then there's something about the right to a lawyer. Can you help with this one, meathead? Yo! meathead. What's the bit about the lawyer? I've seen it on television a million times.'

Meathead Klickman cracked his window so he could breathe. Nassar glanced at the shoes and almost laughed. The criminal sat low in the rear seat with his legs crossed.

'Poor meathead. Can't even read me my rights. This car stinks, meathead. Why don't you clean this car? It smells like cigarette smoke.'

'I hear you like cigarette smoke,' Klickman said, and felt much better about himself. Nassar giggled to help his friend. They'd taken enough crap off this brat.

Mark saw a crowded parking lot next to a tall building. Patrol cars were parked in rows next to the building. Nassar turned into the lot and parked in the driveway.

They rushed him through the entrance doors and down a long hallway. He had finally stopped talking. He was on their turf. Cops were everywhere. Signs directed traffic to the DUI Holding Tank, the Jail, the Visitors' Room, the Receiving Room. Plenty of signs and rooms. They stopped at a desk with a row of closed-circuit monitors behind it, and Nassar signed some papers. Mark studied the surroundings. Klickman almost felt sorry for him. He looked even smaller.

They were off again. The elevator took them to the fourth floor, and again they stopped at a desk. A sign on the wall pointed to the Juvenile Wing, and Mark figured he was getting close.

A uniformed lady with a clipboard and a plastic tag declaring her to be Doreen stopped them. She looked at some papers, then at the clipboard. 'Says here Judge Roosevelt wants Mark Sway in a private room,' she said.

'I don't care where you put him,' Nassar said. 'Just take him.'

She was frowning and looking at her clipboard. 'Of course, Roosevelt wants all juveniles in private rooms. Thinks this is the Hilton.'

'It's not?'

She ignored this, and pointed at a piece of paper for Nassar to sign. He scribbled his name hurriedly and said, 'He's all yours. God help you.'

Klickman and Nassar left without a word.

'Empty your pockets, Mark,' the lady said as she handed him a large metal container. He pulled out a dollar bill, some change, and a pack of gum. She counted it and wrote something on a card, which she then inserted on the end of the metal box. In a corner above the desk, two cameras captured Mark, and he could see himself on one of the dozen screens on the wall. Another lady in a uniform was stamping papers.

'Is this the jail?' Mark asked, cutting his eyes in all directions.

'We call it a detention center,' she said.

'What's the difference?'

This seemed to irritate her. 'Listen, Mark, we get all kinds of smart mouths up here, okay. You'll get along much better if you keep your mouth shut.' She leaned into his face with these words of warning, and her breath was stale cigarettes and black coffee.

'I'm sorry,' he said, and his eyes watered. It suddenly hit him. He was about to be locked in a room far away from his mother, far away from Reggie.

'Follow me,' Doreen said, proud of herself for restoring a little authority to the relationship. She whisked away with a ring of keys dangling and rattling from her waist. They opened a heavy, wooden door and started through a hallway with gray metal doors spaced evenly apart on both sides of the corridor. Each little room had a number beside it. Doreen stopped at Number 16, and unlocked it with one of her keys. 'In here,' she said.

Mark walked in slowly. The room was about twelve feet wide and twenty feet long. The lights were bright and the carpet was clean. Two bunk beds were to his right. Doreen patted the top bunk. 'You can have either bed,' she said, ever the hostess. 'Walls are cinder block and windows are nonbreakable, so don't try anything.' There were two windows – one in the door and one above the lavatory, and neither was big enough to stick his head through. 'Toilet's over there, stainless steel. Can't use ceramic anymore. Had a kid break one and slice his wrists with a piece of it. But that was in the old building. This place is much nicer, don't you think?'

It's gorgeous, Mark almost said. But he was sinking fast. He sat on the bottom bunk and rested his elbows on his knees. The carpet was pale green, the same type of commercial blend he'd been studying at the hospital.

'You okay, Mark?' Doreen asked without the slightest trace of sympathy. This was her job.

'Can I call my mother?'

'Not yet. You can make a few calls in about an hour.'

'Well, can you call her and just tell her I'm okay? She's worried sick.'

Doreen smiled and the make-up cracked around her eyes. She patted his head. 'Can't do it, Mark. Regulations. But she knows you're fine. My goodness, you'll be in court in a couple of hours.'

'How long do kids stay in here?'

'Not long. A few weeks occasionally, but this is sort of a holding area until the kids are processed and either sent back home or to a training school.' She was rattling her keys. 'Listen, I have to go now. The door locks automatically when it's closed, and if it opens without my little key here, then an alarm goes off and there's big trouble. So don't get any ideas, okay, Mark?'

'Yes ma'am.'

'Can I get you anything?'

'A telephone.'

'In just a little while, okay.'

Doreen closed the door behind her. There was a loud click, then silence.

He stared at the doorknob for a long time. This didn't seem like jail. There were no bars on the windows. The beds and floor were clean. The cinder block walls were painted a pleasant shade of yellow. He'd seen worse, in the movies.

There was so much to worry about. Ricky groaning like that again, the fire. Dianne slowly unraveling, cops and reporters glued to him. He didn't know where to start.

He stretched on the top bunk and studied the ceiling. Where in the world was Reggie?

# CHAPTER TWENTY-TWO

The chapel was cold and damp. It was a round building stuck to the side of a mausoleum like a cancerous growth. It was raining outside, and two television crews from New Orleans huddled beside their vans and hid under umbrellas.

The crowd was respectable, especially for a man with no family. His remains were packaged tastefully in a porcelain urn sitting on a mahogany table. Hidden speakers from above brought forth one dreary dirge after another as the lawyer and judges and a few clients ventured in and sat near the rear. Barry The Blade strutted down the aisle with two thugs in tow. He was properly dressed in a black double-breasted suit with a black shirt and a black tie. Black lizard shoes. His ponytail was immaculate. He arrived late, and enjoyed the stares from the mourners. After all, he'd known Jerome Clifford for a long time.

Four rows back, the Right Reverend Roy Foltrigg sat with Wally Boxx and scowled at the ponytail. The lawyers and judges looked at Muldanno, then at Foltrigg, then back at Muldanno. Strange, seeing them in the same room.

The music stopped, and a minister of some generic faith appeared in the small pulpit behind the urn. He started with a lengthy obituary of Walter Jerome Clifford, and threw in everything but the names of his childhood pets. This was not unexpected because when the obituary was over there would be little to say.

It was a brief service, just as Romey had asked for in his note. The lawyers and judges glanced at their watches. Another mournful lamentation started from above, and the minister excused everyone.

Romey's last hurrah was over in fifteen minutes. There were no tears. Even his secretary kept her composure. His daughter was not present. Very sad. He lived forty-four years and no one cried at his funeral.

Foltrigg kept his seat and scowled at Muldanno as he strutted down the aisle and out the door. Foltrigg waited until the chapel was empty, then made an exit with Wally behind him. The cameras were there, and that's exactly what he wanted. Earlier, Wally had leaked a juicy tidbit about the great Roy Foltrigg attending the service, and also that there was a chance Barry The Blade Muldanno would be present. Neither Wally nor Roy had any idea whether Muldanno would attend, but it was only a leak so who cared if it was accurate. It was working.

A reporter asked for a couple of minutes, and Foltrigg did what he always did. He glanced at his watch, looked terribly frustrated by this intrusion, and sent Wally after the van. Then he said what he always said, 'Okay, but make it quick. I'm due in court in fifteen minutes.' He hadn't been to court in three weeks. He usually went about once a month, but to hear him talk he lived in courtrooms, battling the bad guys, protecting the interests of the American taxpayers. A hard-charging crimebuster.

He squeezed under an umbrella and looked at the mini-cam. The reporter waved a microphone in his face. 'Jerome Clifford was a rival. Why did you attend his memorial service?'

He was suddenly sad. 'Jerome was a fine lawyer, and a friend of mine. We faced each other many times, but always respected each other.' What a guy. Gracious even in death. He hated Jerome Clifford and Jerome Clifford hated him, but the camera saw only the heartbreak of a grieving pal.

'Mr. Muldanno has hired a new lawyer and filed a motion for a continuance. What is your response to this?'

'As you know, Judge Lamond has scheduled a hearing on the continuance request for tomorrow morning at 10 A.M. The decision will be his. The United States will be ready for trial whenever he sets it.'

'Do you expect to find the body of Senator Boyette before trial?'

'Yes. I think we're getting close.'

'Is it true you were in Memphis just hours after Mr. Clifford shot himself?'

'Yes.' he sort of shrugged as if it was no big deal.

'There are news reports in Memphis that the kid who was with Mr. Clifford when he shot himself may know something about the Boyette case. Any truth to this?'

He smiled sheepishly, another trademark. When the answer was yes, but he couldn't say it, but he wanted to send the message anyway, he just grinned at the reporters and said, 'I can't comment on that.'

'I can't comment on that,' he said, glancing around as if time was up and his busy trial calendar was calling.

'Does the boy know where the body is?'

'No comment,' he said with irritation. The rain grew harder, and splashed on his socks and shoes. 'I have to be going.'

After an hour in jail, Mark was ready to escape. He inspected both windows. The one above the lavatory had some wire in it, but that did not matter. What was troubling, though, was the fact that any object exiting through this window, including a boy, would fall directly down at least fifty feet, and the fall would be stopped by a concrete sidewalk lined with chain-link fencing and barbed wire. Also, both windows were thick and too small for escape, he determined.

He would be forced to make his break when they transported him, maybe take a hostage or two. He'd seen some great movies about jail-breaks. His favorite was *Escape from Alcatraz* with Clint Eastwood. He'd figure it out.

Doreen knocked on the door, jangled her keys, and stepped inside. She held a directory and a black phone, which she plugged into the wall. 'It's yours for ten minutes. No long distance.' Then she was gone, the door clicking loudly behind her, the cheap perfume floating heavy in the air and burning his eyes.

He found the number for St. Peter's, asked for Room 943, and was informed that no calls were being put through to that room. Ricky's asleep, he thought. Must be bad. He found Reggie's number, and listened to Clint's voice on the recorder. He called Greenway's office, and was informed the doctor was at the hospital. Mark explained exactly who he was, and the secretary said she believed the doctor was seeing Ricky. He called Reggie again. Same recording. He left an urgent message – 'Get me out of jail, Reggie!' He called her home number, and listened to another recording.

He stared at the phone. With about seven minutes left, he had to do something. He flipped through the directory, and found the listings for the Memphis Police Department. He picked the North Precinct and dialed the number.

'Detective Klickman,' he said.

'Just a minute,' said the voice on the other end. He held for a few seconds, then a voice said, 'Who're you holding for?'

He cleared his throat and tried to sound gruff. 'Detective Klickman.'

'He's on duty.'

'When will he be in?'

'Around lunch.'

'Thanks.' Mark hung up quickly, and wondered if the lines were bugged. Probably not. After all, these phones were used by criminals and people like himself to call their lawyers and talk business. There had to be privacy.

He memorized the precinct phone number and address, then

flipped to the yellow pages under Restaurants. He punched a number, and a friendly voice said, 'Domino's Pizza. May I take your order.'

He cleared his throat and tried to sound hoarse. 'Yes, I'd like to order four of your large supremes.'

'Is that all?'

'Yes. Need them delivered at noon.'

'Your name?'

'I'm ordering them for Detective Klickman, North Precinct.'

'Delivered where?'

'North Precinct – 3633 Allen Road. Just ask for Klickman.'

'We've been there before, believe me. Phone number?'

'It's 555–8989.'

There was a short pause as the adding machine rang it up. 'That'll be forty-eight dollars and ten cents.'

'Fine. Don't need it until noon.'

Mark hung up, his heart pounding. But he'd done it once, and he could do it again. He found the Pizza Hut numbers, there were seventeen in Memphis, and started placing orders. Three said they were too far away from downtown. He hung up on them. One young girl was suspicious, said he sounded too young, and he hung up on her too. But for the most part it was just routine business – call, place the order, give the address and phone number, and allow free enterprise to handle the rest.

When Doreen knocked on the door twenty minutes later, he was ordering Klickman some Chinese food from Wong Boys. He quickly hung up and walked to the bunks. She took great satisfaction in removing the phone, like taking toys away from bad little boys. But she was not quick enough. Detective Klickman had ordered about forty deep dish supreme deluxe large pizzas and a dozen Chinese lunches, all to be delivered around noon, at a cost of somewhere in the neighborhood of five hundred dollars.

For his hangover, Gronke sipped his fourth orange juice of the morning and washed down another headache powder. He stood at the window of his hotel room, shoes off, belt unbuckled, shirt unbuttoned, and listened painfully as Jack Nance reported the disturbing news.

'Happened less than thirty minutes ago,' Nance said, sitting on the dresser, staring at the wall, trying to ignore this goon standing at the window with his back to him.

'Why?' Gronke grunted.

'Has to be youth court. They took him straight to jail. I mean, hell, they can't just pick a kid, or anybody else for that matter, and take him straight to jail. They had to file something in youth court. Cal's there now, checking it out. Maybe we'll have it soon, I don't know. Youth court records are locked up, I think.'

'Get the damned records, okay.'

Nance seethed but bit his tongue. He hated Gronke and his little band of cutthroats, and even though he needed the hundred bucks an hour he was tired of hanging around this dirty, smoky room like a flunky waiting to be barked at. He had other clients. Cal was a nervous wreck.

'We're trying,' he said.

'Try harder,' Gronke said to the window. 'Now I gotta call Barry and tell him the kids been taken away and there's no way to get to him. Got him locked up somewhere, probably with a cop sittin' outside his door.' He finished the orange juice and tossed the can in the general direction of the wastebasket. It missed and rattled along the wall. He glared at Nance. 'Barry'll wanna know if there's a way to get the kid. What would you suggest?'

'I suggest you leave the kid alone. This is not New Orleans, and this is not just some little punk you can rub out and make everything wonderful. This kid's got baggage, lots of it. People are watching him. If you do something stupid, you'll have a hundred Fibbies all over your ass. You won't be able to breathe, and you and Mr. Muldanno will rot in jail. Here, not New Orleans.'

'Yeah, yeah.' Gronke waved both hands at him in disgust and walked back to the window. 'I want you boys to keep watching him. If they move him anywhere, I wanna know it immediately. If they take him to court, I wanna know it. Figure it out, Nance. This is your city. You know the streets and alleys. At least you're supposed to. You're gettin' paid good money.'

'Yes sir,' Nance said loudly, then left the room.

# CHAPTER TWENTY-THREE

For two hours every Thursday morning, Reggie disappeared into the office of Dr. Elliot Levin, her long-time psychiatrist. Levin had been holding her hand for ten years. He was the architect who'd figured out the pieces and helped her put the puzzle back together. Their sessions were never disturbed.

Clint paced nervously in Levin's reception area. Dianne had called twice already. She had read the summons and petition to him over the phone. He had called Judge Roosevelt, and the detention center, and Levin's office, and now he waited impatiently for eleven o'clock. The receptionist tried to ignore him.

Reggie was smiling when Dr. Levin finished with her. She pecked him on the cheek, and they walked hand in hand into his plush reception area where Clint was waiting. She stopped smiling. 'What's the matter?' she asked, certain something terrible had happened.

'We need to go,' Clint said, taking her arm and ushering her through the door. She nodded good-bye to Levin, who was watching with interest and concern.

They were on a sidewalk next to a small parking lot. 'They've picked up Mark Sway. He's in custody.'

'What! Who!'

'Cops. A petition was filed this morning alleging Mark to be a delinquent, and Roosevelt issued an order to take him into custody.' Clint was pointing. 'Let's take your car. I'll drive.'

'Who filed the petition?'

'Foltrigg. Dianne called from the hospital, that's where they got him. She had a big fight with the cops, and scared Ricky again. I've talked to her and assured her you'll go get Mark.'

They opened and slammed doors to Reggie's car, and sped from the parking lot. 'Roosevelt's scheduled a hearing for noon,' Clint explained.

'Noon! You must be kidding. That's fifty-six minutes from now.'

'It's an expedited hearing. I talked to him about an hour ago, and he wouldn't comment on the petition. Had very little to say, really. Where are we going?'

She thought about this for a second. 'He's in the detention center, and I can't get him out. Let's go to Juvenile Court. I want to see the

201

petition, and I want to see Harry Roosevelt. This is absurd, a hearing within hours of filing the petition. The law says between three and seven days, not three and seven hours.'

'But isn't there a provision for expedited hearings?'

'Yeah, but only in extreme matters. They've fed Harry a bunch of crap. Delinquent! What's the kid done? This is crazy. They're trying to force him to talk, Clint, that's all.'

'So you didn't expect this?'

'Of course not. Not here, not in Juvenile Court. I've thought about a grand jury summons for Mark from New Orleans, but not Juvenile Court. He's committed no delinquent act. He doesn't deserve to be taken in.'

'Well, they got him.'

Jason McThune zipped his pants, and hit the lever three times before the antique urinal flushed. The bowl was stained with streaks of brown and the floor was wet, and he thanked God he worked in the Federal Building where everything was polished and spiffy. He'd lay asphalt with a shovel before he'd work in Juvenile Court.

But he was here now, like it or not, wasting time on the Boyette case because K. O. Lewis wanted him here. And K.O. took orders from Mr. F. Denton Voyles, Director of the FBI for forty-two years now. And in his forty-two years, no member of Congress and certainly no U.S. Senator had been murdered. And the fact that the late Boyd Boyette had been hidden so neatly was galling. Mr. Voyles was quite upset, not about the killing itself but about the FBI's inability to solve it completely.

McThune had a strong hunch Ms. Reggie Love would arrive shortly, since her client had been snatched away from right under her nose, and he figured she'd be fuming when he saw her. Maybe she'd understand that these legal strategies were being hatched in New Orleans, not Memphis, and certainly not in his office. Surely she would understand that he, McThune, was just a humble FBI agent taking orders from above and doing what the lawyers told him. Perhaps he could dodge her until they were all in the courtroom.

Perhaps not. As McThune opened the rest room door and stepped into the hallway, he was suddenly face to face with Reggie Love. Clint was a step behind her. She saw him immediately, and within seconds he was backed against the wall and she was in his face. She was agitated.

'Morning, Ms. Love,' he said, forcing a smile.

'It's Reggie, McThune.'

'Morning, Reggie.'

'Who's here with you?' she asked, glaring.

'Beg your pardon.'

'Your gang, your little band, your little group of government conspirators. Who's here?'

This was not a secret. He could discuss this with her. 'George Ord, Thomas Fink from New Orleans, K. O. Lewis.'

'Who's K. O. Lewis?'

'Deputy Director, FBI. From D.C.'

'What's he doing here?' Her questions were clipped and rapid, and aimed like arrows at McThune's eyes. He was pinned to the wall, afraid to move, but gallantly trying to appear nonchalant. If Fink of Ord or heaven forbid K. O. Lewis happened into the hallway and saw him huddled with her like this he'd never recover.

'Well, I, uh – '

'Don't make me mention the tape, McThune,' she said, mentioning the damned thing anyway. 'Just tell me the truth.'

Clint was standing behind her, holding her briefcase and watching the traffic. He appeared a bit surprised by this confrontation and the speed with which it was occurring. McThune shrugged as if he'd forgotten about the tape, and now that she mentioned it, what the hell. 'I think Foltrigg's office called Mr. Lewis and asked him to come down. That's all.'

'That's all? Did you guys have a little meeting with Judge Roosevelt this morning?'

'Yes, we did.'

'Didn't bother to call me, did you?'

'Uh, the judge said he'd call you.'

'I see. Are you planning to testify during this little hearing?' She took a step back when she asked this and McThune breathed easier.

'I'll testify if I'm called as a witness.'

She stuck a finger in his face. The nail on the end of it was long, curved, carefully manicured, and painted red, and McThune watched it fearfully. 'You stick with the facts, okay. One lie, however small, or one bit of unsolicited self-serving crap to the judge, or one cheap shot remark that hurts my client, and I'll slice your throat, McThune. You understand?'

He kept smiling, glancing up and down the hall as if she were a pal and they were just having a tiny disagreement. 'I understand,' he said, grinning.

Reggie turned and walked away with Clint by her side. McThune turned and darted back into the rest room, though he knew she wouldn't hesitate to follow him in if she wanted something.

'What was that all about?' Clint asked.

'Just keeping him honest.' They wove through crowds of litigants – paternity defendants, delinquent fathers, kids in trouble – and their lawyers huddled in small packs along the hallway.

'What's the bit about the tape?'

'I didn't tell you about it?'

'No.'

'I'll play it for you later. It's hysterical.' She opened the door with JUDGE HARRY M. ROOSEVELT painted on it, and they entered a small cramped room with four desks in the center and rows of file cabinets around the walls. Reggie went straight for the first desk on the left where a pretty black girl was typing. The plate on her desk gave the name as Marcia Riggle. She stopped typing and smiled. 'Hello, Reggie,' she said.

'Hi, Marcia. Where's His Honor?'

On her birthdays, Marcia received flowers from the law offices of Reggie Love, and chocolates at Christmas. She was the right arm of Harry Roosevelt, a man so overworked he had no time to remember such things as speaking commitments and appointments and anniversaries. But Marcia always remembered. Reggie had handled her divorce two years ago. Momma Love had cooked lasagne for her.

'He's on the bench. Should be off in a few minutes. You're on for noon, you know.'

'That's what I hear.'

'He's tried to call you all morning.'

'Well, he didn't find me. I'll wait in his office.'

'Sure. You want a sandwich? I'm ordering lunch for him now.'

'No, thanks.' Reggie took her briefcase and asked Clint to wait in the hall and watch for Mark. It was twenty minutes before twelve, and he'd be arriving soon.

Marcia handed her a copy of the petition, and Reggie entered the judge's office as if it were hers. She closed the door behind her.

Harry and Irene Roosevelt had also eaten at Momma Love's table. Few, if any, lawyers in Memphis spent as much time in Juvenile Court as Reggie Love, and over the past four years their lawyer–judge relationship had developed from one of mutual respect to one of friendship. About the only asset Reggie had been awarded in the divorce from Joe Cardoni was four season tickets for Memphis State basketball. The threesome – Harry, Irene, and Reggie – had watched many games at the Pyramid, sometimes joined by Elliot Levin, or another male friend of Reggie's. The basketball was usually followed by cheesecake at Café Expresso in The Peabody, or, depending on Harry's mood, maybe a late dinner at Grisanti's in midtown. Harry was always hungry, always planning the next meal. Irene fussed at him about his weight, so he ate more. Reggie occasionally kidded him about it, and each time she mentioned pounds or calories, he immediately asked about Momma Love and her pastas and cheeses and cobblers.

Judges are human. They need friends. He could eat and socialize with Reggie Love or any other lawyer for that matter and maintain his unbiased judicial discretion.

She marveled at the organized debris of his office. The floor was an ancient, pale carpet, most of it covered with neat stacks of briefs and other legal wisdoms all somehow cropped off at the height of twelve inches. Saggy bookshelves lined two walls, but the books could not be seen for the files and more stacks of briefs and memos tucked in front of books with inches hanging perilously in mid-air. Red and manila files were crammed everywhere. Three old wooden chairs sat pitifully before the desk. One had files on it. One had files under it. One was vacant for the moment, but would doubtless be used for some type of storage by the end of the day. She sat on this one and looked at the desk.

Though it was allegedly made of wood, none was visible except for the front and side panels. The top could be leather or chrome, no one would ever know. Harry himself could not remember what the top of his desk looked like. The upper level was another of Marcia's neat rows of legal papers, cropped at eight inches. Twelve inches for the floor, eight for the desk. Underneath and next in depth was a huge daily calendar for 1986, which Harry had once used to draw and doodle while listening to lawyers bore him with their arguments. Under the calendar was no-man's-land. Even Marcia was afraid to go deeper.

She'd stuck a dozen notes on yellow Post-it pads to the back of his chair. Evidently, these were the most urgent of the morning's emergencies.

Despite the chaos of his office, Harry Roosevelt was the most organized judge Reggie had encountered in her four-year career. He was not forced to spend time studying the law because he'd written most of it. He was known for the economy of his words, so his orders and decrees tended to be lean by judicial standards. He didn't tolerate lengthy briefs written by lawyers, and he was abrupt with those who loved to hear themselves talk. He managed his time wisely, and Marcia took care of the rest. His desk and office were somewhat famous in Memphis legal circles, and Reggie suspected he enjoyed this. She admired him immensely, not just for his wisdom and integrity, but also for his dedication to this office. He could've moved up many years ago to a stuffier place on the bench with a fancy desk, and clerks and paralegals, and clean carpet, and dependable airconditioning.

She flipped through the petition. Foltrigg and Fink were the petitioners, their signatures at the bottom. Nothing detailed, just broad, sweeping allegations about the juvenile, Mark Sway, obstructing a federal investigation by refusing to cooperate with the FBI and the U.S. Attorney's office for the Southern District of Louisiana. She despised Foltrigg every time she saw his name.

But it could be worse. Foltrigg's name could be at the bottom of a grand jury subpoena demanding the appearance of Mark Sway in New Orleans. It would be perfectly legal and proper for Foltrigg to do this, and she was a bit surprised he had chosen Memphis as his forum. New Orleans would be next if this didn't work.

The door opened, and a massive black robe lumbered in with Marcia in pursuit, holding a list and clicking off things that had to be done immediately. He listened without looking at her, unzipped the robe and threw it at a chair, the one with the files under it.

'Good morning, Reggie,' he said with a smile. He patted her on the shoulder as he walked behind her. 'That'll be all,' he said calmly to Marcia, who closed the door and left. He picked the little yellow notes from his chair without reading them, then fell in it.

'How's Momma Love?' he asked.

'She's fine. And you?'

'Marvelous. Not surprised to see you here.'

'You didn't have to sign a custody order. I would've brought him here, Harry, you know that. He fell asleep last night in the swing on Momma Love's porch. He's in good hands.'

Harry smiled and rubbed his eyes. Very few lawyers called him Harry in his office. But he rather enjoyed it when it came from her. 'Reggie, Reggie. You never believe your clients should be taken into custody.'

'That's not true.'

'You think all's well if you can just take them home and feed them.'

'It helps.'

'Yes, it does. But according to Mr. Ord and the FBI, little Mark Sway could be in a world of danger.'

'What'd they tell you?'

'It'll come out during the hearing.'

206

'They must've been pretty convincing, Harry. I get an hour's notice of the hearing. That has to be a record.'

'I thought you'd like that. We can do it tomorrow if you'd prefer. I don't mind making Mr. Ord wait.'

'Not with Mark in custody. Release him to my custody, and we'll do the hearing tomorrow. I need some time to think.'

'I'm afraid to release him until I hear proof.'

'Why?'

'According to the FBI, there are some very dangerous people now in the city who may want to shut him up. Do you know a Mr. Gronke, and his pals Bono and Pirini? Ever hear of these guys?'

'No.'

'Neither had I, until this morning. It seems that these gentlemen have arrived in our fair city from New Orleans, and that they're close associates of Mr. Barry Muldanno, or The Blade, as I believe he's known down there. Thank god organized crime never found Memphis. This scares me, Reggie, really scares me. These men do not play games.'

'Scares me too.'

'Has he been threatened?'

'Yes. It happened yesterday at the hospital. He told me about it, and he's been with me ever since.'

'So now you're a bodyguard.'

'No, I'm not. But I don't think the code gives you the authority to order custody of children who may be in danger.'

'Reggie, dear, I wrote the code. I can issue a custody order for any child alleged to be delinquent.'

True, he wrote the law. And the appellate courts had long since ceased second-guessing Harry Roosevelt.

'And according to Foltrigg and Fink, what are Mark's sins?'

Harry snatched two tissues from a drawer and blew his nose. He smiled at her again. 'He can't keep quiet, Reggie. If he knows something, he must tell them. You know that.'

'You're assuming he knows something.'

'I'm not assuming anything. The petition makes certain allegations, and these allegations are based partly on fact and partly on assumption. Same as all petitions, I guess. Wouldn't you say? We never know the truth until we have the hearing.'

'How much of Slick Moeller's crap do you believe?'

'I believe nothing, Reggie, until it is told to me, under oath, in my courtroom, and then I believe about ten percent of it.'

There was a long pause as the judge debated whether to ask the question. 'So, Reggie, what does the kid know?'

'You know it's privileged, Harry.'

He smiled. 'So, he knows more than he should.'

'You could say that.'

'If it's crucial to the investigation, Reggie, then he must tell.'

'What if he refuses?'

'I don't know. We'll deal with that when it happens. How smart is this kid?'

'Very. Broken home, no father, working mother, grew up on the streets. The usual. I talked to his fifth-grade teacher yesterday, and he makes all A's except for math. He's very bright, besides being street smart.'

'No prior trouble.'

'None. He's a great kid, Harry. Remarkable, really.'

'Most of your clients are remarkable, Reggie.'

'This one is special. He's here through no fault of his own.'

'I hope he'll be fully advised by his lawyer. The hearing could get rough.'

'Most of my clients are fully advised.'

'They certainly are.'

There was a brief knock at the door and Marcia appeared. 'Your client is here, Reggie. Witness Room C.'

'Thanks.' She stood and walked to the door. 'I'll see you in a few minutes, Harry.'

'Yes. Listen to me. I'm tough on kids who don't obey me.'

'I know.'

He sat in a chair leaning against the wall, with his arms folded across his chest and a frustrated look on his face. He'd been treated like a convict for three hours now, and he was getting used to it. He felt safe. He hadn't been beaten by the cops or by his fellow inmates.

The room was tiny with no windows and bad lighting. Reggie entered and moved a folding chair near him. She'd been in this room under these circumstances many times. He smiled at her, obviously relieved.

'So how's jail?' she asked.

'They haven't fed me yet. Can we sue them?'

'Maybe. How's Doreen, the lady with the keys?'

'A real snot. How do you know her?'

'I've been there many times, Mark. It's my job. Her husband is serving thirty years in prison for bank robbery.'

'Good. I'll ask her about him if I see her again. Am I going back there, Reggie? I'd like to know what's going on, you know.'

'Well, it's very simple. We'll have a hearing before Judge Harry Roosevelt in a few moments, in his courtroom, that may last a couple of hours. The U.S. Attorney and the FBI are claiming you possess important information, and I think we can expect them to ask the judge to make you talk.'

'Can the judge make me talk?'

Reggie was speaking very slowly and carefully. He was an eleven-year-old child, a smart one with plenty of street sense, but she'd seen many like him and knew that, at this moment, he was nothing but a scared little boy. He might hear her words, and he might not. Or, he might hear what he wanted to hear, so she had to be careful.

'No one can make you talk.'

'Good.'

'But the judge can put you back in the same little room if you don't talk.'

'Back in jail!'

'That's right.'

'I don't understand. I haven't done a damned thing wrong, and I'm in jail. I just don't understand this.'

'It's very simple. If, and I emphasize the word *if*, Judge Roosevelt instructs you to answer certain questions, and *if* you refuse, then he can hold you in contempt of court for not answering, for disobeying him. Now, I've never known an eleven-year-old kid to be held in contempt, but if you were an adult and you refused to answer the judge's questions, then you'd go to jail for contempt.'

'But I'm a kid.'

'Yes, but I don't think he'll allow you to go free if you refuse to answer the questions. You see, Mark, the law is very clear in this area. A person who has knowledge of information crucial to a criminal investigation cannot withhold this information because he feels threatened. In other words, you can't keep quiet because you're afraid of what might happen to you or your family.'

'That's a stupid law.'

'I don't really agree with it either, but that's not important. It is the law, and there are no exceptions, not even for kids.'

'So I get thrown in jail for contempt?'

'It's very possible.'

'Can we sue the judge, or do something else to get me out?'

'No. You can't sue the judge. And Judge Roosevelt is a very good and fair man.'

'I can't wait to meet him.'

'It won't be long now.'

Mark thought about all this. His chair rocked methodically against the wall. 'How long would I be in jail?'

'Assuming, of course, you're sent there, probably until you decide to comply with the judge's orders. Until you talk.'

'Okay. What if I decide not to talk. How long will I stay in jail? A month? A year? Ten years?'

'I can't answer that, Mark. No one knows.'

'The judge doesn't know?'

'No. If he sends you to jail for contempt, I doubt if he has any idea how long he'll make you stay.'

Another long pause. He'd spent three hours in Doreen's little room, and it wasn't such a bad place. He'd seen movies about prison in which gangs fought and rampaged and homemade weapons were used to kill snitches. Guards tortured inmates. Inmates attacked each other. Hollywood at its finest. But this place wasn't so bad.

And look at the alternative. With no place to call home, the Sway family now lived in Room 943 of St. Peter's Charity Hospital. But the thought of Ricky and his mother all alone and struggling without him was unbearable. 'Have you talked to my mother?' he asked.

'No, not yet. I will after the hearing.'

'I'm worried about Ricky.'

'Do you want your mother present in the courtroom when we have this hearing? She needs to be here.'

'No. She's got enough stuff on her mind. You and I can handle this mess.'

She touched his knee, and wanted to cry. Someone knocked on the door, and she said loudly, 'Just a minute.'

'The judge is ready,' came the reply.

Mark breathed deeply and stared at her hand on his knee. 'Can I just take the Fifth Amendment?'

'No. It won't work, Mark. I've already thought about it. The questions will not be asked to incriminate you. They will be asked for the purpose of gathering information you may have.'

'I don't understand.'

'I don't blame you. Listen to me carefully, Mark. I'll try to explain it. They want to know what Jerome Clifford told you before he died. They will ask you some very specific questions about the events immediately before the suicide. They will ask you what, if anything, Clifford told you about Senator Boyette. Nothing you tell them with your answers will in any way incriminate you in the murder of Senator Boyette. Understand? You had nothing to do with it. And, you had nothing to do with the suicide of Jerome Clifford. You broke no laws, okay? You're not a suspect in any crime or wrongdoing. Your answers cannot incriminate you. So, you cannot hide under the protection of the Fifth Amendment.' She paused and watched him closely. 'Understand?'

'No. If I didn't do anything wrong, why was I picked up by the cops and taken to jail? Why am I sitting here waiting for a hearing?'

'You're here because they think you know something valuable, and because, as I stated, every person has a duty to assist law enforcement officials in the course of their investigation.'

'I still say it's a stupid law.'

'Maybe so. But we can't change it today.'

He rocked forward and sat the chair on all fours. 'I need to know something, Reggie. Why can't I just tell them I know nothing? Why can't I say that me and old Romey talked about suicide and going to heaven and hell, you know, stuff like that.'

'Tell lies?'

'Yeah. It'll work, you know. Nobody knows the truth but Romey, me, and you. Right? And Romey, bless his heart, ain't talking.'

'You can't lie in court, Mark.' She said this with all the sincerity she could muster. Hours of sleep had been lost trying to formulate the answer to this inevitable question. She wanted so badly to say 'Yes! That's it! Lie, Mark, lie!'

Her stomach ached and her hands almost shook, but she held firm. 'I cannot allow you to lie to the court. You'll be under oath, so you must tell the truth.'

'Then it was a mistake to hire you, wasn't it?'

'I don't think so.'

'Sure it was. You're making me tell the truth, and in this case the truth might get me killed. If you weren't around, I'd march in there and lie my little butt off and me and Mom and Ricky would all be safe.'

'You can fire me if you like. The court will appoint another lawyer.'

He stood and walked to the darkest corner of the room, and began crying. She watched his head sink and his shoulders sag. He covered his eyes with the back of his right hand, and sobbed loudly.

Though she'd seen it many times, the sight of a child scared and suffering was unbearable. She couldn't keep from crying too.

# CHAPTER TWENTY-FOUR

Two deputies escorted him into the courtroom from a side door, away from the main hallway where the curious were known to lurk, but Slick Moeller anticipated this little maneuver and watched it all from behind a newspaper just a few feet away.

Reggie followed her client and the deputies. Clint waited outside. It was almost a quarter after noon, and the jungle of Juvenile Court had quieted a bit for lunch.

The courtroom was of a shape and design Mark had never seen on television. It was so small! And empty. There were no benches or seats for spectators. The judge sat behind an elevated structure between two flags with the wall just behind him. Two tables were in the center of the room, facing the judge, and one was already occupied with men in dark suits. To the judge's right was a tiny table where an older woman was flipping through a stack of papers, very bored with it all, it seemed, until he entered the room. A gorgeous young lady sat ready with a stenographic machine directly in front of the judge's bench. She wore a short skirt and her legs were attracting a lot of attention. She couldn't be older than sixteen, he thought as he followed Reggie to their table. A bailiff with a gun on his hip was the final actor in the play.

Mark took his seat, very much aware that everyone was staring at him. His two deputies left the room, and when the door closed behind them the judge picked up the file again and flipped through it. They had been waiting on the juvenile and his lawyer, and now it was time for everyone to wait for the judge again. Rules of courtroom etiquette must be followed.

Reggie pulled a single legal pad from her briefcase and began writing notes. She held a tissue in one hand, and dabbed her eyes with it. Mark stared at the table, eyes still wet but determined to suck it up and be tough through this ordeal. People were watching.

Fink and Ord stared at the court reporter's legs. The skirt was halfway between knee and hip. It was tight and seemed to slide upward just a fraction of an inch every minute or so. The tripod holding her recording machine sat firmly between her knees. In the coziness of Harry's courtroom, she was fewer than ten feet away, and the last thing they needed was a distraction. but they kept staring. There! It slipped upward another quarter of an inch.

Baxter L. McLemore, a young attorney fresh from law school, sat nervously at the table with Mr. Fink and Mr. Ord. He was a lowly asssistant with the county Attorney General's office, and it had fallen to his lot to prosecute on this day in Juvenile Court. This was certainly not the glamorous end of prosecution, but sitting next to George Ord was quite a thrill. He knew nothing about the Sway case, and Mr. Ord had explained in the hallway just minutes earlier that Mr. Fink would handle the hearing. With the court's permission, of course. Baxter was expected to sit there and look nice, and keep his mouth shut.

'Is the door locked?' the judge finally asked in the general direction of the bailiff.

'Yes sir.'

'Very well. I have reviewed the petition, and I am ready to proceed. For the record, I note the child is present along with counsel, and that the child's mother, who is alleged to be his custodial parent, was served with a copy of the petition and a summons this morning. However, the child's mother is not present in the courtroom, and this concerns me.' Harry paused for a moment and seemed to read from the file.

Fink decided this was the appropriate time to establish himself in this matter, and he stood slowly, buttoning his jacket, and addressed the court. 'Your Honor, if I may, for the record, I'm Thomas Fink, Assistant U.S. Attorney for the Southern District of Louisiana.'

Harry's gaze slowly left the file and settled on Fink, who was standing stiff-backed, very formal, frowning intelligently as he spoke, still fiddling with the top button of his jacket.

Fink continued. 'I am one of the petitioners in this matter, and, if I may, I would like to address the issue of the presence of the child's mother.' Harry said nothing, just stared as if in disbelief. Reggie couldn't help but smile. She winked at Baxter McLemore.

Harry leaned forward, and rested on his elbows as if intrigued by these great words of wisdom flowing from this gifted legal mind.

Fink had found an audience. 'Your Honor, it's our position, the position of the petitioners, that this matter is of a nature so urgent that this hearing must take place immediately. The child is represented by counsel, quite competent counsel I might add, and none of the child's legal rights will be prejudiced by the absence of his mother. From what we understand, the mother's presence is required by the bedside of her youngest son, and so, well, who knows when she might be able to attend a hearing. We just think it's important, Your Honor, to proceed immediately with this hearing.'

213

'You don't say?' Harry asked.

'Yes sir. This is our position.'

'Your position, Mr. Fink,' Harry said very slowly and very loudly with a pointed finger, 'is in that chair right there. Please sit, and listen to me very carefully, because I will only say this once. And if I have to say it again, I will do so as they are putting the handcuffs on you and taking you away for a night in our splendid jail.'

Fink fell into his chair, mouth open, gaping in disbelief.

Harry scowled over his reading glasses and looked straight down at Thomas Fink. 'Listen to me, Mr. Fink. This is not some fancy courtroom in New Orleans, and I am not one of your federal judges. This is my little private courtroom, and I make the rules, Mr. Fink. Rule number one is that you speak only in my courtroom when you are first spoken to by me. Rule number two is that you do not grace His Honor with unsolicited speeches, comments, or remarks. Rule number three is that His Honor does not like to hear the voices of lawyers. His Honor has been hearing these voices for twenty years, and His Honor knows how lawyers love to hear themselves talk. Rule number four is that you do not stand in my courtroom. You sit at that table and say as little as possible. Do you understand these rules, Mr. Fink?'

Fink stared blankly at Harry and tried to nod.

Harry wasn't finished. 'This is a tiny courtroom, Mr. Fink, designed by myself a long time ago for pivate hearings. We can all see and hear each other just fine, so just keep your mouth shut and your butt in you seat, and we'll get along fine.'

Fink was still trying to nod. He gripped the arms of the chair, determined never to rise again. Behind him, McThune, the lawyer hater, barely suppressed a smile.

'Mr. McLemore, I understand Mr. Fink wants to handle this case for the prosecution. Is this agreeable?'

'Okay with me, Your Honor.'

'I'll allow it. But try and keep him in his seat.'

Mark was terrified. He had hoped for a kind, gentle old man with lots of love and sympathy. Not this. He glanced at Mr. Fink, whose neck was crimson and whose breathing was loud and heavy, and he almost felt sorry for him.

'Ms. Love,' the judge said, suddenly very warm and compassionate, 'I understand you may have an objection on behalf of the child.'

'Yes, Your Honor.' She leaned forward and spoke deliberately in the direction of the court reporter. 'We have several objections we'd like to make at this time, and I want them in the record.'

'Certainly,' Harry said, as if Reggie Love could have anything she wanted. Fink sank lower and felt even dumber. So much for impressing the court with an initial burst of eloquence.

Reggie glanced at her notes. 'Your Honor, I request the transcript of these proceedings be typed and prepared as soon as possible to facilitate an emergency appeal if necessary.'

'So ordered.'

'I object to this hearing on several grounds. First, inadequate notice has been given to the child, his mother, and to his lawyer. About three hours have passed since the petition was served upon the child's mother, and though I have represented the child for three days now, and everyone involved has known this, I was not notified of this hearing until seventy-five minutes ago. This is unfair, absurd, and an abuse of discretion by the court.'

'When would you like to have the hearing, Ms. Love?' Harry asked.

'Today's Thursday,' she said. 'What about Tuesday or Wednesday of next week?'

'That's fine. Say Tuesday at nine.' Harry looked at Fink, who still hadn't moved and was afraid to respond to this. 'Of course, Ms. Love, the child will remain in custody until then.'

'The child does not belong in custody, Your Honor.'

'But I've signed a custody order, and I will not rescind it while we wait on a hearing. Our laws, Ms. Love, provide for the immediate taking of alleged delinquents, and your client is being treated no differently from others. Plus, there are other considerations for Mark Sway, and I'm sure these will be discussed shortly.'

'Then I cannot agree on a continuance if my client will remain in custody.'

'Very well,' His Honor said properly. 'Let the record reflect a continuance was offered by the court and declined by the child.'

'And let the record also reflect the child declined a continuance because the child does not wish to remain in the Juvenile Detention Center any longer than he has to.'

'So noted,' Harry said with a slight grin. 'Please proceed, Ms. Love.'

'We also object to this hearing because the child's mother is not present. Due to extreme circumstances, her presence is not possible at this time, and keep in mind, Your Honor, the poor woman was first notified barely three hours ago. The child here is eleven years old and deserves the assistance of his mother. As you know, Your Honor, our laws strongly favor the presence of the parents in these hearings, and to proceed without Mark's mother is unfair.'

215

'When can Ms. Sway be available?'

'No one knows, Your Honor. She is literally confined to the hospital room with her son who's suffering from post-traumatic stress. Her doctor allows her out of the room only for minutes at a time. It could be weeks before she's available.'

'So you want to postpone this hearing indefinitely?'

'Yes sir.'

'All right. You've got it. Of course, the child will remain in custody pending the hearing.'

'The child does not belong in custody. The child will make himself available anytime the court wants. There's nothing to be gained by keeping the child locked up until a hearing.'

'There are complicating factors in this case, Ms. Love, and I'm not inclined to release this child before we have this hearing and it's determined how much he knows. It's that simple. I'm afraid to release him at this time. If I did so, and if something happened to him, I'd carry the guilt to my grave. Do you understand this, Ms. Love?'

She understood, though she wouldn't admit it. 'I'm afraid you're making this decision based on facts not in evidence.'

'Maybe so. But I have wide discretion in these matters, and until I hear the proof I'm not inclined to release him.'

'That'll look good on appeal,' she snapped, and Harry didn't like it.

'Let the record reflect a continuance was offered to the child until his mother could be present, and the continuance was declined by the child.'

To which Reggie quickly responded, 'And also let the record reflect the child declined the continuance because the child does not wish to remain in the Juvenile Detention Center any longer than he has to.'

'So noted, Ms. Love. Please continue.'

'The child moves this court to dismiss the petition filed against him on the grounds that the allegations are without merit and the petition has been filed in an effort to explore things the child *might* know. The petitioners, Fink and Foltrigg, are using this hearing as a fishing expedition for their desperate criminal investigation. Their petition is a hopeless mishmash of maybes and what ifs, and filed under oath without the slightest hint of the real truth. They're desperate, Your Honor, and they're here shooting in the dark hoping they hit something. The petition should be dismissed, and we should all go home.'

Harry glared down at Fink, and said, 'I'm inclined to agree with her, Mr. Fink. What about it?'

Fink had settled into his chair and watched with comfort as Reggie's first two objections had been shot down by His Honor. His breathing almost returned to normal and his face had gone from crimson to pink, when suddenly the judge was agreeing with her and staring at him.

Fink bolted to the edge of his chair, almost stood but caught himself, and started stuttering. 'Well, uh, Your Honor, we, uh, can prove our allegations if given the chance. We, uh, believe what we've said in the petition – '

'I certainly hope so,' Harry sneered.

'Yes sir, and we know that this child is impeding an investigation. Yes sir, we are confident we can prove what we've alleged.'

'And if you can't?'

'Well, I, uh, we, feel sure that – '

'You realize, Mr. Fink, that if I hear the proof in this case and find you're playing games, I can hold you in contempt. And, knowing Ms. Love the way I do, I'm sure there will be retribution from the child.'

'We intend to file suit first thing in the morning, Your Honor,' Reggie added helpfully. 'Against both Mr. Fink and Roy Foltrigg. They're abusing this court and the juvenile laws of the state of Tennessee. My staff is working on the lawsuit right now.'

Her staff was sitting outside in the hallway eating a Snickers bar and sipping a diet cola. But the threat sounded ominous in the courtroom.

Fink glanced at George Ord, his co-counsel, who was sitting next to him making a list of things to do that afternoon, and nothing on the list had anything to do with Mark Sway or Roy Foltrigg. Ord supervised twenty-eight lawyers working thousands of cases, and he just didn't care about Barry Muldanno and the body of Boyd Boyette. It wasn't in his jurisdiction. Ord was a busy man, too busy to waste valuable time playing gofer for Roy Foltrigg.

But Fink was no featherweight. He'd seen his share of nasty trials and hostile judges and skeptical juries. He was rallying quite nicely. 'Your Honor, the petition is much like an indictment. Its truth cannot be ascertained without a hearing, and if we can get on with it we can prove our allegations.'

Harry turned to Reggie. 'I'll take this motion to dismiss under advisement, and I'll hear the petitioners' proof. If it falls short, then I'll grant the motion and we'll go from there.'

Reggie shrugged as if she expected this.

'Anything else, Ms. Love?'

'Not at this time.'

'Call your first witness, Mr. Fink,' Harry said. 'And make it brief. Get right to the point. If you waste time, I'll jump in with both feet and speed things along.'

'Yes sir. Sergeant Milo Hardy of the Memphis Police is our first witness.'

Mark had not moved during these preliminary skirmishes. He wasn't sure if Reggie had won them all, or lost them all, and for some reason he didn't care. There was something unfair about a system in which a little kid was brought into a courtroom and surrounded by lawyers arguing and sniping at each other under the scornful eye of a judge, the referee, and somehow in the midst of this barrage of laws and code sections and motions and legal talk the kid was supposed to know what was happening to him. It was hopelessly unfair.

And so he just sat and stared at the floor near the court reporter. His eyes were still wet and he couldn't make them stay dry.

The courtroom was silent as Sergeant Hardy was fetched. His Honor relaxed in his chair and removed his reading glasses. 'I want this on the record,' he said. He glared at Fink again. 'This is a private and confidential matter. This hearing is closed for a reason. I defy anyone to repeat any word uttered in this room today, or to discuss any aspect of this proceeding. Now, Mr. Fink, I realize you must report to the U.S. Attorney in New Orleans, and I realize Mr. Foltrigg is a petitioner and has a right to know what happens here. And when you talk to him, please explain that I am very upset by his absence. He signed the petition, and he should be here. You may explain these proceedings to him, and only to him. No one else. And you are to tell him to keep his big mouth shut, do you understand, Mr. Fink?'

'Yes, Your Honor.'

'Will you explain to Mr. Foltrigg that if I get wind of any breach in the confidentiality of these proceedings that I will issue a contempt order and attempt to have him jailed?'

'Yes, Your Honor.'

He was suddenly staring at McThune and K. O. Lewis. They were seated immediately behind Fink and Ord.

'Mr. McThune and Mr. Lewis, you may now leave the courtroom,' Harry said abruptly. They grabbed the armrests as their feet hit the floor. Fink turned and stared at them, then looked at the judge.'

'Uh, Your Honor, would it be possible for these gentlemen to remain in the – '

'I told them to leave, Mr. Fink,' Harry said loudly. 'If they're gonna be witnesses, we'll call them later. If they're not witnesses, they have no business here and they can wait in the hall with the rest of the herd. Now, move along, gentlemen.'

McThune was practically jogging for the door, without the slightest hint of wounded pride, but K. O. Lewis was pissed. He buttoned his jacket and stared at His Honor, but only for a second. No one had ever won a staring contest with Harry Roosevelt, and K. O. Lewis was not about to try. He strutted for the door, which was already open as McThune dashed through it.

Seconds later, Sergeant Hardy entered and sat in the witness chair. He was in full uniform. He shifted his wide ass in the padded seat, and waited. Fink was frozen, afraid to begin without being told to do so.

Judge Roosevelt rolled his chair to the end of the bench and peered down at Hardy. Something had caught his attention, and Hardy sat like a fat toad on a stool until he realized His Honor was just inches away.

'Why are you wearing the gun?' Harry asked.

Hardy looked up, startled, then jerked his head to his right hip as if the gun was a complete surprise to him also. He stared at it as if the damned thing had somehow stuck itself to his body.

'Well, I – '

'Are you on duty or off, Sergeant Hardy?'

'Well, off.'

'Then why are you wearing a uniform, and why in the world are you wearing a gun in my courtroom?'

Mark smiled for the first time in hours.

The bailiff had caught on and was rapidly approaching the witness stand as Hardy jerked at his belt and removed the holster. The bailiff carried it away as if it were a murder weapon.

'Have you ever testified in court?' Harry asked.

Hardy smiled like a child and said, 'Yes sir, many times.'

'You have?'

'Yes sir. Many times.'

'And how many times have you testified while wearing your gun?'

'Sorry, Your Honor.'

Harry relaxed, looked at Fink, and waved at Hardy as if it was now permissible to get on with it. Fink had spent many hours in courtrooms during the past twenty years, and took great pride in his trial skills. His record was impressive. He was glib and smooth, quick on his feet.

But he was slow on his ass, and this sitting while interrogating a witness was such a radical way of finding truth. He almost stood again, caught himself again, and grabbed his legal pad. His frustration was apparent.

'Would you state your name for the record?' he asked in a short, rapid burst.

'Sergeant Milo Hardy, Memphis Police Department.'

'And what is your address?'

Harry held up a hand to cut off Hardy. 'Mr. Fink, why do you need to know where this man lives?'

Fink stared in disbelief. 'I guess, Your Honor, it's just a routine question.'

'Do you know how much I hate routine questions, Mr. Fink?'

'I'm beginning to understand.'

'Routine questions lead us nowhere, Mr. Fink. Routine questions waste hours and hours of valuable time. I do not want to hear another routine question. Please.'

'Yes, Your Honor. I'll try.'

'I know it's hard.'

Fink looked at Hardy and tried desperately to think of a brilliantly original question. 'Last Monday, Sergeant, were you dispatched to the scene of a shooting?'

Harry held up his hand again, and Fink slumped in his seat. 'Mr. Fink, I don't know how you folks do things in New Orleans, but here in Memphis we make our witnesses swear to tell the truth before they start testifying. It's called, "Placing them under oath." Does that sound familiar?'

Fink rubbed his temples and said, 'Yes sir. Could the witness please be sworn?'

The elderly woman at the desk suddenly came to life. She sprang to her feet and yelled at Hardy, who was less than fifteen feet away. 'Raise your right hand!'

Hardy did this, and was sworn to tell the truth. She returned to her seat, and to her nap.

'Now, Mr. Fink, you may proceed,' Harry said with a nasty little smile, very pleased that he'd caught Fink with his pants down. He relaxed in his massive seat, and listened intently to the rapid question and answer routine that followed.

Hardy spoke in a chatty voice, eager to help, full of little details. He described the scene of the suicide, the position of the body, the condition of the car. There were photographs, if His Honor would like to see them. His Honor declined. They were completely irrelevant. Hardy produced a typed transcript of the 911 call made by Mark, and offered to play the recording if His Honor would like to hear it. No, His Honor said.

Then Hardy explained with great joy the capture of young Mark in the woods near the scene, and of their ensuing conversations in his car, at the Sway trailer, en route to the hospital, and over dinner in the cafeteria. He described his gut feelings that young Mark was not telling the complete truth. The kid's story was flimsy, and through skillful interrogation with just the right touch of subtlety, he, Hardy, was able to poke all sorts of holes in it.

The lies were pathetic. The kid said he and his brother stumbled upon the car and the dead body; that they did not hear any gunshots; that they were just a couple of kids playing in the woods, minding their own business, and somehow they found this body. Of course, none of Mark's story was true, and Hardy was quick to catch on.

With great detail, Hardy described the condition of Mark's face, the swollen eye and puffy lip, the blood around the mouth. Kid said he'd been in a fight at school. Another sad little lie.

After thirty minutes, Harry grew restless and Fink took the hint. Reggie had no cross-examination, and when Hardy stepped down and left the room there was no doubt that Mark Sway was a liar who'd tried to deceive the cops. Things would get worse.

When His Honor had asked Reggie if she had any questions for Sergeant Hardy, she simply said, 'I've had no time to prepare for this witness.'

McThune was called as the next witness. He gave his oath to tell the truth and sat in the witness chair. Reggie slowly reached into her briefcase and withdrew a cassette tape. She held it casually in her hand, and when McThune glanced at her she tapped it softly on her legal pad. He closed his eyes.

She carefully placed the tape on the pad, and began tracing its edges with her pen.

Fink was quick, to the point, and by now fairly adept at avoiding even vaguely routine questions. It was a new experience for him, this efficient use of words, and the more he did it the more he liked it.

McThune was as dry as cornmeal. He explained the fingerprints they found all over the car, and on the gun and the bottle, and on the rear bumper. He speculated about the kids and the garden hose, and showed Harry the Virginia Slims cigarette butts found under the tree. He also showed Harry the suicide note left behind by Clifford, and again gave his thoughts about the additional words added by a different pen. He showed Harry the Bic pen found in the car, and said there was no doubt Mr. Clifford had used this pen to scrawl these words. He talked about the speck of blood found on Clifford's hand. It wasn't Clifford's blood, but was of the same type as Mark

Sway's, who just happened to have a busted lip and a couple of wounds from the affair.

'You think Mr. Clifford struck the child at some point during all this?' Harry asked.

'I think so, Your Honor.'

McThune's thoughts and opinions and speculations were objectionable, but Reggie kept quiet. She'd been through many of these hearings with Harry, and she knew he would hear it all and decide what to believe. Objecting would do no good.

Harry asked how the FBI obtained a fingerprint from the child to match those found in the car. McThune took a deep breath, and told about the Sprite can at the hospital, but was quick to point out that they were not investigating the child as a suspect when this happened, just as a witness, and so therefore they felt it was okay to lift the print. Harry didn't like this at all, but said nothing. McThune emphasized that if the child had been an actual suspect, they would never have dreamed of stealing a print. Never.

'Of course you wouldn't,' Harry said with enough sarcasm to make McThune blush.

Fink walked him through the events of Tuesday, the day after the suicide, when young Mark hired a lawyer. They tried desperately to talk with him, then to his lawyer, and things just deteriorated.

McThune behaved himself and stuck to the facts. He left the room in a quick dash for the door, and he left behind the undeniable fact that young Mark was quite a liar.

From time to time, Harry watched Mark during the testimony of Hardy and McThune. The kid was impassive, hard to read, preoccupied with an invisible spot somewhere on the floor. He sat low in his seat and ignored Reggie for the most part. His eyes were wet, but he was not crying. He looked tired and sad, and occasionally glanced at the witness when his lies were emphasized.

Harry had watched Reggie many times under these circumstances, and she usually sat very close to her young clients and whispered to them as the hearings progressed. She would pat them, squeeze their arms, give reassurances, lecture them if necessary. Normally, she was in constant motion, protecting her clients from the harsh reality of a legal system run by adults. But not today. She glanced at her client occasionally as if waiting for a signal, but he ignored her.

'Call your next witness,' Harry said to Fink, who was resting on his elbows, trying not to stand. He looked at Ord for help, then at His Honor.

'Well, Your Honor, this may sound a bit strange, but I'd like to testify next.'

Harry ripped off his reading glasses and glared at Fink. 'You're confused, Mr. Fink. You're the lawyer, not a witness.'

'I know that, sir, but I'm also the petitioner, and, I know this may be a bit out of order, but I think my testimony could be important.'

'Thomas Fink, petitioner, lawyer, witness. You wanna play bailiff, Mr. Fink? Maybe take down a bit of stenography? Perhaps wear my robe for a while? This is not a courtroom, Mr. Fink, it's a theater. Why don't you just choose any role you like?'

Fink stared blankly at the bench without making eye contact with His Honor. 'I can explain, sir,' he said meekly.

'You don't have to explain, Mr. Fink. I'm not blind. You boys have rushed in here half-ass prepared. Mr. Foltrigg should be here, but he's not, and now you need him. You figured you could throw together a petition, bring in some FBI brass, hook in Mr. Ord here, and I'd be so impressed I'd just roll over and do anything you asked. Can I tell you something, Mr. Fink?'

Fink nodded.

'I'm not impressed. I've seen better work at high school mock trial competitions. Half the first-year law students at Memphis State could kick your butt, and the other half could kick Mr. Foltrigg's.'

Fink was not agreeing, but he kept nodding for some reason. Ord slid his chair a few inches away from Fink's.

'What about it, Ms. Love?' Harry asked.

'Your Honor, our rules of procedure and ethics are quite clear. An attorney trying a case cannot participate in the same trial as a witness. It's simple.' She sounded bored and frustrated, as if everyone should know this.

'Mr. Fink?'

Fink was regaining himself. 'Your Honor, I would like to tell the court, under oath, certain facts regarding Mr. Clifford's actions prior to the suicide. I apologize for this request, but under the circumstances it cannot be helped.'

There was a knock on the door, and the bailiff opened it slightly. Marcia entered carrying a plate covered with a thick roast beef sandwich and a tall plastic glass of ice tea. She sat it before His Honor, who thanked her, and she was gone.

It was almost one o'clock, and suddenly everyone was starving. The roast beef and horseradish and pickles, and the side order of onion rings, emitted an appetizing aroma that wafted around the room. All eyes were on the kaiser roll, and as Harry picked it up to take a huge bite, he saw young Mark Sway watching his every move. He stopped the sandwich in mid-air, and noticed that Fink and Ord, and Reggie, and even the bailiff were staring in helpless anticipation.

Harry placed the sandwich onto the plate, and slid it to one side. 'Mr. Fink,' he said, jabbing a finger in Fink's direction, 'stay where you are. Do you swear to tell the truth?'

'I do.'

'You'd better. You're now under oath. You have five minutes to tell me what's bugging you.'

'Yes, thank you, Your Honor.'

'You're so welcome.'

'You see, Jerome Clifford and I were in law school together, and we knew each other for many years. We had many cases together, always on opposite sides, of course.'

'Of course.'

'After Barry Muldanno was indicted, the pressure began to mount and Jerome began acting strange. Looking back, I think he was slowly cracking up, but at the time I didn't think much about it. I mean, you see, Jerome was always a strange one.'

'I see.'

'I was working on the case every day, many hours a day, and I talked to Jerome Clifford several time a week. We had preliminary motions and such, so I saw him in court occasionally. He looked awful. He gained a lot of weight, and was drinking too much. He was always late for meetings. Rarely bathed. Often, he failed to return phone calls, which was unusual for Jerome. About a week before he died he called me at home one night, really drunk, and rambled on for almost an hour. He was crazy. Then, he called me at the office first thing the next morning and apologized. But he wouldn't get off the phone. He kept fishing around as if he was afraid he'd said too much the night before. At least twice he mentioned the Boyette body, and I became convinced Jerome knew where it was.'

Fink paused to allow this to sink in, but Harry was waiting impatiently.

'Well, he called me several times after that, kept talking about the body. I led him on. I implied that he'd said too much when he was drunk. I told him that we were considering an indictment against him for obstruction of justice.'

'Seems to be one of your favorites,' Harry said dryly.

'Anyway, Jerome was drinking heavily and acting bizarre. I confessed to him that the FBI was trailing him around the clock, which was not altogether true, but he seemed to believe it. He grew very paranoid, and called me several times a day. He'd get drunk and call me late at night. He wanted to talk about the body, but was afraid to tell everything. During our last phone conversation, I suggested that maybe we could cut a deal. If he'd tell us where the body was, then we'd help him bail out with no record, no conviction, nothing. He was terrified of his client, and he never once denied knowing where the body was.'

'Your Honor,' Reggie interrupted, 'this, of course, is pure hearsay and quite self-serving. There's no way to verify any of this.'

'You don't believe me?' Fink snapped at her.

'No, I don't.'

'I'm not sure I do either, Mr. Fink,' Harry said. 'Nor am I sure why any of this has any relevance to this hearing.'

'My point, Your Honor, is that Jerome Clifford knew about the body and he was talking about it. Plus, he was cracking up.'

'I'll say he cracked up, Mr. Fink. He put a gun in his mouth. Sounds crazy to me.'

Fink sort of hung in the air with his mouth open, uncertain if he should say anything else.

'Any more witnesses, Mr. Fink?' Harry asked.

'No sir. We do, however, Your Honor, feel that, due to the unusual circumstances of this case, the child should take the stand and testify.'

Harry ripped off the reading glasses again, and leaned toward Fink. If he could have reached him, he might have gone for his neck.

'You what!'

'We, uh, feel that – '

'Mr. Fink, have you studied the juvenile laws for this jurisdiction?'

'I have.'

'Great. Will you please tell us, sir, under which code section the petitioner has the right to force the child to testify?'

'I was merely stating our request.'

'That's great. Under which code section is the petitioner allowed to make such a request?'

Fink dropped his head a few inches and found something on his legal pad to examine.

'This is not a kangaroo court, Mr. Fink. We do not create new rules as we go. The child cannot be forced to testify, same as any other criminal or Juvenile Court proceeding. Surely you understand this.'

Fink studied the legal pad with great intensity.

'Ten-minute recess!' His Honor barked. 'Everyone out of the courtroom, except Ms. Love. Bailiff, take Mark to a witness room.' Harry was standing as he growled these instructions.

Fink, afraid to stand but nonetheless trying, hesitated for a split second too long, and this upset the judge. 'Out of here, Mr. Fink,' he said rudely, pointing to the door.

Fink and Ord stumbled over each other as they clawed for the door. The court reporter and clerk followed them. The bailiff escorted Mark away, and when he closed the door Harry unzipped his robe and threw it on a table. He took his lunch and sat it on the table before Reggie.

'Shall we dine?' he said, tearing the sandwich in two and placing half of it on a napkin for her. He slid the onion rings next to her legal pad. She took one and nibbled around the edges.

'Are you going to allow the kid to testify?' he asked with a mouth full of roast beef.

'I don't know, Harry. What do you think?'

'I think Fink's a dumbass, that's what I think.'

Reggie took a small bite of the sandwich and wiped her mouth.

'If you put him on,' Harry said, crunching, 'Fink'll ask him some very pointed questions about what happened in the car with Clifford.'

'I know. That's what worries me.'

'How will the kid answer the questions?'

'I honestly don't know. I've advised him fully. We've talked about it at length. And I have no idea what he'll do.'

Harry took a deep breath, and realized the ice tea was still on the bench. He took two paper cups from Fink's table, and poured them full of tea.

'It's obvious, Reggie, that he knows something. Why did he tell so many lies?'

'He's a kid, Harry. He was scared to death. He heard more than he should have. He saw Clifford blow his brains out. It scared him to death. Look at his poor little brother. It was a terrible thing to witness, and I think Mark initially thought he might get in trouble. So he lied.'

'I don't really blame him,' Harry said, taking an onion ring. Reggie bit into a pickle.

'What are you thinking?' she asked.

He wiped his mouth, and thought about this for a long time. This child was now his, one of Harry's Kids, and each decision from now on would be based on what was best for Mark Sway.

'If I can assume the child knows something very relevant to the investigation in New Orleans, then several things might happen. First, if you put him on the stand and he gives the information Fink wants, then this matter is closed as far as my jurisdiction is concerned. The kid walks out of here, but he's in great danger. Second, if you put him on the stand, and he refuses to answer Fink's questions, then I will be forced to make him answer. If he refuses, he'll be in contempt. He cannot remain silent if he has crucial information. Either way, if this hearing is concluded here today without satisfactory answers by the child, I strongly suspect Mr. Foltrigg will move quickly. He'll get a grand jury subpoena for Mark, and away you go to New Orleans. If he refuses to talk to the grand jury, he'll certainly be held in contempt by the federal judge, and I suspect he'll be incarcerated.'

Reggie nodded. She was in complete agreement. 'So what do we do, Harry?'

'If the kid goes to New Orleans, I lose control of him. I'd rather keep him here. If I were you, I'd put him on the stand and advise him not to answer the crucial questions. At least not for now. He can always do it later. He can do it tomorrow, or the next day. I'd advise him to withstand the pressure from the judge, and keep his mouth shut, at least for now. He'll go back to our Juvenile Detention Center, which is probably much safer than anything in New Orleans. By doing this, you protect the child from the New Orleans thugs, who scare even me, until the Feds can arrange something better. And you buy yourself some time to see what Mr. Foltrigg will do in New Orleans.'

'You think he's in great danger?'

'Yes, and even if I didn't, I wouldn't take chances. If he spills his guts now, he could get hurt. I'm not inclined to release him today, under any circumstances.'

'What if Mark refuses to talk, and Foltrigg presents him with a grand jury subpoena?'

'I won't allow him to go.'

Reggie's appetite was gone. She sipped her tea from the paper cup and closed her eyes. 'This is so unfair to this boy, Harry. He deserves more from the system.'

'I agree. I'm open to suggestions.'

'What if I don't put him on the stand?'

'I'm not going to release him, Reggie. At least not today. Maybe tomorrow. Maybe the next day. This is happening awfully fast, and I suggest we take the safest route and see what happens in New Orleans.'

'You didn't answer my question. What if I don't put him on the stand?"

'Well, based on the proof I've heard, I'll have no choice but to find him to be a delinquent, and I'll send him back to Doreen. Of course, I could reverse myself tomorrow. Or the next day.'

'He's not a delinquent.'

'Maybe not. But if he knows something, and he refuses to tell, then he's obstructing justice.' There was a long pause. 'How much does he know, Reggie? If you'll tell me, I'll be in a better position to help him.'

'I can't tell you, Harry. It's privileged.'

'Of course it is,' he said with a smile. 'But it's rather obvious he knows plenty.'

'Yes, I guess it is.'

He leaned forward, and touched her arm. 'Listen to me, dear. Our little pal is in a world of trouble. So let's get him out of it. I say we take it one day at a time, keep him in a safe place where we call the shots, and in the meantime start talking to the Feds about their witness protection program. If that falls into place for the kid and his family, then he can tell these awful secrets and be protected.'

'I'll talk to him.'

# CHAPTER TWENTY-FIVE

Under the stern supervision of the bailiff, a man named Grinder, they were reassembled and directed to their positions. Fink glanced about fearfully, uncertain whether to sit, stand, speak, or crawl under the table. Ord picked at the cuticle on a thumb. Baxter McLemore had moved his chair as far away from Fink as possible.

His Honor sipped the remains of the tea and waited until all was still. 'On the record,' he said in the general direction of the court reporter. 'Ms. Love, I need to know if young Mark will testify.'

She was sitting a foot behind her client, and she looked at the side of his face. His eyes were still wet.

'Under the circumstances,' she said, 'he doesn't have much of a choice.'

'Is that a yes or a no?'

'I will allow him to testify,' she said, 'but I will not tolerate abusive questioning by Mr. Fink.'

'Your Honor, please,' Fink said.

'Quiet, Mr. Fink. Remember rule number one? Don't speak until spoken to.'

Fink glared at Reggie. 'A cheap shot,' he snarled.

'Knock it off, Mr. Fink,' Harry said. All was quiet.

His Honor was suddenly all warmth and smiles. 'Mark, I want you to remain in your seat, next to your lawyer, while I ask you some questions.'

Fink winked at Ord. Finally, the kid would talk. This could be the moment.

'Raise your right hand, Mark,' His Honor said, and Mark slowly obeyed. The right hand, as well as the left, was trembling.

The elderly lady stood in front of Mark and properly swore him. He did not stand, but inched closer to Reggie.

'Now, Mark, I'm going to ask you some questions. If you don't understand anything I ask, please feel free to talk to your lawyer. Okay?'

'Yes sir.'

'I'll try to keep the questions clear and simple. If you need a break to step outside and talk to Reggie, Ms. Love, just let me know. Okay?'

'Yes sir.'

Fink turned his chair to face Mark and sat like a hungry puppy awaiting his Alpo. Ord finished his nails, and was ready with his pen and legal pad.

Harry reviewed his notes for a second, then smiled down at the witness. 'Now, Mark, I want you to explain to me exactly how you and your brother discovered Mr. Clifford on Monday.'

Mark gripped the arms of his chair and cleared his throat. This was not what he expected. He'd never seen a movie in which the judge asked the questions.

'We sneaked off into the woods behind the trailer park, to smoke a cigarette,' he began, and slowly led to the point where Romey stuck the water hose in the tail pipe the first time and got in the car.

'What'd you do then?' His Honor asked anxiously.

'I took it out,' he said, and told the story about his trips through the weeds to remove Romey's suicide device. Although he'd told this before, once or twice to his mother and Dr. Greenway, and once or twice to Reggie, it had never seemed amusing to him. But as he told it now, the judge's eyes began to sparkle and his smile widened. He chuckled softly. The bailiff thought it was funny. The court reporter, always noncommittal, was enjoying it. Even the old woman at the clerk's desk was listening with her first smile of the proceedings.

But the humor turned sour as Mr. Clifford grabbed him, slapped him around, and threw him in the car. Mark relived this with a straight face, staring at the brown pumps of the court reporter.

'So you were in the car with Mr. Clifford before he died?' His honor asked cautiously, very serious now.

'Yes sir.'

'And what did he do once he got you in the car?'

'He slapped me some more, yelled at me a few times, threatened me.' And Mark told all that he remembered about the gun, the whiskey bottle, the pills.

The small courtroom was deathly still, and the smiles were long gone. Mark's words were deliberate. His eyes avoided all others. He spoke as if in a trance.

'Did he fire the gun?' Judge Roosevelt asked.

'Yes sir,' he answered, and told them all about it.

When he finished this part of the story, he waited for the next question. Harry thought about it for a long minute.'

'Where was Ricky?'

'Hiding in the bushes. I saw him sneak through the weeds, and I sort of figured he'd removed the water hose again. He did, I found out later. Mr. Clifford kept saying he could feel the gas, and he asked me over and over if I could feel it. I said yes, twice I think, but I knew Ricky had come through.'

'And he didn't know about Ricky?' It was a throwaway question, irrelevant, but asked because Harry couldn't think of a better one at the moment.

'No sir.'

Another long pause.

'So you talked with Mr. Clifford while you were in the car?'

Mark knew what was coming, as did everyone in the courtroom, so he jumped in quickly in an attempt to divert it.

'Yes sir. He was out of his mind, kept talking about floating off to see the Wizard of Oz, off to La La Land, and then he would yell at me for crying, then he would apologize for hitting me.'

There was a pause as Harry waited to see if he was finished. 'Is that all he said?'

Mark glanced at Reggie, who was watching him carefully. Fink inched closer. The court reporter was frozen.

'What do you mean?' Mark asked, stalling.

'Did Mr. Clifford say anything else?'

Mark thought about this for a second, and decided he hated Reggie. He could simply say 'No,' and the ballgame was over. 'No sir, Mr. Clifford did not say anything else. He just rambled on like an idiot for about five minutes, then fell asleep, and I ran like hell.' If he'd never met Reggie, and had not heard her lecture about being under oath and telling the truth, then he would simply say 'No sir.' And go home, or back to the hospital, or wherever.

Or would he? One day in the fourth grade the cops put on a show about police work, and one of them demonstrated a polygraph. He wired up Joey McDermant, the biggest liar in the class, and they watched as the needle went berserk every time Joey opened his mouth. 'We catch criminals lying every time,' the cop had boasted.

With cops and FBI agents swarming around him, could the polygraph be far away? He'd lied so much since Romey killed himself, and he was really tired of it.

'Mark, I asked you if Mr. Clifford said anything else.'

'Like what?'

'Like, did he mention anything about Senator Boyd Boyette?'

'Who?'

Harry flashed a sweet little smile, then it was gone. 'Mark, did Mr. Clifford mention anything about a case of his in New Orleans involving a Mr. Barry Muldanno or the late Senator Boyd Boyette?'

A tiny spider was crawling next to the court reporter's brown pumps, and Mark watched it until it disappeared under the tripod. He thought about that damned polygraph again. Reggie said she would fight to keep it away from him, but what if the judge ordered it?

The long pause before his response said it all. Fink's heart was laboring and his pulse had tripled. Aha! The little bastard *does* know!

'I don't think I want to answer that question,' he said, staring at the floor, waiting for the spider to reappear.

Fink looked hopefully at the judge.

'Mark, look at me,' Harry said like a gentle grandfather. 'I want you to answer the question. Did Mr. Clifford mention Barry Muldanno or Boyd Boyette?'

'Can I take the Fifth Amendment?'

'No.'

'Why not? It applies to kids, doesn't it?'

'Yes, but not in this situation. You're not implicated in the death of Senator Boyette. You're not implicated in any crime.'

'Then why did you put me in jail?'

'I'm going to send you back there if you don't answer my questions.'

'I take the Fifth Amendment anyway.'

They were glaring at each other, witness and judge, and the witness blinked first. His eyes watered and he sniffed twice. He bit his lip, fighting hard not to cry. He clenched the armrests and squeezed until his knuckles were white. Tears dropped on to his cheeks, but he kept staring up into the dark eyes of the Honorable Harry Roosevelt.

The tears of an innocent little boy. Harry turned to his side and pulled a tissue from a drawer under the bench. His eyes were wet too.

'Would you like to talk to your attorney, in private?' he asked.

'We've already talked,' he said in a fading voice. He wiped his cheeks with a sleeve.

Fink was near cardiac arrest. He had so much to say, so many questions for this brat, so many suggestions for the court on how to handle this matter. The kid knew, dammit! Let's make him talk!

'Mark, I don't like to do this, but you must answer my questions. If you refuse, then you're in contempt of court. Do you understand this?'

'Yes sir. Reggie's explained it to me.'

'And did she explain that if you're in contempt, then I can send you back to the Juvenile Detention Center?'

'Yes sir. You can call it jail if you like, it doesn't bother me.'

'Thank you. Do you want to go back to jail?'

'Not really, but I have no place else to go.' His voice was stronger and the tears had stopped. The thought of jail was not as frightening now that he'd seen the inside of it. He could tough it out for a few days. In fact, he figured he could take the heat longer than the judge. He was certain his name would appear in the paper again in the very near future. And the reporters would undoubtedly learn he was locked up by Harry Roosevelt for not talking. And surely the judge would catch hell for locking up a little kid who'd done nothing wrong.

Reggie'd told him he could change his mind anytime he got tired of jail.

'Did Mr. Clifford mention the name Barry Muldanno to you?'

'Take the Fifth.'

'Did Mr. Clifford mention the name Boyd Boyette to you?'

'Take the Fifth.'

'Did Mr. Clifford say anything about the murder of Boyd Boyette?'

'Take the Fifth.'

'Did Mr. Clifford say anything about the present location of the body of Boyd Boyette?'

'Take the Fifth.'

Harry removed his reading glasses for the tenth time, and rubbed his face. 'You can't take the Fifth, Mark.'

'I just did.'

'I'm ordering you to answer these questions.'

'Yes sir. I'm sorry.'

Harry took a pen and began writing.

'Your Honor,' Mark said. 'I respect you and what you're trying to do. But I cannot answer these questions because I'm afraid of what might happen to me or my family.'

'I understand, Mark, but the law does not allow private citizens to withhold information that might be crucial to a criminal investigation. I'm following the law, not picking on you. I'm holding you in contempt. I'm not angry with you, but you leave me no choice. I'm ordering you to return to the Juvenile Detention Center where you will remain as long as you're in contempt.'

'How long will that be?'

'It's up to you, Mark.'

'What if I decide never to answer the questions?'

'I don't know. Right now we'll take it one day at a time.' Harry flipped through his calendar, found a spot, and made a note. 'We'll meet again at noon tomorrow, if that's agreeable with everyone.'

Fink was crushed. He stood, and was about to speak when Ord grabbed his arm and pulled him down. 'Your Honor, I don't think I can be here tomorrow,' he said. 'As you know, my office is in New Orleans, and – '

'Oh, you'll be here tomorrow, Mr. Fink. You and Mr. Foltrigg together. You chose to file your petition here in Memphis, in my court, and now I have jurisdiction over you. As soon as you leave here, I suggest you call Mr. Foltrigg and tell him to be here at noon tomorrow. I want both petitioners, Fink and Foltrigg, right here at twelve o'clock sharp tomorrow. And if you're not here, I'll hold you in contempt, and tomorrow it'll be you and your boss being hauled off to jail.'

Fink's mouth was open but nothing came out. Ord spoke for the first time. 'Your Honor, I believe Mr. Foltrigg has a hearing in federal court in the morning. Mr. Muldanno has a new lawyer who's asking for a continuance, and the judge down there has set the hearing for tomorrow morning.'

'Is that true, Mr. Fink?'

'Yes sir.'

'Then tell Mr. Foltrigg to fax me a copy of the judge's order setting the hearing for tomorrow. I'll excuse him. But as long as Mark is in jail for contempt, I intend to bring him back here every other day to see if he wants to talk. I'll expect both petitioners to be here.'

'That's quite a hardship on us, Your Honor.'

'Not as hard as it's gonna be if you don't show up. You picked this forum, Mr. Fink. Now you gotta live with it.'

Fink had flown to Memphis six hours earlier without a toothbrush or change of underwear. Now it appeared as though he might be forced to lease an apartment with bedrooms for himself and Foltrigg.

The bailiff had eased his way to the wall behind Reggie and Mark, and was watching His Honor and waiting for a signal.

'Mark, I'm going to excuse you now,' Harry said, scribbling on a form, 'and I'll see you again tomorrow. If you have any problems in the detention center, you inform me tomorrow and I'll take care of it. Okay?'

Mark nodded. Reggie squeezed his arm, and said, 'I'll talk to your mother, and I'll come see you in the morning.'

'Tell Mom I'm fine,' he whispered in her ear. 'I'll try and call her tonight.' He stood and left with the bailiff.

'Send in those FBI people,' Harry said to the bailiff as he was closing the door.

'Are we excused, Your Honor?' Fink asked. There was sweat on his forehead. He was anxious to leave this room and call Foltrigg with the horrible news.

'What's the hurry, Mr. Fink?'

'Uh, no hurry, Your Honor.'

'Then relax. I want to talk, off the record, with you boys and the FBI people. Just take a minute.' Harry excused the court reporter and the old woman. McThune and Lewis entered and took their seats behind the lawyers.

Harry unzipped his robe, but did not remove it. He wiped his face with a tissue and sipped the last of the tea. They watched and waited.

'I do not intend to keep this child in jail,' he said, looking at Reggie. 'Maybe for a few days, but not long. It's apparent to me that he has some critical information, and he's duty bound to divulge it.'

Fink started nodding.

'He's scared, and we can all certainly understand that. Perhaps we can convince him to talk if we can guarantee his safety, and that of his mother and brother. I'd like for Mr. Lewis to help us on this. I'm open to suggestions.'

K. O. Lewis was ready. 'Your Honor, we have taken preliminary steps to place him in our witness protection program.'

'I've heard of it, Mr. Lewis, but I'm not familiar with the details.'

'It's quite simple. We move the family to another city. We provide new identities. We find a good job for the mother, and get them a nice place to live. Not a trailer or an apartment, but a house. We make sure the boys are in a good school. There's some cash up front. And we stay close by.'

'Sounds tempting, Ms. Love,' Harry said.

It certainly did. At the moment, the Sways had no home. Dianne worked in a sweatshop. There were no relatives in Memphis.

'They're not mobile right now,' she said. 'Ricky is confined to the hospital.'

'We've already located a children's psychiatric hospital in Portland that can take him right away,' Lewis explained. 'It's a private one, not a charity outfit like St. Peter's, and it's one of the best in the country. They'll take him whenever we ask, and, of course, we'll pay for it. After he's released, we'll move the family to another city.'

'How long will it take to place the entire family into the program?' Harry asked.

'Less than a week,' Lewis answered. 'Director Voyles has given it top priority. The paperwork takes a few days, new driver's license, Social Security numbers, birth certificates, credit cards, things like this. The family has to make the decision to do it, and the mother must tell us where she wants to go. We'll take over from there.'

'What do you think, Ms. Love?' Harry asked. 'Will Ms. Sway go for it?'

'I'll talk to her. She's under enormous stress right now. One kid in a coma, the other in jail, and she lost everything in the fire last night. The idea of running away in the middle of the night could be a hard sell, at least for now.'

'But you'll try?'

'I'll see.'

'Do you think she could be in court tomorrow? I'd like to talk to her.'

'I'll ask the doctor.'

'Good. This meeting is adjourned. I'll see you folks at noon tomorrow.'

The bailiff handed Mark to two Memphis policemen in plain clothes, and they took him through a side door into the parking lot. When they were gone, the bailiff climbed the stairs to the second floor and darted into an empty rest room. Empty, except for Slick Moeller.

They stood before the urinals, side by side, and stared at the graffiti.

'Are we alone?' asked the bailiff.

'Yep. What happened?' Slick had unzipped his pants and had both hands on his waist. 'Be quick.'

'Kid wouldn't talk, so he's going back to jail. Contempt.'

'What does he know?'

'I'd say he knows everything. It's rather obvious. He said he was in the car with Clifford, they talked about this and that, and when Harry pressed him on the New Orleans stuff the kid took the Fifth Amendment. Tough little bastard.'

'But he knows?'

'Oh sure. But he's not telling. Judge wants him back tomorrow at noon to see if a night in the slammer changes his mind.'

Slick zipped his pants and stepped away from the urinal. He took a folded one-hundred-dollar bill from his pocket and handed it to the bailiff.

'You didn't hear it from me,' the bailiff said.

'You trust me, don't you?'

'Of course.' And he did. Mole Moeller never revealed a source.

Moeller had three photographers poised at various places around the Juvenile Court Building. He knew the routines better than the cops themselves, and he figured they'd use the side door near the loading dock for a quick getaway with the kid. That's exactly what they did, and they almost made it to their unmarked car before a heavy woman in fatigues jumped from a parked van and nailed them straight on with her Nikon. The cops yelled at her, and tried to hide the kid behind them, but it was too late. They rushed him to their car, and pushed him into the backseat.

Just great, thought Mark. It was not yet 2 P.M., and so far this day had brought the burning of their trailer, his arrest at the hospital, his new home at the jail, a hearing with Judge Roosevelt, and now, another damned photographer shooting at him for what would undoubtedly be another front page story.

As the car squealed tires and raced away, he sunk low in the backseat. His stomach ached, not from hunger, but from fear. He was alone again.

# CHAPTER TWENTY-SIX

Foltrigg watched the traffic on Poydras Street and waited on the call from Memphis. He was tired of pacing and checking his watch. He had tried to return phone calls and dictate letters, but it was hopeless. His mind could not leave the wonderful image of Mark Sway sitting in a witness chair somewhere in Memphis telling all his splendid secrets. Two hours had passed since the hearing was scheduled to start, and surely they'd take a recess along the way so Fink could dash to a phone and call him.

Larry Trumann was on standby, waiting for the call so they could swing into action with a posse of corpse hunters. They had become quite proficient in digging for bodies during the past eight months. They just hadn't found any.

But today would be different. Roy would take the call, walk to Trumann's office, and off they'd go to find the late Boyd Boyette. Foltrigg talked to himself, not a whisper or a mumble, but a full-blown speech in which he addressed the media with the thrilling announcement that, yes, they had indeed found the Senator, and, yes, he died of six bullet wounds to the head. The gun was a .22, and the bullet fragments were definitely, without the slightest doubt, fired from the same handgun that had been so meticulously traced to the defendant, Mr. Barry Muldanno.

It would be a wonderful moment, this press conference.

Someone knocked slightly and the door opened before Roy could turn around. It was Wally Boxx, the only person allowed such casual entries.

'Heard anything?' Wally asked, walking to the window and standing next to his boss.

'No. Not a word. I wish Fink would get to a phone. He has specific orders.'

They stood in silence and watched the street.

'What's the grand jury doing?' Roy asked.

'The usual. Routine indictments.'

'Who's in there?'

'Hoover. He's finishing up with the drug bust in Gretna. Should be through this afternoon.

'Are they scheduled to work tomorrow?'

'No. They've had a hard week. We promised them yesterday they could take off tomorrow. What're you thinking?'

Foltrigg shifted weight slightly and scratched his chin. His eyes had a faraway look, and he watched the cars below but didn't see them. Heavy thinking was sometimes painful for him. 'Think about this. If, for some reason, the kid doesn't talk, and if Fink drills a dry hole with the hearing, what do we do then? I say we go to the grand jury, get subpoenas for both the kid and his lawyer, and drag them down here. The kid's gotta be scared right now, and he's still in Memphis. He'll be terrified when he has to come here.'

'Why would you subpoena his lawyer?'

'To scare her. Pure harassment. Shake 'em both up. We get the subpoenas today, keep them sealed, sit on them until late tomorrow afternoon when everything's closing for the weekend, then we serve the kid and his lawyer. The subpoenas will require their presence before our grand jury at 10 A.M. Monday morning. They won't have a chance to run to court and quash the subpoenas because it's the weekend and everything's shut down and all the judges are out of town. They'll be too scared not to show up here Monday morning, on our turf, Wally. Right down the hall here, in our building.'

'What if the kid doesn't know anything?'

Roy shook his head in frustration. They'd had this conversation a dozen times in the last forty-eight hours. 'I thought that was established.'

'Maybe. And maybe the kid's talking right now.'

'He probably is.'

A secretary squeaked through on the intercom and announced that Mr. Fink was holding on line one. Foltrigg walked to his desk and grabbed the phone. 'Yes!'

'The hearing's over, Roy,' Fink reported. He sounded relieved and tired.

Foltrigg hit the switch for the speakerphone, and fell into his chair. Wally perched his tiny butt on the corner of the desk. 'Wally's here with me, Tom. Tell us what happened.'

'Nothing much. The kid's back in jail. He wouldn't talk, so the judge found him in contempt.'

'What do you mean, he wouldn't talk?'

'He wouldn't talk. The judge handled both the direct and cross-examinations, and the kid admitted being in the car and talking with Clifford. But when the judge asked questions about Boyette and Muldanno, the kid took the Fifth Amendment.'

'The Fifth Amendment!'

'That's right. He wouldn't budge. Said jail wasn't so bad after all, and that he had no other place to go.'

'But he knows, doesn't he, Tom? The little punk knows.'

'Oh, there's no question about it. Clifford told him everything.'

Foltrigg slapped his hands together. 'I knew it! I knew it! I knew it! I've been telling you boys this for three days now.' He jumped to his feet and squeezed his hands together. 'I knew it!'

Fink continued. 'The judge has scheduled another hearing for noon tomorrow. He wants the kid brought back in to see if he's changed his mind. I'm not too optimistic.'

'I want you at that hearing, Tom.'

'Yes, and the judge wants you too, Roy. I explained you had a hearing on the continuance motion in the morning, and he insisted that you fax him a copy of the hearing order. He said he'd excuse you under those circumstances.'

'Is he some kind of nut?'

'No. He's not a nut. He said he plans to hold these little hearings quite often next week, and he expects both of us, as petitioners, to be there.'

'Then he is a nut.'

Wally rolled his eyes and shook his head. These local judges could be such fools.

'After the hearing, the judge talked to us about placing the kid and his family in witness protection. He thinks he can convince the kid to talk if we can guarantee his safety.'

'That could take weeks.'

'I think so too, but K.O. told the judge it could be done in a matter of days. Frankly, Roy, I don't think the kid will talk until we can make some guarantees. He's a tough little guy.'

'What about his lawyer?'

'She played it cool, didn't say much, but she and the judge are pretty tight. I got the impression the kid's getting a lot of advice. She's no dummy.'

Wally just had to say something. 'Tom, it's me, Wally. What do you think will happen over the weekend?'

'Who knows? As I said, I don't think this kid'll change his mind overnight, and I don't think the judge plans to release him. The judge knows about Gronke and the Muldanno boys, and I get the impression he wants the kid locked up for his own protection. Tomorrow's Friday, so it looks like the kid will stay where he is over the weekend. And I'm sure the judge will call us back in on Monday for another chat.'

'Are you coming in, Tom?' Roy asked.

'Yeah, I'll catch a flight out in a couple of hours, and fly back here in the morning.' Fink's voice was now very tired.

'I'll be waiting for you here tonight, Tom. Good work.'

'Yeah.'

Fink faded away and Roy hit the switch.

'Get the grand jury ready,' he snapped at Wally, who bounced off the desk and headed for the door. 'Tell Hoover to take a break. This won't take but a minute. Get me the Mark Sway file. Inform the clerk that the subpoenas will be sealed until they are served late tomorrow.'

Wally was through the door and gone. Foltrigg returned to the window, mumbling to himself, 'I knew it. I just knew it.'

The cop in the suit signed Doreen's clipboard, and left with his partner. 'Follow me,' she said to Mark as if he'd sinned again and her patience was wearing thin. He followed her, watching her wide rear end rock from side to side in a pair of tight, black polyester pants. A thick, shiny belt squeezed her narrow waist and held an assortment of key rings, two black boxes which he assumed to be pagers, and a pair of handcuffs. No gun. Her shirt was official white with markings up and down the sleeves and gold trim around the collar.

The hall was empty as she opened his door and motioned for him to return to his little room. She followed him in and eased around the walls like a dope dog sniffing at the airport. 'Sort of surprised to see you back here,' she said, inspecting the toilet.

He could think of nothing to say to this, and he was not in the mood for a conversation. As he watched her stoop and bend, he thought about her husband serving thirty years for bank robbery, and if she insisted on chatting he might just bring this up. That would quiet her down and send her on her way.

'Must've upset Judge Roosevelt,' she said, looking through the windows.

'I guess so.'

'How long are you in for?'

'He didn't say. I have to go back tomorrow.'

She walked to the bunks and began patting the blanket. 'I've been reading about you and your little brother. Pretty strange case. How's he doing?'

Mark stood by the door, hoping she would just go away. 'He's probably gonna die,' he said sadly.

'No!'

'Yeah, it's awful. He's in a coma, you know, sucking his thumb, grunting and slobbering every now and then. His eyes have rolled back into his head. Won't eat.'

'I'm sorry I asked.' Her heavily decorated eyes were wide open, and she had stopped touching everything.

Yeah, I'll bet you're sorry you asked, Mark thought. 'I need to be there with him,' Mark said. 'My mom's there, but she's all stressed out. Taking a lot of pills, you know.'

'I'm so sorry.'

'It's awful. I've been feeling dizzy myself. Who knows, I could end up like my brother.'

'Can I get you anything?'

'No. I just need to lie down.' He walked to the bottom bunk and fell into it. Doreen knelt beside him, deeply troubled now.

'Anything you want, honey, you just let me know, okay?'

'Okay. Some pizza would be nice.'

She stood and thought about this for a second. He closed his eyes as if in deep pain.

'I'll see what I can do.'

'I haven't had lunch, you know.'

'I'll be right back,' she said, and she left. The door clicked loudly behind her. Mark bolted to his feet and listened to it.

# CHAPTER TWENTY-SEVEN

The room was dark as usual; the lights off, the door shut, the blinds drawn, the only illumination the moving blue shadows of the muted television high on the wall. Dianne was mentally drained and physically beat from lying in bed with Ricky for eight hours, patting and hugging and cooing and trying to be strong in this damp, dark little cell.

Reggie had stopped by two hours ago, and they'd sat on the edge of the foldaway bed and talked for thirty minutes. She explained the hearing, assured her Mark was being fed and in no physical danger, described his room at the detention center because she'd seen one before, told her he was safer there than here, and talked about Judge Roosevelt and the FBI and their witness protection program. At first, and under the circumstances, the idea was attractive – they would simply move to a new city with new names and a new job and a decent place to live. They could run from this mess and start over. They could pick a large city with big schools and the boys would get lost in the crowd. But the more she lay there curled on one side and stared above Ricky's little head at the wall, the less she liked the idea. In fact, it was a horrible idea – living on the run forever, always afraid of an unexpected knock on the door, always in a panic when one of the boys was late getting home, always lying about their past.

This little plan was forever. What if, she began asking herself, one day, say five or ten years from now, long after the trial in New Orleans, some person she's never met lets something slip and it's heard by the wrong ears, and their trails are quickly traced? And when Mark is, say, a senior in high school, somebody waits on him after a ballgame and sticks a gun to his head? His name wouldn't be Mark, but he would be dead nonetheless.

She had almost decided to veto the idea of witness protection when Mark called her from the jail. He said he'd just finished a large pizza, was feeling great, nice place and all, was enjoying it more than the hospital, food was better, and he chatted so eagerly she knew he was lying. He said he was already plotting his escape, and would soon be out. They talked about Ricky, and the trailer, and the hearing today and the hearing tomorrow. He said he was trusting Reggie's advice, and Dianne agreed this was best. He apologized for not being there to help with Ricky, and she fought tears when he tried to sound so mature. He apologized again for all this mess.

Their conversation had been brief. She found it difficult to talk to him. She had little motherly advice, and felt like a failure because her eleven-year-old son was in jail and she couldn't get him out. She couldn't go see him. She couldn't go talk to the judge. She couldn't tell him to talk or to remain quiet because she was scared too. She couldn't do a damned thing but stay here in this narrow bed and stare at the walls and pray that she would wake up and the nightmare would be over.

It was 6 P.M., time for the local news. She watched the silent face of the anchorperson and hoped it wouldn't happen. But it didn't take long. After two dead bodies were carried from a landfill, a black-and-white still photo of Mark and the cop she'd slapped this morning was suddenly on the screen. She turned up the volume.

The anchorperson gave the basics about the taking of Mark Sway, careful not to call it an arrest, then went to a reporter standing in front of the Juvenile Court Building. He rattled on a few seconds about a hearing he knew nothing about, gushed breathlessly that the child, Mark Sway, had been taken back to the Juvenile Detention Center, and that another hearing would be held tomorrow in Judge Roosevelt's courtroom. Back in the studio, the anchorperson brought 'em up to date on young Mark and the tragic suicide of Jerome Clifford. They ran a quick clip of the mourners leaving the chapel that morning in New Orleans, and had a second or two of Roy Foltrigg talking to a reporter under an umbrella. Back quickly to the anchorperson, who began quoting Slick Moeller's stories, and the suspicion mounted. No comments from the Memphis Police, the FBI, the U.S. Attorney's office, or the Shelby County Juvenile Court. The ice got thinner as she skated into the vast, murky world of unnamed sources, all of whom were short on facts but long on speculation. When she mercifully finished and broke for a commercial, the uninformed could easily believe that young Mark Sway had shot not only Jerome Clifford but Boyd Boyette as well.

Dianne's stomach ached, and she hit the power button. The room was even darker. She had not taken a single bite of food in ten hours. Ricky twitched and grunted, and this irritated her. She eased from the bed, frustrated with him, frustrated with Greenway for the lack of progress, sick of this hospital with its dungeon-like decor and lighting, horrified at a system that allowed children to be jailed for being children, and, above all, scared of these lurking shadows who'd threatened Mark and burned the trailer and obviously were quite willing to do more. She closed the bathroom door behind her, sat on the edge of the bathtub, and smoked a Virginia Slim. Her hands trembled and her thoughts were a blur. A migraine was forming at the base of her skull, and by midnight she would be paralyzed. Maybe the pills would help.

She flushed the skinny cigarette butt, and sat on the edge of Ricky's bed. She had vowed to get through this ordeal one day at a time, but damned if the days weren't getting worse. She couldn't take much more.

Barry The Blade had picked this dumpy little bar because it was quiet, dark, and he remembered it from his teenage years as a young and aspiring hoodlum on the streets of New Orleans. It was not one he routinely frequented, but it was deep in the Quarter, which meant he could park off Canal and dart through the tourists on Bourbon and Royal, and there was no way the Feds could follow him.

He found a tiny table in the back, and sipped a vodka gimlet while waiting for Gronke.

He wanted to be in Memphis himself, but he was out on bond and his movements were restricted. Permission was required before he could leave the state, and he knew better than to ask. Communication with Gronke had been difficult. The paranoia was eating him alive. For eight months now, every curious stare was another cop watching his every move. A stranger behind him on the sidewalk was another Fibbie hiding in the darkness. His phones were tapped. His car and house were bugged. He was afraid to speak half the time because he could almost feel the sensors and hidden mikes.

He finished the gimlet and ordered another one. A double. Gronke arrived twenty minutes late, and crowded his bulky frame into a chair in the corner. The ceiling was seven feet above them.

'Nice place,' Gronke said. 'How you doin'?'

'Okay.' Barry snapped his fingers and the waiter walked over.

'Beer. Grolsch,' Gronke said.

'Did they follow you?' Barry asked.

'I don't think so. I've zigzagged through half the Quarter, you know.'

'What's happening up there?'

'Memphis?'

'No. Milwaukee, you dumbass,' Barry said with a smile. 'What's happening with the kid?'

'He's in jail, and he ain't talkin'. They took him in this morning, had some kinda hearing at lunch before the youth court, then took him back to jail.'

The bartender carried a heavy tray of dirty beer mugs through the swinging doors into the dirty, cramped kitchen, and when he cleared the doors, two FBI agents in jeans stopped him. One flashed a badge while the other took the tray.

'What the hell?' the bartender asked, backing to the wall while staring at the badge just inches from the tip of his wide nose.

'FBI. Need a favor,' said Special Agent Scherff calmly, all business. The other agent pressed forward. The bartender owned two felony convictions, and had been enjoying his freedom for less than six months. He became eager.

'Sure. Anything.'

'What's your name?' asked Scherff.

'Uh, Dole. Link Dole.' He'd used so many names over the years it was difficult keeping them straight.

The agents inched forward even more and Link began to fear an attack. 'Okay, Link. Can you help us?'

Link nodded rapidly. The cook stirred a pot of rice, with a cigarette barely hanging from his lips. He glanced their way once but had other things on his mind.

'There are two men out there having a drink in the rear corner, on the right side where the ceiling is low.'

'Yeah, okay, sure. I'm not involved, am I?'

'No, Link. Just listen.' Scherff pulled a matching set of salt and pepper shakers from his pocket. 'Put these on a tray with a bottle of ketchup. Go to the table, just routine, you know, and switch these with the ones sitting there now. Ask these guys if they want something to eat, or another drink. You understand?'

Link was nodding but not understanding. 'Uh, what's in these?'

'Salt and pepper,' Scherff said. 'And a little bug that allows us to hear what these guys are saying. They're criminals, okay, Link, and we have them under surveillance.'

'I really don't want to get involved,' Link said, knowing full well that if they threatened even slightly he'd bust his ass to get involved.

'Don't make me angry,' Scherff said, waving the shakers.

'Okay, okay.'

A waiter kicked open the swinging doors and shuffled behind them with a stack of dirty dishes. Link took the shakers. 'Don't tell anyone,' he said, trembling.

'It's a deal, Link. This is our little secret. Now, is there an empty closet around here?' Scherff asked this while looking around the cramped and cluttered kitchen. The answer was obvious. There had not been an empty square foot in this dump in fifty years.

Link thought a second or two, very anxious to help his new friends. 'No, but there's a little office right above the bar.'

'Great, Link. Go exchange these, and we'll set up some equipment in the office.' Link held them gingerly as if they might explode, and returned to the bar.

A waiter placed a heavy green bottle of Grolsch in front of Gronke and disappeared.

'The little bastard knows something, doesn't he?' The Blade said.

'Of course. Otherwise, this wouldn't be happening. Why would he get himself a lawyer? Why would he clam up like this?' Gronke drained half his Grolsch with one, thirsty gulp.

Link approached them with a tray loaded with a dozen salt and pepper shakers and bottles of ketchup and mustard. 'You guys eating dinner?' he asked, all business, as he swapped the shakers and bottles on their table.

Barry waved him off. Gronke said, 'No.' And Link was gone. Fewer than thirty feet away, Scherff and three more agents crowded over a small desk and flipped open heavy briefcases. One of the agents grabbed earphones and stuck them to his head. He smiled.

'This kid scares me, man,' Barry said. 'He's told his lawyer, so that makes two more who know.'

'Yeah, but he ain't talkin', Barry. Think about it. We got to him. I showed him the picture. We took care of the trailer. The kid is scared to death.'

'I don't know. Is there any way to get him?'

'Not right now. I mean, hell, the cops have him. He's locked up.'

'There are ways, you know. I doubt if security is tight at a jail for kids.'

'Yeah, but the cops are scared too. They're all over the hospital. Got guards sittin' in the hallway. Fibbies dressed like doctors runnin' all over the place. These people are terrified of us.'

'But they can make him talk. They can put him in the mouse program, throw a buncha money at his mother. Hell, buy them a fancy new house trailer, maybe a double-wide or something. I'm just nervous as hell, Paul. If this kid was clean we would've never heard about him.'

'We can't hit the kid, Barry.'

'Why not?'

'Because he's a kid. Because everybody's watching him right now. Because if we do, a million cops'll hound us to our graves. it won't work.'

'What about his mother or his brother?'

Gronke took another shot of beer, and shook his head in frustration. He was a tough thug who could threaten with the best of them, but, unlike his friend, he was not a killer. This random search for victims scared him. He said nothing.

'What about his lawyer?' Barry asked.

'Why would you kill her?'

'Maybe I hate lawyers. Maybe it'll scare the kid so bad he'll go in to a coma like his brother. I don't know.'

'And maybe killing innocent people in Memphis is not such a good idea. The kid'll just get another lawyer.'

'We'll kill the next one too. Think about it, Paul, this could do wonders for the legal profession,' Barry said with a loud laugh. Then he leaned forward as if a terribly private thought hit him. His chin was inches from the salt shaker. 'Think about it, Paul. If we knock off the kid's lawyer, then no lawyer in his right mind would represent him. Get it?'

'You're losin' it, Barry. You're crackin' up.'

'Yeah, I know. But it's a great thought, ain't it? Smoke her, and the kid won't talk to his own mother. What's her name, Rollie or Ralphie?'

'Reggie. Reggie Love.'

'What the hell kinda name is that for a broad?'

'Don't ask me.'

Barry drained his glass and snapped again for the waiter. 'What's she sayin' on the phone?' he asked, in low again, just above the shaker.

'Don't know. We couldn't go in last night.'

The Blade was suddenly angry. 'You what!' The wicked eyes were fierce and glowing.

'Our man is doing it tonight, if all goes well.'

'What kinda place has she got?'

'Small office in a tall building downtown. It should be easy.'

Scherff pressed the earphone closer to his head. Two of his pals did likewise. The only sound in the room was a slight clicking noise from the recorder.

'Are these guys any good?'

'Nance is pretty smooth and cool under pressure. His partner, Cal Sisson, is a loose cannon. Afraid of his shadow.'

'I want the phones fixed tonight.'

'It'll be done.'

Barry lit an unfiltered Camel and blew smoke at the ceiling. 'Are they protecting the lawyer?' He asked this as his eyes narrowed. Gronke looked away.

'I don't think so.'

'Where does she live? What kinda place?'

'She's got a cute little apartment behind her mother's house.'

'She live alone?'

'I think so.'

'She'd be easy, wouldn't she? Break in, take her out, steal a few things. Just another house burglary gone sour. What do you think?'

Gronke shook his head and studied a young blonde at the bar.

'What do you think?' Barry repeated.

'Yeah, it'd be easy.'

'Then let's do it. Are you listening to me, Paul?'

Paul was listening, but avoiding the evil eyes. 'I'm not in the mood to kill anyone,' he said, still staring at the blonde.

'That's fine. I'll get Pirini to do it.'

Several years earlier, a detainee, as they're called in the Juvenile Detention Center, a twelve-year-old, died in the room next to Mark's from an epileptic seizure. A ton of bad press and a nasty lawsuit followed, and though Doreen had not been on duty when it happened, she had nonetheless been shaken by it. An investigation followed. Two people were terminated. And a new set of regulations came down.

Doreen's shift ended at five, and the last thing she did was check on Mark. She'd stopped by on the hour throughout the afternoon, and watched with growing concern as his condition worsened. He was withdrawing before her very eyes, saying less with each visit, just lying there in bed staring at the ceiling. At five, she brought a county paramedic with her. Mark was given a quick physical, and pronounced alive and well. Vital signs were strong. When she left, she rubbed his temples like a sweet little grandmother and promised to return bright and early tomorrow, Friday. And she sent more pizza.

Mark told her he thought he could make it until then. He'd try to survive the night. Evidently she left instructions, because the next floor supervisor, a short plump little woman named Telda, immediately knocked on his door and introduced herself. For the next four hours, Telda knocked repeatedly and entered the room, staring wildly at his eyes as if he were crazy and something was about to snap.

Mark watched television, no cable, until the news started at ten, then brushed his teeth and turned off the lights. The bed was quite comfortable, and he thought of his mother trying to sleep on that rickety cot the nurses had rolled into Ricky's room.

The pizza was from Domino's, not some leathery slab of cheese someone threw in a microwave, but a real pizza Doreen had probably paid for. The bed was warm, the pizza was real, and the door was locked. He felt safe, not only from the other inmates and the gangs and violence certain to be close by, but especially from the man with the switchblade who knew his name and had the picture. The man who'd burned the trailer. He'd thought about this guy every moment of every hour since he dashed from the elevator early yesterday morning. He'd thought about him on Momma Love's porch last night, and sitting in the courtroom this afternoon listening to Hardy and McThune. He'd worried about him hanging around the hospital where Dianne was unaware.

Sitting in a parked car on Third Street in downtown Memphis at midnight was not Cal Sisson's idea of safe fun, but the doors were locked and there was a gun under the seat. His felony convictions forbade him from owning or possessing a firearm, but this was Jack Nance's car. It was parked behind a delivery van near Madison, a couple of blocks from the Sterick Building. There was nothing suspicious about the car. Traffic was light.

Two uniformed cops on foot strolled along the sidewalk and stopped fewer than five feet from Cal. They stared at him. He glanced in the mirror, and saw another pair. Four cops! One of them sat on the trunk, and the car shook. Had the parking meter run out on him? No, he'd paid for an hour and been here less than ten minutes. Nance said it was a thirty-minute job.

Two more cops joined the two on the sidewalk, and Cal started sweating. The gun worried him, but a good lawyer could convince his probation officer that the gun was not his. He was merely driving for Nance.

An unmarked police car parked behind him, and two cops in plain clothes joined the others. Eight cops!

One in jeans and a sweatshirt bent at the waist and stuck his badge to Cal's window. There was a radio on the seat next to his leg, and thirty seconds ago he should have punched the blue button and warned Nance. But now it was too late. The cops had materialized from nowhere.

He slowly rolled down his window. The cop leaned forward and their faces were inches apart. 'Evening, Cal. I'm Lieutenant Byrd, Memphis PD.'

The fact that he called him Cal made him shudder. He tried to remain calm. 'What can I do for you, Officer?'

'Where's Jack?'

Cal's heart stopped and sweat popped through his skin. 'Jack who?'

Jack who. Byrd glanced over his shoulder and smiled at his partner. The uniformed cops had surrounded the car. 'Jack Nance. Your good friend. Where is he?'

'I haven't seen him.'

'Well, what a coincidence. I haven't seen him either. At least not for the past fifteen minutes. In fact, the last time I saw Jack was at the corner of Union and Second, less than a half an hour ago, and he was getting out of this car here. And you drove away, and, surprise, here you are.'

Cal was breathing, but it was difficult. 'I don't know what you're talking about.'

Byrd unlocked the door and opened it. 'Get out, Cal,' he demanded, and Cal complied. Byrd slammed the door and shoved him against it. Four of the cops surrounded him. The other three were looking in the direction of the Sterick Building. Byrd was in his face.

'Listen to me, Cal. Accomplice to breaking and entering carries seven years. You have three prior convictions, so you'll be charged as a habitual offender, and guess how much time you're looking at.'

His teeth were chattering and his body was shaking. He shook his head, as if he didn't understand and wanted Byrd to tell him.

'Thirty years, no parole.'

He closed his eyes and slumped. His breathing was heavy.

'Now,' Byrd continued, very cool, very cruel. 'We're not worried about Jack Nance. When he finishes with Ms. Love's phones, we've got some boys waiting for him outside the building. He'll be arrested, booked, and in due course sent away. But we don't figure he'll talk much. You follow?'

Cal nodded quickly.

'But, Cal, we figure you might want to cut a deal. Help us a little, know what I mean?'

He was still nodding, only faster.

'We figure you'll tell us what we need to know, and in return, we'll let you walk.'

Cal stared at him desperately. His mouth was open, his chest pounding away.

Byrd pointed to the sidewalk on the other side of Madison. 'You see that sidewalk, Cal?'

Cal took a long, hopeful look at the empty sidewalk. 'Yeah,' he said eagerly.

'Well, it's all yours. Tell me what I want to hear, and you walk. Okay? I'm offering you thirty years of freedom, Cal. Don't be stupid.'
'Okay.'.
'When does Gronke return from New Orleans?'
'In the morning, around ten.'
'Where's he staying?'
'Holiday Inn Crowne Plaza.'
'Room number?'
'It's 782.'
'Where are Bono and Pirini?'
'I don't know.'
'Please, Cal, we're not idiots. Where are they?'
'They're in 783 and 784.'
'Who else from New Orleans is here?'
'That's it. That's all I know.'
'Can we expect more people from New Orleans?'
'I swear I don't know.'
'Do they have any plans to hit the boy, his family, or his lawyer?'
'It's been discussed, but no definite plans. I wouldn't be a part of it, you know.'
'I know, Cal. Any plans to bug more phones?'
'No. I don't think so. Just the lawyer.'
'What about the lawyer's house?'
'No, not to my knowledge.'
'No other bugs or wires or phone taps?'
'Not to my knowledge.'
'No plans to kill anybody?'
'No.'
'If you're lying, I'll come get you, Cal, and it's thirty years.'
'I swear it.'

Suddenly, Byrd slapped him on the left side of his face, then grabbed his collar and squeezed it together. Cal's mouth was open and his eyes showed absolute terror. 'Who burned the trailer?' Byrd snarled at him as he pushed him harder against the car.
'Bono and Pirini,' he said without the slightest hesitation.
'Were you in on it, Cal?'
'No. I swear.'
'Any more fires planned?'
'Not to my knowledge.'
'Then what the hell are they doing here, Cal?'
'They're just waiting, listening, you know, just in case they're needed for something else. Depends on what the kid does.'

Byrd squeezed tighter. He showed him his teeth and twisted the collar. 'One lie, Cal, and I'm all over your ass, okay?'

'I'm not lying, I swear,' Cal said in a shrill voice.

Byrd turned him loose and nodded at the sidewalk. 'Go, and sin no more.' The wall of cops opened, and Cal walked through them and into the street. He hit the sidewalk at full stride, and was last seen jogging into the darkness.

# CHAPTER TWENTY-EIGHT

Friday morning. Reggie sipped strong, black coffee in the darkness of predawn, and waited for another unpredictable day as counsel for Mark Sway. It was a cool, clear morning, the first of many in September, and the first hint that the hot, sticky days of the Memphis summer were coming to an end. She sat in a wicker rocker on the small balcony stuck to the rear of her apartment, and tried to unscramble the past five hours of her life.

The cops had called her at one-thirty, said there was an emergency at her office, and asked her to come down. She'd called Clint, and together they had gone to her office where a half dozen cops were waiting. They had allowed Jack Nance to finish his dirty work and leave the building before they nailed him. They showed Reggie and Clint the three phones and the tiny transmitters glued into the receivers, and they said Nance did pretty good work.

As she watched, they carefully removed the transmitters and kept them for evidence. They explained how Nance entered, and more than once they commented on her lack of security. She said she wasn't that concerned about security. There were no real assets in the office.

She'd checked her files, and everything appeared to be in order. The Mark Sway file was in her briefcase at home, and she kept it there when she slept. Clint examined his desk and said there was a chance Nance went through his files. But Clint's desk was not well organized to begin with, so he couldn't be certain.

The police had known Nance was coming, they had explained, but they wouldn't say how they knew. He was allowed easy access into the building – unlocked doors, absent security guards, etc. – and they had a dozen men watching him. He was in custody now, and so far had said nothing. One cop had taken her aside, and in hushed confidence explained about Nance's connection to Gronke, and to Bono and Pirini. They had been unable to find the latter two; their hotel rooms had been abandoned. Gronke was in New Orleans, and they had him under surveillance.

Nance would serve a couple of years, maybe more. For an instant, she'd wanted the death penalty.

The cops had gradually left. Around three, she and Clint were left alone with the empty offices and the startling knowledge that a professional had entered and laid his traps. A man hired by killers had been there, gathering information so there could be more killings, if necessary. The place made her nervous, and she and Clint had left shortly after the cops and found a coffee shop in midtown.

And so with three hours' sleep and a nerve-racking day about to begin, she sipped her coffee and watched the eastern sky turn orange. She thought about Mark, and how he'd arrived in her office on Wednesday, barely two days ago, wet from the rain and scared to death, and told her about being threatened by a man with a switchblade. This man was big and ugly, and waved the knife and produced a photo of the Sway family. She had listened with horror as this small, shivering child described the switchblade. It was a frightening event to hear about, but it had happened to someone else. She was not directly involved. The knife was not pointed at her.

But that was Wednesday, and this was Friday, and the same bunch of thugs had now violated her, and things were a helluva lot more dangerous. Her little client was safely tucked away in a nice jail with security guards at his beck and call, and here she was sitting alone in the darkness thinking about Bono and Pirini and who knew who else might be out there.

Though it couldn't be seen from Momma Love's house, an unmarked car was parked in the street not far away. Two FBI agents were on guard, just in case. Reggie had agreed to this.

She pictured a hotel room, clouds of cigarette smoke hanging along the ceiling, empty beer bottles littering the floor, curtains drawn, and a small group of badly dressed hoodlums hovering over a small table listening to a tape recorder. She was on the tape recorder, talking to clients, to Dr. Levin, to Momma Love, just chatting away as if everything were private. The hoods were bored for the most part, but occasionally one would chuckle and grunt.

Mark didn't use her office phones, and the strategy of bugging them was ridiculous. These people obviously believed Mark knew about Boyette, and that he and his lawyer were stupid enough to discuss this knowledge over the phone.

The phone in the kitchen rang, and Reggie jumped. She checked her watch – six-twenty. It had to be more trouble because no one called at this hour. She walked inside and caught it after the fourth ring. 'Hello.'

It was Harry Roosevelt. 'Good morning, Reggie. Sorry to wake you.'

'I was awake.'

'Have you seen the paper?'

She swallowed hard. 'No. What is it?'

'It's a front page spread with two big pictures of Mark, one as he's leaving the hospital, under arrest as it says, and the other as he's leaving court yesterday, cop on both sides. Slick Moeller wrote it, and he knows all about the hearing. He's got his facts straight, for a change. He says Mark refused to answer my questions about his knowledge of Boyette and such, and that I found him in contempt and sent him to jail. Makes me sound like Hitler.'

'But how does he know this?'

'Cites unnamed sources.'

She was counting the people in the courtroom during the hearing. 'Was it Fink?'

'I doubt it. Fink would have nothing to gain by leaking this, and the risks are too great. It has to be someone who's not too bright.'

'That's why I said Fink.'

'Good point, but I doubt it was a lawyer. I plan to issue a sub-poena for Mr. Moeller to appear in my court at noon today. I'll demand he give me his source, or I'll throw him in jail for contempt.'

'Wonderful idea.'

'It shouldn't take long. We'll have Mark's little hearing afterward. Okay?'

'Sure, Harry. Listen, there's something you should know. It's been a long night.'

'I'm listening,' he said. Reggie gave him the quick version of the bugging of her office, with particular emphasis on Bono and Pirini and the fact that they had not been found.

'Good Lord,' he said. 'These people are crazy.'

'And dangerous.'

'Are you scared?'

'Of course I'm scared. I've been violated, Harry, and it's frightening to know they've been watching.'

There was a long pause on the other end. 'Reggie, I'm not going to release Mark under any circumstances, not today anyway. Let's see what happens over the weekend. He's much safer where he is.'

'I agree.'

'Have you talked to his mother?'

'Yesterday. She was lukewarm on the idea of witness protection. It might take some time. Poor thing is nothing but ragged nerves.'

'Work on her. Can she be present in court today? I'd like to see her.'

'I'll try.'

'See you at noon.'

She poured another cup of coffee and returned to the balcony. Axle slept under the rocker. The first light of dawn crept through the trees. She held the warm mug with both hands and tucked her bare feet under the heavy bathrobe. She sniffed the aroma and thought about how much she despised the press. So now the world would know about the hearing. So much for confidentiality. Her little client was suddenly more vulnerable. It was obvious now, the fact that he knew something he shouldn't know. If not, why wouldn't he simply have talked when the judge instructed him to?

This game was growing more dangerous by the hour. And she, Reggie Love, Attorney and Counselor-at-Law, was supposed to have all the answers and dispense perfect advice. Mark would look at her with those scared blue eyes, and ask what to do next. How the hell was she supposed to know?

They were after her too.

Doreen woke Mark early. She'd fixed blueberry muffins for him, and she nibbled on one and watched him with great concern. Mark sat in a chair, holding a muffin but not eating it, just staring blankly at the floor. He slowly raised the muffin to his mouth, took a tiny bite, then lowered it to his lap. Doreen watched every move.

'Are you okay, sweetheart?' she asked him.

Mark nodded slowly. 'Oh, I'm fine,' he said in a hollow, hoarse voice.

Doreen patted his knee, then his shoulder. Her eyes were narrow and she was very troubled. 'Well, I'll be around all day,' she said as she stood and walked to the door. 'And I'll be checking on you.'

Mark ignored her, and took another small bite of his muffin. The door slammed and clicked, and suddenly he crammed the rest of it in his mouth and reached for another.

He turned on the television, but with no cable he was forced to watch Bryant Gumbel. No cartoons. No old movies. Just Willard in a hat eating corn on the cob and sweet potato sticks.

Doreen returned twenty minutes later. The keys jangled outside, the lock popped, and the door opened. 'Mark, come with me,' she said. 'You have a visitor.'

He was suddenly still again, detached, lost in another world. He moved slowly. 'Who?' he said in that voice.

'Your lawyer.'

He stood and followed her into the hallway. 'Are you sure you're okay?' she asked, squatting in front of him. He nodded slowly, and they walked to the stairs.

Reggie was waiting in a small conference room one floor below.

She and Doreen exchanged pleasantries, old acquaintances, and the door was locked. They sat on opposite sides of a small, round table.

'Are we buddies?' she asked with a smile.

'Yeah. I'm sorry about yesterday.'

'You don't need to apologize, Mark. Believe me, I understand. Did you sleep well?'

'Yeah. Much better than at the hospital.'

'Doreen says she's worried about you.'

'I'm fine. I'm much better off than Doreen.'

'Good.' Reggie pulled a newspaper from her briefcase and placed the front page on the table. He read it very slowly.

'You've made the front page three days in a row,' she said, trying to coax a smile.

'It's getting old. I thought the hearing was private.'

'Supposed to be. Judge Roosevelt called me early this morning. He's very upset about the story. He plans to bring in the reporter and grill him about it.'

'It's too late for that, Reggie. The story is right here in print. Everybody sees it. It's pretty obvious I'm the kid who knows too much.'

'Right.' She waited as he read it again and studied the pictures of himself.

'Have you talked to your mother?' she asked.

'Yes ma'am. Yesterday afternoon around five. She sounded tired.'

'She is. I saw her before you called, and she's hanging in there. Ricky had a bad day.'

'Yeah. Thanks to those stupid cops. Let's sue them.'

'Maybe later. We need to talk about something. After you left the courtroom yesterday, Judge Roosevelt talked to the lawyers and the FBI. He wants you, your mother, and Ricky placed in the Federal Witness Protection Program. He thinks it's the best way to protect you, and I tend to agree.'

'What is it?'

'The FBI moves you to a new location, a very secret one, far away from here, and you have new names, new schools, new everything. Your mother has a new job, one that pays a lot more than six dollars an hour. After a few years there, they might move you again, just to be safe. They'll place Ricky in a much better hospital until he's better. Government pays for everything, of course.'

'Do I get a new bike?'

'Sure.'

'Just kidding. I saw this once in a movie. A Mafia movie. This informant ratted on the Mafia, and the FBI helped him vanish. He had plastic surgery. They found him a new wife, you know, the works. Sent him off to Brazil or some place.'

'What happened?'

'It took them about a year to find him. They killed his wife too.'

'It was just a movie, Mark. You really have no choice. It's the safest thing to do.'

'Of course, I have to tell them everything before they do all these wonderful things for us.'

'That's part of the deal.'

'The Mafia never forgets, Reggie.'

'You've watched too many movies, Mark.'

'Maybe so. But has the FBI ever lost a witness in this program?'

The answer was yes, but she couldn't cite a specific example. 'I don't know, but we'll meet with them and you can ask all the questions you want.'

'What if I don't want to meet with them? What if I want to stay in my little cell here until I'm twenty years old and Judge Roosevelt finally dies? Then can I get out?'

'Fine. What about your mother and Ricky? What happens to them when he's released from the hospital and they have no place to go?'

'They can move in with me. Doreen'll take care of us.'

Damn, he was quick for an eleven-year-old. She paused for a moment and smiled at him. He glared at her.

'Listen, Mark, do you trust me?'

'Yes, Reggie. I do trust you. You're the only person in the world I trust right now. So please help me.'

'There's no easy way out, okay.'

'I know that.'

'Your safety is my only concern. The safety of you and your family. Judge Roosevelt feels the same way. Now, it'll take a few days to work out the details of the witness program. The judge instructed the FBI yesterday to start working on it immediately, and I think it's the best thing to do.'

'Did you discuss it with my mother?'

'Yes. She wants to talk about it some more. I think she liked the idea.'

'But how do you know it'll work, Reggie? Is it totally safe?'

'Nothing is totally safe, Mark. There are no guarantees.'

'Wonderful. Maybe they'll find us, maybe they won't. That'll make life exciting, won't it.'

'Do you have a better idea?'

'Sure. It's very simple. We collect the insurance money from the trailer. We find another one, and we move into it. I keep my mouth shut and we live happily ever after. I don't really care if they ever find this body, Reggie. I just don't care.'

'I'm sorry, Mark, but that can't happen.'

'Why not?'

'Because you happen to be very unlucky. You have some important information, and you'll be in trouble until you give it up.'

'And then I could be dead.'

'I don't think so, Mark.'

He crossed his arms over his chest and closed his eyes. There was a slight bruise high on his left cheek, and it was turning brown. This was Friday. He'd been slapped by Clifford on Monday, and though it seemed like weeks ago the bruise reminded her that things were happening much too fast. The poor kid still bore the wounds of the attack.

'Where would we go?' he asked softly, his eyes still closed.

'Far away. Mr. Lewis with the FBI mentioned a children's psychiatric hospital in Portland that's supposed to be one of the best. They'll place Ricky in it with the best of everything.'

'Can't they follow us?'

'The FBI can handle it.'

He stared at her. 'Why do you suddenly trust the FBI?'

'Because there's no one else to trust.'

'How long will all this take?'

'There are two problems. The first is the paperwork and details. Mr. Lewis said it could be done within a week. The second is Ricky. It might be a few days before Dr. Greenway will allow him to be moved.'

'So I'm in jail for another week?'

'Looks like it. I'm sorry.'

'Don't be sorry, Reggie. I can handle this place. In fact, I could stay here for a long time if they'd leave me alone.'

'They're not going to leave you alone.'

'I need to talk to my mother.'

'She might be at the hearing today. Judge Roosevelt wants her there. I suspect he'll have a meeting, off the record, with the FBI people and discuss the witness protection program.'

'If I'm gonna stay in jail, why have the hearing?'

'In contempt matters, the judge is required to bring you back into court periodically to allow you to purge yourself of contempt, in other words, to do what he wants you to do.'

'The law stinks, Reggie. It's silly, isn't it?'

'Oftentimes, yes.'

'I had a wild thought last night as I was trying to go to sleep. I thought – what if the body is not where Clifford said it is. What if Clifford was just crazy and talking out of his head? Have you thought about that, Reggie?'

'Yes. Many times.'

'What if all this is a big joke?'

'We can't take that chance, Mark.'

He rubbed his eyes and slid his chair back. He began walking around the small room, suddenly very nervous. 'So we just pack up and leave our lives behind, right? That's easy for you to say, Reggie. You're not the one who'll have the nightmares. You'll go on like nothing ever happened. You and Clint. Momma Love. Nice little law office. Lots of clients. But not us. We'll live in fear for the rest of our lives.'

'I don't think so.'

'But you don't know, Reggie. It's easy to sit here and say everything'll be fine. Your neck's not on the line.'

'You have no choice, Mark.'

'Yes I do. I could lie.'

It was just a motion for a continuance, normally a rather boring and routine legal skirmish, but nothing was boring when Barry The Blade Muldanno was the defendant and Willis Upchurch was the mouthpiece. Throw in the enormous ego of the Reverend Roy Foltrigg and the press manipulation skills of Wally Boxx, and this innocuous little hearing for a continuance took on the air of an execution. The courtroom of the Honorable James Lamond was crowded with the curious, the press, and a small army of jealous lawyers who had more important things to do but just happened to be in the neighborhood. They milled about and spoke in grave tones while keeping anxious eyes on the media. Cameras and reporters attract lawyers like blood attracts sharks.

Beyond the railing that separated the players from the spectators, Foltrigg stood in the center of a tight circle of his assistants and whispered, frowning as if they were planning an invasion. He was decked out in his Sunday best – dark three-piece suit, white shirt, red-and-blue silk tie, hair perfect, shoes shined to a glow. He faced the audience, but of course was much too preoccupied to notice anyone. Across the way, Muldanno sat with his back to the gaggle of onlookers and pretended to ignore everyone. He was dressed in black. The ponytail was perfect and arched down to the bottom of his collar.

Willis Upchurch sat on the edge of the defense table, also facing the press while engaging himself in a highly animated conversation with a paralegal. If it was humanly possible, Upchurch loved the attention more than Foltrigg.

Muldanno did not yet know of the arrest of Jack Nance eight hours earlier in Memphis. He did not know Cal Sisson had spilled his guts. He had not heard from either Bono or Pirini, and he had sent Gronke back to Memphis this morning in complete ignorance of the night's events.

Foltrigg, on the other hand, was feeling quite smug. Based on the taped conversation gathered from the salt shaker, he would obtain on Monday indictments against Muldanno and Gronke for obstruction of justice. Convictions would be easy. He had them in the bag. He had Muldanno facing five years.

But Roy didn't have the body. And trying Barry The Blade on obstruction charges would not generate anywhere near the publicity of a nasty murder trial complete with color glossies of the decomposed corpse and pathologists' reports about bullet entries and trajectories and exits. Such a trial would last for weeks, and Roy would shine on the evening news every night. He could just see it.

He'd sent Fink back to Memphis early this morning with the grand jury subpoenas for the kid and his lawyer. That should liven things up a bit. He should have the kid talking by Monday afternoon, and maybe, with just a little luck, he'd have the remains of Boyette by Monday night. This thought had kept him at the office until three in the morning. He strutted to the clerk's desk for nothing in particular, then strutted back, glaring at Muldanno, who ignored him.

The courtroom deputy stopped in front of the bench and yelled instructions for all to sit. Court was now in session, the Honorable James Lamond presiding. Lamond appeared from a side door, and was escorted to the bench by an assistant carrying a stack of heavy files. In his early fifties, Lamond was a baby among federal judges. One of countless Reagan appointees, he was typical – all business, no smiles, cut the crap and let's get on with it. He had been the U.S. Attorney for the Southern District of Louisiana immediately prior to Roy Foltrigg, and he hated his successor as much as anyone. Six months after taking the job, Foltrigg had embarked upon a speaking tour of the district in which he presented charts and graphs to Rotarians and Civitans and declared with statistical evidence that his office was now much more efficient than it had been in prior years. Indictments were up. Dope dealers were behind bars. Public officials were running scared. Crime was in trouble, and the public's interest was now being fiercely protected because he, Roy Foltrigg, was now the chief federal prosecutor in the district.

It was a stupid thing to do because it insulted Lamond and angered the other judges. They had little use for the Reverend.

Lamond gazed at the crowded courtroom. Everyone was seated. 'My goodness,' he started. 'I'm delighted at the interest shown here today, but honestly, it's just a hearing on a simple motion.' He glared at Foltrigg, who sat in the middle of six assistants. Upchurch had a local lawyer on each side, and two paralegals sitting behind him.

'The court is ready to proceed upon the motion of the defendant, Barry Muldanno, for a continuance. The court notes that this matter is set for trial three weeks from next Monday. Mr. Upchurch, you filed the motion, so you may proceed. Please be brief.'

To the surprise of everyone, Upchurch was indeed brief. He simply stated what was common knowledge about the late Jerome Clifford, and explained to the court that he had a trial in federal court in St. Louis beginning three weeks from Monday. He was glib, relaxed, and completely at home in this strange courtroom. A continuance was necessary, he explained with remarkable efficiency, because he needed time to prepare a defense for what would undoubtedly be a long trial. He finished in ten minutes.

'How much time do you need?' Lamond asked.

'Your Honor, I have a busy trial calendar, and I'll be happy to show it to you. In all fairness, six months would be a reasonable delay.'

'Thank you. Anything else?'

'No sir. Thank you, Your Honor.' Upchurch took his seat as Foltrigg was leaving his and heading for the podium directly in front of the bench. He glanced at his notes and was about to speak when Lamond beat him to it.

'Mr. Foltrigg, surely you don't deny that the defense is entitled to more time, in light of the circumstances?'

'No, Your Honor, I don't deny this. But I think six months is entirely too much time.'

'So how much would you suggest?'

'A month or two. You see, Your Honor, I – '

'I'm not going to sit up here and listen to a haggle over two months or six or three or four, Mr. Foltrigg. If you concede the defendant is entitled to a delay, then I'll take this matter under advisement and set this case for trial whenever my calendar will allow.'

Lamond knew Foltrigg needed a delay worse than Muldanno. He just couldn't ask for it. Justice must always be on the attack. Prosecutors are incapable of asking for more time.

'Well, yes, Your Honor,' Foltrigg said loudly. 'But it's our position that needless delays should be avoided. This matter has dragged on long enough.'

'Are you suggesting this court is dragging its feet, Mr. Foltrigg?'

'No, Your Honor, but the defendant is. He's filed every frivolous motion known to American jurisprudence to stall this prosecution. He's tried every tactic, every – '

'Mr. Foltrigg. Mr. Clifford is dead. He can't file any more motions. And now the defendant has a new lawyer, who, as I see it, has only filed one motion.'

Foltrigg looked at his notes and started a slow burn. He had not expected to prevail in this little matter, but he certainly hadn't expected to get kicked in the teeth.

'Do you have anything relevant to say?' His Honor asked, as if Foltrigg had yet to say anything of substance.

He grabbed his legal pad and stormed back to his seat. A rather pitiful performance. He should've sent an underling.

'Anything else, Mr. Upchurch?' Lamond asked.

'No sir.'

'Very well. Thanks to all of you for your interest in this matter. Sorry it has been so brief. Maybe we'll do more next time. An order for a new trial setting will be forthcoming.'

Lamond stood just minutes after he'd sat, and was gone. The reporters filed out, and of course were followed by Foltrigg and Upchurch, who walked to opposite ends of the hallway and held impromptu press conferences.

# CHAPTER TWENTY-NINE

Though Slick Moeller had reported jailhouse riots, rapes, and beatings, and though he'd stood on the safe side of the doors and bars, he'd never actually, physically, been inside a jail cell. And though this thought was heavy on his mind, he kept his cool and projected the aura of the surefooted reporter and confident believer in the First Amendment. He had a lawyer on each side, high-paid studs from a hundred-man firm that had represented the *Memphis Press* for decades, and they had assured him a dozen times in the past two hours that the Constitution of the United States of America was his friend and on this day would be his shield. Slick wore jeans, a safari jacket, and hiking boots, very much the weather-beaten reporter.

Harry was not impressed with the aura being projected by this weasel. Nor was he impressed with the silk-stocking, blue-blooded Republican mouthpieces who'd never before darkened the doors to his courtroom. Harry was upset. He sat on his bench and read for the tenth time Slick's morning story. He also reviewed applicable First Amendment cases dealing with reporters and their confidential sources. And he took his time so Slick would sweat.

The doors were locked. The bailiff, Slick's friend Grinder, stood quite nervously by the bench. Following the judge's order, two uniformed deputies sat directly behind Slick and his lawyers, and seemed poised and ready for action. This bothered Slick and his lawyers, but they tried not to show it.

The same court reporter with an even shorter skirt filed her nails and waited for the words to start flowing. The same grouchy old woman sat at her table and flipped through the *National Enquirer*. They waited and waited. It was almost twelve-thirty. As usual, the docket was packed and things were behind schedule. Marcia had a club sandwich waiting for Harry between hearings. The Sway hearing was next.

He leaned forward on his elbows and glared down at Slick, who at a hundred and thirty pounds weighed probably a third of what Harry did. 'On the record,' he barked at the stenographer, and she started pecking away.

Cool as he was, Slick jerked with these first words and sat upright.

'Mr. Moeller, I've brought you here under summons because you've violated a section of the Tennessee Code regarding the confidentiality of my proceedings. This is a very grave matter because we're dealing with the safety and well-being of a small child. Unfortunately, the law does not provide criminal penalties, only contempt.'

He removed his reading glasses and began rubbing them with a handkerchief. 'Now, Mr. Moeller,' he said like a frustrated grandfather, 'as upset as I am with you and your story, I am much more troubled by the fact that someone leaked this information to you. Someone who was in this courtroom during the hearing yesterday. Your source troubles me greatly.'

Grinder leaned against the wall and pressed his calves against it to keep his knees from shaking. He would not look at Slick. His first heart attack had been only six years ago, and if he didn't control himself this might be the big one.

'Please sit in the witness chair, Mr. Moeller,' Harry instructed with a sweep of the hand. 'Be my guest.'

Slick was sworn by the old grouch. He placed one hiking boot on one knee, and looked at his attorneys for reassurance. They were not looking at him. Grinder studied the ceiling tiles.

'You are under oath, Mr. Moeller,' Harry reminded him just seconds after he'd been sworn.

'Yes sir,' he uttered and feebly attempted to smile at this huge man who was sitting high above him and peering down over the railing of the bench.

'Did you in fact write the story in today's paper with your name on it?'

'Yes sir.'

'Did you write it by yourself, or did someone assist you?'

'Well, Your Honor, I wrote every word, if that's what you mean.'

'That's what I mean. Now, in the fourth paragraph of this story, you write, and I quote, "Mark Sway refused to answer questions about Barry Muldanno or Boyd Boyette." End quote. Did you write that, Mr. Moeller?'

'Yes sir.'

'And were you present during the hearing yesterday when the child testified?'

'No sir.'

'Were you in this building?'

'Uh, yes sir. I was. Nothing wrong with that, is there?'

'Be quiet, Mr. Moeller. I'll ask the questions, and you answer them. Do you understand the relationship here?'

'Yes sir.' Slick pleaded with his eyes to his lawyers, but both were deep into reading at this moment. He felt alone.

'So you weren't present. Now, Mr. Moeller, how did you learn that the child refused to answer my questions about Barry Muldanno or Boyd Boyette?'

'I had a source.'

Grinder had never thought of himself as a source. He was just a low-paid courtroom bailiff with a uniform and a gun, and bills to pay. He was about to be sued by Sears for his wife's credit card. He wanted to wipe the sweat from his forehead but was afraid to move.

'A source,' Harry repeated, mocking Slick. 'Of course you had a source, Mr. Moeller. I assumed this. You weren't here. Someone told you. This means you had a source. Now, who was your source?'

The lawyer with the grayest hair quickly stood to speak. He was dressed in standard big-firm attire – charcoal suit, white button-down, red tie but with a daring yellow stripe on it, and black shoes. His name was Alliphant. He was a partner who normally avoided courtrooms. 'Your Honor, if I may.'

Harry grimaced, and he slowly turned from the witness. His mouth was open as if he were shocked at this daring interruption. He scowled at Alliphant, who repeated himself. 'If I may, Your Honor.'

Harry let him hang there for an eternity, then said, 'You haven't been in my courtroom before, have you, Mr. Alliphant?'

'No sir,' he answered, still standing.

'I didn't think so. Not one of your usual hangouts. How many lawyers are in your firm, Mr. Alliphant?'

'A hundred and seven, at last count.'

Harry whistled and shook his head. 'That's a buncha lawyers. Do any of them practice in Juvenile Court?'

'Well, I'm sure some do, Your Honor.'

'Which ones?'

Alliphant stuck one hand in one pocket while running a loose finger along the edge of his legal pad. He did not belong here. His legal world was one of boardrooms and thick documents, of fat retainers and fancy lunches. He was rich because he billed three hundred dollars an hour and had thirty partners doing the same. His firm prospered because it paid seventy associates fifty thousand a year and expected them to bill five times that. He was here ostensibly because he was chief counsel for the paper, but actually because no one in the firm's litigation section could make the hearing on two hours' notice.

Harry despised him, his firm, and their ilk. He did not trust the corporate types who came down from the tall buildings to mingle with the lower class only when necessary. They were arrogant and afraid to get their hands dirty.

'Sit down, Mr. Alliphant,' he said, pointing. 'You do not stand in my courtroom. Sit.'

Alliphant awkwardly backed in to his chair.

'Now what are you trying to say, Mr. Alliphant?'

'Well, Your Honor, we object to these questions, and we object to the court's interrogation of Mr. Moeller on the grounds that his story is protected free speech under the First Amendment of the Constitution. Now – '

'Mr. Alliphant, have you read the applicable code section dealing with closed hearings in juvenile matters? Surely you have.'

'Yes sir, I have. And, frankly, Your Honor, I have some real problems with this section.'

'Oh you do? Go on.'

'Yes, sir. It's my opinion that this code section is unconstitutional, as written. I have some cases here from other – '

'Unconstitutional?' Harry asked with raised eyebrows.

'Yes sir,' Alliphant answered firmly.

'Do you know who wrote the code section, Mr. Alliphant?'

Alliphant turned to his associate as if he knew everything. But he shook his head.

'I wrote it, Mr. Alliphant,' Harry said loudly. 'Me. *Moi*. Yours truly. And if you knew anything about juvenile law in this state, you would know that I am the expert because I wrote the law. Now, what can you say about that?'

Slick slid down in his chair. He'd covered a thousand trials. He'd seen lawyers hammered by angry judges, and he knew their clients usually suffered.

'I contend it's unconstitutional, Your Honor,' Alliphant said gallantly.

'And the last thing I intend to do, Mr. Alliphant, is to get into a long, hot-air debate with you about the First Amendment. If you don't like the law, then take it up on appeal and get it changed. I honestly don't care. But right now, while I'm missing lunch, I want your client to answer the question.' He turned back to Slick, who was waiting in terror. 'Now, Mr. Moeller, who was your source?'

Grinder was about to vomit. He stuck his thumbs under his belt and pressed against his stomach. By reputation, Slick was a man of his word. He always protected his sources.

'I cannot reveal my source,' Slick said in an effort at great drama, the martyr willing to face death. Grinder took a deep breath. Such sweet words.

Harry immediately motioned for the two deputies. 'I find you in contempt, Mr. Moeller, and order you to jail.' The deputies stood beside Slick, who looked around wildly for help.

'Your Honor,' Alliphant said, standing without thinking. 'We object to this! You cannot – '

Harry ignored Alliphant. He spoke to the deputies. 'Take him to the city jail. No special treatment. No favors. I'll bring him back Monday for another try.'

They yanked Slick up and handcuffed him. 'Do something!' he yelled at Alliphant, who was saying, 'This is protected speech, Your Honor. You can't do this.'

'I'm doing it, Mr. Alliphant,' Harry yelled. 'And if you don't sit down, you'll be in the same cell with your client.'

Alliphant dropped into his chair.

They dragged Slick to the door, and as they opened it, Harry had one final thing to say. 'Mr. Moeller, if I read one word in your paper written by you while in jail, I'll let you sit there for a month before I bring you back. You understand.'

Slick couldn't speak. 'We'll appeal, Slick,' Alliphant promised as they shoved him through and closed the door. 'We'll appeal.'

Dianne Sway sat in a heavy wood chair, holding her oldest son and watching the sunlight filter through the dusty, broken blinds of Witness Room B. The tears were gone and words had failed them.

After five days and four nights of involuntary confinement in the psychiatric ward, she at first had been happy to leave it. But happiness these days came in tiny spurts, and she now longed to return to Ricky's bed. Now that she'd seen Mark, and held him and cried with him, she knew he was safe. Under the circumstances, that was all a mother could ask.

She didn't trust her instincts or judgment. Five days in a cave takes away any sense of reality. The endless series of shocks had left her drained and stunned. The drugs – pills to sleep and pills to wake up and pills to get through it – deadened the mind so that her life was a series of snapshots thrown on the table one at a time. The brain worked, but in slow motion.

'They want us to go to Portland,' she said, rubbing his arm.

'Reggie talked to you about it.'

'Yes, we had a long talk yesterday. There's a good place for Ricky out there, and we can start over.'

'Sounds good, but it scares me.'

'Scares me too, Mark. I don't want to live the next forty years looking over my shoulder. I read a story one time in some magazine about a Mafia informant who helped the FBI and they agreed to hide him. Just like they want us to do. I think it took two years before the Mafia found him and blew him up in his car.'

'I think I saw the movie.'

'I can't live like that, Mark.'

'Can we get another trailer?'

'I think so. I talked to Mr. Tucker this morning, and he says he had the trailer covered with plenty of insurance. He said he had another one for us. And I still have my job. In fact, they delivered my paycheck to the hospital this morning.'

Mark smiled at the thought of returning to the trailer park and hanging out with the kids. He even missed school.

'These people are deadly, Mark.'

'I know. I've met them.'

She thought for a second, then asked, 'You what?'

'I guess it's something else I forgot to tell you.'

'I'd like to hear it.'

'It happened a couple of days ago at the hospital. I don't know which day. They're all running together.' He took a deep breath. He told her about his encounter with the man and the switchblade and their family portrait. Normally, she, or any mother, would have been shocked. But for Dianne, it was just another event in this horrible week.

'Why didn't you tell me?' she asked.

'Because I didn't want to worry you.'

'You know, we might not be in this trouble if you'd told me everything up front.'

'Don't fuss at me, Mom. I can't take it.'

She couldn't take it either, so she dropped it. Reggie knocked on the door and it opened. 'We need to go,' she said. 'The judge is waiting.'

They followed her through the hall and around a corner. Two deputies trailed behind. 'Are you nervous?' Dianne whispered. 'No. It's no big deal, Mom.'

Harry was munching on the sandwich and flipping through the file when they entered the courtroom. Fink, Ord, and Baxter McLemore, the Juvenile Court prosecutor-of-the-day, were all seated together at their table, all quiet and subdued, all bored and waiting for what would undoubtedly be a quick appearance by the kid. Fink and Ord were captivated by the court reporter's legs and skirt. Her figure was obscene – tiny waist, healthy breasts, slender legs. She was the only redeeming element in this rinky-dink courtroom, and Fink had to admit to himself that he'd thought about her on the flight to New Orleans yesterday. And he'd thought about her all the way back to Memphis. She was not disappointing him. The skirt was at mid-thigh and inching upward.

Harry looked at Dianne and gave his best smile. His large teeth were perfect and his eyes were warm. 'Hello, Ms. Sway,' he said sweetly. She nodded and tried to smile.

'It is a pleasure meeting you, and I'm sorry it has to be under these circumstances.'

'Thank you, Your Honor,' she said softly to the man who'd ordered her son to jail.

Harry looked at Fink with contempt. 'I trust everyone has read this morning's *Memphis Press*. It has a fascinating story about our proceedings yesterday, and the man who wrote the story is now in jail. I intend to investigate this matter further, and I am confident I will find the leak.'

Grinder, by the door, was suddenly ill again.

'And when I find it, I intend to fix it with a contempt order. So, ladies and gentlemen, keep your mouths shut. Not a word to anyone.' He took the file. 'Now, Mr. Fink, where's Mr. Foltrigg?'

Sitting firmly in place, Fink answered, 'He's in New Orleans, Your Honor. I have a copy of the court order you requested.'

'Fine. I'll take your word for it. Madam Clerk, swear the witness.'

Madam Clerk threw her hand in the air, and barked at Mark, 'Raise your right hand.' Mark stood awkwardly, and was sworn.

'You can remain in your seat,' Harry said. Reggie was on his right, Dianne on the left.

'Mark, I'm going to ask you some questions, okay?'

'Yes sir.'

'Prior to his death, did Mr. Clifford say anything to you about a Mr. Barry Muldanno?'

'I'm not going to answer that.'

'Did Mr. Clifford mention the name of Boyd Boyette.'

'I'm not going to answer that.'

'Did Mr. Clifford say anything about the murder of Boyd Boyette?'

'I'm not going to answer that.'

'Did Mr. Clifford say anything about the present location of the body of Boyd Boyette?'

'I'm not going to answer that.'

Harry paused and looked at his notes. Dianne had stopped breathing and was staring blankly at Mark. 'It's okay, Mom,' he whispered to her.

'Your Honor,' he said in a strong, confident voice. 'I want you to understand that I'm not answering for the same reasons I gave yesterday. I'm just scared, that's all.'

Harry nodded but gave no expression. He was neither angry nor pleased. 'Mr. Bailiff, take Mark back to the witness room, and keep him there until we finish. He can talk to his mother before he's transported to the detention center.'

Grinder's knees were putty, but he managed to lead Mark from the courtroom.

Harry unzipped his robe. 'Let's go off the record. Madam Clerk, you and Ms. Gregg can go to lunch.' It was not an offer, but a demand. Harry wanted fewer ears in the courtroom.

Ms. Gregg swung her legs toward Fink, and his heart stopped. He and Ord watched with their mouths open as she stood, took her purse, and pranced from the courtroom.

'Get the FBI, Mr. Fink,' Harry instructed.

McThune and a weary K. O. Lewis were fetched and took seats behind Ord. Lewis was a busy man with a thousand important items stacked on his desk in Washington, and he'd asked himself a hundred times in the past twenty-four hours why he'd come to Memphis. Of course, Director Voyles wanted him here, which clarified his priorities immensely.

'Mr. Fink, you indicated before the hearing there is an urgent matter that I should know about.'

'Yes sir. Mr. Lewis would like to address it.'

'Mr. Lewis. Please be brief.'

'Yes, Your Honor. We've had Barry Muldanno under surveillance for several months, and yesterday we obtained by electronic means a conversation between Muldanno and Paul Gronke. It took place in a bar in the French Quarter, and I think you need to hear it.'

'You have the tape?'

'Yes sir.'

'Then let it roll.' Harry was suddenly unconcerned with time.

McThune quickly assembled a tape player and speaker on the desk in front of Fink, and Lewis inserted a micro-cassette. 'The first voice you'll hear is that of Muldanno,' he explained like a chemist preparing a demonstration. 'Then Gronke.'

The courtroom was still and quiet as the scratchy but very clear voices squawked from the speaker. The entire conversation was captured; the suggestion by Muldanno of hitting the kid, and Gronke's doubts about getting to him; the idea of hitting the kid's mother or brother, and Gronke's protests of killing innocent people; Muldanno's talk of killing his lawyer, and the laughter about it doing wonders for the legal profession; the boasting of Gronke about taking care of the trailer; and finally the plans to bug the lawyer's phones that night.

It was chilling. Fink and Ord had heard it ten times already, so they were noncommittal. Reggie closed her eyes when the taking of her life was so nonchalantly bantered about. Dianne was rigid with fear. Harry stared at the speaker as if he could see their faces, and when the tape was finished and Lewis punched the button, he simply said, 'Play it again.'

They listened to it the second time, and the shock began to wear off. Dianne was trembling. Reggie held her arm and tried to be brave, but the easy talk of killing the kid's lawyer made her blood run cold. Dianne's skin broke out in goose pimples, and her eyes began to water. She thought of Ricky, who at this moment was being watched by Greenway and a nurse, and prayed he was safe.

'I've heard enough,' Harry said when the tape stopped. Lewis took his seat, and they waited for His Honor to give direction. He wiped his eyes with a handkerchief, then took a long drink of ice tea. He smiled at Dianne. 'Now, Ms. Sway, do you understand why we've placed Mark in the detention center?'

'I think so.'

'Two reasons. The first is that he refused to answer my questions, but at the moment, that's not nearly as important as the second. He's in great danger, as you've just heard. What would you like for me to do next?'

It was an unfair question posed to a scared, deeply troubled, and irrational person, and she didn't like him asking it. She just shook her head. 'I don't know,' she mumbled.

Harry spoke slowly, and there was no doubt he knew exactly what should be done next. 'Reggie has told me that she's discussed the witness protection program with you. Tell me what you think.'

Dianne raised her head and bit her lip. She thought for a few seconds and tried to focus on the tape recorder. 'I do not want those people,' she said deliberately, nodding at the recorder, 'following me and my children for the rest of our lives. And I'm afraid that will happen if Mark gives you what you want.'

'You'll have the protection of the FBI and every necessary agency of the U.S. Government.'

'But no one can completely guarantee our safety. These are my children, Your Honor, and I'm a single parent. There's no one else. If I make a mistake, I could lose, well, I can't even imagine it.'

'I think you'll be safe, Ms. Sway. There are thousands of government witnesses now being protected.'

'But some have been found, haven't they?'

It was a quiet question that hit hard. Neither McThune nor Lewis could deny the fact that witnesses had been lost. There was a long silence.

'Well, Ms. Sway,' Harry finally said with a great deal of compassion, 'what's the alternative?'

'Why can't you arrest these people? Lock them up somewhere. I mean, it looks as if they're just roaming free terrorizing me and my family, and also Reggie here. What're the damned cops doing?'

'It's my understanding, Ms. Sway, that one arrest was made last night. The police here are looking for the two men who burned your trailer, two thugs from New Orleans named Bono and Pirini, but they haven't found them. Is that correct, Mr. Lewis?'

'Yes sir. We think they're still in the city. And I might add, Your Honor, that the U.S. Attorney in New Orleans intends to indict Muldanno and Gronke early next week on charges of obstruction of justice. So they'll be in custody very soon.'

'But this is the Mafia, isn't it?' Dianne asked.

Every idiot who could read the newspapers knew it was the Mafia. It was a Mafia killing by a Mafia gunman whose family had been Mafia hoods in New Orleans for four decades. Her question was so simple, yet it implied the obvious: the Mafia is an invisible army with plenty of soldiers.

Lewis did not wish to answer the question, so he waited for His Honor, who likewise hoped it would simply go away. There was a long, awkward silence.

Dianne cleared her throat and spoke in a much stronger voice. 'Your Honor, when you guys can show me a way to completely protect my children, then I'll help you. But not until then.'

'So you want him to stay in jail,' Fink blurted.

She turned and glared at Fink, less than ten feet away. 'Sir, I'd rather have him in a detention center than in a grave.'

Fink slumped in his chair and stared at the floor. Seconds ticked away. Harry looked at his watch, and zipped his robe. 'I suggest we meet again Monday at noon. Let's take things one day at a time.'

# CHAPTER THIRTY

Paul Gronke finished his unexpected trip to Minneapolis as the Northwest 727 lifted off the runway and started for Atlanta. From Atlanta, he hoped to catch a direct flight to New Orleans, and once home he had no plans to leave for a long time. Maybe years. Regardless of his friendship with Muldanno, Gronke was tired of this mess. He could break a thumb or a leg when necessary, and he could huff and puff and scare almost anybody. But he did not particularly enjoy stalking little kids and waving switchblades at them. He made a nice living off his clubs and beer joints, and if The Blade needed help, he'd just have to lean on his family. Gronke was not family. He was not Mafia. And he was not going to kill anyone for Barry Muldanno.

He'd made two phone calls this morning as soon as his flight arrived at the Memphis airport. The first call spooked him because no one answered. He then dialed a backup number for a recorded message, and again there was no answer. He walked quickly to the Northwest ticket counter and paid cash for a one-way ticket to Minneapolis. Then he found the Delta counter and paid cash for a one-way ticket to Dallas–Fort Worth. Then he bought a ticket to Chicago, on United. He roamed the concourses for an hour, watching his back and seeing nothing, and at the last second hopped on Northwest.

Bono and Pirini had strict instructions. The two phone calls meant one of two things: either the cops had them, or they were forced to pull up stakes and haul ass. Neither thought was comforting.

The flight attendant brought two beers. It was a few minutes after one, too early to start drinking, but he was edgy, and what the hell. It was 5 P.M. somewhere.

Muldanno would flip out and start throwing things. He'd run to his uncle and borrow some more thugs. They'd descend upon Memphis and start hurting people. Finesse was not Barry's long suit.

Their friendship had started in high school, in the tenth grade, their last year of formal education before they dropped out and began hustling on the streets of New Orleans. Barry's route to crime was preordained by family. Gronke's was a bit more complicated. Their first venture had been a fencing operation that had been wildly successful. The profits, however, were siphoned off by Barry and sent to the family. They peddled some drugs, ran some numbers, managed a whorehouse, all cash-rich ventures. But Gronke saw little of the cash. After ten years of this lopsided partnership, he told Barry he wanted a place of his own. Barry helped him buy a topless bar, then a porno house. Gronke made money and was able to keep it. At about this point in their careers, Barry started his killing, and Gronke established more distance between them.

But they remained friends. A month or so after Boyette disappeared, the two of them spent a long weekend at Johnny Sulari's house in Acapulco with a couple of strippers. After the girls had passed out one night, they went for a long walk on the beach. Barry was drinking tequila and talking more than usual. His name had just surfaced as a suspect. He bragged to his friend about the killing.

The landfill in Lafourche Parish was worth millions to the Sulari family. Johnny's scheme was to eventually route most of the garbage from New Orleans to it. Senator Boyette had been an unexpected enemy. His antics had attracted lots of negative publicity for the dump, and the more ink Boyette received the crazier he'd become. He'd launched federal investigations. He'd called in dozens of EPA bureaucrats who'd prepared massive volumes of studies, most of which condemned the landfill. In Washington, he'd hounded the Justice Department until it initiated its own investigation into the allegations of mob involvement. Senator Boyette became the biggest obstacle to Johnny's gold mine.

The decision had been made to hit Boyette.

Sipping from a bottle of Cuervo Gold, Barry laughed about the killing. He stalked Boyette for six months, and was pleasantly surprised to learn that the Senator, who was divorced, had an affinity with young women. Cheap young women, the kind he could find in a bordello and buy for fifty bucks. His favorite place was a seedy roadhouse halfway between New Orleans and Houma, the site of the landfill. It was in oil country, and frequented by offshore roustabouts and the cute little whores they attracted. Evidently, the Senator knew the owner and had a special arrangement. He always parked behind a garbage dumpster, away from the gravel lot crowded with monster pickups and Harleys. He always used the rear entrance by the kitchen.

The Senator's trips to Houma became more frequent. He was raising hell in town meetings and holding press conferences every week. And he enjoyed the drives back to New Orleans with his little quickies at the roadhouse.

The hit was easy, Barry said as they sat on the beach with foamy saltwater rushing around them. He trailed Boyette for twenty miles after a rowdy landfill meeting in Houma, and waited patiently in the darkness behind the roadhouse. When Boyette emerged after his little liaison, he hit him in the head with a nightstick and quickly threw him in the backseat. He stopped a few miles down the road and pumped four bullets in his head. The body was wrapped in garbage bags and placed in the trunk.

Imagine that, Barry had marveled, a U.S. Senator snatched from the darkness of a run-down bordello. He'd served for twenty-one years, chaired powerful committees, eaten at the White House, trotted around the globe searching for ways to spend taxpayers' money, had eighteen assistants and gofers working for him, and, bam!, just like that, got caught with his pants down. Barry thought it was hilarious. One of his easiest jobs, he said, as if there'd been hundreds.

A state trooper had stopped Barry for speeding ten miles outside of New Orleans. Imagine that, he said, chatting with a cop with a warm body in the trunk. He talked football and avoided a ticket. But then he panicked, and decided to hide the body in a different place. Gronke was tempted to ask where, but thought better of it.

The case against him was shaky. The trooper's records placed Barry in the vicinity at the time of the disappearance. But with no body, there was no proof of the time of death. One of the prostitutes saw a man who resembled Barry in the shadows of the parking lot while the Senator was being entertained. She was now under government protection, but not expected to make a good witness. Barry's car had been cleaned and sanitized. No blood samples, no fibers or hair. The star of the government's case was a Mafia informant, a man who'd spent twenty of his forty-two years in jail, and who was not expected to live to testify. A .22 caliber Ruger had been seized from the apartment of one of Barry's girlfriends, but, again, with no corpse it was impossible to determine the cause of death. Barry's fingerprints were on the gun. It was a gift, said the girlfriend.

Juries are hesitant to convict without first knowing for certain that the victim is indeed dead. And Boyette was such an eccentric character that rumors and gossip had produced all sorts of wild speculation about his disappearance. One published report detailed his recent history of psychiatric problems, and thus had given rise to a popular theory that he'd gone nuts and run off with a teenage hooker. He had gambling debts. He drank too much. His ex-wife had sued him for fraud in the divorce. And on and on.

Boyette had plenty of reasons to disappear.

And now, an eleven-year-old kid in Memphis knew where he was buried. Gronke opened the second beer.

Doreen held Mark's arm and walked him to his room. His steps were measured and he stared at the floor in front of them as if he'd just witnessed a car bomb in a crowded marketplace.

'Are you okay, baby?' she asked, the wrinkles around her eyes bunched together with terrible concern.

He nodded and plodded along. She quickly unlocked the door, and placed him on the bottom bunk.

'Lie right here, sweetheart,' she said, pulling back the covers and swinging his legs onto the bed. She knelt beside him and searched his eyes for answers. 'Are you sure you're okay?'

He nodded but could say nothing.

'Do you want me to call a doctor?'

'No,' he managed to say in a hollow voice. 'I'm fine.'

'I think I'll get a doctor,' she said. He grabbed her arm and squeezed tightly.

'I just need some rest,' he mumbled. 'That's all.'

She unlocked the door with the key and slowly eased out, her eyes never leaving Mark. When the door closed and clicked, he swung his feet to the floor.

At three Friday afternoon, Harry Roosevelt's legendary patience was gone. His weekend would be spent in the Ozarks, fishing with his two sons, and as he sat on the bench and looked at the courtroom still crowded with deadbeat dads awaiting sentencing for nonpayment, his mind kept wandering to thoughts of long sleepy mornings and cool mountain streams. At least two dozen men filled the pews of the main courtroom, and most had either current wives or current girlfriends sitting anxiously at their elbows. A few had brought their lawyers, though there was no legal relief available at this moment. All of them would soon be serving weekend sentences at the Shelby County Penal Farm for failing to pay child support.

Harry wanted to adjourn by four, but it looked doubtful. His two sons waited in the back row. Outside, the Jeep was packed, and when the gavel finally rapped for the last time, they would rush His Honor from the building and whisk him away to the Buffalo River. That was the plan anyway. They were bored, but they had been here before many times.

In spite of the chaos in the front of the courtroom – clerks hauling bundles of files in and out, lawyers whispering as they waited, deputies standing by, defendants being shuffled to the bench then out the door – Harry's assembly line moved with determined efficiency. He glared at each deadbeat, scolded a bit, sometimes a quick lecture, then he signed an order and moved on to the next one.

Reggie eased into the courtroom and made her way to the clerk seated next to the bench. They whispered for a minute with Reggie pointing to a document she'd brought with her. She laughed at something that was probably not that funny, but Harry heard her and motioned her to the bench.

'Something wrong?' he asked with his hand over the microphone.

'No. Mark's fine, I guess. I need a quick favor. It's another case.'

Harry smiled and turned off the mike. Typical Reggie. Her cases were always the most important and needed immediate attention. 'What is it?' he asked.

The clerk handed Harry the file while Reggie handed him an order. 'It's another snatch and run by the Welfare Department,' she said in a low voice. No one was listening. No one cared.

'Who's the kid?' he asked, flipping through the file.

'Ronald Allan Thomas the Third. Also known as Trip Thomas. He was taken into custody last night by Welfare and placed in a foster home. His mother hired me an hour ago.'

'Says here he's been abandoned and neglected.'

'Not true, Harry. It's a long story, but I assure you this kid has good parents and a clean home.'

'And you want the kid released?'

'Immediately. I'll pick him up myself, and take him home to Momma Love if I have to.'

'And feed him lasagne.'

'Of course.'

Harry scanned the order and signed his name at the bottom. 'I'll have to trust you, Reggie.'

'You always do. I saw Damon and Al back there. They look rather bored.'

Harry handed the order to the clerk who stamped it. 'So am I. When I get this riffraff cleared from my courtroom, we're going fishing.'

'Good luck. I'll see you Monday.'

'Have a nice weekend, Reggie. You'll check on Mark, won't you?'

'Of course.'

'Try and talk some sense into his mother. The more I think about it, the more I'm convinced these people must cooperate with the

Feds and enter the witness program. Hell, they have nothing to lose by starting over. Convince her they'll be protected.'

'I'll try. I'll spend some time with her this weekend. Maybe we can wrap it up Monday.'

'I'll see you then.'

Reggie winked at him, and backed away from the bench. The clerk handed her a copy of the order, and she left the courtroom.

# CHAPTER THIRTY-ONE

Thomas Fink, fresh from another exciting flight from Memphis, entered Foltrigg's office at four-thirty Friday afternoon. Wally Boxx sat like a faithful lapdog on the sofa, writing what Fink presumed to be another speech for their boss, or perhaps a press release for upcoming indictments. Roy's shoeless feet were on his desk and the phone was cradled on his shoulder. He was listening with his eyes closed. The day had been a disaster. Lamond had embarrassed him in a crowded courtroom. Roosevelt had failed to make the kid talk. He'd had it with judges.

Fink removed his jacket and sat down. Foltrigg ended his phone chat and hung up. 'Where are the grand jury subpoenas?' he asked.

'I hand-delivered them to the U.S. marshal in Memphis, and gave him strict instructions not to serve them until he heard from you.'

Boxx left the sofa and sat next to Fink. It would be a shame if he were excluded from a conversation.

Roy rubbed his eyes and ran his fingers through his hair. Frustrating, very frustrating. 'So what's the kid gonna do, Thomas? You were there. You saw the kid's mother. You heard her voice. What's gonna happen?'

'I don't know. It's obvious the kid has no plans to talk anytime soon. He and his mother are terrified. They've watched too much television, seen to many Mafia informants blown to bits. She's convinced they won't be safe in witness protection. She's really scared. The woman's been through hell this week.'

'That's real touching,' Boxx mumbled.

'I have no choice but to use the subpoenas,' Foltrigg said gravely, pretending to be troubled by this thought. 'They leave me no choice. We were fair and reasonable. We asked the youth court in Memphis to help us with the kid, and it simply has not worked. It's time we got these people down here, on our turf, in our courtroom, in front of our people, and made them talk. Don't you agree, Thomas?'

Fink was not in full agreement.' Jurisdiction worries me. The kid is under the jurisdiction of the Juvenile Court up there, and I'm not sure what'll happen when he gets the subpoena.'

Roy was smiling. 'That's right, but the court is closed for the weekend. We've done some research, and I think federal law supersedes state law on this one, don't you, Wally?'

'I think so. Yes,' said Wally.

'And I've talked to the marshal's office here. I've told them I want the boys in Memphis to pick the kid up tomorrow and bring him here so he can face the grand jury Monday. I don't think the locals in Memphis will interfere with the U.S. marshal's office. We've made arrangements to house him here in the Juvenile Wing at city jail. Should be a piece of cake.'

'What about the lawyer?' asked Fink. 'You can't make her testify. If she knows anything, she learned it in the course of her representation of the kid. It's privileged.'

'Pure harassment,' Foltrigg admitted with a smile. 'She and the kid will be scared to death on Monday. We'll be calling the shots, Thomas.'

'Speaking of Monday. Judge Roosevelt wants us in his courtroom at noon.'

Roy and Wally had a good laugh at this. 'He'll be a lonely judge, won't he,' Foltrigg said with a chuckle. 'You, me, the kid, and the kid's lawyer will all be down here. What a fool.'

Fink did not join their laughter.

At five, Doreen knocked on the door, and rattled keys until it opened. Mark was on the floor playing checkers against himself, and immediately became a zombie. He sat on his feet, and stared at the checkerboard as if in a trance.

'Are you okay, Mark?'

Mark didn't answer.'

'Mark, honey, I'm really worried about you. I think I'll call the doctor. You might be going into shock, just like your little brother.'

He shook his head slowly, and looked at her with mournful eyes. 'No, I'm okay. I just need some rest.'

'Could you eat something?'

'Maybe some pizza.'

'Sure, baby. I'll get one ordered. Look, honey, I get off duty in five minutes, but I'll tell Telda to watch you real close, okay. Will you be all right till I get back in the morning?'

'Maybe,' he moaned.

'Poor child. You got no business in here.'

'I'll make it.'

Telda was much less concerned than Doreen. She checked on Mark twice. On her third visit to his room, around eight o'clock, she brought visitors. She knocked and opened the door slowly, and Mark was about to do his trance routine when he saw the two large men in suits.

'Mark, these men are U.S. marshals,' Telda said nervously. Mark stood near the toilet. The room was suddenly tiny.

'Hi, Mark,' said the first one. 'I'm Vern Duboski, deputy U.S. marshal.' His words were crisp and precise. A Yankee. But that was all Mark noticed. He was holding some papers.

'You are Mark Sway?'

He nodded, unable to speak.

'Don't be afraid, Mark. We just have to give you these papers.'

He looked at Telda for help, but she was clueless. 'What are they?' he asked nervously.

'It's a grand jury subpoena, and it means that you have to appear before a federal grand jury on Monday in New Orleans. Now, don't worry, we're gonna come get you tomorrow afternoon and drive you down.'

A nervous pain shot through his stomach and he was weak. His mouth was dry. 'Why?' he asked.

'We can't answer that, Mark. It's none of our business, really. We're just following orders.'

Mark stared at the papers Vern was waving. New Orleans! 'Have you told my mother?'

'Well, you see, Mark, we're required to give her a copy of these same papers. We'll explain everything to her, and we'll tell her you'll be fine. In fact, she can go with you if she wants.'

'She can't go with me. She can't leave Ricky.'

The marshals looked at each other. 'Well, anyway, we'll explain everything to her.'

'I have a lawyer, you know. Have you told her?'

'No. We're not required to notify the attorneys, but you're welcome to call her if you like.'

'Does he have access to a telephone?' the second one asked Telda.

'Only if I bring him one,' she said.

'You can wait thirty minutes, can't you?'

'If you say so,' Telda said.

'So, Mark, in about thirty minutes you can call your lawyer.' Duboski paused and looked at his sidekick. 'Well, good luck to you, Mark. Sorry if we scared you.'

They left him standing near the toilet, leaning on the wall for support, more confused than ever, scared to death. And angry. The system was rotten. He was sick of laws and lawyers and courts, of cops and agents and marshals, of reporters and judges and jailers. Dammit!

He yanked a paper towel from the wall and wiped his eyes, then sat on the toilet.

He swore to the walls that he would not go to New Orleans.

Two other deputy marshals would serve Dianne, and two more would serve Ms. Reggie Love at home, and all this serving of subpoenas was carefully coordinated to happen at roughly the same time. In reality, one deputy marshal, or one unemployed concrete worker for that matter, could have served all three subpoenas at a leisurely pace and completed the job in an hour. But it was more fun to use six men in three cars with radios and telephones and guns, and to strike quickly under cover of darkness like a Special Forces assault unit.

They knocked on Momma Love's kitchen door, and waited until the porch light came on and she appeared behind the screen. She instantly knew they were trouble. During the nightmare of Reggie's divorce and commitments and legal warfare with Joe Cardoni, there had been several deputies and men in dark suits standing at her doorway at odd hours. These guys always brought trouble.

'Can I help you?' she asked with a forced smile.

'Yes ma'am. We're looking for one Reggie Love.'

They even talked like cops. 'And who are you?' she asked.

'I'm Mike Hedley, and this is Terry Flagg. We're U.S. marshals.'

'U.S. marshals, or deputy U.S. marshals? Let me see some ID.'

This shocked them, and in perfect synchronization they reached into their pockets for their badges. 'We're deputy U.S. marshals, ma'am.'

'That's not what you said,' she said, examining the badges held up to the screen door.

Reggie was sipping coffee on the tiny balcony of her apartment when she heard the car doors slam. She was now peeking around the corner and looking down at the two men standing under the light. She could hear the voices, but could not understand what they were saying.

'Sorry, ma'am,' Hedley said.

'Why do you want one Reggie Love?' Momma Love asked with a suspicious frown.

'Does she live here?'

'Maybe, maybe not. What do you want?'

Hedley and Flagg looked at each other. 'We're supposed to serve her with a subpoena.'

'A subpoena for what?'

'May I ask who you are?' Flagg said.

'I'm her mother. Now what's the subpoena for?'

'It's a grand jury subpoena. She's supposed to appear before a grand jury in New Orleans on Monday. We can just leave it with you, if you like.'

'I'm not accepting service of it,' she said, as if she fought with process servers every week. 'You have to actually serve her, if I'm not mistaken.'

'Where is she?'

'She doesn't live here.'

This irritated them. 'That's her car,' Hedley said, nodding at Reggie's Mazda.

'She doesn't live here,' Momma Love repeated.

'Okay, but is she here now?'

'No.'

'Do you know where she is?'

'Have you tried her office? She works all the time.'

'But why is her car here?'

'Sometimes she rides with Clint, her secretary. They may be having dinner, or something.'

They gave each other frustrated stares. 'I think she's here,' Hedley said, suddenly aggressive.

'You're not paid to think, son. You're paid to serve those damned papers, and I'm telling you she's not here.' Momma Love raised her voice when she said this, and Reggie heard it.

'Can we search the house?' Flagg asked.

'If you have a warrant, you can search the house. If you don't have a warrant, it's time to get off my property.'

They both took a step back, and stopped. 'I hope you're not obstructing the service of a federal subpoena,' Hedley said gravely. It was supposed to have an ominous, dire ring to it, but Hedley failed miserably.

'And I hope you're not trying to threaten an old woman.' Her hands were on her hips and she was ready for combat.

They surrendered and backed away. 'We'll be back,' Hedley promised as he opened his car door.

'I'll be here,' she shouted angrily, opening the front door. She stood on the small porch and watched as they backed into the street. She waited for five minutes, and when she was certain they were gone, she went to Reggie's apartment over the garage.

Dianne took the subpoena from the polite and apologetic gentleman

285

without comment. She read it by the light of the dim lamp next to Ricky's bed. It contained no instructions, just a command for Mark to appear before the grand jury at 10 A.M. at the address below. There was no hint of how he was to get there; no clue as to when he might return; no warning of what could happen if he failed to comply or failed to talk.

She called Reggie, but there was no answer.

Though Clint's apartment was only fifteen minutes away, the drive took almost an hour. She zigzagged through midtown, then raced around the interstate going nowhere in particular, and when she was certain she was not being followed, she parked on a street crowded with empty cars. She walked four blocks to his apartment.

His nine o'clock date had been abruptly canceled, and it was a date with a lot of promise. 'I'm sorry,' Reggie said as he opened the door and she eased through it.

'That's okay. Are you all right?' He took her bag and waved at the sofa. 'Sit down.'

Reggie was no stranger to the apartment. She found a diet Coke in the refrigerator and sat on a bar stool. 'It was the U.S. marshal's office with a grand jury subpoena. Ten o'clock Monday morning in New Orleans.'

'But they didn't serve you?'

'No. Momma Love ran them off.'

'Then you're off the hook.'

'Yeah, unless they find me. There's no law against dodging subpoenas. I need to call Dianne.'

Clint handed her a phone, and she punched the numbers from memory. 'Relax, Reggie,' he said, and kissed her gently on the cheek. He picked up stray magazines and turned on the stereo. Dianne was on the phone, and Reggie managed three words before she was forced to listen. Subpoenas were everywhere. One for Reggie, one for Dianne, and one for Mark. Reggie tried to calm her. Dianne had called the detention center, but couldn't get through to Mark. Phones were unavailable at this hour, she'd been told. They talked for five minutes. Reggie, badly shaken herself, tried to convince Dianne everything was fine. She, Reggie, was in control. She promised to call her in the morning, then hung up.

'They can't take Mark,' Clint said. 'He's under the jurisdiction of our Juvenile Court.'

'I need to talk to Harry. But he's out of town.'

'Where is he?'

'Fishing somewhere with his sons.'

'This is more important than fishing, Reggie. Let's find him. He can stop it, can't he?'

She was thinking of a hundred things at once. 'This is pretty slick, Clint. Think about it. Foltrigg waits until late Friday to serve subpoenas for Monday morning.'

'How can he do this?'

'It's easy. He just did it. In a criminal case like this, a federal grand jury can subpoena any witness from anywhere, regardless of time and distance. And the witness must appear unless he or she can first quash the subpoena.'

'How do you quash one?'

'You file a motion in federal court to void the subpoena.'

'Lemme guess, federal court in New Orleans?'

'That's right. We're forced to find the trial judge early Monday morning in New Orleans and beg him to allow an emergency hearing to quash the subpoena.'

'It won't work, Reggie.'

'Of course it won't work. That's the way Foltrigg planned it.' She gulped the diet coke. 'Do you have any coffee?'

'Sure.' He began opening drawers.

Reggie was thinking out loud. 'If I can dodge the subpoena until Monday, Foltrigg will be forced to issue another one. Then maybe I'll have time to quash. The problem is Mark. They're not after me, because they know they can't force me to talk.'

'Do you know where the damned body is, Reggie?'

'No.'

'Does Mark?'

'Yes.'

He froze for a moment, then ran water in the pot.

'We have to figure out a way to keep Mark here, Clint. We can't allow him to go to New Orleans.'

'Call Harry.'

'Harry's fishing in the mountains.

'Then call Harry's wife. Find out where he's fishing in the mountains. I'll go get him if necessary.'

'You're right.' She grabbed the phone and started calling.

# CHAPTER THIRTY-TWO

Final room check at the Juvenile Detention Center was 10 P.M., when they made sure all lights and televisions were off. Mark heard Telda rattling keys and giving commands across the hall. His shirt was soaked, unbuttoned, and sweat ran to his navel and puddled around the zipper of his jeans. The television was off. His breathing was heavy. His thick hair was watery and rows of sweat ran to his eyebrows and dripped from the tip of his nose. She was next door. His face was crimson and hot.

Telda knocked, then unlocked Mark's door. The light was on and this immediately irritated her. She took a step inside, glanced at the bunks, but he wasn't there.

Then she saw his feet beside the toilet. He was curled tightly with his knees on his chest, motionless except for rapid, heavy breathing. His eyes were closed and his left thumb was in his mouth.

'Mark!' she shouted, suddenly terrified. 'Mark! Oh my god!' She ran from the room to get help, and was back within seconds with Denny, her partner, who took a quick look.

'Doreen was worried about this,' Denny said, touching the sweat on Mark's stomach. 'Damn, he's soaking wet.'

Telda was pinching his wrist. 'His pulse is crazy. Look at him breathe. Call an ambulance!'

'The poor kid's in shock, isn't he?'

'Go call an ambulance!'

Denny lumbered from the room and the floor shook. Telda picked Mark up and carefully placed him on the bottom bunk, where he curled again and brought his knees to his chest. The thumb never left his mouth. Denny was back with a clipboard. 'This must be Doreen's handwriting. Says here to check on him every half hour, and if there's any doubt, to rush him to St. Peter's and call Dr. Greenway.'

'This is all my fault,' Telda said. 'I shouldn't have allowed those damned marshals in here. Scared the poor boy to death.'

Denny knelt beside her, and with a thick thumb peeled back the right eyelid. 'Damn! His eyes have rolled back. This kid's in trouble,' he said with all the gravity of a brain surgeon.

'Get a washcloth over here,' Telda said, and Denny did as told. 'Doreen was telling me this is what happened to his little brother. They saw that shooting on Monday, both of them, and the little one's been in shock ever since.' Denny handed her the cloth and she wiped Mark's forehead.'

'Damn, his heart's gonna explode,' Denny said, on his knees again next to Telda. 'He's breathing like crazy.'

'Poor kid. I should've run those marshals off,' Telda said.

'I would have. They got no right coming on this floor.' He jabbed another thumb into the left eye, and Mark groaned and twitched. Then he started the moaning, just like Ricky, and this scared them even more. A low, dull, pitchless sound from deep in the throat. He sucked hard on the thumb.

A paramedic from the main jail three floors down ran into the room, followed by another jailer. 'What's up?' he asked as Telda and Denny moved.

'I think it's called traumatic shock or stress or something,' Telda said. 'He's been acting strange all day, then about an hour ago two U.S. marshals were here to give him a subpoena.' The paramedic was not listening. He gripped a wrist and found the pulse. Telda rattled on. 'They scared him to death, and I think it sent him into shock. I should've watched him after that, but I got busy.'

'I would've run those damned marshals off,' Denny said. They stood side by side behind the paramedic.

'This is what happened to his little brother, you know, the one who's been in the newspaper all week. The shooting and all.'

'He's gotta go,' the paramedic said, standing, frowning, and talking into his radio. 'Hurry up with the stretcher to the fourth floor,' he barked into it. 'Got a kid in bad shape.'

Denny stuck the clipboard in front of the paramedic. 'Says here to take him to St. Peter's. Dr. Greenway.'

'That's where his brother is,' Telda added. 'Doreen told me all about it. She was worried this might happen. Said she almost sent for an ambulance this afternoon. Said he's been slipping away all day. I should've been more careful.'

The stretcher arrived with two more paramedics. Mark was quickly laid on it and covered with a blanket. A strap was placed across his thighs and another on his chest. His eyes never opened, but he managed to keep the thumb in his mouth.

And he managed to emit the painful, monotonous groan that frightened the paramedics and sped the stretcher along. It rolled quickly past the front station, and into an elevator.

'You ever seen this before?' one paramedic mumbled under his breath to the other.

'Not that I recall.'

'He's burning up.'

'The skin is normally cool and clammy with shock. I've never seen this.'

'Yeah. Maybe traumatic shock is different. Check out that thumb.'

'Is this the kid the mob's after?'

'Yeah. Front page today and yesterday.'

'I guess he's gone over the edge.'

The elevator stopped, and they pushed the stretcher hurriedly through a series of short hallways, all busy and filled with the usual Friday night madness of city jail. A set of double doors flew open, and they were at the ambulance.

The ride to St. Peter's took less than ten minutes, half as long as the wait once they arrived. Three other ambulances were in the process of depositing their occupants. St. Peter's received the vast majority of Memphis knife wounds, gunshot victims, beaten wives, and mangled bodies from weekend car wrecks. The pace was hectic twenty-four hours a day, but from sunset Friday until late Sunday, the place was in chaos.

They rolled him through the bay and onto the white-tiled floors where the stretcher stopped and the paramedics waited and filled out forms. A small army of nurses and doctors scrambled around a new patient and all yelled at the same time. People ran in every direction. A half dozen cops milled about. Three more stretchers were parked haphazardly in the wide hallway.

A nurse ventured by, stopped for a second, and asked the paramedics, 'What is it?' One of them handed her a form.

'So he's not bleeding,' she said, as if nothing mattered except flowing blood.

'No. Looks like stress or shock or something. Runs in the family.'

'He can wait. Roll him to Intake. I'll be back in a minute.' And she was off.

They wove the stretcher through heavy traffic, and stopped in a small room off the main hallway. The forms were presented to another nurse, who scribbled something without looking at Mark. 'Where's Dr. Greenway?' she asked the paramedics.

They looked at each other, and shrugged at the nurse.

'You haven't called him?' she asked.

'Well, no.'

'Well, no,' she repeated to herself and rolled her eyes. What a couple of dumbasses. 'Look, this is a war zone, okay. We're talking blood and guts. We've lost two people in that hallway right there in the past thirty minutes. Psychiatric emergencies do not get top priority around here.'

'You want us to shoot him?' one of them said, nodding at Mark, and this really pissed her off.

'No. I want you to leave. I'll take care of him, but you guys just get the hell out of here.'

'You signed the forms, lady. He's all yours.' They smiled at her, and headed for the door.

'Is there a policeman with him?' she asked.

'Nope. He's just a juvenile.' They were gone.

Mark managed to roll onto his left side and bring his knees to his chest. The straps were not tight. His eyes opened slightly. A black man was lying across three chairs in one corner of the room. An empty stretcher with blood on the sheets was by a green door next to a water fountain. The nurse answered the phone, said a few words, and left the room. Mark quickly unhooked the straps and jumped to the floor. There was no crime in walking around. He was a nut case now, so what if she caught him on his feet.

The forms she'd been holding were on the counter. He grabbed them, and pushed the stretcher through the green door, which led to a cramped corridor with small rooms on both sides. He abandoned the stretcher and threw the forms in a garbage can. The exit signs led to a door with a window in it. It opened into the madhouse of Admissions.

Mark smiled to himself. He'e been here before. He watched the chaos through the window and picked the spot where he and Hardy had stood after Greenway and Dianne disappeared with Ricky. He eased through the door, and casually made his way through the snarled throng of sick and wounded trying anxiously to get admitted. Running and darting might attract attention, so he played it cool. He rode his favorite escalator to the basement, and found an empty wheelchair by the stairs. It was adult-size, but he worked the wheels and rolled himself past the cafeteria to the morgue.

Clint had fallen asleep on the sofa. Letterman was almost over when the phone rang. Reggie grabbed it. 'Hello.'

'Hi, Reggie. It's me, Mark.'

'Mark! How are you, dear?'

'Doing great, Reggie. Just wonderful.'

'How'd you find me?' she asked, turning off the TV.

'I called Momma Love and woke her. She gave me this number. It's Clint's place, right?'

'Right. How'd you get to a phone? It's awful late.'

'Well, I'm not in jail anymore.'

291

She stood and walked to the snack bar. 'Where are you, dear?'

'At the hospital. St. Peter's.'

'I see. And how'd you get there?'

'They brought me in an ambulance.'

'Are you okay?'

'Great.'

'Why'd they take you in an ambulance?'

'I had an attack of post-traumatic stress syndrome, and they rushed me over.'

'Should I come see you?'

'Maybe. What's this grand jury stuff?'

'Nothing but an attempt to scare you into talking.'

'Well, it worked. I'm more scared than ever.'

'You sound fine.'

'Nervous energy, Reggie. I'm scared to death.'

'I mean, you don't sound like you're in shock or anything.'

'I recovered real quick. I faked them out, Reggie, okay? I jogged in my little cell for half an hour, and when they found me I was soaking wet and in bad shape, as they say.'

Clint sat up on the sofa and listened intently.

'Have you seen a doctor?' she asked, frowning at Clint.

'Not exactly.'

'What does that mean?'

'It means I walked out of the emergency room. It means I've escaped, Reggie. It was so easy.'

'Oh my god!'

'Relax. I'm fine. I'm not going back to jail, Reggie. And I'm not going to see the grand jury in New Orleans. They'll just lock me up down there, won't they?'

'Listen, Mark, you can't do this. You can't escape. You must – '

'I've already escaped, Reggie. And you know something?'

'What?'

'I doubt if anyone knows it yet. This place is so crazy, I doubt if they've missed me yet.'

'What about the cops?'

'What cops?'

'Didn't a cop go with you to the hospital?'

'No. I'm just a kid, Reggie. I had two huge paramedics, but I'm just a little kid and at the time I was in a coma, sucking my thumb, moaning and groaning, just like Ricky. You'd have been proud. It was like something out of a movie. Once I got here, they turned their backs, and just like that, I walked away.'

'You can't do this, Mark.'

'It's done, okay? And I'm not going back.'

'What about your mother?'

'Oh, I talked to her about an hour ago, by phone of course. She freaked out, but I convinced her I was fine. She didn't like it, told me to come to Ricky's room. We had a big fight over the phone, but she settled down. I think she's on pills again.'

'But you're at the hospital?'

'That's right.'

'Where? In which room?'

'Are you still my lawyer?'

'Of course I'm your lawyer.'

'Good. So if I tell you something, you can't repeat it, right?'

'Right.'

'Are you my friend, Reggie?'

'Of course I'm your friend.'

'That's good, because right now you're the only friend I have. Will you help me, Reggie? I'm really scared.'

'I'll do anything, Mark. Where are you?'

'In the morgue. There's a little office in the corner, and I'm hiding under the desk. The lights are off. If I hang up real quick, you'll know somebody walked in. They've brought in two bodies while I've been here, but so far no one's come to the office.'

'The morgue?'

Clint bolted to his feet and stood beside her.

'Yeah. I've been here before. I know this place pretty well, remember.'

'Sure.'

'Who's in the morgue?' Clint whispered. She frowned at him and shook her head.

'Mom said they have a subpoena for you too, Reggie. Is this true?'

'Yes, but they haven't served me. That's why I'm here at Clint's. If they don't hand me the subpoena, then I don't have to go.'

'So you're hiding too?'

'I guess.'

Suddenly his end clicked and the dial tone followed. She stared at the receiver, then quickly placed it on the phone. 'He hung up,' she said.

'What the hell's going on!' Clint asked.

'It's Mark. He's escaped from jail.'

'He what!'

'He's hiding in the morgue at St. Peter's.' She said this as if she didn't believe it. The phone rang, and she snatched it. 'Hello.'

'Sorry about that. The door to the morgue opened, then closed. I thought they were bringing in another body.'

'Are you safe, Mark?'

'Hell no, I'm not safe. But I'm a kid, okay. And now I'm a psychiatric case. So if they catch me, I'll just go into shock again and they'll put me in a room. Then I'll figure out another way to escape, maybe.'

'You can't hide forever.'

'Neither can you.'

She marveled once again at his quick tongue. 'You're right, Mark. So what do we do?'

'I don't know. I really would like to leave Memphis. I'm sick of cops and jails.'

'Where do you want to go?'

'Well, let me ask you something. If you come and get me, and we leave town together, then you could get in trouble for helping me escape. Right?'

'Yes. I'd be an accomplice.'

'What would they do to you?'

'We'll worry about that later. I've done worse things.'

'So you'll help me?'

'Yes, Mark. I'll help you.'

'And you won't tell anybody?'

'We may need Clint.'

'Okay, you can tell Clint. But nobody else, okay?'

'You have my word.'

'And you won't try to talk me into going back to jail?'

'I promise.'

There was a long pause. Clint was near panic.

'Okay, Reggie. You know the main parking lot, the one next to that big green building?'

'Yes.'

'Drive into it, just like you're looking for a place to park. Go real slow. I'll be hiding between some cars.'

'That place is dark and dangerous, Mark.'

'It's Friday night, Reggie. Everything around here is dark and dangerous.'

'But there's a guard in the exit booth.'

'That guard sleeps half the time. It's a guard, not a cop. I know what I'm doing, okay?'

'Are you sure?'

'No. But you said you'd help me.'

'I will. When should I be there?'

294

'As fast as you can.'

'I'll be in Clint's car. It's a black Honda Accord.'

'Good. Hurry.'

'I'm on my way. Be careful, Mark.'

'Relax, Reggie. This is just like the movies.'

She hung up, and took a deep breath.

'My car?' Clint asked.

'They're looking for me too.'

'You're crazy, Reggie. This is insane. You can't run away with an escaped, I don't know, whatever the hell he is. They'll arrest you for contributing. You'll be indicted. You'll lose your license.'

'Where's my bag?'

'In the bedroom.'

'I need your keys, and your credit cards.'

'My credit cards! Look, Reggie, I love you, sweetheart, but my car and my plastic?'

'How much cash do you have?'

'Forty bucks.'

'Give it here. I'll pay you back.' She headed for the bedroom.

'You've lost your mind.'

'I've lost it before, remember.'

'Come on, Reggie.'

'Get a grip, Clint. We're not blowing anything. I've got to help Mark. He's sitting in a dark office in the morgue at St. Peter's begging for help. What am I supposed to do?'

'Well, hell! I think you should attack the place with a shotgun and blow people away. Anything for Mark Sway.'

She threw her toothbrush in a canvas bag. 'Give me the credit cards and the cash, Clint. I'm in a hurry.'

He reached in his pockets. 'You're nuts. This is ridiculous.'

'Stay by the phone. Do not leave this place, okay. I'll call you later.' She grabbed his keys, cash, and two credit cards – Visa and Texaco.

He followed her to the door. 'Take it easy with the Visa. It's almost to the limit.'

'Why am I not surprised?' She kissed him on the cheek. 'Thanks, Clint. Take care of Momma Love.'

'Call me,' he said, thoroughly defeated.

She eased through the door and disappeared in the darkness.

# CHAPTER THIRTY-THREE

From the moment Mark jumped into the car and hid on the floor, Reggie became an accomplice to his escape. But, unless he murdered someone before they were caught, it was doubtful her crime would be punishable by incarceration. She was thinking more along the lines of community service, perhaps a bit of restitution, and forty years of probation. Hell, she'd give them all the probation they wanted. It would be her first offense. She, and her lawyer, could make a strong argument that the kid was being hunted by the Mafia, and he was all alone, and, well, dammit, somebody had to do something! She couldn't worry about legal niceties when her client was out there begging for help. Maybe she could pull strings and keep her license to practice.

She paid the parking guard fifty cents, and refused eye contact. She had circled through the lot one time. The guard was in another world. Mark was rolled into a tight coil somewhere in the darkness under the dashboard, and he remained there until she turned on Union and headed for the river.

'Is it safe now?' he asked nervously.

'I think so.'

He sprang into the seat, and surveyed the landscape. The digital clock gave the time as twelve-fifty. The six lanes of Union Avenue were deserted. She drove three blocks, catching red lights at each one, while waiting for Mark to speak.

'So where are we going?' she finally asked.

'The Alamo.'

'The Alamo?' she repeated without a trace of a smile.

He shook his head. Adults could be so dumb at times. 'It's a joke, Reggie.'

'Sorry.'

'I take it you haven't seen *Pee-Wee's Big Adventure*.'

'Is that a movie?'

'Forget it. Just forget it.' They waited for another red light.

'I like your car better,' he said, rubbing his hand along the Accord's console and taking a sudden interest in the radio.

'That's good, Mark. This street is about to stop at the river, and I think we should discuss exactly where it is you want to go.'

'Well, right now, I just want to leave Memphis, okay? I really don't care where we go, I just want to get out of Dodge.'

'And once we leave Memphis, where might we be going? A destination would be nice.'

'Let's cross the bridge by the Pyramid, okay?'

'Fair enough. You want to go to Arkansas?'

'Why not? Yeah, sure, let's go to Arkansas.'

'Fair enough.'

With that decision out of the way, he leaned forward and carefully inspected the radio. He pushed a button, turned a knob, and Reggie braced for a loud burst of rap or heavy metal. He made adjustments with both hands. Just a kid with a new toy. He should be home in a warm bed, and he should sleep late since it's Saturday. And fresh from bed he should watch cartoons, then, still in pajamas, play Nintendo with all its buttons and gadgets, much like he was doing right then with the radio. The Four Tops finished a song.

'You listen to oldies?' she asked, genuinely surprised.

'Sometimes. I thought you'd like it. It's almost one o'clock in the morning, not the best time for the loud stuff, you know.'

'Why do you think I like oldies?'

'Well, Reggie, to be perfectly honest, I can't see you at a rap concert. And besides, the radio in your car was on this station last time I rode in it.'

Union Avenue stopped at the river, and they sat at another red light. A police car stopped next to them, and the cop behind the wheel frowned at Mark.

'Don't look at him,' Reggie scolded.

The light changed, and she turned right onto Riverside Drive. The cop followed. 'Don't turn around,' she said under her breath. 'Just act normal.'

'Damn, Reggie, why is he following us?'

'I have no idea. Just be cool.'

'He recognized me. My face has been plastered all over the newspapers this week, and the cop recognized me. This is just great, Reggie. We make our big escape, and ten minutes later the cops nail us.'

'Be quiet, Mark. I'm trying to drive and watch him at the same time.'

He eased downward, sliding slowly until his butt was on the edge of the seat and his head was just above the door handle. 'What's he doing?' he whispered.

Her eyes darted back and forth from the mirror to the street. 'Just following. No, wait. Here he comes.'

The police car eased by them, then sped away. 'He's gone,' she said, and Mark breathed again.

They entered I-40 at the downtown ramp, and were on the bridge over the Mississippi River. He gazed at the brightly lit Pyramid to the right, then spun around to admire the Memphis skyline fading in the distance. He stared in awe, as if he'd never seen it before. Reggie wondered if the poor child had ever left Memphis.

An Elvis song started. 'You like Elvis?' he asked.

'Mark, believe it or not, when I was a teenager growing up in Memphis, a bunch of us girls would ride over to Elvis's house on Sundays and watch him play touch football. This was before he was really famous, and he still lived at home with his parents in a nice little house. He went to Humes High School, which is now Northside.'

'I live in north Memphis. At least I did. I don't know where I live now.'

'We'd go to his concerts, and we'd see him hanging out around town. He was just an average guy, at first, then things changed. He got so famous he couldn't live a normal life.'

'Just like me, Reggie,' he said with a sudden smile. 'Think of it. Me and Elvis. Pictures on the front page. Photographers everywhere. All sorts of people looking for us. It's tough being famous.'

'Yeah, and wait till tomorrow, in the Sunday paper. I can see the headlines now, big, bold letters – "SWAY ESCAPES".'

'It's great! And they'll have my smiling face on the front page again with cops all around me like I'm some kind of serial killer. And those same cops will sound so stupid trying to explain how an eleven-year-old kid escaped from jail. I wonder if I'm the youngest kid to ever escape from jail.'

'Probably.'

'I do feel sorry for Doreen, though. Do you think she'll get in trouble?'

'Was she on duty?'

'No. It was Telda and Denny. Wouldn't bother me if they got fired.'

'Doreen's probably okay. She's been there a long time.'

'I faked her out, you know. I started acting like I was going into shock, just fading away to La La Land as Romey called it. Every time she checked on me, I acted weirder and weirder; quit talking to her, just stared at the ceiling and groaned. She knows all about Ricky, and she became convinced it was happening to me too. Yesterday, she brought in a medic from the jail, and he examined me. Said I was fine. But Doreen was worried. I guess I used her.'

'How'd you get out?'

'Played like I was in shock, you know. I worked up a good sweat running around my little cell, then curled up in a ball and sucked my thumb. It scared them so bad, they called the ambulance. I knew if I could make it to St. Peter's, I was home free. That place is a zoo.'

'And you just disappeared?'

'They had me on this stretcher, and when they turned their backs I got up and, yeah, just disappeared. Look, Reggie, there were people dying right and left, so no one was concerned with me. It was easy.'

They were over the bridge and into Arkansas. The highway was flat and lined on both sides by truck stops and motels. He turned to admire the Memphis skyline once more, but it was gone.

'What are you looking for?' she asked.

'Memphis. I like to look at the tall buildings downtown. A teacher told me once that people actually live in those tall buildings. It's hard to believe.'

'Why is it hard to believe?'

'I saw a movie once about this little rich kid who lived in a tall building in a city, and he roamed around the streets just having a great time. He knew the cops by their first names. He stopped taxis when he wanted to go somewhere. And at night, he'd sit on the balcony and watch the streets below. I've always thought that would be a wonderful way to live. No cheap house trailers. No trashy neighbors. No pickups parked in the street in front of your house.'

'You can have it, Mark. It's yours, if you want it.'

He gave her a long look. 'How?'

'Right now the FBI will give you whatever you want. You can live in a tall building in a big city, or you can live in a cabin in the mountains. You pick the place.'

'I've been thinking about that.'

'You can live on a beach and play in the ocean, or you can live in Orlando and go to Disney World every day.'

'That'd be okay for Ricky. I'm too old. I've heard the tickets are too expensive.'

'You'd probably get a lifetime pass, if you asked for it. Right now, Mark, you and your mom can get anything you want.'

'Yeah, but, Reggie, who wants it if you're afraid of your shadow. For three nights now, I've had nightmares about these people, Reggie. I don't want to be scared for the rest of my life. They'll get me one day, I know they will.'

'So what do you do, Mark?'

'I don't know, but I've been thinking real hard about something.'

'I'm listening.'

'One good thing about jail is that it allows you to think a lot.' He placed one foot on one knee and wrapped his fingers around it. 'Think about this, Reggie. What if Romey told me a lie? He was drunk, taking pills, out of his mind. Maybe he was just talking to hear himself talk. I was there, remember. The man was crazy. Said all sorts of weird things, and at first I believed all of it. I was scared to death, and I wasn't thinking clearly. My head was hurting where he'd slapped me. But now, well, I'm not so sure. All week I've been remembering crazy stuff he said and did, and maybe I was too eager to believe everything.'

She was driving exactly fifty-five miles per hour and hanging on every word. She had no idea where he was going with this, and she had no idea where the car was going either.

'But I couldn't take a chance, right? I mean, what if I'd told the cops everything and they found the body right where Romey said? Everybody's happy but the Mafia, and who knows what would happen to me. And what if I'd told the cops everything, but Romey was lying and they found no body. I'm off the hook, right, because in reality I didn't know anything at all. What a joker, that Romey. But it was too big of a risk.' He paused for half a mile. The Beach Boys sang 'California Girls.' 'So I've had a brainstorm.'

By now, she could almost feel this brainstorm. Her heart stopped and she managed to keep the wheels between the white lines of the right lane. 'And what might that be?' she asked nervously.

'I think we should see if Romey was lying or not.'

She cleared her dry throat. 'You mean, go find the body.'

'That's right.'

She wanted to laugh at this innocent humor of a hyperactive mind, but at the moment she didn't have the strength. 'You must be kidding.'

'Well, let's talk about it. You and I are both expected to be in New Orleans Monday morning, right?'

'I guess. I haven't seen a subpoena.'

'But I'm your client, and I've got a subpoena. So even if they didn't give you one, you'd still have to go with me, right?'

'That's true.'

'And now we're on the run, right? Just you and me, Bonnie and Clyde, running from the cops.'

'I guess you could say that.'

'Where's the last place they'd look for us? Think about it, Reggie. Where's the last place in the world they'd expect us to run to?'

'New Orleans.'

300

'Right. Now, I don't know anything about hiding out, but since you're dodging a subpoena and you're a lawyer and all, and you deal with criminals all the time, I figure you could get us to New Orleans and no one would know it. Right?'

'I suppose so.' She was beginning to agree with him, and she was shocked by her own words.

'And if you can get us to New Orleans, then we'll find Romey's house.'

'Why Romey's house?'

'That's where the body's supposed to be.'

This was the last thing in the world she wanted to know. She slowly removed her glasses and rubbed her eyes. A slight headache was forming between her temples, and it would only get worse.

Romey's house? The home of Jerome Clifford, deceased? He had said this very slowly, and she had heard it very slowly. She glared at taillights in front of them but there was nothing but a red blur. Romey's house? The victim of the murder was buried at the home of the accused's lawyer. This was beyond bizarre. Her mind raced wildly in circles asking itself a hundred questions and answering none of them. She glanced in the mirror, and was suddenly aware that he was staring at her with a curious smile.

'Now you know, Reggie,' he said.

'But how, why – '

'Don't ask because I don't know. It's crazy, isn't it? That's why I think Romey could've made it up. A crazy mind created this weird story about the body being at his house.'

'So, you don't think it's really there?' she asked, seeking reassurance.'

'We won't know until we look. If it's not there, I'm off the hook and life returns to normal.'

'But what if it's there?'

'We'll worry about that when we find it.'

'I don't like your brainstorm.'

'Why not?'

'Look, Mark, son, client, friend, if you think I'm going to New Orleans to dig up a dead body, then you're crazy.'

'Of course I'm crazy. Me and Ricky, just a couple of nut cases.'

'I won't do it.'

'Why not, Reggie?'

'It's much too dangerous, Mark. It's insane, and it could get us killed. I won't go, and I can't let you do it.'

'Why is it dangerous?'

301

'Well, it's just dangerous. I don't know.'

'Think about it, Reggie. We check on the body, okay. Then if it's not where Romey said, I'm home free. We'll tell the cops to drop everything against us, and in return I'll tell them what I know. And since I don't know where the body really is, the Mafia couldn't care less about me. We walk.'

We walk. Too much television. 'And if we find the body?'

'Good question. Think about this slowly, Reggie. Try and think like a kid. If we find the body, and then you call the FBI and tell them you know exactly where it is because you've seen it with your own eyes, then they'll give us anything we want.'

'And what exactly do you want?'

'Probably Australia. A nice house, plenty of money for my mother. New car. Maybe some plastic surgery. I saw that once in a movie. They rearranged this guy's entire face. He was dog ugly to start with, and he snitched on some drug dealers just so he could get a new face. Looked like a movie star when it was over. About two years later, the drug dealers gave him another new face.'

'You're serious?'

'About the movie?'

'No, about Australia.'

'Maybe.' He paused and looked out the window. 'Maybe.'

They listened to the radio and didn't speak for several miles. Traffic was light, Memphis was farther away.

'Let's make a deal,' he said, looking out his window.

'Maybe.'

'Let's go to New Orleans.'

'I'm not digging for a body.'

'Okay, okay. But let's go there. No one will expect us. We'll talk about the body when we get there.'

'We've already talked about it.'

'Just go to New Orleans, okay?'

The highway intersected another one, and they were on top of an overpass. She pointed to her right. Ten miles away, the Memphis skyline glowed and flickered under a half-moon. 'Wow,' he said in awe. 'It's beautiful.'

Neither of them could know that it would be his last look at Memphis.

They stopped in Forrest City, Arkansas, for gas and snacks. Reggie paid for cupcakes, a large coffee, and a Sprite, while Mark hid on the floor. Minutes later, they were back on the interstate headed for Little Rock.

Steam poured from the Styrofoam cup as she drove and watched him inhale four cupcakes. He ate like a kid – crumbs on his pants and in the seat, cream filling on his fingers, which he licked as if he hadn't seen food in a month. It was almost two-thirty. The road was empty except for convoys of tractor-trailer rigs. She set the cruise control on sixty-five.

'Do you think they're chasing us yet?' he asked, finishing the last cupcake and opening the Sprite. There was a certain excitement in his voice.

'I doubt it. I'm sure the police are searching the hospital, but why would they suspect we're together?'

'I'm worried about Mom. I called her, you know, before I called you. Told her about the escape, and that I was hiding in the hospital. She got real mad. But I think I convinced her I'm safe. I hope they don't give her a hard time.'

'They won't. But she'll worry herself sick.'

'I know. I don't mean to be cruel, but I think she can handle it. Look at what she's already been through. My mom's pretty tough.'

'I'll tell Clint to call her later today.'

'Are you going to tell Clint where we're going?'

'I'm not sure where we're going.'

He thought about this as two trucks roared by and the Honda veered to the right.

'What would you do, Reggie?'

'For starters, I don't think I would have escaped.'

'That's a lie.'

'I beg your pardon.'

'Sure it is. You're dodging a subpoena, aren't you? I'm doing the same thing. So what's the difference? You don't want to face the grand jury. I don't want to face the grand jury, so here we are on the run. We're in the same boat, Reggie.'

'There's only one difference. You were in jail, and you escaped. That's a crime.'

'I was in a jail for juveniles, and juveniles do not commit crimes. Isn't that what you told me? Juveniles are rowdy, or delinquent, or in need of supervision, but juveniles do not commit crimes. Right?'

'If you say so. But it was wrong to escape.'

'It's done. I can't undo it. It's wrong for you to dodge the law too, isn't it?'

'Absolutely not. There's no crime in avoiding a subpoena. I was doing fine until I picked you up.'

'Then stop the car and let me out.'

'Oh sure. Please be serious, Mark.'

'I am serious.'

'Right. And what'll you do when you get out?'

'Oh, I don't know. I'll go as far as I can, and if I get caught then I'll just go into shock and they'll send me back to Memphis. I'll claim I was crazy, and they'll never know you were involved. Just stop any-time you feel like it, and I'll get out.' He leaned forward and punched the seek button on the radio. For five minutes they listened to Con-way Twitty and Tammy Wynette.

'I hate country music,' she said, and he turned it off.

'Can I ask you something?' she said.

'Sure.'

'Suppose we go to New Orleans and find the body. And, according to your plan, we then cut a deal with the FBI and you go into their witness protection plan. You, Dianne, and Ricky then fly off into the sunset to Australia or wherever, right?'

'I guess.'

'Then, why not cut a deal and tell them now?'

'Now you're thinking, Reggie,' he said, patronizingly, as if she'd finally awakened and was beginning to see the light.

'Thank you so much,' she said.

'It took me a while to figure it out. The answer is easy. I don't com-pletely trust the FBI. Do you?'

'Not completely.'

'And I'm not willing to give them what they want until me, my mother, and my brother are already far away. You're a good lawyer, Reggie, and you wouldn't allow your client to take any chances, would you?'

'Go on.'

'Before I tell these clowns anything, I want to make sure we are safely put away somewhere. It'll take some time to move Ricky. If I told them now, the bad guys might find out before we can disappear. It's too risky.'

'But what if you told them now, and they didn't find the body? What if Clifford was, as you say, joking?'

'I would never know, would I? I'd be undercover somewhere, get-ting a nose job, changing my name to Tommy or something, and all of it would be for nothing. It makes more sense to know now, Reggie, if Romey told me the truth.'

She shook her bewildered head. 'I'm not sure I follow you.'

'I'm not sure I follow me, either. But one thing is for certain: I'm not going to New Orleans with the U.S. marshals. I'm not going to face the grand jury on Monday and refuse to answer questions so they can throw my little butt in jail down there.'

'Good point. So how do we spend our weekend?'

'How far is it to New Orleans?'

'Five or six hours.'

'Let's go. We can always chicken out once we get there.'

'How much trouble will it be to find the body?'

'Probably not much.'

'Can I ask where it is at Clifford's house?'

'Well, it's not hanging in a tree or lying in the bushes. It'll take a little work.'

'This is completely crazy, Mark.'

'I know. It's been a bad week.'

# CHAPTER THIRTY-FOUR

So much for a quiet Saturday morning with the kids. Jason McThune studied his feet on the rug next to his bed, and tried to focus on the clock on the wall by the bathroom door. It was almost six, still dark outside, and the cobwebs from a late night bottle of wine blurred his eyes. His wife rolled over and grunted something he could not understand.

Twenty minutes later, he found her deep under the covers and kissed her good-bye. He might not be home for a week, he said, but doubted if she heard. Saturdays at work and days out of town were the norm. Nothing unusual.

But today would be unusual. He opened the door and the dog ran into the backyard. How could an eleven-year-old kid simply disappear? The Memphis Police had no idea. He just vanished, the lieutenant said.

Not surprisingly, traffic was light in the predawn hours as he headed for the Federal Building downtown. He punched numbers on his car phone. Agents Brenner, Latchee, and Durston were roused from sleep and instructed to meet him immediately. He flipped through his black book and found the Alexandria number for K. O. Lewis.

K.O. was not asleep, but neither was he in the mood to be disturbed. He was eating his oatmeal, enjoying his coffee, chatting with his wife, and just how in the hell could an eleven-year-old kid disappear while in police custody? he demanded. McThune told him what he knew, which was nothing, and asked him to be ready to come to Memphis. It could be a long weekend. K.O. said he would make a couple of calls, find the jet, and call him back at the office.

At the office McThune called Larry Trumann in New Orleans, and was delighted when Trumann answered the phone disoriented and obviously trying to sleep. This was Trumann's case, though McThune had worked on it all week. And just for fun, he called George Ord and asked him to come on down with the rest of the gang. McThune explained he was hungry, and could George please bring some Egg McMuffins.

By seven, Brenner, Latchee, and Durston were in his office gulping coffee and speculating wildly. Ord arrived next without the food, then two uniformed Memphis policemen knocked on the door to the outer office. Ray Trimble, Deputy Chief of Police and a legend in Memphis law enforcement, was with them.

They assembled in McThune's office, and Trimble, in fluent cop-talk, got right to the point. 'Subject was transported from the detention center by ambulance to St. Peter's around ten-thirty last night. Subject was signed in by the paramedics at St. Peter's ER, at which time the paramedics left. Subject was not accompanied by Memphis Police or jail personnel. Paramedics are certain a nurse, one Gloria Watts, female white, signed subject in, but no paperwork can be found. Ms. Watts has stated she had subject in ER Intake Room, and was called out of room for an undetermined reason. She was absent for no more than ten minutes, and upon her return, subject was gone. The paperwork was gone too, and Ms. Watts assumed subject had been taken to ER for examination and treatment.' Trimble slowed a bit and cleared his throat as if this was somehow unpleasant. 'At approximately five this morning, Ms. Watts was evidently preparing to leave her shift, and she checked the Intake records. She thought of the subject, and began asking questions. Subject could not be found in ER, and Admissions had no record of his arrival. Hospital Security was called, then Memphis PD. At this time, a thorough search of the hospital is under way.'

'Six hours,' McThune said in disbelief.

'I beg your pardon,' Trimble said.

'It took six hours to realize the kid was missing.'

'Yes sir, but we don't run the hospital, you see.'

'Why was the kid transported to the hospital without security?'

'I can't answer that. An investigation will be undertaken. It looks like an oversight.'

'Why was the kid taken to the hospital?'

Trimble took a file from a briefcase, and handed McThune a copy of Telda's report. He read it carefully. 'Says he went into shock after the U.S. marshals left. What the hell were the marshals doing there?'

Trimble opened the file again, and handed McThune the subpoena. He read it carefully, then handed it to George Ord.

'Anything else, Chief?' he said to Trimble, who had never taken a seat and had never stopped pacing slightly. He was anxious to leave.

'No sir. We'll complete the search, and call you immediately if we find anything. We've got about four dozen men there right now, and we've been checking for a little over an hour.'

'Have you talked to the kid's mother?'

'No sir. Not yet. She's still asleep. We're watching the room in case he tries to get to her.'

'I'll talk to her first, Chief. I'll be over in about an hour. Make sure no one sees her before I do.'

'No problem.'

'Thank you, Chief.' Trimble clicked his heels together, and for an instant looked as though he wanted to salute. He was gone, along with his officers.

McThune looked at Brenner and Latchee. 'You guys call every available agent. Get them here right now. Immediately.' They bolted from the room.

'What about the subpoena?' he asked Ord, who was still holding it.

'I can't believe it. Foltrigg's lost his mind.'

'You knew nothing about it?'

'Of course not. This kid is under the jurisdiction of the Juvenile Court. I wouldn't think of trying to reach him. Would you want to piss off Harry Roosevelt?'

'I don't think so. We need to call him. I'll do it, and you call Reggie Love. I'd rather not talk to her.'

Ord left the room to find a phone. 'Call the U.S. marshal,' McThune snapped at Durston. 'Get the scoop on this subpoena. I want to know everything about it.'

Durston left, and suddenly McThune was alone. He raced through a phone book until he found the Roosevelts. But there was no Harry. If he had a number, it was unlisted, and that was perfectly understandable with no less than fifty thousand single mothers trying to collect unpaid child support. McThune made three quick calls to lawyers he knew, and the third one said that Harry lived on Kensington Street. He would send an agent when he could spare one.

Ord returned shaking his head. 'I talked to Reggie Love's mother, but she asked more questions than I did. I don't think she's there.'

'I'll send two men as soon as possible. I guess you'd better call Foltrigg, the dumbass.'

'Yeah, I guess you're right.' Ord turned and left the office again.

At eight, McThune left the elevator on the ninth floor of St. Peter's with Brenner and Durston following close behind. Three more agents, decked out in a splendid variety of hospital garb, met him at the elevator and walked with him to Room 943. Three massive security guards stood near the door. McThune knocked gently, and motioned for his small squadron to back away. He didn't want to scare the poor woman.

The door opened slightly. 'Yes,' came a weak voice from the darkness.

'Ms. Sway, I'm Jason McThune, Special Agent, FBI. I saw you in court yesterday.'

The door opened wider, and Dianne stepped into the crack. She said nothing, just waited for his next words.

'Can I talk to you in private?'

She glanced to her left – three security guards, two agents, and three men in scrubs and lab jackets. 'In private?' she said.

'We can walk this way,' he said, nodding toward the end of the hall.

'Is something the matter?' she asked, as if nothing else could possibly go wrong.

'Yes ma'am.'

She took a deep breath, and disappeared. Seconds later, she eased through the door with her cigarettes, and closed it gently behind her. They walked slowly in the center of the empty hall.

'I don't suppose you've talked to Mark,' McThune said.

'He called me yesterday afternoon from the jail,' she said, sticking a cigarette between her lips. It was not a lie; Mark had indeed called her from the jail.

'Since then?'

'No,' she lied. 'Why?'

'He's missing.'

She hesitated for a step, then continued. 'What do you mean, he's missing?' She was surprisingly calm. She's probably just numb to all this, McThune thought. He gave her a quick version of Mark's disappearance. They stopped at the window and looked at downtown.

'My god, do you think the Mafia's got him?' she asked, and her eyes watered immediately. She held the cigarette with a trembling hand, unable to light it.

McThune shook his head confidently. 'No. They don't even know. We're keeping a lid on it. I think he just walked away. Right here, in the hospital. We figured he might have tried to contact you.'

'Have you searched this place? He knows it really well, you know.'

'They've been searching for three hours, but it looks doubtful. Where would he go?'

She finally lit the cigarette and took a long drag, then exhaled a small cloud. 'I have no idea.'

'Well, let me ask you something. What do you know about Reggie Love? Is she in town this weekend? Was she planning a trip?'

'Why?'

'We can't find her either. She's not at home. Her mother ain't saying much. You received a subpoena last night, right?'

'That's right.'

'Well, Mark got one, and they tried to serve one on Reggie Love, but they haven't found her yet. Is it possible Mark's with her?'

I hope so, Dianne thought. She hadn't thought about this. In spite of the pills she hadn't slept fifteen minutes since he'd called. But Mark on the loose with Reggie was a new idea. A much more pleasant idea.

'I don't know. It's possible, I guess.'

'Where would they be, you know, the two of them together?'

'How the hell am I supposed to know? You're the FBI. I hadn't thought about that until five seconds ago, and now you're asking me where they are. Give me a break.'

McThune felt stupid. It was not a bright question, and she was not as frail as he thought.

Dianne puffed her cigarette, and watched the cars crawl along the streets below. Knowing Mark, he was probably changing diapers in the nursery or assisting with surgery in orthopedics, or maybe scrambling eggs in the kitchen. St. Peter's was the largest hospital in the state. There were thousands of people under its varied roofs. He'd roamed the halls and made dozens of friends, and it would take them days to find him. She expected him to call any minute.

'I need to get back,' she said, sticking the filter in an ashtray.

'If he contacts you, I need to know it.'

'Sure.'

'And if you hear from Reggie Love, I'd appreciate a call. I'll leave two men here on this floor, in case you need them.'

She walked away.

By eight-thirty, Foltrigg had assembled in his office the usual crew of Wally Boxx, Thomas Fink, and Larry Trumann, who arrived last with his hair still wet from a quick shower.

Foltrigg was dressed like a fraternity pledge in his pressed chinos, starched cotton button-down, and shiny loafers. Trumann wore a jogging suit. 'The lawyer's missing too,' he announced as he poured coffee from a thermos.

'When did you hear this?' Foltrigg asked.

'Five minutes ago, on my car phone. McThune called me. They went to her house to serve her around eight, but couldn't find her. She's disappeared.'

'What else did McThune say?'

'They're still searching the hospital. The kid spent three days there and knows it very well.'

'I doubt if he's there,' Foltrigg said with his customary quick command of unknown facts.

'Does McThune think the kid's with the lawyer?' Boxx asked.

'Who in hell knows? She'd be kind of stupid to help the kid escape, wouldn't she?'

'She's not that bright,' Foltrigg said scornfully.

Neither are you, thought Trumann. You're the idiot who issued the subpoenas that started this latest episode. 'McThune's spoken twice this morning with K. O. Lewis. He's on standby. They plan to search the hospital until noon, then give up. If the kid's not found by then, Lewis will zip to Memphis.'

'You think Muldanno's involved?' Fink asked.

'I doubt it. Looks like the kid strung them along until he got to the hospital, and at that point he was on home turf. I'll bet he called the lawyer, and now they're hiding somewhere in Memphis.'

'I wonder if Muldanno knows,' Fink said, looking at Foltrigg.

'His people are still in Memphis,' Trumann said. 'Gronke's here, but we haven't seen Bono or Pirini. Hell, they might have a dozen boys up there by now.'

'Has McThune called in the dogs?' Foltrigg asked.

'Yeah. He's got everyone in his office working on it. They're watching her house, her secretary's apartment, they've even sent two men to find Judge Roosevelt, who's fishing somewhere in the mountains. Memphis PD has the hospital choked off.'

'What about the phones?'

'Which phones?'

'The phones in the hospital room. He's a kid, Larry, you know he'll try to call his mother.'

'It takes approval from the hospital. McThune said they're working on it. But it's Saturday, and the necessary people are not in.'

Foltrigg stood behind his desk, and walked to the window. 'The kid had six hours before anyone realized he was missing, right?'

'That's what they said.'

'Have they found the lawyer's car?'

'No. They're still looking.'

'I'll bet they don't find it in Memphis. I'll bet the kid and Ms. Love are in the car.'

'Oh really.'

'Yeah. Haulin' ass.'

'And where might they be haulin' ass to?'

'Somewhere far away.'

At nine-thirty, a Memphis policeman called in the tag number of an

311

illegally parked Mazda. It belonged to one Reggie Love. The message was quickly sent to Jason McThune at his office in the Federal Building.

Ten minutes later, two FBI agents knocked on the door to apartment Number 28 at Bellevue Gardens. They waited, and knocked again. Clint hid in the bedroom. If they kicked the door down, then he would simply be sleeping on this lovely and peaceful Saturday morning. They knocked the third time, and the phone started to ring. It startled him, and he almost lunged for it. But his answering machine was on. If the cops would come to his apartment, then they would certainly not hesitate to call. After the tone, he heard Reggie's voice. He lifted the receiver, and quickly whispered, 'Reggie, call me right back.' He hung up.

They knocked the fourth time, and left. The lights were off and the curtains covered every window. He stared at the phone for five minutes, and it finally rang. The answering machine gave its message, then the tone. Again, it was Reggie.

'Hello,' he said quickly.

'Good morning, Clint,' she said cheerfully. 'How are things in Memphis?'

'Oh, the usual, you know, cops watching my apartment, banging on the door. Typical Saturday.'

'Cops?'

'Yeah. For the past hour, I've been sitting in my closet watching my little television. The news is all over the place. They haven't mentioned you, yet, but Mark's on every channel. Right now, it's simply a disappearance, not an escape.'

'Have you talked to Dianne?'

'I called her about an hour ago. The FBI had just told her he was missing. I explained he was with you, and this calmed her a bit. Frankly, Reggie, she's been shocked so much I don't think it registered. Where are you?'

'We've checked into a motel in Metairie.'

'I'm sorry. Did you say Metairie? As in Louisiana? Right outside of New Orleans?'

'That's the place. We drove all night.'

'Why the hell are you down there, Reggie? Of all the places to hide, why did you pick a suburb of New Orleans? Why not Alaska?'

'Because it's the last place we'd be expected. We're safe, Clint. I paid cash and registered under another name. We'll sleep a bit, then see the city.'

'See the city? Come on, Reggie, what's going on?'

'I'll explain it later. Have you talked to Momma Love?'

'No. I'll call her right now.'

'Do that. I'll call back this afternoon.'

'You're crazy, Reggie. Do you know that? You've lost your mind.'

'I know. But I've been crazy before. Good-bye now.'

Clint placed the phone on the table, and stretched on the unmade bed. She had indeed been crazy before.

# CHAPTER THIRTY-FIVE

Barry the Blade entered the warehouse alone. Gone was the swaggering strut of the quickest gun in town. Gone was the smirking scowl of the cocky street hood. Gone were the flashy suit and Italian loafers. The earrings were in a pocket. The ponytail was tucked under his collar. He'd shaved just an hour ago.

He climbed the rusted steps to the second level, and thought about playing on these same stairs as a child. His father was alive then, and after school he'd hang around here until dark, watching containers come and go, listening to the stevedores, learning their language, smoking their cigarettes, looking at their magazines. It was a wonderful place to grow up, especially for a boy who wanted to be nothing but a gangster.

Now, the warehouse was not as busy. He walked along the runway next to the dirty, painted windows overlooking the river. His steps echoed through the vast emptiness below. A few dusty containers were scattered about, and hadn't been moved in years. His uncle's black Cadillacs were parked together near the docks. Tito, the faithful chauffeur, polished a fender. He glanced up at the sound of footsteps, and waved at Barry.

Though he was quite anxious, he walked deliberately, trying not to strut. Both hands were stuck deep in his pockets. He watched the river through the ancient windows. An imitation paddle wheeler hauled tourists downriver for a breathtaking tour of more warehouses and perhaps a barge or two. The runway stopped at a metal door. He pushed a button and looked directly into the camera above his head. A loud click, and the door opened. Mo, a former stevedore who'd given him his first beer when he was twelve, stood there, wearing a dreadful suit. Mo had at least four guns either on him or within reach. He nodded at Barry, and waved him on. Mo had been a friendly guy until he'd started wearing suits, which happened about the same time he saw *The Godfather*, and he hadn't smiled since.'

Barry walked through a room with two empty desks, and knocked on a door. He took a deep breath. 'Come in,' a voice said gently, and he entered his uncle's office.

Johnny Sulari was aging nicely. A big man, in his seventies, he stood straight and moved quickly. His hair was brilliantly gray, and not a fraction of the hairline had receded. His forehead was small, and the hair started two inches above the eyebrows and was slicked back in shiny waves. As usual, he wore a dark suit, with the jacket hanging on a rack by the window. The tie was navy and terribly boring. The red suspenders were his trademark. He smiled at Barry and waved to a worn leather chair, the same one Barry had sat in as a child.

Johnny was a gentleman, one of the last in a declining business being quickly overrun by younger men who were greedier and nastier. Men like his nephew here.

But it was a forced smile. This was not a social call. They'd talked more in the past three days than in the past three years.

'Bad news, Barry?' Johnny asked, knowing the answer.

'You might say so. The kid's disappeared in Memphis.'

Johnny stared icily at Barry, who, for one of the few times in his life, did not stare back. The eyes failed him. The lethal, legendary eyes of Barry The Blade Muldanno were blinking and watching the floor.

'How could you be so stupid?' Johnny asked calmly. 'Stupid to leave the body around here. Stupid to tell your lawyer. Stupid. Stupid. Stupid.'

The eyes blinked faster and he shifted his weight. He nodded in agreement, now penitent. 'I need help, okay.'

'Of course you need help. You've done a very stupid thing, and now you need someone to rescue you.'

'It concerns all of us, I think.'

Johnny's eyes flashed pure anger, but he controlled himself. He was always under control. 'Oh, really. Is that a threat, Barry? You're coming into my office to ask for help and you're threatening me? Are you planning to do some talkin'? Come on, boy. If you're convicted, you'll take it to your grave.'

'That's true, but I'd rather not be convicted, you know. There's still time.'

'You're a dumbass, Barry. Have I ever told you that?'

'I think so.'

'You stalked the man for weeks. You caught him sneaking out of a dirty little whorehouse. All you had to do was hit him over the head, coupla bullets, clean out his pockets, leave the body for the whores to trip over, and the cops would say it's just another cheap murder. They woulda never suspected anybody. But, no, Barry, you're too dumb to keep it simple.'

Barry shifted again and watched the floor.

Johnny glared at him and unwrapped a cigar. 'Answer my

questions slowly, okay? I don't wanna know too much, you understand?'

'Yeah.'

'Is the body here in the city?'

'Yeah.'

Johnny clipped the end of the cigar and licked it slowly. He shook his head in disgust. 'How stupid. Is it easy to get to?'

'Yeah.'

'Have the Feds been close to it?'

'I don't think so.'

'Is it underground?'

'Yeah.'

'How long will it take to dig it up or whatever you have to do?'

'An hour, maybe two.'

'So it's not in dirt?'

'Concrete.'

Johnny lit the cigar with a match, and relaxed the wrinkles above his eyes. 'Concrete,' he repeated. Maybe the boy wasn't quite as stupid as he thought. Forget it. He was plenty stupid. 'How many men?'

'Two or three. I can't do it. They're watching every move I make. If I go near the place, I'll just lead them to it.'

Plenty stupid, all right. He blew a smoke ring. 'A parking lot? A sidewalk?'

'Under a garage.' Barry shifted again, and kept his eyes on the floor.

Johnny blew another smoke ring. 'A garage. A parking garage?'

'A garage behind a house.'

He studied the thin layer of ashes at the end of the cigar, then slowly placed it between his teeth. He wasn't stupid, he was dumb. He puffed it twice. 'When you say house, do you mean a house on a street with other houses near it?'

'Yeah.' At the time of the burial, Boyd Boyette had been in his truck for twenty-five hours. Options were limited. He was near panic, and was afraid to leave the city. It wasn't such a bad idea, at the time.

'And these other houses have people living in them, right? People with ears and eyes?'

'I haven't met them, you know, but I would assume so.'

'Don't get cute with me.'

Barry slid an inch in his chair. 'Sorry,' he said.

Johnny stood and walked slowly to the tinted windows directly above the river. He shook his head in disbelief, and puffed his cigar in frustration. Then he turned and walked back to his seat. He placed the cigar in the ashtray and leaned forward on his elbows. 'Whose house?' he asked, stonefaced and ready to explode.

Barry swallowed hard and recrossed his legs. 'Jerome Clifford's.'

There was no eruption. Johnny was known to have ice water in his veins, and took great pride in staying cool. He was a rarity in this profession, but his level head had made him lots of money. And kept him alive. He placed his left hand completely over his mouth as if there was no way he could believe this. 'Jerome Clifford's house,' he repeated.

Barry nodded. At the time, Clifford had been skiing in Colorado, and Barry knew this because Clifford had invited him to go. He lived alone in a big house with dozens of shady trees. The garage was a separate structure sitting by itself in the backyard. It was a perfect place, he had thought, because no one would ever suspect it.

And he'd been right – it was a perfect place. The Feds hadn't been near it. It was not a mistake. He'd planned to move it later. The mistake had been to tell Clifford.

'And you want me to send in three men to dig it up, without making a sound, and dispose of it properly?'

'Yes sir. It could save my ass.'

'Why do you say this?'

'Because I'm afraid this kid knows where it is, and he's disappeared. Who knows what he's doing? It's just too risky. We gotta move the body, Johnny. I'm begging you.'

'I hate beggars, Barry. What if we get caught? What if a neighbor hears something and calls the cops, and they show up, just checkin' on a prowler, you know, and, son of a bitch, there's three boys diggin' up a corpse.'

'They won't get caught.'

'How do you know! How'd you do it? How'd you bury him in concrete without getting caught?'

'I've done it before, okay.'

'I wanna know!'

Barry straightened himself a bit, and recrossed his legs. 'The day after I hit him, I unloaded six bags of ready-mix at the garage. I was in a truck with bogus tags, dressed like a yard boy, you know. No one seemed to notice. The nearest house is a good thirty yards away, and there's trees everywhere. I went back at midnight in the same truck and unloaded the body in the garage. Then I left. There's a ditch behind the garage, and a park on the other side of the ditch. I just walked through the trees, climbed across the ditch, and sneaked into the garage. Took about thirty minutes to dig a shallow grave, put the body in it, and mix the concrete. The floor of the garage is gravel, white rock, you know. I went back the next night, after the stuff had dried, and covered it with the gravel. He's got this old boat, and so I rolled the boat back over it. When I left, everything was perfect. Clifford never had a clue.'

'Until you told him, of course.'

'Yeah, until I told him. It was a mistake, I admit.'

'Sounds like a lot of hard work.'

'I've done it before, okay. It's easy. I was gonna move it later, but then the Feds got involved and they've followed me for eight months.'

Johnny was nervous now. He relit the cigar and returned to the window. 'You know, Barry,' he said, looking at the water, 'you've got some talent, boy, but you're an idiot when it comes to removing the evidence. We've always used the Gulf out there. Whatever happened to barrels and chains and weights?'

'I promise it won't happen again. Just help me now, and I'll never make this mistake again.'

'There won't be a next time, Barry. If you somehow survive this, I'm gonna let you drive a truck for a while, then maybe run a fence for a year or so. I don't know. Maybe you can go to Vegas and spend a little time with Rock.'

Barry stared at the back of the silver head. He'd lie for the moment, but he would not drive a truck or fence or kiss Rock's ass. 'Whatever you say, Johnny. Just help me.'

Johnny returned to his seat behind the desk. He pinched the bridge of his nose. 'I guess it's urgent.'

'Tonight. This kid's on the loose. He's scared, and it's just a matter of time before he tells someone.'

Johnny closed his eyes and shook his head.

Barry continued. 'Give me three men. I'll tell them exactly how to do it, and I promise they won't get caught. It'll be easy.'

Johnny nodded slowly, painfully. Okay. Okay. He stared at Barry. 'Now get the hell outta here.'

After seven hours of searching, chief Trimble declared St. Peter's to be free of Mark Sway. He huddled in the lobby near Admissions with his officers, and pronounced the search over. They would continue to patrol the tunnels and walkways and corridors, and stand guard at the elevators and stairwells, but they were all now convinced the kid had eluded them. Trimble called McThune at his office with the news.

McThune was not surprised. He had been briefed periodically throughout the morning as the search fizzled out. And there was no sign of Reggie. Momma Love had been bothered twice, and now she refused to answer the door. She'd told them to either produce a search warrant, or get the hell off her property. There was no probable cause for a search warrant, and he suspected Momma Love knew this. The hospital had consented to the wiring of the phone in Room 943. Less than thirty minutes earlier, two agents, posing as orderlies, had entered the room while Dianne was down the hall talking to the Memphis Police. Instead of inserting the device, they simply switched phones. They were in the room less than a minute. The child, they reported, was asleep and never moved. The line was direct to the outside, and tapping in through the hospital switchboard would've taken at least two hours and involved other people.

Clint had not been found, but there was no valid reason to obtain a search warrant for his apartment, so they simply watched it.

Harry Roosevelt had been located in a rented boat somewhere along the Buffalo River in Arkansas. McThune had talked to him around eleven. Harry was livid, to say the least, and was now en route back to the city.

Ord had called Foltrigg twice during the morning, but, uncharacteristically, the great man had little to say. The brilliant strategy of ambush by subpoena had blown up in his face, and he was plotting some serious damage control.

K. O. Lewis was already on board Director Voyles's jet, and two agents had been dispatched to meet him at the airport. He would arrive around two.

An All-Points-Bulletin for Mark Sway had been on the national wire since early morning. McThune was reluctant to add the name of Reggie Love to it. Though he hated lawyers, he found it difficult to believe one would actually help a child escape. But as the morning dragged on and there was no sign of her, he became convinced that their disappearances were more than coincidental. At eleven, he added her name to the APB, along with a physical description and a comment that she was probably traveling with Mark Sway. If they were in fact together, and if they had crossed a state line, the offense would be federal and he'd have the pleasure of nailing her.

There was little to do but wait. He and George Ord feasted on cold sandwiches and coffee for lunch. Another phone call, another reporter asking questions. No comment.

Another phone call, and Agent Durston walked into the office and held up three fingers. 'Line three,' he said. 'It's Brenner at the hospital.' McThune hit the button. 'Yeah,' he barked at the phone.

Brenner was in Room 945, next door to Ricky. He spoke in a guarded voice. 'Jason, listen, we just heard a phone call from Clint Van Hooser to Dianne Sway. He told her he had just talked to Reggie, that she and Mark were in New Orleans, and everything was fine.'

'New Orleans!'

'That's what he said. No indication of exactly where, just New Orleans. Dianne said almost nothing, and the entire conversation lasted under two minutes. He said he was calling from his girlfriend's apartment in East Memphis, and he promised to call back later.'

'Where in East Memphis?'

'We can't determine that, and he didn't say. We'll try and trace it next time. He hung up too quick. I'll send the tape over.'

'Do that.' McThune punched another button, and Brenner was gone. He immediately called Larry Trumann in New Orleans.

# CHAPTER THIRTY-SIX

The house was in the bend of an old, shady street, and as they approached it Mark instinctively slid downward in the seat until only his eyes and the top of his head were visible in the window. He was wearing a black-and-gold Saints cap Reggie had bought him at a Wal-Mart along with a pair of jeans and two sweatshirts. A street map was folded badly and stuffed beside the hand brake.

'It's a big house,' he said from under the cap as they drove through the bend without the slightest decrease in speed. Reggie saw as much as she could, but she was driving on a strange street and trying desperately not to appear suspicious. It was 3 P.M., hours before dark, and they could drive and look for the rest of the afternoon if they wished. She, too, wore a Saints cap, solid black, and it covered her short gray hair. Her eyes hid behind large sunglasses.

She held her breath as they passed the mailbox with the name Clifford on the side in small, gold, stick-on lettering. It certainly was a big house, but nothing spectacular for this neighborhood. It was of English Tudor design, with dark wood and dark brick, and ivy covering all of one side and most of the front. It was not particularly pretty, she thought as she remembered the newspaper article in which Clifford was described as a divorced father of one. It was obvious, to her at least, that the house did not have the advantage of a woman living in it. Though she could glance at it only as she made the bend and cut her eyes in all directions, looking at once for neighbors, cops, thugs, the garage, and the house, she noticed there were no flowers in the beds and the hedges needed trimming. The windows were covered with dark, drab curtains.

It was not pretty, but it was certainly peaceful. It sat in the center of a large lot with dozens of heavy oaks around it. The driveway ran along a thick hedge and disappeared somewhere around back. Though Clifford had been dead for five days, the grass was neatly trimmed. There was no clue that the house was now uninhabited. There was no hint of any suspicion. Perhaps it was the perfect place to hide a body.

'There's the garage,' Mark said, peeking now. It was a separate structure, fifty or so feet from the house, obviously built much later. A small sidewalk led to the house. A red Triumph Spitfire was on blocks next to the garage.

Mark jerked and stared at the house through the rear window as they eased down the street. 'What do you think, Reggie?'

'Looks awfully quiet, doesn't it?'

'Yeah.'

'Is it what you expected?' she asked.

'I don't know. I watch all those cop shows, you know, and for some reason I could just see Romey's house with yellow police line tape strung all over the place.'

'Why? No crime was committed there. It's just the home of a man who committed suicide. Why would the cops be interested?'

The house was out of sight, and Mark turned around and sat straight in the seat. 'Do you think they've searched it?' he asked.

'Probably. I'm sure they got a search warrant for his house and office, but what could they find? He carried his little secret with him.'

They stopped at an intersection, then continued their tour of the neighborhood.

'What happens to his house?' Mark asked.

'I'm sure he had a will. His heirs will get the house and his assets.'

'Yeah. You know, Reggie, I guess I need a will. With everybody after me and all. What do you think?'

'What, exactly, do you own?'

'Well, now that I'm famous and all, I figure the Hollywood people will be knocking on my door. I realize we don't have a door at the present time, but something's gotta happen about that, Reggie, don't you think? I mean, we gotta have a door, of some sort? Anyway, they'll want to do this big movie about the kid who knew too much, and, I hate to say this for obvious reasons, but if these goons put me away, then the movie will be huge and Mom and Ricky will be on easy street. Follow me?'

'I think so. You want a will so Dianne and Ricky will get the movie rights to your life story?'

'Exactly.'

'You don't need one.'

'Why not?'

'They'll get all your assets anyway.'

'Just as well. Saves me attorney's fees.'

'Could we talk about something other than wills and death?'

He shut up and watched the houses on his side of the street. He'd slept most of the night in the backseat, then napped for five hours in the motel room. She, on the other hand, had driven all night and napped less than two hours. She was tired, scared, and beginning to snap at him.

They zigzagged at a leisurely pace through the tree-lined streets. The weather was warm and clear. At every house, people were either mowing grass or pulling weeds or painting shutters. Spanish moss hung from stately oaks. It was Reggie's first tour of New Orleans, and she wished the circumstances were better.

'Are you getting tired of me, Reggie?' he asked without looking at her.

'Of course not. Are you tired of me?'

'No, Reggie. Right now, you're my only friend in the entire world. I just hope I'm not bugging you.'

'I promise.'

Reggie had studied the street map for two hours. She completed a wide loop, and now they were on Romey's street again. They eased by the house without slowing, both gawking at the double garage with a pitched gable above the retractable doors. It needed painting. The concrete drive stopped twenty feet from the doors and turned to the rear of the house. A ragged hedgerow over six feet high ran along one side of the garage and blocked the view of the nearest house, which was at least a hundred feet away. Behind the garage, the small rear lawn stopped at a chain-link fence, and beyond the fence was a heavily wooded area.

They said nothing during the second viewing of Romey's house. The black Accord wandered aimlessly through the neighborhood and stopped near a tennis court in an open area called West Park. Reggie unfolded the street map, and twisted and flipped it until it covered most of the front seat. Mark watched two heavy housewives engage in truly horrible tennis. But they were cute, with their pink and green socks and matching sun visors. A biker approached on a narrow asphalt trail, then disappeared deep into the woods.

Once again, Reggie attempted to fold the map. 'This is the place,' she said.

'Do you want to chicken out?' he asked.

'Sort of. What about you?'

'I don't know. We've come this far. Seems kinda silly to run away now. The garage looked harmless to me.'

She was still folding the map. 'I guess we can try, and if we get spooked, we'll just run back here.'

'Where are we now?'

She opened her door. 'Let's go for a walk.'

The bike trail ran beside a soccer field, then cut through a dense section of woods. The branches of the trees met above it, giving a tunnel-like darkness. The bright sunlight flickered through intermittently. An occasional biker forced them from the asphalt for a few seconds.

The walk was refreshing. After three days in the hospital, two days in jail, seven hours in the car, and six hours in the motel, Mark could barely restrain himself as they rambled through the woods. He missed his bike, and he thought how nice it would be if he and Ricky were here on this trail, racing through the trees without a worry in the world. Just kids again. He missed the crowded streets of the trailer park with kids running everywhere and games of all sorts materializing without a moment's notice. He missed the private little trails of his own wood around Tucker Wheel Estates and the long, solitary walks he had enjoyed all his life. And, strange as it seemed, he missed his hiding places under his own personal trees and beside creeks that belonged to him where he could sit and think, and, yes, sneak a cigarette or two. He hadn't touched one since Monday.

'What am I doing here?' he asked, barely audible.

'It was your idea,' she said, hands stuck deep in her new jeans, also from Wal-Mart.

'It's been my favorite question this week – "What am I doing here?" I've asked it everywhere, the hospital, the jail, the courtroom. Everywhere.'

'You want to go home, Mark?'

'What's home?'

'Memphis. I'll take you back to your mother.'

'Yeah, but I won't stay with her, will I? In fact, we probably wouldn't even make it to Ricky's room before they grabbed me, and off I'd go, back to jail, back to court, back to see Harry, who'd really be ticked, wouldn't he?'

'Yeah, but I can work on Harry.'

Nobody worked on Harry, Mark had decided. He could see himself sitting in court trying to explain why he'd escaped. Harry would send him back to the detention center where his sweetheart Doreen would be a different person. No pizza. No television. They'd probably put leg chains on him and throw him in solitary.

'I can't go back, Reggie. Not now.'

They had discussed their various options until both were tired of the subject. Nothing had been settled. Each new idea immediately raised a dozen problems. Each course of action ran in all directions and eventually led to disaster. They had both reached, through different routes, the unmistakable conclusion that there was no simple solution. There was no reasonable thing to do. There was no plan even remotely attractive.

But neither believed they would actually dig for the body of Boyd Boyette. Something would happen along the way to spook them, and they'd run back to Memphis. This was yet to be admitted by either.

Reggie stopped at the half-mile marker. To the left was an open, grassy area with a pavilion in the center for picnics. To the right, a small foot trail ventured deeper into the trees. 'Let's try this,' she said, and they left the bike route.

He followed close behind. 'Do you know where you're going?'

'No. But follow me anyway.'

The trail widened a bit, then suddenly gave out and disappeared. Empty beer bottles and chip bags littered the ground. They wove through trees and brush until they found a small clearing. The sun was suddenly bright. Reggie shielded her eyes with her hand and looked at a straight row of trees stretching before them.

'I think that's the creek,' she said.

'What creek?'

'According to the map, Clifford's street borders West Park, and there's a little green line that appears to be a creek or bayou or something running behind his house.'

'It's nothing but trees.'

She shuffled sideways for a few feet, then stopped and pointed. 'Look, there are roofs on the other side of those trees. I think it's Clifford's street.'

Mark stood beside her and strained on tiptoes. 'I see them.'

'Follow me,' she said, and they headed for the row of trees.'

It was a beautiful day. They were out for a stroll in the park. This was public property. Nothing to be afraid of.

The creek was nothing but a dry bed of sand and litter. They picked their way down through the vines and brush, and stood where the water once ran many years before. Even the mud had dried. They climbed the opposite bank, a much steeper one but with more vines and saplings to grab on to.

Reggie was breathing hard when they stopped on the other side of the creek bed. 'Are you scared?' she asked.

'No. Are you?'

'Of course, and you are too. Do you want to keep going?'

'Sure, and I'm not afraid. We're just out for a hike, that's all.' He was terrified and wanted to run, but they had made it this far without incident. And there was a certain thrill in sneaking through the jungle like this. He'd done it a thousand times around the trailer park. He knew to watch for snakes and poison ivy. He'd learned how to line up three trees ahead of him to keep from getting lost. He'd played hide-and-seek in rougher terrain than this. He suddenly crouched low and darted ahead. 'Follow me.'

'This is not a game,' she said.

'Just follow me, unless, of course, you're scared.'

'I'm terrified. I'm fifty-two years old, Mark. Now slow down.'

The first fence they saw was made of cedar, and they stayed in the trees and moved behind the houses. A dog barked in their general direction, but they could not be seen from the house. Then a chain-link fence, but it was not Clifford's. The woods and underbrush thickened, but from nowhere came a small trail that ran parallel to the fence row.

Then, they saw it. On the other side of a chain-link fence, the red Triumph Spitfire sat alone and abandoned next to Romey's garage. The edge of the woods stopped less than twenty feet from the fence, and between it and the rear wall of the garage a dozen or so oaks and elms with Spanish moss shaded the backyard.

Not surprisingly, Romey was a slob. He had piled boards and bricks, buckets and rakes, all sorts of debris behind the garage and out of sight of the street.

There was a small gate in the chain-link fence. The garage had a window and a door in the rear wall. Sacks of unused and ruined fertilizer were stacked against it. An old lawn mower with the handles off was parked by the door. On the whole, the yard was overgrown and had been for some time. Weeds along the fence were knee-high.

They squatted in the trees and stared at the garage. They would get no closer. The neighbor's patio and charcoal grill were a stone's throw away.

Reggie tried to catch her breath, but it was not possible She clutched Mark's hand, and found it impossible to believe that the body of a United State Senator was buried less than a hundred feet from where she was now hiding.

'Are we gonna go in there?' Mark asked. It was almost a challenge, though she detected a trace of fear. Good, she thought, he is scared.

She caught her breath long enough to whisper. 'No. We've come far enough.'

He hesitated for a long time, then said, 'It'll be easy.'

'It's a big garage,' she said.

'I know exactly where it is.'

'Well, I haven't pressed you on this, but don't you think it's time to share it with me?'

'It's under the boat.'

'He told you this?'

'Yes. He was very specific. It's buried under the boat.'

'What if there's no boat.'

'Then we haul ass.'

He was finally sweating and breathing hard. She'd seen enough. She stayed low and began backing away. 'I'm leaving now,' she said.

K. O. Lewis never left the plane. McThune and company were waiting when it landed, and they rushed aboard as it refueled. Thirty minutes later, they left for New Orleans where Larry Trumann now waited anxiously.

Lewis didn't like it. What the hell was he supposed to do in New Orleans? It was a big city. They had no idea what she was driving. In fact, they didn't know if Reggie and Mark had driven, flown, or taken a bus or a train. It was a tourist and convention city with thousands of hotel rooms and crowded streets. Until they made a mistake, it would be impossible to find them.

But Director Voyles wanted him on the scene, and so off he went to New Orleans. Find the kid and make him talk – those were his instructions. Promise him anything.

# CHAPTER THIRTY-SEVEN

Two of the three, Leo and Ionucci, were veteran leg-breakers for the Sulari family, and were actually related by blood to Barry The Blade, though they often denied it. The third, a huge kid with massive biceps, a wide neck, and thick waist, was known simply as the Bull, for obvious reasons. He'd been sent on this unusual errand to perform most of the grunt work. Barry assured them it would not be difficult. The concrete was thin. The body was small. Chip a little here, and chip a little there, and before they knew it they'd see a black garbage bag.

Barry had diagrammed the floor of the garage, and marked with exact confidence the position of the grave. He had drawn a map with a line starting at the parking lot of West Park and running between the tennis courts, across the soccer field, through a patch of trees, then across another field with a picnic pavilion, then along the bike route for a ways until a footpath led to the ditch. It would be easy, he had assured them all afternoon.

The bike trail was deserted, and with good reason. It was ten minutes after eleven, Saturday night. The air was muggy, and by the time they reached the footpath they were breathing heavily and sweating. The Bull, much younger and fitter, followed the other two and smiled to himself as they bitched quietly in the blackness about the humidity. They were in their late thirties, he guessed, chain-smokers of course, abusive drinkers, sloppy eaters. They were griping about sweating, and they hadn't walked a mile yet.

Leo was in charge of this expedition, and he carried the flashlight. They were dressed in solid black. Ionucci followed like a bloodhound with heartworms, head down, breathing hard, lethargic, mad at the world for being here. 'Careful,' Leo said as they eased down the ditch bank in heavy weeds. They were not exactly woodsy types. This place had been frightening enough at 6 P.M. when they first walked it off. Now it was terrifying. The Bull expected at any moment to step on a thick, squirming snake. Of course, if he was bitten, he could turn around with justification, and, he hoped, find the car. His two buddies would then be forced to go it alone. He tripped on a log, but kept his balance. He almost wished for a snake.

'Careful,' Leo said for the tenth time, as if saying it made things safer. They eased along the dark and weedy creek bed for two hundred yards, then climbed the other bank. The flashlight was turned off, and they crouched low through the brush until they were behind Clifford's chain-link fence. They rested on their knees.

'This is stupid, you know,' Ionucci said between loud breaths. 'Since when do we dig up bodies?'

Leo was surveying the darkness of Clifford's backyard. Not a single light. They had driven by only minutes earlier, and noticed a small gas light burning in a globe near the front door, but the rear was complete darkness. 'Shut up,' he said without moving his head.

'Yeah, yeah,' Ionucci mumbled. 'It's stupid.' His screaming lungs were almost audible. Sweat dripped from his chin. The Bull knelt behind them, shaking his head at their unfitness. They were used primarily as bodyguards and drivers, occupations that required little exertion. Legend held that Leo did his first killing when he was seventeen, but was forced to quit a few years later when he served time. The Bull had heard that Ionucci had been shot twice over the years, but this was unconfirmed. The people who generated these stories were not known for telling the truth.

'Let's go,' Leo said like a field marshal. They scooted across the grass to the gate in Clifford's fence, then through it. They darted between the trees until they landed against the rear wall of the garage. Ionucci was in pain. He fell to all fours and heaved mightily. Leo crawled to a corner and looked for movement next door. Nothing. Nothing but the sounds of Ionucci's impending cardiac arrest. The Bull peeked around the other corner and watched the rear of Clifford's house.

The neighborhood was asleep. Even the dogs had called it a night.

Leo stood and tried to open the rear door. It was locked. 'Stay here,' he said, and slid low around the garage until he came to the front door. It was locked also. Back to the rear, he said, 'We gotta break some glass. It's locked too.'

Ionucci produced a hammer from a pouch on his waist, and Leo began tapping lightly on the dirty pane just above the doorknob. 'Watch that corner,' he said to the Bull, who crawled behind him and looked in the direction of the Ballantine home next door.

Leo pecked and pecked until the pane was broken. He carefully removed broken pieces and tossed them aside. When the jagged edges were clear, he slid his left arm through and unlocked the door. He turned on the flashlight, and the three eased inside.

Barry said he remembered the place being a mess, and Clifford obviously had been too busy to tidy things up before he passed on. The first thing they noticed was that the floor was gravel, not concrete.

Leo kicked at the white rocks beneath his feet. If Barry had told them about the gravel flooring, he didn't remember it.

The boat was in the center of the garage. It was a sixteen-foot outboard ski rig with a heavy layer of dust over it. Three of the four trailer tires were flat. This boat had not touched water in years. Layers of junk were piled against it. Garden tools, sacks of aluminum cans, stacks of newspapers, rusted patio furniture. Romey didn't need a garbage service. Hell, he had a garage. Thick spiderwebs were strung in every corner. Unused tools hung from the walls.

Clifford, for some reason, had been a prodigious collector of wire clothes hangers. Thousands of them hung on strands of wire above the boat. Rows and rows of clothes hangers. At some point, he'd grown weary of running the wire, so he'd simply driven long nails into the wall studs and packed hundreds of hangers on them. Romey, the environmentalist, had also collected cans and plastic containers, obviously with the lofty goal of recycling. But he'd been a busy man, and so a small mountain of green garbage bags stuffed with cans and bottles filled half of the garage. He'd been such a slob, he'd even thrown some of the bags into the boat.

Leo aimed the small light at a point directly under the main beam of the trailer. He motioned for the Bull, who eased onto all fours and began brushing away the white rock gravel. From the waist pouch, Ionucci produced a small trowel. The Bull took it and scraped away more gravel. His two partners stood over his shoulders.

Two inches down, the scraping sound changed when he struck concrete. The boat was in the way. The Bull stood, slowly lifted the hitch, and with a mighty strain rolled the front of the trailer five feet to the side. The side of the trailer brushed against the mountain of aluminum cans, and there was a prolonged racket. The men froze, and listened.

'You gotta be careful.' Leo whispered the obvious. 'Stay here, and don't move.' He left them standing in the dark beside the boat, and eased through the rear door. He stood beside a tree behind the garage and watched the Ballantine house next door. It was dark and quiet. A patio light cast a dim glow around the grill and flower beds, but nothing moved. Leo watched and waited. He doubted the neighbors could hear a jackhammer. He crept back inside the garage and aimed the flashlight at the spot of concrete under the gravel. 'Let's clear it off,' he said, and the Bull returned to his knees.

Barry had explained that he'd first dug a shallow grave, approximately six feet by two feet, and no more than eighteen inches deep. Then he'd stuffed the body into it. Then he'd packed the pre-mix concrete around the body, which was wrapped in black plastic garbage bags. Then he'd added water to his little recipe. He'd returned the next day to cover it all with gravel and put the boat in place.

He'd done a fine job. Given Clifford's talent for organization, it would be another five years before the boat was moved. Barry had explained that this was just a temporary grave. He'd planned to move it, but the Feds started trailing him. Leo and Ionucci had disposed of a few bodies, usually in weighted barrels over water, but they were impressed with Barry's temporary hiding place.

The Bull scraped and brushed, and soon the entire concrete surface was clear. Ionucci knelt on the other side of it, and he and the Bull began chipping away with chisels and hammers. Leo placed the flashlight on the gravel beside them, and eased again through the rear door. He crouched low and moved to the front of the garage. All was quiet. The chiseling could be heard, all right. He walked quickly to the rear of Clifford's house, maybe fifty feet away, and the sounds were barely audible. He smiled to himself. Had the Ballantines been awake, they could not have heard it.

He darted back to the garage, and sat in the darkness between a corner and the Spitfire. He could see the empty street. A small, black car eased around the bend in front of the house, and was gone. No other traffic. Through the hedge, he could see the outline of the Ballantine house. Nothing moved. The only sounds were the muffled chippings of concrete from the grave of Boyd Boyette.

Clint's Accord stopped near the tennis courts. A red Cadillac was parked near the street. Reggie turned off the lights and the engine.

They sat in silence and stared through the windshield at the dark soccer field. This is a wonderful place to get mugged, she thought to herself, but didn't mention it. There was plenty of fear without thinking of muggers.

Mark hadn't said much since dark. They had napped, together on one bed, for an hour after the pizza had been delivered to their motel room. They had watched television. He had asked her repeatedly about the time, as if he had an appointment with a firing squad. At ten, she was convinced he would chicken out. At eleven, he was pacing around the room, and going back and forth to the bathroom.

But here they were at eleven-forty, sitting in a hot car on a dark night, planning an impossible mission that neither really wanted.

'Do you think anybody knows we're here?' he asked softly.

She looked at him. His gaze was lost somewhere beyond the soccer field. 'You mean, here in New Orleans?'

'Yeah. Do you think anyone knows we're in New Orleans?'

'No. I don't think so.'

This seemed to satisfy him. She'd talked to Clint around seven. A Memphis TV station had reported that she was missing as well, but things appeared to be quiet. Clint hadn't left his bedroom in twelve hours, he said, so would they please hurry up and do whatever the hell they were planning. He'd called Momma Love. She was worried, but doing okay under the circumstances.

They left the car and walked along the bike trail.

'Are you sure you want to do this?' she asked, looking around nervously. The trail was pitch black, and in places only the asphalt beneath their feet kept them from wandering into the trees. They walked slowly, side by side, and held hands.

As she took one uncertain step after another, Reggie asked herself what she was doing here on this trail, in these woods of this city, at this moment, with this kid whom she loved dearly but was not willing to die for. She clutched his hand and tried to be brave. Surely, she prayed, something would happen very soon and they would dash back to the car and leave New Orleans.

'I've been thinking,' Mark said.

'Why am I not surprised?'

'It might be too hard to actually find the body, you know. So, this is what I've decided. You'll stay in the trees close to the ditch, you see, and I'll sneak through the backyard and into the garage. I'll look under the boat, you know, just to make sure it's there, then we'll get out of here.'

'You think you can just look under the boat and see the body?'

'Maybe I can see where it is, you know?'

She squeezed his hand tighter. 'Listen to me, Mark. We're sticking together, okay. If you go to the garage, then I'm going too.' Her voice was remarkably firm. Surely, they wouldn't make it to the garage.

There was a break in the trees. A light on a pole revealed the picnic pavilion to their left. The footpath started to the right. Mark pressed a switch, and the beam from a small flashlight hit the ground in front of them. 'Follow me,' he said. 'Nobody can see us out here.'

He moved deftly through the woods without a sound. Back in the motel room, he had recounted many stories of his late night walks through the woods around the trailer park, and of the games the boys played in the darkness. Jungle games, he called them. With the light in his hand, he moved faster now, brushing past limbs and dodging saplings.

'Slow down, Mark,' she said more than once.

He held her hand and helped her down the ditch bank. They climbed to the other side, and crept through the woods and under-brush until they found the mysterious trail that had surprised them hours earlier. The fences started. They moved slowly, quietly, and Mark turned off the flashlight.

They were in the dense trees directly behind Clifford's house. They knelt and caught their breath. Through the brush and weeds they could see the outline of the rear of the garage.

'What if we don't see the body?' she asked. 'What then?'

'We'll worry about that when it happens.'

This was not the moment for another long discussion about his options. On all fours, he crawled to the edge of the thick underbrush. She followed. They stopped twenty feet from the gate in thick, wet weeds. The backyard was dark and still. Not a light or sound or movement. The entire street was sound asleep.

'Reggie, I want you to stay here. Keep your head down. I'll be back in a minute.'

'No sir!' she whispered loudly. 'You can't do this, Mark!'

He was already moving. This was a game to him, just another jungle game with his little buddies giving chase and shooting guns with colored water. He slid through the grass like a lizard, and opened the gate just wide enough to slide through.

Reggie followed on all fours through the weeds, then stopped. He was already out of sight. He stopped behind the first tree, and listened. He crawled to the next one, and heard something. Chink! Chink! He froze on his hands and knees. The sounds were coming from the garage. Chink! chink! Very slowly, he peeked around the tree and stared at the rear door. Chink! Chink! He glanced back at Reggie, but the woods and underbrush were black. She was nowhere in sight. He looked at the door again. Something was different. He crawled to the next tree, ten feet closer. The sounds were louder. The door was open slightly, and a windowpane was missing.

Somebody was in there! Chink! Chink! Chink! Somebody was hid-ing in there with the lights off, and he was digging! Mark breathed deeply, and crawled behind a pile of debris less then ten feet from the rear door. He hadn't made a sound, and he knew it. The grass was taller around the debris, and he crawled through it like a chameleon, very slowly. Chink! Chink!

He crouched low, and started for the rear door. The ragged end of a rotted two-by-four caught his ankle and he tripped. The pile of debris rattled and an empty paint bucket fell to the ground.

Leo bounced to his feet and darted to the rear of the garage. He yanked a .38 with a silencer from his waist, and scooted in the darkness until he was at the corner where he squatted and listened. The chiseling had stopped inside. Ionucci peeked through the rear door.

Reggie heard the racket behind the garage, and fell to her stomach in the wet grass. She closed her eyes and said a prayer. What the hell was she doing here?

Leo sneaked to the pile of debris, then cut around it with the gun drawn and ready to fire. He squatted again, and patiently studied the darkness. The fence was barely visible. Nothing moved. He slid next to a tree fifteen feet behind the garage, and waited. Ionucci watched him closely. Long seconds passed without a sound. Leo stood upright and crept slowly toward the gate. A twig snapped under his foot, freezing him in place for a second.

He moved around the backyard, bolder now but with the gun still ready, and leaned against a tree, a thick oak with limbs hanging low near the Ballantine property line. In the unkempt hedgerow less than twelve feet away, Mark crouched on all fours and held his breath. He watched the dark figure move between the trees in the darkness, and he knew if he kept still he would not be found. He exhaled slowly, his eyes glued to the silhouette of the man by the tree.

'What is it?' a deep voice asked from the garage. Leo slid the gun into the waist of his pants and eased backward. Ionucci was standing outside the door. 'What is it?' he repeated.

'I don't know,' Leo said in a half-whisper. 'Maybe just a cat or something. Get back to work.'

The door closed softly, and Leo paced silently back and forth behind the garage for five minutes. Five minutes, but it seemed like an hour to Mark.

Then the dark figure eased around the corner and was gone. Mark watched every move. He slowly counted to one hundred, then crawled along the hedgerow until it stopped at the fence. He paused at the gate and counted to thirty. All was quiet except for the distant, muffled chiseling. Then he darted to the edge of the brush where Reggie was crouching in terror. She grabbed him as they ducked into the heavier undergrowth.

'They're in there!' he said, out of breath.

'Who?!'

'I don't know! They're digging up the body!'

'What happened!?'

He was breathing rapidly. His head bobbed up and down as he swallowed and tried to speak. 'I tripped on something, and this one guy, I think he had a gun, almost found me. God I was scared!'

'You're still scared. And so am I! Let's get outta here!'

'Listen, Reggie. Wait a minute. Listen! Can you hear it?'

'No! Hear what?'

'That chinking noise. I can't hear it either. We're too far away.'

'And I say we get farther away. Let's go.'

'Just wait a minute, Reggie. Dammit!'

'They're killers, Mark. They're Mafia people. Let's get the hell out of here!'

He breathed through his teeth, and glared at her. 'Settle down, Reggie. Just settle down, okay. Look, no one can see us here. You can't even see these trees from the garage. I tried, okay. Now settle down.'

She fell to her knees, and they stared at the garage. He placed his finger to his lips. 'We're safe here, okay,' he whispered. 'Listen.'

They listened, but the sounds could not be heard.

'Mark, these are Muldanno's people. They know you've escaped. They're panicking. They've got guns and knives and who knows what else. Let's go. They beat us. It's all over. They win.'

'We can't let them take the body, Reggie. Think about it. If they get away with it, it'll never be found.'

'Good. You're off the hook, and the Mafia forgets about you. Now let's go.'

'No, Reggie. We gotta do something.'

'What! You want to pick a fight with Mafia thugs? Come on, Mark. This is crazy.'

'Just wait a minute.'

'Okay. I'll wait exactly one minute, then I'm gone.'

He turned and smiled at her. 'You won't leave me, Reggie. I know you better than that.'

'Don't push me, Mark. Now I know how Ricky felt when you were playing around with Clifford and his little water hose.'

'Just be quiet, okay. I'm thinking.'

'That's what scares me.'

She sat on her butt with her legs crossed in front of her. Leaves and vines rubbed her face and neck. He rocked gently on all fours like a lion ready to kill, and finally said, 'I've got an idea.'

'Of course you do.'

'Stay here.'

She suddenly grabbed the back of his neck and pulled his face to hers. 'Listen, buster, this is not one of your little jungle games where you shoot rubber darts and throw dirt clods. Those are not your little buddies in there playing hide-and-seek, or GI Joe, or whatever the hell you play. This is life and death, Mark. You just made one mistake, and you got lucky. One more, and you'll be dead. Now let's get the hell outta here! Now!'

He was still for a few seconds as she scolded him, then he jerked viciously away. 'Stay here, and don't move,' he said with stiff jaws. He crept from the brush, through the grass to the fence.

Just inside the gate was an abandoned flower bed outlined with sunken timbers and covered with weeds. He crawled to it, and picked out three rocks with all the fussiness of a chef selecting tomatoes at the market. He watched both corners of the garage, then made a silent retreat into the darkness.

Reggie was waiting, and she had not moved a muscle. He knew she could not find her way to the car. He knew she needed him. They huddled again in the brush.

'Mark, this is insane, son,' she pleaded. 'Please. These people are not playing games.'

'They're too busy to worry about us, okay. We're safe here, Reggie. Look, if they came tearing out of that door right now, they could never find us. We're safe here, Reggie. Trust me.'

'Trust you! You'll get yourself killed.'

'Stay here.'

'What! Please, Mark! No more games!'

He ignored her and pointed to a spot near three trees, about thirty feet away. 'I'll be right back,' he said, and he disappeared.

He crawled through the brush until he was behind the Ballantine house. He could barely see the edge of Romey's garage. Reggie was lost in the dark undergrowth.

The patio was small and dimly lit. There were three white wicker chairs and a charcoal grill. A large plate-glass window overlooked it, and it was this window that attracted his attention. He stood behind a tree, and measured the distance, which he estimated to be the length of two house trailers. The rock would have to be low enough to miss the branches, yet high enough to clear a row of hedges. He took a deep breath, and threw it as hard as he could.

Leo jumped at the sound from next door. He crept in front of the garage and peeked through the hedge. The patio was quiet and still. It sounded like a rock landing on wooden decking and rattling around next to the brick. Maybe it was just a dog. He watched for a long time, and nothing happened. They were safe. Another false alarm.

Mr. Ballantine rolled over and stared at the ceiling. He was in his early sixties, and sleep had been difficult since the removal of the disc a year and a half ago. He had just dozed off, and was awakened by a sound. Or was it a sound? No place was safe in New Orleans any-more, and he'd paid two thousand dollars for an alarm system six months earlier. Crime was everywhere. They were thinking about moving.

He rolled to one side, and had just closed his eyes when the win-dow crashed. He bolted to the door, turned on the bedroom light, and yelled, 'Get up, Wanda! Get up!' Wanda was reaching for her robe, and Mr. Ballantine was grabbing the shotgun from the closet. The alarm was wailing. They raced down the hall, yelling at each other and flipping on light switches. The glass had scattered through-out the den, and Mr. Ballantine aimed the shotgun at the window as if to prevent another attack. 'Call the police!' he barked at her. '911!'

'I know the number!'

'Hurry up!' He tiptoed in his house shoes around the glass, crouch-ing low with the gun as if a burglar had chosen to enter the house through the window. He fought his way to the kitchen where he punched numbers on a control panel, and the sirens stopped.

Leo had just resettled into his guard post next to the Spitfire when the crash shattered the stillness. He bit a hole in his tongue as he scrambled to his feet and darted once again to the hedge. A siren screamed briefly, then stopped. A man in a red nightshirt down to his knees was running onto the patio with a shotgun.

Leo crept quickly to the rear door of the garage. Ionucci and the Bull were crouched in terror beside the boat. Leo stepped on a rake, and the handle landed on a bag full of aluminum cans. The three stopped breathing. Voices could be heard next door.

'What the hell is it?' Ionucci demanded through clenched teeth. He and the Bull were shiny with sweat. Their shirts were stuck to their bodies. Their heads were soaking wet.

'I don't know,' Leo bristled, spitting blood, inching toward the window facing the hedge that separated the Ballantine property. 'Something went through a window, I think. I don't know. Crazy bastard's got a shotgun!'

'A what!' Ionucci almost shrieked. He and the Bull slowly raised their heads to the window and joined Leo there. The crazy man with the shotgun was stomping around his backyard, yelling at the trees.

Mr. Ballantine was sick of New Orleans and sick of drugs and sick of punks trying to rob and pillage, and he was sick of crime and living in fear like this, and he was just so damned sick of it all he raised his shotgun and fired once at the trees for good measure. That'll teach the slimy little bastards that he meant business. Come back to his house, and you'll leave in a hearse. BOOM!

Mrs. Ballantine stood in the doorway in her pink robe, and screamed when he fired and wounded the trees.

The three heads in the garage next door hit the dirt when the shooting started. 'Sumbitch is crazy!' Leo screeched. Slowly, they raised their heads again in perfect unison, and at precisely that instant, the first police car pulled into the Ballantine driveway with blue and red lights flashing wildly.

Ionucci was the first one out the door, followed by the Bull, then Leo. They were in a huge hurry, but at the same time careful not to attract attention from the idiots next door. They scooted along, close to the ground, dashing from tree to tree, trying desperately to make it to the woods before there was more gunfire. The retreat was orderly.

Mark and Reggie huddled deep in the brush. 'You're crazy,' she kept muttering, and it was not idle talk. She honestly believed that her client was mentally unbalanced. But she hugged him anyway, and they squeezed close together. They didn't see the three silhouettes scampering along until they crossed through the fence.

'There they are,' Mark whispered, pointing. Not thirty seconds earlier, he had told her to watch the gate.

'Three of them,' he whispered. The three leaped into the underbrush, less than twenty feet from where they were hiding, and disappeared into the woods.

They squeezed closer together. 'You're crazy,' she said again.

'Maybe so. But it's working.'

The shotgun blast had almost sent Reggie over the edge. She'd been trembling when they arrived here. She'd been mortified when he returned with news that someone was in the garage. She'd damned near screamed when he threw the rock through the window. But the shotgun was the final straw. Her heart was pounding and her hands were trembling.

And oddly, at this moment, she knew they couldn't run. The three grave robbers were now between them and their car. There was no escape.

The shotgun blast brought the neighborhood to life. Floodlights filled backyards as men and women in bathrobes walked onto patios and looked in the direction of the Ballantines'. Voices shouted inquiries across fences. Dogs came to life. Mark and Reggie withdrew deeper into the brush.

Mr. Ballantine and one of the cops walked along the rear fence, searching perhaps for more felonious rocks. It was hopeless. Reggie and Mark could hear voices, but they could not understand what was being said. Mr. Ballantine yelled a lot.

The cops settled him down, then helped him tape clear plastic over the window. The red and blue lights were turned off, and after twenty minutes, the cops left.

Reggie and Mark waited, trembling and holding hands. Bugs crawled over their skin. The mosquitoes were brutal. The weeds and burrs stuck to their dark sweatshirts. The lights in the Ballantine house finally went off, and they waited some more.

# CHAPTER THIRTY-EIGHT

A few minutes after one, the clouds broke and the half-moon lightened Romey's backyard and garage for a moment. Reggie glanced at her watch. Her legs were numb from squatting. Her back ached from sitting on her tail. Oddly, though, she had become accustomed to her little spot in the jungle, and after surviving the thugs, the cops, and the idiot with the shotgun, she was feeling remarkably safe. Her breathing and pulse were normal. She was not sweating, though her jeans and shirt were still wet from exertion and humidity. Mark swatted and slapped mosquitoes, and said little. He was eerily calm. He chewed on a weed, watched the fence row, and acted as if he and he alone knew precisely when to make the next move.

'Let's go for a little walk,' he said, rising from his knees.

'Where to? The car?'

'No. Just down the trail. My leg is about to cramp.'

Her right leg was numb below the knee. Her left leg was dead below the hip, and she stood with great difficulty. She followed him through the brush until they were on the small trail parallel to the creek. He moved deftly through the darkness without the benefit of the flashlight, swatting mosquitoes and stretching his legs.

They stopped deep in the woods, out of sight of the fence rows of Romey's neighbors.

'I really think we should leave now,' she said, a bit louder since the houses were no longer in view. 'I have this fear of snakes, you see, and I don't want to step on one.'

He did not look at her, but stared in the direction of the ditch. 'I don't think it's a good idea to leave now,' he whispered.

She knew he had a reason for saying this. She'd not won an argument in the past six hours. 'Why?'

'Because those men could still be around here. In fact, they could be close by waiting for things to settle down so they can return. If we head for the car, we might meet them.'

'Mark, I can't take any more of this, okay? This may be fun and games for you, but I'm fifty-two years old and I've had it. I can't believe I'm hiding in this jungle at one o'clock in the morning.'

He put his forefinger over his lips. 'Shhhhhh. You're talking too loud. And this isn't a game.'

'Dammit, I know it's not a game! Don't lecture me.'

'Keep your cool, Reggie. We're safe now.'

'Safe my ass! I won't feel safe until I lock the door at the motel.'

'Then leave. Go on. Find your way back to the car, and leave.'

'Sure, and let me guess. You'll stay here, right?'

The moonlight disappeared, and suddenly the woods were darker. He turned his back to her and began walking toward their hiding place. She instinctively followed him, and this irritated her because at this moment she was depending on an eleven-year-old. But she followed him anyway, along a trail invisible to her, through the dense woods to the undergrowth, to about the same point where they'd waited before. The garage was barely visible.

The blood had returned to her legs, though they were very stiff. Her lower back throbbed. She could rub her hand across her forearm and feel the bumps from the mosquito bites. There was a thin sliver of blood on the back of her left hand, probably from a sticker in the brush or perhaps a weed. If she ever made it back to Memphis, she vowed to join a health club and get in shape. Not that she planned any more ventures like this, but she was tired of aching and gasping for breath.

Mark lowered onto one knee, stuck another weed in his mouth to chew on, and watched the garage.

They waited, almost in silence, for an hour. When she'd reached the point of leaving him and running wildly through the woods, Reggie said, 'Okay, Mark, I'm leaving. Do what you've got to do, because I'm leaving now.' But she didn't move.

They crouched together, and he pointed at the garage as if she didn't know where it was. 'I'm crawling up there, okay, with the flashlight, and I'm looking at the body, or the grave, or whatever they were digging at, okay?'

'No.'

'It won't take but a second, maybe. If I'm lucky, I'll be right back.'

'I'm going with you,' she said.

'No. I want you to stay here. I'm worried that those guys are watching too, somewhere along the tree line. If they come after me, I want you to start yelling and run like crazy.'

'No. No way, sweetheart. If you're looking at the body, then I'm looking at the body, and I'm not arguing about it. That's final.'

He looked at her eyes, four or five inches away, and decided not to argue. Her head was shaking and her jaw was tight. She looked cute under the cap.

'Then follow me, Reggie. Stay low, and listen. Always listen, okay.'

'All right, all right. I'm not totally helpless. In fact, I'm getting pretty good at crawling.'

They attacked from the brush on all fours again, two figures sliding in the still darkness. The grass was wet and cool. The gate, still open from the hasty retreat of the grave robbers, squeaked slightly when Reggie hooked it with a foot. Mark glared at her. They stopped behind the first tree, then eased to the next. Not a sound from anywhere. It was 2 A.M., and the neighborhood was silent. Mark, however, was worried about the nut next door with the gun. He doubted the man would sleep well with a thin sheet of plastic over the window, and he could envision him sitting in the kitchen watching the patio and waiting for the snap of a twig before he began blasting away again. They stopped at the next tree, then crawled to the junk pile.

She nodded once, taking small, quick breaths. They crouched and darted to the rear door of the garage, which was slightly open. Mark stuck his head inside. He turned on the flashlight and aimed it at the floor. Reggie eased in behind him.

The odor was thick and pungent, like a dead animal rotting in the sun. Reggie instinctively covered her nose and mouth. Mark breathed deeply, then held his breath.

The only open space in the cluttered room was in the center, where the boat had been parked. They crouched over the concrete slab. 'I'm getting sick,' Reggie said, barely opening her mouth.

Another ten minutes, and the body would have been out. They had started in the center, somewhere around the torso, and chipped away at each side. The black garbage bags, partially decomposed by the cement, had been ripped away. A ragged little trench had been cut away toward the feet and knees.

Mark had seen enough. He picked up a chisel, one that had been left behind, and jabbed it into black plastic.

'Don't!' Reggie whispered loudly, backing away but still seeing it all.

He ripped through the garbage bag with the chisel, and followed it closely with the light. He made a slow turn, then pulled the plastic with his hand. He bolted upright in horror, then slowly placed the light squarely into the decaying face of the late Senator Boyd Boyette.

Reggie took another step backward, and fell onto a pile of bags filled with aluminum cans. The racket was deafening in the still air. She scrambled and fought to get up in the darkness, but the thrashing and kicking created more noise. Mark grabbed a hand, and pulled her toward the boat. 'I'm sorry!' she whispered, standing two feet from the corpse without thinking about it.

'Shhhhh,' Mark said as he stepped onto a box and peeked through the window. A light came on next door. The shotgun could not be far behind.

'Let's go,' he said. 'Stay low.'

They eased through the rear door, and Mark closed it behind them. A door slammed at the neighbor's. He hit his hands and knees and slid around the debris pile, past the trees, and through the gate. Reggie was on his heels. They stopped crawling when they reached the brush. They crouched low and scampered like squirrels until they found the trail. Mark turned on the flashlight, and they didn't slow until they were at the creek. He ducked into some weeds, and turned off the light.

'What's the matter?' she asked, breathing hard, terrified, and damned sure not willing to pause in this getaway.

'Did you see his face?' Mark asked, in awe of what they'd just done.

'Of course I saw his face. Now let's go.'

'I want to see it again.'

She almost slapped him. Then she stood upright, hands on hips, and started walking toward the creek.

Mark ran beside her with the flashlight. 'I was just kidding.' She stopped and glared at him, then he took her hand and led her down the bank to the creek bed.

They entered the expressway by the Superdome and headed for Metairie. Traffic was light, though heavier than in most cities at two-thirty on a Sunday morning. Not a word had been spoken since they'd jumped in the car at West Park and left the area. And the silence bothered neither.

Reggie contemplated how close she'd been to death. Mafia hoods, snakes, crazy neighbors, police, guns, shock, heart attack – it would've made no difference. She was indeed fortunate to be here, racing along the expressway, soaked with perspiration, covered with insect bites, bloody from the wounds of nature, and dirty from a night in the jungle. It could've been so much worse. She'd take a hot shower at the motel, maybe sleep a little, then worry about the next move. She was exhausted from the fear and sudden shocks. She was in pain from the crawling and stooping. She was too old for this non-sense. The things lawyers do.

Mark gently scratched the bites on his left forearm, and watched the lights of New Orleans thin as they left downtown. 'Did you see that brown stuff on his face?' he asked without looking at her.

Though the face was now forever seared into her memory, she could not, at the moment, recall any brown stuff on it. It was a small, shriveled, partially decayed face, and one that she wished she could forget.

'I saw only the worms,' she said.

'The brown stuff was blood,' he said with the authority of a medical examiner.

She did not wish to pursue this conversation. There were more important things to discuss now that the silence was broken.

'I think we need to talk about your plans, now that this little escapade is behind us,' she said, glancing at him.

'We need to move fast, Reggie. Those guys will be back to get the body, don't you think?'

'Yes. For once I agree. They might be back now, for all we know.'

He scratched the other forearm, and placed an ankle on a knee. 'I've been thinking.'

'I'm sure you have.'

'There are two things I don't like about Memphis. The heat, and the flat land. There are no hills or mountains, you know what I mean? I've always thought it would be so nice to live in the mountains where the air is cool and the snow is deep in the wintertime. Wouldn't that be fun, Reggie?'

She smiled to herself and changed lanes. 'Sounds wonderful. Any particular mountain?'

'Out west somewhere. I love to watch those old 'Bonanza' reruns with Hoss and Little Joe. Adam was okay, but it really ticked me off when he left. I've watched them since I was a little kid, and I've always thought it would be neat to live out there.'

'What happened to the tall buildings and the crowded city?'

'That was yesterday. Today, I'm thinking about mountains.'

'Is that where you want to go, Mark?'

'I think so. Can I?'

'It can be arranged. Right now, they'll agree to almost anything.'

He stopped scratching and locked his fingers around his knee. His voice was tired. 'I can't go back to Memphis, can I, Reggie?'

'No,' she said softly.

'I didn't think so.' He thought about this for a few seconds. 'It's just as well, I guess. There's not much left there.'

'Think of it as yet another adventure, Mark. A new home, new school, new job for your mother. You'll have a much nicer place to live, new friends, mountains all around you if that's what you want.'

'Be honest with me, Reggie. Do you think they'll ever find me?'

She had to say no. At this moment, he had no choice. She would run and hide with him no more. They had to either call the FBI and strike a deal, or call the FBI and turn themselves in. This little trip was about to be over.

'No, Mark. They'll never find you. You have to trust the FBI.'

'I don't trust the FBI, and you don't either.'

'I don't completely distrust them. But right now, they've got the only game in town.'

'And I have to play along with them?'

'Unless you have a better idea.'

Mark was in the shower. Reggie dialed Clint's number, and listened as the phone rang a dozen times before he answered. It was almost 3 A.M.

'Clint, it's me.'

His voice was thick and slow. 'Reggie?'

'Yes, me, Reggie. Listen to me, Clint. Turn on the light, put your feet on the floor, and listen to me.'

'I'm listening.'

'Jason McThune's phone number is listed in the Memphis directory. I want you to call him, and tell him you need Larry Trumann's home phone number in New Orleans. Got that?'

'Why don't you look in the New Orleans phone book?'

'Don't ask questions, Clint. Just do as I say. Trumann's not listed down here.'

'What's going on, Reggie?' His words were much quicker.

'I'll call you back in fifteen minutes. Make some coffee. This could be a long day.' She hung up and unlaced her muddy sneakers.

Mark finished a quick shower, and ripped open a new package of underwear. He'd been embarrassed when Reggie bought them, but now it seemed so unimportant. He slipped into a new, yellow tee shirt, and pulled on his new but dirty Wal-Mart jeans. No socks. He wasn't going anywhere for a while, according to his attorney.

He left the tiny bathroom. Reggie was lying on the bed, shoes off, weeds and grass on the cuffs of her jeans. He sat on the edge of her bed, and stared at the wall.

'Feel better?' she asked.

He nodded, said nothing, then lay beside her. She pulled him close to her body, and placed an arm under his wet head. 'I'm all messed up, Reggie,' he said softly. 'I don't know what happens next any-more.'

The tough little boy who threw rocks through windows and out-smarted killers and cops and raced fearlessly through dark woods began to cry. He bit his lip and squinted his eyes, but couldn't stop the tears. She held him closer. Then he broke, finally, and sobbed loudly with no attempt to hold it back, no effort at being tough now. He cried without shame or embarrassment. His body shook and he squeezed her arm.

'It's okay, Mark,' she whispered in his ear. 'Everything's okay.' With her free hand, she wiped tears from her cheeks, and squeezed him even closer. Now it was up to her. She had to be the lawyer again, the counselor who moved daringly and called the shots. His life was once again in her hands.

The television was on but the sound was off. Its gray and blue shadows cast a dim light over the small room with its double beds and cheap furniture.

Jo Trumann grabbed the phone and searched the darkness for the clock. Ten minutes before four. She handed it to her husband, who took it and sat in the center of the bed. 'Hello,' he grunted.

'Hi, Larry. It's me, Reggie Love, remember?'

'Yeah. Where are you?'

'Here in New Orleans. We need to talk, and the sooner the better.'

He almost said something smart about the hour of the day, but thought better of it. It was important, or she wouldn't be calling. 'Sure. What's going on, Reggie?'

'Well, we've found the body, for starters.'

Trumann was suddenly on his feet and sliding into his house shoes. 'I'm listening.'

'I've seen the body, Larry. About two hours ago. I saw it with my own eyes. Smelled it too.'

'Where are you?' Trumann pressed a button on the recorder by the phone.

'I'm at a pay phone, so no cute stuff, okay?'

'Okay.'

'The people who buried the body tried to retrieve it last night, but they were unable to do so. Long story, Larry. I'll explain it later. I'm willing to bet they'll try again very soon.'

'Is the kid with you?'

'Yes. He knew where it was, and we came, we saw, and we conquered. You'll have it by noon today if you do as I say.'

'Anything.'

'That's the spirit, Larry. The kid wants to cut a deal. So we need to talk.'

'When and where?'

346

'Meet me in the Raintree Inn on Veterans Boulevard in Metairie. There's a grill that's open all night. How long will it take?'

'Give me forty-five minutes.'

'The sooner you get here, the sooner you'll get the body.'

'Can I bring someone with me?'

'Who?'

'K. O. Lewis.'

'He's in town?'

'Yeah. We knew you were here, so Mr. Lewis flew in a few hours ago.'

There was hesitation on her end. 'How'd you know I was here?'

'We have ways.'

'Who have you wired, Trumann? Talk to me. I want a straight answer.' Her voice was firm, yet with a trace of panic.

'Can I explain it when we meet?' he asked, kicking himself in the ass for opening this can of worms.

'Explain it now,' she commanded.

'I'll be happy to explain when – '

'Listen, asshole. I'm canceling the meeting unless you tell me right now who's been wired. Talk, Trumann.'

'Okay. We bugged the kid's mother's room at the hospital. It was a mistake. I didn't do it, okay. Memphis did it.'

'What'd they hear?'

'Not much. Your man Clint called yesterday afternoon and told her you guys were in New Orleans. That's all, I swear.'

'Would you lie to me, Trumann?' she asked, thinking of the tape from their first encounter.

'I'm not lying, Reggie,' Trumann insisted, thinking of the same damned tape.

There was a long pause in which he heard nothing but her breathing. 'Just you and K. O. Lewis,' she said. 'No one else. If Foltrigg shows up, all deals are off.'

'I swear.'

She hung up. Trumann immediately called K. O. Lewis at the Hilton. Then he called McThune in Memphis.

347

# CHAPTER THIRTY-NINE

Exactly forty-five minutes later, Trumann and Lewis walked nervously into the near empty grill at the Raintree Inn. Reggie waited at a table in the corner, far away from anyone. Her hair was wet and she wore no make-up. A bulky tee shirt with LSU TIGERS in purple letters was tucked into a pair of faded jeans. She sipped black coffee, and neither stood nor smiled as they approached and sat opposite her.

'Good morning, Ms. Love,' Lewis said in an attempt to be nice.

'It's Reggie, okay, and it's too early for pleasantries. Are we alone?'

'Of course,' Lewis said. At that moment eight FBI agents were guarding the parking lot, and more were on the way.

'No bugs, wire, body mikes, salt shakers, or ketchup bottles?'

'None.'

A waiter appeared, and they ordered coffee.

'Where's the kid?' Trumann asked.

'He's around. You'll see him soon enough.'

'Is he safe?'

'Of course he's safe. You boys couldn't catch him if he was on the streets begging for food.'

She handed Lewis a piece of paper. 'These are the names of three psychiatric hospitals that specialize in children. Battenwood in Rockford, Illinois. Ridgewood in Tallhassee. And Grant's Clinic in Phoenix. Any one of the three will do.'

Their eyes went slowly from her face to the list. They focused and studied it. 'But we've already checked with the clinic in Portland,' Lewis said, puzzled.

'I don't care where you've checked, Mr. Lewis. Take this list, and check again. I suggest you do it quickly. Call Washington, get them out of bed, and get it done.'

He folded the list and placed it under his elbow. 'You, uh, you say you've seen the body,' he asked, trying to sound authoritative but failing miserably.

She smiled. 'I have. Less than three hours ago. Muldanno's men were trying to get it, but we scared them off.'

'We?'

'Mark and I.'

348

They both studied her intently, and waited for the precious details of this wild, impossible little story. The coffee arrived, and they ignored both it and the waiter.

'We're not eating,' Reggie said rudely, and the waiter left.

'Here's the deal,' she said. 'There are a few provisions, none of which are in the least bit negotiable. Do it my way, do it now, and you might get the body before Muldanno carries it away and drops it in the ocean. If you blow it, gentlemen, I doubt you'll ever get this close again.'

They nodded furiously.

'Did you fly here on a private jet?' she asked Lewis.

'Yes. It's the Director's.'

'How many does it seat?'

'Twenty or so.'

'Good. Send it back to Memphis right now. I want you to pick up Dianne and Ricky Sway, along with his doctor and Clint. Fly them here immediately. McThune is welcome to come. We'll meet them at the airport, and when Mark is safely on board and the plane is gone, I'll tell you where the body is. How about it so far?'

'No problem,' Lewis said. Trumann was speechless.

'The entire family enters the witness protection plan. First, they pick the hospital, and when Ricky is able to move, they'll pick the city.'

'No problem.'

'Complete change of identification, nice little house, the works. This woman needs to stay home and raise her kids for a while, so I'd suggest a monthly allowance in the sum of four thousand dollars, guaranteed for three years. Plus an initial cash outlay of twenty-five thousand. They lost everything in the fire, remember?'

'Of course. These things are easy.' Lewis was so eager, she wished she'd asked for more.

'If, at some point, she wants to return to work, then I'd suggest a nice, cushy government job with no responsibilities, short hours, and a fat salary.'

'We have plenty of those.'

'Should they desire to move at any time, and to any place, they'll be allowed to do so, at your expense, of course.'

'We do it all the time.'

Trumann was smiling now, though he was trying not to.

'She'll need a car.'

'No problem.'

'Ricky may need extended treatment.'

'We'll cover it.'

'I want Mark examined by a psychiatrist, though I suspect he's in better shape than we are.'

'Done.'

'There are a couple of other minor matters, and they'll be covered in the agreement.'

'What agreement?'

'The agreement I'm having typed as we speak. It'll be signed by myself, Dianne Sway, Judge Harry Roosevelt, and you, Mr. Lewis, on behalf of Director Voyles.'

'What else is in the agreement?' Lewis asked.

'I want your assurance that you'll do everything in your power to compel the attendance of Roy Foltrigg before the Juvenile Court of Shelby County, Tennessee. Judge Roosevelt will want to discuss a few matters with him, and I'm sure Foltrigg will resist. If a subpoena is issued for him, I want it served by you, Mr. Trumann.'

'Gladly,' Trumann said with a nasty smile.

'We'll do what we can,' Lewis added, a bit confused.

'Good. Go make your phone calls. Get the plane in the air. Call McThune and tell him to pick up Clint Van Hooser and take him to the hospital. Get that damned bug off her phone, because I need to talk to her.'

'No problem.' They jumped to their feet.

'We'll meet right here in thirty minutes.'

Clint hammered away on his ancient Royal portable. His third cup of coffee shook each time he slapped the return and rattled the kitchen table. He studied his hurried chicken-scratch handwriting on the back of an *Esquire*, and tried to remember each provision as she'd spouted it over the phone. If he finished it, it would be, without a doubt, the sloppiest legal document ever prepared. He cursed and grabbed the Liquid Paper.

A knock on the door startled him. He ran his fingers through his unkempt and unwashed hair, and walked to the door. 'Who is it?'

'FBI.'

Not so loud, he almost said. He could hear the neighbors now, gossiping about him and his predawn arrest. Probably drugs, they would say.

He cracked the door and peeked under the safety chain. Two agents with puffy eyes stood in the darkness. 'We were told to come get you,' one said apologetically.

'I need some ID.'

They stuck their badges near the door. 'FBI,' the first one said.

Clint opened the door wider, and waved them in. 'I'll be a few more minutes. Have a seat.'

They stood awkwardly in the center of the den and he returned to the table and the typewriter. He pecked slowly. The chicken scratch failed him, and he ad-libbed the rest. The important points were there, he hoped. She always found something to change in his typing at the office, but this would have to do. He pulled it carefully from the Royal, and placed it in a small briefcase.

'Let's go,' he said.

At five-forty, Trumann returned alone to the table where Reggie waited. He brought two cellular phones. 'Thought we might need these,' he said.

'Where'd you get them?' Reggie asked.

'They were delivered to us here.'

'By some of your men?'

'That's right.'

'Just for fun, how many men do you have right now within a quarter of a mile of this place?'

'I don't know. Twelve or thirteen. It's routine, Reggie. They might be needed. We'll send a few to protect the kid, if you'll tell me where he is. I assume he's alone.'

'He's alone, and he's fine. Did you talk to McThune?'

'Yes. They've already picked up Clint.'

'That was fast.'

'Well, to be honest, we've had men watching his apartment for twenty-four hours now. We simply woke them up, and told them to knock on his door. We found your car, Reggie, but we couldn't find Clint's.'

'I'm driving it.'

'That's what I figured. Pretty slick, but we would've found you within twenty-four hours.'

'Don't be so cocky, Trumann. You've been looking for Boyette for eight months.'

'True. How'd the kid escape?'

'It's a long story. I'll save it for later.'

'You could be implicated, you know.'

'Not if you guys sign our little agreement.'

'We'll sign it, don't worry.' One of the phones rang, and Trumann grabbed it. As he listened, K. O. Lewis hurried to the table and brought his own cellular phone. He jumped into his chair, and leaned across the table, his eyes glowing with excitement. 'Talked to Washington. We're checking the hospitals right now. Everything looks fine. Director Voyles will call here in a minute. He'll probably want to talk to you.'

'How about the plane?'

Lewis checked his watch. 'It's leaving now, should be in Memphis by six-thirty.'

Trumann placed a hand over his phone. 'This is McThune. He's at the hospital waiting for Dr. Greenway and the administrator. They've made contact with Judge Roosevelt, and he's on his way down there.'

'Have you de-bugged her phone?' Reggie asked.

'Yes.'

'Removed the salt shakers?'

'No salt shakers. Everything's clean.'

'Good. Tell him to call back in twenty minutes,' she said.

Trumann mumbled into the phone and flipped a switch. Within seconds, K.O.'s phone beeped. He stuck it to his head, and broke into a large smile. 'Yes sir,' he said, most respectfully. 'Just a second.'

He jabbed the phone at Reggie. 'It's Director Voyles. He'd like to speak with you.'

Reggie took it slowly, and said, 'This is Reggie Love.' Lewis and Trumann watched like two kids waiting for ice cream.

A deep and very clear voice came from the other end. Though Denton Voyles had never been fond of the press during his forty-two years as Director of the FBI, they occasionally captured a brief word or two. The voice was familiar. 'Ms. Love, this is Denton Voyles. How are you?'

'Just fine. The name's Reggie, okay.'

'Sure, Reggie. Listen, K.O. just brought me up to date, and I want to assure you the FBI will do anything you want to protect this kid and his family. K.O. has full authority to act for me. We'll also protect you if you wish.'

'I'm more concerned about the child, Denton.'

Trumann and Lewis glanced at each other. She had just called him Denton, a feat no one had dared to attempt before. And she was not the least disrespectful.

'If you want, you can fax me the agreement here and I'll sign it myself,' he said.

'That won't be necessary, but thanks.'

'And my plane is at your disposal.'

'Thank you.'

'And I promise that we'll see to it that Mr. Foltrigg has to face the music in Memphis. We had nothing to do with the grand jury subpoenas, you understand?'

'Yes, I know.'

'Good luck to you, Reggie. You guys work out the details. Lewis can move mountains. Call me if you need me. I'll be at the office all day.'

'Thank you,' she said, and handed the phone back to K. O. Lewis, the mountain mover.

The assistant night manager of the grill, a young man of no more than nineteen with a peach fuzz mustache and an attitude, walked to the table. These people had been here for an hour, and from all indications they had set up camp. There were three phones in the center of the table. Some papers were lying about. The woman wore a sweatshirt and jeans. One of the men wore a cap and no socks. 'Excuse me,' he said curtly, 'can I be of assistance?'

Trumann glanced over his shoulder, and snapped, 'No.'

He hesitated, and took a step closer. 'I'm the assistant night manager, and I demand to know what you're doing here.'

Trumann snapped his fingers loudly, and two gentlemen reading the Sunday paper at a table not far away jumped to their feet and whipped badges from their pockets. They stuck them into the face of the assistant night manager. 'FBI,' they said together as they each took an arm and led him away. He did not return. The grill was still deserted.

A phone rang, and Lewis took it. He listened carefully. Reggie opened the Sunday New Orleans paper. At the bottom of the front page was her face. The picture was taken from the bar registry, and it was next to Mark's fourth-grade class photo. Side by side. Escaped. Disappeared. On the run. Boyette and all that. She turned to the comics.

'That was Washington,' Lewis reported as he placed the phone on the table. 'The clinic in Rockford is full. They're checking on the other two.'

Reggie nodded and sipped her coffee. The sun was making its first efforts of the day. Her eyes were red and her head was hurting, but the adrenaline was pumping. With a little luck, she would be home by dark.

'Look, Reggie, could you give us an idea how long it'll take to get to the body?' Trumann asked with great caution. He didn't want to press; didn't want to upset her. But he needed to start planning.

'Muldanno's still out there, and if he gets it first, we're all up a creek.' He paused and waited for her to say something. 'It's in the city, right?'

'If you don't get lost, you should be able to find it in fifteen minutes.'

'Fifteen minutes,' he repeated slowly, as if this was too good to be true. Fifteen minutes.

# CHAPTER FORTY

Clint hadn't smoked a cigarette in four years, but he found himself puffing nervously on a Virginia Slim. Dianne had one too, and they stood at the end of the hall and watched as the day broke over downtown Memphis. Greenway was in the room with Ricky. Next door, Jason McThune, the hospital administrator, and a small collection of FBI agents waited. Both Clint and Dianne had talked to Reggie in the past thirty minutes.

'The Director has given his word,' Clint said, sucking hard on the narrow cigarette, trying to extract a little smoke. 'There's no other choice, Dianne.'

She stared through the window with one arm across her chest and the other hand holding the cigarette near her mouth. 'We just leave, right? We just get on the plane and fly off into the sunset, and everybody lives happily ever after?'

'Something like that.'

'What if I don't want to, Clint?'

'You can't say no.'

'Why not?'

'It's very simple. Your son has made the decision to talk. He's also made the decision to enter the witness protection program, so like it or not, you have to go too. You and Ricky.'

'I'd like to talk to my son.'

'You can talk to him in New Orleans. If you can change his mind, then the deal's off. Reggie's not dropping the big news until you guys are on the plane and in the air.'

Clint was trying to be firm, yet compassionate. She was scared, weak, and vulnerable. Her hands trembled as she placed the filter between her lips.

'Ms. Sway,' a heavy voice said from behind. They turned to find the Honorable Harry M. Roosevelt standing behind them in a massive, bright blue jogging suit with Memphis State Tigers emblazoned across the front. It had to be a triple extra-large, and it stopped six inches above the ankles. A pair of ancient but seldom used running shoes covered his long feet. He was holding the two-page agreement Clint had typed.

She acknowledged his presence but said nothing.

'Hello, Your Honor,' Clint said quietly.

'I just talked to Reggie,' he said to Dianne. 'I'd say they've had a rather eventful trip.' He stepped between them and ignored Clint. 'I've read this agreement, and I'm inclined to sign it. I think it's in the best interests of Mark for you to do the same.'

'Is that an order?' she asked.

'No. I do not have the power to bind you to this agreement,' he said, then flashed a huge, warm smile. 'But, I would if I could.'

She placed the cigarette in an ashtray on the windowsill, and stuck both hands deep into the pockets of her jeans. 'And if I don't?'

'Then Mark will be returned here, placed back in detention, and beyond that, who knows. He will eventually be forced to talk. the situation is much more urgent now.'

'Why?'

'Because we now know for a fact that Mark knows where the body is. So does Reggie. They could be in great danger. You're at the point, Ms. Sway, where you have to trust people.'

'That's easy for you to say.'

'Indeed it is. But if I were you, I'd sign this and get on the plane.'

Dianne slowly took the agreement from His Honor. 'Let's go talk to Dr. Greenway.'

They followed her down the hall to the room next to Ricky's.

Twenty minutes later, the ninth floor of St. Peter's was sealed off by a dozen FBI agents. The waiting room was evacuated. The nurses were told to remain at their station. Three of the elevators were stopped on the ground floor. The other was held in place on the ninth by an agent.

The door to Room 943 opened, and little Ricky Sway, drugged and sound asleep, was wheeled into the hallway on a stretcher pushed by Jason McThune and Clint Van Hooser. On this, his sixth day of confinement, he was no better than when he first arrived. Greenway walked along one side, Dianne the other. Harry followed along for a few steps, then stopped.

The stretcher was pushed into the waiting elevator, which decended to the fourth floor, also secured by FBI agents. It was rushed a short distance to a service elevator, where Agent Durston held the door, then taken to the second floor, also secured. Ricky never moved. Dianne held his arm and jogged beside the stretcher.

They maneuvered through a series of short corridors and metal doors, and were suddenly on a flat roof. A helicopter was waiting. Ricky was loaded quickly, and Dianne, Clint, and McThune climbed aboard.

Minutes later, the helicopter landed near a hangar at Memphis International Airport. A half dozen FBI agents guarded the pad as Ricky was rolled to a nearby jet.

At ten minutes before seven, a cellular phone rang at the corner table of the Raintree Grill, and Trumann grabbed it. He listened and checked his watch. 'They're in the air,' he announced and set the phone down. Lewis was talking to Washington again.

Reggie breathed deeply and smiled at Trumann. 'The body's in concrete. You'll need a few hammers and chisels.'

Trumann choked on his orange juice. 'Okay. Anything else?'

'Yeah. Place a couple of your boys near the intersection of St. Joseph and Carondelet.'

'Close by?'

'Just do it, okay.'

'Done. Anything else?'

'I'll be back in a minute.' Reggie walked to the registration desk, and asked the clerk to check the fax machine. The clerk returned with a copy of the two-page agreement, which Reggie read closely. The typing was horrible, but the words were perfect. She returned to the table. 'Let's get Mark,' she said.

Mark finished brushing his teeth for the third time, and sat on the edge of the bed. His black-and-gold Saints canvas bag was packed with dirty clothes and new underwear. Cartoons were on, but he was not interested.

He heard a car door, then footsteps, then a knock. 'Mark, it's me,' Reggie said.

He opened the door, but she did not step inside. 'Are you ready to go?'

'I guess.' The sun was up and the parking lot was visible. A familiar face was behind her. It was one of the FBI agents from the first meeting at the hospital. Mark grabbed his bag, and stepped out into the parking lot. Three cars were waiting. A man opened the rear door of the middle car, and Mark and his attorney got in.

The little motorcade sped away.

'Everything's fine,' Reggie said, taking his hand. The two men in the front seat stared straight ahead. 'Ricky and your mother are on the plane. They'll be here in about an hour. Are you okay?'

'I guess. Have you told them?' he whispered.

'Not yet,' she answered. 'Not until you're on the plane and in the air.'

'Are all these guys FBI agents?'

She nodded and patted his hand. He suddenly felt important, sitting in the rear of his own black car, being rushed to the airport to board a private jet, cops all around just to protect him. He crossed his legs and sat a bit straighter.

He'd never flown before.

# CHAPTER FORTY-ONE

Barry paced nervously before the tinted windows in Johnny's office, and watched the tugs and barges on the river. His nasty eyes were red, but not from booze or partying. He hadn't slept. He'd waited here at the warehouse for the body to be delivered to him, and when Leo and company arrived around one without it, he had called his uncle.

Johnny, on this fine Sunday morning, was wearing neither tie nor suspenders. He paced slowly behind his desk, puffing blue smoke from his third cigar of the day. A thick cloud hung not far above his head.

The screaming and ass chewing had ended hours ago. Barry had cursed Leo and Ionucci and the Bull, and Leo had cursed back. But with time, the panic subsided. Throughout the night, Leo had periodically driven by Clifford's house, always in a different vehicle, and seeing nothing unusual. The body was still there.

Johnny decided to wait twenty-four hours and try again. They would watch the place during the day, and attack with full force after dark. The Bull assured him he could have the body out of the concrete in ten minutes.

Just be cool, Johnny had told everyone. Just be cool.

Roy Foltrigg finished the Sunday paper on the patio of his suburban split-level, and walked barefooted across the wet grass with a cup of cold coffee. He had slept little. He had waited in the darkness on his front porch for the paper to arrive, then ran to fetch it in his pajamas and bathrobe. He had called Trumann, but, strangely, Mrs. Trumann wasn't sure where her husband had gone.

He inspected his wife's rosebushes along the back fence, and asked himself for the hundredth time where Mark Sway would run to. There was no doubt, at least in his mind, that Reggie had helped him escape. She'd obviously gone crazy again, and run off with the kid. He smiled to himself. He'd have the pleasure of busting her ass.

The hangar was a quarter of a mile from the main terminal, in a row of identical buildings all drab gray and sitting quietly together. The words GULF AIR were painted in orange letters above the tall double doors, which were opening as the three cars stopped in front of the hangar. The floor was sparkling concrete, painted green without a speck of dirt and covered with nothing but two private jets side by side in a far corner. A few lights were on, and their reflections glowed in the green floor. The building was big enough for a stock car race, Mark thought as he stretched his neck for a glimpse of the two jets.

With the doors out of the way, the entire front of the hangar was now open. Three men walked hurriedly along the back wall as if searching for something. Two more stood by one door. Outside, another half dozen moved slowly about, keeping their distance from the cars that had just parked.

'Who are these people?' Mark asked, in the general direction of the front seat.

'They're with us,' Trumann said.

'They're FBI agents,' Reggie clarified.

'Why so many?'

'They're just being careful,' she said. 'How much longer, do you think?' she asked Trumann.

He glanced at his watch. 'Probably thirty minutes.'

'Let's walk around,' she said, opening her door. As if on cue, the other eleven doors in the little parade opened and the cars emptied. Mark looked around at the other hangars, and the terminal, and a plane landing on the runway in front of them. This had become terribly exciting. Not three weeks ago, he'd beaten the crap out of a subdivision kid at school after the kid taunted him because he'd never flown. If they could only see him now. Rushed to the airport by private car, waiting for his private jet to take him anywhere he wanted to go. No more trailers. No more fights with subdivision kids. No more notes to Mom, because now she would be at home. He'd decided, sitting alone in the motel room, that this was a wonderful idea. He'd come to New Orleans and out-smarted the Mafia in its own backyard, and he could do it again.

He caught a few stares from the agents by the door. They cut their eyes quickly at him, then looked away. Just checking him out. Maybe he'd sign some autographs later.

He followed Reggie into the vast hangar, and the two private jets caught his attention. They were like small, shiny toys sitting under the Christmas tree waiting to be played with. One was black, the other silver, and Mark stared at them.

A man in an orange shirt with Gulf Air on a patch above the pocket closed the door to a small office inside the hangar and walked in their direction. K. O. Lewis met him, and they talked quietly. The man waved at the office, and said something about coffee.

Larry Trumann knelt beside Mark, still staring at the jets. 'Mark, do you remember me?' he asked with a smile.

'Yes sir. I met you at the hospital.'

'That's right. My name's Larry Trumann.' He offered his hand, and Mark shook it slowly. Children are not supposed to shake hands with adults. 'I'm an FBI agent here in New Orleans.'

Mark nodded and kept staring at the jets.

'Would you like to look at them?' Trumann asked.

'Can I?' he asked, suddenly friendly to Trumann.

'Sure.' Trumann stood and placed a hand on Mark's shoulder. They walked slowly across the gleaming concrete, the sounds of Trumann's steps echoing upward. They stopped in front of the black jet. 'Now this is a Lear Jet,' Trumann began.

Reggie and K. O. Lewis left the small office with tall cups of steaming coffee. The agents who'd escorted them here had slipped into the shadows of the hangar. They sipped what must've been their tenth cups of this long morning, and watched as Trumann and the kid inspected the jets.

'He's a brave kid,' Lewis said.

'He's remarkable,' Reggie said. 'At times he thinks like a terrorist, then he cries like a little child.'

'He is a child.'

'I know. But don't tell him. It may upset him, and, hell, who knows what he might do.' She took a long sip. 'Truly remarkable.'

K.O. blew into his cup, then took a tiny sip. 'We've pulled some strings. There's a room waiting for Ricky at Grant's Clinic in Phoenix. We need to know if that's the destination. The pilot called five minutes ago. He has to get clearance, file a flight plan, you know.'

'Phoenix it is. Complete confidentiality, okay? Register the kid under another name. Same for the mother and Mark. Keep some of your boys nearby. I want you to pay for his doctor's trip out there and for a few days of work.'

'No problem. The people in Phoenix have no idea what's coming. Have you guys talked about a permanent home?'

'A little, not much. Mark says he wants to live in the mountains.'

'Vancouver's nice. We vacationed there last summer. Absolutely gorgeous.'

'Out of the country?'

'No problem. Director Voyles said they can go anywhere. We've placed a few witnesses outside the States, and I think the Sways are perfect candidates. These people will be taken care of, Reggie. You have my word.'

The man in the orange shirt joined Mark and Trumann, and was now in charge of the tour. He lowered the steps to the black Lear, and the three disappeared inside.

'I must confess,' Lewis said after he swallowed another scalding dose of coffee, 'I was never convinced the kid knew.'

'Clifford told him everything. He knew exactly where it was.'

'Did you?'

'No. Not until yesterday. When he first came to my office, he told me that he knew, but he didn't tell me where it was. Thank god for that. He kept it to himself until we were near the body yesterday afternoon.'

'Why'd you come here? Seems awfully risky.'

Reggie nodded at the jets. 'You'll have to ask him. He insisted we find the body. If Clifford lied to him, then he figured he was off the hook.'

'And so you just drove down here and looked for the body? Just like that?'

'It was a bit more involved. It's a long story, K.O., and I'll give you all the details over a long dinner.'

'I can't wait.'

Mark's small head was now in the cockpit, and Reggie half expected the engines to start, the plane to taxi slowly from the hangar, out onto the runway, and Mark to dazzle them with a perfect take-off. She knew he could do it.

'Are you concerned about your own safety?' Lewis asked.

'Not really. I'm just a humble lawyer. What would they gain by coming after me?'

'Retribution. You don't understand the way they think.'

'Indeed I don't.'

'Director Voyles would like for us to stick close for a few months, at least until the trial is over.'

'I don't care what you do, I just don't want to see anyone who's watching me, okay?'

'Fine. We have ways.'

The tour moved to the second jet, a silver Citation, and for the moment Mark Sway had forgotten about dead bodies and bad guys lurking in shadows. The steps came down, and he climbed aboard with Trumann in tow.

An agent with a radio walked to Reggie and Lewis, and said, 'They're on final approach.' They followed him to the opening of the hangar near the cars. A minute later Mark and Trumann joined them, and as they watched the sky to the north a tiny plane appeared.

'That's them,' Lewis said. Mark inched his way next to Reggie and took her hand. The plane grew larger as it approached the runway. It, too, was black, but much larger than the jets in the hangar. Agents, some in suits and some in jeans, began moving around as the plane taxied to them. It stopped a hundred feet away, and the engines died. A full minute passed before the door opened and the stairs hit the ground.

Jason McThune trotted down first, and when he stepped onto the tarmac a dozen FBI agents had the plane surrounded. Dianne and Clint were next. They joined McThune, and together the three walked briskly toward the hangar.

Mark released Reggie's hand and ran to meet his mother. Dianne grabbed and hugged him, and for an awkward second or two everyone else either watched or looked at the terminal in the distance.

They said nothing as they embraced. He squeezed her tightly around the neck, and finally said, through tears, 'I'm sorry, Mom. I'm so sorry.' She clutched his head and pressed it to her shoulder, and at the same time thought of strangling him and of never letting go.

Reggie led them into the small but clean office, and offered Dianne coffee. She declined. Trumann, McThune, Lewis, and the gang waited nervously outside the door. Trumann, especially, was anxious. What if they changed their minds? What if Muldanno got the body? What if? He paced and fidgeted, glanced at the locked door, asked Lewis a hundred questions. Lewis sipped coffee and tried to remain calm. It was now twenty minutes before eight. The sun was bright, the air humid.

Mark sat in his mother's lap, and Reggie, the lawyer, sat behind the desk. Clint stood by the door.

'I'm glad you came,' Reggie said to Dianne.

'I didn't have much of a choice.'

'You do now. You can change your mind, if you want. You can ask me anything.'

'Do you realize how fast all this is happening, Reggie? Six days ago, I came home and found Ricky curled in his bed sucking his thumb. Then Mark and the cop showed up. Now I'm being asked to become someone else and run away to another world. My god.'

'I understand,' Reggie said. 'But we can't stop things.'

'Are you mad at me, Mom?' he asked.

'Yeah. No cookies for a week.' She stroked his hair. There was a long pause.

'How's Ricky?' Reggie asked.

'About the same. Dr. Greenway is trying to bring him around so he can enjoy the plane ride. But they had to drug him slightly when we left the hospital.'

'I'm not going back to Memphis, Mom,' Mark said.

'The FBI has contacted a children's psychiatric hospital in Phoenix, and they're waiting for you now,' Reggie explained. 'It's a good one. Clint checked it out Friday. It's been highly recommended.'

'So we're going to live in Phoenix?' Dianne asked.

'Only until Ricky is released. Then you go wherever you want. Canada. Australia. New Zealand. It's up to you. Or you can stay in Phoenix.'

'Let's go to Australia, Mom. They still have real cowboys down there. Saw it in a movie once.'

'No more movies for you, Mark,' Dianne said, still rubbing his head. 'We wouldn't be here if you hadn't watched so many movies.'

'What about TV?'

'No. From now on, you'll do nothing but read books.'

The office was silent for a long time. Reggie had nothing else to say. Clint was dead tired and about to fall asleep on his feet. Dianne's mind was moving clearly now, for the first time in a week. Frightened as she was, she had escaped the dungeon at St. Peter's. She had seen sunlight and smelled real air. She was holding her lost son, and the other one would improve. All these people were trying to help. The lamp factory was history. Employment was now a thing of the past. No more cheap trailers. No more worries about past due child support and unpaid bills. She could watch the boys grow up. She could join the PTA. She could buy some clothes and do her nails. Good gosh, she was only thirty years old. With a little effort and a little money, she could be attractive again. There were men out there.

As dark and treacherous as the future seemed, it could not be as horrible as the past six days. Something had to give. She was due a break. Have a little faith, baby.

'I guess we'd better get to Phoenix,' she said.

Reggie grinned with relief. She pulled the agreement from a briefcase Clint brought with him. It had been signed by Harry and McThune. Reggie added her signature, and handed the pen to Dianne. Mark, now bored with hugs and tears, walked to the wall and admired a series of framed color photos of jets. 'On second thought, I might be a pilot,' he said to Clint.

Reggie took the agreement. 'I'll be back in a minute,' she said, opening the door and closing it behind her.

Trumann jumped when it opened. Hot coffee splashed from his trembling cup and burned his right hand. He cursed, and slung at the floor, then wiped it on his pants.

'Relax, Larry,' Reggie said. 'Everything's fine. Sign here.' She stuck the agreement in his face, and Trumann scrawled his name. K.O. did the same.

'Get the plane ready,' Reggie said. 'They're going to Phoenix.'

'K.O. turned and flashed a hand signal at the agents by the hangar entry. McThune jogged toward them with more instructions. Reggie returned to the office and closed the door.

K.O. and Trumann shook hands and smiled goofily. They stared at the door to the office.

'What now?' Trumann mumbled.

'She's a lawyer,' K.O. said. 'Nothing's ever easy with lawyers.'

McThune walked to Trumann and handed him an envelope. 'It's a subpoena for the Reverend Roy Foltrigg,' he said with a smile. 'Judge Roosevelt issued it this morning.'

'On Sunday morning?' Trumann asked, taking the envelope.

'Yeah. He called his clerk, and they met at his office. He's very excited about seeing Foltrigg back in Memphis.'

The three chuckled at this. 'It'll be served upon the Reverend this morning,' Trumann said.

After a minute, the door opened. Clint, Dianne, Mark, then Reggie filed out and headed for the tarmac. The engines were started. Agents scurried about. Trumann and Lewis escorted them to the hangar doors, and stopped.

K.O., ever the diplomat, offered his hand to Dianne, and said, 'Good luck, Ms. Sway. Jason McThune will escort you to Phoenix, and handle things once you get there. You are completely safe. And if we can do anything to help, please let us know.'

Dianne gave a sweet smile and shook his hand. Mark offered his, and said, 'Thanks, K.O. You've been a real pain in the ass.' But he was smiling, and it struck everyone as being funny.

K.O. laughed. 'Good luck to you, Mark, and I assure you, son, you've been a bigger pain.'

'Yeah, I know. Sorry about all this.' He shook hands with Trumann, and walked away with his mother and McThune. Reggie and Clint remained by the hangar door.

At some point, about halfway to the jet, Mark stopped. As if suddenly scared, he froze in place and watched as Dianne climbed the steps to the plane. At no time during the past twenty-four hours had it occurred to him that Reggie would be left behind. He had simply assumed, for whatever reason, that she would stay with them until this ordeal was over. She would fly off with them, and hang around the new hospital until they were safe. And as he stood there, a tiny figure on the vast tarmac, motionless and stunned, he realized she was not beside him. She was back there with Clint and the FBI.

He turned slowly, and stared at her in terror as this reality sunk in. He took two steps toward her, then stopped. Reggie left her small group and walked to him. She knelt on the tarmac, and looked into his panicked eyes.

He bit his lip. 'You can't come with us, can you?' he asked slowly in a frightened voice. Though they had talked for hours, this subject was never touched.

She shook her head as her eyes watered.

He wiped his eyes with the back of his hand. The FBI agents were close by, but not watching. For once in his life, he was not ashamed to cry in public. 'But I want you to go,' he said.

'I can't, Mark.' She leaned forward, took both of his shoulders, and hugged him gently. 'I can't go.'

Tears flooded his cheeks. 'I'm sorry about all this. You didn't deserve it.'

'But if it hadn't happened, Mark, I never would've met you.' She kissed him on the cheek, and held his shoulders tight. 'I love you, Mark. I'll miss you.'

'I'll never see you again, will I?' His lip quivered and tears dripped off his chin. His voice was frail.

She gritted her teeth and shook her head. 'No, Mark.'

Reggie took a deep breath, and stood. She wanted to grab him, and take him home to Momma Love. He could have the bedroom upstairs, and all the spaghetti and ice cream he could eat.

Instead, she nodded at the plane where Dianne was standing in the door, waiting patiently. He wiped his cheeks again. 'I'll never see you again,' he said, almost to himself. He turned, and made a feeble attempt to straighten his shoulders, but he couldn't. He walked slowly to the steps, and glanced back for one last look.

# CHAPTER FORTY-TWO

Minutes later, as the plane taxied to the end of the runway, Clint eased to her side and took her hand. They watched silently as it took off and finally disappeared in the clouds.

She wiped tears from both cheeks. 'I think I'll become a real estate lawyer,' she said. 'I can't take any more of this.'

'He's quite a kid,' Clint said.

'It hurts, Clint.'

He squeezed her hand harder. 'I know.'

Trumann appeared quietly beside her, and the three of them looked at the sky. She noticed him, and pulled the micro-cassette tape from her pocket. 'It's yours,' she said. He took it.

'The body is in the garage behind Jerome Clifford's house,' she said, still wiping tears, '886 East Brookline.'

Trumann turned to his left and stuck a radio to his mouth. The agents bolted for their cars. Reggie and Clint did not move.

'Thanks, Reggie,' Trumann said, now suddenly anxious to leave.

She nodded at the distant clouds. 'Don't thank me,' she said. 'Thank Mark.'

# The Firm

*To Renée*

# CHAPTER ONE

The senior partner studied the résumé for the hundredth time and again found nothing he disliked about Mitchell Y. McDeere, at least not on paper. He had the brains, the ambition, the good looks. And he was hungry; with his background, he had to be. He was married, and that was mandatory. The firm had never hired an unmarried lawyer, and it frowned heavily on divorce, as well as womanizing and drinking. Drug testing was in the contract. He had a degree in accounting, passed the CPA exam the first time he took it and wanted to be a tax lawyer, which of course was a requirement with a tax firm. He was white, and the firm had never hired a black. They managed this by being secretive and clubbish and never soliciting job applications. Other firms solicited, and hired blacks. This firm recruited, and remained lily white. Plus, the firm was in Memphis, of all places, and the top blacks wanted New York or Washington or Chicago. McDeere was a male, and there were no women in the firm. That mistake had been made in the mid-seventies when they recruited the number one grad from Harvard, who happened to be a she and a wizard at taxation. She lasted four turbulent years and was killed in a car wreck.

He looked good, on paper. He was their top choice. In fact, for this year there were no other prospects. The list was very short. It was McDeere or no one.

The managing partner, Royce McKnight, studied a dossier labeled Mitchell Y. McDeere – Harvard." An inch thick with small print and a few photographs, it had been prepared by some ex-CIA agents in a private intelligence outfit in Bethesda. They were clients of the firm and each year did the investigating for no fee. It was easy work, they said, checking out unsuspecting law students. They learned, for instance, that he preferred to leave the Northeast, that he was holding three job offers, two in New York and one in Chicago, and that the highest offer was $76,000 and the lowest was $68,000. He was in demand. He had been given the opportunity to cheat on a securities exam during his second year. He declined, and made the highest grade in the class. Two months ago he had been offered cocaine at a law school party. He said no and left when everyone began snorting. He drank and occasional beer, but drinking was expensive and he had no money. He owed close to $23,000 in student loans. He was hungry.

Royce McKnight flipped through the dossier and smiled. McDeere was their man.

Lamar Quin was thirty-two and not yet a partner. He had been brought along to look young and act young and project a youthful image for Bendini, Lambert & Locke, which in fact was a young firm, since most of the partners retired in their late forties or early fifties with money to burn. He would make partner in this firm. With a six-figure income guaranteed for the rest of his life, Lamar could enjoy the twelve-hundred-dollar tailored suits that hung so comfortably from his tall athletic frame. He strolled nonchalantly across the thousand-dollar-a-day suite and poured another cup of decaf. He checked his watch. He glanced at the two partners sitting at the small conference table near the windows.

Precisely at two-thirty someone knocked on the door. Lamar looked at the partners, who slid the résumé and dossier into an open briefcase. All three reached for their jackets. Lamar buttoned his top button and opened the door.

'Mitchell McDeere?' he asked with a huge smile and a hand thrust forward.

'Yes.' They shook hands violently.

'Nice to meet you, Mitchell. I'm Lamar Quin.'

'My pleasure. Please call me Mitch.' He stepped inside and quickly surveyed the spacious room.

'Sure, Mitch.' Lamar grabbed his shoulder and led him across the suite, where the partners introduced themselves. They were exceedingly warm and cordial. They offered him coffee, then water. They sat around a shiny mahogany conference table and exchanged pleasantries. McDeere unbuttoned his coat and crossed his legs. He was now a seasoned veteran in the search for employment, and he knew they wanted him. He relaxed. With three job offers from three of the most prestigious firms in the country, he did not need this interview, this firm. He could afford to be a little overconfident now. He was there out of curiosity. And he longed for warmer weather.

Oliver Lambert, the senior partner, leaned forward on his elbows and took control of the preliminary chitchat. He was glib and engaging with a mellow, almost professional baritone. At sixty-one, he was the grandfather of the firm and spent most of his time administering and balancing the enormous egos of some of the richest lawyers in the country. He was the counselor, the one the younger associates went to with their troubles. Mr. Lambert also handled the recruiting, and it was his mission to sign Mitchell Y. McDeere.

'Are you tired of interviewing?' asked Oliver Lambert.

'Not really. It's part of it.'

Yes, yes, they all agreed. Seemed like yesterday they were interviewing and submitting résumés and scared to death they wouldn't find a job and three years of sweat and torture would be down the drain. They knew what he was going through, all right.

'May I ask a question?' Mitch asked.

'Certainly.'

'Sure.'

'Anything.'

'Why are we interviewing in this hotel room? The other firms interview on campus through the placement office.'

'Good question.' They all nodded and looked at each other and agreed it was a good question.

'Perhaps I can answer that, Mitch,' said Royce McKnight, the managing partner. 'You must understand our firm. We are different, and we take pride in that. We have forty-one lawyers, so we are small compared with other firms. We don't hire too many people; about one every other year. We offer the highest salary and fringes in the country, and I'm not exaggerating. So we are very selective. We selected you. The letter you received last month was sent after we screened over two thousand third year law students at the best schools. Only one letter was sent. We don't advertise openings and we don't solicit applications. We keep a low profile, and we do things differently. That's our explanation.'

'Fair enough. What kind of firm is it?'

'Tax. Some securities, real estate and banking, but eighty percent is tax work. That's why we wanted to meet you, Mitch. You have an incredibly strong tax background.'

'Why'd you go to Western Kentucky?' asked Oliver Lambert.

'Simple. They offered me a full scholarship to play football. Had it not been for that, college would've been impossible.'

'Tell us about your family.'

'Why is that important?'

'It's very important to us, Mitch,' Royce McKnight said warmly.

They all say that, thought McDeere. 'Okay, my father was killed in the coal mines when I was seven years old. My mother remarried and lives in Florida. I had two brothers. Rusty was killed in Vietnam. I have a brother named Ray McDeere.'

'Where is he?'

'I'm afraid that's none of your business.' He stared at Royce McKnight and exposed a mammoth chip on his shoulder. The dossier, oddly, was silent on Ray.

'I'm sorry,' the managing partner said softly.

'Mitch, our firm is in Memphis,' Lamar said. 'Does that bother you?'

'Not at all. I'm not fond of cold weather.'

'Have you ever been to Memphis?'

'No.'

'We'll have you down soon. You'll love it.'

Mitch smiled and nodded and played along. Were these guys serious? How could he consider such a small firm in such a small town when Wall Street was waiting?

'How are you ranked in your class?' Mr. Lambert asked.

'Top five.' Not top five percent, but top five. That was enough of an answer for all of them. Top five out of three hundred. He could have said number three, a fraction away from number two, and within striking distance of number one. But he didn't. They came from inferior schools – Chicago, Columbia and Vanderbilt, as he re-called from a cursory examination of Martindale-Hubbell's Legal Directory. He knew they would not dwell on academics.

'Why did you select Harvard?'

'Actually, Harvard selected me. I applied at several schools and was accepted everywhere. Harvard offered more financial assistance. I thought it was the best school. Still do.'

'You've done quite well here, Mitch,' Mr. Lambert said, admiring the résumé. The dossier was in the briefcase, under the table.

'Thank you. I've worked hard.'

'You made extremely high grades in your tax and securities courses.'

'That's where my interest lies.'

'We've reviewed your writing sample, and it's quite impressive.'

'Thank you. I enjoy research.'

They nodded and acknowledged this obvious lie. It was part of the ritual. No law student or lawyer in his right mind enjoyed research, yet, without fail, every prospective associate professed a deep love for the library.

'Tell us about your wife,' Royce McKnight said, almost meekly. They braced for another reprimand. But it was a standard, non-sacred area explored by every firm.

'Her name is Abby. She has a degree in elementary education from Western Kentucky. We graduated one week and got married the next. For the past three years she's taught at a private kindergarten near Boston College.'

'And is the marriage –'

'We're very happy. We've known each other since high school.'

'What position did you play?' asked Lamar, in the direction of less sensitive matters.

'Quarterback. I was heavily recruited until I messed up a knee in my last high school game. Everyone disappeared except Western Kentucky. I played off and on for four years, even started some as a junior, but the knee would never hold up.'

'How'd you make straight As and play football?'

'I put the books first.'

'I don't imagine Western Kentucky is much of an academic school,' Lamar blurted with a stupid grin, and immediately wished he could take it back. Lambert and McKnight frowned and acknowledged the mistake.

'Sort of like Kansas State,' Mitch replied. They froze, all of them froze, and for a few seconds stared incredulously at each other. This guy McDeere knew Lamar Quin went to Kansas State. He had never met Lamar Quin and had no idea who would appear on behalf of the firm and conduct the interview. Yet he knew. He had gone to Martindale-Hubbell's and checked them out. He had read the biographical sketches of all of the forty-one lawyers in the firm, and in a split second he had recalled that Lamar Quin, just one of the forty-one, had gone to Kansas State. Damn, they were impressed.

'I guess that came out wrong,' Lamar apologized.

'No problem.' Mitch smiled warmly. It was forgotten.

Oliver Lambert cleared his throat and decided to get personal again. 'Mitch, our firm frowns on drinking and chasing women. We're not a bunch of Holy Rollers, but we put business ahead of everything. We keep low profiles and we work very hard. And we make plenty of money.'

'I can live with all that.'

'We reserve the right to test any member of the firm for drug use.'

'I don't use drugs.'

'Good. What's your religious affiliation?'

'Methodist.'

'Good. You'll find a wide variety in our firm. Catholics, Baptists, Episcopalians. It's really none of our business, but we like to know. We want stable families. Happy lawyers are productive lawyers. That's why we ask these questions.'

Mitch smiled and nodded. He'd heard this before.

The three looked at each other, then at Mitch. This meant they had reached the point in the interview where the interviewee was supposed to ask one or two intelligent questions. Mitch recrossed his legs. Money, that was the big question, particularly how it compared to his other offers. If it isn't enough, thought Mitch, then it was nice to meet you fellas. If the pay is attractive, *then* we can discuss families and marriages and football and churches. But, he knew, like all the other firms they had to shadowbox around the issue until things got awkward and it was apparent they had discussed everything in the world but money. So, hit them with a soft question first.

'What type of work will I do initially?'

They nodded and approved of the question. Lambert and McKnight looked at Lamar. This answer was his.

'We have something similar to a two-year apprenticeship, although we don't call it that. We'll send you all over the country to tax seminars. Your education is far from over. You'll spend two weeks next winter in Washington at the American Tax Institute. We take great pride in our technical expertise, and the training is continual, for all of us. If you want to pursue a master's in taxation, we'll pay for it. As far as practicing law, it won't be very exciting for the first two years. You'll do a lot of research and generally boring stuff. But you'll be paid handsomely.'

'How much?'

Lamar looked at Royce McKnight, who eyed Mitch and said, 'We'll discuss the compensation and other benefits when you come to Memphis.'

'I want a ballpark figure or I may not come to Memphis.' He smiled, arrogant but cordial. He spoke like a man with three job offers.

The partners smiled at each other, and Mr. Lambert spoke first. 'Okay. A base salary of eighty thousand the first year, plus bonuses. Eighty-five thousand the second year, plus bonuses. A low-interest mortgage so you can buy a home. Two country club memberships. And a new BMW. You pick the color, of course.'

They focused on his lips, and waited for the wrinkles to form on his cheeks and the teeth to break through. He tried to conceal a smile, but it was impossible. He chuckled.

'That's incredible,' he mumbled. Eighty thousand in Memphis equaled a hundred and twenty thousand in New York. Did the man say BMW! His Mazda hatchback had a million miles on it and for the moment had to be jump-started while he saved for a rebuilt starter.

'Plus a few more fringes we'll be glad to discuss in Memphis.'

Suddenly he had a strong desire to visit Memphis. Wasn't it by the river?

The smile vanished and he regained his composure. He looked sternly, importantly at Oliver Lambert and said, as if he'd forgotten about the money and the home and the BMW, 'Tell me about your firm.'

'Forty-one lawyers. Last year we earned more per lawyer than any firm our size or larger. That includes every big firm in the country. We take only rich clients – corporations, banks and wealthy people who pay our healthy fees and never complain. We've developed a specialty in international taxation, and it's both exciting and very profitable. We deal only with people who can pay.'

'How long does it take to make partner?'

'On the average, ten years, and it's a hard ten years. It's not unusual for our partners to earn half a million a year, and most retire before they're fifty. You've got to pay your dues, put in eighty-hour weeks, but it's worth it when you make partner.'

Lamar leaned forward. 'You don't have to be a partner to earn six figures. I've been with the firm seven years, and went over a hundred thousand four years ago.'

Mitch thought about this for a second and figured by the time he was thirty he could be well over a hundred thousand, maybe close to two hundred thousand. At the age of thirty!

They watched him carefully and knew exactly what he was calculating.

'What's an international tax firm doing in Memphis?' he asked.

That brought smiles. Mr. Lambert removed his reading glasses and twirled them. 'Now that's a good question. Mr. Bendini founded the firm in 1944. He had been a tax lawyer in Philadelphia and had picked up some wealthy clients in the South. He got a wild hair and landed in Memphis. For twenty-five years he hired nothing but tax lawyers, and the firm prospered nicely down there. None of us are from Memphis, but we have grown to love it. It's a very pleasant old Southern town. By the way, Mr. Bendini died in 1970.'

'How many partners in the firm'

'Twenty, active. We try to keep a ratio of one partner for each associate. That's high for the industry, but we like it. Again, we do things differently.'

'All of our partners are multi-millionaires by the age of forty-five,' Royce McKnight said.

'All of them?'

'Yes, sir. We don't guarantee it, but if you join our firm, put in ten hard years, make partner and put in ten more years, and you're not a millionaire at the age of forty-five, you'll be the first in twenty years.'

'That's an impressive statistic.'

'It's an impressive firm, Mitch,' Oliver Lambert said, 'and we're very proud of it. We're a close-knit fraternity. We're small and we take care of each other. We don't have the cut-throat competition the big firms are famous for. We're very careful whom we hire, and our goal is for each new associate to become a partner as soon as possible. Toward that end we invest an enormous amount of time and money in ourselves, especially our new people. It is a rare, extremely rare occasion when a lawyer leaves our firm. It is simply unheard of. We go the extra mile to keep careers on track. We want our people happy. We think it is the most profitable way to operate.'

'I have another impressive statistic,' Mr. McKnight added. 'Last year, for firms our size or larger, the average turnover rate among associates was twenty-eight percent. At Bendini, Lambert & Locke, it was zero. Year before, zero. It's been a long time since a lawyer left our firm.'

They watched him carefully to make sure all of this sank in. Each term and each condition of the employment was important, but the permanence, the finality of his acceptance overshadowed all other items on the checklist. They explained as best they could, for now. Further explanation would come later.

Of course, they knew much more than they could talk about. For instance, his mother lived in a cheap trailer park in Panama City Beach, remarried to a retired truck driver with a violent drinking problem. They knew she had received $41,000 from the mine explosion, squandered most of it, then went crazy after her oldest son was killed in Vietnam. They knew he had been neglected, raised in poverty by his brother Ray (whom they could not find) and some sympathetic relatives. The poverty hurt, and they assumed, correctly, it had bred the intense desire to succeed. He had worked thirty hours a week at an all night convenience store while playing football and making perfect grades. They knew he seldom slept. They knew he was hungry. He was their man.

'Would you like to come visit us?' asked Oliver Lambert.

'When?' asked Mitch, dreaming of a black 318i with a sunroof.

The ancient Mazda hatchback with three hubcaps and a badly cracked windshield hung in the gutter with its front wheels sideways, aiming at the curb, preventing a roll down the hill. Abby grabbed the door handle on the inside, yanked twice and opened the door. She inserted the key, pressed the clutch and turned the wheel. The Mazda began a slow roll. As it gained speed, she held her breath, released the clutch and bit her lip until the unmuffled rotary engine began whining.

With three job offers on the table, a new car was four months away. She could last. For three years they had endured poverty in a two-room student apartment on a campus covered with Porsches and little Mercedes convertibles. For the most part they had ignored the snubs from the classmates and co-workers in this bastion of East Coast snobbery. They were hillbillies from Kentucky, with few friends. But they had endured and succeeded quite nicely all to themselves.

She preferred Chicago to New York, even for a lower salary, largely because it was further from Boston and closer to Kentucky. But Mitch remained noncommittal, characteristically weighing it all carefully and keeping most of it to himself. She had not been invited to visit New York and Chicago with her husband. And she was tired of guessing. She wanted an answer.

She parked illegally on the hill nearest the apartment and walked two blocks. Their unit was one of thirty in a two-story red-brick rectangle. Abby stood outside her door and fumbled through the purse looking for keys. Suddenly, the door jerked open. He grabbed her, yanked her inside the tiny apartment, threw her on the sofa and attacked her neck with his lips. She yelled and giggled as arms and legs thrashed about. They kissed, one of those long, wet, ten minute embraces with groping and fondling and moaning, the kind they had enjoyed as teenagers when kissing was fun and mysterious and the ultimate.

'My goodness,' she said when they finished. 'What's the occasion?'

'Do you smell anything?' Mitch asked.

She looked away and sniffed. 'Well, yes. What is it?'

'Chicken chow mein and egg foo yung. From Wong Boys.'

'Okay, what's the occasion?'

'Plus an expensive bottle of Chablis. It's even got a cork.'

'What have you done, Mitch?'

'Follow me.' On the small, painted kitchen table, among the legal pads and casebooks, sat a large bottle of wine and a sack of Chinese food. They shoved the law school paraphernalia aside and spread the food. Mitch opened the wine and filled two plastic wineglasses.

'I had a great interview today,' he said.

'Who?'

'Remember that firm in Memphis I received a letter from last month?'

'Yes. You weren't too impressed.'

'That's the one. I'm very impressed. It's all tax work and the money looks good.'

'How good?'

He ceremoniously dipped chow mein from the container onto both plates, then ripped open the tiny packages of soy sauce. She waited for an answer. He opened another container and began dividing the egg foo yung. He sipped his wine and smacked his lips.

'How much?' she repeated.

'More than Chicago. More than Wall Street.'

She took a long, deliberate drink of wine and eyed him suspiciously. Her brown eyes narrowed and glowed. The eyebrows lowered and the forehead wrinkled. She waited.

'How much?'

'Eighty thousand, first year, plus bonuses. Eighty-five, second year, plus bonuses.' He said this nonchalantly while studying the celery bits in the chow mein.

'Eighty thousand,' she repeated.

'Eighty thousand, babe. Eighty thousand bucks in Memphis, Tennessee, is about the same as a hundred and twenty thousand bucks in New York.'

'Who wants New York?' she asked.

'Plus a low-interest mortgage loan.'

That word – mortgage – had not been uttered in the apartment in a long time. In fact, she could not, at the moment recall the last discussion about a home or anything related to one. For months now it had been accepted that they would *rent* some place until some distant, unimaginable point in the future when they achieved affluence and would then qualify for a large mortgage.

She sat her glass of wine on the table and said matter-of-factly, 'I didn't hear that.'

'A low-interest mortgage loan. The firm loans enough money to buy a house. It's very important to these guys that their associates look prosperous, so they give us the money at a much lower rate.'

'You mean as in a *home*, with grass around it and shrubs?'

'Yep. Not some overpriced apartment in Manhattan, but a three-bedroom house in the suburbs with a driveway and a two-car garage where we can park the BMW.'

The reaction was delayed by a second or two, but she finally said, 'BMW? Whose BMW?'

'Ours, babe. Our BMW. The firm leases a new one and gives us the keys. It's sort of like a signing bonus for a first-round draft pick. It's worth another five thousand a year. We pick the color, of course. I think black would be nice. What do you think?'

'No more clunkers. No more leftovers. No more hand-me-downs,' she said as she slowly shook her head.

He crunched on a mouthful of noodles and smiled at her. She was dreaming, he could tell, probably of furniture, and wallpaper, and perhaps a pool before too long. And babies, little dark eyed children with light brown hair.

'And there are some other benefits to be discussed later.'

'I don't understand, Mitch. Why are they so generous?'

'I asked that question. They're very selective, and they take a lot of pride in paying top dollar. They go for the best and don't mind shelling out the bucks. Their turnover rate is zero. Plus, I think it costs more to entice the top people to Memphis.'

'It would be closer to home,' she said without looking at him.'

'I don't have a home. It would be closer to your parents, and that worries me.'

She deflected this, as she did most of his comments about her family. 'You'd be closer to Ray.'

He nodded, bit into an egg roll and imagined her parents' first visit, that sweet moment when they pulled into the driveway in their well-used Cadillac and stared in shock at the new French colonial with two new cars in the garage. They would burn with envy and wonder how the poor kid with no family and no status could afford all this at twenty-five and fresh out of law school. They would force painful smiles and comment on how nice everything was, and before long Mr. Sutherland would break down and ask how much the house cost and Mitch would tell him to mind his own business and it would drive the old man crazy. They'd leave after a short visit and return to Kentucky, where all their friends would hear how great the daughter and the son-in-law were doing down in Memphis. Abby would be sorry they couldn't get along but wouldn't say much. From the start they had treated him like a leper. He was so unworthy they had boycotted the small wedding.

'Have you ever been to Memphis?' he asked.

'Once when I was a little girl. Some kind of convention for the church. All I remember is the river.'

'They want us to visit.'

'Us! You mean I'm invited?'

'Yes. They insist on you coming.'

'When?'

'Couple of weeks. They'll fly us down Thursday afternoon for the weekend.'

'I like this firm already.'

# CHAPTER TWO

The five-story building had been built a hundred years earlier by a cotton merchant and his sons after the Reconstruction, during the revival of cotton trading in Memphis. It sat in the middle of Cotton Row on Front Street near the river. Through its halls and doors and across its desks, millions of bales of cotton had been purchased from the Mississippi and Arkansas deltas and sold around the world. Deserted, neglected, then renovated time and time again since the first war, it had been purchased for good in 1951 by an aggressive tax lawyer named Anthony Bendini. He renovated it yet again and began filling it with lawyers. He renamed it the Bendini Building.

He pampered the building, indulged it, coddled it, each year adding another layer of luxury to his landmark. He fortified it, sealing doors and windows and hiring armed guards to protect it and its occupants. He added elevators, electronic surveillance, security codes, closed-circuit television, a weight room, a steam room, locker rooms and a partners' dining room on the fifth floor with a captivating view of the river.

In twenty years he built the richest law firm in Memphis, and, indisputably, the quietest. Secrecy was his passion. Every associate hired by the firm was indoctrinated in the evils of the loose tongue. Everything was confidential. Salaries, perks, advancement and, most especially, clients. Divulging firm business, the young associates were warned, could delay the awarding of the holy grail – a partnership. Nothing left the fortress on Front Street. Wives were told not to ask, or were lied to. The associates were expected to work hard, keep quiet and spend their healthy paychecks. They did, without exception.

With forty-one lawyers, the firm was the fourth largest in Memphis. Its members did not advertise or seek publicity. They were clannish and did not fraternize with other lawyers. Their wives played tennis and bridge and shopped among themselves. Bendini, Lambert & Locke was a big family, of sorts. A rather rich family.

At 10 A.M. on a Friday, the firm limo stopped on Front Street and Mr. Mitchell Y. McDeere emerged. He politely thanked the driver, and admired the vehicle as it drove away. His first limo ride. He stood on the sidewalk next to a streetlight and admired the quaint, picturesque, yet somehow imposing home of the quiet Bendini firm. It was

384

a far cry from the gargantuan steel-and-glass erections inhabited by New York's finest or the enormous cylinder he had visited in Chicago. But he instantly knew he would like it. It was less pretentious. It was more like himself.

Lamar Quin walked through the front door and down the steps. He yelled at Mitch and waved him over. He had met them at the airport the night before and checked them into the Peabody – 'the South's Grand Hotel'.

'Good morning, Mitch! How was your night?' They shook hands like lost friends.

'Very nice. It's a great hotel.'

'We knew you'd like it. Everybody likes the Peabody.'

They stepped into the front foyer, where a small billboard greeted Mr. Mitchell Y. McDeere, the guest of the day. A well-dressed, but unattractive receptionist smiled warmly and said her name was Sylvia and if he needed anything while he was in Memphis just let her know. He thanked her. Lamar led him to a long hallway where he began the guided tour. He explained the layout of the building and introduced Mitch to various secretaries and paralegals as they walked. In the main library on the second floor a crowd of lawyers circled the mammoth conference table and consumed pastries and coffee. They became silent when the guest entered.

Oliver Lambert greeted Mitch and introduced him to the gang. There were about twenty in all, most of the associates in the firm, and most barely older than the guest. The partners were too busy, Lamar had explained, and would meet him later at a private lunch. He stood at the end of the table as Mr. Lambert called for quiet.

'Gentlemen, this is Mitchell McDeere. You've all heard about him, and here he is. He is our number one choice this year, our number one draft pick, so to speak. He is being romanced by the big boys in New York and Chicago and who knows where else, so we have to sell him on our little firm here in Memphis.' They smiled and nodded their approval. The guest was embarrassed.

'He will finish at Harvard in two months and will graduate with honors. He's an associate editor of the *Harvard Law Review*.' This made an impression, Mitch could tell. 'He did his undergraduate work at Western Kentucky, where he graduated summa cum laude.' This was not quite as impressive. 'He also played football for four years, starting as quarterback in his junior year.' Now they were really impressed. A few appeared to be in awe, as if staring at Joe Namath.

The senior partner continued his monologue while Mitch stood awkwardly beside him. He droned on about how selective they had always been and how well Mitch would fit in. Mitch stuffed his hands in his pockets and quit listening. He studied the group. They were young, successful and affluent. The dress code appeared to be strict, but no different than New York or Chicago. Dark gray or navy wool suits, white or blue cotton button downs, medium starch, and silk ties. Nothing bold or nonconforming. Maybe a couple of bow ties, but nothing more daring. Neatness was mandatory. No beards, mustaches or hair over the ears. There were a couple of wimps, but good looks dominated.

Mr. Lambert was winding down. 'Lamar will give Mitch a tour of our offices, so you'll have a chance to chat with him later. Let's make him welcome. Tonight he and his lovely, and I do mean lovely, wife, Abby, will eat ribs at the Rendezvous, and of course tomorrow night is the firm dinner at my place. I'll ask you to be on your best behavior.' He smiled and looked at the guest. 'Mitch, if you get tired of Lamar, let me know and we'll get someone more qualified.'

He shook hands with each one of them again as they left, and tried to remember as many names as possible.

'Let's start the tour,' Lamar said when the room cleared. 'This, of course, is a library, and we have identical ones on each of the first four floors. We also use them for large meetings. The books vary from floor to floor, so you never know where your research will lead you. We have two full-time librarians, and we use microfilm and microfiche extensively. As a rule, we don't do any research outside the building. There are over a hundred thousand volumes, including every conceivable tax reporting service. That's more than some law schools. If you need a book we don't have, just tell a librarian.'

They walked past the lengthy conference table and between dozens of rows of books. 'A hundred thousand volumes,' Mitch mumbled.

'Yeah, we spend almost half a million a year on upkeep, supplements and new books. The partners are always griping about it, but they wouldn't think of cutting back. It's one of the largest private law libraries in the country, and we're proud of it.'

'It's pretty impressive.'

'We try to make research as painless as possible. You know what a bore it is and how much time can be wasted looking for the right materials. You'll spend a lot of time here the first two years, so we try to make it pleasant.'

Behind a cluttered workbench in a rear corner, one of the librarians introduced himself and gave a brief tour of the computer room, where a dozen terminals stood ready to assist with the latest computerized research. He offered to demonstrate the latest, truly incredible software, but Lamar said they might stop by later.

'He's a nice guy,' Lamar said as they left the library. 'We pay him forty thousand a year just to keep up with the books. It's amazing.'

Truly amazing, thought Mitch.

The second floor was virtually identical to the first, third and fourth. The center of each floor was filled with secretaries, their desks, file cabinets, copiers and the other necessary machines. On one side of the open area was the library, and on the other was a configuration of smaller rooms and offices.

'You won't see any pretty secretaries,' Lamar said softly as they watched them work. 'It seems to be an unwritten firm rule. Oliver Lambert goes out of his way to hire the oldest and homeliest ones he can find. Of course, some have been here for twenty years and have forgotten more law than we learned in law school.'

'They seem kind of plump,' Mitch observed, almost to himself.

'Yeah, it's part of the overall strategy to encourage us to keep our hands in our pockets. Philandering is strictly forbidden, and to my knowledge has never happened.'

'And if it does?'

'Who knows. The secretary would be fired, of course. And I suppose the lawyer would be severely punished. It might cost a partnership. No one wants to find out, especially with this bunch of cows.'

'They dress nice.'

'Don't get me wrong. We hire only the best legal secretaries and we pay more than any other firm in town. You're looking at the best, not necessarily the prettiest. We require experience and maturity. Lambert won't hire anyone under thirty.'

'One per lawyer?'

'Yes, until you're a partner. Then you'll get another, and by then you'll need one. Nathan Locke has three, all with twenty years' experience, and he keeps them jumping.'

'Where's his office?'

'Fourth floor. It's off limits.'

Mitch started to ask, but didn't.

The corner offices were 25 by 25, Lamar explained, and occupied by the most senior partners. Power offices, he called them, with great admiration. They were decorated to each individual's taste with no expense spared and vacated only at retirement or death, then fought over by the younger partners.

Lamar flipped a switch in one and they stepped inside, closing the door behind them. 'Nice view, huh,' he said as Mitch walked to the windows and looked at the river moving ever so slowly beyond Riverside Drive.

'How do you get this office?' Mitch asked as he admired a barge inching under the bridge leading to Arkansas.

'Takes time, and when you get here you'll be very wealthy, and very busy, and you won't have time to enjoy the view.'

'Whose is it?'

'Victor Milligan. He's head of tax, and a very nice man. Originally from New England, he's been here for twenty-five years and calls Memphis home.' Lamar stuck his hands in his pockets and walked around the room. 'The hardwood floors and ceilings came with the building, over a hundred years ago. Most of the building is carpeted, but in a few spots the wood was not damaged. You'll have the option of rugs and carpet when you get here.'

'I like the wood. What about the rug?'

'Some kind of antique Persian. I don't know its history. The desk was used by his great-grandfather, who was a judge of some sort in Rhode Island, or so he says. He's full of crap, and you never know when he's blowing smoke.'

'Where is he?'

'Vacation, I think. Did they tell you about vacations?'

'No.'

'You get two weeks a year for the first five years. Paid, of course. Then three weeks until you become a partner, then you take whatever you want. The firm has a chalet in Vail, a cabin on a lake in Manitoba and two condos on Seven Mile Beach on Grand Cayman Island. They're free, but you need to book early. Partners get priority. After that it's first come. The Caymans are extremely popular in the firm. It's an international tax haven and a lot of our trips are written off. I think Milligan's there now, probably scuba diving and calling it business.'

Through one of his courses, Mitch had heard of the Cayman Islands and knew they were somewhere in the Caribbean. He started to ask exactly where, but decided to check it himself.

'Only two weeks?' he asked.

'Uh, yeah. Is that a problem?'

'No, not really. The firms in New York are offering at least three.' He spoke like a discriminating critic of expensive vacations. He wasn't. Except for the three-day weekend they referred to as a honeymoon, and an occasional drive through New England, he had never participated in a vacation and had never left the country.

'You can get an additional week, unpaid.'

Mitch nodded as though this was acceptable. They left Milligan's office and continued the tour. The hallway ran in a long rectangle with the attorneys' offices to the outside, all with windows, sunlight, views. Those with views of the river were more prestigious, Lamar explained, and usually occupied by partners. There were waiting lists.

The conference rooms, libraries and secretarial desks were on the inside of the hallway, away from the windows and distractions.

The associates' offices were smaller – 15 by 15 – but richly decorated and much more imposing than any associates' offices he had seen in New York or Chicago. The firm spent a small fortune on design consultants, Lamar said. Money, it seemed, grew on trees. The younger lawyers were friendly and talkative and seemed to welcome the interruption. Most gave brief testimonials to the greatness of the firm and of Memphis. The old town kind of grows on you, they kept telling him, but it takes time. They, too, had been recruited by the big boys in Washington and on Wall Street, and they had no regrets.

The partners were busier, but just as nice. He had been carefully selected, he was told again and again, and he would fit in. It was his kind of firm. They promised to talk more during lunch.

An hour earlier, Kay Quin had left the kids with the baby nurse and the maid and met Abby for brunch at the Peabody. She was a small-town girl, much like Abby. She had married Lamar after college and lived in Nashville for three years while he studied law at Vanderbilt. Lamar made so much money she quit work and had two babies in fourteen months. Now that she had retired and finished her child-bearing, she spent most of her time with the garden club and the heart fund and the country club and the PTA and the church. Despite the money and the affluence, she was modest and unpretentious, and apparently determined to stay that way regardless of her husband's success. Abby found a friend.

After croissants and eggs Benedict, they sat in the lobby of the hotel, drinking coffee and watching the ducks swim in circles around the fountain. Kay had suggested a quick tour of Memphis with a late lunch near her home. Maybe some shopping.

'Have they mentioned the low-interest loan?' she asked.

'Yes, at the first interview.'

'They'll want you to buy a house when you move here. Most people can't afford a house when they leave law school, so the firm loans you the money at a lower rate and holds the mortgage.'

'How low?'

'I don't know. It's been seven years since we moved here, and we've bought another house since then. It'll be a bargain, believe me. The firm will see to it that you own a home. It's sort of an unwritten rule.'

'Why is it so important?'

'Several reasons. First of all, they want you down here. This firm is very selective, and they usually get who they want. But Memphis is not exactly in the spotlight, so they have to offer more. Also, the firm is very demanding, especially on the associates. There's pressure, overwork, eighty-hour weeks and time away from home. It won't be easy on either of you, and the firm knows it. The theory is that a strong marriage means a happy lawyer, and the happy lawyer is a productive lawyer, so the bottom line is profits. Always profits.

'And there's another reason. These guys – all guys, no women – take a lot of pride in their wealth, and everyone is expected to look and act affluent. It would be an insult to the firm if an associate was forced to live in an apartment. They want you in a house, and after five years in a bigger house. If we have some time this afternoon, I'll show you some of the partners' homes. When you see them, you won't mind the eighty-hour weeks.'

'I'm used to them now.'

'That's good, but law school doesn't compare with this. Sometimes they'll work a hundred hours a week during tax season.'

Abby smiled and shook her head as if this impressed her a great deal. 'Do you work?'

'No. Most of us don't work. The money is there, so we're not forced to, and we get little help with the kids from our husbands. Of course, working is not forbidden.'

'Forbidden by whom?'

'The firm.'

'I would hope not.' Abby repeated the word 'forbidden' to herself, but let it pass.

Kay sipped her coffee and watched the ducks. A small boy wandered away from his mother and stood near the fountain.

'Do you plan to start a family?' Kay asked.

'Maybe in a couple of years.'

'Babies are encouraged.'

'By whom?'

'The firm.'

'Why should the firm care if we have children?'

'Again, stable families. A new baby is a big deal around the office. They send flowers and gifts to the hospital. You're treated like a queen. Your husband gets a week off, but he'll be too busy to take it.

They put a thousand dollars in a trust fund for college. It's a lot of fun.'

'Sounds like a big fraternity.'

'It's more like a big family. Our social life revolves around the firm, and that's important because none of us are from Memphis. We're all transplants.'

'That's nice, but I don't want anyone telling me when to work and when to quit and when to have children.'

'Don't worry. They're very protective of each other, but the firm does not meddle.'

'I'm beginning to wonder.'

'Relax, Abby. The firm is like a family. They're great people, and Memphis is a wonderful old town to live in and raise kids. The cost of living is much lower and life moves at a slower pace. You're probably considering the bigger towns. So did we, but I'll take Memphis any day over the big cities.'

'Do I get the grand tour?'

'That's why I'm here. I thought we'd start downtown, then head out east and look at the nicer neighborhoods, maybe look at some houses and eat lunch at my favorite restaurant.'

'Sounds like fun.'

Kay paid for the coffee, as she had the brunch, and they left the Peabody in the Quin family's new Mercedes.

The dining room, as it was simply called, covered the west end of the fifth floor above Riverside Drive and high above the river in the distance. A row of eight-foot windows lined the wall and provided a fascinating view of the tugboats, paddle-wheelers, barges, docks and bridges.

The room was protected turf, a sanctuary for those lawyers talented and ambitious enough to be called partners in the quiet Bendini firm. They gathered each day for lunches prepared by Jessie Frances, a huge, temperamental old black woman, and served by her husband, Roosevelt, who wore white gloves and an odd-fitting, faded, wrinkled hand-me-down tux given to him by Mr. Bendini himself shortly before his death. They also gathered for coffee and doughnuts some mornings to discuss firm business and, occasionally, for a glass of wine in the late afternoon to celebrate a good month or an exceptionally large fee. It was for partners only, and maybe an occasional guest such as a blue chip client or prospective recruit. The associates could dine there twice a year, only twice – and records were kept – and then only at the invitation of a partner.

Adjacent to the dining room was a small kitchen where Jessie Frances performed, and where she had cooked the first meal for Mr. Bendini and a few others twenty-six years earlier. For twenty-six years she had cooked Southern food and ignored requests to experiment and try dishes she had trouble pronouncing. 'Don't eat it if you don't like it,' was her standard reply. Judging from the scraps Roosevelt collected from the tables, the food was eaten and enjoyed immensely. She posted the week's menu on Monday, asked that reservations be made by ten each day and held grudges for years if someone canceled or didn't show. She and Roosevelt worked four hours each day and were paid a thousand each month.

Mitch sat at a table with Lamar Quin, Oliver Lambert and Royce McKnight. The entrée was prime ribs, served with fried okra and boiled squash.

'She laid off the grease today,' Mr. Lambert observed.

'It's delicious,' Mitch said.

'Is your system accustomed to grease?'

'Yes. They cook this way in Kentucky.'

'I joined this firm in 1955,' Mr. McKnight said, 'and I come from New Jersey, right? Out of suspicion, I avoided most Southern dishes as much as possible. Everything is battered and fried in animal fat, right? Then Mr. Bendini decides to open up this little café. He hires Jessie Frances, and I've had heartburn for the past twenty years. Fried ripe tomatoes, fried green tomatoes, fried eggplant, fried okra, fried squash, fried anything and everything. One day Victor Milligan said too much. He's from Connecticut, right? And Jessie Frances had whipped up a batch of fried dill pickles. Can you imagine? Fried dill pickles! Milligan said something ugly to Roosevelt and he reported it to Jessie Frances. She walked out the back door and quit. Stayed gone for a week. Roosevelt wanted to work, but she kept him at home. Finally, Mr. Bendini smoothed things over and she agreed to return if there were no complaints. But she also cut back on the grease. I think we'll all live ten years longer.'

'It's delicious,' said Lamar as he buttered another roll.

'It's always delicious,' added Mr. Lambert as Roosevelt walked by. 'Her food is rich and fattening, but we seldom miss lunch.'

Mitch ate cautiously, engaged in nervous chitchat and tried to appear completely at ease. It was difficult. Surrounded by eminently successful lawyers, all millionaires, in their exclusive, lavishly ornamented dining suite, he felt as if he was on hallowed ground. Lamar's presence was comforting, as was Roosevelt's.

When it was apparent Mitch had finished eating, Oliver Lambert wiped his mouth, rose slowly and tapped his tea glass with his spoon. 'Gentlemen, could I have your attention.'

The room became silent as the twenty or so partners turned to the head table. They laid their napkins down and stared at the guest. Somewhere on each of their desks was a copy of the dossier. Two months earlier they had voted unanimously to make him their number one pick. They knew he ran four miles a day, did not smoke, was allergic to sulfites, had no tonsils, had a blue Mazda, had a crazy mother and once threw three interceptions in one quarter. They knew he took nothing stronger than aspirin even when he was sick, and that he was hungry enough to work a hundred hours a week if they asked. They liked him. He was good-looking, athletic-looking, a man's man with a brilliant mind and a lean body.

'As you know, we have a very special guest today, Mitch McDeere. He will soon graduate with honors from Harvard –'

'Hear! Hear!' said a couple of Harvard alumni.

'Yes, thank you. He and his wife, Abby, are staying at the Peabody this weekend as our guests. Mitch will finish in the top five out of three hundred and has been heavily recruited. We want him here, and I know you will speak to him before he leaves. Tonight he will have dinner with Lamar and Kay Quin, and then tomorrow night is the dinner at my place. You are all expected to attend.' Mitch smiled awkwardly at the partners as Mr. Lambert rambled on about the greatness of the firm. When he finished, they continued eating as Roosevelt served bread pudding and coffee.

Kay's favorite restaurant was a chic East Memphis hangout for the young affluent. A thousand ferns hung from everywhere and the jukebox played nothing but early sixties. The daiquiris were served in tall souvenir glasses.

'One is enough,' Kay warned.

'I'm not much of a drinker.'

They ordered the quiche of the day and sipped daiquiris.

'Does Mitch drink?'

'Very little. He's an athlete and very particular about his body. An occasional beer or glass of wine, nothing stronger. How about Lamar?'

'About the same. He really discovered beer in law school, but he has trouble with his weight. The firm frowns on drinking.'

'That's admirable, but why is it their business?'

'Because alcohol and lawyers go together like blood and vampires. Most lawyers drink like fish, and the profession is plagued with alcoholism. I think it starts in law school. At Vanderbilt, someone was always tapping a keg of beer. Probably the same at Harvard. The job has a lot of pressure, and that usually means a lot of booze. These guys aren't a bunch of teetotalers, mind you, but they keep it under control. A healthy lawyer is a productive lawyer.'

'I guess that makes sense. Mitch says there's no turnover.'

'It's rather permanent. I can't recall anyone leaving in the seven years we've been here. The money's great and they're careful about whom they hire. They don't want anyone with family money.'

'I'm not sure I follow.'

'They won't hire a lawyer with other sources of income. They want them young and hungry. It's a question of loyalty. If all your money comes from one source, then you tend to be very loyal to that source. The firm demands extreme loyalty. Lamar says there's never talk of leaving. They're all happy, and either rich or getting that way. And if one wanted to leave, he couldn't find as much money with another firm. They'll offer Mitch whatever it takes to get you down here. They take great pride in paying more.'

'Why no female lawyers?'

'They tried it once. She was a real bitch and kept the place in an uproar. Most women lawyers walk around with chips on their shoulders looking for fights. They're hard to deal with. Lamar says they're afraid to hire one because they couldn't fire her if she didn't work out, with affirmative action and all.'

The quiche arrived and they declined another round of daiquiris. Hundreds of young professionals crowded under the clouds of ferns, and the restaurant grew festive. Smokey Robinson sang softly from the jukebox.

'I've got a great idea,' Kay said. 'I know a realtor. Let's call her and go look at some houses.'

'What kind of houses?'

'For you and Mitch. For the newest associate at Bendini, Lambert & Locke. She can show you several in your price range.'

'I don't know our price range.'

'I'd say a hundred to a hundred and fifty thousand. The last associate bought in Oakgrove, and I'm sure he paid something like that.'

Abby leaned forward and almost whispered, 'How much would the notes be?'

'I don't know. But you'll be able to afford it. Around a thousand a month, maybe a little more.'

Abby stared at her and swallowed hard. The small apartments in Manhattan were renting for twice that. 'Let's give her a call.'

As expected, Royce McKnight's office was a power one with a great view. It was in one of the prized corners on the fourth floor, down the hall from Nathan Locke. Lamar excused himself, and the managing partner asked Mitch to have a seat at a small conference table next to the sofa. A secretary was sent for coffee.

McKnight asked him about his visit so far, and Mitch said he was quite impressed.

'Mitch, I want to nail down the specifics of our offer.'

'Certainly.'

'The base salary is eighty thousand for the first year. When you pass the bar exam you receive a five thousand dollar raise. Not a bonus, but a raise. The exam is given sometime in August and you'll spend most of your summer reviewing for it. We have our own bar study courses and you'll receive extensive tutoring from some of the partners. This is done primarily on firm time. As you know, most firms put you to work and expect you to study on your own time. Not us. No associate of this firm has ever flunked the bar exam, and we're not worried about you breaking with tradition. Eighty thousand initially, up to eighty-five in six months. Once you've been here a year, you'll be raised to ninety thousand, plus you'll get a bonus each December based on the profits and performance during the prior twelve months. Last year the average bonus for associates was nine thousand. As you know, profit sharing with associates is extremely rare for law firms. Any questions about the salary?'

'What happens after the second year?'

'Your base salary is raised about ten percent a year until you become a partner. Neither the raises nor the bonuses are guaranteed. They are based on performance.'

'Fair enough.'

'As you know, it is very important to us that you buy a home. It adds stability and prestige and we're very concerned about these things, especially with our associates. The firm provides a low-interest mortgage loan, thirty years, fixed rate, nonassumable should you decide to sell in a few years. It's a one shot deal, available only for your first home. After that you're on your own.'

'What kind of rate?'

'As low as possible without running afoul with the IRS. Current market rate is around ten, ten and a half. We should be able to get you a rate of seven to eight percent. We represent some banks, and they assist us. With this salary, you'll have no trouble qualifying. In fact, the firm will sign on as a guarantor if necessary.'

'That's very generous, Mr. McKnight.'

'It's important to us. And we don't lose any money on the deal.

Once you find a house, our real estate section handles everything. All you have to do is move in.'

'What about the BMW?'

Mr. McKnight chuckled. 'We started that about ten years ago and it's proved to be quite an inducement. It's very simple. You pick out a BMW, one of the smaller ones, we lease it for three years and give you the keys. We pay for tags, insurance, maintenance. At the end of three years you buy it from the leasing company for the fair market value. It's also a one shot deal.'

'That's very tempting.'

'We know.'

Mr. McKnight looked at his legal pad. 'We provide complete medical and dental coverage for the entire family. Pregnancies, checkups, braces, everything. Paid entirely by the firm.'

Mitch nodded, but was not impressed. This was standard.

'We have a retirement plan second to none. For every dollar you invest, the firm matches it with two, provided, however, you invest at least ten percent of your base pay. Let's say you start at eighty, and the first year you set aside eight thousand. The firm kicks in sixteen, so you've got twenty-four after the first year. A money pro in New York handles it and last year our retirement earned nineteen percent. Not bad. Invest for twenty years and you're a millionaire at forty-five, just off retirement. One stipulation: if you bail out before twenty years, you lose everything but the money you put in, with no income earned on that money.'

'Sounds rather harsh.'

'No, actually it's rather generous. Find me another firm or company matching two to one. There are none, to my knowledge. It's our way of taking care of ourselves. Many of our partners retire at fifty, some at forty-five. We have no mandatory retirement, and some work into their sixties and seventies. To each his own. Our goal is simply to ensure a generous pension and make early retirement an option.'

'How many retired partners do you have?'

'Twenty or so. You'll see them around here from time to time. They like to come in and have lunch and a few keep office space. Did Lamar cover vacations?'

'Yes.'

'Good. Book early, especially for Vail and the Caymans. You buy the air fare, but the condos are free. We do a lot of business in the Caymans and from time to time we'll send you down for two or three days and write the whole thing off. Those trips are not counted as vacation, and you'll get one every year or so. We work hard, Mitch, and we recognize the value of leisure.'

'Mitch nodded his approval and dreamed of lying on a sun-drenched beach in the Caribbean, sipping on a pina colada and watching string bikinis.

'Did Lamar mention the signing bonus?'

'No, but it sounds interesting.'

'If you join our firm we hand you a check for five thousand. We prefer that you spend the bulk of it on a new wardrobe. After seven years of jeans and flannel shirts, your inventory of suits is probably low, and we realize it. Appearance is very important to us. We expect our attorneys to dress sharp and conservative. There's no dress code, but you'll get the picture.'

Did he say five thousand dollars? For clothes? Mitch currently owned two suits, and he was wearing one of them. He kept a straight face and did not smile.

'Any questions?'

'Yes. The large firms are infamous for being sweatshops where the associates are flooded with tedious research and locked away in some library for the first three years. I want no part of that. I don't mind doing my share of research and I realize I will be the low man on the pole. But I don't want to research and write briefs for the entire firm. I'd like to work with real clients and their real problems.'

Mr. McKnight listened intently and waited with his rehearsed answer. 'I understand, Mitch. You're right, it is a real problem in the big firms. But not here. For the first six weeks you'll do little but study for the bar exam. When that's over, you begin practicing law. You'll be assigned to a partner, and his clients will become your clients. You'll do most of his research and, of course, your own, and occasionally you'll be asked to assist someone else with the preparation of a brief or some research. We want you happy. We take pride in our zero turnover rate, and we go the extra mile to keep careers on track. If you can't get along with your partner, we'll find another one. If you discover you don't like tax, we'll let you try securities or banking. It's your decision. The firm will soon invest a lot of money in Mitch McDeere, and we want him to be productive.'

Mitch sipped his coffee and searched for another question. Mr. McKnight glanced at his checklist.

'We pay all moving expenses to Memphis.'

'That won't be much. Just a small rental truck.'

'Anything else, Mitch?'

'No, sir. I can't think of anything.'

The checklist was folded and placed in the file. The partner rested both elbows on the table and leaned forward. 'Mitch, we're not push-ing, but we need an answer as soon as possible. If you go elsewhere, we must then continue to interview. It's a lengthy process, and we'd like our new man to start by July 1.'

'Ten days soon enough?'

'That's fine. Say by March 30?'

'Sure, but I'll contact you before then.' Mitch excused himself, and found Lamar waiting in the hall outside McKnight's office. They agreed on seven for dinner.

# CHAPTER THREE

There were no law offices on the fifth floor of the Bendini Building. The partners' dining room and kitchen occupied the west end, some unused and unpainted storage rooms sat locked and empty in the center, then a thick concrete wall sealed off the remaining third of the floor. A small metal door with a button beside it and a camera over it hung in the center of the wall and opened into a small room where an armed guard watched the door and monitored a wall of closed circuit screens. A hallway zigzagged through a maze of cramped offices and workrooms where an assortment of characters went secretly about their business of watching and gathering information. The windows to the outside were sealed with paint and covered with blinds. The sunlight stood no chance of penetrating the fortress.

DeVasher, head of security, occupied the largest of the small, plain offices. The lone certificate on his bare walls recognized him for thirty years of dedicated service as a detective with the New Orleans Police Department. He was of medium build with a slight belly, thick shoulders and chest and a huge, perfectly round head that smiled with great reluctance. His wrinkled shirt was mercifully unbuttoned at the collar, allowing his bulging neck to sag unrestricted. A thick polyester tie hung on the coat-rack with a badly worn blazer.

Monday morning after the McDeere visit, Oliver Lambert stood before the small metal door and stared at the camera over it. He pushed the button twice, waited and was finally cleared through security. He walked quickly through the cramped hallway and entered the cluttered office. DeVasher blew smoke from a Dutch Masters into a smokeless ashtray and shoved papers in all directions until wood was visible on his desk.

'Mornin', Ollie. I guess you want to talk about McDeere.'

DeVasher was the only person in the Bendini Building who called him Ollie to his face.

'Yes, among other things.'

'Well, he had a good time, was impressed with the firm, liked Memphis okay and will probably sign on.'

'Where were your people?'

'We had the rooms on both sides at the hotel. His room was wired, of course, as was the limo and the phone and everything else. The usual, Ollie.'

'Let's get specific.'

'Okay. Thursday night they checked in late and went to bed. Little discussion. Friday night he told her all about the firm, the offices, the people, said you were a real nice man. I thought you'd like that.'

'Get on with it.'

'Told her about the fancy dining room and his little lunch with the partners. Gave her the specifics on the offer and they were ecstatic. Much better than his other offers. She wants a home with a driveway and a sidewalk and trees and a backyard. He said she could have one.'

'Any problems with the firm?'

'Not really. He commented on the absence of blacks and women, but it didn't seem to bother him.'

'What about his wife?'

'She had a ball. She likes the town, and she and Quin's wife hit it off. They looked at houses Friday afternoon, and she saw a couple she liked.'

'You get any addresses?'

'Of course, Ollie. Saturday morning they called the limo and rode all over town. Very impressed with the limo. Our driver stayed away from the bad sections, and they looked at more houses. I think they decided on one, 1231 East Meadowbrook. It's empty. Realtor by the name of Betsy Bell walked them through it. Asking one-forty, but will take less. Need to move it.'

'That's a nice part of town. How old is the house?'

'Ten, fifteen years. Three thousand square feet. Sort of a colonial-looking job. It's nice enough for one of your boys, Ollie.'

'Are you sure that's the one they want?'

'For now anyway. They discussed maybe coming back in a month or so to look at some more. You might want to fly them back as soon as they accept. That's normal procedure, ain't it?'

'Yes. We'll handle that. What about the salary?'

'Most impressed. Highest one so far. They talked and talked about the money. Salary, retirement, mortgage, BMW, bonus, everything. They couldn't believe it. Kids must really be broke.'

'They are. You think we got him, huh?'

'I'd bet on it. He said once that the firm may not be as prestigious as the ones on Wall Street, but the lawyers were just as qualified and a lot nicer. I think he'll sign on, yeah.'

'Any suspicions?'

'Not really. Quin evidently told him to stay away from Locke's office. He told his wife that no one ever went in there but some secretaries and a handful of partners. But he said Quin said Locke was eccentric and not that friendly. I don't think he's suspicious, though. She said the firm seemed concerned about some things that were none of its business.'

'Such as?'

'Personal matters. Children, working wives, etc. She seemed a bit irritated, but I think it was more of an observation. She told Mitch Saturday morning that she would be damned if any bunch of lawyers would tell her when to work and when to have babies. But I don't think it's a problem.'

'Does he realize how permanent this place is?'

'I think so. There was no mention of putting in a few years and moving on. I think he got the message. He want's to be a partner, like all of them. He's broke and wants the money.'

'What about the dinner at my place?'

'They were nervous, but had a good time. Very impressed with your place. Really liked your wife.'

'Sex?'

'Every night. Sounded like a honeymoon in there.'

'What'd they do?'

'We couldn't see, remember. Sounded normal. Nothing kinky. I thought of you and how much you like pictures, and I kept telling myself we should've rigged up some cameras for old Ollie.'

'Shut up, DeVasher.'

'Maybe next time.'

They were silent as DeVasher looked at a notepad. He stubbed his cigar in the ashtray and smiled to himself.

'All in all,' he said, 'it's a strong marriage. They seemed to be very intimate. Your driver said they held hands all weekend. Not a cross word for three days. That's pretty good, ain't it? But who am I? I've been married three times myself.'

'That's understandable. What about children?'

'Couple of years. She wants to work some, then get pregnant.'

'What's your opinion of this guy?'

'Very good, very decent young man. Also very ambitious. I think he's driven and he won't quit until he's at the top. He'll take some chances, bend some rules if necessary.'

Ollie smiled. 'That's what I wanted to hear.'

'Two phone calls. Both to her mother in Kentucky. Nothing remarkable.'

'What about his family?'

'Never mentioned.'

'No word on Ray?'

'We're still looking, Ollie. Give us some time.'

DeVasher closed the McDeere file and opened another, much thicker one. Lambert rubbed his temples and stared at the floor. 'What's the latest?' he asked softly.

'It's not good, Ollie. I'm convinced Hodge and Kozinski are working together now. Last week the FBI got a warrant and checked Kozinski's house. Found our wiretaps. They told him his house was bugged, but of course they don't know who did it. Kozinski tells Hodge last Friday while they're hiding in the third-floor library. We got a bug nearby, and we pick up bits and pieces. Not much, but we know they talked about the wiretaps. They're convinced everything is bugged, and they suspect us. They're very careful where they talk.'

'Why would the FBI bother with a search warrant?'

'Good question. Probably for our benefit. To make things look real legal and proper. They respect us.'

'Which agent?'

'Tarrance. He's in charge, evidently.'

'Is he good?'

'He's okay. Young, green, overzealous, but competent. He's no match for our men.'

'How often has he talked to Kozinski?'

'There's no way to know. They figure we're listening, so everybody's real careful. We know of four meetings in the last month, but I suspect more.'

'How much has he spilled?'

'Not much, I hope. They're still shadow-boxing. The last conversation we got was a week ago and he didn't say much. He's bad scared. They're coaxing a lot, but not getting much. He hasn't yet made the decision to cooperate. They approached him, remember. At least we think they approached him. They shook him up pretty bad and he was ready to cut a deal. Now he's having second thoughts. But he's still in contact with them, and that's what worries me.'

'Does his wife know?'

'I don't think so. She knows he's acting strange, and he tells her it's office pressure.'

'What about Hodge?'

'Still ain't talked to the Fibbies, as far as we know. He and Kozinski talk a lot, or whisper I should say. Hodge keeps saying he's scared to death of the FBI, that they don't play fair and they cheat and play dirty. He won't move without Kozinski.'

'What if Kozinski is eliminated?'

'Hodge will be a new man. But I don't think we've reached that point. Dammit, Ollie, he ain't some hotshot thug who gets in the way. He's a very nice young man, with kids and all that.'

'Your compassion is overwhelming. I guess you think I enjoy this. Hell, I practically raised these boys.'

'We'll get them back in line, then, before this thing goes too far. New York's getting suspicious, Ollie. They're asking a lot of questions.'

'Who?'

'Lazarov.'

'What have you told them, DeVasher?'

'Everything. That's my job. They want you in New York day after tomorrow, for a full briefing.'

'What do they want?'

'Answers. And plans.'

'Plans for what?'

'Preliminary plans to eliminate Kozinski, Hodge and Tarrance, should it become necessary.'

'Tarrance! Are you crazy, DeVasher? We can't eliminate a cop. They'll send in the troops.'

'Lazarov is stupid, Ollie. You know that. He's an idiot, but I don't think we should tell him.'

'I think I will. I think I'll go to New York and tell Lazarov he's a complete fool.'

'You do that, Ollie. You do that.'

Oliver Lambert jumped from his seat and headed for the door. 'Watch McDeere for another month.'

'Sure, Ollie. You betcha. He'll sign. Don't worry.'

# CHAPTER FOUR

The Mazda was sold for two hundred dollars, and most of the money was immediately invested in a twelve-foot U-Haul rental truck. He would be reimbursed in Memphis. Half of the odd assortment of furniture was given or thrown away, and when loaded the truck held a refrigerator, a bed, a dresser and chest of drawers, a small color television, boxes of dishes, clothes and junk and an old sofa which was taken out of sentiment and would not last long in the new location.

Abby held Hearsay, the mutt, as Mitch worked his way through Boston and headed south, far south toward the promise of better things. For three days they drove the back roads, enjoyed the countryside, sang along with the radio, slept in cheap motels and talked of the house, the BMW, new furniture, children, affluence. They rolled down the windows and let the wind blow as the truck approached top speeds of almost forty-five miles per hour. At one point, somewhere in Pennsylvania, Abby mentioned that perhaps they could stop in Kentucky for a brief visit. Mitch said nothing, but chose a route through the Carolinas and Georgia, never venturing within two hundred miles of any point on the Kentucky border. Abby let it pass.

They arrived in Memphis on a Thursday morning, and, as promised, the black 318i sat under the carport as though it belonged there. He stared at the car. She stared at the house. The lawn was thick, green and neatly trimmed. The hedges had been manicured. The marigolds were in bloom.

The keys were found under a bucket in the utility room, as promised.

After the first test drive, they quickly unloaded the truck before the neighbors could inspect the sparse belongings. The U-Haul was returned to the nearest dealer. Another test drive.

An interior designer, the same one who would do his office, arrived after noon and brought with her samples of carpet, paint, floor coverings, curtains, drapes, wallpaper. Abby found the idea of a designer a bit hilarious after their apartment in Cambridge, but played along. Mitch was immediately bored, and excused himself for another test drive. He toured the tree-lined, quiet, shady streets of this handsome neighborhood of which he was now a member. He smiled as boys on bicycles stopped and whistled at his new car. He waved at the postman walking down the sidewalk sweating profusely. Here he was,

Mitchell Y. McDeere, twenty-five years old and one week out of law school, and he had arrived.

At three, they followed the designer to an upscale furniture store where the manager politely informed them that Mr. Oliver Lambert had already made arrangements for their credit, if they so chose, and there was in fact no limit on what they could buy and finance. They bought a houseful. Mitch frowned from time to time, and twice vetoed items as too expensive, but Abby ruled the day. The designer complimented her time and again on her marvelous taste, and said she would see Mitch on Monday, to do his office. Marvelous, he said.

With a map of the city, they set out for the Quin residence. Abby had seen the house during the first visit, but did not remember how to find it. It was in a section of town called Chickasaw Gardens, and she remembered the wooded lots, huge houses and professionally land-scaped front yards. They parked in the driveway behind the new Mercedes and the old Mercedes.

The maid nodded politely, but did not smile. She led them to the living room, and left them. The house was dark and quiet – no children, no voices, no one. They admired the furniture and waited. They mumbled quietly, then grew impatient. Yes, they agreed, they had in fact been invited to dinner on this night, Thursday, June 25, at 6 P.M. Mitch checked his watch again and said something about it being rude. They waited.

From the hallway, Kay emerged and attempted to smile. Her eyes were puffy and glazed, with mascara leaking from the corners. Tears flowed freely down her cheeks, and she held a handkerchief over her mouth. She hugged Abby and sat next to her on the sofa. She bit the handkerchief and cried louder.

Mitch knelt before her. 'Kay, what's happened?'

She bit harder and shook her head. Abby squeezed her knee, and Mitch patted the other one. They watched her fearfully, expecting the worst. Was it Lamar or one of the kids?

'There's been a tragedy,' she said through the quiet sobbing.

'Who is it?' Mitch asked.

She wiped her eyes and breathed deeply. 'Two members of the firm, Marty Kozinski and Joe Hodge, were killed today. We were very close to them.'

'Mitch sat on the coffee table. He remembered Marty Kozinski from the second visit in April. He had joined Lamar and Mitch for lunch at a deli on Front Street. He was next in line for a partnership, but had seemed less than enthused. Mitch could not place Joe Hodge.

'What happened?' he asked.

She had stopped crying, but the tears continued. She wiped her face again and looked at him. 'We're not sure. They were on Grand Cayman, scuba diving. There was some kind of an explosion on a boat, and we think they drowned. Lamar said details were sketchy. There was a firm meeting a few hours ago, and they were all told about it. Lamar barely made it home.'

'Where is he?'

'By the pool. He's waiting for you.'

He sat in a white metal lawn chair next to a small table with a small umbrella, a few feet from the edge of the pool. Near a flower bed, a circular lawn sprinkler rattled and hissed and spewed forth water in a perfect arc which included the table, umbrella, chair and Lamar Quin. He was soaked. Water dripped from his nose, ears and hair. The blue cotton shirt and wool pants were saturated. He wore no socks or shoes.

He sat motionless, never flinching with each additional dousing. He had lost touch. Some distant object on the side fence attracted and held his attention. An unopened bottle of Heineken sat in a puddle on the concrete beside his chair.

Mitch surveyed the back lawn, in part to make sure the neighbors could not see. They could not. An eight-foot cypress fence ensured complete privacy. He walked around the pool and stopped at the edge of the dry area. Lamar noticed him, nodded, attempted a weak smile and motioned to a wet chair. Mitch pulled it a few feet away and sat down, just as the next barrage of water landed.

His stare returned to the fence, or whatever it was in the distance. For an eternity they sat and listened to the thrashing sound of the sprinkler. Lamar would sometimes shake his head and attempt to mumble. Mitch smiled awkwardly, unsure of what, if anything, needed to be said.

'Lamar, I'm very sorry,' he finally offered.

He acknowledged this and looked at Mitch. 'Me too.'

'I wish I could say something.'

His eyes left the fence, and he cocked his head sideways in Mitch's direction. His dark hair was soaked and hung in his eyes. The eyes were red and pained. He stared, and waited until the next round of water passed over.

'I know. But there's nothing to say. I'm sorry it had to happen now, today. We didn't feel like cooking.'

'That should be the least of your concern. I lost my appetite a moment ago.'

'Do you remember them?' he asked, blowing water from his lips.

'I remember Kozinski, but not Hodge.'

'Marty Kozinski was one of my best friends. From Chicago. He joined the firm three years ahead of me and was next in line for a partnership. A great lawyer, one we all admired and turned to. Probably the best negotiator in the firm. Very cool and dry under pressure.'

He wiped his eyebrows and stared at the ground. When he talked the water dripped from his nose and interfered with his enunciation. 'Three kids. His twin girls are a month older than our son, and they've always played together.' He closed his eyes, bit his lip and started crying.

Mitch wanted to leave. He tried not to look at his friend. 'I'm very sorry, Lamar. Very sorry.'

After a few minutes, the crying stopped, but the water continued. Mitch surveyed the spacious lawn in search of the outside faucet. Twice he summoned the courage to ask if he could turn off the sprinkler, and twice he decided he could last if Lamar could. Maybe it helped. He checked his watch. Darkness was an hour and a half away.

'What about the accident?' Mitch finally asked.

'We weren't told much. They were scuba diving and there was an explosion on the boat. The dive captain was also killed. A native of the islands. They're trying to get the bodies home now.'

'Where were their wives?'

'At home, thankfully. It was a business trip.'

'I can't picture Hodge.'

'Joe was a tall blond-headed guy who didn't say much. The kind you meet but don't remember. He was a Harvard man like yourself.'

'How old was he?'

'He and Marty were both thirty-four. He would've made partner after Marty. They were very close. I guess we're all close, especially now.'

With all ten fingernails he combed his hair straight back. He stood and walked to dry ground. Water poured from his shirt-tail and the cuffs of his pants. He stopped near Mitch and looked blankly at the treetops next door. 'How's the BMW?'

'It's great. A fine car. Thanks for delivering it.'

'When did you arrive?'

'This morning. I've already put a thousand miles on it.'

'Did the interior woman show up?'

'Yeah. She and Abby spent next year's salary.'

'That's nice. Nice house. We're glad you're here, Mitch. I'm just sorry about the circumstances. You'll like it here.'

'You don't have to apologize.'

'I still don't believe it. I'm numb, paralyzed. I shudder at the thought of seeing Marty's wife and the kids. I'd rather be lashed with a bullwhip than go over there.'

The women appeared, walked across the wooden patio deck and down the steps to the pool. Kay found the faucet and the sprinkler was silenced.

They left Chickasaw Gardens and drove west with the traffic toward downtown, into the fading sun. They held hands, but said little. Mitch opened the sunroof and rolled down the windows. Abby picked through a box of old cassettes and found Springsteen. The stereo worked fine. 'Hungry Heart' blew from the windows as the little shiny roadster made its way toward the river. The warm, sticky, humid Memphis summer air settled in with the dark. Softball fields came to life as teams of fat men with tight polyester pants and lime-green and fluorescent-yellow shirts laid chalk lines and prepared to do battle. Cars full of teenagers crowded into fast-food joints to drink beer and gossip and check out the opposite sex. Mitch began to smile. He tried to forget about Lamar, and Kozinski and Hodge. Why should he be sad? They were not his friends. He was sorry for their families, but he did not really know these people. And he, Mitchell Y. McDeere, a poor kid with no family, had much to be happy about. Beautiful wife, new house, new car, new job, new Harvard degree. A brilliant mind and a solid body that did not gain weight and needed little sleep. Eighty thousand a year, for now. In two years he could be in six figures, and all he had to do was work ninety hours a week. Piece of cake.

He pulled into a self-serve and pumped fifteen gallons. He paid inside and bought a six-pack of Michelob. Abby opened two, and they darted back into the traffic. He was smiling now.

'Let's eat,' he said.

'We're not exactly dressed,' she said.

He stared at her long, brown legs. She wore a white cotton skirt, above the knees, with a white cotton button-down. He had shorts, deck shoes and a faded black polo. 'With legs like that, you could get us into any restaurant in New York.'

'How about the Rendezvous? The dress seemed casual.'

'Great idea.'

They paid to park in a lot downtown and walked two blocks to a narrow alley. The smell of barbecue mixed with the summer air and hung like a fog close to the pavement. The aroma filtered gently through the nose, mouth and eyes and caused a rippling sensation deep in the stomach. Smoke poured into the alley from vents running underground into the massive ovens where the best pork ribs were barbecued in the best barbecue restaurant in a city known for world-class barbecue. The Rendezvous was downstairs, beneath the alley, beneath an ancient red-brick building that would have been demolished decades earlier had it not been for the famous tenant in the basement.

There was always a crowd and a waiting list, but Thursdays were slow, it seemed. They were led through the cavernous, sprawling, noisy restaurant and shown a small table with a red checked table-cloth. There were stares along the way. Always stares. Men stopped eating, froze with ribs hanging from their teeth, as Abby McDeere glided by like a model on a runway. She had stopped traffic from a sidewalk in Boston. Whistles and catcalls were a way of life. And her husband was used to it. He took great pride in his beautiful wife.

An angry black man with a red apron stood before them. 'Okay, sir,' he demanded.

The menus were mats on the tables, and completely unnecessary. Ribs, ribs and ribs.

'Two whole orders, cheese plate, pitcher of beer,' Mitch shot back at him. The waiter wrote nothing, but turned and screamed in the direction of the entrance: 'Gimme two whole, cheese, pitcher!'

When he left, Mitch grabbed her leg under the table. She slapped his hand.

'You're beautiful,' he said. 'When was the last time I told you that you are beautiful?'

'About two hours ago.'

'Two hours! How thoughtless of me!'

'Don't let it happen again.'

He grabbed her leg again and rubbed the knee. She allowed it. She smiled seductively at him, dimples forming perfectly, teeth shining in the dim light, soft pale brown eyes glowing. Her dark brunet hair was straight and fell perfectly a few inches below her shoulders.

The beer arrived and the waiter filled two mugs without saying a word. Abby took a small drink and stopped smiling.

'Do you think Lamar's okay?' she asked.

'I don't know. I thought at first he was drunk. I felt like an idiot sitting there watching him get soaked.'

'Poor guy. Kay said the funerals will probably be Monday, if they can get the bodies back in time.'

'Let's talk about something else. I don't like funerals, any funeral, even when I'm there out of respect and don't know the deceased. I've had some bad experiences with funerals.'

The ribs arrived. They were served on paper plates with aluminum foil to catch the grease. A small dish of slaw and one of baked beans sat around a foot long slab of dry ribs sprinkled heavily with the secret sauce. They dug in with fingers.

'What would you like to talk about?' she asked.

'Getting pregnant.'

'I thought we were going to wait a few years.'

'We are. But I think we should practice diligently until then.'

'We've practiced in every roadside motel between here and Boston.'

'I know, but not in our new home.' Mitch ripped two ribs apart, slinging sauce into his eyebrows.

'We just moved in this morning.'

'I know. What're we waiting for?'

'Mitch, you act as though you've been neglected.'

'I have, since this morning. I suggest we do it tonight, as soon as we get home, to sort of christen our new house.'

'We'll see.'

'Is it a date? Look, did you see that guy over there? He's about to break his neck trying to see some leg. I oughta go over and whip his ass.'

'Yes. It's a date. Don't worry about those guys. They're staring at you. They think you're cute.'

'Very funny.'

Mitch stripped his ribs clean and ate half of hers. When the beer was gone, he paid the check and they climbed into the alley. He drove carefully across town and found the name of a street he recognized from one of his many road trips of the day. After two wrong turns, he found Meadowbrook, and then the home of Mr. and Mrs. Mitchell Y. McDeere.

The mattress and box springs were stacked on the floor of the master bedroom, surrounded by boxes. Hearsay hid under a lamp on the floor and watched as they practiced.

Four days later, on what should have been his first day behind his new desk, Mitch and his lovely wife joined the remaining thirty-nine members of the firm, and their lovely wives, as the paid their last respects to Martin S. Kozinski. The cathedral was full. Oliver Lambert offered a eulogy so eloquent and touching not even Mitchell

McDeere, who had buried a father and a brother, could resist chill bumps. Abby's eyes watered at the sight of the widow and the children.

That afternoon, they met again in the Presbyterian church in East Memphis to say farewell to Joseph M. Hodge.

# CHAPTER FIVE

The small lobby outside Royce McKnight's office was empty when Mitch arrived precisely at eight-thirty, on schedule. He hummed and coughed and began to wait anxiously. From behind two file cabinets an ancient blue-haired secretary appeared and scowled in his general direction. When it was apparent he was not welcome, he introduced himself and explained he was to meet Mr. McKnight at this appointed hour. She smiled and introduced herself as Louise, Mr. McKnight's personal secretary, for thirty-one years now. Coffee? Yes, he said, black. She disappeared and returned with a cup and saucer. She notified her boss through the intercom and instructed Mitch to have a seat. She recognized him now. One of the other secretaries had pointed him out during the funerals yesterday.

She apologized for the somber atmosphere around the place. No one felt like working, she explained, and it would be days before things were normal. They were such nice young men. The phone rang and she explained that Mr. McKnight was in an important meeting and could not be disturbed. It rang again, she listened, and escorted him into the managing partner's office.

Oliver Lambert and Royce McKnight greeted Mitch and introduced him to two other partners, Victor Milligan and Avery Tolleson. They sat around a small conference table. Louise was sent for more coffee. Milligan was head of tax, and Tolleson, at forty-one, was one of the younger partners.

'Mitch, we apologize for such a depressing beginning,' McKnight said. 'We appreciate your presence at the funerals yesterday, and we're sorry your first day as a member of our firm was one of such sadness.'

'I felt I belonged at the funerals,' Mitch said.

'We're very proud of you, and we have great plans for you. We've just lost two of our finest lawyers, both of whom did nothing but tax, so we'll be asking more of you. All of us will have to work a little harder.'

Louise arrived with a tray of coffee. Silver coffee server, fine china.

'We are quite saddened, ' said Oliver Lambert. 'So please bear with us.'

They all nodded and frowned at the table. Royce McKnight looked at some notes on a legal pad.

'Mitch, I think we've covered this before. At this firm, we assign each associate to a partner, who acts as a supervisor and mentor. These relationships are very important. We try to match you with a partner with whom you will be compatible and able to work closely, and we're usually right. We have made mistakes. Wrong chemistry, or whatever, but when that happens we simply reassign the associate. Avery Tolleson will be your partner.'

Mitch smiled awkwardly at his new partner.

'You will be under his direction, and the cases and files you work on will be his. Virtually all of it will be tax work.'

'That's fine.'

'Before I forget it, I'd like to have lunch today,' Tolleson said.

'Certainly,' Mitch said.

'Take my limo,' Mr. Lambert said.

'I had planned to,' said Tolleson.

'When do I get a limo?' Mitch asked.

They smiled, and seemed to appreciate the relief. 'In about twenty years,' said Mr. Lambert.

'I can wait.'

'How's the BMW?' asked Victor Milligan.

'Great. It's ready for the five-thousand-mile service.'

'Did you get moved in okay?'

'Yes, everything's fine. I appreciate the firm's assistance in everything. You've made us feel very welcome and Abby and I are extremely grateful.'

McKnight quit smiling and returned to the legal pad. 'As I've told you, Mitch, the bar exam has priority. You've got six weeks to study for it and we assist in every way possible. We have our own review courses directed by our members. All areas of the exam will be covered and your progress will be closely watched by all of us, especially Avery. At least half of each day will be spent on bar review, and most of your spare time as well. No associate in this firm has ever failed the exam.'

'I won't be the first'

'If you flunk it, we take away the BMW,' Tolleson said with a slight grin.

'Your secretary will be a lady named Nina Huff. She's been with the firm more that eight years. Sort of temperamental, not much to look at, but very capable. She knows a lot of law and has a tendency to give advice, especially to the newer attorneys. It'll be up to you to keep her in place. If you can't get along with her, we'll move her.'

'Where's my office?'

'Second floor, down the hall from Avery. The interior woman will be here this afternoon to pick out the desk and furnishings. As much as possible, follow her advice.'

Lamar was also on the second floor, and at the moment that thought was comforting. He thought of him sitting by the pool, soaking wet, crying and mumbling incoherently.

McKnight spoke. 'Mitch, I'm afraid I neglected to cover something that should've been discussed during the first visit here.'

He waited, and finally said, 'Okay, what is it?'

The partners watched McKnight intently. 'We've never allowed an associate to begin his career burdened with student loans. We prefer that you find other things to worry about, and other ways to spend your money. How much do you owe?'

Mitch sipped his coffee and thought rapidly. 'Almost twenty-three thousand.'

'Have the documents on Louise's desk first thing in the morning.'

'You, uh, mean the firm satisfies the loans?'

'That's our policy. Unless you object.'

'No objection. I don't quite know what to say.'

'You don't have to say anything. We've done it for every associate for the past fifteen years. Just get the paperwork to Louise.'

'That's very generous, Mr. McKnight.'

'Yes, it is.'

Avery Tolleson talked incessantly as the limo moved slowly through the noontime traffic. Mitch reminded him of himself, he said. A poor kid from a broken home, raised by foster families throughout southwest Texas, then put on the streets after high school. He worked the night shift in a shoe factory to finance junior college. An academic scholarship to UTEP opened the door. He graduated with honors, applied to eleven law schools and chose Stanford. he finished number two in his class and turned down offers from every big firm on the West Coast. He wanted to do tax work, nothing but tax work. Oliver Lambert had recruited him sixteen years ago, back when the firm had fewer than thirty lawyers.

He had a wife and two kids, but said little about the family. He talked about money. His passion, he called it. The first million was in the bank. The second was two years away. At four hundred thousand a year gross, it wouldn't take long. His specialty was forming partnerships to purchase supertankers. He was the premier specialist in his field and worked at three hundred an hour, sixty, sometimes seventy hours a week.

Mitch would start at a hundred bucks an hour, at least five hours a day until he passed the bar and got his license. Then eight hours a day would be expected, at one-fifty an hour. Billing was the lifeblood of the firm. Everything revolved around it. Promotions, raises, bonuses, survival, success, everything revolved around how well one was billing. Especially the new guys. The quickest route to a reprimand was to neglect the daily billing records. Avery could not remember such a reprimand. It was simply unheard of for a member of the firm to ignore his billing.

The average for associates was one-seventy-five per hour. For partners, three hundred. Milligan got four hundred an hour from a couple of his clients, and Nathan Locke once got five hundred an hour for some tax work that involved swapping assets in several foreign countries. Five hundred bucks an hour! Avery relished the thought, and computed five hundred per hour by fifty hours per week at fifty weeks per year. One million two hundred fifty thousand a year! That's how you make money in this business. You get a bunch of lawyers working by the hour and you build a dynasty. The more lawyers you get, the more money the partners make.

Don't ignore the billing, he warned. That's the first rule of survival. If there were no files to bill on, immediately report to his office. He had plenty. On the tenth day of each month the partners review the prior month's billing during one of their exclusive luncheons. It's a big ceremony. Royce McKnight reads out each lawyer's name, then the total of his monthly billing. The competition among the partners is intense, but good-spirited. They're all getting rich, right? It's very motivational. As for the associates, nothing is said to the low man unless it's his second straight month. Oliver Lambert will say something in passing. No one has ever finished low for three straight months. Bonuses can be earned by associates for exorbitant billing. Partnerships are based on one's track record for generating fees. So don't ignore it, he warned again. It must always have priority – after the bar exam, of course.

The bar exam was a nuisance, an ordeal that must be endured, a rite of passage, and nothing any Harvard man should fear. Just concentrate on the review courses, he said, and try to remember everything he had just learned in law school.

The limo wheeled into a side street between two tall buildings and stopped in front of a small canopy that extended from the curb to a black metal door. Avery looked at his watch and said to the driver, 'Be back at two.'

Two hours for lunch, thought Mitch. That's over six hundred dollars in billable time. What a waste.

The Manhattan Club occupied the top floor of a ten-story office building which had last been fully occupied in the early fifties. Avery referred to the structure as a dump, but was quick to point out that the club was the most exclusive lunch and dinner refuge in the city. It offered excellent food in an all-white rich-male, plush environment. Powerful lunches for powerful people. Bankers, lawyers, executives, entrepreneurs, a few politicians and a few aristocrats. A gold-plated elevator ran nonstop past the deserted offices and stopped on the elegant tenth floor. The maître d' called Mr. Tolleson by name and asked about his good friends Oliver Lambert and Nathan Locke. He expressed sympathies for the loss of Mr. Kozinski and Mr. Hodge. Avery thanked him and introduced the newest member of the firm. The favorite table was waiting in the corner. A courtly black man named Ellis delivered the menus.

'The firm does not allow drinking at lunch,' Avery said as he opened his menu.

'I don't drink during lunch.'

'That's good. What'll you have?'

'Tea, with ice.'

'Iced tea, for him,' Avery said to the waiter. 'Bring me a Bombay martini on the rocks with three olives.'

Mitch bit his tongue and grinned behind the menu.

'We have too many rules,' Avery mumbled.

The first martini led to a second, but he quit after two. He ordered for both of them . Broiled fish of some sort. The special of the day. He watched his weight carefully, he said. He also worked out daily at a health club, his own health club. He invited Mitch to come sweat with him. Maybe after the bar exam. There were the usual questions about football in college and the standard denials of any greatness.

Mitch asked about the children. He said they lived with their mother.

The fish was raw and the baked potato was hard. Mitch picked at his plate, ate his salad slowly and listened as his partner talked about most of the other people present for lunch. The mayor was seated at a large table with some Japanese. One of the firm's bankers was at the next table. There were some other big-shot lawyers and corporate types, all eating furiously and importantly, powerfully. The atmosphere was stuffy. According to Avery, every member of the club was a compelling figure, a potent force both in his field and in the city. Avery was at home.

They both declined dessert and ordered coffee. He would be expected to be in the office by nine each morning, Avery explained as he lit a Montesino. The secretaries would be there at eight-thirty. Nine to five, but no one worked eight hours a day. Personally, he was in the office by eight, and seldom left before six. He could bill twelve hours each day, every day, regardless of how many hours he actually worked. Twelve a day, five days a week, at three hundred an hour, for fifty weeks. Nine hundred thousand dollars! In billable time! That was his goal. Last year he had billed seven hundred thousand but there had been some personal problems. The firm didn't care if Mitch came in at 6 A.M. or 9 A.M., as long as the work was done.

'What time are the doors unlocked?' Mitch asked.

Everyone has a key, he explained, so he could come and go as he pleased. Security was tight, but the guards were accustomed to workaholics. Some of the work habits were legendary. Victor Milligan, in his younger days, worked sixteen hours a day, seven days a week, until he made partner. Then he quit working on Sundays. He had a heart attack and gave up Saturdays. His doctor put him on ten-hour days, five days a week, and he hasn't been happy since. Marty Kozinski knew all the janitors by first name. He was a 9 A.M. man who wanted to have breakfast with the kids. He would come in at nine and leave at midnight. Nathan Locke claims he can't work well after the secretaries arrive, so he comes in at six. It would be a disgrace to start later. Here's a man sixty-one years old, worth ten million, and works from six in the morning until eight at night five days a week and then a half day on Saturday. If he retired, he'd die.

Nobody punched a clock, the partner explained. Come and go as you please. Just get the work done.

Mitch said he got the message. Sixteen hours a day would be nothing new.

Avery complimented him on the new suit. There was an unwritten dress code, and it was apparent Mitch had caught on. Avery had a tailor, an old Korean in South Memphis, he would recommend when Mitch could afford it. Fifteen hundred a suit. Mitch said he would wait a year or two.

An attorney from one of the bigger firms interrupted and spoke to Avery. He offered his sympathies and asked about the families. He and Joe Hodge had worked together on a case last year, and he couldn't believe it. Avery introduced him to Mitch. He was at the funeral, he said. They waited for him to leave, but he rambled on and on about how sorry he was. It was obvious he wanted details. Avery offered none, and he finally left.

By two, the power lunches were losing steam, and the crowd thinned. Avery signed the check, and the maître d' led them to the door. The chauffeur stood patiently by the rear of the limo. Mitch crawled into the back and sank into the heavy leather seat. He watched the buildings and the traffic. He looked at the pedestrians scurrying along the hot sidewalks and wondered how many of them had seen the inside of a limo or the inside of the Manhattan Club. How many of them would be rich in ten years? He smiled, and felt good. Harvard was a million miles away. Harvard with no student loans. Kentucky was in another world. His past was forgotten. He had arrived.

The decorator was waiting in his office. Avery excused himself and asked Mitch to be in his office in an hour to begin work. She had books full of office furniture and samples of everything. He asked for suggestions, listened with as much interest as he could muster, then told her he trusted her judgment and she could pick out whatever she felt was appropriate. She liked the solid cherry work desk, no drawers, burgundy leather wing chairs and a very expensive oriental rug. Mitch said it was marvelous.

She left and he sat behind the old desk, one that looked fine and would have suited him except that it was considered used and therefore not good enough for a new lawyer at Bendini, Lambert & Locke. The office was fifteen by fifteen, with two six-foot windows facing north and staring directly into the second floor of the old building next door. Not much of a view. With a strain, he could see a glimpse of the river to the northwest. The walls were sheet-rock and bare. She had picked out some artwork. He determined that the Ego Wall would face the desk, behind the wing chairs. The diplomas, etc., would have to be mounted and framed. The office was big, for an associate. Much larger than the cubbyholes where the rookies were placed in New York and Chicago. It would do for a couple of years. Then on to one with a better view. Then a corner office, one of those power ones.

Miss Nina Huff knocked on the door and introduced herself as the secretary. She was a heavyset woman of forty-five, and with one glance it was not difficult to understand why she was still single. With no family to support, it was evident she spent her money on clothes and make-up – all to no avail. Mitch wondered why she did not invest in a fitness counselor. She informed him forthrightly that she had been with the firm eight and a half years now and knew all there was to know about office procedure. If he had a question, just ask her. He thanked her for that. She had been in the typing pool and was grateful for the return to general secretarial duties. He nodded as

418

though he understood completely. She asked if he knew how to operate the dictating equipment. Yes, he said. In fact, the year before he had worked for a three-hundred-man firm on Wall Street and that firm owned the very latest in office technology. But if he had a problem he would ask her, he promised.

'What's your wife's name?' she asked.

'Why is that important?' he asked.

'Because when she calls, I would like to know her name so that I can be real sweet and friendly to her on the phone.'

'Abby.'

'How do you like your coffee?'

'Black, but I'll fix it myself.'

'I don't mind fixing your coffee for you. It's part of my job.'

'I'll fix it myself.'

'All the secretaries do it.'

'If you ever touch my coffee, I'll see to it that you're sent to the mail room to lick stamps.'

'We have an automated licker. Do they lick stamps on Wall Street?'

'It was a figure of speech.'

'Well, I've memorized your wife's name and we've settled the issue of coffee, so I guess I'm ready to start.'

'In the morning. Be here at eight-thirty.'

'Yes, boss.' She left and Mitch smiled to himself. She was a real smart-ass, but she would be fun.

Lamar was next. He was late for a meeting with Nathan Locke, but he wanted to stop by and check on his friend. He was pleased their offices were close. He apologized again for last Thursday's dinner. Yes, he and Kay and the kids would be there at seven to inspect the new house and furniture.

Hunter Quin was five. His sister Holly was seven. They both ate the spaghetti with perfect manners from the brand-new dining table and dutifully ignored the grown-up talk circulating around them. Abby watched the two and dreamed of babies. Mitch thought they were cute, but was not inspired. He was busy recalling the events of the day.

The women ate quickly, then left to look at the furniture and talk about the remodeling. The children took Hearsay to the backyard.

'I'm a little surprised they put you with Tolleson,' Lamar said, wiping his mouth.

'Why is that?'

'I don't think he's ever supervised an associate.'

'Any particular reason?'

'Not really. He's a great guy, but not much of a team player. Sort of a loner. Prefers to work by himself. He and his wife are having some problems, and there's talk that they've separated. But he keeps it to himself.'

Mitch pushed his plate away and sipped the iced tea. 'Is he a good lawyer?'

'Yes, very good. They're all good if they make partner. A lot of his clients are rich people with millions to put in tax shelters. He sets up limited partnerships. Many of his shelters are risky, and he's known for his willingness to take chances and fight with the IRS later. Most of his clients are big-time risk takers. You'll do a lot of research looking for ways to bend the tax laws. It'll be fun.'

'He spent half of lunch lecturing on billing.'

'It's vital. There's always the pressure to bill more and more. All we have to sell is our time. Once you pass the bar your billing will be monitored weekly by Tolleson and Royce McKnight. It's all computerized and they can tell down to the dime how productive you are. You'll be expected to bill thirty to forty hours a week for the first six months. Then fifty for a couple of years. Before they'll consider you for partner, you've got to hit sixty hours a week consistently over a period of years. No active partner bills less than sixty a week – most of it at the maximum rate.'

'That's a lot of hours.'

'Sounds that way, but it's deceptive. Most good lawyers can work eight or nine hours a day and bill twelve. It's called padding. It's not exactly fair to the client, but it's something everybody does. The great firms have been built by padding files. It's the name of the game.'

'Sounds unethical.'

'So is ambulance chasing by plaintiff's lawyers. It's unethical for a dope lawyer to take his fee in cash if he has a reason to believe the money is dirty. A lot of things are unethical. What about the doctor who sees a hundred Medicare patients a day? Or the one who performs unnecessary surgery? Some of the most unethical people I've met have been my own clients. It's easy to pad a file when your client is a multimillionaire who wants to screw the government and wants you to do it legally. We all do it.'

'Do they teach it?'

'No. You just sort of learn it. You'll start off working long, crazy hours, but you can't do it forever. So you start taking shortcuts.

Believe me, Mitch, after you've been with us a year you'll know how to work ten hours and bill twice that much. It's sort of a sixth sense lawyers acquire.'

'What else will I acquire?'

Lamar rattled his ice cubes and thought for a moment. 'A certain amount of cynicism. This business works on you. When you were in law school you had some noble idea of what a lawyer should be. A champion of individual rights; a defender of the Constitution; a guardian of the oppressed; an advocate for your client's principles. Then after you practice for six months you realize we're nothing but hired guns. Mouthpieces for sale to the highest bidder, available to anybody, any crook, any sleazebag with enough money to pay our outrageous fees. Nothing shocks you. It's supposed to be an honorable profession, but you'll meet so many crooked lawyers you'll want to quit and find an honest job. Yeah, Mitch, you'll get cynical. And it's sad, really.'

'You shouldn't be telling me this at this stage of my career.'

'The money makes up for it. It's amazing how much drudgery you can endure at two hundred thousand a year.'

'Drudgery? You make it sound terrible.'

'I'm sorry. It's not that bad. My perspective on life changed radically last Thursday.'

'You want to look at the house? It's marvelous.'

'Maybe some other time. Let's just talk.'

# CHAPTER SIX

At five A.M. the alarm clock exploded on the new bed table under the new lamp, and was immediately silenced. Mitch staggered through the dark house and found Hearsay waiting at the back door. He released him into the backyard and headed for the shower. Twenty minutes later he found his wife under the covers and kissed her goodbye. She did not respond.

With no traffic to fight, the office was ten minutes away. He had decided his day would start at five-thirty, unless someone could top that, then he would be there at five, or four-thirty, or whenever it took to be first. Sleep was a nuisance. He would be the first lawyer to arrive at the Bendini Building on this day, and every day until he became a partner. If it took the others ten years, he could do it in seven. He would become the youngest partner in the history of the firm, he had decided.

The vacant lot next to the Bendini Building had a ten-foot chain link fence around it and a guard by the gate. There was a parking place inside with his name sprayed between the yellow lines. He stopped by the gate and waited. The uniformed guard emerged from the darkness and approached the driver's door. Mitch pushed a button, lowered the window and produced a plastic card with his picture on it.

'You must be the new man,' the guard said as he held the card.

'Yes. Mitch McDeere.'

'I can read. I should've known by the car.'

'What's your name?' Mitch asked.

'Dutch Hendrix. Worked for the Memphis Police Department for thirty-three years.'

'Nice to meet you, Dutch.'

'Yeah. Same to you. You start early, don't you?'

Mitch smiled and took the ID card. 'No, I thought everyone would be here.'

Dutch managed a smile. 'You're the first. Mr. Locke will be along shortly.'

The gate opened and Dutch ordered him through. He found his name in white on the asphalt and parked the spotless BMW all by itself on the third row from the building. He grabbed his empty burgundy eel-skin attaché case from the rear seat and gently closed the door. Another guard waited by the rear entrance. Mitch introduced himself and watched as the door was unlocked. He checked his watch. Exactly five-thirty. He was relieved that this hour was early enough. The rest of the firm was still asleep.

He flipped on the light switch in his office, and laid the attaché case on the temporary desk. He headed for the coffee room down the hall, turning on lights as he went. The coffee-pot was one of those industrial sizes with multi-levels, mutli-burners, multi-pots and no apparent instructions on how to operate any of it. He studied this machine for a moment as he emptied a pack of coffee into the filter. He poured water through one of the holes in the top and smiled when it began dripping in the right place.

In one corner of his office were three cardboard boxes full of books, files, legal pads and class notes he had accumulated in the previous three years. He sat the first one on his desk and began removing its contents. The materials were categorized and placed in neat little piles around the desk.

After two cups of coffee, he found the bar review materials in box number three. He walked to the window and opened the blinds. It was still dark. He did not notice the figure suddenly appear in the doorway.

'Good morning!'

Mitch spun from the window and gawked at the man. 'You scared me,' he said, and breathed deeply.

'I'm sorry. I'm Nathan Locke. I don't believe we've met.'

'I'm Mitch McDeere. The new man.' They shook hands.

'Yes, I know. I apologize for not meeting you earlier. I was busy during your earlier visits. I think I saw you at the funerals Monday.'

Mitch nodded and knew for certain he had never been within a hundred yards of Nathan Locke. He would have remembered. It was the eyes, the cold black eyes with layers of black wrinkles around them. Great eyes. Unforgettable eyes. His hair was white and thin on top with thickets around the ears, and the whiteness contrasted sharply with the rest of his face. When he spoke, the eyes narrowed and the black pupils glowed fiercely. Sinister eyes. Knowing eyes.

'Maybe so,' Mitch said, captivated by the most evil face he had ever encountered. 'Maybe so.'

'I see you're an early riser.'

'Yes, sir.'

'Well, good to have you.'

Nathan Locke withdrew from the doorway and disappeared. Mitch checked the hall, then closed the door. No wonder they keep him on the fourth floor away from everyone, he thought. Now he understood why he didn't meet Nathan Locke before he signed on. He might have had second thoughts. Probably hid him from all the prospective recruits. He had, without a doubt, the most ominous, evil presence Mitch had ever felt. It was the eyes, he said to himself again, as he propped his feet on the desk and sipped coffee. The eyes.

As Mitch expected, Nina brought food when she reported at eight-thirty. She offered Mitch a doughnut, and he took two. She inquired as to whether she should bring enough food every morning, and Mitch said he thought it would be nice of her.

'What's that?' she asked, pointing at the stacks of files and notes on the desk.

'That's our project for the day. We need to get this stuff organized.'

'No dictating?'

'Not yet. I meet with Avery in a few minutes. I need this mess filed away in some order.'

'How exciting,' she said as she headed for the coffee room.

Avery Tolleson was waiting with a thick, expandable file, which he handed to Mitch. 'This is the Capps file. Part of it. Our client's name is Sonny Capps. He lives in Houston now, but grew up in Arkansas. Worth about thirty million and keeps his thumb on every penny of it. His father gave him an old barge line just before he died, and he turned it into the largest towing service on the Mississippi River. Now he has ships, or boats, as he calls them, all over the world. We do eighty percent of his legal work, everything but the litigation. He wants to set up another limited partnership to purchase another fleet of tankers, this one from the family of some dead Chink in Hong Kong. Capps is usually the general partner, and he'll bring in as many as twenty-five limited partners to spread the risk and pool their resources. This deal is worth about sixty-five million. I've done several limited partnerships for him and they're all different, all complicated. And he is extremely difficult to deal with. He's a perfectionist and thinks he knows more than I do. You will not be talking to him. In fact, no one here talks to him but me. That file is a portion of the last partnership I did for him. It contains, among other things, a prospectus, an agreement to form a partnership, letters of intent, disclosure statements and the limited partnership agreement itself. Read every word of it. Then I want you to prepare a rough draft of the partnership agreement for this venture.'

The file suddenly grew heavier. Perhaps five-thirty was not early enough.

The partner continued. 'We have about forty days, according to Capps, so we're already behind. Marty Kozinski was helping with this one, and as soon as I review his file I'll give it to you. Any questions?'

'What about the research?'

'Most of it is current, but you'll need to update it. Capps earned over nine million last year and paid a pittance in taxes. He doesn't believe in paying taxes, and holds me personally responsible for every dime that's sent in. It's all legal, of course, but my point is that this is high-pressure work. Millions of dollars in investment and tax savings are at stake. The venture will be scrutinized by the governments of at least three countries. So be careful.'

Mitch flipped through the documents. 'How many hours a day do I work on this?'

'As many as possible. I know the bar exam is important, but so is Sonny Capps. He paid us almost a half a million last year in legal fees.'

'I'll get it done.'

'I know you will. As I told you, your rate is one hundred an hour. Nina will go over the time records with you today. Remember, don't ignore the billing.'

'How could I forget?'

Oliver Lambert and Nathan Locke stood before the metal door on the fifth floor and stared at the camera above. Something clicked loudly and the door opened. A guard nodded. DeVasher waited in his office.

'Good morning, Ollie,' he said quietly while ignoring the other partner.

'What's the latest?' Locke snapped in DeVasher's direction without looking at him.

'From where?' DeVasher asked calmly.

'Chicago.'

'They're very anxious up there, Nat. Regardless of what you believe, they don't like to get their hands dirty. And, frankly, they just don't understand why they have to.'

'What do you mean?'

'They're asking some tough questions, like why can't we keep our people in line?'

'And what're you telling them?'

'That everything's okay. Wonderful. The great Bendini firm is solid. The leaks have been plugged. Business as usual. No problems.'

'How much damage did they do?' asked Oliver Lambert.

'We're not sure. We'll never be sure, but I don't think they ever talked. They had decided to, no doubt about that, but I don't think they did. We've got it from a pretty good source there were FBI agents en route to the island the day of the accident, so we think they planned to rendezvous to spill their guts.'

'How do you know this?' asked Locke.

'Come on, Nat. We've got our sources. Plus, we had people all over the island. We do good work, you know.'

'Evidently.'

'Was it messy?'

'No, no. Very professional.'

'How'd the native get in the way?'

'We had to make it look good, Ollie.'

'What about the authorities down there?'

'What authorities? It's a tiny, peaceful island, Ollie. Last year they had one murder and four diving accidents. As far as they're concerned, it's just another accident. Three accidental drownings.'

'What about the FBI?' asked Locke.

'Don't know.'

'I thought you had a source.'

'We do. But we can't find him. We've heard nothing as of yesterday. Our people are still on the island and they've noticed nothing unusual.'

'How long will you stay there?'

'Couple of weeks.'

'What happens if the FBI shows up?' asked Locke.

'We watch them real close. We'll see them when they get off the plane. We'll follow them to their hotel rooms. We may even bug their phones. We'll know what they eat for breakfast and what they talk about. We'll assign three of our guys for every one of theirs, and when they go to the toilet we'll know it. There ain't nothing for them to find, Nat. I told you it was a clean job, very professional. No evidence. Relax.'

'This makes me sick, DeVasher,' Lambert said.

'You think I like it, Ollie? What do you want us to do? Sit back and let them talk? Come on, Ollie, we're all human. I didn't want to do it, but Lazarov said do it. You wanna argue with Lazarov, go ahead. They'll find you floating somewhere. Those boys were up to no good. They should've kept quiet, driven their little fancy cars and played big-shot lawyers. No, they gotta get sanctimonious.'

Nathan Locke lit a cigarette and blew a heavy cloud of smoke in the general direction of DeVasher. The three sat in silence for a moment as the smoke settled across his desk. He glared at Black Eyes but said nothing.

Oliver Lambert stood and stared at the black wall next to the door. 'Why did you want to see us?' he asked.

DeVasher took a deep breath. 'Chicago wants to bug the home phones of all nonpartners.'

'I told you,' Lambert said to Locke.

'It wasn't my idea, but they insist on it. They're very nervous up there, and they wanna take some extra precautions. You can't blame them.'

'Don't you think it's going a bit too far?' asked Lambert.

'Yeah, it's totally unnecessary. But Chicago doesn't think so.'

'When?' asked Locke.

'Next week or so. It'll take a few days.'

'All of them?'

'Yes. That's what they said.'

'Even McDeere?'

'Yes. Even McDeere. I think Tarrance will try again, and he might start at the bottom this time.'

'I met McDeere this morning,' said Locke. 'He was here before me.'

'Five thirty-two,' answered DeVasher.

The law school memorabilia were removed to the floor and the Capps file spread across the desk. Nina brought a chicken salad sandwich back from lunch, and he ate it as he read and as she filed away the junk on the floor. Shortly after one, Wally Hudson, or J. Walter Hudson as the firm letterhead declared him, arrived to begin the study for the bar exam. Contracts were his specialty. He was a five-year member of the firm and the only Virginia man, which he found odd because Virginia had the best law school in the country, in his opinion. He had spent the last two years developing a new review course for the contracts section of the exam. He was quite anxious to try it on someone, and McDeere happened to be the man. He handed Mitch a heavy three-ring notebook that was at least four inches thick and weighed as much as the Capps file.

The exam would last for four days and consist of three parts, Wally explained. The first day would be a four-hour multiple-choice exam on ethics. Gill Vaughn, one of the partners, was the resident expert on ethics and would supervise that portion of the review. The second day would be an eight-hour exam known simply as multi-state. It covered most areas of the law common to all states. It, too, was multiple choice and the questions were very deceptive. Then the heavy action. Days three and four would be eight hours each and cover fifteen areas of substantive law. Contracts, Uniform Commercial Code, real estate, torts, domestic relations, wills, estates, taxation, workmen's compensation, constitutional law, federal trial procedure, criminal procedure, corporations, partnerships, insurance and debtor–creditor relations. All answers would be in essay form, and the questions would emphasize Tennessee law. The firm had a review plan for each of the fifteen sections.

'You mean fifteen of these?' Mitch asked as he lifted the notebook.

Wally smiled. 'Yes. We're very thorough. No one in this firm has ever flunked –'

'I know. I know. I won't be the first.'

'You and I will meet at least once a week for the next six weeks to go through the materials. Each session will last about two hours, so you can plan accordingly. I would suggest each Wednesday at three.'

'Morning or afternoon?'

'Afternoon.'

'That's fine.'

'As you know, contracts and the Uniform Commercial Code go hand in hand, so I've incorporated the UCC into those materials. We'll cover both, but it'll take more time. A typical bar exam is loaded with commercial transactions. Those problems make great essay questions, so that notebook will be very important. I've included actual questions from old exams, along with the model answers. It's fascinating reading.'

'I can't wait.'

'Take the first eighty pages for next week. You'll find some essay questions you'll need to answer.'

'You mean homework?'

'Absolutely. I'll grade it next week. It's very important to practice these questions each week.'

'This could be worse than law school.'

'It's much more important than law school. We take it very seriously. We have a committee to monitor your progress from now until you sit for the exam. We'll be watching very closely.'

'Who's on the committee?'

'Myself, Avery Tolleson, Royce McKnight, Randall Dunbar and Kendall Mahan. We'll meet each Friday to assess your progress.'

Wally produced a smaller, letter-sized notebook and laid it on the

desk. 'This is your daily log. You are to record the hours spent studying for the exam and the subjects studied. I'll pick it up every Friday
morning before the committee meets. Any questions?'

'I can't think of any,' Mitch said as he laid the notebook on top of
the Capps file.'

'Good. See you next Wednesday at three.'

Less than ten seconds after he left, Randall Dunbar walked in with
a thick notebook remarkably similar to the one left behind by Wally.
In fact, it was identical, but not quite as thick. Dunbar was head of
real estate and had handled the purchase and sale of the McDeere
home in May. He handed Mitch the notebook, labeled *Real Estate
Law*, and explained how his specialty was the most critical part of the
exam. Everything goes back to property, he said. He had carefully
prepared the materials himself over the past ten years and confessed
that he had often thought of publishing them as an authoritative
work on property rights and land financing. He would need at least
one hour a week, preferably on Tuesday afternoon. He talked for an
hour about how different the exam was thirty years ago when he took
it.

Kendall Mahan added a new twist. He wanted to meet on Saturday mornings. Early, say seven-thirty.

'No problem,' Mitch said as he took the notebook and placed it
next to the others. This one was for constitutional law, a favorite of
Kendall's, although he seldom got to use it, he said. It was the most
important section of the exam, or at least it had been when he took it
five years ago. He had published an article on First Amendment
rights in the *Columbia Law Review* in his senior year there. A copy of it
was in the notebook, in case Mitch wanted to read it. He promised to
do so almost immediately.

The procession continued throughout the afternoon until half of
the firm had stopped by with notebooks, assignments of homework
and requests for weekly meetings. No fewer than six reminded him
that no member of the firm had ever failed the bar exam.

When his secretary said goodbye at five, the small desk was
covered with enough bar review materials to choke a ten-man firm.
Unable to speak, he simply smiled at her and returned to Wally's
version of contract law. Food crossed his mind an hour later. Then,
for the first time in twelve hours, he thought of Abby. He called her.

'I won't be home for a while,' he said.

'But I'm cooking dinner.'

'Leave it on the stove,' he said, somewhat shortly.

There was a pause. 'When will you be home?' she asked with slow,
precise words.

'In a few hours.'

'A few hours. You've already been there half the day.'

'That's right, and I've got much more to do.'

'But it's your first day.'

'You wouldn't believe it if I told you.'

'Are you all right?'

'I'm fine. I'll be home later.'

The starting engine awakened Dutch Hendrix, and he jumped to his feet. The gate opened and he waited by it as the last car left the lot. It stopped next to him.

'Evenin', Dutch,' Mitch said.

'You just now leaving?'

'Yeah, busy day.'

Dutch flashed his light at his wrist and checked the time. Eleven-thirty.

'Well, be careful,' Dutch said.

'Yeah. See you in a few hours.'

The BMW turned onto Front Street and raced away into the night. A few hours, thought Dutch. The rookies were indeed amazing. Eighteen, twenty hours a day, six days a week. Sometimes seven. They all planned to be the world's greatest lawyer and make a million dollars overnight. Sometimes they worked around the clock, slept at their desks. He had seen it all. But they couldn't last. The human body was not meant for such abuse. After about six months they lost steam. They would cut back to fifteen hours a day, six days a week. Then five and a half. Then twelve hours a day.

No one could work a hundred hours a week for more than six months.

# CHAPTER SEVEN

One secretary dug through a file cabinet in search of something Avery needed immediately. The other secretary stood in front of his desk with a steno pad, occasionally writing down the instructions he gave when he stopped yelling into the receiver of his phone and listened to whoever was on the other end. Three red lights were blinking on the phone. When he spoke into the receiver the secretaries spoke sharply to each other. Mitch walked slowly into the office and stood by the door.

'Quiet!' Avery yelled to the secretaries.

The one in the file cabinet slammed the drawer and went to the next file cabinet, where she bent over and pulled the bottom drawer. Avery snapped his fingers at the other one and pointed at his desk calendar. He hung up without saying goodbye.

'What's my schedule for today?' he asked pulling a file from his credenza.

'Ten A.M. meeting with the IRS downtown. One P.M. meeting with Nathan Locke on the Spinosa file. Three-thirty, partners' meeting. Tomorrow you're in tax court all day, and you're supposed to prepare all day today.'

'Great. Cancel everything. Check the flights to Houston Saturday afternoon and the return flights Monday, early Monday.'

'Yes, sir.'

'Mitch! Where's the Capps file?'

'On my desk.'

'How much have you done?'

'I've read through most of it.'

'We need to get in high gear. That was Sonny Capps on the phone. I wants to meet Saturday morning in Houston, and he wants a rough draft of the limited partnership agreement.'

Mitch felt a nervous pain in his empty stomach. If he recalled correctly, the agreement was a hundred and forty some pages long.

'Just a rough draft,' Avery said as he pointed to a secretary.

'No problem,' Mitch said with as much confidence as he could muster. 'It may not be perfect, but I'll have a rough draft.'

'I need it by noon Saturday, as perfect as possible. I'll get one of my secretaries to show Nina where the form agreements are in the memory bank. That will save some dictation and typing. I know this is unfair, but there's nothing fair about Sonny Capps. He's very demanding. He told me the deal must close in twenty days or it's dead. Everything is waiting on us.'

'I'll get it done.'

'Good. Let's meet at eight in the morning to see where we are.'

Avery punched one of the blinking lights and began arguing into the receiver. Mitch walked to his office and looked for the Capps file under the fifteen notebooks. Nina stuck her head in the door.

'Oliver Lambert wants to see you.'

'When?' Mitch asked.

'As soon as you can get there.'

Mitch looked at his watch. Three hours at the office and he was ready to call it a day. 'Can it wait?'

'I don't think so. Mr. Lambert doesn't usually wait for anybody.'

'I see.'

'You'd better go.'

'What does he want?'

'His secretary didn't say.'

He put on his coat, straightened his tie and raced upstairs to the fourth floor, where Mr. Lambert's secretary was waiting. She introduced herself and informed him she had been with the firm for thirty-one years. In fact, she was the second secretary hired by Mr. Anthony Bendini after he moved to Memphis. Ida Renfroe was her name, but everyone called her Mrs. Ida. She showed him into the big office and closed the door.

Oliver Lambert stood behind his desk and removed his reading glasses. He smiled warmly and laid his pipe in the brass holder. 'Good morning, Mitch,' he said softly, as if time meant nothing. 'Let's sit over there.' He waved to the sofa.

'Would you like coffee?' Mr. Lambert asked.

'No, thanks.'

Mitch sank into the couch and the partner sat in a stiff wing chair, two feet away and three feet higher. Mitch unbuttoned his coat and tried to relax. He crossed his legs and glanced at his new pair of Cole-Haans. Two hundred bucks. That was an hour's work for an associate at this money-printing factory. He tried to relax. But he could feel the panic in Avery's voice and see the desperation in his eyes when he held the phone and listened to this Capps fellow on the other end. This, his second full day on the job, and his head was pounding and his stomach hurting.

Mr. Lambert smiled downward with his best sincere grandfatherly smile. It was time for a lecture of some sort. He wore a brilliant white shirt, button-down, all-cotton, pinpoint, with a small, dark silk bow tie which bestowed upon him a look of extreme intelligence and wisdom. As always, he was tanned beyond the usual midsummer Memphis scorched bronzeness. His teeth sparkled like diamonds. A sixty-year-old model.

'Just a couple of things, Mitch,' he said. 'I understand you've become quite busy.'

'Yes, sir, quite.'

'Panic is a way of life in a major law firm, and clients like Sonny Capps can cause ulcers. Our clients are only assets, so we kill ourselves for them.'

Mitch smiled and frowned at the same time.

'Two things, Mitch. First, my wife and I want you and Abby to have dinner with us Saturday. We dine out quite often, and we enjoy having our friends with us. I am somewhat of a chef myself, and I appreciate fine food and drink. We usually reserve a large table at one of our favorite restaurants in town, invite our friends and spend the evening with a nine-course meal and the rarest of wines. Will you and Abby be free on Saturday?'

'Of course.'

'Kendall Mahan, Wally Hudson, Lamar Quin and their wives will also be there.'

'We'd be delighted.'

'Good. My favorite place in Memphis is Justine's. It's an old French restaurant with exquisite cuisine and an impressive wine list. Say seven Saturday?'

'We'll be there.'

'Second, there's something we need to discuss. I'm sure you're aware of it, but it's worth mentioning. It's very important to us. I know they taught you at Harvard that there exists a confidential relationship between yourself, as a lawyer, and your client. It's a privileged relationship and you can never be forced to divulge anything a client tells you. It's strictly confidential. It's a violation of our ethics if we discuss our client's business. Now, this applies to every lawyer, but at this firm we take this professional relationship very seriously. We don't discuss a client's business with anyone. Not other lawyers. Not spouses. Sometimes, not even each other. As a rule, we don't talk at home, and our wives have learned not to ask. The less you say, the better off you are. Mr. Bendini was a great believer in secrecy, and he taught us well. You will never hear a member of this firm mention even so much as a client's name outside this building. That's how serious we are.'

Where's he going with this? Mitch asked himself. Any second-year

433

law student could give this speech. 'I understand that, Mr. Lambert, and you don't have to worry about me.'

'"Loose tongues lose lawsuits." That was Mr. Bendini's motto, and he applied it to everything. We simply do not discuss our clients' business with anyone, and that includes our wives. We're very quiet, very secretive, and we like it that way. You'll meet other lawyers around town and sooner or later they'll ask something about our firm, or about a client. We don't talk, understand?'

'Of course, Mr. Lambert.'

'Good. We're very proud of you, Mitch. You'll make a great lawyer. And a very rich lawyer. See you Saturday.'

Mrs. Ida had a message for Mitch. Mr. Tolleson needed him at once. He thanked her and raced down the stairs, down the hallway, past his office, to the big one in the corner. There were now three secretaries digging and whispering to each other while the boss yelled into the telephone. Mitch found a safe spot in a chair by the door and watched the circus. The women pulled files and notebooks and mumbled in strange tongues among themselves. Occasionally Avery would snap his fingers and point here and there and they would jump like scared rabbits.

After a few minutes he slammed the phone down, again without saying goodbye. He glared at Mitch.

'Sonny Capps again. The Chinese want seventy-five million and he's agreed to pay it. There will be forty-one limited partners instead of twenty-five. We have twenty days, or the deal is off.'

Two of the secretaries walked over to Mitch and handed him thick expandable files.

'Can you handle it?' Avery asked, almost with a sneer. The secretaries looked at him.

Mitch grabbed the files and headed for the door. 'Of course I can handle it. Is that all?'

'It's enough. I don't want you to work on anything but that file between now and Saturday, understand?'

'Yes, boss.'

'In his office he removed the bar review materials, all fifteen notebooks, and piled them in a corner. The Capps file was arranged neatly across the desk. He breathed deeply and began reading. There was a knock at the door.

'Who is it?'

Nina stuck her head through. 'I hate to tell you this, but your new furniture is here.'

He rubbed his temples and mumbled incoherently.

'Perhaps you could work in the library for a couple of hours.'

'Perhaps.'

They repacked the Capps file and moved the fifteen notebooks into the hall, where two large black men waited with a row of bulky cardboard boxes and an oriental rug.

Nina followed him to the second floor library.

'I'm supposed to meet with Lamar Quin at two to study for the bar exam. Call him and cancel. Tell him I'll explain later.'

'You have a two o'clock meeting with Gill Vaughn,' she said.

'Cancel that one too.'

'He's a partner.'

'Cancel it. I'll make it up later.'

'It's not wise.'

'Just do as I say.'

'You're the boss.'

'Thank you.'

The paperhanger was a short muscle-bound woman advanced in years but conditioned to hard work and superbly trained. For almost forty years now, she explained to Abby, she had hung expensive paper in the finest homes in Memphis. She talked constantly, but wasted no motion. She cut precisely, like a surgeon, then applied glue like an artist. While it dried, she removed her tape measure from her leather work belt and analyzed the remaining corner of the dining room. She mumbled numbers which Abby could not decipher. She gauged the length and height in four different places, then committed it all to memory. She ascended the stepladder and instructed Abby to hand her a roll of paper. It fit perfectly. She pressed it firmly to the wall and commented for the hundredth time on how nice the paper was, how expensive, how long it would look good and last. She liked the color too. It blended wonderfully with the curtains and the rug. Abby had long since grown tired of saying thanks. She nodded and looked at her watch. It was time to start dinner.

When the wall was finished, Abby announced it was quitting time and asked her to return at nine the next morning. The lady said certainly, and began cleaning up her mess. She was being paid twelve dollars an hour, cash, and was agreeable to almost anything. Abby admired the room. They would finish it tomorrow, and the wall-papering would be complete except for two bathrooms and the den. The painting was scheduled to begin next week. The glue from the paper and the wet lacquer for the mantel and the newness of the furniture combined for a wonderful fresh aroma. Just like a new house.

Abby said goodbye to the paperhanger and went to the bedroom where she undressed and lay across her bed. She called her husband, spoke briefly to Nina and was told he was in a meeting and would be a while. Nina said he would call. Abby stretched her long, sore legs and rubbed her shoulders. The ceiling fan spun slowly above her. Mitch would be home eventually. He would work a hundred hours a week for a while, then cut back to eighty. She could wait.

She awoke an hour later and jumped from the bed. It was almost six. Veal piccata. Veal piccata. She stepped into a pair of khaki walking shorts and slipped on a white polo. She ran to the kitchen, which was finished except for some paint and a set of curtains due in next week. She found the recipe in a pasta cookbook and arranged the ingredients neatly on the countertop. There had been little red meat in law school, maybe an occasional hamburger steak. When she cooked, it had been chicken this or chicken that. There had been a lot of sandwiches and hot dogs.

But now, with all this sudden affluence, it was time to learn to cook. In the first week she prepared something new every night, and they ate whenever he got home. She planned the meals, studied the cookbooks, experimented with the sauces. For no apparent reason, Mitch liked Italian food, and with spaghetti and pork capellini tried and perfected, it was time for veal piccata. She pounded the veal scallops with a mallet until they were thin enough, then laid them in flour seasoned with salt and pepper. She put a pan of water on the burner for the linguine. She poured a glass of Chablis and turned on the radio. She had called the office twice since lunch, and he had not found time to return the calls. She thought of calling again, but said no. It was his turn. Dinner would be fixed, and they would eat whenever he got home.

The scallops were sautéed in hot oil for three minutes until the veal was tender; then removed. She poured the oil from the pan and added wine and lemon juice until it was boiling. She scraped and stirred the pan to thicken the sauce. She returned the veal to the pan, and added mushrooms and artichokes and butter. She covered the pan and let it simmer.

She fried bacon, sliced tomatoes, cooked linguine and poured another glass of wine. By seven, dinner was ready; bacon and tomato salad with tubettini, veal piccatea and garlic bread in the oven. He had not called. She took her wine to the patio and looked around the backyard. Hearsay ran from under the shrubs. Together they walked the length of the yard, surveying the Bermuda and stopping under the two large oaks. The remains of a long-abandoned tree house were scattered among the middle branches of the largest oak. Initials were carved on its trunk. A piece of rope hung from the other. She found a rubber ball, threw it and watched as the dog chased it. She listened for the phone though the kitchen window. It did not ring.

Hearsay froze, then growled at something next door. Mr. Rice emerged from a row of perfectly trimmed box hedges around his patio. Sweat dripped from his nose and his cotton undershirt was soaked. He removed his green gloves, and noticed Abby across the chain-link fence, under her tree. He smiled. He looked at her brown legs and smiled. He wiped his forehead with a sweaty forearm and headed for the fence.

'How are you?' he asked, breathing heavy. His thick gray hair dripped and clung to his scalp.

'Just fine, Mr. Rice. How are you?'

'Hot. Must be a hundred degrees.'

Abby slowly walked to the fence to chat. She had caught his stares for a week now, but did not mind. He was at least seventy and probably harmless. Let him look. Plus, he was a living, breathing, sweating human who could talk and maintain a conversation to some degree. The paperhanger had been her only source of dialogue since Mitch left before dawn.

'Your lawn looks great,' she said.

He wiped again and spat on the ground. 'Great? You call this great? This belongs in a magazine. I've never seen a puttin' green look this good. I deserve garden of the month, but they won't give it to me. Where's your husband?'

'At the office. He's working late.'

'It's almost eight. He must've left before sun-up this morning. I take my walk at six-thirty, and he's already gone. What's with him?'

'He likes to work.'

'If I had a wife like you, I'd stay at home. Couldn't make me leave.'

Abby smiled at the compliment. 'How is Mrs. Rice?'

He frowned, then yanked a weed out of the fence. 'Not too good, I'm afraid. Not too good.' He looked away and bit his lip. Mrs. Rice was almost dead with cancer. There were no children. She had a year, the doctors said. A year at the most. They had removed most of her stomach, and the tumors were now in the lungs. She weighed ninety pounds and seldom left the bed. During their first visit across the fence his eyes watered when he talked of her and of how he would be alone after fifty-one years.

'Naw, they won't give me garden of the month. Wrong part of

town. It always goes to those rich folks who hire yard boys to do all the work while they sit by the pool and sip daiquiris. It does look good, doesn't it?'

'It's incredible. How many times a week do you mow?'

'Three or four. Depends on the rain. You want me to mow yours?'

'No. I want Mitch to mow it.'

'He ain't got time, seems like. I'll watch it, and if it needs a little trim, I'll come over.'

Abby turned and looked at the kitchen window. 'Do you hear the phone?' she asked, walking away. Mr. Rice pointed to his hearing aid.

She said goodbye and ran to the house. The phone stopped when she lifted the receiver. It was eight-thirty, almost dark. She called the office, but no one answered. Maybe he was driving home.

An hour before midnight, the phone rang. Except for it and the light snoring, the second floor office was without a sound. His feet were on the new desk, crossed at the ankles and numb from lack of circulation. The rest of his body slouched comfortable in the thick leather executive chair. He slumped to one side and intermittently exhaled the sounds of a deep sleep. The Capps file was strewn over the desk and one formidable looking document was held firmly against his stomach. His shoes were on the floor, next to the desk, next to a pile of documents from the Capps file. An empty potato chip bag was between the shoes.

After a dozen rings he moved, then jumped to the phone. It was his wife.

'Why haven't you called?' she asked, coolly, yet with a slight touch of concern.

'I'm sorry. I fell asleep. What time is it?' He rubbed his eyes and focused on his watch.

'Eleven. I wish you would call.'

'I did call. No one answered.'

'When?'

'Between eight and nine. Where were you?'

She did not answer. She waited. 'Are you coming home?'

'No. I need to work all night.'

'All night? You can't work all night, Mitch.'

'Of course I can work all night. Happens all the time around here. It's expected.'

'I expected you home, Mitch. And the least you could've done was call. Dinner is still on the stove.'

'I'm sorry. I'm up to my ears in deadlines and I lost track of time. I apologize.'

There was silence for a moment as she considered the apology. 'Will this become a habit, Mitch?'

'It might.'

'I see. When do you think you might be home?'

'Are you scared?'

'No, I'm not scared. I'm going to bed.'

'I'll come in around seven for a shower.'

'That's nice. If I'm asleep, don't wake me.'

She hung up. He looked at the receiver, then put it in place. On the fifth floor a security agent chuckled to himself. '"Don't wake me." That's good,' he said as he pushed a button on the computerized recorder. He punched three buttons and spoke into a small mike. 'Hey, Dutch, wake up down there.'

Dutch woke up and leaned to the intercom. 'Yeah, what is it?'

'This is Marcus upstairs, I think our boy plans to stay all night.'

'What's his problem?'

'Right now it's his wife. He forgot to call her and she fixed a real nice supper.'

'Aw, that's too bad. We've heard that before, ain't we?'

'Year, every rookie does it the first week. Anyway, he told her he ain't coming home till in the morning. So go back to sleep.'

Marcus pushed some more buttons and returned to his magazine.

Abby was waiting when the sun peeked between the oak trees. She sipped coffee and held the dog and listened to the quiet sounds of her neighborhood stirring to life. Sleep had been fitful. A hot shower had not eased the fatigue. She wore a white terry-cloth bathrobe, one of his, and nothing else. Her hair was wet and pulled straight back.

A car door slammed and the dog pointed inside the house. She heard him unlock the kitchen door, and moments later the sliding door to the patio opened. He laid his coat on a bench near the door and walked over to her.

'Good morning,' he said, then sat down across the wicker table.

She gave him a fake smile. 'Good morning to you.'

'You're up early,' he said in an effort at friendliness. It did not work. She smiled again and sipped her coffee.

He breathed deeply and gazed across the yard. 'Still mad about last night, I see.'

'Not really. I don't carry a grudge.'

'I said I was sorry, and I meant it. I tried to call once.'

'You could've called again.'

'Please don't divorce me, Abby. I swear it will never happen again. Just don't leave me.'

She managed a genuine grin. 'You look terrible,' she said.

'What's under the robe?'

'Nothing.'

'Let's see.'

'Why don't you take a nap? You look haggard.'

'Thanks. But I've got a nine o'clock meeting with Avery. And a ten o'clock meeting with Avery.'

'Are they trying to kill you the first week?'

'Yes, but they can't do it. I'm too much of a man. Let's go take a shower.'

'I've taken one.'

'Naked?'

'Yes.'

'Tell me about it. Tell me every detail.'

'If you'd come home at a decent hour you wouldn't feel depraved.'

'I'm sure it'll happen again, dear. There will be plenty of all-nighters. You didn't complain in law school when I studied around the clock.'

'It was different. I endured law school because I knew it would soon end. But now you're a lawyer and you will be for a long time. Is this part of it? Will you always work a thousand hours a week?'

'Abby, this is my first week.'

'That's what worries me. It will only get worse.'

'Sure it will. That's part of it, Abby. It's a cutthroat business where the weak are eaten and the strong get rich. It's a marathon. He who endures wins the gold.'

'And dies at the finish line.'

'I don't believe this. We moved here a week ago, and you're already worried about my health.'

She sipped the coffee and rubbed the dog. She was beautiful. With tired eyes, no make-up, and wet hair, she was beautiful. He stood, walked behind her and kissed her on the cheek. 'I love you,' he whispered.

She clutched his hand on her shoulder. 'Go take a shower. I'll fix breakfast.'

The table was arranged to perfection. Her grandmother's china was taken from the cabinet and used for the first time in the new home. Candles were lit in silver candlesticks. Grapefruit juice was poured in the crystal tea glasses. Linen napkins that matched the tablecloth were folded on the plates. When he finished his shower and changed into a new Burberry glen plaid, he walked to the dining room and whistled.

'What's the occasion?'

'It's a special breakfast, for a special husband.'

He sat and admired the china. The food was warming in a covered silver dish. 'What'd you cook?' he asked, smacking his lips. She pointed and he removed the lid. He stared at it.

'What's this?' he asked without looking at her.

'Veal piccata.'

'Veal what?'

'Veal piccata.'

'He glanced at his watch. 'I thought it was breakfast time.'

'I cooked it for dinner last night, and I suggest you eat it.'

'Veal piccata for breakfast?'

She grinned firmly and shook her head slightly. He looked again at the dish, and for a second or two analyzed the situation.

Finally, he said, 'Smells good.'

# CHAPTER EIGHT

Saturday morning. He slept in and didn't get to the office until seven. He didn't shave, wore jeans, an old button-down, no socks and Bass loafers. Law school attire.

The Capps agreement had been printed and reprinted late Friday. He made some further revisions, and Nina ran it again at eight Friday night. He assumed she had little or no social life, so he didn't hesitate to ask her to work late. She said she didn't mind overtime, so he asked her to work Saturday morning.

She arrived at nine, wearing a pair of jeans that would fit a nose guard. He handed her the agreement, all two hundred and six pages, with his latest changes, and asked her to run it for the fourth time. He was to meet with Avery at ten.

The office changed on Saturday. All of the associates were there, as well as most of the partners and a few of the secretaries. There were no clients, thus no dress code. There was enough denim to launch a cattle drive. No ties. Some of the preppier ones wore their finest starched Duckheads with heavily starched button-downs and seemed to crackle when they walked.

But the pressure was there, at least for Mitchell Y. McDeere, the newest associate. He had canceled his bar review meetings on Thursday, Friday and Saturday, and the fifteen notebooks sat on the shelf, gathering dust and reminding him that he would indeed become the first member to flunk the bar exam.

At ten the fourth revision was complete, and Nina ceremoniously laid it on Mitch's desk and left for the coffee room. It had grown to two hundred and nineteen pages. He had read every word four times and researched the tax code provisions until they were memorized. He marched down the hall to his partner's office and laid it on the desk. A secretary was packing a mammoth briefcase while the boss talked on the phone.

'How many pages?' Avery asked when he hung up.

'Over two hundred.'

'This is quite impressive. How rough is it?'

'Not very. That's the fourth revision since yesterday morning. It's almost perfect.'

'We'll see. I'll read it on the plane, then Capps will read it with a magnifying glass. If he finds one mistake he'll raise hell for an hour and threaten not to pay. How many hours are in this?'

'Fifty-four and a half, since Wednesday.'

'I know I've pushed, and I apologize. You've had a tough first week. But our clients sometimes push hard, and this won't be the last time we break our necks for someone who pays us two hundred dollars an hour. It's part of the business.'

'I don't mind it. I'm behind on the bar review, but I can catch up.'

'Is that Hudson twerp giving you a hard time?'

'No.'

'If he does, let me know. He's only a five-year man, and he enjoys playing professor. Thinks he's a real academic. I don't particularly like him.'

'He's no problem.'

Avery placed the agreement in the briefcase. 'Where are the prospectus and other documents?'

'I've done a very rough draft of each. You said we had twenty days.'

'We do, but let's get it done. Capps starts demanding things long before their deadlines. Are you working tomorrow?'

'I hadn't planned on it. In fact, my wife has sort of insisted we go to church.'

Avery shook his head. 'Wives can really get in the way, can't they?' He said this without expecting a reply.

Mitch did not respond.

'Let's have Capps finished by next Saturday.'

'Fine. No problem,' Mitch said.

'Have we discussed Koker-Hanks?' Avery asked while rummaging through a file.

'No.'

'Here it is. Koker-Hanks is a big general contractor out of Kansas City. Keeps about a hundred million under contract, all over the country. An outfit out of Denver called Holloway Brothers has offered to buy Koker-Hanks. They want to swap some stock, some assets, some contracts, and throw in some cash. Pretty complicated deal. Familiarize yourself with the file, and we'll discuss it Tuesday morning when I get back.'

'How much time do we have?'

'Thirty days.'

It was not quite as thick as the Capps file, but just as imposing. 'Thirty days,' Mitch mumbled.

'The deal is worth eighty million, and we'll rake off two hundred grand in fees. Not a bad deal. Every time you look at that file, charge it for an hour. Work on it whenever you can. In fact, if the name

Koker-Hanks crosses your mind while you're driving to work, stick it for an hour. The sky's the limit on this one.'

Avery relished the thought of a client who would pay regardless of the charges. Mitch said goodbye and returned to his office.

About the time the cocktails were finished, while they studied the wine list and listened to Oliver Lambert's comparison of the nuances, the subtleties, the distinctions of each of the French wines, about the time Mitch and Abby realized they would much rather be home eating a pizza and watching TV, two men with the correct key entered the shinny black BMW in the parking lot of Justine's. They wore coats and ties and looked inconspicuous. They sped away innocently and drove across midtown to the new home of Mr. and Mrs. McDeere. They parked the BMW where it belonged, in the carport. The driver produced another key, and the two entered the house. Hearsay was locked in a closet in the washroom.

In the dark, a small leather attaché case was placed on the dining table. Thin disposable rubber gloves were pulled and stretched over the hands, and each took a small flashlight.

'Do the phones first,' one said.

They worked quickly, in the dark. The receiver from the kitchen phone was unplugged and laid on the table. The microphone was unscrewed and examined. A tiny drop-in transmitter, the size of a raisin, was glued in the cavity of the receiver and held firmly in place for ten seconds. When the glue became firm, the microphone was replaced and the receiver was plugged into the phone and hung on the kitchen wall. The voices, or signals, would be transmitted to a small receiver to be installed in the attic. A larger transmitter next to the receiver would send the signals across town to an antenna on top of the Bendini Building. Using the AC lines as a power source, the small bugs in the phones would transmit indefinitely.

'Get the one in the den.'

The attaché case was moved to a sofa. Above the recliner they drove a small nail into a ridge in the paneling, then removed it. A thin black cylinder, one twentieth of an inch by one inch, was carefully placed in the hole. It was cemented in place with a dab of black epoxy. The microphone was invisible. A wire, the thickness of a human hair, was gently fitted into the seam of the paneling and run to the ceiling. It would be connected to a receiver in the attic.

Identical mikes were hidden in the walls of each bedroom. The men found the retractable stairs in the main hallway and climbed into the attic. One removed the receiver and transmitter from the case while the other painstakingly pulled the tiny wires from the walls. When he gathered them, he wrapped them together and laid them under the insulation and ran them to a corner where his partner was placing the transmitter in an old cardboard box. An AC line was spliced and wired to the unit to provide power and transmission. A small antenna was raised to within an inch of the roof decking.

Their breathing became heavier in the sweltering heat of the dark attic. The small plastic casing of an old radio was fitted around the transmitter, and they scattered insulation and old clothing around it. It was in a remote corner and not likely to be noticed for months, maybe years. And if it was noticed, it would appear to be only worthless junk. It could be picked up and thrown away without suspicion. They admired their handiwork for a second, then descended the stairs.

They meticulously covered their tracks and were finished in ten minutes.

Hearsay was realised from the closet, and the men crept into the carport. They backed quickly out the driveway and sped into the night.

As the baked pompano was served, the BMW parked quietly next to the restaurant. The driver fished through his pockets and found the key to a maroon Jaguar, property of Mr. Kendall Mahan, attorney-at-law. The two technicians locked the BMW and slid into the Jag. The Mahans lived much closer than the McDeeres, and judging from the floor plans, the job would be quicker.

On the fifth floor of the Bendini Building, Marcus stared at a panel of blinking lights and waited for some signal from 1231 East Meadowbrook. The dinner party had broken up thirty minutes earlier, and it was time to listen. A tiny yellow light flashed weakly, and he draped a headset over his ears. He pushed a button to record. He waited. A green light beside the code McD6 began flashing. It was the bedroom wall. The signals grew clearer, voices, at first faint, then very clear. He increased the volume. And listened.

'Jill Mahan is a bitch,' the female, Mrs. McDeere, was saying. 'The more she drank, the bitchier she got.'

'I think she's a blue blood of some sort,' Mr. McDeere replied.

'Her husband is okay, but she's a real snot,' Mrs. McDeere said.

'Are you drunk?' asked Mr. McDeere.

'Almost. I'm ready for passionate sex.'

Marcus increased the volume and leaned toward the blinking lights.

'Take your clothes off,' demanded Mrs. McDeere.

'We haven't done this for a while,' said Mr. McDeere.

Marcus stood and hovered above the switches and lights.

'And whose fault is that?' she asked.

'I haven't forgotten how. You're beautiful.'

'Get in the bed,' she said.

Marcus turned the dial marked VOLUME until it would go no further. He smiled at the lights and breathed heavily. He loved these associates, fresh from law school and full of energy. He smiled at the sounds of their lovemaking. He closed his eyes and watched them.

# CHAPTER NINE

The Capps crisis passed in two weeks without disaster, thanks largely to a string of eighteen-hour days by the newest member of the firm, a member who had not yet passed the bar exam and who was too busy practicing law to worry about it. In July he billed an average of fifty-nine hours a week, a firm record for a nonlawyer. Avery proudly informed the partners at the monthly meeting that McDeere's work was remarkable for a rookie. The Capps deal was closed three days ahead of schedule, thanks to McDeere. The documents totaled four hundred pages, all perfect, all meticulously researched, drafted and redrafted by McDeere. Koker-Hanks would close within a month, thanks to McDeere, and the firm would earn close to a quarter of a mill. He was a machine.

Oliver Lambert expressed concern over his study habits. The bar exam was less than three weeks away, and it was obvious to all that McDeere was not ready. He had canceled half his review sessions in July and had logged less than twenty hours. Avery said not to worry, his boy would be ready.

Fifteen days before the exam, Mitch finally complained. He was about to flunk it, he explained to Avery over lunch at the Manhattan Club, and he needed time to study. Lots of time. He could cram it in for the next two weeks and pass by the hair of his ass. But he had to be left alone. No deadlines. No emergencies. No all-nighters. He pleaded. Avery listened carefully, and apologized. He promised to ignore him for the next two weeks. Mitch said thanks.

On the first Monday in August, a firm meeting was called in the main library on the first floor. It was the meeting room, the largest of the four libraries, the showplace. Half the lawyers sat around the antique cherry conference table with twenty chairs under it. The rest stood next to the shelves of thick leather law books which had not been opened in decades. Every member was present, even Nathan Locke. He arrived late and stood next to the door by himself. He spoke to no one, and no one looked at him. Mitch stole a glance at Black Eyes when possible.

The mood was somber. No smiles. Beth Kozinski and Laura Hodge were escorted through the door by Oliver Lambert. They were seated at the front of the room facing a wall where two veiled portraits hung. They held hands and tried to smile. Mr. Lambert stood with his back to the wall and faced the small audience.

447

He spoke softly, his rich baritone exuding sympathy and compassion. He almost whispered at first, but the power of his voice made every sound and every syllable clear throughout the room. He looked at the two widows and told of the deep sadness the firm felt, how they would always be taken care of as long as there was a firm. He talked of Marty and Joe, of their first few years with the firm, of their importance to the firm, of the vast voids their deaths created. He spoke of their love for their families, their dedication to their homes.

The man was eloquent. He spoke in prose, with no forethought as to what the next sentence would be. The widows cried softly and wiped their eyes. And then some of the closer ones, Lamar Quin and Doug Turney, began to sniffle.

When he had said enough, he unveiled the portrait of Martin Kozinski. It was an emotional moment. There were more tears. There would be a scholarship established at the Chicago Law School in his name. The firm would set up trusts for his children's education. The family would be taken care of. Beth bit her lip, but cried louder. The seasoned, hardened, tough-as-nails negotiators of the great Bendini firm swallowed rapidly and avoided looking at each other. Only Nathan Locke was unmoved. He glared at the wall with his penetrating lasers and ignored the ceremony.

Then the portrait of Joe Hodge, and a similar biography, similar scholarship and trust funds. Mitch had heard a rumor that Hodge purchased a two-million-dollar life insurance policy four months before his death.

When the eulogies were complete, Nathan Locke disappeared through the door. The lawyers surrounded the widows and offered quiet words and embraces. Mitch did not know them and had nothing to say. He walked to the front wall and examined the paintings. Next to those of Kozinski and Hodge were three slightly smaller, but equally dignified portraits. The one of the woman caught his attention. The brass plate read: 'Alice Knauss 1948–1977.'

'She was a mistake,' Avery said under his breath as he stepped next to his associate.

'What do you mean?' Mitch asked.

'Typical female lawyer. Came here from Harvard, number one in her class and carrying a chip because she was a female. Thought every man alive was a sexist and it was her mission in life to eliminate discrimination. Super-bitch. After six months we all hated her but couldn't get rid of her. She forced two partners into early retirement. Milligan still blames her for his heart attack. He was her partner.'

'Was she a good lawyer?'

'Very good, but it was impossible to appreciate her talents. She was so contentious about everything.'

'What happened to her?'

'Car wreck. Killed by a drunk driver. It was really tragic.'

'Was she the first woman?'

'Yes, and the last, unless we get sued.'

Mitch nodded to the next portrait. 'Who was he?'

'Robert Lamm. He was a good friend of mine. Emory Law School in Atlanta. He was about three years ahead of me.'

'What happened?'

'No one knows. He was an avid hunter. We hunted moose in Wyoming one winter. In 1970 he was deer hunting in Arkansas and turned up missing. They found him a month later in a ravine with a hole through his head. Autopsy said the bullet entered through the rear of his skull and blew away most of his face. They speculate the shot was fired from a high-powered rifle at long range. It was probably an accident, but we'll never know. I could never imagine anyone wanting to kill Bobby Lamm.'

The last portrait was of John Mickel, 1940–1984. 'What happened to him?' Mitch whispered.

'Probably the most tragic of all. He was not a strong man, and the pressure got to him. He drank a lot, and started drugs. Then his wife left him and they had a bitter divorce. The firm was embarrassed. After he had been here ten years, he began to fear he would not become a partner. The drinking got worse. We spent a small fortune on treatment, shrinks, everything. But nothing worked. He became depressed, then suicidal. He wrote a seven-page suicide note and blew his brains out.'

'That's terrible.'

'Sure was.'

'Where'd they find him?'

Avery cleared his throat and glanced around the room. 'In your office.'

'What!'

'Yeah, but they cleaned it up.'

'You're kidding!'

'No, I'm serious. It was years ago, and the office has been used since then. It's okay.'

Mitch was speechless.

'You're not superstitious, are you?' Avery asked with a nasty grin.

'Of course not.'

'I guess I should've told you, but it's not something we talk about.'
'Can I change offices?'
'Sure. Just flunk the bar exam and we'll give you one of those para-
legal offices in the basement.'
'If I flunk it, it'll be because of you.'
'Yes, but you won't flunk it, will you?'
'If you can pass it, so can I.'

From 5A.M. to 7A.M. the Bendini building was empty and quiet.
Nathan Locke arrived around six, but went straight to his office and
locked the door. At seven, the associates began appearing and voices
could be heard. By seven-thirty the firm had a quorum, and a handful of secretaries punched in. By eight the halls were full and it was
chaos as usual. Concentration became difficult. Interruptions were
routine. Phones beeped incessantly. By nine, all lawyers, paralegals,
clerks and secretaries were either present or accounted for.

Mitch treasured the solitude of the early hours. He moved his clock
up thirty minutes and began waking Dutch at five, instead of five-
thirty. After making two pots of coffee, he roamed the dark halls flipping light switches and inspecting the building. Occasionally, on a
clear morning, he would stand before the window in Lamar's office
and watch the dawn break over the mighty Mississippi below. He
would count the barges lined neatly before their tugboats plowing
slowly upriver. He watched the trucks inch across the bridge in the
distance. But he wasted little time. He dictated letters, briefs, summaries, memorandums and a hundred other documents for Nina to
type and Avery to review. He crammed for the bar exam.

The morning after the ceremony for the dead lawyers, he found
himself in the library on the first floor looking for a treatise when he
again noticed the five portraits. He walked to the wall and stared at
them, remembering the brief obituaries given by Avery. Five dead
lawyers in fifteen years. It was a dangerous place to work. On a legal
pad he scribbled their names and the years they died. It was five-
thirty.

Something moved in the hallway, and he jerked to his right. In the
darkness he saw Black Eyes watching. He stepped forward to the
door and glared at Mitch. 'What are you doing?' he demanded.

Mitch faced him and attempted a smile. 'Good morning to you. It
happens I am studying for the bar exam.'

Locke glanced at the portraits and then stared at Mitch. 'I see.
Why are you so interested in them?'

'Just curious. This firm has had its share of tragedy.'

'They're all dead. A real tragedy will occur if you don't pass the bar exam.'

'I intend to pass it.'

'I've heard otherwise. Your study habits are causing concern among the partners.'

'Are the partners concerned about my excessive billing?'

'Don't get smart. You were told the bar exam has priority over everything. An employee with no license is of no use to the firm.'

Mitch thought of a dozen smart retorts, but let it pass. Locke stepped backward and disappeared. In his office with the door closed, Mitch hid the names and dates in a drawer and opened a review book on constitutional law.

# CHAPTER TEN

The Saturday after the bar exam Mitch avoided his office and his house and spent the morning digging in the flower beds and waiting. With the remodeling complete, the house was now presentable, and of course the first guests had to be her parents. Abby had cleaned and polished for a week, and it was now time. She promised they wouldn't stay long, no more than a few hours. He promised to be as nice as possible.

Mitch had washed and waxed both new cars and they looked as if they had just left the showroom. The lawn had been manicured by a kid down the street. Mr. Rice had applied fertilizer for a month and it looked like a puttin' green, as he liked to say.

At noon they arrived, and he reluctantly left the flower beds. He smiled and greeted them and excused himself to go clean up. He could tell they were uncomfortable, and he wanted it that way. He took a long shower as Abby showed them every piece of furniture and every inch of wallpaper. These things impressed the Sutherlands. Small things always did. They dwelt on the things others did or did not have. He was the president of a small county bank that had been on the verge of collapse for ten years. She was too good to work and had spent all of her adult life seeking social advancement in a town where there was none to be had. She had traced her ancestry to royalty in one of the old countries, and this had always impressed the coal miners in Danesboro, Kentucky. With so much blue blood in her veins, it had fallen her duty to do nothing but drink hot tea, play bridge, talk of her husband's money, condemn the less fortunate and work tirelessly in the Garden Club. He was a stuffed shirt who jumped when she barked and lived in eternal fear of making her mad. As a team they had relentlessly pushed their daughter from birth to be the best, achieve the best, but most importantly, marry the best. Their daughter had rebelled and married a poor kid with no family except a crazy mother and a criminal brother.

'Nice place you've got here, Mitch,' Mr. Sutherland said in an effort to break the ice. They sat for lunch and began passing dishes.

'Thanks.' Nothing else, just thanks. He concentrated on the food. There would be no smiles from him at lunch. The less he said, the more uncomfortable they would be. He wanted then to feel awkward, guilty, wrong. He wanted them to sweat, to bleed. It had been their

452

decision to boycott the wedding. It had been their stones cast, not his.

'Everything is so lovely,' her mother gushed in his direction.

'Thanks.'

'We're so proud of it, Mother,' Abby said.

The conversation immediately went to the remodeling. The men ate in silence as the women chattered on and on about what the decorator did to this room and that one. At times, Abby was almost desperate to fill in the gaps with words about whatever came to mind. Mitch almost felt sorry for her, but he kept his eyes on the table. The butter knife could have cut the tension.

'So you've found a job?' Mrs. Sutherland asked.

'Yes. I start a week from Monday. I'll be teaching third-graders at St. Andrew's Episcopal School.'

'Teaching doesn't pay much,' her father blurted.

He's relentless, thought Mitch.

'I'm not concerned with money, Dad. I'm a teacher. To me, it's the most important profession in the world. If I wanted money, I would've gone to medical school.'

'Third-graders,' her mother said. 'That's such a cute age. You'll be wanting children before long.'

Mitch had already decided that if anything would attract these people to Memphis on a regular basis, it was grandchildren. And he had decided he could wait a long time. He had never been around children. There were no nieces or nephews, except maybe a few unknown ones Ray had scattered around the country. And he had developed no affinity with children.

'Maybe in a few years, Mother.'

Maybe after they're both dead, thought Mitch.

'You want children, don't you Mitch?' asked the mother-in-law.

'Maybe in a few years.'

Mr. Sutherland pushed his plate away and lit a cigarette. The issue of smoking had been repeatedly discussed in the days before the visit. Mitch wanted it banned completely from his house, especially by these people. They had argued vehemently, and Abby won.

'How was the bar exam?' the father-in-law asked.

This could be interesting, Mitch thought. 'Grueling.' Abby chewed her food nervously.

'Do you think you passed?'

'I hope so.'

'When will you know?'

'Four to six weeks.'

'How long did it last?'

'Four days.'

'He's done nothing but study and work since we moved here. I haven't seen much of him this summer,' Abby said.

Mitch smiled at his wife. The time away from home was already a sore subject, and it was amusing to hear her condone it.

'What happens if you don't pass it?' her father asked.

'I don't know. I haven't thought about it.'

'Do they give you a raise when you pass?'

Mitch decided to be nice, as he had promised. But it was difficult. 'Yes, a nice raise and a nice bonus.'

'How many lawyers are in the firm?'

'Forty.'

'My goodness,' said Mrs. Sutherland. She lit up one of hers. 'There's not that many in Dane County.'

'Where's your office?' he asked.

'Downtown.'

'Can we see it?' she asked.

'Maybe some other time. It's closed to visitors on Saturdays.' Mitch amused himself with his answer. Closed to visitors, as if it was a museum.

Abby sensed disaster and began talking about the church they had joined. It had four thousand members, a gymnasium and bowling alley. She sang in the choir and taught eight-year-olds in Sunday school. Mitch went when he was not working but he'd been working most Sundays.

'I'm happy to see you've found a church home, Abby,' her father said piously. For years he had led the prayer each Sunday at the First Methodist Church in Danesboro, and the other six days he had tirelessly practiced greed and manipulation. According to Ray, he had also steadily but discreetly pursued whiskey and women.

An awkward silence followed as the conversation came to a halt. He lit another one. Keep smoking, old boy, Mitch thought. Keep smoking.

'Let's have dessert on the patio,' Abby said. She began clearing the table.

They bragged about his gardening skills, and he accepted the credit. The same kid down the street had pruned the trees, pulled the weeds, trimmed the hedges and edged the patio. Mitch was proficient only in pulling weeds and scooping dog crap. He could also operate the lawn sprinkler, but usually let Mr. Rice do it.

Abby served strawberry shortcake and coffee. She looked helplessly at her husband, but he was noncommittal.

'This is a real nice place you've got here,' her father said for the third time as he surveyed the backyard. Mitch could see his mind working. He had taken the measure of the house and neighborhood, and the curiosity was becoming unbearable. How much did the place cost, dammit?' That's what he wanted to know. How much down? How much a month? Everything. He would keep pecking away until he could work in the questions somewhere.

'This is a lovely place,' her mother said for the tenth time.

'When was it built?' her father asked.

Mitch laid his plate on the table and cleared his throat. He could sense it coming. 'It's about fifteen years old,' he answered.

'How many square feet?'

'About twenty-two hundred,' Abby answered nervously. Mitch glared at her. His composure was vanishing.

'It's a lovely neighborhood,' her mother added helpfully.

'New loan, or did you assume one?' her father asked, as if he were interviewing a loan applicant with weak collateral.

'It's a new loan,' Mitch said, then waited. Abby waited and prayed.

He didn't wait, couldn't wait. 'What'd you pay for it?'

Mitch breathed deeply and was about to say, 'Too much.' Abby was quicker. 'We didn't pay too much, Daddy,' she said firmly with a frown. 'We're quite capable of managing our money.'

Mitch managed a smile while biting his tongue.

Mrs. Sutherland was on her feet. 'Let's go for a drive, shall we? I want to see the river and that new pyramid they've built beside it. Shall we? Come on, Harold.'

Harold wanted more information about the house, but his wife was now tugging on his arm.

'Great idea,' Abby said.

They loaded into the shiny new BMW and went to see the river. Abby asked them not to smoke in the new car. Mitch drove in silence and tried to be nice.

# CHAPTER ELEVEN

Nina entered the office in a rush with a stack of paperwork and laid it before her boss. 'I need signatures,' she demanded, and handed him his pen.

'What is all this?' Mitch asked as he dutifully scribbled his name.

'Don't ask. Just trust me.'

'I found a misspelled word in the Landmark Partners agreement.'

'It's the computer.'

'Okay. Get the computer fixed.'

'How late are you working tonight?'

Mitch scanned the documents and signed off on each. 'I don't know. Why?'

'You look tired. Why don't you go home early, say around ten or ten-thirty, and get some rest. Your eyes are beginning to look like Nathan Locke's.'

'Very funny.'

'Your wife called.'

'I'll call her in a minute.'

When he finished she restacked the letters and documents.

'It's five o'clock. I'm leaving. Oliver Lambert is waiting on you in the first-floor library.'

'Oliver Lambert! Waiting on me?'

'That's what I said. He called not more than five minutes ago. Said it was very important.'

Mitch straightened his tie and ran down the hall, down the stairs, and walked casually into the library. Lambert, Avery and what appeared to be most of the partners sat around the conference table. All of the associates were present, standing behind the partners. The seat at the head of the table was empty, and waiting. The room was quiet, almost solemn. There were no smiles. Lamar was close by and refused to look at him. Avery was sheepish, sort of embarrassed. Wally Hudson twirled the end of his bow tie and slowly shook his head.

'Sit down, Mitch,' Mr. Lambert said gravely. 'We have something to discuss with you.' Doug Turney closed the door.

He sat and searched for any small sign of reassurance. None. The partners rolled their chairs in his direction, squeezing together in the process. The associates surrounded him and glared downward.

'What is it?' he asked meekly, looking helplessly at Avery. Small beads of sweat surfaced above his eyebrows. His heart pounded like a jackhammer. His breathing was labored.

Oliver Lambert leaned across the edge of the table and removed his reading glasses. He frowned sincerely, as if this would be painful. 'We've just received a call from Nashville, Mitch, and we wanted to talk with you about it.'

The bar exam. The bar exam. The bar exam. History had been made. An associate of the great Bendini firm had finally flunked the bar exam. He glared at Avery, and wanted to scream, 'It's all your fault!' Avery pinched his eyebrows as if a migraine had hit and avoided eye contact. Lambert eyed the other partners suspiciously and returned to McDeere.

'We were afraid this would happen, Mitch.'

He wanted to speak, to explain that he deserved just one more chance, that the exam would be given again in six months and he would ace it, that he would not embarrass them again. A thick pain hit below the belt.

'Yes, sir,' he said humbly, in defeat.

Lambert moved in for the kill. 'The folks in Nashville told us that you made the highest score on the bar exam. Congratulations, Counselor.'

The room exploded with laughter and cheers. They gathered around and shook his hand, patted his back and laughed at him. Avery rushed forward with a handkerchief and wiped his forehead. Kendal Mahan slammed three bottles of champagne on the table and began popping corks. A round was poured into plastic wineglasses. He finally breathed and broke into a smile. He slugged the champagne, and they poured him another glass.

Oliver Lambert placed his arm gently around Mitch's neck and spoke. 'Mitch, we are very proud of you. You're the third member of our firm to win the gold medal, and we think that calls for a little bonus. I have here a firm check in the amount of two thousand dollars, which I am presenting to you as a small reward for this achievement.'

There were whistles and catcalls.

'This is, of course, in addition to the substantial raise you have just earned.'

More whistles and catcalls. Mitch took the check but did not look at it.

Mr. Lambert raised his hand and asked for quiet. 'On behalf of the firm, I would like to present you with this.' Lamar handed him a package wrapped in brown paper. Mr. Lambert peeled it off and threw it on the table.

'It's a plaque which we prepared in anticipation of this day. As you can also see, it is a bronzed replica of a piece of firm stationery, complete with every name. As you can see, the name of Mitchell Y. McDeere has been added to the letterhead.'

Mitch stood and awkwardly received the award. The color had returned to his face, and the champagne was beginning to feel good. 'Thank you,' he said softly.

Three days later the Memphis paper published the names of the attorneys who passed the bar exam. Abby clipped the article for the scrapbook and sent copies to her parents and Ray.

Mitch had discovered a deli three blocks from the Bendini Building between Front Street and Riverside Drive, near the river. It was a dark hole in the wall with few customers and greasy chili dogs. He liked it because he could sneak away and proofread a document while he ate. Now that he was a full-blown associate, he could eat a hot dog for lunch and bill a hundred and fifty an hour.

A week after his name was in the paper, he sat by himself at a table in the rear of the deli and ate a chili dog with a fork. The place was empty. He read a prospectus an inch thick. The Greek who ran the place was asleep behind the cash register.

A stranger approached his table and stopped a few feet away. He unraveled a piece of Juicy Fruit, making as much noise as possible. When it was apparent he was not being seen, he walked to the table and sat down. Mitch looked across the red-checkered tablecloth and laid the document next to the iced tea.

'Can I help you?' he asked.

The stranger glanced at the counter, glanced at the empty tables and glanced behind him. 'You're McDeere, aren't you?'

It was a rich brogue, undoubtedly Brooklyn. Mitch studied him carefully. He was about forty, with a short military haircut on the sides and a wisp of gray hair hanging almost to his eyebrows. The suit was a three-piece, navy in color, made of at least ninety percent polyester. The tie was cheap imitation silk. He wasn't much of a dresser, but there was a certain neatness about him. And an air of cockiness.

'Yeah. Who are you?' Mitch asked.

He grabbed his pocket and whipped out a badge. 'Tarrance, Wayne Tarrance, special agent, FBI.' He raised his eyebrows and waited for a response.

'Have a seat,' Mitch said.

'Don't mind if I do.'

'Do you want to frisk me?'

'Not till later. I just wanted to meet you. Saw your name in the paper and heard you were the new man at Bendini, Lambert & Locke.'

'Why should that interest the FBI?'

'We watch that firm pretty close.'

Mitch lost interest in the chili dog and slid the plate to the center of the table. He added more sweetener to his tea in a large styrofoam cup.

'Would you like something to drink?' Mitch asked.

'No thanks.'

'Why do you watch the Bendini firm?'

Tarrance smiled and looked toward the Greek. 'I can't really say at this point. We got our reasons, but I didn't come here to talk about that. I came here to meet you, and to warn you.'

'To warn me?'

'Yes, to warn you about the firm.'

'I'm listening.'

'Three things. Number one, don't trust anyone. There's not a single person in that firm you can confide in. Remember that. It will become important later on. Number two, every word you utter, whether at home, at the office or anywhere in the building, is likely to be recorded. They might even listen to you in your car.'

Mitch watched and listened intently. Tarrance was enjoying this.

'And number three?' Mitch asked.

'Number three, money don't grow on trees.'

'Would you care to elaborate?'

'I can't right now. I think you and I will become very close. I want you to trust me, and I know I'll have to earn your trust. So I don't want to move too fast. We can't meet at your office, or my office, and we can't talk on the phone. So from time to time I'll come find you. In the meantime, just remember those three things, and be careful.'

Tarrance stood and reached for his wallet. 'Here's my card. My home number is on the back. Use it only from a pay phone.'

Mitch studied the card. 'Why should I be calling you?'

'You won't need to for a while. But keep the card.'

Mitch placed it in his shirt pocket.

'There's one other thing,' Tarrance said. 'We saw you at the funerals of Hodge and Kozinski. Sad, really sad. Their deaths were not accidental.'

He looked down at Mitch with both hands in his pockets and smiled.

'I don't understand.'

Tarrance started for the door. 'Gimme a call sometime, but be careful. Remember, they're listening.'

A few minutes after four a horn honked and Dutch bolted to his feet. He cursed and walked in front of the headlights.

'Dammit, Mitch. It's four o'clock. What're you doing here?'

'Sorry, Dutch. Couldn't sleep. Rough night.' The gate opened.

By seven-thirty he had dictated enough work to keep Nina busy for two days. She bitched less when her nose was glued to the monitor. His immediate goal was to become the first associate to justify a second secretary.

At eight o'clock he parked himself in Lamar's office and waited. He proofed a contract and drank coffee, and told Lamar's secretary to mind her own business. He arrived at eight-fifteen.

'We need to talk,' Mitch said as he closed the door. If he believed Tarrance, the office was bugged and the conversation would be recorded. He was not sure whom to believe.

'You sound serious,' Lamar said.

'Ever hear of a guy named Tarrance, Wayne Tarrance?'

'No.'

'FBI.'

Lamar closed his eyes. 'FBI,' he mumbled.

'That's right. He had a badge and everything.'

'Where did you meet him?'

'He found me at Lansky's Deli on Union. He knew who I was, knew I'd just been admitted. Says he knows all about the firm. They watch us real close.'

'Have you told Avery?'

'No. No one but you. I'm not sure what to do.'

Lamar picked up the phone. 'We need to tell Avery. I think this has happened before.'

'What's going on, Lamar?'

Lamar talked to Avery's secretary and said it was an emergency. In a few seconds he was on the other end. 'We've got a small problem, Avery. An FBI agent contacted Mitch yesterday. He's in my office.'

Lamar listened, then said to Mitch, 'He's got me on hold. Said he was calling Lambert.'

'I take it this is pretty serious,' Mitch said.

'Yes, but don't worry. There's an explanation. It's happened before.'

Lamar held the receiver closer and listened to the instructions. He hung up. 'They want us in Lambert's office in ten minutes.'

Avery, Royce McKnight, Oliver Lambert, Harold O'Kane and Nathan Locke were waiting. They stood nervously around the small conference table and tried to appear calm when Mitch entered the office.

'Have a seat,' Nathan Locke said with a short, plastic smile. 'We want you to tell us everything.'

'What's that?' Mitch pointed to a tape recorder in the center of the table.

'We don't want to miss anything,' Locke said, and pointed to an empty chair. Mitch sat and stared across the table at Black Eyes. Avery sat between them. No one made a sound.

'Okay. I was eating lunch yesterday at Lansky's Deli on Union. This guy walks up and sits across my table. He knows my name. Shows me a badge and says his name is Wayne Tarrance, special agent, FBI. I look at the badge, and it's real. He tells me he wants to meet because we'll get to know each other. They watch this firm real close and he warns me not to trust anyone. I ask him why, and he said he doesn't have time to explain, but he will later. I don't know what to say, so I just listen. He says he will contact me later. He gets up to leave and tells me they saw me at the funerals. Then he says the deaths of Kozinski and Hodge were not accidents. And he leaves. The entire conversation lasted less than five minutes.'

Black Eyes glared at Mitch and absorbed every word. 'Have you ever seen this man before?'

'Never.'

'Whom did you tell?'

'Only Lamar. I told him first thing this morning.'

'Your wife?'

'No.'

'Did he leave you a phone number to call?'

'No.'

'I want to know every word that was said,' Lock demanded.

'I've told you what I remember. I can't recall it verbatim.'

'Are you certain?'

'Let me think a minute.' A few things he would keep to himself. He stared at Black Eyes, and knew that Locke suspected more.

'Let's see. He said he saw my name in the paper and knew I was the new man here. That's it. I've covered everything. It was a very brief conversation.'

'Try to remember everything,' Locke persisted.

'I asked him if he wanted some of my tea. He declined.'

The tape recorder was turned off, and the partners seemed to relax a little. Locke walked to the window. 'Mitch, we've had trouble with the FBI, as well as the IRS. It's been going on for a number of years. Some of our clients are high rollers – wealthy individuals who make millions, spend millions and expect to pay little or no taxes. They pay us thousands of dollars to legally avoid taxes. We have a reputation for being very aggressive, and we don't mind taking chances if our clients instruct us to. We're talking about very sophisticated businessmen who understand risks. They pay dearly for our creativeness. Some of the shelters and write-offs we set up have been challenged by the IRS. We've slugged it out with them in tax litigation for the past twenty years. They don't like us, we don't like them. Some of our clients have not always possessed the highest degree of ethics, and they have been investigated and harassed by the FBI. For the past three years, we, too, have been harassed.

'Tarrance is a rookie looking for a big name. He's been here less than a year and has become a thorn. You are not to speak to him again. Your brief conversation yesterday was probably recorded. He is dangerous, extremely dangerous. He does not play fair, and you'll learn soon enough that most of the feds don't play fair.'

'How many of these clients have been convicted?'

'Not a single one. And we've won our share of litigation with the IRS.'

'What about Kozinski and Hodge?'

'Good question,' answered Oliver Lambert. 'We don't know what happened. It first appeared to be an accident, but now we're not sure. There was a native of the islands on board with Marty and Joe. He was the captain and divemaster. The authorities down there now tell us they suspect he was a key link in a drug ring based in Jamaica and perhaps the explosion was aimed at him. He died, of course.'

'I don't think we'll ever know,' Royce McKnight added. 'The police down there are not that sophisticated. We've chosen to protect the families, and as far as we're concerned, it was an accident. Frankly, we're not sure how to handle it.'

'Don't breathe a word of this to anyone,' Locke instructed. 'Stay away from Tarrance, and if he contacts you again, let us know immediately. Understand?'

'Yes, sir.'

'Don't even tell your wife,' Avery said.

Mitch nodded.

The grandfather's warmth returned to Oliver Lambert's face. He smiled and twirled his reading glasses. 'Mitch, we know this is frightening, but we've grown accustomed to it. Let us handle it, and trust us. We are not afraid of Mr. Tarrance, the FBI, the IRS or anybody else because we've done nothing wrong. Anthony Bendini built this firm by hard work, talent and uncompromising ethics. It has been drilled into all of us. Some of our clients have not been saints, but no lawyer can dictate morals to his client. We don't want you worrying about this. Stay away from this guy – he is very, very dangerous. If you feed him, he'll get bolder and become a nuisance.'

Locke pointed a crooked finger at Mitch. 'Further contact with Tarrance will jeopardize your future with this firm.'

'I understand,' Mitch said.

'He understands,' Avery said defensively. Locke glared at Tolleson.

'That's all we have, Mitch,' Mr. Lambert said. 'Be cautious.'

Mitch and Lamar hit the door and found the nearest stairway.

'Get DeVasher,' Locke said to Lambert, who was on the phone. Within two minutes the two senior partners had been cleared and were sitting before DeVasher's cluttered desk.

'Did you listen?' Locke asked.

'Of course I listened to it, Nat. We heard every word the boy said. You handled it real well. I think he's scared and will run from Tarrance.'

'What about Lazarov?'

'I gotta tell him. He's the boss. We can't pretend it didn't happen.'

'What will they do?'

'Nothing serious. We'll watch the boy around the clock and check all his phone calls. And wait. He's not gonna move. It's up to Tarrance. He'll find him again, and the next time we'll be there. Try to keep him in the building as much as possible. When he leaves, let us know, if you can. I don't think it's that bad, really.'

'Why would they pick McDeere?' said Locke.

'New strategy, I guess. Kozinski and Hodge went to them, remember. Maybe they talked more than we thought. I don't know. Maybe they figure McDeere is the most vulnerable because he's fresh out of school and full of rookie idealism. And ethics – like our ethical friend Ollie here. That was good, Ollie, real good.'

'Shut up, DeVasher.'

DeVasher quit smiling and bit his bottom lip. He let it pass. He looked at Locke. 'You know what the next step is, don't you?' If Tarrance keeps pushing, that idiot Lazarov will call me one day and tell me to remove him. Silence him. Put him in a barrel and drop him in the Gulf. And when that happens, all of you honorable esquires will take your early retirement and leave the country.'

'Lazarov wouldn't order a hit on an agent.'

'Oh, it would be a foolish move, but then Lazarov is a fool. He's very anxious about the situation down here. He calls a lot and asks all sorts of questions. I give him all sorts of answers. Sometimes he listens, sometimes he cusses. Sometimes he says he's gotta talk to the board. But if he tells me to take out Tarrance, then we'll take out Tarrance.'

'This makes me sick at my stomach,' Lambert said.

'You wanna get sick, Ollie. You let one of your little Gucci-loafered counselors get chummy with Tarrance and start talking, you'll get a helluva lot worse than sick. Now, I suggest you boys keep McDeere so busy he won't have time to think about Tarrance.'

'My God, DeVasher, he works twenty hours a day. He started like fire and he hasn't slowed down.'

'Just watch him close. Tell Lamar Quin to get real tight with him so if he's got something on his mind, maybe he'll unload.'

'Good idea,' said Locke. He looked at Ollie. 'Let's have a long talk with Quin. He's closest to McDeere, and maybe he can get closer.'

'Look, boys,' DeVasher said, 'McDeere is scared right now. He won't make a move. If Tarrance contacts him again, he'll do what he did today. He'll run straight to Lamar Quin. He showed us who he confides in.'

'Did he tell his wife last night?' asked Locke.

'We're checking the tapes now. It'll take about an hour. We've got so damned many bugs in this city it takes six computers to find anything.'

Mitch stared through the window in Lamar's office and selected his words carefully. He said little. Suppose Tarrance was correct. Suppose everything was being recorded.

'Do you feel better?' Lamar asked.

'Yeah, I guess. It makes sense.'

'It's happened before, just like Locke said.'

'Who? Who was approached before?'

'I don't remember. Seems like it was three or four years ago.'

'But you don't remember who it was?'

'No. Why is that important?'

'I'd just like to know. I don't understand why they would pick me, the new man, the one lawyer out of forty who knows the least about this firm and its clients. Why would they pick me?'

'I don't know, Mitch. Look, why don't you do as Locke suggested? Try to forget about it and run from this guy Tarrance. You don't have to talk to him unless he's got a warrant. Tell him to get lost if he shows up again. He's dangerous.'

'Yeah, I guess you're right.' Mitch forced a smile and headed for the door. 'We're still on for dinner tomorrow night?'

'Sure. Kay wants to grill steaks and eat by the pool. Make it late, say around seven-thirty.'

'See you then.'

# CHAPTER TWELVE

The guard called his name, frisked him and led him to a large room where a row of small booths was occupied with visitors talking and whispering through thick metal screens.

'Number fourteen,' the guard said, and pointed. Mitch walked to his booth and sat down. A minute later Ray appeared and sat between his dividers on the other side of the screen. Were it not for a scar on Ray's forehead and a few wrinkles around the eyes, they could pass for twins. Both were six-two, weighed about one-eighty, with light brown hair, small blue eyes, high cheekbones and large chins. They had always been told there was Indian blood in the family, but the dark skin had been lost through years in the coal mines.

Mitch had not been to Brushy Mountain in three years. Three years and three months. They'd exchanged letters twice a month, every month, for eight years now.

'How's your French?' Mitch finally asked. Ray's Army test scores had revealed an amazing aptitude for languages. He had served two years as a Vietnamese interpreter. He had mastered German in six months while stationed there. Spanish had taken four years, but he was forced to learn it from a dictionary in the prison library. French was his latest project.

'I'm fluent, I guess,' Ray answered. 'It's kinda hard to tell in here. I don't get much practice. Evidently they don't teach French in the projects, so most of these brothers here are unilingual. It's undoubtedly the most beautiful language.'

'Is it easy?'

'Not as easy as German. Of course, it was easier to learn German since I was living there and everybody spoke it. Did you know that fifty percent of our language comes from German through Old English?'

'No, I didn't know that.'

'It's true. English and German are first cousins.'

'What's next?'

'Probably Italian. It's a Romance language like French and Spanish and Portuguese. Maybe Russian. Maybe Greek. I've been reading about the Greek isles. I plan to go there soon.'

Mitch smiled. Ray was at least seven years away from parole.

'You think I'm kidding, don't you?' Ray asked. 'I'm checking out of here, Mitchell, and it won't be long.'

'What are your plans?'

'I can't talk. But I'm working on it.'

'Don't do it, Ray.'

'I'll need some help on the outside, and enough money to get me out of this country. A thousand should do it. You can handle that, can't you? You won't be implicated.'

'Aren't they listening to us?'

'Sometimes.'

'Let's talk about something else.'

'Sure. How's Abby?'

'She's fine.'

'Where is she?'

'Right now she's in church. She wanted to come, but I told her she wouldn't get to see you.'

'I'd like to see her. Your letters sound like y'all are doing real well. New house, cars, country club. I'm very proud of you. You're the first McDeere in two generations to amount to a damned thing.'

'Our parents were good people, Ray. They had no opportunities and a lot of bad luck. They did the best they could.'

Ray smiled and looked away. 'Yeah, I guess so. Have you talked to Mom?'

'It's been a while.'

'Is she still in Florida?'

'I think so.'

They paused and studied their fingers. They thought of their mother. Painful thoughts for the most part. There had been happier times, when they were small and their father was alive. She never recovered from his death, and after Rusty was killed the aunts and uncles put her in an institution.

Ray took his finger and followed the small metal rods in the screen. He watched his finger. 'Let's talk about something else.'

Mitch nodded in agreement. There was so much to talk about, but it was all in the past. They had nothing in common but the past, and it was best to leave it alone.

'You mentioned in a letter that one of your ex-cellmates is a private investigator in Memphis.'

'Eddie Lomax. He was a Memphis cop for nine years, until he got sent up for rape.'

'Rape?'

'Yeah. He had a tough time here. Rapists are not well regarded around this place. Cops are hated. They almost killed him until I stepped in. He's been out about three years now. He writes me all the time. Does mainly divorce investigations.'

'Is he in the phone book?'

'969-3838. Why do you need him?'

'I've got a lawyer buddy whose wife is fooling around, but he can't catch her. Is this guy good?'

'Very good, so he says. He's made some money.'

'Can I trust him?'

'Are you kidding? Tell him you're my brother and he'll kill for you. He's gonna help me get out of here, he just doesn't know it. You might mention it to him.'

'I wish you'd stop that.'

A guard walked behind Mitch. 'Three minutes,' he said.

'What can I send you?' Mitch asked.

'I'd like a real favor, if you don't mind.'

'Anything.'

'Go to a bookstore and look for one of those cassette courses on how to speak Greek in twenty-four hours. That plus a Greek-to-English dictionary would be nice.'

'I'll send it next week.'

'How about Italian too?'

'No problem.'

'I'm undecided about whether to go to Sicily or the Greek isles. It's really got me tore up. I asked the prison minister about it, and he was of no help. I've thought of going to the warden. What do you think?'

Mitch chuckled and shook his head. 'Why don't you go to Australia?'

'Great idea. Send me some tapes in Australian and a dictionary.'

They both smiled, then stopped. They watched each other carefully and waited for the guard to call time. Mitch looked at the scar on Ray's forehead and thought of the countless bars and countless fights that led to the inevitable killing. Self-defense, Ray called it. For years he had wanted to cuss Ray for being so stupid, but the anger had passed. Now he wanted to embrace him and take him home and help him find a job.

'Don't feel sorry for me,' Ray said.

'Abby wants to write you.'

'I'd like that. I barely remember her as a small girl in Danesboro, hanging around her daddy's bank on Main Street. Tell her to send me a picture. And I'd like a picture of your house. You're the first McDeere in a hundred years to own real estate.'

'I gotta go.'

'Do me a favor. I think you need to find Mom, just to make sure she's alive. Now that you're out of school, it would be nice to reach out to her.'

'I've thought about that.'

'Think about it some more, okay?'

'Sure. I'll see you in a month or so.'

DeVasher sucked on a Roi-Tan and blew a lungful of smoke into his air purifier. 'We found Ray McDeere,' he announced proudly.

'Where?' asked Ollie.

'Brushy Mountain State Prison. Convicted of second-degree murder in Nashville eight years ago and sentenced to fifteen years with no parole. Real name is Raymond McDeere. Thirty-one years old. No family. Served three years in the Army. Dishonorable discharge. A real loser.'

'How'd you find him?'

'He was visited yesterday by his kid brother. We happened to be following. Twenty-four-hour surveillance, remember.'

'His conviction is public record. You should've found this earlier.'

'We would have, Ollie, if it was important. But it's not important. We do our job.'

'Fifteen years, huh? Who'd he kill?'

'The usual. A buncha drunks in a bar fighting over a woman. No weapon, though. Police and autopsy report say he hit the victim twice with his fists and cracked his skull.'

'Why the dishonorable discharge?'

'Gross insubordination. Plus, he assaulted an officer. I don't know how he avoided a court-martial. Looks like a nasty character.'

'You're right, it's not important. What else do you know?'

'Not much. We've got the house wired, right? He has not mentioned Tarrance to his wife. In fact, we listen to this kid around the clock, and he ain't mentioned Tarrance to anyone.'

Ollie smiled and nodded his approval. He was proud of McDeere. What a lawyer.

'What about sex?'

'All we can do is listen, Ollie. But we listen real close, and I don't think they've had any in two weeks. Of course, he's here sixteen hours a day going through the workaholic rookie counselor routine that you guys instill. It sounds like she's getting tired of it. Could be the usual rookie's wife syndrome. She calls her mother a lot – collect, so he won't know. She told her mom that he's changing and all that crap. She thinks he'll kill himself working so hard. That's what we're hearing. So I don't have any pictures, Ollie, and I'm sorry because I know how much you enjoy them. First chance we get, we'll have you some pictures.'

Ollie glared at the wall but said nothing.

'Listen, Ollie, I think we need to send the kid with Avery to Grand Cayman on business. See if you can arrange it.'

'That's no problem. May I ask why?'

'Not right now. You'll know later.'

The building was in the low-rent section of downtown, a couple of blocks from the shadows of the modern steel-and-glass towers which were packed together as if land was scarce in Memphis. A sign on a door directed one's attention upstairs, where Eddie Lomax, private investigator, maintained an office. Hours by appointment only. The door upstairs advertised investigations of all types – divorces, accidents, missing relatives, surveillance. The ad in the phone book mentioned the police expertise, but not the ending of that career. It listed eavesdropping, countermeasures, child custody, photographs, courtroom evidence, voice-stress analysis, location of assets, insurance claims and premarital background review. Bonded, insured, licensed and available twenty-four hours a day. Ethical, reliable, confidential, peace of mind.

Mitch was impressed with the abundance of confidence. The appointment was for 5P.M., and he arrived a few minutes early. A shapely platinum blond with a constricting leather skirt and matching black boots asked for his name and pointed to an orange vinyl chair next to a window. Eddie would be a minute. He inspected the chair, and noticing a fine layer of dust and several spots of what appeared to be grease, he declined and said his back was sore. Tammy shrugged and returned to her gum chewing and typing of some document; Mitch speculated whether it was a premarital report, or maybe a surveillance summary, or perhaps a countermeasure attack plan. The ashtray on her desk was filled with butts smeared with pink lipstick. While typing with her left hand, the right one instantly and precisely picked another cigarette from the pack and thrust it between her sticky lips. With remarkable coordination, she flicked something with her left hand and a flame shot to the tip of a very skinny and incredibly long liberated cigarette. When the flame disappeared, the lips instinctively compacted and hardened around the tiny protrusion, and the entire body began to inhale. Letters became words, words became sentences, sentences became paragraphs as she tried desperately to fill her lungs. Finally, with an inch of the cigarette hanging as ashes, she swallowed, picked it from her lips with two brilliant red fingernails and exhaled mightily. The smoke billowed toward the stained plaster ceiling, where it upset an existing cloud and swirled around a hanging fluorescent light. She coughed, a hacking, irritating cough which reddened her face and gyrated her huge breasts until they bounced dangerously close to the typewriter keys. She grabbed a nearby cup and lapped up something, then reinserted the filter-tip 1000 and pecked away.

After two minutes, Mitch began to fear the carbon monoxide. He spotted a small hole in the window, in a pane that for some reason the spiders had not draped with cobwebs. He walked to within inches of the shredded, dust-laden curtains and tried to inhale in the direction of the opening. He felt sick. There was more hacking and wheezing behind him. He tried to open the window, but layers of cracked paint had long since welded it shut.

Just when he began to feel dizzy the typing and smoking stopped. 'You a lawyer?'

Mitch turned from the window and looked at the secretary. She was now sitting on the edge of her desk, legs crossed, with the black leather skirt well above her knees. She sipped a Diet Pepsi.

'Yes.'

'In a big firm?'

'Yes.'

'I thought so. I could tell by your suit and your cute little preppie button-down with a silk paisley tie. I can always spot the big-firm lawyers, as opposed to the ham-and-eggers who hang around the City Court.'

The smoke was clearing and Mitch was breathing easier. He admired her legs, which for the moment were positioned just so and demanded to be admired. She was now looking at his shoes.

'You like the suit, huh?' he said.

'It's expensive, I can tell. So's the tie. I'm not so sure about the shirt and shoes.'

Mitch studied the leather boots, the legs, the skirt and the tight sweater around the large breasts and tried to think of something cute to say. She enjoyed this gazing back and forth, and again sipped on her Diet Pepsi.

When she'd had enough, she nodded at Eddie's door and said, 'You can go in now. Eddie's waiting.'

The detective was on the phone, trying to convince some poor old man that his son was in fact a homosexual. A very active homosexual. He pointed to a wooden chair, and Mitch sat down. He saw two windows, both wide open, and breathed easier.

Eddie looked disgusted and covered the receiver. 'He's crying,' he whispered to Mitch, who smiled obligingly, as if he was amused.

He wore blue lizard-skin boots with pointed toes, Levi's, a well-starched peach button-down, which was unbuttoned well into the dark chest hair and exposed two heavy gold chains and one which appeared to be turquoise. He favored Tom Jones or Humperdinck or one of those bushy-headed, dark-eyed singers with thick sideburns and solid chins.

'I've got photographs,' he said, and yanked the receiver from his ear when the old man screamed. He pulled five glossy eight-by-tens from a file and slid them across the desk into Mitch's lap. Yes, indeed, they were homosexuals, whoever they were. Eddie smiled at him proudly. The bodies were somewhere on a stage in what appeared to be a queer club. He laid them on the desk and looked at the window. They were of high quality, in color. Whoever took them had to have been in the club. Mitch thought of the rape conviction. A cop sent up for rape.

He slammed the phone down. 'So you're Mitchell McDeere! Nice to meet.'

They shook hands across the desk. 'My pleasure,' Mitch said. 'I saw Ray Sunday.'

'I feel like I've known you for years. You look just like Ray. He told me you did. Told me all about you. I guess he told you about me. The police background. The conviction. The rape. Did he explain to you it was statutory rape, and that the girl was seventeen years old, looked twenty-five, and that I got framed?'

'He mentioned it. Ray doesn't say much. You know that.'

'He's a helluva guy. I owe him my life, literally. They almost killed me in prison when they found out I was a cop. He stepped in and even the blacks backed down. He can hurt people when he wants to.'

'He's all the family I have.'

'Yeah, I know. You bunk with a guy for years in an eight-by-twelve cell and you learn all about him. He's talked about you for hours. When I was paroled you were thinking about law school.'

'I finished in June of this year and went to work for Bendini, Lambert & Locke.'

'Never heard of them.'

'It's a tax and corporate firm on Front Street.'

'I do a lot of sleazy divorce work for lawyers. Surveillance, taking pictures, like those, and gathering filth for court.' He spoke quickly, with short, clipped words and sentences. The cowboy boots were placed gingerly on the desk for display. 'Plus, I've got some lawyers I run cases for. If I dig up a good car wreck or personal-injury suit, I'll shop around to see who'll give me the best cut. That's how I bought this building. That's where the money is – personal injury. These lawyers take forty percent of the recovery. Forty percent!' He shook his head in disgust as if he couldn't believe greedy lawyers actually lived and breathed in this city.

'You work by the hour?' Mitch asked.

'Thirty bucks, plus expenses. Last night I spent six hours in my van outside a Holiday Inn waiting for my client's husband to leave his room with his whore so I could take some pictures. Six hours. That's a hundred eighty bucks for sitting on my ass looking at dirty magazines and waiting. I also charged her for dinner.'

Mitch listened intently, as if he wished he could do it.

Tammy stuck her head in the door and said she was leaving. A stale cloud followed her and Mitch looked at the windows. She slammed the door.

'She's a great gal,' Eddie said. 'She's got trouble with her husband. He's a truck driver who thinks he's Elvis. Got the jet-black hair, ducktail, lamb-chop sideburns. Wears those thick gold sunglasses Elvis wore. When he's not on the road he sits around the trailer listening to Elvis albums and watching those terrible movies. They moved here from Ohio just so this clown can be near the King's grave. Guess what his name is.'

'I have no idea.'

'Elvis. Elvis Aaron Hemphill. Had his name legally changed after the King died. He does an impersonation routine in dark nightclubs around the city. I saw him one night. He wore a white skintight jumpsuit unbuttoned to his navel, which would've been okay except he's got this gut that hangs out and looks like a bleached watermelon. It was pretty sad. His voice is hilarious, sounds like one of those old Indian chiefs chanting around the campfire.'

'So what's the problem?'

'Women. You would not believe the Elvis nuts who visit this city. They flock to watch this buffoon act like the King. They throw panties at him, big panties, panties made for heavy, wide lardasses, and he wipes his forehead and throws them back. They give him their room numbers, and we suspect he sneaks around and tries to play the big stud, just like Elvis. I haven't caught him yet.'

Mitch could not think of any response to all this. He grinned like an idiot, like this was truly an incredible story. Lomax read him well.

'You got trouble with your wife?'

'No. Nothing like that. I need some information about four people. Three are dead, one is alive.'

'Sounds interesting. I'm listening.'

Mitch pulled the notes from a pocket. 'I assume this is strictly confidential.'

'Of course it is. As confidential as you are with your client.'

Mitch nodded in agreement, but thought of Tammy and Elvis and wondered why Lomax told him that story.

'It must be confidential.'

'I said it would be. You can trust me.'

'Thirty bucks an hour?'

'Twenty for you. Ray sent you, remember?'

'I appreciate that.'

'Who are these people?'

'The three dead ones were once lawyers in our firm. Robert Lamm was killed in 1970 in a hunting accident somewhere in Arkansas. Somewhere in the mountains. He was missing for about two weeks and they found him with a bullet in the head. There was an autopsy. That's all I know. Alice Knauss died in 1977 in a car wreck here in Memphis. Supposedly a drunk driver hit her. John Mickel committed suicide in 1984. His body was found in his office. There was a gun and a note.'

'That's all you know?'

'That's it.'

'What're you looking for?'

'I want to know as much as I can about how these people died. What were the circumstances surrounding each death? Who investigated each death? Any unanswered questions or suspicions.'

'What do you suspect?'

'At this point, nothing. I'm just curious.'

'You're more than curious.'

'Okay, I'm more than curious. But for now, let's leave it at that.'

'Fair enough. Who's the fourth guy?'

'A man named Wayne Tarrance. He's an FBI agent here in Memphis.'

'FBI!'

'Does that bother you?'

'Yes, it bothers me. I get forty an hour for cops.'

'No problem.'

'What do you want to know?'

'Check him out. How long has he been here? How long has he been an agent? What's his reputation?'

'That's easy enough.'

Mitch folded the paper and stuck it in his pocket. 'How long will this take?'

'About a month.'

'That's fine.'

'Say, what was the name of your firm?'

'Bendini, Lambert & Locke.'

'Those two guys who got killed last summer – '

'They were members.'

'Any suspicions?'

'No.'

'Just thought I'd ask.'

'Listen, Eddie. You must be very careful with this. Don't call me at home or the office. I'll call you in about a month. I suspect I'm being watched very closely.'

'By whom?'

'I wish I knew.'

# CHAPTER THIRTEEN

Avery smiled at the computer printout. 'For the month of October you billed an average of sixty-one hours per week.'

'I thought it was sixty-four,' Mitch said.

'Sixty-one is good enough. In fact, we've never had a first-year man average so high in one month. Is it legitimate?'

'No padding. In fact, I could've pushed it higher.'

'How many hours are you working a week?'

'Between eighty-five and ninety. I could bill seventy-five if I wanted to.'

'I wouldn't suggest it, at least not now. It could cause a little jealousy around here. The younger associates are watching you very closely.'

'You want me to slow down?'

'Of course not. You and I are a month behind right now. I'm just worried about the long hours. A little worried, that's all. Most associates start like wildfire – eighty- and ninety-hour weeks – but they burn out after a couple of months. Sixty-five to seventy is about average. But you seem to have unusual stamina.'

'I don't require much sleep.'

'What does your wife think about it?'

'Why is that important?'

'Does she mind the long hours?'

Mitch glared at Avery, and for a second thought of the argument the previous night when he arrived home for dinner at three minutes before midnight. It was a controlled fight, but the worst one yet, and it promised to be followed by others. No ground was surrendered. Abby said she felt closer to Mr. Rice next door than to her husband.

'She understands. I told her I would make partner in two years and retire before I was thirty.'

'Looks likes you're trying.'

'You're not complaining, are you? Every hour I billed last month was on one of your files, and you didn't seem too concerned about overworking me.'

Avery laid the printout on his credenza and frowned at Mitch. 'I just don't want you to burn out or neglect things at home.'

It seemed odd receiving marital advice from a man who had left his wife. He looked at Avery with as much contempt as he could generate. 'You don't need to worry about what happens at my house. As long as I produce around here you should be happy.'

Avery leaned across the desk. 'Look, Mitch, I'm not very good at this sort of thing. This is coming from higher up. Lambert and McKnight are worried that maybe you're pushing a bit too hard. I mean, five o'clock in the morning, every morning, even some Sundays. That's pretty intense, Mitch.'

'What did they say?'

'Nothing much. Believe it or not, Mitch, those guys really care about you and your family. They want happy lawyers with happy wives. If everything is lovely, then the lawyers are productive. Lambert is especially paternalistic. He's planning to retire in a couple of years, and he's trying to relive his glory years through you and the other guys. If he asks too many questions or gives a few lectures, take it in stride. He's earned the right to be the grandfather around here.'

'Tell them I'm fine, Abby's fine, we're all happy and I'm very productive.'

'Fine, now that that's out of the way, you and I leave for Grand Cayman a week from tomorrow. I've got to meet with some Caymanian bankers on behalf of Sonny Capps and three other clients. Mainly business, but we always manage to work in a little scuba diving and snorkeling. I told Royce McKnight you were needed, and he approved the trip. He said you probably needed the R and R. Do you want to go?'

'Of course. I'm just a little surprised.'

'It's business, so our wives won't be going. Lambert was a little concerned that it may cause a problem at home.'

'I think Mr. Lambert worries too much about what happens at my home. Tell him I'm in control. No problems.'

'So you're going?'

'Sure, I'm going. How long will we be there?'

'Couple of days. We'll stay in one of the firm's condos. Sonny Capps may stay in the other one. I'm trying to get the firm plane, but we may have to fly commercial.'

'No problem with me.'

Only two of the passengers on board the Cayman Airways 727 in Miami wore ties, and after the first round of complimentary rum punch Avery removed his and stuffed it in his coat pocket. The punch was served by beautiful brown Caymanian stewardesses with blue eyes and comely smiles. The women were great down there, Avery said more than once.

Mitch sat by the window and tried to conceal the excitement of his first trip out of the country. He had found a book on the Cayman Islands in the library. There were three islands, Grand Cayman, Little Cayman and Cayman Brac. The two smaller ones were sparsely populated and seldom visited. Grand Cayman had eighteen thousand people, twelve thousand registered corporations and three hundred banks. The population was twenty percent white, twenty percent black, and the other sixty percent wasn't sure and didn't care. Georgetown, the capital, in recent years had become an international tax haven with bankers as secretive as the Swiss. There were no income taxes, corporate taxes, capital-gains taxes, estate or gift taxes. Certain companies and investments were given guarantees against taxation for fifty years. The islands were a dependent British territory with an unusually stable government. Revenue from import duties and tourism funded whatever government was necessary. There was no crime or unemployment.

Grand Cayman was twenty-three miles long and eight miles wide in places, but from the air it looked much smaller. It was a small rock surrounded by clear, sapphire water.

The landing almost occurred in a lagoon, but at the last second a small asphalt strip came forth and caught the plane. They disembarked and sang their way through customs. A black boy grabbed Mitch's bags and threw them with Avery's into the trunk of a 1972 Ford LTD. Mitch tipped him generously.

'Seven Mile Beach!' Avery commanded as he turned up the remnants of his last rum punch.

'Okay, mon,' the driver drawled. He gunned the taxi and laid rubber in the direction of Georgetown. The radio blared reggae. The driver shook and gyrated and kept a steady beat with his fingers on the steering wheel. He was on the wrong side of the road, but so was everybody else. Mitch sank into the worn seat and crossed his legs. The car had no air conditioning except for the open windows. The muggy tropical air rushed across his face and blew his hair. This was nice.

The island was flat, and the road into Georgetown was busy with small, dusty European cars, scooters and bicycles. The homes were small one-stories with tin roofs and neat, colorful paint jobs. The lawns were tiny with little grass, but the dirt was neatly swept. As they neared the town the houses became shops, two- and three-story white frame buildings where tourists stood under the canopies and took refuge from the sun. The driver made a sharp turn and suddenly they were in the midst of a downtown crowded with modern bank buildings.

Avery assumed the role of tour guide. 'There are banks here from everywhere. Germany, France, Great Britain, Canada, Spain, Japan, Denmark. Even Saudi Arabia and Israel. Over three hundred, at last count. It's become quite a tax haven. The bankers here are extremely quiet. They make the Swiss look like blabbermouths.'

The taxi slowed in heavy traffic, and the breeze stopped. 'I see a lot of Canadian banks.' Mitch said.

'That building right there is the Royal Bank of Montreal. We'll be there at ten in the morning. Most of our business will be with Canadian banks.'

'Any particular reason?'

'They're very safe, and very quiet.'

The crowded street turned and dead-ended into another one. Beyond the intersection the glittering blue of the Caribbean rose to the horizon. A cruise ship was anchored in the bay.

'That's Hogsty Bay,' Avery said. 'That's where the pirates docked their ships three hundred years ago. Blackbeard himself roamed these islands and buried his loot. They found some of it a few years ago in a cave east of here near Bodden Town.'

Mitch nodded as if he believed this tale. The driver smiled in the rearview mirror.

Avery wiped the sweat from his forehead. 'This place has always attracted pirates. Once it was Blackbeard, now it's modern-day pirates who form corporations and hide their money here. Right, mon?'

'Right, mon,' the driver replied.

'That's Seven Mile Beach,' Avery said. 'One of the most beautiful and most famous in the world. Right, mon?'

'Right, mon.'

'Sand as white as sugar. Warm, clear water. Warm, beautiful women. Right, mon?'

'Right, mon.'

'Will they have the cookout tonight at the Palms?'

'Yes, mon. Six o'clock.'

'That's next door to our condo. The Palms is a popular hotel with the hottest action on the beach.'

Mitch smiled and watched the hotels pass. He recalled the interview at Harvard when Oliver Lambert preached about how the firm frowned on divorce and chasing women. And drinking. Perhaps Avery had missed those sermons. Perhaps he hadn't.

The condos were in the center of Seven Mile Beach, next door to another complex and the Palms. As expected, the units owned by the

479

firm were spacious and richly decorated. Avery said they would sell
for at least half a million each, but they weren't for sale. They were
not for rent. They were sanctuaries for the weary lawyers of Bendini,
Lambert & Locke. And a few very favored clients.

From the balcony off the second-floor bedroom, Mitch watched the
small boats drift aimlessly over the sparkling sea. The sun was beginning its descent and the small waves reflected its rays in a million
directions. The cruise ship moved slowly away from the island.
Dozens of people walked the beach, kicking sand, splashing in the
water, chasing sand crabs and drinking rum punch and Jamaican
Red Stripe beer. The rhythmic beat of Caribbean music drifted from
the Palms, where a large open-air thatched-roof bar attracted the
beachcombers like a magnet. From a grass hut nearby they rented
snorkeling gear, catamarans and volleyballs.

Avery walked to the balcony in a pair of brilliant orange-and-
yellow flowered shorts. His body was lean and hard, with no flab. He
owned part interest in a health club in Memphis and worked out
every day. Evidently there were some tanning beds in the club. Mitch
was impressed.

'How do you like my outfit?' Avery asked.

'Very nice. You'll fit right in.'

'I've got another pair if you'd like.'

'No, thanks. I'll stick to my Western Kentucky gym shorts.'

Avery sipped on a drink and took in the scenery. 'I've been here a
dozen times, and I still get excited. I've thought about retiring down
here.'

'That would be nice. You could walk the beach and chase the sand
crabs.'

'And play dominoes and drink Red Stripe. Have you ever had a
Red Stripe?'

'Not that I recall.'

'Let's go get one.'

The open-air bar was called Rumheads. It was packed with thirsty
tourists and a few locals who sat together around a wooden table and
played dominoes. Avery fought through the crowd and returned with
two bottles. They found a seat next to the domino game.

'I think this is what I'll do when I retire. I'll come down here and
play dominoes for a living. And drink Red Stripe.'

'It's good beer.'

'And when I get tired of dominoes, I'll throw some darts.'

'He nodded to a corner where a group of drunk Englishmen were
tossing darts at a board and cursing each other. 'And when I get tired

of darts, well, who knows what I'll do. Excuse me.' He headed for a table on the patio where two string bikinis had just sat down. He introduced himself, and they asked him to have a seat. Mitch ordered another Red Stripe and went to the beach. In the distance he could see the bank buildings of Georgetown. He walked in that direction.

The food was placed on folding tables around the pool. Grilled grouper, barbecue shark, pompano, fried shrimp, turtle and oysters, lobster and red snapper. It was all from the sea, and all fresh. The guests crowded around the tables and served themselves while waiters scurried back and forth with gallons of rum punch. They ate on small tables in the courtyard overlooking Rumheads and the sea. A reggae band tuned up. The sun dipped behind a cloud, then over the horizon.

Mitch followed Avery through the buffet and, as expected, to a table where the two women were waiting. They were sisters, both in their late twenties, both divorced, both half drunk. The one named Carrie had fallen in heat with Avery, and the other one, Julia, immediately began making eyes at Mitch. He wondered what Avery had told them.

'I see you're married,' Julia whispered as she moved next to him.

'Yes, happily.'

She smiled as if to accept the challenge. Avery and his woman winked at each other. Mitch grabbed a glass of punch and gulped it down.

He picked at his food and could think of nothing but Abby. This would be hard to explain, if an explanation became necessary. Having dinner with two attractive women who were barely dressed. It would be impossible to explain. The conversation became awkward at the table, and Mitch added nothing. A waiter set a large pitcher on the table, and it quickly was emptied. Avery became obnoxious. He told the women Mitch had played for the New York Giants, had two Super Bowl rings. Made a million bucks a year before a knee injury ruined his career. Mitch shook his head and drank some more. Julia drooled at him and moved closer.

The band turned up the volume, and it was time to dance. Half the crowd moved to a wooden floor under two trees, between the pool and the beach. 'Let's dance!' Avery yelled, and grabbed his woman. They ran through the tables and were soon lost in the crowd of jerking and lunging tourists.

He felt her move closer, then her hand was on his leg. 'Do you wanna dance?' she asked.

'No.'

'Good. Neither do I. What would you like to do?' She rubbed her breasts on his biceps and gave her best seductive smile, only inches away.

'I don't plan to do anything.' He removed her hand.

'Aw, come on. Let's have some fun. Your wife will never know.'

'Look, you're a very lovely lady, but you're wasting your time with me. It's still early. You've got plenty of time to pick up a real stud.'

'You're cute.'

The hand was back, and Mitch breathed deeply. 'Why don't you get lost.'

'I beg your pardon.' The hand was gone.

'I said, Get lost.''

She backed away. 'What's wrong with you?'

'I have an aversion to communicable diseases. Get lost.'

'Why don't you get lost.'

'That's a wonderful idea. I think I will get lost. Enjoyed dinner.'

Mitch grabbed a glass of rum punch and made his way through the dancers to the bar. He ordered a Red Stripe and sat by himself in a dark corner of the patio. The beach in front of him was deserted. The lights of a dozen boats moved slowly across the water. Behind him were the sounds of the Barefoot Boys and the laughter of the Caribbean night. Nice, he thought, but it would be nicer with Abby. Maybe they would vacation here next summer. They needed time together, away from home and the office. There was a distance between them – distance he could not define. Distance they could not discuss but both felt. Distance he was afraid of.

'What are you watching?' The voice startled him. She walked to the table and sat next to him. She was a native, dark skin with blue or hazel eyes. It was impossible to tell in the dark. But they were beautiful eyes, warm and uninhibited. Her dark curly hair was pulled back and hung almost to her waist. She was an exotic mixture of black, white and probably Latin. And probably more. She wore a white bikini top cut very low and barely covering her large breasts and a long, brightly colored skirt with a slit to the waist that exposed almost everything when she sat and crossed her legs. No shoes.

'Nothing really,' Mitch said.

She was young, with a childish smile that revealed perfect teeth. 'Where are you from?' she asked.

'The States.'

She smiled and chuckled. 'Of course you are. Where in the States?' It was the soft, gentle, precise, confident English of the Caribbean.

'Memphis.'

'A lot of people come here from Memphis. A lot of divers.'

'Do you live here?' he asked.

'Yes. All my life. My mother is a native. My father is from England. He's gone now, back to where he came from.'

'Would you like a drink?' he asked.

'Yes. Rum and soda.'

He stood at the bar and waited for the drinks. A dull, nervous something throbbed in his stomach. He could slide into the darkness, disappear into the crowd and find his way to the safety of the condo. He could lock the door and read a book on international tax havens. Pretty boring. Plus, Avery was there by now with his hot little number. The girl was harmless, the rum and Red Stripe told him. They would have a couple of drinks and say good night.

He returned with the drinks and sat across from the girl, as far away as possible. They were alone on the patio.

'Are you a diver?' she asked.

'No. Believe it or not, I'm here on business. I'm a lawyer, and I have meetings with some bankers in the morning.'

'How long will you be here?'

'Couple of days.' He was polite, but short. The less he said, the safer he would be. She recrossed her legs and smiled innocently. He felt weak.

'How old are you?' he asked.

'I'm twenty, and my name is Eilene. I'm old enough.'

'I'm Mitch.' His stomach flipped and he felt light-headed. He sipped rapidly on his beer. He glanced at his watch.

She watched with that same seductive smile. 'You're very handsome.'

This was unraveling in a hurry. Keep cool, he told himself, just keep cool.

'Thank you.'

'Are you an athlete?'

'Sort of. Why do you ask?'

'You look like an athlete. You're very muscular and firm.' It was the way she emphasized 'firm' that made his stomach flip again. He admired her body and tried to think of some compliment that would not be suggestive. Forget it.

'Where do you work?' he asked, aiming for less sensual areas.

'I'm a clerk in a jewelry store in town.'

'Where do you live?'

'In Georgetown. Where are you staying?'

'A condo next door.' He nodded in the direction, and she looked to her left. She wanted to see the condo, he could tell. She sipped on her drink.

'Why aren't you at the party?' she asked.

'I'm not much on parties.'

'Do you like the beach?'

'It's beautiful.'

'It's prettier in the moonlight.' That smile, again.

He could say nothing to this.

'There's a better bar about a mile down the beach,' she said. 'Let's go for a walk.'

'I don't know, I should get back. I've got some work to do before morning.'

She laughed and stood. 'No one goes in this early in the Caymans. Come on. I owe you a drink.'

'No. I'd better not.'

She grabbed his hand, and he followed her off the patio onto the beach. They walked in silence until the Palms was out of sight and the music was growing dimmer. The moon was overhead and brighter now, and the beach was deserted. She unsnapped something and removed her skirt, leaving nothing but a string around her waist and a string running between her legs. She rolled up her skirt and placed it around his neck. She took his hand.

Something said run. Throw the beer bottle in the ocean. Throw the skirt in the sand. And run like hell. Run to the condo. Lock the door. Lock the windows. Run. Run. Run.

And something said to relax. It's harmless fun. Have a few more drinks. If something happens, enjoy it. No one will ever know. Memphis is a thousand miles away. Avery won't know. And what about Avery? What could he say? Everybody does it. It had happened once before when he was in college, before he was married but after he was engaged. He had blamed it on too much beer, and had survived with no major scars. Time took care of it. Abby would never know.

Run. Run. Run.

They walked for a mile and there was no bar in sight. The beach was darker. A cloud conveniently hid the moon. They had seen no one since Rumheads. She pulled his hand toward two plastic beach chairs next to the water. 'Let's rest,' she said. He finished his beer.

'You're not saying much,' she said.

'What would you like for me to say?'

'Do you think I'm beautiful?'

'You are very beautiful. And you have a beautiful body.'

She sat on the edge of her chair and splashed her feet in the water. 'Let's go for a swim.'

'I, uh, I'm not really in the mood.'

'Come on, Mitch. I love the water.'

'Go ahead. I'll watch.'

She knelt beside him in the sand and faced him, inches away. In slow motion, she reached behind her neck. She unhooked her bikini top, and it fell off, very slowly. Her breasts, much larger now, lay on his left forearm. She handed the top to him. 'Hold this for me.' It was soft and white and weighed less than a millionth of an ounce. He was paralyzed and his breathing, heavy and labored only seconds ago, had now ceased altogether.

She walked slowly into the water. The white string covered nothing from the rear. Her long, dark, beautiful hair hung to her waist. She waded knee deep, then turned to the beach.

'Come on, Mitch. The water feels great.'

She flashed a brilliant smile and he could see it. He rubbed the bikini top and knew this would be his last chance to run. But he was dizzy and weak. Running would require more strength than he could possibly muster. He wanted to just sit and maybe she would go away. Maybe she would drown. Maybe the tide would suddenly materialize and sweep her out to sea.

'Come on, Mitch.'

He removed his shirt and waded into the water. She watched him with a smile, and when he reached her, she took his hand and led him to deeper water. She locked her hands around his neck, and they kissed. He found the strings. They kissed again.

She stopped abruptly and, without speaking, started for the beach. He watched her. She sat on the sand, between the two chairs, and removed the rest of her bikini. He ducked under the water and held his breath for an eternity. When he surfaced, she was reclining, resting on her elbows in the sand. He surveyed the beach and, of course, saw no one. At that precise instant, the moon ducked behind another cloud. There was not a boat or a catamaran or a dinghy or a swimmer or a snorkeler or anything or anybody moving on the water.

'I can't do this,' he muttered through clenched teeth.

'What did you say, Mitch?'

'I can't do this!' he yelled.

'But I want you.'

'I can't do it.'

'Come on, Mitch. No one will ever know.'

No one will ever know. No one will ever know. He walked slowly toward her. No one will ever know.

There was complete silence in the rear of the taxi as the lawyers rode into Georgetown. They were late. They had overslept and missed breakfast. Neither felt particularly well. Avery looked especially haggard. His eyes were bloodshot and his face was pale. He had not shaved.

The driver stopped in heavy traffic in front of the Royal Bank of Montreal. The heat and humidity were already stifling.

Randolph Osgood was the banker, a stuffy British type with a navy double-breasted suit, horn-rimmed glasses, a large shiny forehead and a pointed nose. He greeted Avery like an old friend and introduce himself to Mitch. They were led to a large office on the second floor with a view of Hogsty Bay. Two clerks where waiting.

'Exactly what do you need, Avery?' Osgood asked through his nose.

'Let's start off with some coffee. I need summaries of all the accounts of Sonny Capps, Al Coscia, Dolph Hemmba, Ratzlaff Partners and Greene Group.'

'Yes, and how far back would you like to go?'

'Six months. Every account.'

Osgood snapped his fingers at one of the clerks. She left and returned with a tray of coffee and pastries. The other clerk took notes.

'Of course, Avery, we'll need authorization and powers of attorney for each of these clients,' Osgood said.

'They're on file,' Avery said as he unpacked his briefcase.

'Yes, but they've expired. We'll need current ones. Every account.'

'Very well.' Avery slid a file across the table. 'They're in there. Everything's current.' He winked at Mitch.

A clerk took the file and spread the documents over the table. Each instrument was scrutinized by both clerks, then by Osgood himself. The lawyers drank coffee and waited.

Osgood smiled and said, 'It all appears to be in order. We'll get the records. What else do you need?'

'I need to establish three corporations. Two for Sonny Capps and one for Greene Group. We'll follow the usual procedure. The bank will serve as registered agent, etc.'

'I'll procure the necessary documents,' Osgood said, and looked at a clerk. 'What else?'

'That's all for now.'

'Very well. We should have these records within thirty minutes. Will you be joining me for lunch?'

'I'm sorry, Randolph. I must decline. Mitch and I have a prior commitment. Maybe tomorrow.'

Mitch knew nothing of a prior commitment, at least none he was involved in.

'Perhaps,' replied Osgood. He left the room with the clerks.

Avery closed the door and removed his jacket. He walked to the window and sipped coffee. 'Look, Mitch. I'm sorry about last night. Very sorry. I got drunk and quit thinking. I was wrong to push that woman on you.'

'Apology accepted. Don't let it happen again.'

'It won't. I promise.'

'Was she good?'

'I think so. I don't remember too much. What did you do with her sister?'

'She told me to get lost. I hit the beach and took a walk.'

Avery bit into a pastry and wiped his mouth. 'You know I'm separated. We'll probably get a divorce in a year or so. I'm very discreet because the divorce could get nasty. There's an unwritten rule in the firm – what we do away from Memphis stays away from Memphis. Understand?'

'Come on, Avery. You know I wouldn't tell.'

'I know. I know.'

Mitch was glad to hear of the unwritten rule, although he awakened with the security that he had committed the perfect crime. He had thought of her in bed, the shower, the taxi, and now he had trouble concentrating on anything. He had caught himself looking at jewelry stores when they reached Georgetown.

'I've got a question,' Mitch said.

Avery nodded and ate the pastry.

'When I was recruited a few months ago by Oliver Lambert and McKnight and the gang, it was impressed upon me repeatedly that the firm frowned on divorce, women, booze, drugs, everything but hard work and money. That's why I took the job. I've seen the hard work and money, but now I'm seeing other things. Where did you go wrong? Or do all the guys do it?'

'I don't like your question.'

'I knew you wouldn't. But I'd like an answer. I deserve an answer. I feel like I was misled.'

'So what are you going to do? Leave because I got drunk and laid up with a whore?'

'I haven't thought about leaving.'

'Good. Don't.'

'But I'm entitled to an answer.'

'Okay. Fair enough. I'm the biggest rogue in the firm, and they'll come down hard when I mention the divorce. I chase women now and then, but no one knows it. Or at least they can't catch me. I'm sure it's done by other partners, but you'd never catch them. Not all of them, but a few. Most have very stable marriages and are forever faithful to their wives. I've always been the bad boy, but they've tolerated me because I'm so talented. They know I drink during lunch and sometimes in the office, and they know I violate some more of their sacred rules, but they made me a partner because they need me. And now that I'm a partner, they can't do much about it. I'm not that bad of a guy, Mitch.'

'I didn't say you were.'

'I'm not perfect. Some of them are, believe me. They're machines, robots. They live, eat and sleep for Bendini, Lambert & Locke. I like to have a little fun.'

'So you're the exception –'

'Rather than the rule, yes. And I don't apologize for it.'

'I didn't ask for an apology. Just a clarification.'

'Clear enough?'

'Yes. I've always admired your bluntness.'

'And I admire your discipline. It's a strong man who can remain faithful to his wife with the temptations you had last night. I'm not that strong. Don't want to be.'

Temptations. He had thought of inspecting the downtown jewelry shops during lunch.

'Look, Avery, I'm not a Holy Roller, and I'm not shocked. I'm not one to judge – I've been judged all my life. I was just confused about the rules, that's all.'

'The rules never change. They're cast in concrete. Carved in granite. Etched in stone. Violate too many and you're out. Or violate as many as you want, but just don't get caught.'

'Fair enough.'

Osgood and a group of clerks entered the room with computer printouts and stacks of documents. They made neat piles on the table and alphabetized it all.

'This should keep you busy for a day or so,' Osgood said with a forced smile. He snapped his fingers and the clerks disappeared. 'I'll be in my office if you need something.'

'Yes, thanks,' Avery said as he hovered over the first set of documents. Mitch removed his coat and loosened his tie.

'Exactly what are we doing here?' he asked.

'Two things. First, we'll review the entries into all of these accounts. We're looking primarily for interest earned, what rate, how much, etc. We'll do a rough audit of each account to make sure the interest is going where it is supposed to go. For example, Dolph

Hemmba sends his interest to nine different banks in the Bahamas. It's stupid, but it makes him happy. It's also impossible for anyone to follow, except me. He has about twelve million in this bank, so it's worth keeping up with. He could do this himself, but he feels better if I do it. At two-fifty an hour, I don't mind. We'll check the interest this bank is paying on each account. The rate varies depending on a number of factors. It's discretionary with the bank, and this is a good way to keep them honest.'

'I thought they were honest.'

'They are, but they're bankers, remember.'

'You're looking at close to thirty accounts here, and when we leave we'll know the exact balance, the interest earned and where the interest is going. Second, we have to incorporate three companies under Caymanian jurisdiction. It's fairly easy legal work and could be done in Memphis. But the clients think we must come here to do it. Remember, we're dealing with people who invest millions. A few thousand in legal fees doesn't bother them.'

Mitch flipped through a printout in the Hemmba stack. 'Who's this guy Hemmba? I haven't heard of him.'

'I've got a lot of clients you haven't heard of. Hemmba is a big farmer in Arkansas, one of the state's largest landowners.'

'Twelve million dollars?'

'That's just in this bank.'

'That's a lot of cotton and soybeans.'

'Let's just say he has other ventures.'

'Such as?'

'I really can't say.'

'Legal or illegal?'

'Let's just say he's hiding twenty million plus interest in various Caribbean banks from the IRS.'

'Are we helping him?'

Avery spread the documents on one end of the table and began checking entries. Mitch watched and waited for an answer. The silence grew heavier and it was obvious there would not be one. He could press, but he had asked enough questions for one day. He rolled up his sleeves and went to work.

At noon he learned about Avery's prior commitment. His woman was waiting at the condo for a little rendezvous. He suggested they break for a couple of hours and mentioned a café downtown Mitch could try.

Instead of a café, Mitch found the Georgetown Library four blocks from the bank. On the second floor he was directed to the periodicals, where he found a shelf full of old editions of *The Daily Caymanian*. He dug back six months and pulled the one dated June 27. He laid it on a small table by a window overlooking the street. He glanced out the window, then looked closer. There was a man he had seen only moments earlier on the street by the bank. He was behind the wheel of a battered yellow Chevette parked in a narrow drive across from the library. He was a stocky, dark-haired, foreign-looking type with a gaudy green-and-orange shirt and cheap touristy sunglasses.

The same Chevette with the same driver had been parked in front of the gift shop next to the bank, and now, moments later, it was parked four blocks away. A native on a bicycle stopped next to him and took a cigarette. The man in the car pointed at the library. The native left his bicycle and walked quickly across the street.

Mitch folded the newspaper and stuck it in his coat. He walked past the rows of shelves, found a *National Geographic* and sat down at a table. He studied the magazine and listened carefully as the native climbed the stairs, noticed him, walked behind him, seemed to pause as if to catch a glimpse of what he was reading, then disappeared down the stairs. Mitch waited for a moment, then returned to the window. The native was taking another cigarette and talking to the man in the Chevette. He lit the cigarette and rode away.

Mitch spread the newspaper on the table and scanned the headline story of the two American lawyers and their dive guide who had been killed in a mysterious accident the day before. He made mental notes and returned the paper.

The Chevette was still watching. He walked in front of it, made the block and headed in the direction of the bank. The shopping district was squeezed tightly between the bank buildings and Hogsty Bay. The streets were narrow and crowded with tourists on foot, tourists on scooters, tourists in rented compacts. He removed his coat and ducked into a T-shirt shop with a pub upstairs. He climbed the stairs, ordered a Coke, and sat on the balcony.

Within minutes the native with the bicycle was at the bar drinking a Red Stripe and watching from behind a hand-printed menu.

Mitch sipped on the Coke and scanned the congestion below. No sign of the Chevette, but he knew it was close by. He saw another man stare at him from the street, then disappear. Then a woman. Was he paranoid? Then the Chevette turned the corner two blocks away and moved slowly beneath him.

He went to the T-shirt store and bought a pair of sunglasses. He walked for a block, then darted into an alley. He ran through the dark shade to the next street, then into a gift shop. He left through the back door, into an alley. He saw a large clothing store for tourists and entered though a side door. He watched the street closely and saw nothing. The racks were full of shorts and shirts of all colors – clothes the natives would not buy but the Americans loved. He stayed conservative – white shorts with a red knit pullover. He found a pair of straw sandals that sort of matched the hat he liked. The clerk giggled and showed him to a dressing room. He checked the street again. Nothing. The clothes fit, and he asked her if he could leave his suit and shoes in the back for a couple of hours. 'No problem, mon,' she said. He paid in cash, slipped her a ten and asked her to call a cab. She said he was very handsome.

He watched the street nervously until the cab arrived. He darted across the sidewalk, into the back seat. 'Abanks Dive Lodge,' he said.

'That's a long way, mon.'

Mitch threw a twenty over the seat. 'Get moving. Watch your mirror. If someone is following, let me know.'

He grabbed the money. 'Okay, mon.'

Mitch sat low under his new hat in the back seat as his driver worked his way down Shedden Road, out of the shopping district, around Hogsty Bay, and headed east, past Red Bay, out of the city of Georgetown and onto the road to Bodden Town.

'Who are you running from, mon?'

Mitch smiled and rolled down his window. 'The Internal Revenue Service.' He thought that was cute, but the driver seemed confused. There were no taxes and no tax collectors in the islands, he remembered. The driver continued in silence.

According to the paper, the dive guide was Philip Abanks, son of Barry Abanks, the owner of the dive lodge. He was nineteen when he was killed. The three had drowned when an explosion of some sort hit their boat. A very mysterious explosion. The bodies had been found in eighty feet of water in full scuba gear. There were no witnesses to the explosion and no explanations why it occurred two miles offshore in an area not known for diving. The article said there were many unanswered questions.

Bodden Town was a small village twenty minutes from Georgetown. The dive lodge was south of town on an isolated stretch of beach.

'Did anyone follow us?' Mitch asked.

The driver shook his head.

'Good job. Here's forty bucks.' Mitch looked at his watch. 'It's almost one. Can you be here at exactly two-thirty?'

'No problem, mon.'

The road ended at the edge of the beach and became a white rock parking area shaded by dozens of royal palms. The front building of the lodge was a large, two-story home with a tin roof and an outer stairway leading to the center of the second floor. The Grand House, it was called. It was painted a light blue with neat white trim, and it was partially hidden by bay vines and spider lilies. The handwrought fretwork was painted pink. The solid wooden shutters were olive. It was the office and eating room of Abanks Dive Lodge. To its right the palm trees thinned and a small driveway curved around the Grand House and sloped downward to a large open area of white rock. On each side was a group of a dozen or so thatched-roof huts where divers roomed. A maze of wooden sidewalks ran from the huts to the central point of the lodge, the open-air bar next to the water.

Mitch headed for the bar to the familiar sounds of reggae and laughter. It was similar to Rumheads, but without the crowd. After a few minutes, the bartender, Henry, delivered a Red Stripe to Mitch.

'Where's Barry Abanks?' Mitch asked.

He nodded to the ocean and returned to the bar. Half a mile out, a boat cut slowly through the still water and made its way toward the lodge. Mitch ate the cheeseburger and watched the dominoes.

The boat docked at a pier between the bar and a larger hut with the words DIVE SHOP hand painted over a window. The divers jumped from the boat with their equipment bags and, without exception, headed for the bar. A short, wiry man stood next to the boat and barked orders at the deckhands, who were unloading empty scuba tanks onto the pier. He wore a white baseball cap and not much else. A tiny black pouch covered his crotch and most of his rear end. From the looks of his brown leathery skin he hadn't worn much in the past fifty years. He checked in at the dive shop, yelled at the dive captains and deckhands and made his way to the bar. He ignored the crowd and went to the freezer, where he picked up a Heineken, removed the top and took a long drink.

The bartender said something to Abanks and nodded toward Mitch. He opened another Heineken and walked to Mitch's table.

He did not smile. 'Are you looking for me?' It was almost a sneer.

'Are you Mr. Abanks?'

'That's me. What do you want?'

'I'd like to talk to you for a few minutes.'

He gulped his beer and gazed at the ocean. 'I'm too busy. I have a dive boat leaving in forty minutes.'

'My name is Mitch McDeere. I'm a lawyer from Memphis.'

'Abanks glared at him with tiny brown eyes. Mitch had his attention. 'So?'

'So, the two men who died with your son were friends of mine. It won't take but a few minutes.'

Abanks sat on a stool and rested on his elbows. 'That's not one of my favorite subjects.'

'I know. I'm sorry.'

'The police instructed me not to talk to anyone.'

'It's confidential. I swear.'

Abanks squinted and stared at the brilliant blue water. His face and arms bore the scars of a life at sea, a life spent sixty feet down guiding novices through and around coral reefs and wrecked ships.

'What do you want to know?' he asked softly.

'Can we talk somewhere else?'

'Sure. Let's take a walk.' He yelled at Henry and spoke to a table of divers as he left. They walked on the beach.

'I'd like to talk about the accident.' Mitch said.

'You can ask. I may not answer.'

'What caused the explosion?'

'I don't know. Perhaps an air compressor. Perhaps some fuel. We are not certain. The boat was badly damaged and most of the clues went up in flames.'

'Was it your boat?'

'Yes. One of my small ones. A thirty-footer. Your friends had chartered it for the morning.'

'Where were the bodies found?'

'In eighty feet of water. There was nothing suspicious about the bodies, except that there were no burns or other injuries that would indicate they had been in the explosion. So I guess that makes the bodies very suspicious.'

'The autopsies said they drowned.'

'Yes, they drowned. But your friends were in full scuba gear, which was later examined by one of my divemasters. It worked perfectly. They were good divers.'

'What about your son?'

'He was not in full gear. But he could swim like a fish.'

'Where was the explosion?'

'They had been scheduled to dive along a series of reef formations at Roger's Wreck Point. Are you familiar with the island?'

'No.'

'It's around the East Bay on Northeastern Point. Your friends had never dived there and my son suggested they try it. We knew your friends well. They were experienced divers and took it seriously. They always wanted a boat by themselves and didn't mind paying for it. And they always wanted Philip as their dive captain. We don't know if they made any dives on the Point. The boat was found burning two miles at sea, far from any of our dive sites.'

'Could the boat have drifted?'

'Impossible. If there had been engine trouble, Philip would have used the radio. We have modern equipment, and our divemasters are always in touch with the dive shop. There's no way the explosion could have occurred at the Point. No one saw it or heard it, and there's always someone around. Secondly, a disabled boat could not drift two miles in that water. And, most importantly, the bodies were not on the boat, remember. Suppose the boat did drift, how do you explain the drifting of the bodies eighty feet below. They were found within twenty meters of the boat.'

'Who found them?'

'My men. We caught the bulletin over the radio, and I sent a crew. We knew it was our boat, and my men started diving. They found the bodies within minutes.'

'I know this is difficult to talk about.'

Abanks finished his beer and threw the bottle in a wooden garbage box. 'Yes, it is. But time takes away the pain. Why are you so interested?'

'The families have a lot of questions.'

'I am sorry for them. I met their wives last year. They spent a week with us. Such nice people.'

'Is it possible they were simply exploring new territory when it happened?'

'Possible, yes. But not likely. Our boats report their movements from one dive site to the next. That's standard procedure. No exceptions. I have fired a dive captain for not clearing a site before going to the next. My son was the best captain on the island. He grew up in these waters. He would never fail to report his movements at sea. It's that simple. The police believe that is what happened, but they have to believe something. It's the only explanation they have.'

'But how do they explain the condition of the bodies?'

'They can't. It's simply another diving accident as far as they're concerned.'

'Was it an accident?'

'I think not.'

The sandals had rubbed blisters by now, and Mitch removed them. They turned and started back to the lodge.

'If it wasn't an accident, what was it?'

Abanks walked and watched the ocean crawl along the beach. He smiled for the first time. 'What are the other possibilities?'

'There's a rumor in Memphis that drugs could have been involved.'

'Tell me about this rumor.'

'We've heard that your son was active in a drug ring, that possibly he was using the boat that day to meet a supplier at sea, that there was a dispute and my friends got in the way.'

Abanks smiled again and shook his head. 'Not Philip. To my knowledge he never used drugs, and I know he didn't trade in them. He wasn't interested in money. Just women and diving.'

'Not a chance?'

'No, not a chance. I've never heard this rumor, and I doubt if they know more in Memphis. This is a small island, and I would have heard it by now. It's completely false.'

The conversation was over and they stopped near the bar. 'I'll ask you a favor,' Abanks said. 'Do not mention any of this to the families. I cannot prove what I know to be true, so it's best if no one knows. Especially the families.'

'I won't tell anyone. And I will ask you not to mention our conversation. Someone might follow me here and ask questions about my visit. Just say we talked about diving.'

'As you wish.'

'My wife and I will be here next spring for our vacation. I'll be sure to look you up.'

# CHAPTER FOURTEEN

St. Andrew's Episcopal School was located behind the church of the same name on a densely wooded and perfectly manicured five-acre estate in the middle of midtown Memphis. The white and yellow brick was occasionally visible where the ivy had for some reason turned and pursued another course. Symmetrical rows of clipped boxwoods lined the sidewalks and the small playground. It was a one-story L-shaped building sitting quietly in the shadows of a dozen ancient oaks. Cherished for its exclusivity, St. Andrew's was the most expensive private school in Memphis for grades kindergarten through six. Affluent parents signed the waiting list shortly after birth.

Mitch stopped the BMW in the parking lot between the church and the school. Abby's burgundy Peugeot was three spaces down, sitting innocently. He was unexpected. The plane had landed an hour earlier, and he had stopped by the house to change into something lawyerly. He would see her, then back to his desk for a few hours at one hundred and fifty per hour.

He wanted to see her here, at the school, unannounced. A surprise attack. A countermove. He would say hello. He missed her. He couldn't wait to see her, so he stopped by the school. He would be brief, the first touch and feel and words after that incident on the beach. Could she tell just by looking at him? Maybe she could read his eyes. Would she notice a slight strain in his voice? Not if she was surprised. Not if she was flattered by his visit.

He squeezed the steering wheel and stared at her car. What an idiot! A stupid fool! Why didn't he run? Just throw her skirt in the sand and run like hell. But, of course, he didn't. He said what the hell, no one will ever know. So now he was supposed to shrug it off and say what the hell, everybody does it.

On the plane he laid his plans. First, he would wait until late this night and tell her the truth. He would not lie, had no desire to live a lie. He would admit it and tell her exactly what happened. Maybe she would understand. Why, almost any man – hell, virtually every man would have taken the dive. His next move would depend on her reaction. If she was cool and showed a trace of compassion, he would tell her he was sorry, so very sorry, and that it would never happen again. If she fell all to pieces, he would beg, literally beg for forgiveness and swear on the Bible that it was a mistake and would never happen again. He would tell her how much he loved her and worshipped her, and please just give him one more chance. And if she started packing her bags, he would probably at that point realize he should not have told her.

Deny. Deny. Deny. His criminal-law professor at Harvard had been a radical named Moskowitz, who had made a name for himself defending terrorists and assassins and child fondlers. His theory of defense was simply: Deny! Deny! Deny! Never admit one fact or one piece of evidence that would indicate guilt.

He remembered Moskowitz as they landed in Miami, and began working on Plan B, which called for this surprise visit at the school and a late-night romantic dinner at her favorite place. And no mention of anything but hard work in the Caymans. He opened the car door, thought of her beautiful smiling, trusting face and felt nauseous. A thick, dull pain hammered deep in his stomach. He walked slowly in the late autumn breeze to the front door.

The hallway was empty and quiet. To his right was the office of the headmaster. He waited for a moment in the hall, waited to be seen, but no one was there. He walked quietly ahead until, at the third classroom, he heard the wonderful voice of his wife. She was plowing through multiplication tables when he stuck his head in the door and smiled. She froze, then giggled. She excused herself, told them to stay in their seats and read the next page. She closed the door.

'What're you doing here?' she asked as he grabbed her and pinned her to the wall. She glanced nervously up and down the hall.

'I missed you,' he said with conviction. He bear-hugged her for a good minute. He kissed her neck and tasted the sweetness of her perfume. And then the girl returned. You piece of scum, why didn't you run?

'When did you get in?' she asked, straightening her hair and glancing down the hall.

'About an hour ago. You look wonderful.'

Her eyes were wet. Those wonderfully honest eyes. 'How was your trip?'

'Okay. I missed you. It's no fun when you're not around.'

Her smile widened and she looked away. 'I missed you too.'

They held hands and walked toward the front door. 'I'd like a date tonight,' he said.

'You're not working?'

'No. I'm not working. I'm going out with my wife to her favorite restaurant. We'll eat and drink expensive wine and stay out late, and then get naked when we get home.'

'You did miss me.' She kissed him again, on the lips, then looked down the hall. 'But you better get out of here before someone sees you.'

They walked quickly to the front door without being seen.

He breathed deeply in the cool air and walked quickly to his car. He did it. He looked into those eyes, held her and kissed her like always. She suspected nothing. She was touched and even moved.

DeVasher paced behind his desk and sucked nervously on a Roi-Tan. He sat in his worn swivel chair and tried to concentrate on a memo, then he jumped to his feet and paced again. He checked his watch. He called his secretary. He called Oliver Lambert's secretary. He paced some more.

Finally, seventeen minutes after he was supposed to arrive, Ollie was cleared through security and walked into DeVasher's office.

DeVasher stood behind his desk and glared at Ollie. 'You're late!'

'I'm very busy,' Ollie answered as he sat in a worn Naugahyde chair. 'What's so important?'

DeVasher's face instantly changed into a sly, evil smile. He dramatically opened a desk drawer and proudly threw a large manila envelope across the desk into Ollie's lap. 'Some of the best work we've ever done.'

Lambert opened the envelope and gaped at the eight by ten black-and-white photographs. He stared at each one, holding them inches from his nose, memorizing each detail. DeVasher watched proudly.

Lambert reviewed them again and began breathing heavily. 'These are incredible.'

'Yep. We thought so.'

'Who's the girl?' Ollie asked, still staring.

'A local prostitute. Looks pretty good, doesn't she? We've never used her before, but you can bet we'll use her again.'

'I want to meet her, and soon.'

'No problem. I kinda figured you would.'

'This is incredible. How'd she do it?'

'It looked difficult at first. He told the first girl to get lost. Avery had the other one, but your man wanted no part of her friend. He left and went to that little bar on the beach. That's when our girl there showed up. She's a pro.'

'Where were your people?'

'All over the place. Those were shot from behind a palm tree, about eighty feet away. Pretty good, aren't they?'

'Very good. Give the photographer a bonus. How long did they roll in the sand?'

'Long enough. They were very compatible.'

'I think he really enjoyed himself.'

'We were lucky. The beach was deserted and the timing was perfect.'

Lambert raised the photograph toward the ceiling, in front of his eyes. 'Did you make me a set?' he asked from behind it.

'Of course, Ollie. I know how much you enjoy these things.'

'I thought McDeere would be tougher than that.'

'He's tough, but he's human. He's no dummy either. We're not sure, but we think he knew we were watching him the next day during lunch. He seemed suspicious and began darting around the shopping district. Then he disappeared. He was an hour late for his meeting with Avery at the bank.'

'Where'd he go?'

'We don't know. We were just watching out of curiosity, nothing serious. Hell, he might've been in a bar downtown for all we know. But he just disappeared.'

'Watch him carefully. He worries me.'

DeVasher waved another manila envelope. 'Quit worrying, Ollie. We own him now! He would kill for us if he knew about these.'

'What about Tarrance?'

'Not a sign. McDeeere ain't mentioned it to anybody, at least not to anybody we're listening to. Tarrance is hard to trail sometimes, but I think he's staying away.'

'Keep your eyes open.'

'Don't worry about my end, Ollie. You're the lawyer, the counselor, the esquire, and you get your eight-by-tens. You run the firm. I run the surveillance.'

'How are things at the McDeere house?'

'Not too good. She was very cool to the trip.'

'What'd she do when he was gone?'

'Well, she ain't one to sit around the house. Two nights she and Quin's wife went out to eat at a couple of those yuppie joints. Then to the movies. She was out one night with a schoolteacher friend. She shopped a little.

'She also called her mother a lot, collect. Evidently there's no love lost between our boy and her parents, and she wants to patch things up. She and her mom are tight and it really bothers her because they can't be a big happy family. She wants to go home to Kentucky for Christmas, and she's afraid he won't go for it. There's a lot of friction. A lot of undercurrents. She tells her mom he works too much, and her mom says it's because he wants to show them up. I don't like the sound of it, Ollie. Bad vibes.'

'Just keep listening. We've tried to slow him down, but he's a machine.'

'Yeah, at a hundred and fifty an hour I know you want him to slack off. Why don't you cut all your associates back to forty hours a week so they can spend more time with their families? You could cut your salary, sell a Jag or two, hock your old lady's diamonds, maybe sell your mansion and buy a smaller house by the country club.'

'Shut up, DeVasher.'

Oliver Lambert stormed out of the office. DeVasher turned red with his high-pitched laughter, then, when his office was empty, he locked the photos in a file cabinet. 'Mitchell McDeere,' he said to himself with an immense smile, 'now you are ours.'

# CHAPTER FIFTEEN

On a Friday, at noon, two weeks before Christmas, Abby said good-bye to her students and left St. Andrew's for the holidays. At one, she parked in a lot full of Volvos and BMWs and Saabs and more Peugeots and walked hurriedly through the cold rain into the crowded terrarium where the young affluent gathered to eat quiche and *fajitas* and black bean soup among the plants. This was Kay Quin's current hot spot of the year, and this was the second lunch they'd had in a month. Kay was late, as usual.

It was a friendship still in the initial stages of development. Cautious by nature, Abby had never been one to rush into chumminess with a stranger. The three years at Harvard had been friendless, and she had learned a great deal of independence. In six months in Memphis she had met a handful of prospects at church and one at school, but she moved cautiously.

At first Kay Quin had pushed hard. She was at once a tour guide, shopping consultant and even a decorator. But Abby had moved slowly, learning a little with each visit and watching her new friend carefully. They had eaten several times in the Quin home. They had seen each other at firm dinners and functions, but always in a crowd. And they had enjoyed each other's company over four long lunches at whatever happened to be the hottest gathering place at that moment for the young and beautiful Gold MasterCard holders in Memphis. Kay noticed cars and homes and clothes, but pretended to ignore it all. Kay wanted to be a friend, a close friend, a confidante, and intimate. Abby kept the distance, slowly allowing her in.

The reproduction of a 1950s jukebox sat below Abby's table on the first level near the bar, where a standing-room crowd sipped and waited for tables. After ten minutes and two Roy Orbisons, Kay emerged from the crowd at the front door and looked upward to the third level. Abby smiled and waved.

They hugged and pecked each other properly on the cheeks, without transferring lipstick.

'Sorry I'm late,' Kay said.

'That's okay. I'm used to it.'

'This place is packed,' Kay said, looking around in amazement. It was always packed. 'So you're out of school?'

'Yes. As of an hour ago. I'm free until January 6.'

501

They admired each other's outfits and commented on how slim and in general how beautiful and young they were.

Christmas shopping at once became the topic, and they talked of stores and sales and children until the wine arrived. Abby ordered scampi in a skillet, but Kay stuck with the old fern bar standby of broccoli quiche.

'What're your plans for Christmas?' Kay asked.

'None yet. I'd like to go to Kentucky to see my folks, but I'm afraid Mitch won't go. I've dropped a couple of hints, both of which were ignored.'

'He still doesn't like your parents?'

'There's been no change. In fact, we don't discuss them. I don't know how to handle it.'

'With great caution, I would imagine.'

'Yeah, and great patience. My parents were wrong, but I still need them. It's painful when the only man I've ever loved can't tolerate my parents. I pray every day for a small miracle.'

'Sounds like you need a rather large miracle. Is he working as hard as Lamar says?'

'I don't know how a person could work any harder. It's eighteen hours a day Monday through Friday, eight hours on Saturday, and since Sunday is a day of rest, he puts in only five or six hours. He reserves a little time for me on Sunday.'

'Do I hear a touch of frustration?'

'A lot of frustration, Kay. I've been patient, but it's getting worse. I'm beginning to feel like a widow. I'm tired of sleeping on the couch waiting for him to get home.'

'You're there for food and sex, huh?'

'I wish. He's too tired for sex. It's not a priority anymore. And this is a man who could never get enough. I mean, we almost killed each other in law school. Now, once a week if I'm lucky. He comes home, eats if he has the energy and goes to bed. If I'm really lucky, he might talk to me for a few minutes before he passes out. I'm starved for adult conversation, Kay. I spend seven hours a day with eight-year-olds, and I crave words with more than three syllables. I try to explain this to him and he's snoring. Did you go through this with Lamar?'

'Sort of. He worked seventy hours a week for the first year. I think they all do. It's kind of like initiation into the fraternity. A male ritual in which you have to prove your manliness. But most of them run out of gas after a year, and cut back to sixty or sixty-five hours. They still work hard, but not the kamikaze routine of the rookie year.'

'Does Lamar work every Saturday?'

'Most Saturdays, for a few hours. Never on Sunday. I've put my foot down. Of course, if there's a big deadline or it's tax season, then they all work around the clock. I think Mitch has them puzzled.'

'He's not slowing down any. In fact, he's possessed. Occasionally he won't come home until dawn. Then it's just a quick shower, and back to the office.'

'Lamar says he's already a legend around the office.'

Abby sipped her wine and looked over the rail at the bar. 'That's great. I'm married to a legend.'

'Have you thought about children?'

'It requires sex, remember?'

'Come on, Abby, it can't be that bad.'

'I'm not ready for children. I can't handle being a single parent. I love my husband, but at this point in his life, he would probably have a terribly important meeting and leave me alone in the labor room. Eight centimeters dilated. He thinks of nothing but that damned law firm.'

Kay reached across the table and gently took Abby's hand. 'It'll be okay,' she said with a firm smile and a wise look. 'The first year is the hardest. It gets better, I promise.'

'Abby smiled. 'I'm sorry.'

The waiter arrived with their food, and they ordered more wine. The scampi simmered in the butter-and-garlic sauce and produced a delicious aroma. The cold quiche was all alone on a bed of lettuce with a sickly tomato wedge.

Kay picked a glob of broccoli and chewed on it. 'You know, Abby, the firm encourages children.'

'I don't care. Right now I don't like the firm. I'm competing with the firm, and I'm losing badly. So I couldn't care less what they want. They will not plan my family for me. I don't understand why they are so interested in things which are none of their business. That place is eerie, Kay. I can't put my finger on it, but those people make my skin crawl.'

'They want happy lawyers with stable families.'

'And I want my husband back. They're in the process of taking him away, so the family is not so stable. If they'd get off his back, perhaps we could be normal like everyone else and have a yard full of children. But not now.'

The wine arrived, and the scampi cooled. She ate it slowly and drank her wine. Kay searched for less sensitive areas.

'Lamar said Mitch went to the Caymans last month.'

'Yes. He and Avery were there for three days. Strictly business, or so he says. Have you been there?'

'Every year. It's a beautiful place with gorgeous beaches and warm water. We go in June of each year, when school is out. The firm owns two huge condos right on the beach.'

'Mitch wants to vacation there in March, during my spring break.'

'You need to. Before we had kids, we did nothing but lie on the beach, drink rum and have sex. That's one reason the firm furnishes the condos and, if you're lucky, the airplane. They work hard, but they appreciate the need for leisure.'

'Don't mention the firm to me, Kay, I don't want to hear about what they like or dislike, or what they do or don't do, or what they encourage or discourage.'

'It'll get better, Abby. I promise. You must understand that your husband and my husband are both very good lawyers, but they could not earn this kind of money anywhere else. And you and I would be driving new Buicks instead of new Peugeots and Mercedes-Benzes.'

Abby cut a shrimp in half and rolled it through the butter and garlic. She stabbed a portion with a fork, then pushed her plate away. The wineglass was empty. 'I know, Kay, I know. but there is a hell of a lot more to life than a big yard and a Peugeot. No one around here seems to be aware of that. I swear, I think we were happier living in a two-room student apartment in Cambridge.'

'You've only been here a few months. Mitch will slow down eventually, and you'll get into your routine. Before long there will be little McDeeres running around the backyard, and before you know it, Mitch will be a partner. Believe me, Abby, things will get better. You're going through a period we've all been through, and we made it.'

'Thanks, Kay, I certainly hope you're right.'

The park was a small one, two or three acres on a bluff above the river. A row of cannons and two bronze statues memorialized those brave Confederates who had fought to save the river and the city. Under the monument to a general and his horse a wino tucked himself away. His cardboard box and ragged quilt provided little shelter from the bitter cold and the tiny pellets of frozen rain. Fifty yards below, the evening traffic rushed along Riverside Drive. It was dark.

Mitch walked to the row of cannons and stood gazing at the river and the bridges leading to Arkansas. He zipped his raincoat and flipped the collar around his ears. He looked at his watch. He waited.

The Bendini Building was almost visible six blocks away. He had parked in a garage in midtown and taken a taxi back to the river. He was sure he had not been followed. He waited.

The icy wind blowing up from the river reddened his face and reminded him of the winters in Kentucky after his parents were gone. Cold, bitter winters. Lonely, desolate winters. He had worn someone else's coats, passed down from a cousin or a friend, and they had never been heavy enough. Secondhand clothes. He dismissed those thoughts.

The frozen rain turned to sleet and the tiny pieces of ice stuck in his hair and bounced on the sidewalk around him. He looked at his watch.

There were footsteps and a figure in a hurry walking toward the cannons. Whoever it was stopped, then approached slowly.

'Mitch?' It was Eddie Lomax, dressed in jeans and a full-length rabbit coat. With his thick mustache and white cowboy hat he looked like an ad for a cigarette. The Marlboro Man.

'Yeah, it's me.'

Lomax walked closer, to the other side of the cannon. They stood like Confederate sentries watching the river.

'Have you been followed?' Mitch asked.

'No, I don't think so. You?'

'No.'

Mitch stared at the traffic on Riverside Drive, and beyond, to the river. Lomax thrust his hands deep into his pockets. 'You talked to Ray, lately?' Lomax asked.

'No.' The answer was short, as if to say, 'I'm not standing here in the sleet to chitchat.'

'What'd you find?' Mitch asked, without looking.

Lomax lit a cigarette, and now he *was* the Marlboro Man. 'On the three lawyers, I found a little info. Alice Knauss was killed in a car wreck in 1977. Police report said she was hit by a drunk driver, but oddly enough, no such driver was ever found. The wreck happened around midnight on a Wednesday. She had worked late down at the office and was driving home. She lived out east, in Sycamore View, and about a mile from her condo she gets hit head-on by a one-ton pickup. Happened on New London Road. She was driving a fancy little Fiat and it was blown to pieces. No witnesses. When the cops got there, the truck was empty. No sign of a driver. They ran the plates and found that the truck had been stolen in St. Louis three days earlier. No fingerprints or nothing.'

'They dusted for prints?'

'Yeah. I know the investigator who handled it. They were suspicious but had zero to go on. There was a broken bottle of whiskey on the floorboard, so they blamed it on a drunk driver and closed the file.'

'Autopsy?'

'No. It was pretty obvious how she died.'

'Sounds suspicious.'

'Very much so. All three of them are suspicious. Robert Lamm was the deer hunter in Arkansas. He and some friends had a deer camp in Izard County in the Ozarks. They went over two or three times a year during the season. After a morning in the woods, everyone returned to the cabin but Lamm. They searched for two weeks and found him in a ravine, partially covered with leaves. He had been shot once through the head, and that's about all they know. They ruled out suicide, but there was simply no evidence to begin an investigation.'

'So he was murdered?'

'Apparently so. Autopsy showed an entry at the base of the skull and an exit wound that removed most of his face. Suicide would have been impossible.'

'It could have been an accident.'

'Possibly. He could have caught a bullet intended for a deer, but it's unlikely. He was found a good distance from the camp, in an area seldom used by hunters. His friends said they neither heard nor saw other hunters the morning he disappeared. I talked to the sheriff, who is now the ex-sheriff, and he's convinced it was murder. He claims there was evidence that the body had been covered intentionally.'

'Is that all?'

'Yeah, on Lamm.'

'What about Mickel?'

'Pretty sad. He committed suicide in 1984 at the age of thirty-four. Shot himself in the right temple with a Smith & Wesson .357. He left a lengthy farewell letter in which he told his ex-wife he hoped she would forgive him and all that crap. Said goodbye to the kids and his mother. Real touching.'

'Was it his handwriting?'

'Not exactly. It was typed, which was not unusual, because he typed a good bit. He had an IBM Selectric in his office, and the letter came from it. He had a terrible handwriting.'

'So what's suspicious?'

'The gun. He never bought a gun in his life. No one knows where it came from. No registration, no serial number, nothing. One of his friends in the firm allegedly said something to the effect that Mickel had told him he had bought a gun for protection. Evidently he was having some emotional problems.'

'What do you think?'

Lomax threw his cigarette butt in the frozen rain on the sidewalk. He cupped his hands over his mouth and blew in them. 'I don't know. I can't believe a tax lawyer with no knowledge of guns could obtain one without registration or serial number. If a guy like that wanted a gun, he would simply go to a gun shop, fill out the papers and buy a nice, shiny new piece. This gun was at least ten years old and had been sanitized by professionals.'

'Did the cops investigate?'

'Not really. It was open and shut.'

'Did he sign the letter?'

'Yeah, but I don't know who verified the signature. He and his wife had been divorced for a year, and she had moved back to Baltimore.'

Mitch buttoned the top button of his overcoat and shook the ice from his collar. The sleet was heavier, and the sidewalk was covered. Tiny icicles were beginning to form under the barrel of the cannon. The traffic slowed on Riverside as wheels began to slide and spin.

'So what do you think of our little firm?' Mitch asked as he stared at the river in the distance.

'It's a dangerous place to work. They've lost five lawyers in the past fifteen years. That's not a very good safety record.'

'Five?'

'If you include Hodge and Kozinski. I've got a source telling me there are some unanswered questions.'

'I didn't hire you to investigate those two.'

'And I'm not charging you for it. I got curious, that's all.'

'How much do I owe you?'

'Six-twenty.'

'I'll pay cash. No records, okay?'

'Suits me. I prefer cash.'

Mitch turned from the river and gazed at the tall buildings three blocks from the park. He was cold now, but in no hurry to leave. Lomax watched him from the corner of his eye.

'You've got problems, don't you, pal?'

'Wouldn't you say so?' Mitch answered.

'I wouldn't work there. I mean, I don't know all that you do, and I suspect you know a lot you're not telling. But we're standing here in the sleet because we don't want to be seen. We can't talk on the phone. We can't meet in your office. Now you don't want to meet in my office. You think you're being followed all the time. You tell me to be careful and watch my rear because they, whoever they are, may be following me. You've got five lawyers in that firm who've died under very suspicious circumstances, and you act like you may be next. Yeah, I'd say you got problems. Big problems.'

'What about Tarrance?'

'One of the best agents; transferred in here about two years ago.'

'From where?'

'New York.'

The wino rolled from under the bronze horse and fell to the sidewalk. He grunted, staggered to his feet, retrieved his cardboard box and quilt and left in the direction of downtown. Lomax jerked around and watched anxiously. 'It's just a tramp,' Mitch said. They both relaxed.

'Who are we hiding from?' Lomax asked.

'I wish I knew.'

Lomax studied his face carefully. 'I think you know.'

Mitch said nothing.

'Look, Mitch, you're not paying me to get involved. I realize that. But my instincts tell me you're in trouble, and I think you need a friend, someone to trust. I can help, if you need me. I don't know who the bad guys are, but I'm convinced they're very dangerous.'

'Thanks,' Mitch said softly without looking, as if it was time for Lomax to leave and let him stand there in the sleet for a while.

'I would jump in that river for Ray McDeere, and I can certainly help his little brother.'

Mitch nodded slightly, but said nothing. Lomax lit another cigarette and kicked the ice from his lizard-skins. 'Just call me anytime. And be careful. They're out there, and they play for keeps.'

# CHAPTER SIXTEEN

At the intersection of Madison and Cooper in midtown, the old two-story buildings had been renovated into singles bars and watering holes and gift shops and a handful of good restaurants. The intersection was known as Overton Square, and it provided Memphis with its best nightlife. A playhouse and a bookstore added a touch of culture. Trees lined the narrow median on Madison. The weekends were rowdy with college students and sailors from the Navy base, but on week nights the restaurants were full but quiet and uncrowded. Paulette's, a quaint French place in a white stucco building, was noted for its wine list and desserts and the gentle voice of the man at the Steinway. With sudden affluence came a collection of credit cards, and the McDeeres had used theirs in a quest for the best restaurants in town. Paulette's was the favorite, so far.

Mitch sat in the corner of the bar, drinking coffee and watching the front door. He was early, and had planned it that way. He had called her three hours earlier and asked if he could have a date for seven. She asked why, and he said he would explain later. Since the Caymans he had known someone was following, watching, listening. For the past month he had spoken carefully on the phone, had caught himself watching the rearview mirror, had even chosen his words around the house. Someone was watching and listening, he was sure.

Abby rushed in from the cold and glanced around the parlor for her husband. He met her in the front of the bar and pecked her on the cheek. She removed her coat, and they followed the maître d' to a small table in a row of small tables which were all full with people within earshot. Mitch glanced around for another table, but there were none. He thanked him and sat across from his wife.

'What's the occasion?' she asked suspiciously.

'Do I need a reason to have dinner with my wife?'

'Yes. It's seven o'clock on Monday night, and you're not at the office. This is indeed a special occasion.'

A waiter squeezed between their table and the next, and asked if they wanted a drink. Two white wines, please. Mitch glanced around the dining room again and caught a glimpse of a gentleman sitting alone five tables away. The face looked familiar. When Mitch looked again, the face slid behind a menu.

'What's the matter, Mitch?'

He laid his hand on hers and frowned. 'Abby, we gotta talk.'

Her hand flinched slightly and she stopped smiling. 'About what?'

He lowered his voice. 'About something very serious.'

She exhaled deeply and said, 'Can we wait for the wine? I might need it.'

Mitch looked again at the face behind the menu. 'We can't talk here.'

'Then why are we here?'

'Look, Abby, you know where the rest rooms are? Down the hall over there, to your right?'

'Yes, I know.'

'There's a rear entrance at the end of the hall. It goes out to the side street behind the restaurant. I want you to go to the rest room, then out the door. I'll be waiting next to the street.'

She said nothing. Her eyebrows lowered and the eyes narrowed. Her head leaned slightly to the right.

'Trust me, Abby. I can explain later. I'll meet you outside and we'll find another place to eat. I can't talk in here.'

'You're scaring me.'

'Please,' he said firmly, squeezing her hand. 'Everything is fine. I'll bring your coat.'

She stood with her purse and left the room. Mitch looked over his shoulder at the man with the familiar face, who suddenly stood and welcomed an elderly lady to his table. He did not notice Abby's exit.

In the street behind Paulette's, Mitch draped the coat over Abby's shoulders and pointed eastward. 'I can explain,' he said more than once. A hundred feet down the street, they walked between two buildings and came to the front entrance of the Bombay Bicycle Club, a singles bar with good food and live blues. Mitch looked at the headwaiter, then surveyed the two dining rooms, then pointed to a table in the rear corner. 'That one,' he said.

Mitch sat with his back to the wall and his face toward the dining room and the front door. The corner was dark. Candles lit the table. They ordered more wine.

Abby sat motionless, staring at him, watching every move and waiting.

'Do you remember a guy named Rick Acklin from Western Kentucky?'

'No,' she said without moving her lips.

'He played baseball, lived in the dorm. I think you may have met him once. A very nice guy, real clean-cut, good student. I think he was from Bowling Green. We weren't good friends, but we knew each other.'

She shook her head and waited.

'Well, he finished a year before we did and went to law school at Wake Forest. Now he's with the FBI. And he's working here in Memphis.' He watched her closely to see if 'FBI' would have an impact. It did not. 'And today I'm eating lunch at Obloe's hot-dog place on Main Street, when Rick walks up out of nowhere and says hello. Just like it was a real coincidence. We chat for a few minutes, and another agent, guy by the name of Tarrance, walks up and has a seat. It's the second time Tarrance has chased me down since I passed the bar.'

'The second . . . ?'

'Yes. Since August.'

'And these are . . . FBI agents?'

'Yes, with badges and everything. Tarrance is a veteran agent from New York. Been here about two years. Acklin is a rookie they brought in three months ago.'

'What do they want?'

The wine arrived and Mitch looked around the club. A band was tuning up on a small stage in a far corner. The bar was crowded with well-dressed professional types chitting and chatting relentlessly. The waiter pointed to the unopened menus. 'Later,' Mitch said rudely.

'Abby, I don't know what they want. The first visit was in August, right after my name was printed in the paper for passing the bar.' He sipped his wine and detailed play by play the first Tarrance visit at Lansky's Deli on Union, the warnings about whom not to trust and where not to talk, the meeting with Locke and Lambert and the other partners. He explained their version of why the FBI was so interested in the firm and said that he discussed it with Lamar and believed every word Lock and Lambert had said.

Abby hung on every word, but waited to start asking.

'And now, today, while I'm minding my own business, eating a foot-long with onions, this guy I went to college with walks up and tells me that they, the FBI, know for a fact that my phones are bugged, my home is wired and somebody down at Bendini, Lambert & Locke knows when I sneeze and take a crap. Think of it, Abby, Rick Acklin was transferred here after I passed the bar exam. Nice coincidence, huh?'

'But what do they want?'

'They won't say. They can't tell me, yet. They want me to trust them, and all that routine. I don't know, Abby. I have no idea what they're after. But they've chosen me for some reason.'

'Did you tell Lamar about this visit?'

'No. I haven't told anyone. Except you. And I don't plan to tell anyone.'

She gulped the wine. 'Our phones are tapped?'

'According to the FBI. But how do they know?'

'They're not stupid, Mitch. If the FBI told me my phones were tapped, I'd believe them. You don't?'

'I don't know whom to believe. Locke and Lambert were so smooth and believable when they explained how the firm fights with the IRS and the FBI. I want to believe them, but so much of it doesn't add up. Look at it this way – if the firm had a rich client who was shady and worthy of FBI scrutiny, why would the FBI pick me, the rookie, the one who knows the least, and begin following me? What do I know? I work on files someone else hands me. I have no clients of my own. I do as I'm told. Why not go after one of the partners?'

'Maybe they want you to squeal on the clients.'

'No way. I'm a lawyer and sworn to secrecy about the affairs of clients. Everything I know about a client is strictly confidential. The feds know that. No one expects a lawyer to talk about his clients.'

'Have you seen any illegal deals?'

He cracked his knuckles and gazed around the dining room. He smiled at her. The wine had settled and was taking effect. 'I'm not supposed to answer that question, even from you, Abby. But the answer is no. I've worked on files for twenty of Avery's clients and a few other ones here and there, and I've seen nothing suspicious. Maybe a couple of risky tax shelters, but nothing illegal. I've got a few questions about the bank accounts I saw in the Caymans, but nothing serious.' Caymans! His stomach dropped as he thought of the girl on the beach. He felt sick.

The waiter loitered nearby and stared at the menus. 'More wine,' Mitch said, pointing at the glasses.

Abby leaned forward, near the candles, and looked bewildered. 'Okay, who tapped our phones?'

'Assuming they're tapped, I have no idea. At the first meeting in August, Tarrance implied it was someone from the firm. I mean, that's the way I took it. He said not to trust anyone at the firm, and that everything I said was subject to being heard and recorded. I assumed he meant they were doing it.'

'And what did Mr. Locke say about that?'

'Nothing. I didn't tell him. I kept a few things to myself.'

'Someone has tapped our phones and wired our house?'

'And maybe our cars. Rick Acklin made a big deal of it today. He kept telling me not to say anything I didn't want recorded.'

'Mitch, this is incredible. Why would a law firm do that?'

He shook his head slowly and looked into the empty wineglass. 'I have no idea, babe. No idea.'

The waiter set two new wineglasses on the table and stood with his hands behind him. 'Will you be ordering?' he asked.

'In a few minutes,' Abby said.

'We'll call you when we're ready,' Mitch added.

'Do you believe it, Mitch?'

'I think something's up. There's more to the story.'

She slowly folded her hands on the table and stared at him with a look of utter fear. He told the story of Hodge and Kozinski, starting with Tarrance at the deli, then to the Caymans and being followed and the meeting with Abanks. He told her everything Abanks had said. Then Eddie Lomax and the deaths of Alice Knauss, Robert Lamm and John Mickel.

'I've lost my appetite,' she said when he finished.

'So have I. But I feel better now that you know.'

'Why didn't you tell me sooner?'

'I hoped it would go away. I hoped Tarrance would leave me alone and find someone else to torment. But he's here to stay. That's why Rick Acklin was transferred to Memphis. To work on me. I have been selected by the FBI for a mission I know nothing about.'

'I feel weak.'

'We have to be careful, Abby. We must continue to live as if we suspect nothing.'

'I don't believe this. I'm sitting here listening to you, but I don't believe what you're telling me. This is not real, Mitch. You expect me to live in a house that's wired and the phones are tapped and someone, somewhere is listening to everything we say.'

'Do you have a better idea?'

'Yeah. Let's hire this Lomax guy to inspect our house.'

'I've thought of that. But what if he finds something? Think about it. What if we know for sure the house is wired? What then? What if he breaks a device that's been planted? They, whoever in hell they are, will know that we know. It's too dangerous, for now anyway. Maybe later.'

'This is crazy, Mitch. I guess we're supposed to run out in the backyard to have a conversation.'

'Of course not. We could use the front yard.'

'At this moment, I don't appreciate your sense of humor.'

'Sorry. Look, Abby, let's be normal and patient for a while. Tarrance has convinced me he's serious and he's not going to forget about me. I can't stop him. He finds me, remember. I think they follow me and wait in ambush. For the time being, it's important that we carry on as usual.'

'Usual? Come to think of it, there's not much conversation around the house these days. I sort of feel sorry for them if they're waiting to hear meaningful dialogue. I talk to Hearsay a lot.'

# CHAPTER SEVENTEEN

The snow cleared long before Christmas, leaving the ground wet and making way for the traditional Southern holiday weather of gray skies and cold rain. Memphis had seen two white Christmases in the past ninety years, and the experts predicted no more in the century.

There was snow in Kentucky, but the roads were clear. Abby called her parents early Christmas morning after she packed. She was coming, she said, but she would be alone. They were disappointed, they said, and suggested that perhaps she should stay if it was causing trouble. She insisted. It was a ten-hour drive. Traffic would be light, and she would be there by dark.

Mitch said very little. He spread the morning paper on the floor next to the tree and pretended to concentrate as she loaded her car. The dog hid nearby under a chair, as if waiting for an explosion. Their gifts had been opened and arranged neatly on the couch. Clothes and perfume and albums, and for her, a full-length fox coat. For the first time in the young marriage, there was money to spend at Christmas.

She draped the coat over her arm and walked to the paper. 'I'm leaving now,' she said softly, but firmly.

He stood slowly and looked at her.

'I wish you would come with me,' she said.

'Maybe next year.' It was a lie, and they knew it. But it sounded good. It was promising.

'Please be careful.'

'Take care of my dog.'

'We'll be fine.'

He took her shoulders and kissed her on the cheek. He looked at her and smiled. She was beautiful, much more so than when they married. At twenty-four, she looked her age, but the years were becoming very generous.

They walked to the carport, and he helped her into the car. They kissed again, and she backed down the driveway.

Merry Christmas, he said to himself. Merry Christmas, he said to the dog.

After an hour of watching the walls, he threw two changes of clothes in the BMW, placed Hearsay in the front seat and left town. He drove south on Interstate 55, out of Memphis, into Mississippi. The road was deserted, but he kept an eye on the rearview mirror. The dog whimpered precisely every sixty minutes, and Mitch would stop on the shoulder – if possible, just over a hill. He would find a cluster of trees where he could hide and watch the traffic while Hearsay did his business. He noticed nothing. After five stops, he was sure he was not being followed. They evidently took off Christmas Day.

In six hours he was in Mobile, and two hours later he crossed the bay at Pensacola and headed for the Emerald Coast of Florida. Highway 98 ran through the coastal towns of Navarre, Fort Walton Beach, Destin and Sandestin. It encountered clusters of condominiums and motels, miles of shopping centers, then strings of run-down amusement parks and low rent T-shirt shops, most of which had been locked and neglected since Labor Day. Then it went for miles with no congestion, no sprawl, just an awesome view of the snowy-white beaches and brilliant emerald waters of the Gulf. East of Sandestin, the highway narrowed and left the coast, and for an hour he drove alone on the two-lane with nothing to look at but the woods and an occasional self-serve gas station or quick-shop convenience store.

At dusk, he passed a high rise, and a sign said Panama City Beach was eight miles ahead. The highway found the coast again at a point where it forked and offered a choice between the bypass to the north and the scenic route straight ahead on what was called the Miracle Strip. He chose the scenic route next to the beach – the strip that ran for fifteen miles by the water and was lined on both sides with condos, cheap motels, trailer parks, vacation cottages, fast-food joints and T-shirt shops. This was Panama City Beach.

Most of the ten zillion condos were empty, but there were a few cars parked about and he assumed that some families vacationed on the beach for Christmas. A hot-weather Christmas. At least they're together, he said to himself. The dog barked, and they stopped by a pier where men from Pennsylvania and Ohio and Canada fished and watched the dark waters.

They cruised the Miracle Strip by themselves. Hearsay stood on the door and took in the sights, barking at the occasional flashing neon of a cinder-block motel advertising its openness and cheap rates. Christmas on the Miracle Strip closed everything but a handful of diehard coffee shops and motels.

He stopped for gas at an all-night Texaco with a clerk who seemed uncommonly friendly.

'San Luis Street?' Mitch asked.

'Yes, yes,' the clerk said with an accent and pointed to the west. 'Second traffic light to the right. First left. That's San Luis.'

The neighborhood was a disorganized suburb of antique mobile homes. Mobile, yes, but it was apparent they had not moved in decades. The trailers were packed tightly together like rows of dominoes. The short, narrow driveways seemed inches apart and were filled with old pickups and rusted lawn furniture. The streets were crowded with parked cars, junk cars, abandoned cars. Motorcycles and bicycles leaned on the trailer hitches and lawn-mower handles protruded from beneath each home. A sign called the place a retirement village – 'San Pedro Estates – A Half Mile from the Emerald Coast.' It was more like a slum on wheels, or a project with a trailer hitch.

He found San Luis Street and suddenly felt nervous. It was winding and narrow with smaller trailers in worse shape than the other 'retirement homes'. He drove slowly, anxiously watching street numbers and observing the multitude of out-of-state license plates. The street was empty except for the parked and abandoned cars.

The home at 486 San Luis was one of the oldest and smallest. It was scarcely bigger than a camper. The original paint job looked to be silver, but the paint was cracked and peeling, and a dark green layer of mold covered the top and inched downward to a point just above the windows. The screens were missing. One window above the trailer hitch was badly cracked and held together with gray electrical tape. A small covered porch surrounded the only entrance. The storm door was open, and through the screen Mitch could see a small color television and the silhouette of a man walking by.

This was not what he wanted. By choice, he had never met his mother's second husband, and now was not the time. He drove on, wishing he had not come.

He found on the Strip the familiar marquee of a Holiday Inn. It was empty, but open. He hid the BMW away from the highway, and registered under the name of Eddie Lomax of Danesboro, Kentucky. He paid cash for a single room with an ocean view.

The Panama City Beach phone book listed three Waffle Huts on the Strip. He lay across the motel bed and dialed the first number. No luck. He dialed the second number, and again asked for Ida Ainsworth. Just a minute, he was told. He hung up. It was 11 P.M. He had slept for two hours.

The taxi took twenty minutes to arrive at the Holiday Inn, and the driver began by explaining that he had been home enjoying leftover turkey with his wife and kids and kinfolks when the dispatcher called, and how it was Christmas and he hoped to be with his family all day and not worry about work for one day of the year. Mitch threw a twenty over the seat and asked him to be quiet.

'What's at the Waffle Hut, man?' the driver asked.

'Just drive.'

'Waffles, right?' He laughed and mumbled to himself. He adjusted the radio volume and found his favorite soul station. He glanced in the mirror, looked out the windows, whistled a bit, then said, 'What brings you down here on Christmas?'

'Looking for someone.'

'Who?'

'A woman.'

'Ain't we all. Anyone in particular?'

'An old friend.'

'She at the Waffle Hut?'

'I think so.'

'You some kinda private eye or something?'

'No.'

'Seems mighty suspicious to me.'

'Why don't you just drive.'

The Waffle Hut was a small, rectangular, boxlike building with a dozen tables and a long counter facing the grill, where everything was cooked in the open. Large plate-glass windows lined one side next to the tables so the customers could take in the Strip and the condos in the distance while they enjoyed their pecan waffles and bacon. The small parking lot was almost full, and Mitch directed the driver to an empty slot near the building.

'Ain't you getting out?' the driver asked.

'No. Keep the meter running.'

'Man, this is strange.'

'You'll get paid.'

'You got that right.'

Mitch leaned forward and rested his arms on the front seat. The meter clicked softly and he studied the customers inside. The driver shook his head, slumped in the seat, but watched out of curiosity.

In the corner, next to the cigarette machine a table of fat tourists with long shirts, white legs and blacke socks drank coffee, and all talked at the same time while glancing at the menus. The leader, the one with an unbuttoned shirt, a heavy gold chain draped upon his chest hair, thick gray sideburns and a Phillies baseball cap, looked repeatedly toward the grill, in search of a waitress.

'You see her?' asked the driver.

Mitch said nothing, then leaned forward and frowned. She appeared from nowhere and stood at the table with her pen and order book. The leader said something funny, and the fat people laughed. She never smiled, just kept writing. She was frail and much thinner. Almost too thin. The black-and-white uniform fit snugly and squeezed her tiny waist. Her gray hair was pulled tightly and hidden under the Waffle Hut bonnet. She was fifty-one, and from the distance she looked her age. Nothing worse. She seemed sharp. When she finished scribbling she snatched the menus from their hands, said something polite, almost smiled, then disappeared. She moved quickly among the tables, pouring coffee, handing ketchup bottles and giving orders to the cook.

Mitch relaxed. The meter ticked slowly.

'Is that her?' asked the driver.

'Yes.'

'What now?'

'I don't know.'

'Well, we found her, didn't we?'

Mitch followed her movements and said nothing. She poured coffee for a man sitting alone. He said something, and she smiled. A wonderful, gracious smile. A smile he had seen a thousand times in the darkness staring at the ceiling. His mother's smile.

A light mist began to fall and the intermittent wipers cleaned the windshield every ten seconds. It was almost midnight, Christmas Day.

The driver tapped the wheel nervously and fidgeted. He sank lower in the seat, then changed stations. 'How long we gonna sit here?'

'Not long.'

'Man, this is weird.'

'You'll be paid.'

'Man, money ain't everything. It's Christmas. I got kids at home, kinfolks visiting, turkey and wine to finish off, and here I am sitting at the Waffle Hut so you can look at some old woman through the window.'

'It's my mother.'

'Your what!'

'You heard me.'

'Man, oh man. I get all kinds.'

'Just shut up, okay?'

'Okay. Ain't you gonna talk to her? I mean it's Christmas, and you found your momma. You gotta go see her, don't you?'

'No. Not now.'

Mitch sat back in the seat and looked at the dark beach across the highway. 'Let's go.'

At daybreak, he dressed in jeans and a sweatshirt, no socks or shoes, and took Hearsay for a walk on the beach. They walked east, toward the first glow of orange peeking above the horizon. The waves broke gently thirty yards out and rolled quietly onto shore. The sand was cool and wet. The sky was clear and full of sea gulls talking incessantly among themselves. Hearsay ran boldly into the sea, then retreated furiously when the next wave of white foam approached. For a house dog, the endless stretch of sand and water demanded exploration. He ran a hundred yards ahead of Mitch.

After two miles they approached a pier, a large concrete structure running two hundred feet from the beach into the ocean. Hearsay, fearless now, darted onto it and ran to a bucket of bait next to two men standing motionless and staring down at the water. Mitch walked behind them, to the end of the pier, where a dozen fishermen talked occasionally to each other and waited for their lines to jump. The dog rubbed himself on Mitch's leg and grew still. A brilliant return of the sun was in progress, and for miles the water glistened and turned from black to green.

Mitch leaned on the railing and shivered in the cool wind. His bare feet were frozen and gritty. For miles along the beach in both directions, the hotels and condos sat quietly and waited for the day. There was no one on the beach. Another pier jutted into the water miles away.

The fishermen spoke with the sharp, precise words of those from the North. Mitch listened long enough to learn the fish were not biting. He studied the sea. Looking southeast, he thought of the Caymans, and Abanks. And the girl for a moment, then she was gone. He would return to the islands in March, for a vacation with his wife. Damn the girl. Surely he would not see her. He would dive with Abanks and cultivate a friendship. They would drink Heineken and Red Stripe at his bar and talk of Hodge and Kozinski. He would follow whoever was following him. Now that Abby was an accomplice, she would assist him.

The man waited in the dark beside the Lincoln Town Car. He nervously checked his watch and glanced at the dimly lit sidewalk that disappeared in front of the building. On the second floor a light was turned off. A minute later, the private eye walked from the building toward the car. The man walked up to him.

'Are you Eddie Lomax?' he asked anxiously.

Lomax slowed, then stopped. They were face to face. 'Yeah. Who are you?'

The man kept his hands in his pockets. It was cold and damp, and he was shaking. 'Al Kilbury. I need some help, Mr. Lomax. Real bad. I'll pay you right now in cash, whatever you want. Just help me.'

'It's late, pal.'

'Please. I've got the money. Name the price. You gotta help, Mr. Lomax.' He pulled a roll of cash from his left pants pocket and stood ready to count.

Lomax looked at the money, then glanced over his shoulder. 'What's the problem?'

'My wife. In an hour she's supposed to meet a man at a motel in South Memphis. I've got the room number and all. I just need you to go with me and take pictures of them coming and going.'

'How do you know this?'

'Phone taps. She works with the man, and I've been suspicious. I'm a wealthy man, Mr. Lomax, and it's imperative I win the divorce. I'll pay you a thousand in cash now.' He quickly peeled off ten bills and offered them.

Lomax took the money. 'Okay. Let me get my camera.'

'Please hurry. Everything's in cash okay? No records.'

'Suits me,' said Lomax as he walked toward the building.

Twenty minutes later, the Lincoln rolled through the crowded parking lot of a Days Inn. Kilbury pointed to a second-floor room on the back side of the motel, then to a parking space next to a brown Chevy van. Lomax backed carefully alongside the van and parked his Town Car. Kilbury again pointed to the room, again checked his watch and again told Lomax how much he appreciated his services. Lomax thought of the money. A thousand bucks for two hours' work. Not bad. He unpacked a camera, loaded the film and gauged the light. Kilbury watched nervously, his eyes darting from the camera to the room across the parking lot. He looked hurt. He talked of his wife and their wonderful years together, and why, oh why was she doing this?

Lomax listened and watched the rows of parked cars in front of him. He held his camera.

He did not notice the door of the brown van. It quietly and slowly slid open, just three feet behind him. A man in a black turtleneck wearing black gloves crouched low in the van and waited. When the parking lot was still, he jumped from the van, yanked open the left rear door of the Lincoln and fired three times into the back of Eddie's head. The shots, muffled with a silencer, could not be heard outside the car.

Eddie slumped against the wheel, already dead. Kilbury bolted from the Lincoln, ran to the van and sped away with the assassin.

# CHAPTER EIGHTEEN

After three days of unbillable time, of no production, of exile from their sanctuaries, of turkey and ham and cranberry sauce and new toys that came unassembled, the rested and rejuvenated lawyers of Bendini, Lambert & Locke returned to the fortress on Front Street with a vengeance. The parking lot was full by seven-thirty. They sat fixed and comfortable behind their heavy desks, drank coffee by the gallons, meditated over mail and correspondence and documents and mumbled incoherently and furiously into their Dictaphones. They barked orders at secretaries and clerks and paralegals, and at each other. There were a few 'How was your Christmas?' greetings in the halls and around the coffeepots, but small talk was cheap and unbillable. The sounds of typewriters, intercoms and secretaries all harmonized into one glorious hum as the mint recovered from the nuisance of Christmas. Oliver Lambert walked the halls, smiling with satisfaction and listening, just listening to the sounds of wealth being made by the hour.

At noon, Lamar walked into the office and leaned across the desk. Mitch was deep into an oil and gas deal in Indonesia.

'Lunch?' Lamar asked.

'No, thanks. I'm behind.'

'Aren't we all. I thought we could run down to the Front Street Deli for a bowl of chili.'

'I'll pass. Thanks.'

Lamar glanced over his shoulder at the door and leaned closer as if he had extraordinary news to share. 'You know what today is, don't you?'

Mitch glanced at his watch. 'The twenty-eighth.'

'Right. And do you know what happens on the twenty-eighth of December of every year?'

'You have a bowel movement.'

'Yes. And what else?'

'Okay. I give up. What happens?'

'At this very moment, in the dining room on the fifth floor, all the partners are gathered for a lunch of roast duck and French wine.'

'Wine, for lunch?'

'Yes. It's a special occasion.'

'Okay?'

523

'After they eat for an hour, Roosevelt and Jessie Frances will leave and Lambert will lock the door. Then it's all the partners, you see. Only the partners. And Lambert will hand out a financial summary for the year. It's got all the partners listed, and beside each name is a number that represents their total billing for the year. Then on the next page is a summary of the net profits after expenses. Then, based on production they divide the pie!'

Mitch hung on every word. 'And?'

'And, last year the average piece of pie was three hundred and thirty thousand. And, of course, it's expected to be even higher this year. Goes up every year.'

'Three hundred and thirty thousand,' Mitch repeated slowly.

'Yep. And that's just the average. Locke will get close to a million. Victor Milligan will run a close second.'

'And what about us?'

'We get a piece too. A very small piece. Last year it was around nine thousand, on the average. Depends on how long you've been here and production.'

'Can we go watch?'

'They wouldn't sell a ticket to the President. It's supposed to be a secret meeting, but we all know about it. Word will begin drifting down late this afternoon.'

'When do they vote on who to make the next partner?'

'Normally, it would be done today. But, according to rumor, there may not be a new partner this year because of Marty and Joe. I think Marty was next in line, then Joe. Now, they might wait a year or two.'

'So who's next in line?'

Lamar stood straight and smiled proudly. 'One year from today, my friend, I will become a partner in Bendini, Lambert & Locke. I'm next in line, so don't get in my way this year.'

'I heard it was Massengill – a Harvard man, I might add.'

'Massengill doesn't have a prayer. I intend to bill a hundred and fourty hours a week for the next fifty-two weeks, and those birds will beg me to become a partner. I'll go to the fourth floor, and Massingill will go the basement with the paralegals.'

'I'm putting my money on Massengill.'

'He's a wimp. I'll run him into the ground. Let's go eat a bowl of chili, and I'll reveal my strategy.'

'Thanks, but I need to work.'

Lamar strutted from the office and passed Nina, who was carrying a stack of papers. She laid them on a cluttered corner of the desk. 'I'm going to lunch. Need anything?'

'No. Thanks. Yes, a Diet Coke.'

The halls quietened during lunch as the secretaries escaped the building and walked toward downtown to a dozen small cafés and delicatessens nearby. With half the lawyers on the fifth floor counting their money, the gentle roar of commerce took an intermission.

Mitch found an apple on Nina's desk and rubbed it clean. He opened a manual on IRS regulations, laid it on the copier behind her desk and touched the green PRINT button. A red warning lit up and flashed the message: INSERT FILE NUMBER. He backed away and looked at the copier. Yes, it was a new one. Next to the PRINT button was another that read BYPASS. He stuck his thumb on it. A shrill siren erupted from within the machine, and the entire panel of buttons turned bright red. He looked around helplessly, saw no one and frantically grabbed the instruction manual.

'What's going on here?' someone demanded over the wailing of the copier.

'I don't know!' Mitch yelled, waving the manual.

Lela Pointer, a secretary too old to walk from the building for lunch, reached behind the machine and flipped a switch. The siren died.

'What the hell?' Mitch said, panting.

'Didn't they tell you?' she demanded, grabbing the manual and placing it back in its place. She drilled a hole in him with her tiny fierce eyes, as if she had caught him in her purse.

'Obviously not. What's the deal?'

'We have a new copying system,' she lectured downward through her nose. 'It was installed the day after Christmas. You must code in the file number before the machine will copy. Your secretary was supposed to tell you.'

'You mean this thing will not copy unless I punch in a ten digit number?'

'That's correct.'

'What about copies in general, with no particular file?'

'Can't be done. Mr. Lambert says we lose too much money on unbilled copies. So, from now on, every copy is automatically billed to a file. You punch in the number first. The machine records the number of copies and sends it to the main terminal, where it goes on the client's billing account.'

'What about personal copies?'

Lela shook her head in total frustration. 'I can't believe your secretary didn't tell you all this.'

'Well, she didn't, so why don't you help me out.'

'You have a four-digit access number for yourself. At the end of each month you'll be billed for your personal copies.'

Mitch stared at the machine and shook his head. 'Why the damned alarm system?'

'Mr. Lambert says that after thirty days they will cut off the alarms. Right now, they're needed for people like you. He's very serious about this. Says we've been losing thousands on unbilled copies.'

'Right. And I suppose every copier in the building has been re-placed.'

She smiled with satisfaction. 'Yes, all seventeen.'

'Thanks.' Mitch returned to his office in search of a file number.

At three that afternoon, the celebration on the fifth floor came to a joyous conclusion, and the partners, now much wealthier and slightly drunker, filed out of the dining room and descended to their offices below. Avery, Oliver Lambert and Nathan Locke walked the short hallway to the security wall and pushed the button. DeVasher was waiting.

He waved at the chairs in his office and told them to sit down: Lambert passed around hand wrapped Hondurans, and everyone lit up.

'Well, I see we're all in a festive mood,' DeVasher said with a sneer. 'How much was it? Three hundred and ninety thousand, aver-age?'

'That's correct, DeVasher,' Lambert said. 'It was a very good year.' He puffed slowly and blew smoke rings at the ceiling.

'Did we all have a wonderful Christmas?' DeVasher asked.

'What's on your mind?' Locke demanded.

'Merry Christmas to you too, Nat. Just a few things. I met with Lazarov two days ago in New Orleans. He does not celebrate the birth of Christ, you know. I brought him up to date on the situation down here, with emphasis on McDeere and the FBI. I assured him there had been no further contact since the initial meeting. He did not quite believe this and said we would check with their sources within the Bureau. I don't know what that means, but who am I to ask questions? He instructed me to trail McDeere twenty-four hours a day for the next six months. I told him we were already doing so, sort of. He does not want another Hodge-Kozinski situation. He's very distressed about that. McDeere is not to leave the city on firm business unless at least two of us go with him.'

'He's going to Washington in two weeks,' Avery said.

'What for?'

'American Tax Institute. It's a four-day seminar that we require of all new associates. It's been promised to him, and he'll be very suspicious if it's canceled.'

'We made his reservations in September,' Ollie added.

'I'll see if I can clear it with Lazarov,' DeVasher said. 'Give me the dates, flights and hotel reservations. He won't like this.'

'What happened Christmas?' Locke asked.

'Not much. His wife went to her home in Kentucky. She's still there. McDeere took the dog and drove to Panama City Beach, Florida. We think he went to see his mom, but we're not sure. Spent one night at a Holiday Inn on the beach. Just he and the dog. Pretty boring. Then he drove to Birmingham, stayed in another Holiday Inn, then early yesterday morning he drove to Brushy Mountain to visit his brother. Harmless trip.'

'What's he said to his wife?' asked Avery.

'Nothing, as far as we can tell. It's hard to hear everything.'

'Who else are you watching?' asked Avery.

'We're listening to all of them, sort of sporadically. We have no real suspects, other than McDeere, and that's just because of Tarrance. Right now all's quiet.'

'He's got to go to Washington, DeVasher,' Avery insisted.

'Okay, okay. I'll get it cleared with Lazarov. He'll make us send five men for surveillance. What an idiot.'

Ernie's Airport Lounge was indeed near the airport. Mitch found it after three attempts and parked between two four-wheel-drive swampmobiles with real mud caked on the tires and headlights. The parking lot was full of such vehicles. He looked around and instinctively removed his tie. It was almost eleven. The lounge was deep and long and dark with colorful beer signs flashing in the painted windows.

He looked at the note again, just to be sure. 'Dear Mr. McDeere: Please meet me at Ernie's Lounge on Winchester tonight – late. It's about Eddie Lomax. Very important. Tammy Hemphill, his secretary.'

The note had been tacked on the door to the kitchen when he arrived home. He remembered her from the one visit to Eddie's office, back in November. He remembered the tight leather skirt, huge breasts, bleached hair, red sticky lips and smoke billowing from her nose. And he remembered the story about her husband, Elvis.

The door opened without incident, and he slid inside. A row of pool tables covered the left half of the room. Through the darkness and black smoke, he could make out a small dance floor in the rear. To the right was a long saloon-type bar crowded with cowboys and cowgirls, all drinking Bud longnecks. No one seemed to notice him. He walked quickly to the end of the bar and slid onto the stool. ' Bud longneck,' he told the bartender.

Tammy arrived before the beer. She was sitting and waiting on a crowded bench by the pool tables. She wore tight washed jeans, faded denim shirt and kinky red high-heels. The hair had just received a fresh bleaching.

'Thanks for coming,' she said into his face. 'I've been waiting for four hours. I knew of no other way to find you.'

Mitch nodded and smiled as if to say, 'It's okay. You did the right thing.'

'What's up?' he said.

She looked around. 'We need to talk, but not here.'

'Where do you suggest?'

'Could we maybe drive around?'

'Sure, but not in my car. It, uh, it may not be a good idea.'

'I've got a car. It's old, but it'll do.'

Mitch paid for the beer and followed her to the door. A cowpoke sitting near the door said, 'Getta loada this. Guy shows up with a suit and picks her up in thirty seconds.' Mitch smiled at him and hurried out the door. Dwarfed in a row of massive mud-eating machinery was a well-worn Volkswagen Rabbit. She unlocked it, and Mitch doubled over and squeezed into the cluttered seat. She pumped the accelerator five times and turned the key. Mitch held his breath until it started.

'Where would you like to go?' she asked.

Where we can't be seen, Mitch thought. 'You're driving.'

'You're married, aren't you?' she asked.

'Yes. You?'

'Yes. and my husband would not understand this situation right here. That's why I chose that dump back there. We never go there.'

She said this as if she and her husband were discriminating critics of dark redneck dives.

'I don't think my wife would understand either. She's out of town, though.'

Tammy drove in the direction of the airport. 'I've got an idea,' she said. She clutched the steering wheel tightly and spoke nervously.

'What's on your mind?' Mitch asked.

'Well, you heard about Eddie.'

'Yes.'

'When did you last see him?'

'We met ten days or so before Christmas. It was sort of a secret meeting.'

'That's what I thought. He kept no records of the work he was doing for you. Said you wanted it that way. He didn't tell me much. But me and Eddie, well, we, uh, we were . . . close.'

Mitch could think of no response.

'I mean, we were very close. Know what I mean?'

Mitch grunted and sipped the longneck.

'And he told me things I guess he wasn't supposed to tell me. Said you had a real strange case, that some lawyers in your firm had died under suspicious circumstances. And that you always thought somebody was following and listening. That's pretty weird for a law firm.'

So much for the confidentiality, thought Mitch. 'That it is.'

She turned, made the exit to the airport and headed for the acres of parked cars.

'And after he finished his work for you, he told me once, just once, in bed, that he thought he was being followed. This was three days before Christmas. And I asked him who it was. He said he didn't know, but mentioned your case and something about it was probably related to the same people who were following you. He didn't say much.'

She parked in the short-term section near the terminal.

'Who else would follow him?' Mitch asked.

'No one. He was a good investigator who left no trail. I mean, he was an ex-cop and an ex-con. He was very street-smart. He got paid to follow people and collect dirt. No one followed him. Never.'

'So who killed him?'

'Whoever was following him. The paper made like he got caught snooping on some rich guy and was wasted. It's not true.'

Suddenly, from out of nowhere, she produced a filter-tip 1000 and shot a frame at the end. Mitch rolled down the window.

'Mind if I smoke?' she asked.

'No, just blow it that way,' he said, pointing to her window.

'Anyway, I'm scared. Eddie was convinced the people following you are extremely dangerous and extremely smart. Very sophisticated, was what he said. And if they killed him, what about me? Maybe they think I know something. I haven't been to the office since the day he was killed. Don't plan to go back.'

'I wouldn't if I were you.'

'I'm not stupid. I worked for him for two years and learned a lot. There's a lot of nuts out there. We saw all kinds.'

'How did they shoot him?'

'He's got a friend in Homicide. Guy told me confidentially that Eddie got hit three times in the back of the head, point blank range, with a .22 pistol. And they don't have a clue. He told me it was a very clean, professional job.'

Mitch finished the longneck and laid the bottle on the floorboard with a half dozen empty beer cans. A very clean, professional job.

'It doesn't make sense,' she repeated. 'I mean, how could anyone sneak up behind Eddie, somehow get in the back seat and shoot him three times in the back of the head? And he wasn't even supposed to be there.'

'Maybe he fell asleep and they ambushed him.'

'No. He took all kinds of speed when he worked late at night. Stayed wired.'

'Are there any records at the office?'

'You mean about you?'

'Yeah, about me.'

'I doubt it. I never saw nothing in writing. He said you wanted it that way.'

'That's right,' Mitch said with relief.

'They watched a 727 lift off to the north. The parking lot vibrated. 'I'm really scared, Mitch. Can I call you Mitch?'

'Sure. Why not?'

'I think he got killed because of the work he did for you. That's all it could be. And if they'd kill him because he knew something, they probably assume I know it too. What do you think?'

'I wouldn't take any chances.'

'I might disappear for a while. My husband does a little nightclub work, and we can get mobile if we have to. I haven't told him all this, but I guess I have to. What do you think?'

'Where would you go?'

'Little Rock, St. Louis, Nashville. He's laid off, so we can move around, I guess.' Her words trailed off. She lit another one.

A very clean, professional job, Mitch repeated to himself. He glanced at her and noticed a small tear on her cheek. She was not ugly, but the years in lounges and nightclubs were taking their toll. Her features were strong, and minus the bleach and heavy makeup she would be somewhat attractive for her age. About forty, he guessed.

She took a mighty drag and sent a cloud of smoke surging from the Rabbit. 'I guess we're in the same boat, aren't we? I mean, they're after both of us. They've killed all those lawyers, now Eddie, and I guess we're next.'

Don't hold back, baby, just blurt it out. 'Look, let's do this. We need to keep in touch. You can't call me on the phone, and we can't be seen together. My wife knows everything, and I'll tell her about this little meeting. Don't worry about her. Once a week, write me a note and tell me where you are. What's your mother's name?'

'Doris.'

'Good. That's your code name. Sign the name Doris on anything you send me.'

'Do they read your mail too?'

'Probably so, Doris, probably so.'

# CHAPTER NINETEEN

At five P.M., Mitch turned off the light in his office, grabbed both briefcases and stopped at Nina's desk. Her phone was glued to one shoulder while she typed on the IBM. She saw him and reached in a drawer for an envelope. 'This is your confirmation at the Capital Hilton,' she said into the receiver.

'The dictation is on my desk,' he said. 'See you Monday.' He took the stairs to the fourth floor, to Avery's office in the corner, where a small riot was in progress. One secretary stuffed files into a massive briefcase. Another one spoke sharply to Avery, who was yelling on the phone to someone else. A paralegal shot orders to the first secretary.

Avery slammed the phone down. 'Are you ready!' he demanded at Mitch.

'Waiting for you,' Mitch replied.

'I can't find the Greenmark file,' a secretary snarled at the paralegal.

'It was with the Rocconi file!' said the paralegal.

'I don't need the Greenmark file!' Avery shouted. 'How many times do I have to tell you? Are you deaf?'

The secretary glared at Avery. 'No, I can hear very well. And I distinctly heard you say, "Pack the Greenmark file."'

'The limousine is waiting,' said the other secretary.

'I don't need the damned Greenmark file!' Avery shouted.

'How about Rocconi?' asked the paralegal.

'Yes! Yes! For the tenth time. I need the Rocconi file!'

'The airplane is waiting too,' said the other secretary.

One briefcase was slammed shut and locked. Avery dug through a pile of documents on his desk. 'Where's the Fender file? Where are any of my files? Why can't I ever find a file?'

'Here's Fender,' said the first secretary as she stuffed it into another briefcase.

Avery stared at a piece of notepaper. 'All right. Do I have Fender, Rocconi, Cambridge Partners, Greene Group, Sonny Capps to Otaki, Burton Brothers, Galveston Freight and McQuade?'

'Yes, yes, yes,' said the first secretary.

'That's all of them,' said the paralegal.

'I don't believe it,' Avery said as he grabbed his jacket. 'Let's go.'

He stode through the door with the secretaries, paralegal and Mitch in pursuit. Mitch carried two briefcases, the parallegal had two, and a secretary had one. The other secretary scribbled notes as Avery barked the orders and demands he wanted carried out while he was away. The entourage crowded onto the small elevator for the ride to the first floor. Outside, the chauffeur sprang into action, opening doors and loading it all in the trunk.

Mitch and Avery fell into the back seat.

'Relax, Avery,' Mitch said. 'You're going to the Caymans for three days. Just relax.'

'Right, right. I'm taking with me enough work for a month. I've got clients screaming for my hide, threatening suits for legal malpractice. I'm two months behind, and now you're leaving for four days of boredom at a tax seminar in Washington. You're timing is great, McDeere. Just great.'

Avery opened a cabinet and mixed a drink. Mitch declined. The limo moved around Riverside Drive in the rush-hour traffic. After three swallows of gin, the partner breathed deeply.

'Continuing education. What a joke,' Avery said.

'You did it when you were a rookie. And if I'm not mistaken, you spent a week not long ago at the international tax seminar in Honolulu. Or did you forget?'

'It was work. All work. Are you taking your files with you?'

'Of course, Avery. I'm expected to attend the tax seminar eight hours a day, learn the latest tax revisions Congress has bestowed upon us and in my spare time bill five hours a day.'

'Six, if you can. We're behind, Mitch.'

'We're always behind, Avery. Fix another drink. You need to unwind.'

'I plan to unwind at Rumheads.'

Mitch thought of the bar with its Red Stripe, dominoes, darts and, yes, string bikinis. And the girl.

'Is this your first flight on the Lear?' Avery asked, more relaxed now.

'Yes. I've been here seven months, and I'm just now seeing the plane. If I had known this last March, I'd have gone to work with a Wall Street firm.'

'You're not Wall Street material. You know what those guys do? They've got three hundred lawyers in a firm, right? And each year they hire thirty new associates, maybe more. Everybody wants a job because it's Wall Street, right? And after about a month they get all thirty of them together in one big room and inform them they're expected to work ninety hours a week for five years, and at the end of five years, half of them will be gone. The turnover is incredible. They try to kill the rookies, bill them out at a hundred, hundred-fifty an hour, make a bundle off them, then run them off. That's Wall Street. And the little boys never get to see the firm plane. Or the firm limo. You are truly lucky, Mitch. You should thank God every day that we chose to accept you here at good old Bendini, Lambert & Locke.'

'Ninety hours sounds like fun. I could use the rest.'

'It'll pay off. Did you hear what my bonus was last year?'

'No.'

'Four-eight-five. Not bad, huh? And that's just the bonus.'

'I got six thousand,' Mitch said.

'Stick with me and you'll be in the big leagues soon enough.'

'Yeah, but first I gotta get my continuing legal education.'

Ten minutes later the limo turned into a drive that led to a row of hangars. Memphis Aero, the sign said. A sleek silver Lear 55 taxied slowly toward the terminal. 'That's it,' Avery said.

The briefcases and luggage were loaded quickly onto the plane, and within minutes they were cleared for take-off. Mitch fastened his seat belt and admired the leather-and-brass cabin. It was lavish and luxurious, and he had expected nothing less. Avery mixed another drink and buckled himself in.

An hour and fifteen minutes later, the Lear began its descent into Baltimore-Washington International Airport. After it taxied to a stop, Avery and Mitch descended to the tarmac and opened the baggage door. Avery pointed to a man in a uniform standing near a gate. 'That's your chauffeur. The limo is in front. Just follow him. You're about forty minutes from the Capital Hilton.'

'Another limo?' Mitch asked.

'Yeah. They wouldn't do this for you on Wall Street.'

They shook hands, and Avery climbed back on the plane. The refueling took thirty minutes, and when the Lear took off and turned south, he was asleep again.

Three hours later, it landed in Georgetown, Grand Cayman. It taxied past the terminal to a very small hangar where it would spend the night. A security guard waited on Avery and his luggage and escorted him to the terminal and through customs. The pilot and copilot ran through the post flight ritual. They too were escorted through the terminal.

After midnight, the lights in the hangar were extinguished and the half dozen planes sat in the darkness. A side door opened, and three men, one of them Avery, entered and walked quickly to the Lear 55.

Avery opened the baggage compartment, and the three hurriedly unloaded twenty-five heavy cardboard boxes. In the muggy tropical
heat, the hangar was like an oven. They sweated profusely but said
nothing until all boxes were out of the plane.

'There should be twenty-five. Count them,' Avery said to a
muscle-bound native with a tank top and a pistol on his hip. The
other man held a clipboard and watched intently as if he was a receiving clerk in a warehouse. The native counted quickly, sweat
dripping onto the boxes.

'Yes. Twenty-five.'

'How much?' asked the man with the clipboard.

'Six and a half million.'

'All cash?'

'All cash. U.S. dollars. Hundreds and twenties. Let's get it loaded.'

'Where's it going?'

'QuebecBank. They're waiting for us.'

They each grabbed a box and walked through the dark to the side
door, where a comrade was waiting with an Uzi. The boxes were
loaded into a dilapidated van with CAYMAN PRODUCE stenciled badly
on the side. The armed natives sat with guns drawn as the receiving
clerk drove away from the hangar in the direction of downtown
Georgetown.

Registration began at eight outside the Century Room on the mezzanine. Mitch arrived early, signed in, picked up the heavy notebook of
materials with his name printed on the cover and went inside. He
took a seat near the center of the large room. Registration was limited
to two hundred, the brochure said. A porter served coffee, and Mitch
spread the Washington *Post* before him. The news was dominated by
a dozen stories of the beloved Redskins, who were in the Super Bowl
again.

The room filled slowly as tax lawyers from around the country
gathered to hear the latest developments in tax laws that changed
daily. A few minutes before nine, a clean cut, boyish attorney sat to
Mitch's left and said nothing. Mitch glanced at him and returned to
the paper. When the room was packed, the moderator welcomed
everyone and introduced the first speaker. Congressman something
or other from Oregon, chairman of the House Ways and Means subcommittee. As he took the podium for what was supposed to be a
one-hour presentation, the attorney to Mitch's left leaned over and
offered his hand.

'Hi, Mitch,' he whispered. 'I'm Grant Harbison, FBI.' He handed
Mitch a card.

The congressman started with a joke that Mitch did not hear. He studied the card, holding it near his chest. There were five people seated within three feet of him. He didn't know anyone in the room, but it would be embarrassing if anyone knew he was holding an FBI card. After five minutes, Mitch shot a blank stare at Harbison.

Harbison whispered, 'I need to see you for a few minutes.'

'What if I'm busy?' Mitch asked.

The agent slid a plain white envelope from his seminar notebook and handed it to Mitch. He opened it near his chest. It was handwritten. Across the top, in small but imposing letters, the words read simply: 'Office of the Director – FBI.'

The note read

Dear Mr. McDeere:
I would like to speak with you for a few
moments during lunch. Please follow the
instructions of Agent Harbison. It won't
take long. We appreciate your cooperation.
Thanks.
F. DENTON VOYLES
Director

Mitch folded the letter in the envelope and slowly placed it in his notebook. We appreciate your cooperation. From the Director of the FBI. He realized the importance at this moment of maintaining his composure, of keeping a straight, calm face as if it was simply routine. But he rubbed his temples with both hands and stared at the floor in front of him. He closed his eyes and felt dizzy. The FBI. Sitting next to him! Waiting on him. The Director and hell knows who else. Tarrance would be close at hand.

Suddenly, the room exploded in laughter at the congressman's punch line. Harbison leaned quickly toward Mitch and whispered, 'Meet me in the men's room around the corner in ten minutes.' The agent left his notebooks on the table and exited among the laughter.

Mitch flipped to the first section of the notebook and pretended to study materials. The congressman was detailing his courageous battle to protect tax shelters for the wealthy while at the same time easing the burden on the working class. Under his fearless guidance, the subcommittee had refused to report legislation limiting deductions for oil and gas exploration. He was a one-man army on the Hill.

Mitch waited fifteen minutes, then another five, then began coughing. He needed water, and with hand over mouth he slid between the chairs to the back of the room and out the rear door. Harbison was in the men's room washing his hands for the tenth time.

Mitch walked to the basin next to him and turned on the cold water. 'What are you boys up to?' Mitch asked.

Harbison looked at Mitch in the mirror. 'I'm just following orders. Director Voyles wants to personally meet you, and I was sent to get you.'

'And what might he want?'

'I wouldn't want to steal his thunder, but I'm sure it's rather important.'

Mitch cautiously glanced around the rest room. It was empty. 'And what if I'm too busy to meet with him?'

Harbison turned off the water and shook his hands into the basin. 'The meeting is inevitable, Mitch. Let's not play games. When your little seminar breaks for lunch, you'll find a cab number 8667, outside to the left of the main entrance. It will take you to the Vietnam Veterans Memorial, and we'll be there. You must be careful. Two of them followed you here from Memphis.'

'Two of whom?'

'The boys from Memphis. Just do as we say and they'll never know.'

The moderator thanked the second speaker, a tax professor from New York University, and dismissed them for lunch.

Mitch said nothing to the taxi driver. He sped away like a maniac, and they were soon lost in traffic. Fifteen minutes later, they parked near the Memorial.

'Don't get out yet,' the driver said with authority. Mitch did not move. For ten minutes, he did not move or speak. Finally, a white Ford Escort pulled alongside the cab and honked. It then drove away.

The driver stared ahead and said, 'Okay. Go to the Wall. They'll find you after about five minutes.'

Mitch stepped to the sidewalk, and the cab left. He stuck his hands deep in the pockets of his wool overcoat and walked slowly to the Memorial. Bitter wind gusts from the north scattered leaves in all directions. He shivered and flipped the collar of his coat around his ears.

A solitary pilgrim sat rigidly in a wheelchair and stared at the Wall. He was covered with a heavy quilt. Under his oversized camouflage beret, a pair of aviator's sunglasses covered his eyes. He sat near the end of the wall, near the names of those killed in 1972.

537

Mitch followed the years down the sidewalk until he stopped near the wheelchair. He searched the names, suddenly oblivious to the man.

He breathed deeply and was aware of a numbness in his legs and stomach. He looked slowly downward, and then, near the bottom, there it was. Engraved neatly, matter-of-factly, just like all the others, was the name Rusty McDeere.

A basket of frozen and wilted flowers sat on its side next to the monument, inches under his name. Mitch gently laid them to one side and knelt before the Wall. He touched the engraved letters of Rusty's name. Rusty McDeere. Age eighteen, forever. Seven weeks in Vietnam when he stepped on a land mine. Death was instantaneous, they said. They always said that, according to Ray. Mitch wiped a small tear and stood staring at the length of the Wall. He thought of the fifty-eight thousand families who had been told that death was instantaneous and no one suffered over there.

'Mitch, they're waiting.'

He turned and looked at the man in the wheelchair, the only human in sight. The aviator's glasses stared at the Wall and did not look up. Mitch glanced around in all directions.

'Relax, Mitch. We've got the place sealed off. They're not watching.'

'And who are you?' Mitch asked.

'Just one of the gang. You need to trust us, Mitch. The Director has important words, words that could save your life.'

'Where is he?'

The man in the wheelchair turned his head and looked down the sidewalk. 'Start walking that way. They'll find you.'

Mitch stared for a moment longer at his brother's name and walked behind the wheelchair. He walked past the statue of the three soldiers. He walked slowly, waiting, with hands deep in his pockets. Fifty yards past the monument, Wayne Tarrance stepped from behind a tree and walked beside him. 'Keep walking,' he said.

'Why am I not surprised to see you here?' Mitch said.

'Just keep walking. We know of at least two goons from Memphis who were flown in ahead of you. They're at the same hotel, next door to you. They did not follow you here. I think we lost them.'

'What the hell's going on, Tarrance?'

'You're about to find out. Keep walking. But relax, no one is watching you, except for about twenty of our agents.'

'Twenty?'

'Yeah. We've got the place sealed off. We want to make sure those bastards from Memphis don't show up here. I don't expect them.'

'Who are they?'

'The Director will explain.'

'Why is the Director involved?'

'You ask a lot of questions, Mitch.'

'And you don't have enough answers.'

Tarrance pointed to the right. They left the sidewalk and headed for a heavy concrete bench near a footbridge leading to a small forest. The water on the pond below was frozen white.

'Have a seat,' Tarrance instructed. They sat down. Two men walked across the footbridge. Mitch immediately recognized the shorter one as Voyles. F. Denton Voyles, Director of the FBI under three Presidents. A tough-talking, heavy-handed crime buster with a reputation for ruthlessness.

Mitch stood out of respect when they stopped at the bench. Voyles stuck out a cold hand and stared at Mitch with the same large, round face that was famous around the world. They shook hands and exchanged names. Voyles pointed to the bence. Tarrance and the other agent walked to the footbridge and studied the horizon. Mitch glanced across the pond and saw two men, undoubtedly agents with their identical black trench coats and close haircuts, standing against a tree a hundred yards away.

Voyles sat close to Mitch, their legs touching. A brown fedora rested to one side of his large, bald head. He was at least seventy, but the dark green eyes danced with intensity and missed nothing. Both men sat still on the cold bench with their hands stuck deep in their overcoats.

'I appreciate you coming,' Voyles started.

'I didn't feel as though I had a choice. You folks have been relentless.'

'Yes. It's very important to us.'

Mitch breathed deeply, 'Do you have any idea how confused and scared I am? I'm totally bewildered. I would like an explanation, sir.'

'Mr. McDeere, can I call you Mitch?'

'Sure. Why not.'

'Fine. Mitch, I am a man of very few words. And what I'm about to tell you will certainly shock you. You will be horrified. You may not believe me. But I assure you it's all true, and with your help we can save your life.'

Mitch braced himself and waited.

'Mitch, no lawyer has ever left your law firm alive. Three have tried, and they were killed. Two were about to leave, and they died last summer. Once a lawyer joins Bendini, Lambert & Locke, he never leaves, unless he retires and keeps his mouth shut. And by the time they retire, they are a part of the conspiracy and cannot talk. The firm has an extensive surveillance operation on the fifth floor. Your house and car are bugged. Your phones are tapped. Your desk and office are wired. Virtually every word you utter is heard and recorded on the fifth floor. They follow you, and sometimes your wife. They are here in Washington as we speak. You see, Mitch, the firm is more than a firm. It is a division of a very large business, a very profitable business. A very illegal business. The firm is not owned by the partners.'

Mitch turned and watched him closely. The Director looked at the frozen pond as he spoke.

'You see, Mitch, the law firm of Bendini, Lambert & Locke is owned by the Morolto crime family in Chicago. The Mafia. The Mob. They call the shots from up there. And that's why we're here.' He touched Mitch firmly on the knee and stared at him from six inches away. 'It's Mafia, Mitch, and illegal as hell.'

'I don't believe it,' he said, frozen with fear. His voice was weak and shrill.

The Director smiled. 'Yes you do, Mitch. Yes you do. You've been suspicious for some time now. That's why you talked to Abanks in the Caymans. That's why you hired that sleazy investigator and got him killed by those boys on the fifth floor. You know the firm stinks, Mitch.'

Mitch leaned forward and rested his elbows on his knees. He stared at the ground between his shoes. 'I don't believe it,' he mumbled weakly.

'As far as we can tell, about twenty-five percent of their clients, or I should say your clients, are legitimate. There are some very good lawyers in that firm, and they do tax and securities work for rich clients. It's a very good front. Most of the files you've worked on so far have been legit. That's how they operate. They bring in a new rookie, throw money at him, buy the BMW, the house, all that jazz, wine and dine and go to the Caymans, and they work his ass off with what is really legitimate legal stuff. Real clients. Real lawyer stuff. That goes on for a few years, and the rookie doesn't suspect a thing, right? It's a great firm, great bunch of guys. Plenty of money. Hey, everything's wonderful. Then after five or six years, when the money is really good, when they own your mortgage, when you have a wife and kids and everything is so secure, they drop the bomb and tell the truth. There's no way out. It's the Mafia, Mitch. Those guys don't play games. They'll kill one of your children or your wife, they don't care. You're making more money than you could possible make anywhere else. You're blackmailed because you've got a family that doesn't mean a damned thing to the Mob, so what do you do, Mitch? You stay. You can't leave. If you stay you make a million and retire young with your family intact. If you want to leave, you'll wind up with your picture on the wall in the first-floor library. They're very persuasive.'

Mitch rubbed his temples and began shivering.

'Look, Mitch, I know you must have a thousand questions. Okay. So I'll just keep talking and tell you what I know. The five dead lawyers all wanted out after they learned the truth. We never talked to the first three, because, frankly, we knew nothing about the firm until seven years ago. They've done an excellent job of staying quiet and leaving no trail. The first three just wanted out, probably, so they got out. In coffins. Hodge and Kozinski were different. They approached us, and over the course of a year we had several meetings. They dropped the bomb on Kozinski after he'd been there for seven years. He told Hodge. They whispered between themselves for a year. Kozinski was about to make partner and wanted out before that happened. So he and Hodge made the fatal decision to get out. They never suspected the first three were killed, or at least they never mentioned it to us. We sent Wayne Tarrance to Memphis to bring them in. Tarrance is an organized crime specialist from New York. He and the two were getting real close when that thing happened in the Caymans. These guys in Memphis are very good, Mitch. Don't ever forget that. They've got the money and they hire the best. So after Hodge and Kozinski were killed, I made the decision to get the firm. If we can bust that firm, we can indict every significant member of the Morolto family. There could be over five hundred indictments. Tax evasion, laundering, racketeering, just whatever you want. It could destroy the Morolto family, and that would be the single most devastating blow to organized crime in the past thirty years. And, Mitch, it's all in the files at the quiet little Bendini firm in Memphis.'

'Why Memphis?'

'Ah, good question. Who would suspect a small firm in Memphis, Tennessee? There's no mob activity down there. It's a quiet, lovely, peaceful city by the river. It could've been Durham or Topeka or Wichita Falls. But they chose Memphis. It's big enough, though, to hide a forty-man firm. Perfect choice.'

'You mean every partner . . .' His words trailed off.

'Yes, every partner knows and plays by the rules. We suspect that most of the associates know, but it's hard to tell. There's so much we don't know, Mitch. I can't explain how the firm operates and who's in on it. But we strongly suspect a lot of criminal activity down there.'

'Such as?'

'Tax fraud. They do all the tax work for the Morolto bunch. They file nice, neat, proper-looking tax returns each year and report a fraction of the income. They launder money like crazy. They set up legitimate businesses with dirty money. That bank in St. Louis, big client, what is it?'

'Commercial Guaranty.'

'Right, that's it. Mafia owned. Firm does all its legal work. Morolto takes in an estimated three hundred million a year from gambling, dope, numbers, everything. All cash, right? Most of it goes to those banks in the Caymans. How does it move from Chicago to the islands? Any idea? The plane, we suspect. That gold-plated Lear you flew up here on runs about once a week to Georgetown.'

Mitch sat straight and watched Tarrance, who was out of hearing range and standing now on the footbridge. 'So why don't you get your indictments and bust it all up?'

'We can't. We will, I assure you. I've assigned five agents to the project in Memphis and three here in Washington. I'll get them, Mitch, I promise you. But we must have someone from the inside. They are very smart. They have plenty of money. They're extremely careful, and they don't make mistakes. I am convinced that we must have help from you or another member of the firm. We need copies of files, copies of bank records, copies of a million documents that can only come from within. It's impossible otherwise.'

'And I have been chosen.'

'And you have been chosen. If you decline, then you can go on your way and make plenty of money and in general be a successful lawyer. But we will keep trying. We'll wait for the next new associate and try to pick him off. And if that doesn't work, we'll move in on one of the older associates. One with courage and morals and guts to do what's right. We'll find our man one day, Mitch, and when that happens we'll indict you along with all the rest and ship your rich successful ass off to prison. It will happen, son, believe me.'

At that moment, at that place and time, Mitch believed him. 'Mr. Voyles, I'm cold. Could we walk around?'

'Sure, Mitch.'

They walked slowly to the sidewalk and headed in the direction of the Vietnam Memorial. Mitch glanced over his shoulder. Tarrance and the other agent were following at a distance. Another agent in dark brown sat suspiciously on a park bench up the sidewalk.

THE FIRM

'Who was Anthony Bendini?' Mitch asked.

'He married a Morolto in 1930. The old man's son-in-law. They had an operation in Philadelphia back then, and he was stationed there. Then, in the forties, for some reason, he was sent to Memphis to set up shop. He was a good lawyer, though, from what we know.'

A thousand questions flooded his brain and fought to be asked. He tried to appear calm, under control, skeptical.

'What about Oliver Lambert?'

'A prince of a guy. The perfect senior partner, who just happened to know all about Hodge and Kozinski and the plans to eliminate them. The next time you see Mr. Lambert around the office, try to remember that he is a cold-blooded murderer. Of course, he has no choice. If he didn't cooperate, they'd find him floating somewhere. They're all like that, Mitch. They started off just like you. Young, bright, ambitious, then suddenly one day they were in over their heads with no place to go. So they play along, work hard, do a helluva job putting up a good front and looking like a real respectable little law firm. Each year or so they recruit a bright young law student from a poor background, no family money, with a wife who wants babies, and they throw money at him and sign him up.'

Mitch thought of the money, the excessive salary from a small firm in Memphis, and the car and low-interest mortgage. He was headed for Wall Street and had been sidetracked by the money. Only the money.

'What about Nathan Locke?'

The Director smiled. 'Locke is another story. He grew up a poor kid in Chicago and was running errands for old man Morolto by the time he was ten. He's been a hood all his life. Scratched his way through law school, and the old man sent him South to work with Anthony Bendini in the white-collar-crime division of the family. He was always a favorite of the old man.'

'When did Morolto die?'

'Eleven years ago at the age of eighty-eight. He has two slimy sons, Mickey the Mouth and Joey the Priest. Mickey lives in Las Vegas and has a limited role in the family business. Joey is the boss.'

The sidewalk reached an intersection with another one. In the distance to the left, the Washington Monument reached upward in the bitter wind. To the right, the walkway led to the Wall. A handful of people were now staring at it, searching for the names of sons and husbands and friends. Mitch headed for the Wall. They walked slowly.

Mitch spoke softly. 'I don't understand how the firm can do so

543

much illegal work and keep it quiet. That place is full of secretaries and clerks and paralegals.'

'Good point, and one I cannot fully answer. We think it operates as two firms. One is legitimate, with the new associates, most of the secretaries and support people. Then, the senior associates and partners do the dirty work. Hodge and Kozinski were about to give us plenty of information, but they never made it. Hodge told Tarrance once that there was a group of paralegals in the basement he knew little about. They worked directly for Locke and Milligan and McKnight and a few other partners, and no one was really sure what they did. Secretaries know everything, and we think that some of them are probably in on it. If so, I'm sure they're well paid and too scared to talk. Think about it, Mitch. If you work there making great money with great benefits, and you know that if you ask too many questions or start talking you wind up in the river, what do you do? You keep your mouth shut and take the money.'

They stopped at the beginning of the Wall, at a point where the black granite began at ground level and started its run of 246 feet until it angled into the second row of identical panels. Sixty feet away, and elderly couple stared at the wall and cried softly. They huddled together, for warmth and strength. The mother bent down and laid a framed black-and-white photo at the base of the Wall. The father laid a shoebox full of high school memorabilia next to the photo. Football programs, class pictures, love letters, key rings and a gold chain. They cried louder.

Mitch turned his back to the Wall and looked at the Washington Monument. The Director watched his eyes.

'So what am I supposed to do?' Mitch asked.

'First of all, keep your mouth shut. If you start asking questions, your life could be in danger. Your wife's also. Don't have any kids in the near future. They're easy targets. It's best to play dumb, as if everything is wonderful and you still plan to be the world's greatest lawyer. Second, you must make a decision. Not now, but soon. You must decide if you will cooperate or not. If you choose to help us, we will of course make it worth your while. If you choose not to, then we will continue to watch the firm until we decide to approach another associate. As I said, one of these days we'll find someone with guts and nail those bastards. And the Morolto crime family as we know it will cease to exist. We'll protect you, Mitch, and you'll never have to work again in your life.'

'What life? I'll live in fear forever, if I live. I've heard stories of witnesses the FBI has supposedly hidden. Ten years later, the car explodes as they back out the driveway to go to work. The body is scattered over three blocks. The Mob never forgets, Director. You know that.'

'They never forget, Mitch. But I promise you, you and your wife will be protected.'

The Director looked at his watch. 'You'd better get back or they'll be suspicious. Tarrance will be in touch. Trust him, Mitch. He's trying to save your life. He has full authority to act on my behalf. If he tells you something, it's coming from me. He can negotiate.'

'Negotiate what?'

'Terms, Mitch. What we give you in return for what you give us. We want the Morolto family, and you can deliver. You name your price, and this government, working through the FBI, will deliver. Within reason, of course. And that's coming from me, Mitch.' They walked slowly along the Wall and stopped by the agent in the wheelchair. Voyles stuck out his hand. 'Look, there's a taxi waiting where you came in, number 1073. Same driver. You'd better leave now. We will not meet again, but Tarrance will contact you in a couple of days. Please think about what I said. Don't convince yourself the firm in invincible and can operate forever, because I will not allow it. We will make a move in the near future, I promise that. I just hope you're on our side.'

'I don't understand what I'm supposed to do.'

'Tarrance has the game plan. A lot will depend upon you and what you learn once you're committed.'

'Committed?'

'That's the word, Mitch. Once you commit, there's no turning back. They can be more ruthless than any organization on earth.'

'Why did you pick me?'

'We had to pick someone. No, that's not true. We picked you because you have the guts to walk away from it. You have no family except a wife. No ties, no roots. You've been hurt by every person you ever cared for, except Abby. You raised yourself, and in doing so became self-reliant and independent. You don't need the firm. You can leave it. You're hardened and callused beyond your years. And you're smart enough to pull it off, Mitch. You won't get caught. That's why we picked you. Good day, Mitch. Thanks for coming. You'd better get back.'

Voyles turned and walked quickly away. Tarrance waited at the end of the Wall, and gave Mitch a quick salute, as if to say, 'So long – for now.'

# CHAPTER TWENTY

After making the obligatory stop in Atlanta, the Delta DC9 landed in a cold rain at Memphis International. It parked at Gate 19, and the tightly packed crowd of business travelers quickly disembarked. Mitch carried only his briefcase and an *Esquire*. He saw Abby waiting near the pay phones and moved quickly through the pack. He threw the briefcase and magazine against the wall and bear-hugged her. The four days in Washington seemed like a month. They kissed again and again, and whispered softly.

'How about a date?' he asked.

'I've got dinner on the table and wine in the cooler,' she said. They held hands and walked through the mob pushing down the concourse in the general direction of the luggage pickup.

He spoke quietly. 'Well, we need to talk, and we can't do it at home.'

She gripped his hand tighter. 'Oh?'

'Yes. In fact, we need to have a long talk.'

'What happened?'

'It'll take a while.'

'Why am I suddenly nervous?'

'Just keep cool. Keep smiling. They're watching.'

She smiled and glanced to the right. 'Who's watching?'

'I'll explain in just a moment.'

Mitch suddenly pulled her to his left. They cut through the wave of human traffic and darted into a dark, crowded lounge full of businessmen drinking and watching the television above the bar and waiting for their flights. A small, round table covered with empty beer mugs had just been vacated, and they sat with their backs to the wall and a view of the bar and the concourse. They sat close together, within three feet of another table. Mitch stared at the door and analyzed every face that walked in. 'How long are we going to be here?' she asked.

'Why?'

She slid out of the full length fox and folded it on the chair across the table. 'What exactly are you looking for?'

'Just keep smiling for a moment. Pretend you really missed me. Here, give me a kiss.' He pecked her on the lips, and they smiled into each other's eyes. He kissed her cheek and returned to the door. A waiter rushed to the table and cleaned it off. They ordered wine.

She smiled at him. 'How was your trip?'

'Boring. We were in class eight hours a day, for four days. After the first day, I hardly left the hotel. They crammed six months' worth of tax revisions into thirty-two hours.'

'Did you get to sightsee?'

He smiled and looked dreamily at her. 'I missed you, Abby. More than I've ever missed anyone in my life. I love you. I think you're gorgeous, absolutely stunning. I do not enjoy traveling alone and waking up in a strange hotel bed without you. And I have something horrible to tell you.'

She stopped smiling. He slowly looked around the room. They were three deep at the bar and yelling at the Knicks-Lakers game. The lounge was suddenly louder.

'I'll tell you about it,' he said, 'But there's a very good chance someone is in here right now watching us. They cannot hear, but they can observe. Just smile occasionally, although it will be hard.'

The wine arrived, and Mitch began his story. He left nothing out. She spoke only once. He told her about Anthony Bendini and old man Morolto, and then Nathan Locke growing up in Chicago and Oliver Lambert and the boys on the fifth floor.

Abby nervously sipped her wine and tried valiantly to appear as the normal loving wife who missed her husband and was now enjoying immensely his recollection of the tax seminar. She watched the people at the bar, sipped a little and occasionally grinned at Mitch as he told of the money laundering and the murdered lawyers. Her body ached with fear. Her breath was wildly irregular. But she listened, and pretended.

The waiter brought more wine as the crowd thinned. An hour after he started, Mitch finished in a low whisper.

'And Voyles said Tarrance would contact me in a few days to see if I will cooperate. He said goodbye and walked away.'

'And this was Tuesday?' she asked.

'Yes. The first day.'

'What did you do the rest of the week?'

'I slept little, ate little, walked around with a dull headache most of the time.'

'I think I feel one coming.'

'I'm sorry, Abby. I wanted to fly home immediately and tell you. I've been in shock for three days.'

'I'm in shock now. I'm not believing this, Mitch. This is like a bad dream, only much worse.'

'And this is only the beginning. The FBI is dead serious. Why else would the Director himself meet with me, an insignificant rookie lawyer from Memphis, in fifteen-degree weather on a concrete park bench? He's assigned five agents in Memphis and three in Washington, and he said they'll spend whatever it takes to get the firm. So if I keep my mouth shut, ignore them and go about my business of being a good and faithful member of Bendini, Lambert & Locke, one day they'll show up with arrest warrants and haul everybody away. And if I choose to cooperate, you and I will leave Memphis in the dead of night after I hand the firm to the feds, and we'll go off and live in Boise, Idaho, as Mr. and Mrs. Wilbur Gates. We'll have plenty of money, but we'll have to work to avoid suspicion. After my plasic surgery, I'll get a job driving a forklift in a warehouse, and you can work part time at a day care. We'll have two, maybe three kids and pray every night that people we've never met keep their mouths shut and forget about us. We'll live every hour of every day in morbid fear of being discovered.'

'That's perfect, Mitch, just perfect.' She was trying hard not to cry.

He smiled and glanced around the room. 'We have a third option. We can walk out that door, buy two tickets to San Diego, sneak across the border and eat tortillas for the rest of our lives.'

'Let's go.'

'But they'd probably follow us. With my luck, Oliver Lambert will be waiting in Tijuana with a squad of goons. It won't work. Just a thought.'

'What about Lamar?'

'I don't know. He's been here six or seven years, so he probably knows. Avery's a partner, so he's very much a part of the conspiracy.'

'And Kay?'

'Who knows. It's very likely none of the wives know. I've thought about it for four days, Abby, and it's a marvelous front. The firm looks exactly like it's supposed to look. They could fool anyone. I mean, how would you and I or any other prospective recruit even think of such an operation? It's perfect. Except, now the feds know about it.'

'And now the feds expect you to do their dirty work. Why did they pick you, Mitch? There are forty lawyers in the firm.'

'Because I knew nothing about it. I was a sitting duck. The FBI is not sure when the partners spring the surprise on the associates, so they couldn't take a chance with anyone else. I happened to be the new guy, so they set the trap as soon as I passed the bar exam.'

Abby chewed her lip and held back tears. She looked blankly at the door across the dark room. 'And they listen to everything we say,' she said.

'No. Just every phone call and conversation around the house and the cars. We're free to meet here or in most restaurants, and there's always the patio. But I suggest we move farther away from the sliding door. To be safe, we nead to sneak behind the storage shed and whisper softly.'

'Are you trying to be funny? I hope not. This is no time for jokes. I'm so scared, angry, confused, mad as hell and not sure where to turn. I'm afraid to speak in my own house. I watch every word I utter on the phone, even if it's a wrong number. Every time the phone rings, I jump and stare at it. And now this.'

'You need another drink.'

'I need ten drinks.'

'Mitch grabbed her wrist and squeezed firmly. 'Wait a minute. I see a familiar face. Don't look around.'

She held her breath. 'Where?'

'On the other side of the bar. Smile and look at me.'

Sitting on a barstool and staring intently at the TV was a well-tanned blond with a loud blue-and-white alpine sweater. Fresh from the slopes. But Mitch had seen the tan and the blond bangs and the blond mustache somewhere in Washington. Mitch watched him carefully. The blue light from the tube illuminated his face. Mitch hid in the dark. The man lifted a bottle of beer, hesitated, then, there!, shot a glance into the corner where the McDeeres huddled closely together.

'Are you sure?' Abby asked through clenched teeth.

'Yes. He was in Washington, but I can't place him. In fact, I saw him twice.'

'Is he one of them?'

'How am I supposed to know?'

'Let's get out of here.'

Mitch laid a twenty on the table and they left the airport.

Driving her Peugeot, he raced through the short-term parking lot, paid the attendant and sped away toward midtown. After five minutes of silence, she leaned across and whispered in his ear, 'Can we talk?'

He shook his head. 'Well, how's the weather been while I was away?'

Abby rolled her eyes and looked through the passenger window. 'Cold,' she said. 'Chance of light snow tonight.'

'It was below freezing the entire week in Washington.'

Abby looked flabbergasted at this revelation. 'Any snow?' she asked with raised eyebrows and wide eyes as if enthralled with the conversation.

'No. Just raw cold.'

'What a coincidence! Cold here and cold there.'

Mitch chuckled to himself. They rode silently on the interstate loop. 'So who's gonna win the Super Bowl?' he asked.'

'Oilers.'

'Think so, huh? I'm for the Redskins. That's all they talked about in Washington.'

'My, my. Must be a real fun city.'

More silence. Abby placed the back of her hand over her mouth and concentrated on the tail-lights ahead. At this moment of bewilderment, she would take her chances in Tijuana. Her husband, number three in his class (at Harvard), the one with Wall Street firms rolling out the red carpet, the one who could have gone anywhere, to any firm, had signed up with the . . . Mafia! With five dead lawyers notched on their belts, they most surely wouldn't hesitate with number six. Her husband! Then the many conversations with Kay Quin swirled around her brain. The firm encourages babies. The firm permits wives to work, but not forever. The firm hires no one with family money. The firm demands loyalty to the firm. The firm has the lowest turnover rate in the country. Small wonder.

Mitch watched her carefully. Twenty minutes after they left the airport, the Peugeot parked in the carport next to the BMW. They held hands and walked to the end of the driveway.

'This is crazy, Mitch.'

'Yes, but it's real. It will not go away.'

'What do we do?'

'I don't know, babe. But we gotta do it quick, and we can't make mistakes.'

'I'm scared.'

'I'm terrified.'

Tarrance did not wait long. One week after he waved goodbye to Mitch at the Wall, he spotted him walking hurriedly in the cold in the direction of the Federal Building on North Main, eight blocks from the Bendini Building. He followed him for two blocks, then slid into a small coffee shop with a row of windows facing the street, or the mall, as it was called. Cars were prohibited on Main Street in Memphis. The asphalt had been covered with tile when the boulevard had ceased being a street and had been transformed into the Mid-America Mall. An occasional useless and desolate tree rose from the tile and stretched its barren limbs between the buildings. Winos and urban nomads drifted aimlessly from one side of the mall to the other, begging for money and food.

Tarrance sat at a front window and watched in the distance as Mitch disappeared into the Federal Building. He ordered coffee and a chocolate doughnut. He checked his watch. It was 10 A.M. According to the docket, McDeere had a brief hearing in Tax Court at this moment. It should be very brief, the clerk of the court had informed Tarrance. He waited.

Nothing is ever brief in court. An hour later, Tarrance moved his face closer to the window and studied the scattered bodies walking quickly in the distance. He drained his coffee cup for the third time, laid two dollars on the table and stood hidden in the door. As Mitch approached on the other side of the mall, Tarrance moved swiftly toward him.

Mitch saw him and slowed for a second.

'Hello, Mitch. Mind if I walk with you?'

'Yes, I mind, Tarrance. It's dangerous, don't you think?'

They walked briskly and did not look at each other. 'Look at that store over there,' Tarrance said, pointing to their right. 'I need a pair of shoes.' They ducked into Don Pang's House of Shoes. Tarrance walked to the rear of the narrow store and stopped between two rows of fake Reeboks at $4.99 for two pairs. Mitch followed him and picked up a pair of size tens. Don Pang or some other Korean eyed them suspiciously but said nothing. They watched the front door through the racks.

'The Director called me yesterday,' Tarrance said without moving his lips. 'He asked about you. Said it was time you made a decision.'

'Tell him I'm still thinking.'

'Have you told the boys at the office?'

'No. I'm still thinking.'

'That's good. I don't think you should tell them.' He handed Mitch a business card. 'Keep this. There are two numbers on the back. Use either one from a pay phone. You'll get a recorder, so just leave a message and tell me exactly when and where to meet you.'

Mitch put the card in his pocket.

Suddenly, Tarrance ducked lower. 'What is it!' Mitch demanded.

'I think we've been caught. I just saw a goon walk past the store and look in. Listen to me, Mitch, and listen carefully. Walk with me out of the store right now, and the instant we get out the door, yell at me to get lost and shove me away. I'll act like I want to fight, and you run in the direction of your office.'

'You're gonna get me killed, Tarrance.'

'Just do as I say. As soon as you get to the office, report this incident to the partners. Tell them I cornered you and you got away as soon as possible.'

Outside, Mitch shoved harder than necessary and yelled, 'Get the hell away from me! And leave me alone!' He ran two blocks to Union Avenue, then walked to the Bendini Building. He stopped in the men's room on the first floor to catch his breath. He stared at himself in the mirror and breathed deeply ten times.

Avery was on the phone, with two lights holding and blinking. A secretary sat on the sofa, ready with a steno pad for the onslaught of commands. Mitch looked at her and said, 'Would you step outside, please. I need to speak to Avery in private.' She stood and Mitch escorted her to the door. He closed it.

Avery watched him closely and hung up. 'What's going on?' he asked.

Mitch stood by the sofa. 'The FBI just grabbed me as I was returning from Tax Court.'

'Damn! Who was it?'

'Same agent. Guy by the name of Tarrance.'

Avery picked up the phone and kept talking. 'Where did it happen?'

'On the mall. North of Union. I was just walking alone, minding my own business.'

'Is this the first contact since that other thing?'

'Yes. I didn't recognize the guy at first.'

Avery spoke into the receiver. 'This is Avery Tolleson. I need to speak to Oliver Lambert immediately. . . . I don't care if he's on the phone. Interrupt him, and now.'

'What's going on, Avery?' Mitch asked.

'Hello, Oliver. Avery here. Sorry for the interruption. Mitch McDeere is here in my office. A few minutes ago he was walking back from the Federal Building when the FBI agent approached him on the mall . . . What? Yes, he just walked in my office and told me about it . . . All right, we'll be there in five minutes.' He hung up. 'Relax, Mitch. We've been through this before.'

'I know, Avery, but this does not make sense. Why would they bother with me? I'm the newest man in the firm.'

'It's harassment, Mitch. Pure and simple. Nothing but harassment. Sit down.'

Mitch walked to the window and looked at the river in the distance. Avery was a cool liar. It was now time for the 'they're just picking on us' routine. Relax, Mitch. Relax? With eight FBI agents assigned to the firm and the Director, Mr. Denton Voyles himself, monitoring the case daily? Relax? He'd just been caught whispering to an FBI agent inside a dollar shoe store. And now he was forced to act like he was an ignorant pawn being preyed upon by the evil forces of the federal government. Harassment? Then why was the goon following him on a routine walk to the courthouse? Answer that, Avery.

'You're scared, aren't you?' Avery asked as he put his arm around him and gazed out the window.

'Not really. Locke explained it all last time. I just wish they would leave me alone.'

'It's a serious matter, Mitch. Don't take it lightly. Let's walk over and see Lambert.'

Mitch followed Avery around the corner and down the hall. A stranger in a black suit opened the door for them, then closed it. Lambert, Nathan Locke and Royce McKnight stood near the small conference table. Again, a tape recorder sat on the table. Mitch sat across from it. Black Eyes sat at the head of the table and glared at Mitch.

He spoke with a menacing frown. There were no smiles in the room. 'Mitch, has Tarrance or anyone elso from the FBI contacted you since the first meeting last August?'

'No.'

'Are you certain?'

Mitch slapped the table. 'Dammit! I said no! Why don't you put me under oath?'

Locke was startled. They were all startled. A heavy, tense silence followed for thirty seconds. Mitch glared at Black Eyes, who retreated ever so slightly with a casual movement of his head.

Lambert, ever the diplomat, the mediator, intervened. 'Look, Mitch, we know this is frightening.'

'Damn right it is. I don't like it at all. I'm minding my own business, working my ass off ninety hours a week, trying to be nothing but a good lawyer and member of this firm, and for some unknown reason I keep getting these little visits from the FBI. Now, sir, I would like some answers.'

Locke pressed the red button on the recorder. 'We'll talk about that in a minute. First, you tell us everything that happened.'

'It's very simple, Mr. Locke. I walked to the Federal Building at ten for an appearance before Judge Kofer on the Malcolm Delaney case. I was there about an hour, and I finished my business. I left the Federal Building, and I was walking in the direction of our office – in a hurry, I might add. It's about twenty degrees out there. A block or two north of Union, this guy Tarrance came out of nowhere, grabbed my arm and pushed me into a small store. I started to knock the hell out of him, but, after all, he is an FBI agent. And I didn't want to make a scene. Inside, he tells me he wants to talk for a minute. I pulled away from him, and ran to the door. He followed me, tried to grab me, and I shoved him away. Then I ran here, went straight to Avery's office, and here we are. That's all that was said. Play by play, everything.'

'What did he want to talk about?'

'I didn't give him a chance, Mr. Locke. I have no plans to talk to any FBI agent unless he has a subpoena.'

'Are you sure it's the same agent?'

'I think so. I didn't recognize him at first. I haven't seen him since last August. Once inside the store, he pulled his badge and gave me his name again. At that point, I ran.'

Locke pressed another button and sat back in the chair. Lambert sat behind him and smiled ever so warmly. 'Listen, Mitch, we explained this last time. These guys are getting bolder and bolder. Just last month they approached Jack Aldrich while he was eating lunch in a grill on Second Street. We're not sure what they're up to, but Tarrance is out of his mind. It's nothing but harassment.'

Mitch watched his lips but heard little. As Lambert spoke, he thought of Kozinski and Hodge and their pretty widows and children at the funerals.

Black Eyes cleared his throat. 'It's a serious matter, Mitch. But we have nothing to hide. They could better spend their time investigation our clients if they suspect wrongdoing. We're lawyers. We may represent people who flirt with the law, but we have done nothing wrong. This is very baffling to us.'

Mitch smiled and opened his hands. 'What do you want me to do?' he asked sincerely.

'There's nothing you can do, Mitch,' said Lambert. 'Just stay away from this guy, and run if you see him. If he so much as looks at you, report it immediately.'

'That's what he did,' Avery said defensively.

Mitch looked as pitiful as possible.

'You can go, Mitch' Lambert said. 'And keep us posted.'

He left the office by himself.

DeVasher paced behind his desk and ignored the partners. 'He's lying, I tell you. He's lying. The son of a bitch is lying. I know he's lying.'

# WITH COMPLIMENTS

THE MUSEUM OF SCOTTISH LIGHTHOUSES
KINNAIRD HEAD • FRASERBURGH • AB43 9DU
TEL (01346) 511022 • FAX (01346) 511033
E-MAIL: enquiries@lighthousemuseum.demon.co.uk

'What did your man see?' asked Locke.

'My man saw something different. Slightly different. But very different. He says McDeere and Tarrance walked sort of nonchalantly into the shoe store. No physical intimidation by Tarrance. None at all. Tarrance walks up, they talk, and both sort of duck into the store. My man says they disappear into the back of the store, and they're back there for three, maybe four minutes. Then another one of our guys walks by the store, looks in and sees nothing. Evidently, they saw our man, because within seconds they come flying out of the store with McDeere shoving and yelling. Something ain't right, I tell you.'

'Did Tarrance grab his arm and force him into the store?' Nathan Lock asked slowly, precisely.

'Hell no. And that's the problem. McDeere went voluntarily, and when he said the guy grabbed his arm, he's lying. My man says he thinks they would've stayed in there for a while if they hadn't seen us.'

'But you're not sure of that,' Nathan Locke said.

'I wasn't sure, dammit. They didn't invite me into the store.'

DeVasher kept pacing while the lawyers stared at the floor. He unwrapped a Roi-Tan and crammed it into his fat mouth.

Finally, Oliver Lambert spoke, 'Look, DeVasher, it's very possible McDeere is telling the truth and you man got the wrong signals. It's very possible. I think McDeere is entitled to the benefit of the doubt.'

DeVasher grunted and ignored this.

'Do you know of any contact since last August?' asked Royce McKnight.

'We don't know of any, but that doesn't mean they ain't talked, does it now? We didn't know about those other two until it was almost too late. It's impossible to watch every move they make. Impossible.'

He walked back and forth by his credenza, obviously deep in thought. 'I gotta talk to him,' he finally said.

'Who?'

'McDeere. It's time he and I had a little talk.'

'About what?' Lambert asked nervously.

'You let me handle it, okay?' Just stay out of my way.'

'I think it's a bit premature,' Locke said.

'And I don't give a damn what you think. If you clowns were in charge of security, you'd all be in prison.'

Mitch sat in his office with the door closed and stared at the walls. A migraine was forming at the base of his skull, and he felt sick. There was a knock at the door.

'Come in,' he said softly.

Avery peeked inside, then walked to the desk. 'How about lunch?'

'No, thanks. I'm not hungry.'

The partner slid his hands into his trouser pockets and smiled warmly. 'Look, Mitch, I know you're worried. Let's take a break. I've got to run downtown for a meeting. Why don't you meet me at the Manhattan Club at one. We'll have a long lunch and talk things over. I've reserved the limo for you. It'll be waiting outside at a quarter till.'

Mitch managed a weak smile, as if he was touched by this. 'Sure, Avery. Why not.'

'Good. I'll see you at one.'

At a quarter till, Mitch opened the front door and walked to the limo. The driver opened the door, and Mitch fell in. Company was waiting.

A short, fat, bald-headed man with a huge, bulging, hanging neck sat smugly in the corner of the rear seat. He stuck out a hand. 'Name's DeVasher, Mitch. Nice to meet you.'

'Am I in the right limo?' Mitch asked.

'Sure. Sure. Relax.' The driver pulled away from the curb.

'What can I do for you?' Mitch asked.

'You can listen for a while. We need to have a little talk.' The driver turned on Riverside Drive and headed for the Hernando De Soto Bridge.

'Where are we going?' Mitch asked.

'For a little ride. Just relax, son.'

So I'm number six, thought Mitch. This is it. No, wait a minute. They were much more creative than this with their killing.

'Mitch, can I call you Mitch?'

'Sure.'

'Fine. Mitch, I'm in charge of security for the firm, and – '

'Why does the firm need security?'

'Just listen to me, son, and I'll explain. The firm has an extensive security program, thanks to old man Bendini. He was a nut about security and secrecy. My job is to protect the firm, and quite frankly, we're very concerned about this FBI business.'

'So am I.'

'Yes. We believe the FBI is determined to infiltrate our firm in hopes of collecting information on certain clients.'

'Which clients?'

'Some high rollers with questionable tax shelters.'

Mitch nodded and looked at the river below. They were now in Arkansas, with the Memphis skyline fading behind them. DeVasher recessed the conversation. He sat like a frog with his hands folded across the gut. Mitch waited, until it became apparent that lapses in conversation and awkward silence did not bother DeVasher. Several miles across the river, the driver left the interstate and found a rough county road that circled and ran back to the east. Then he turned on to a gravel road that went for a mile through low-lying bean fields next to the river. Memphis was suddenly visible again, across the water.

'Where are we going?' Mitch asked, with some alarm.

'Relax. I want to show you something.'

A gravesite, thought Mitch. The limo stopped on a cliff that fell ten feet to a sandbar next to the bank. The skyline stood impressively on the other side. The top of the Bendini Building was visible.

'Let's take a walk,' DeVasher said.

'Where to?' Mitch asked.

'Come on. It's okay.' DeVasher opend his door and walked to the rear bumper. Slowly, Mitch followed him.

'As I was saying, Mitch, we are very troubled by this contact with the FBI. If you talk to them, they will get bolder, then who knows what the fools will try. It's imperative that you not speak to them, ever again. Understand?'

'Ycs. I've understood since the first visit in August.'

Suddenly, DeVasher was in his face, nose to nose. He smiled wickedly. 'I have something that will keep you honest.' He reached in his sport coat and pulled out a manila envelope.

'Take a look at these,' he said with a sneer, and walked away.

Mitch leaned on the limo and nervously opened the envelope. There were four photographs, black and white, eight by ten, very clear. On the beach. The girl.

'Oh my god! Who took these?' Mitch yelled at him.

'What difference does it make. It's you, ain't it?'

There was no doubt about who it was. He ripped the photographs into small pieces and threw them in DeVasher's direction.

'We got plenty at the office,' DeVasher said calmly. 'Bunch of them. We don't want to use them, but one more little conversation with Mr. Tarrance or any other Fibbie and we'll mail them to your wife. How would you like that, Mitch? Imagine your pretty little wife going to the mailbox to get her *Redbook* and catalogues and she sees this strange envelope addressed to her. Try to thing of that, Mitch.

The next time you and Tarrance decide to shop for plastic shoes, think about us, Mitch. Because we'll be watching.'

'Who knows about these?' Mitch asked.

'Me and the photographer, and now you. Nobody in the firm knows, and I don't plan to tell them. But if you screw up again, I suspect they'll be passing them around at lunch. I play hardball, Mitch.'

He sat on the trunk and rubbed his temples. DeVasher walked up next to him. 'Listen, son. You're a very bright young man, and you're on your way to big bucks. Don't screw it up. Just work hard, play the game, buy new cars, build bigger homes, the works. Just like all the other guys. Don't try to be no hero. I don't want to use the pictures.'

'Okay, okay.'

# CHAPTER TWENTY-ONE

For seventeen days and seventeen nights, the troubled lives of Mitch and Abby McDeere proceeded quietly without interference from Wayne Tarrance or any of his confederates. The routines returned. Mitch worked eighteen hours a day, every day of the week, and never left the office for any reason except to drive home. Lunch was at the desk. Avery sent other associates to run errands or file motions or appear in court. Mitch seldom left his office, the fifteen-by-fifteen sanctuary where he was certain Tarrance could not get him. If possible, he stayed out of the halls and men's rooms and coffee room. They were watching, he was sure. He was not sure who they were, but there was no doubt that a bunch of folks were vitally interested in his movements. So he stayed at his desk, with the door shut most of the time, working diligently, billing like crazy and trying to forget that the building had a fifth floor and on the fifth floor was a short, fat, mean little bastard named DeVasher who had a collection of photographs that could ruin him.

With each uneventful day, Mitch withdrew even more into his asylum and became even more hopeful that perhaps the last episode in the Korean shoe store had scared Tarrance or maybe gotten him fired. Maybe Voyles would just simply forget the entire operation, and Mich could continue along his happy way of getting rich and making partner and buying everything in sight. But he knew better.

To Abby, the house was a prison, though she could come and go at will. She worked longer hours at school, spent more time walking the malls and made at least one trip each day to the grocery store. She watched everyone, especially men in dark suits who looked at her. She wore black sunglasses so they could not see her eyes. She wore them when it was raining. Late at night, after supper alone while she waited for him, she stared at the walls and resisted the temptation to investigate. The phones could be examined with a magnifying glass. The wires and mikes could not be invisible, she told herself. More than once she thought of finding a book on such devices so she could identify them. But Mitch said no. They were in the house, he assured her, and any attempt to find them could be disastrous.

So she moved silently around her own house, feeling violated and knowing it could not last much longer. They both knew the importance of appearing normal, of sounding normal. They tried to engage in normal talk about how the day went, about the office and her students, about the weather, about this and that. But the conversations were flat, often forced and strained. When Mitch was in law school the love-making had been frequent and rowdy; now it was pratically nonexistent. Someone was listening.

Midnight walks around the block became a habit. After a quick sandwich each night, they would deliver the rehearsed lines about needing exercise and head for the street. They held hands and walked in the cold, talking about the firm and the FBI, and which way to turn; always the same conclusion: there was no way out. None. Seventeen days and seventeen nights.

The eighteenth day brought a new twist. Mitch was exhausted by 9 P.M. and decided to go home. He had worked nonstop for fifteen and a half hours. At two hundred per. As usual, he walked the halls on the second floor, then took the stairs to the third floor. He casually checked each office to see who was still working. No one on the third floor. He followed the stairs to the fourth floor and walked the wide rectangular hallway as if in search of something. All lights except one were off. Royce McKnight was working late. Mitch eased by his office without being seen. Avery's door was closed, and Mitch grabbed the doorknob. It was locked. He walked to the library down the hall, looking for a book he did not need. After two weeks of the casual late-night inspections, he had found no closed circuit cameras above the halls or offices. They just listen, he decided. They do not see.

He said goodbye to Dutch Hendrix at the front gate and drove home. Abby was not expecting him at such an early hour. He quietly unlocked the door from the carport and eased into the kitchen. He flipped on a light switch. She was in the bedroom. Between the kitchen and the den was a small foyer with a rolltop desk where Abby left each day's mail. He laid his briefcase softly on the desk, then saw it. A large brown envelope addressed with a black marker to Abby McDeere. No return address. Scrawled in heavy black letters were the words PHOTOGRAPHS – DO NOT BEND. His heart stopped first, then his breathing. He grabbed the envelope. It had been opened.

A heavy layer of sweat broke across his forehead. His mouth was dry and he could not swallow. His heart returned with the fury of a jackhammer. The breathing was heavy and painful. He was nauseous. Slowly, he backed away from the desk, holding the envelope. She's in bed, he thought. Hurt, sick, devastated and mad as hell. He wiped his forehead and tried to collect himself. Face it like a man, he said.

She was in the bed, reading a book with the television on. The dog was in the backyard. Mitch opened the bedroom door, and Abby bolted upright in horror. She almost screamed at the intruder, until she recognized him.

'You scared me, Mitch!'

Her eyes glowed with fear, then fun. They had not been crying. They looked fine, normal. No pain. No anger. He could not speak.

'Why are you home?' she demanded, sitting up in bed, smiling now.

Smiling? 'I live here,' he said weakly.

'Why didn't you call?'

'Do I have to call before I can come home?' His breathing was now almost normal. She was fine!

'It would be nice. Come here and kiss me.'

He leaned across the bed and kissed her. He handed her the envelope. 'What's this?' he asked nonchalantly.

'You tell me. It's addressed to me, but there was nothing inside. Not a thing.' She closed her book and laid it on the night table.

Not a thing! He smiled at her and kissed her again. 'Are you expecting photographs from anyone?' he asked in complete ignorance.

'Not that I know of. Must be a mistake.'

He could almost hear DeVasher laughing at this very moment on the fifth floor. The fat little bastard was standing up there somewhere in some dark room full of wires and machines with a headset stretched around his massive bowling ball of a head, laughing uncontrollably.

'That's strange,' Mitch said. Abby pulled on a pair of jeans and pointed to the backyard. Mitch nodded. The signal was simple, just a quick point or a nod of the head in the direction of the patio.

Mitch laid the envelope on the rolltop desk and for a second touched the scrawled markings on it. Probably DeVasher's handwriting. He could almost hear him laughing. He could see his fat face and nasty smile. The photographs had probably been passed around during lunch in the partners' dining room. He could see Lambert and McKnight and even Avery gawking admiringly over coffee and dessert.

They'd better enjoy the pictures, dammit. They'd better enjoy the remaining few months of their bright and rich and happy legal careers.

Abby walked by and he grabbed her hand. 'What's for dinner?' he asked for the benefit of those listening.

'Why don't we go out? We could celebrate since you're home at a decent hour.'

They walked through the den. 'Good idea,' said Mitch. They eased through the rear door, across the patio and into the darkness.

'What is it?' Mitch asked.

'You got a letter today from Doris. She said she's in Nashville, but will return to Memphis on the twenty-seventh of February. She says she needs to see you. It's important. It was a very short letter.'

'The twenty-seventh! That was yesterday.'

'I know. I presume she's already in town. I wonder what she wants.'

'Yeah, and I wonder where she is.'

'She said her husband had an engagement here in town.'

'Good. She'll find us,' Mitch said.

Nathan Locke closed his office door and pointed DeVasher in the direction of the small conference table near the window. The two men hated each other and made no attempt to be cordial. But business was business, and they took orders from the same man.

'Lazarov wanted me to talk to you,' DeVasher said. 'I've spent the past two days with him in Vegas, and he's very anxious. They're all anxious, Locke, and he trusts you more than anyone else around here. He likes you more than he likes me.'

'That's understandable,' Locke said with no smile. The ripples of black around his eyes narrowed and focused intensely on DeVasher.

'Anyway, there are a few things he wants us to discuss.'

'I'm listening.'

'McDeere's lying. You know how Lazarov's always bragged about having a mole inside the FBI. Well, I've never believed him, and still don't, for the most part. But according to Lazarov, his little source is telling him that there was some kind of secret meeting involving McDeere and some FBI heavyweights when your boy was in Washington back in January. We were there, and our men saw nothing, but it's impossible to track anyone twenty-four hours a day without getting caught. It's possible he could've slipped away for a little while without our knowledge.'

'Do you believe it?'

'It's not important whether I believe it. Lazarov believes it, and that's all that matters. At any rate, he told me to make preliminary plans to, uh, take care of him.'

'Damn DeVasher! We can't keep eliminating people.'

'Just preliminary plans, nothing serious. I told Lazarov I thought it was much too early and that it would be a mistake. But they are very worried, Locke.'

'This can't continue, DeVasher. I mean, damn! We have reputations to consider. We have a higher casualty rate than oil rigs. People will start talking. We're gonna reach a point where no law student in his right mind would take a job here.'

'I don't think you need to worry about that. Lazarov has put a freeze on hiring. He told me to tell you that. He also wants to know how many associates are still in the dark.'

'Five, I think. Let's see, Lynch, Sorrell, Buntin, Myers and McDeere.'

'Forget McDeere. Lazarov is convinced he knows much more than we think. Are you certain the other four know nothing?'

Locke thought for a moment and mumbled under his breath. 'Well, we haven't told them. You guys are listening and watching. What do you hear?'

'Nothing, from those four. They sound ignorant and act as if they suspect nothing. Can you fire them?'

'Fire them! They're lawyers, DeVasher. You don't fire lawyers. They're loyal members of the firm.'

'The firm is changing, Locke. Lazarov wants to fire the ones who don't know and stop hiring new ones. It's obvious the Fibbies have changed their stategy, and it's time for us to change as well. Lazarov wants to circle the wagons and plug the leaks. We can't sit back and wait for them to pick off our boys.'

'Fire them,' Locke repeated in disbelief. 'This firm has never fired a lawyer.'

'Very touching, Locke. We've disposed of five, but never fired one. That's real good. You've got a month to do it, so start thinking of a reason. I suggest you fire all four at one time. Tell them you lost a big account and you're cutting back.'

'We have clients, not accounts.'

'Okay, fine. Your biggest client is telling you to fire Lynch, Sorrell, Buntin and Myers. Now start making plans.'

'How do we fire those four without firing McDeere?'

'You'll think of something, Nat. You got a month. Get rid of them and don't hire any new boys. Lazarov wants a tight little unit where everyone can be trusted. He's scared, Nat. Scared and mad. I don't have to tell you what could happen if one of your boys spilled his guts.'

'No, you don't have to tell me. What does he plan to do with McDeere?'

'Right now, nothing but the same. We're listening twenty-four hours a day, and the kid has never mentioned a word to his wife or anyone else. Not a word! He's been corralled twice by Tarrance, and reported both incidents to you. I still think the second meeting was somewhat suspicious, so we're being very careful. Lazarov, on the other hand, insists there was a meeting in Washington. He's trying to confirm. He said his sources knew little, but they were digging. If in fact McDeere met with the Fibbies up there and failed to report it, then I'm sure Lazarov will instruct me to move quickly. That's why he wants preliminary plans to take McDeere out.'

'How do you plan to do it?'

'It's too early. I haven't given it much thought.'

'You know he and his wife are going to the Caymans in two weeks for a vacation. They'll stay in one of our condos, the usual.'

'We wouldn't do it there again. Too suspicious. Lazarov instructed me to get her pregnant.'

'McDeere's wife?'

'Yep. He wants them to have a baby, a little leverage. She's on the pill, so we gotta break in, take her little box, match up the pills and replace them with placebos.'

At this, the great black eyes saddened just a touch and looked through the window. 'What the hell's going on, DeVasher?' he asked softly.

'This place is about to change, Nat. It appears as though the feds are extremely interested, and they keep pecking away. One day, who knows, one of your boys may take the bait, and you'll all leave town in the middle of the night.'

'I don't believe that, DeVasher. A lawyer here would be a fool to risk his life and his family for a few promises from the feds. I just don't believe it will happen. These boys are too smart and they're making too much money.'

'I hope you're right.'

# CHAPTER TWENTY-TWO

The leasing agent leaned against the rear of the elevator and admired the black leather miniskirt from behind. He followed it down almost to the knees, where it ended and the seams in the black silk stockings began and snaked downward to black heels. Kinky heels, with little red bows across the toes. He slowly worked his way back up the seams, past the leather, pausing to admire the roundness of her rear, then upward to the red cashmere sweater, which from his vantage point revealed little but from the other side was quite impressive, as he had noticed in the lobby. The hair landed just below the shoulder blades and contrasted nicely with the red. He knew it was bleached, but add the bleach to the leather mini and the seams and the kinky heels and the tight sweater hugging those things around the front, add all that together and he knew this was a woman he could have. He would like to have her in the building. She just wanted a small office. The rent was negotiable.

The elevator stopped. The door opened, and he followed her into the narrow hall. 'This way' – he pointed, flipping on a light switch. In the corner, he moved in front of her and stuck a key in a badly aged wooden door.

'It's just two rooms,' he said, flipping on another switch. 'About two hundred square feet.'

She walked straight to the window. 'The view is okay,' Tammy said, staring into the distance.

'Yes, a nice view. The carpet is new. Painted last fall. Rest room's down the hall. It's a nice place. The entire building's been renovated within the past eight years.' He stared at the black seams as he spoke.

'It's not bad,' Tammy said, not in response to anything he had mentioned. She continued to stare out the window. 'What's the name of this place?'

'The Cotton Exchange Building. One of the oldest in Memphis. It's really a prestigious address.'

'How prestigious is the rent?'

He cleared his throat and held a file before him. He did not look at the file. He was gaping at the heels now. 'Well, it's such a small office. What did you say you needed it for?'

'Secretarial work. Free-lance secretarial.' She moved to the other window, ignoring him. He followed every move.

'I see. How long will you need it?'

'Six months, with an option for a year.'

'Okay, for six months we can lease it for three-fifty a month.'

She did not flinch or look from the window. She slid her right foot out of the shoe and rubbed the left calf with it. The seam continued, he observed, under the heel and along the bottom of the foot. The toenails were . . . red! She cocked her rear to the left and leaned on the windowsill. His file was shaking.

'I'll pay two-fifty a month,' she said with authority.

He cleared his throat. There was no sense being greedy. The tiny rooms were dead space, useless to anyone else, and had not been occupied in years. The building could use a free-lance secretary. Hell, he might even need a free-lance secretary.

'Three hundred, but no less. This building is in demand. Ninety percent occupied right now. Three hundred a month, and that's too low. We're barely covering costs at that.'

She turned suddenly, and there they were. Staring at him. The cashmere was stretched tightly around them. 'The ad said there were furnished offices available,' she said.

'We can furnish this one,' he said, eager to cooperate. 'What do you need?'

She looked around the office. 'I would like a secretarial desk with credenza in here. Several file cabinets. A couple of chairs for clients. Nothing fancy. The other room does not have to be furnished. 'I'll put a copier in there.'

'No problem,' he said with a smile.

'And I'll pay three hundred a month, furnished.'

'Good,' he said as he opened a file and withdrew a blank lease. He laid it on a folding table and began writing.

'Your name?'

'Doris Greenwood.' Her mother was Doris Greenwood, and she had been Tammy Inez Greenwood before she ran up on Buster Hemphill, who later became (legally) Elvis Aaron Hemphill, and life had pretty much been downhill since. Her mother lived in Effingham, Illinois.

'Okay, Doris,' he said with an effort at suaveness, as if they were now on a first name basis and growing closer by the moment. 'Home address?'

'Why do you need that?' she asked with irritation.

'Well, uh, we just need that information.'

'It's none of your business.'

'Okay, okay. No problem.' He dramatically scratched out that portion of the lease. He hovered above it. 'Let's see. We'll run it from today, March 2, for six months until September 2. Is that okay?'

She nodded and lit a cigarette.

He read the next paragraph. 'Okay, we require a three-hundred-dollar deposit and the first month's rent in advance.'

From a pocket in the tight black leather skirt, she produced a roll of cash. She counted six one-hundred-dollar bills and laid them on the table. 'Receipt, please,' she demanded.

'Certainly.' He continued writing.

'What floor are we on?' she asked, returning to the windows.

'Ninth. There's a ten percent late charge past the fifteenth of the month. We have the right to enter at any reasonable time to inspect. Premises cannot be used for any illegal purpose. You pay all utilities and insurance on contents. You get one parking space in the lot across the street, and here are two keys. Any questions?'

'Yeah. What if I work odd hours? I mean, real late at night.'

'No bid deal. You can come and go as you please. After dark the security guard at the Front Street door will let you pass.'

Tammy stuck the cigarette between her sticky lips and walked to the table. She glanced at the lease, hesitated, then signed the name of Doris Greenwood.

They locked up, and he followed her carefully down the hall to the elevator.

By noon the next day, the odd assortment of furniture had been delivered and Doris Greenwood of Greenwood Services arranged the rented typewriter and the rented phone next to each other on the secretarial desk. Sitting and facing the typewriter, she could look slightly to her left out of the window and watch the traffic on Front Street. She filled the desk drawers with typing paper, notepads, pencils, odds and ends. She placed magazines on the filing cabinets and the small table between the two chairs where her clients would sit.

There was a knock at the door. 'Who is it?' she asked.

'It's your copier,' a voice answered.

She unlocked the door and opened it. A short, hyperactive little man named Gordy rushed in, looked around the room and said rudely, 'Okay, where do you want it?'

'In there,' Tammy said, pointing to the eight-by-ten empty room with no door on the hinges. Two young men in blue uniforms pushed and pulled the cart holding the copier.

Gordy laid the paperwork on her desk. 'It's a mighty big copier for this place. We're talking ninety copies a minute with a collator and automatic feed. It's a big machine.'

'Where do I sign?' she asked, ignoring the small talk.

He pointed with the pen. 'Six months, at two-forty a month. That includes service and maintenance and five hundred sheets of paper for the first two months. You want legal or letter sized?'

'Legal.'

'First payment due on the tenth, and same thereafter for five months. Operator's manual is on the rack. Call me if you have any questions.'

The two servicemen gawked at the tight stonewashed jeans and the red heels and slowly left her office. Gordy ripped off the yellow copy and handed it to her. 'Thanks for the business,' he said.

She locked the door behind them. She walked to the window next to her dest and looked north, along Front. Two blocks up on the opposite side, floors four and five of the Bendini Building were visible.

He kept to himself with his nose buried deep in the books and the piles of paperwork. He was too busy for any of them, except Lamar. He was very much aware that his withdrawal was not going unnoticed. So he worked harder. Perhaps they would not be suspicious if he billed twenty hours a day. Perhaps money would insulate him.

Nina left a box of cold pizza when she checked out after lunch. He ate it while he cleared his desk. He called Abby. Said he was going to see Ray and that he would return to Memphis late Sunday. He eased through the side door and into the parking lot.

For three and a half hours, he raced along Interstate 40 with his eyes on the rearview mirror. Nothing. He never saw them. They probably just call ahead, he thought, and wait for him somewhere up there. In Nashville, he made a sudden exit into downtown. Using a map he had scribbled, he darted in and out of traffic, making U-turns wherever possible and in general driving like a nut. To the south of town, he turned quickly into a large apartment complex and cruised between the buildings. It was nice enough. The parking lots were clean and the faces were white. All of them. He parked next to the office and locked the BMW. The pay phone by the covered pool worked. He called a cab and gave an address two blocks away. He ran between the buildings, down a side street and arrived precisely with the cab. 'Greyhound bus station,' he said to the driver. 'And in a hurry. I've got ten minutes.'

'Relax, pal. It's only six blocks away.'

Mitch ducked low in the rear seat and watched the traffic. The driver moved with a slow confidence and seven minutes later turned onto Eighth Street. He stopped in front of the station. Mitch threw two fives over the seat and darted into the terminal. He bought a one way ticket on the four-thirty bus to Atlanta. It was four thirty-one, according to the clock on the wall. The clerk pointed through the swinging doors. 'Bus No. 454,' she said. 'Leaving in a moment.'

The driver slammed the baggage door, took his ticket and followed Mitch onto the bus. The first three rows were filled with elderly blacks. A dozen more passengers were scattered toward the rear. Mitch walked slowly down the aisle, gazing at each face and seeing no one. He took a window seat on the fourth row from the rear. He slipped on a pair of sunglasses and glanced behind him. No one. Dammit! Was it the wrong bus? He stared out the dark windows as the bus moved quickly into traffic. They would stop in Knoxville. Maybe his contact would be there.

When they were on the interstate and the driver reached his cruising speed, a man in blue jeans and madras shirt suddenly appeared and slid into the seat next to Mitch. It was Tarrance. Mitch breathed easier.

'Where have you been?' he asked.

'In the rest room. Did you lose them?' Tarrance spoke in a low voice while surveying the backs of the heads of the passengers. No one was listening. No one could hear.

'I never see them, Tarrance. So I cannot say if I lost them. But I think they would have to be supermen to keep my trail this time.'

'Did you see our man in the terminal?'

'Yes. By the pay phone with the red Falcons cap. Black dude.'

'That's him. He would've signaled if they were following.'

'He gave me the go-ahead.'

Tarrance wore silver reflective sunglasses under a green Michigan State baseball cap. Mitch could smell the fresh Juicy Fruit.

'Sort of out of uniform, aren't you?' Mitch said with no smile. 'Did Voyles give you permission to dress like that?'

'I forgot to ask him. I'll mention it in the morning.'

'Sunday morning?' Mitch asked.

'Of course. He'll wanna know all about our little bus ride. I briefed him for an hour before I left town.'

'Well, first things first. What about my car?'

'We'll pick it up in a few minutes and babysit it for you. It'll be in Knoxville when you need it. Don't worry.'

'You don't think they'll find us?'

'No way. No one followed you out of Memphis, and we detected nothing in Nashville. You're clean as a whistle.'

'Pardon my concern. But after that fiasco in the shoe store, I know you boys are not above stupidity.'

'It was a mistake, all right. We – '

'A big mistake. One that could get me on the hit list.'

'You covered it well. It won't happen again.'

'Promise me, Tarrance. Promise me no one will ever again approach me in public.'

Tarrance looked down the aisle and nodded.

'No, Tarrance. I need to hear it from your mouth. Promise me.'

'Okay, okay. It won't happen again. I promise.'

'Thanks. Now maybe I can eat at a restaurant without fear of being grabbed.'

'You've made your point.'

An old black man with a cane inched toward them, smiled and walked past. The rest-room door slammed. The Greyhound rode the left lane and blew past the lawful drivers.

Tarrance flipped through a magazine. Mitch gazed into the countryside. The man with the cane finished his business and wobbled to his seat on the front row.

'So what brings you here?' Tarrance asked, flipping pages.

'I don't like airplanes. I always take the bus.'

'I see. Where would you like to start?'

'Voyles said you had a game plan.'

'I do. I just need a quarterback.'

'Good ones are very expensive.'

'We've got the money.'

'It'll cost a helluva lot more than you think. The way I figure it, I'll be throwing away a forty-year legal career at, say, an average of half a million a year.'

'That's twenty million bucks.'

'I know. But we can negotiate.'

'That's good to hear. You're assuming that you'll work, or practice, as you say , for forty years. That's a precarious assumption. Just for fun, let's assume that within five years we bust up the firm and indict you along with all your buddies. And that we obtain convictions, and you go off to prison for a few years. They won't keep you long because you're a white-collar type, and of course you've heard how nice the federal pens are. But at any rate, you'll lose your license, your house, your little BMW. Probably your wife. When you get out, you can open up a private investigation service like your old friend Lomax. It's easy work, unless you sniff the wrong underwear.'

'Like I said. It's negotiable.'

'All right. Let's negotiate. How much do you want?'

'For what?'

Tarrance closed the magazine, placed it under his seat and opened a thick paperback. He pretended to read. Mitch spoke from the corner of his mouth with his eyes on the median.

'That's a very good question,' Tarrance said softly, just above the distant grind of the diesel engine. 'What do we want from you? Good question. First, you have to give up your career as a lawyer. You'll have to divulge secrets and records that belong to your clients. That, of course, is enough to get you disbarred, but that won't seem important. You and I must agree that you will hand us the firm on a silver platter. Once we agree, if we agree, the rest will fall into place. Second, and most important, you will give us enough documentation to indict every member of the firm and most of the top Morolto people. The records are in the little building there on Front Street.'

'How do you know this?'

Tarrance smiled. 'Because we spend billions of dollars fighting organized crime. Because we've tracked the Moroltos for twenty years. Because we have sources within the family. Because Hodge and Kozinski were talking when they were murdered. Don't sell us short, Mitch.'

'And you think I can get this information out?'

'Yes, Counselor. You can build a case from the inside that will collapse the firm and break up one of the largest crime families in the country. You gotta lay out the firm for us. Whose office is where? Names of all secretaries, clerks, paralegals. Who works on what files? Who's got which clients? The chain of command. Where on the fifth floor? What's up there? Where are the records kept? Is there a central storage area? How much is computerized? How much is on microfilm? And most important, you gotta bring the stuff out and hand it to us. Once we have probable cause, we can go in with a small army and get everything. But that's an awfully big step. We gotta have a very tight and solid case before we go crashing in with search warrants.'

'Is that all you want?'

'No. You'll have to testify against all of your buddies at their trials. Could take years.'

Mitch breathed deeply and closed his eyes. The bus slowed behind a caravan of mobile homes split in two. Dusk was approaching, and, one at a time, the cars in the westbound lane brightened with headlights. Testifying at trial! This, he had not thought of. With millions to spend for the best criminal lawyers, the trials could drag on forever.

Tarrance actually began reading the paperback, a Louis L'Amour. He adjusted the reading light above them, as if he was indeed a real passenger on a real journey. After thirty miles of no talk, no negotiation, Mitch removed his sunglasses and looked at Tarrance.

'What happens to me?'

'You'll have a lot of money, for what that's worth. If you have any sense of morality, you can face yourself each day. You can live anywhere in the country, with a new identity, of course. We'll find you a job, fix your nose, do anything you want, really.'

Mitch tried to keep his eyes on the road, but it was impossible. He glared at Tarrance. 'Morality? Don't ever mention that word to me again, Tarrance. I'm an innocent victim, and you know it.'

Tarrance grunted with a smart-ass grin.

They rode in silence for a few miles.

'What about my wife?'

'Yeah, you can keep her.'

'Very funny.'

'Sorry. She'll get everything she wants. How much does she know?'

'Everything.' He thought of the girl on the beach. 'Well, almost everything.'

'We'll get her a fat government job with the Social Security Administration anywhere you want. It won't be that bad, Mitch.'

'It'll be wonderful. Until an unknown point in the future when one of your people opens his or her mouth and lets something slip to the wrong person, and you'll read about me or my wife in the paper. The Mob never forgets, Tarrance. They're worse than elephants. And they keep secrets better than your side. You guys have lost people, so don't deny it.'

'I won't deny it. And I'll admit to you that they can be ingenious when they decide to kill.'

'Thanks. So where do I go?'

'It's up to you. Right now we have about two thousand witnesses living all over the country under new names with new homes and new jobs. The odds are overwhelmingly in your favor.'

'So I play the odds?'

'Yes. You either take the money and run, or you play big-shot lawyer and bet that we never infiltrate.'

'That's a hell of a choice, Tarrance.'

'It is. I'm glad it's yours.'

'The female companion of the ancient black man with the cane rose feebly from her seat and began shuffling toward them. She grabbed each aisle seat as she progressed. Tarrance leaned toward

Mitch as she passed. He would not dare speak with this stranger in the vicinity. She was at least ninety, half crippled, probable illiterate, and couldn't care less if Tarrance received his next breath of air. But Tarrance was instantly mute.

Fifteen minutes later, the rest-room door opened and released the sounds of the toilet gurgling downward into the pit of the Greyhound. She shuffled to the front and took her seat.

'Who is Jack Aldrich?' Mitch asked. He suspected a coverup with this one, and he carefully watched the reaction from the corner of his eye. Tarrance looked up from the book and stared at the seat in front of him.

'Name's familiar. I can't place him.'

Mitch returned his gaze to the window. Tarrance knew. He had finched, and his eyes had narrowed too quickly before he answered. Mitch watched the westbound traffic.

'So who is he?' Tarrance finally asked.

'You don't know him?'

'If I knew him, I wouldn't ask who he was.'

'He's a member of our firm. You should've known that, Tarrance.'

'The city's full of lawyers. I guess you know them all.'

'I know the ones at Bendini, Lambert & Locke, the quiet little firm you guys have been studying for ten years. Aldrich is a six-year man who allegedly was approached by the FBI a couple of months ago. True or false?'

'Absolutely false. Who told you this?'

'It doesn't matter. Just a rumor around the office.'

'It's a lie. We've talked to no one but you since August. You have my word. And we have no plans to talk to anyone else, unless, of course, you decline and we must find another prospect.'

'You've never talked to Aldrich?'

'That's what I said.'

Mitch nodded and picked up a magazine. They rode in silence for thirty minutes. Tarrance gave up on his novel, and finally said, 'Look, Mitch, we'll be in Knoxville in an hour or so. We need to strike a deal, if we're going to. Director Voyles will have a thousand questions in the morning.'

'How much money?'

'Half a million bucks.'

Any lawyer worth his salt knew the first offer had to be rejected. Always. He had seen Avery's mouth drop open in shock and his head shake wildly in absolute disgust and disbelief with first offers, re-gardless of how reasonable. There would be counteroffers, and counter-counteroffers, and further negotiations, but always, the first offer was rejected.

So by shaking his head and smiling at the window as if this was what he expected, Mitch said no to half a million.

'Did I say something funny?' Tarrance, the nonlawyer, the non-negotiator, asked.

'That's ridiculous, Tarrance. You can't expect me to walk away from a gold mine for half a million bucks. After taxes, I net three hundred thousand at best.'

'And if we close the gold mine and sent all you Gucci-footed hot-shots to jail?'

'If. If. If. If you knew so much, why haven't you done something? Voyles said you boys have been watching and waiting for ten years. That's real good, Tarrance. Do you always move so fast?'

'Do you wanna take that chance, McDeere? Let's say it takes us another five years, okay? After five years we bust the joint and send your ass to jail. At that point it won't make any difference how long it took us, will it? The result will be the same, Mitch.'

'I'm sorry. I thought we were negotiating, not threatening.'

'I've made you an offer.'

'Your offer is too low. You expect me to make a case that will hand you hundreds of indictments against a group of the sleaziest criminals in America, a case that could easily cost me my life. And you offer a pittance. Three million, at least.'

Tarrance did not flinch or frown. He received the counteroffer with a good, straight poker face, and Mitch, the negotiator, knew it was not out of the ballpark.

'That's a lot of money,' Tarrance said, almost to himself. 'I don't think we've ever paid that much.'

'But you can, can't you?'

'I doubt it. I'll have a talk to the Director.'

'The Director! I thought you had complete authority on this case. Are we gonna run back and forth to the Director until we have a deal?'

'What else do you want?'

'I've got a few things in mind, but we won't discuss them until the money gets right.'

The old man with the cane apparently had weak kidneys. He stood again and began the awkward wobble to the rear of the bus. Tarrance again started his book. Mitch flipped through an old copy of *Field & Stream*.

The Greyhound left the interstate in Knoxville two minutes before eight. Tarrance leaned closer an whispered, 'Take the front door out of the terminal. You'll see a young man wearing an orange University of Tennessee sweat suit standing beside a white Bronco. He'll recognize you and call you Jeffrey. Shake hands like lost friends and get in the Bronco. He'll take you to your car.'

'Where is it?' Mitch whispered.

'Behind a dorm on campus.'

'Have they checked it for bugs?'

'I think so. Ask the man in the Bronco. If they were tracking you when you left Memphis, they might be suspicious by now. You should drive to Henderson. It's about fifty miles this side of Nashville. There's a Holiday Inn there. Spend the night and go see your brother tomorrow. We'll be watching also, and if things look fishy, I'll find you Monday morning.'

'When's the next bus ride?'

'Your wife's birthday is Tuesday. Make reservations for eight at Grisanti's, that Italian place on Airways. At precisely nine, go to the cigarette machine in the bar, insert six quarters and buy a pack of anything. In the tray where the cigarettes are released, you will find a cassette tape. Buy yourself one of those small tape players that joggers wear with earphones and listen to the tape in your car, not at home, and sure as hell not at the office. Use the earphones. Let your wife listen to it. I'll be on the cassette, and I'll give you our top dollar. I'll also explain a few things. After you've listened to it a few times, dispose of it.'

'This is rather elaborate, isn't it?'

'Yes, but we don't need to speak to each other for a couple of weeks. They're watching and listening, Mitch. And they're very good. Don't forget that.'

'Don't worry.'

'What was your football jersey number in high school?'

'Fourteen.'

'And college?'

'Fourteen.'

'Okay. Your code number is 1–4–1–4. Thursday night, from a touch tone pay phone, call 757–6000. You'll get a voice that will lead you through a little routine involving your code number. Once you're cleared, you will hear my recorded voice, and I will ask you a series of questions. We'll go from there.'

'Why can't I just practice law?'

The bus pulled into the terminal and stopped. 'I'm going on to Atlanta,' Tarrance said. 'I will not see you for a couple of weeks. If there's an emergency, call one of the two numbers I gave you before.'

Mitch stood in the aisle and looked down at the agent. 'Three million, Tarrance. Not a penny less. If you guys can spend billions fighting organized crime, surely you can find three million for me. And, Tarrance, I have a third option. I can disappear in the middle of the night, vanish into the air. If that happens, you and the Moroltos can fight each other till hell freezes over, and I'll be playing dominoes in the Caribbean.'

'Sure, Mitch. You might play a game or two, but they'd find you within a week. And we wouldn't be there to protect you. So long, buddy.'

Mitch jumped from the bus and darted through the terminal.

# CHAPTER TWENTY-THREE

At eight-thirty A.M. on Tuesday, Nina formed neat piles out of the rubble and debris on his desk. She enjoyed this early-morning ritual of straightening the desk and planning his day. The appointment book lay unobstructed on a corner of his desk. She read from it. 'You have a very busy day today, Mr. McDeere.'

Mitch flipped through a file and tried to ignore her. 'Every day is busy.'

'You have a meeting at ten o'clock in Mr. Mahan's office on the Delta Shipping appeal.'

'I can't wait,' Mitch mumbled.

'You have a meeting at eleven-thirty in Mr. Tolleson's office on the Greenbriar dissolution, and his secretary informed me it would last at least two hours.'

'Why two hours?'

'I'm not paid to ask those questions, Mr. McDeere. If I do I might get fired. At three-thirty, Victor Milligan wants to meet with you.'

'About what?'

'Again, Mr. McDeere, I'm not supposed to ask questions. And you're due in Frank Mulholland's office downtown in fifteen minutes.'

'Yes, I know. Where is it?'

'The Cotton Exchange Building. Four or five blocks up Front at Union. You've walked by it a hundred times.'

'Fine. What else?'

'Shall I bring you something back from lunch?'

'No, I'll grab a sandwich downtown.'

'Wonderful. Do you have everything for Mulholland?'

He pointed to the heavy black briefcase and said nothing. She left, and seconds later Mitch walked down the hall, down the stairs and out the front door. He paused for a second under a streetlight, then turned and walked quickly toward downtown. The black briefcase was in his right hand, the burgundy eel-skin attaché was in his left hand. The signal.

In front of a green building with boarded windows, he stopped next to a fire hydrant. He waited a second, then crossed Front Street. Another signal.

On the ninth floor of the Cotton Exchange Building, Tammy

Greenwood of Greenwood Services backed away from the window and put on her coat. She locked the door behind her and pushed the elevator button. She waited. She was about to encounter a man who could easily get her killed.

Mitch entered the lobby and went straight to the elevators. He noticed no one in particular. A half dozen businessmen were in the progress of talking as they came and went. A woman was whispering on the pay phone. A security guard loitered near the Union Street entrance. He pushed the elevator button and waited, alone. As the door opened, a young clean cut Merrill Lynch type in a black suit and sparkling wing tips stepped into the elevator. Mitch had hoped for a solitary ride upward.

Mulholland's office was on the seventh floor. Mitch pushed the seven button and ignored the kid in the black suit. As the elevator moved, both men dutifully stared at the blinking numbers above the door. Mitch eased to the rear of the small elevator and set the heavy briefcase on the floor, next to his right foot. The door opened on the fourth floor, and Tammy walked nervously in. The kid glanced at her. Her attire was remarkably conservative. A simple, short knit dress with no plunging necklines. No kinky shoes. Her hair was tinted to a soft shade of red. He glanced again and pushed the CLOSE DOOR button.

Tammy brought aboard a large black briefcase, identical to Mitch's. She ignored his eyes, stood next to him, quietly setting it next to his. On the seventh floor, Mitch grabbed her briefcase and left the elevator. On the eighth floor, the cute young man in the black suit made his departure, and on the ninth floor Tammy picked up the heavy black briefcase full of files from Bendini, Lambert & Locke and took it to her office. She locked and bolted the door, quickly removed her coat and went to the small room where the copier was waiting and running. There were seven files, each at least an inch thick. She laid them neatly on the folding table next to the copier and took the one marked 'Koker-Hanks to East Texas Pipe.' She unhooked the aluminum clasp, removed the contents from the file and carefully placed the stack of documents and letters and notes into the automatic feed. She pushed the PRINT button and watched as the machine made two perfect copies of everything.

Thirty minutes later, the seven files were returned to the briefcase. The new files, fourteen of them, were locked away in a fireproof file cabinet hidden in a small closet, which was also locked. Tammy placed the briefcase near the door, and waited.

Frank Mulholland was a partner in a ten-man firm that specialized in banking and securities. His client was an old man who had founded and built a chain of do-it-yourself hardware stores and at one point had been worth eighteen million before his son and a renegade board of directors took control and forced him into retirement. The old man sued. The company countersued. Everybody sued everybody, and the suits and countersuits had been hopelessly deadlocked for eighteen months. Now that the lawyers were fat and happy, it was time to talk settlement. Bendini, Lambert & Locke handled the tax advice for the son and the new board, and two months earlier Avery had introduced Mitch to the hostilities. The plan was to offer the old man a five-million-dollar package of common stock, convertible warrants and a few bonds.

Mulholland was not impressed with the plan. His client was not greedy, he explained repeatedly, and he knew he would never regain control of the company. His company, remember. But five million was not enough. Any jury of any degree of intelligence would be sympathetic to the old man, and a fool could see the lawsuit was worth at least, well . . . at least twenty million!

After an hour of sliding proposals and offers and counteroffers across Mulholland's desk, Mitch had increased the package to eight million and the old man's lawyer said he might consider fifteen. Mitch politely repacked his attaché case and Mulholland politely escorted him to the door. They promised to meet again in a week. They shook hands like best friends.

The elevator stopped on the fifth floor, and Tammy walked casually inside. It was empty, except for Mitch. When the door closed, he said, 'Any problems?'

'Nope. Two copies are locked away.'

'How long did it take?'

'Thirty minutes.'

It stopped on the fourth floor, and she picked up the empty briefcase. 'Noon tomorrow?' she asked.

'Yes,' he replied. The door opened and she disappeared onto the fourth floor. He rode alone to the lobby, which was empty except for the same security guard. Mitchell McDeere, attorney-at-law, hurried from the building with a heavy briefcase in each hand and walked importantly back to his office.

The celebration of Abby's twenty-fifth birthday was rather subdued. Through the dim candlelight in a dark corner of Grisanti's, they whispered and tried to smile at each other. It was difficult. Somewhere at that moment in the restaurant an invisible FBI agent was holding a cassette tape that he would insert into a cigarette machine in the lounge at precisely nine o'clock, and Mitch was supposed to be there seconds later to retrieve it without being seen or caught by the bad guys, whoever they were and whatever they looked like. And the tape would reveal just how much cold hard cash the McDeeres would receive in return for evidence and a subsequent life on the run.

They picked at their food, tried to smile and carry on an extended conversation, but mainly they fidgeted and glanced at their watches. The dinner was brief. By eight forty-five they were finished with the plates. Mitch left in the direction of the rest room, and he stared into the dark lounge as he walked by. The cigarette machine was in the corner, exactly where it should be.

They ordered coffee, and at exactly nine Mitch returned to the lounge, to the machine, where he nervously inserted six quarters and pulled the lever under Marlboro Lights, in memory of Eddie Lomax. He quickly reached into the tray, took the cigarettes and, fishing around in the darkness, found the cassette tape. The pay telephone next to the machine rang, and he jumped. He turned and surveyed the lounge. It was empty except for two men at the bar watching the television behind and above the bartender. Drunk laughter exploded from a dark corner far away.

Abby watched every step and move until he sat across from her. She raised her eyebrows. 'And?'

'I got it. Your basic black Sony cassette tape.' Mitch sipped coffee and smiled innocently while quickly surveying the crowded dining room. No one was watching. No one cared.

He handed the check and the American Express card to the waiter. 'We're in a hurry,' he said rudely. The waiter returned within seconds. Mitch scribbled his name.

The BMW was indeed wired. Heavily wired. Tarrance's gang had very quietly and very thoroughly examined it with magnifying glasses while waiting for the Greyhound four days earlier. Expertly wired, with terribly expensive equipment capable of hearing and recording the slightest sniffle or cough. But the bugs could only listen and record; they could not track. Mitch thought that was awfully nice of them, just to listen but not to follow the movements of the BMW.

It left the parking lot of Grisanti's with no conversation between its occupants. Abby carefully opened a portable tape recorder and placed the cassette inside. She handed Mitch the earphones, which he stuck onto his head. She pushed the PLAY button. She watched him as he listened and drove aimlessly toward the interstate.

The voice belonged to Tarrance: 'Hello Mitch. Today is Tuesday, February 25, sometime after nine P.M. Happy Birthday to your lovely wife. This tape will run about ten minutes, and I instruct you to listen to it carefully, once or twice, then dispose of it. I had a face-to-face meeting with Director Voyles last Sunday and briefed him on everything. By the way, I enjoyed the bus ride. Director Voyles is very pleased with the way things are going, but he thinks we've talked long enough. He wants to cut a deal, and rather quickly. He explained to me in no uncertain terms that we have never paid three million dollars and we're not about to pay it to you. He cussed a lot but to make a long story short, Director Voyles said we could pay a million cash, no more. He said the money would be deposited in a Swiss bank and no one, not even the IRS, would ever know about it. A million dollars, tax free. That's our best deal, and Voyles said you can go to hell if you said no. We're gonna bust that little firm, Mitch, with or without you.'

Mitch smiled grimly and stared at the traffic racing past them on the I-240 loop. Abby watched for a sign, a signal, a grunt or groan, anything to indicate good news or bad. She said nothing.

The voice continued: 'We'll take care of you, Mitch. You'll have access to FBI protection anytime you think you need it. We'll check on you periodically, if you want. And if you want to move on to another city after a few years, we'll take care of it. You can move every five years if you want, and we'll pick up the tab and find jobs for you. Good jobs with the VA or Social Security or Postal Service. Voyles said we'd even find you a high-paying job with a private government contractor. You name it, Mitch, and it's yours. Of course, we'll provide new identities for you and your wife, and you can change every year if you desire. No problem. Or if you got a better idea, we'll listen. You wanna live in Europe or Australia, just say so. You'll get special treatment. I know we're promising a lot, Mitch, but we're dead serious and we'll put it in writing. We'll pay a million in cash, tax free, and set you up wherever you choose. So that's the deal. And in return, you must hand us the firm, and the Moroltos. We'll talk about that later. For now, your time is up. Voyles is breathing down my neck, and things must happen quickly. Call me at that number Thursday night at nine from the pay phone next to the men's room in Houston's on Poplar. So long, Mitch.'

He sliced a finger across his throat, and Abby pushed the STOP button, then REWIND. He handed her the earphones, and she began to listen intently.

It was an innocent walk in the park, two lovebirds holding hands and stolling casually through the cool, clear moonlight. They stopped by a cannon and gazed at the majestic river inching ever so slowly toward New Orleans. The same cannon where the late Eddie Lomax once stood in a sleet storm and delivered one of his last investigative reports.

Abby held the cassette in her hand and watched the river below. She had listened to it twice and refused to leave it in the car, where who knows who might snatch it. After weeks of practicing silence, and then speaking only outdoors, words were becoming difficult.

'You know, Abby,' Mitch finally said as he tapped the wooden wheel of the cannon, 'I've always wanted to work with the post office. I had an uncle once who was a rural mail carrier. That would be neat.'

It was a gamble, this attempt at humor. But it worked. She hesitated for three seconds, then laughed slightly, and he could tell she indeed thought it was funny. 'Yeah, and I could mop floors in a VA hospital.'

'You wouldn't have to mop floors. You could change bed-pans, something meaningful, something inconspicuous. We'd live in a neat little white frame house on Maple Street in Omaha. I'd be Harvey and you'd be Thelma, and we'd need a short, unassuming last name.'

'Poe,' Abby added.

'That's great. Harvey and Thelma Poe. The Poe family. We'd have a million dollars in the bank but couldn't spend a dime because everyone on Maple Street would know it and then we'd become different, which is the last thing we want.'

'I'd get a nose job.'

'But your nose is perfect.'

'Abby's nose is perfect but what about Thelma's? We'd have to get it fixed, don't you think?'

'Yeah, I suppose.' He was immediately tired of the humor and became quiet. Abby stepped in front of him, and he draped his arms over her shoulders. They watched a tug quietly push a hundred barges under the bridge. An occasional cloud dimmed the moonlight, and the cool winds from the west rose intermittently, then dissipated.

'Do you believe Tarrance?' Abby asked.

'In what way?'

'Let's suppose you do nothing. Do you believe one day they'll eventually infiltrate the firm?'

'I'm afraid not to believe.'

'So we take the money and run?'

'It's easier for me to take the money and run, Abby. I have nothing to leave behind. For you, it's different. You'll never see your family again.'

'Where would we go?'

'I do not know. But I wouldn't want to stay in this country. The feds cannot be trusted entirely. I'll feel safer in another country, but I won't tell Tarrance.'

'What's the next step?'

'We cut a deal, then quickly go about the job of gathering enough information to sink the ship. I have no idea what they want, but I can find it for them. When Tarrance has enough, we disappear. We take our money, get our nose jobs and disappear.'

'How much money?'

'More than a million. They're playing games with the money. It's all negotiable.'

'How much will we get?'

'Two million cash, tax free. Not a dime less.'

'Will they pay it?'

'Yes, but that's not the question. The question is, will we take it and run?'

She was cold, and he draped his coat over her shoulders. He held her tightly. 'It's a rotten deal, Mitch,' she said, 'but at least we'll be together.'

'The name's Harvey, not Mitch.'

'Do you think we'll be safe, Harvey?'

'We're not safe here.'

'I don't like it here. I'm lonely and scared.'

'I'm tired of being a lawyer.'

'Let's take the money and haul ass.'

'You've got a deal, Thelma.'

She handed the cassette tape to him. He glanced at it, then threw it far below, beyond Riverside Drive, in the direction of the river. They held hands and stolled quickly through the park toward the BMW parked on Front Street.

# CHAPTER TWENTY-FOUR

For only the second time in his career, Mitch was allowed to visit the palatial dining room on the fifth floor. Avery's invitation came with the explanation that the partners were all quite impressed with the seventy-one hours per week he averaged in billing for the month of February, and thus they wished to offer the small reward of lunch. It was an invitation no associate could turn down, regardless of schedules and meetings and clients and deadlines and all the other terribly important and urgently critical aspects of careers at Bendini, Lambert & Locke. Never in history had an associate said no to an invitation to the dining room. Each received two invitations per year. Records were kept.

Mitch had two days to prepare for it. His first impulse was to decline, and when Avery first mentioned it a dozen lame excuses crossed his mind. Eating and smiling and chatting and fraternizing with criminals, regardless of how rich and polished, was less attractive than sharing a bowl of soup with a homeless down at the bus station. But to say no would be a grievous breach of tradition. And as things were going, his movements were already suspicious enough.

So he sat with his back to the window and forced smiles and small talk in the direction of Avery and Royce McKnight and, of course, Oliver Lambert. He knew he would eat at the same table with those three. Knew it for two days. He knew they would watch him carefully but nonchalantly, trying to detect any loss of enthusiasm, or cynicism, or hopelessness. Anything, really. He knew they would hang on every word, regardless of what he said. He knew they would lavish praise and promises upon his weary shoulders.

Oliver Lambert had never been more charming. Seventy-one hours a week for a February for an associate was a firm record, he said as Roosevelt served prime ribs. All the partners were amazed, and delighted, he explained softly while glancing around the room. Mitch forced a smile and sliced his serving. The other partners, amazed or indifferent, were talking idly and concentrating on the food. Mitch counted eighteen active partners and seven retirees, those with the khakis and sweaters and relaxed looks about them.

'You have remarkable stamina, Mitch,' Royce McKnight said with a mouthful. He nodded politely. Yes, yes, I practice my stamina all the time, he thought to himself. As much as possible, he kept his

584

mind off Joe Hodge and Marty Kozinski and the other three dead lawyers memorialized on the wall downstairs. But it was impossible to keep his mind off the pictures of the girl in the sand, and he wondered if they all knew. Had they all seen the pictures? Passed them around during one of these little lunches when it was just the partners and no guests? DeVasher had promised to keep them to himself, but what's a promise from a thug? Of course they'd seen them. Voyles said every partner and most of the associates were in on the conspiracy.

For a man with no appetite, he managed the food nicely. He even buttered and devoured an extra roll, just to appear normal. Nothing wrong with his appetite.

'So you and Abby are going to the Caymans next week?' Oliver Lambert said.

'Yes. It's her spring break, and we booked one of the condos two months ago. Looking forward to it.'

'It's a terrible time to go,' Avery said in disgust. 'We're a month behind right now.'

'We're always a month behind, Avery. So what's another week? I guess you want me to take my files with me?'

'Not a bad idea. I always do.'

'Don't do it, Mitch,' Oliver Lambert said in mock protest. 'This place will be standing when you return. You and Abby deserve a week to yourselves.'

'You'll love it down there,' Royce McKnight said, as if Mitch had never been and that thing on the beach didn't happen and no one knew anything about any photographs.

'When do you leave?' Lambert asked.

'Sunday morning. Early.'

'Are you taking the Lear?'

'No. Delta nonstop.'

Lambert and McKnight exchanged quick looks that Mitch was not supposed to see. There were other looks from other tables, occasional quick glances filled with curiosity that Mitch had caught since he entered the room. He was there to be noticed.

'Do you scuba-dive?' asked Lambert, still thinking about the Lear versus the Delta nonstop.

'No, but we plan to do some snorkeling.'

'There's a guy on Rum Point, on the north end, name of Adrian Bench, who's got a great dive lodge and will certify you in one week. It's a hard week, lot of instruction, but it's worth it.'

In other words, stay away from Abanks, Mitch thought. 'What's the name of the lodge?' he asked.

'Rum Point Divers. Great place.'

Mitch frowned intelligently as if making a mental note of this help-ful advice. Suddenly, Oliver Lambert was hit with sadness. 'Be careful, Mitch. It brings back memories of Marty and Joe.'

Avery and McKnight stared at their plates in a split-second memorial to the dead boys. Mitch swallowed hard and almost sneered at Oliver Lambert. But he kept a straight face, even man-aged to look sad with the rest of them. Marty and Joe and their young widows and fatherless children. Marty and Joe, two young wealthy lawyers expertly killed and removed before they could talk. Marty and Joe, two promising sharks eaten by their own. Voyles had told Mitch to think of Marty and Joe whenever he saw Oliver Lambert.

And now, for a mere million bucks, he was expected to do what Marty and Joe were about to do, without getting caught. Perhaps a year from now the next new associate would be sitting here and watching the saddened partners talk about young Mitch McDeere and his remarkable stamina and what a helluva lawyer he would have been but for the accident. How many would they kill?

He wanted two million. Plus a couple of other items.

After an hour of important talk and good food, the lunch began breaking up as partners excused themselves, spoke to Mitch and left the room. They were proud of him, they said. He was their brightest star of the future. The future of Bendini, Lambert & Locke. He smiled and thanked them.

About the time Roosevelt served the banana cream pie and coffee, Tammy Greenwood Hemphill of Greenwood Services parked her dirty brown Rabbit behind the shiny Peugeot in the school parking lot. She left the motor running. She took four steps, stuck a key into the trunk of the Peugeot and removed the heavy black briefcase. She slammed the trunk and sped away in the Rabbit.

From a small window in the teachers' lounge, Abby sipped coffee and stared through the trees, across the playground and into the parking lot in the distance. She could barely see her car. She smiled and checked her watch. Twelve-thirty, as planned.

Tammy weaved her way carefully throught the noon traffic in the direction of downtown. Driving was tedious when watching the rear-view mirror. As usual, she saw nothing. She parked in her designated place across the street from the Cotton Exchange Building.

There were nine files in this load. She arranged them neatly on the folding table and began making copies. Sigalas Partners, Lettie Plunk Trust, HandyMan Hardware and two files bound loosely with a thick rubber band and marked AVERY'S FILES. She ran two copies of every sheet of paper in the files and meticulously put them back together. In a ledger book, she entered the date, time and name of each file. There were now twenty-nine entries. He said there would eventually be about forty. She placed one copy of each file into the locked and hidden cabinet in the closet, then repacked the briefcase with the original files and one copy of each.

Pursuant to his instructions, a week earlier she had rented in her name an eight-by-eight storage room at the Summer Avenue Mini Storage. It was fourteen miles from downtown, and thirty minutes later she arrived and unlocked number 38C. In a small cardboard box she placed the other copies of the nine files and scribbled the date on the end of the flap. She placed it next to three other boxes on the floor.

At exactly 3 P.M., she wheeled into the parking lot, stopped behind the Peugeot, opened its trunk and left the briefcase where she'd found it.

Seconds later, Mitch stepped from the front door of the Bendini Building and stretched his arms. He breathed deeply and gazed up and down Front Street. A lovely spring day. Five blocks to the north and nine floors up, in the window, he noticed the blinds had been pulled all the way down. The signal. Good. Everything's fine. He smiled to himself, and returned to his office.

At three o'clock in the morning, Mitch eased out of bed and quietly pulled on a pair of faded jeans, flannel law school shirt, white insulated socks and a pair of old work boots. He wanted to look like a truck driver. Without a word, he kissed Abby, who was awake, and left the house. East Meadowbrook was deserted, as were all the streets between home and the interstate. Surely they would not follow him at this hour.

He drove Interstate 55 south for twenty-five miles to Senatobia, Mississippi. A busy, all-night truck stop called the 4-55 shone brightly a hundred yards from the four-lane. He darted through the trucks to the rear where a hundred semis were parked for the night. He stopped next to the Truck Wash bay and waited. A dozen eighteen-wheelers inched and weaved around the pumps.

A black guy wearing a Falcons football cap stepped from around the corner and stared at the BMW. Mitch recognized him as the agent in the bus terminal in Knoxville. He killed the engine and stepped from the car.

'McDeere?' the agent asked.

'Of course. Who else? Where's Tarrance?'

'Inside in a booth by the window. He's waiting.'

Mitch opened the door and handed the keys to the agent. 'Where are you taking it?'

'Down the road a little piece. We'll take care of it. You were clean coming out of Memphis. Relax.'

He climbed into the car, eased between two diesel pumps and headed for the interstate. Mitch watched his little BMW disappear as he entered the truck-stop café. It was three forty-five.

The noisy room was filled with heavy middle-aged men drinking coffee and eating store-bought pies. They picked their teeth with colored toothpicks and talked of bass fishing and politics back at the terminal. Many spoke with loud Northern twangs. Merle Haggard wailed from the jukebox.

The lawyer moved awkwardly toward the rear until he saw in an unlit corner a familiar face hidden beneath aviator's sunshades and the same Michigan State baseball cap. Then the face smiled. Tarrance was holding a menu and watching the front door. Mitch slid into the booth.

'Hello, good buddy,' Tarrance said. 'How's the truckin'?'

'Wonderful. I think I prefer the bus, though.'

'Next time we'll try a train or something. Just for variety. Laney get your car?'

'Laney?'

'The black dude. He's an agent, you know.'

'We haven't been properly introduced. Yes, he's got my car. Where's he taking it?'

'Down the interstate. He'll be back in an hour or so. We'll try to have you on the road by five so you can be at the office by six. We'd hate to mess up your day.'

'It's already shot to hell.'

A partially crippled waitress named Dot ambled by and demanded to know what they wanted. Just coffee. A surge of Roadway drivers swarmed in the front door and filled up the café. Merle could barely be heard.

'So how are the boys at the office?' Tarrance asked cheerfully.

'Everything's fine. The meters are ticking as we speak and everyone's getting richer. Thanks for asking.'

'No problem.'

'How's my old pal Voyles doing?' Mitch asked.

'He's quite anxious, really. He called me twice today and repeated for the tenth time his desire to have an answer from you. Said you'd had plenty of time and all that. I told him to relax. Told him about our little roadside rendezvous tonight and he got real excited. I'm supposed to call him in four hours, to be exact.'

'Tell him a million bucks won't do it, Tarrance. You boys like to brag about spending billions fighting organized crime, so I say throw a little my way. What's a couple of million cash to the federal government?'

'So it's a couple of million now?'

'Damned right it's a couple of million. And not a dime less. I want a million now and a million later. I'm in the process of copying all of my files, and I should be finished in a few days. Legitimate files, I think. If I gave them to anyone I'd be permanently disbarred. So when I give them to you, I want the first million. Let's just call it good faith money.'

'How do you want it paid?'

'Deposited in an account in a bank in Zurich. But we'll discuss the details later.'

Dot slid two saucers onto the table and dropped two mismatched cups on them. She poured from a height of three feet and splashed coffee in all directions. 'Free refills,' she grunted, and left.

'And the second million?' Tarrance asked, ignoring the coffee.

'When you and I and Voyles decide I've supplied you with enough documents to get the indictments, then I get half. After I testify for the last time, I get the other half. That's incredibly fair, Tarrance.'

'It is. You've got a deal.'

Mitch breathed deeply, and felt weak. A deal. A contract. An agreement. One that could never be put in writing, but one that was terribly enforceable nonetheless. He sipped the coffee but didn't taste it. They had agreed on the money. He was on a roll. Keep pushing.

'And there's one other thing, Tarrance.'

The head lowered and turned slightly to the right. 'Yeah?'

Mitch leaned closer, resting on his forearms. 'It won't cost you a dime, and you boys can pull it off with no sweat. Okay?'

'I'm listening.'

'My brother Ray is at Brushy Mountain. Seven years until parole. I want him out.'

'That's ridiculous, Mitch. We can do a lot of things, but we damned sure can't parole state prisoners. Federal maybe, but not state. No way.'

'Listen to me, Tarrance, and listen good. If I hit the road with the Mafia on my trail, my brother goes with me. Sort of like a package deal. And I know if Director Voyles wants him out of prison, he'll get out of prison. I know that. Now, you boys just figure out a way to make it happen.'

'But we have no authority to interfere with state prisoners.'

Mitch smiled and returned to his coffee. 'James Earl Ray escaped from Brushy Mountain. And he had help from the outside.'

'Oh, that's great. We attack the prison like commandos and rescue your brother. Beautiful.'

'Don't play dumb with me, Tarrance. It's not negotiable.'

'All right, all right. I'll see what I can do. Anything else? Any more surprises?'

'No, just questions about where we go and what we do. Where do we hide initially? Where do we hide during the trials? Where do we live for the rest of our lives? Just minor questions like that.'

'We can discuss it later.'

'What did Hodge and Kozinski tell you?'

'Not enough. We've got a notebook, a rather thick notebook, in which we've accumulated and indexed everything we know about the Moroltos and the firm. Most of it's Morolto crap, their organization, key people, illegal activities and so on. You need to read it all before we start to work.'

'Which, of course, will be after I've received the first million.'

'Of course. When can we see your files?'

'In about a week. I've managed to copy four files that belong to someone else. I may get my hands on a few more of those.'

'Who's doing the copying?'

'None of your business.'

Tarrance thought for a second and let it pass. 'How many files?'

'Between forty and fifty. I have to sneak them out a few at a time. Some I've worked on for eight months, others only a week or so. As far as I can tell, they're all legitimate clients.'

'How many of these clients have you personally met?'

'Two or three.'

'Don't bet they're all legitimate. Hodge told us about some dummy files, or sweat files as they are known to the partners, that have been around for years and every new associate cuts his teeth on them; heavy files that require hundreds of hours and make the rookies feel like real lawyers.'

'Sweat files?'

'That's what Hodge said. It's any easy game, Mitch. They lure you with the money. They smother you with work that looks legitimate and for the most part probably is legitimate. Then, after a few years, you've unwittingly become a part of the conspiracy. You're nailed, and there's no getting out. Even you, Mitch. You started work in July, eight months ago, and you've probably already touched a few of the dirty files. You didn't know it, had no reason to suspect it. But they've already set you up.'

'Two million, Tarrance. Two million and my brother.'

Tarrance sipped the lukewarm coffee and ordered a piece of coconut pie as Dot came within earshot. He glanced at his watch and surveyed the crowd of truckers, all smoking cigarettes and drinking coffee and talking relentlessly.

'He adjusted the sunglasses. 'So what do I tell Mr. Voyles?'

'Tell him we ain't got a deal until he agrees to get Ray out of prison. No deal, Tarrance.'

'We can probably work something out.'

'I'm confident you can.'

'When do you leave for the Caymans?'

'Early Sunday. Why?'

'Just curious, that's all.'

'Well, I'd like to know how many different groups will be following me down there. Is that asking too much? I'm sure we'll attract a crowd, and frankly, we had hoped for a little privacy.'

'Firm condo?'

'Of course.'

'Forget privacy. It's probably got more wires than a switchboard. Maybe even some cameras.'

'That's comforting. We might stay a couple of nights at Abanks Dive Lodge. If you boys are in the neighborhood, stop by for a drink.'

'Very funny. If we're there, it'll be for a reason. And you won't know it.'

Tarrance ate the pie in three bites. He left two bucks on the table and they walked to the dark rear of the truck stop. The dirty asphalt pavement vibrated under the steady hum of an acre of diesel engines. They waited in the dark.

'I'll talk to Voyles in a few hours,' Tarrance said. 'Why don't you and your wife take a leisurely Saturday-afternoon drive tomorrow?'

'Anyplace in particular?'

'Yeah. There's a town called Holly Springs thirty miles east of here. Old place, full of antebellum homes and Confederate history. Women love to drive around and look at the old mansions. Make your appearance around four o'clock and we'll find you. Our buddy Laney will be driving a bright red Chevy Blazer with Tennessee plates. Follow him. We'll find a place and talk.'

'Is it safe?'

'Trust us. If we see or smell something, we'll break off. Drive around town for an hour, and if you don't see Laney, grab a sandwich and go back home. You'll know they were too close. We won't take chances.'

'Thanks. A great bunch of guys.'

Laney eased around the corner in the BMW and jumped out. 'Everything's clear. No trace of anyone.'

'Good,' Tarrance said. 'See you tomorrow, Mitch. Happy truckin'.' They shook hands.

'It's not negotiable, Tarrance,' Mitch said again.

'You can call me Wayne. See you tomorrow.'

# CHAPTER TWENTY-FIVE

The black thunderheads and driving rain had long since cleared the tourists from Seven Mile Beach when the McDeers, soaked and tired, arrived at the luxury condominium duplex. Mitch backed the rented Mitsubishi jeep over the curb, across the small lawn and up to the front door. Unit B. His first visit had been to Unit A. They appeared to be identical, except for the paint and trim. The key fit, and they grabbed and threw luggage as the clouds burst and the rain grew thicker.

Once inside and dry, they unpacked in the master bedroom upstairs with a long balcony facing the wet beach. Cautious with their words, they inspected the town house and checked out each room and closet. The refrigerator was empty, but the bar was very well stocked. Mitch mixed two drinks, rum and Coke, in honor of the islands. They sat on the balcony with their feet in the rain and watched the ocean churn and spill toward the shore. Rumheads was quiet and barely visible in the distance. Two natives sat at the bar, drinking and watching the sea.

'That's Rumheads over there,' Mitch said, pointing with his drink.

'Rumheads?'

'I told you about it. It's a hot spot where tourists drink and the locals play dominoes.'

'I see.' Abby was unimpressed. She yawned and sank lower into the plastic chair. She closed her eyes.

'Oh, this is great, Abby. Our first trip out of the country, our first real honeymoon, and you're asleep ten minutes after we hit land.'

'I'm tired, Mitch. I packed all night while you were sleeping.'

'You packed eight suitcases – six for you and two for me. You packed every garment we own. No wonder you were awake all night.'

'I don't want to run out of clothes.'

'Run out? How many bikinis did you pack? Ten? Twelve?'

'Six.'

'Great. One a day. Why don't you put one on?'

'What?'

'You heard me. Go put on that little blue one with high legs and a couple of strings around the front, the one that weighs half a gram and cost sixty bucks and your buns hang out when you walk. I wanna see it.'

'Mitch, it's raining. You've brought me here to this island during the monsoon season. Look at those clouds. Dark and thick and extremely stationary. I won't need any bikinis this week.'

Mitch smiled and began rubbing her legs. 'I rather like the rain. In fact, I hope it rains all week. It'll keep us inside, in the bed, sipping rum and trying to hurt each other.'

'I'm shocked. You mean you actually want sex? We've already done it once this month.'

'Twice.'

'I thought you wanted to snorkel and scuba dive all week.'

'Nope. There's probably a shark out there waiting for me.'

The winds blew harder and the balcony was being drenched.

'Let's go take off our clothes,' Mitch said.

After an hour, the storm began to move. The rain slackened, then turned to a soft drizzle, then it was gone. The sky lightened as the dark, low clouds left the tiny island and headed northeast, toward Cuba. Shortly before its scheduled departure over the horizon, the sun suddenly emerged for a brief encore. It emptied the beach cottages and town homes and condos and hotel rooms as the tourists strolled through the sand toward the water. Rumheads was suddenly packed with dart throwers and thirsty beachcombers. The domino game picked up where it had left off. The reggae band next door at the Palms tuned up.

Mitch and Abby walked aimlessly along the edge of the water in the general direction of Georgetown, away from the spot where the girl had been. He thought of her occasionally, and of the photographs. He had decided she was a pro and had been paid by DeVasher to seduce and conquer him in front of the hidden cameras. He did not expect to see her this time.

As if on cue, the music stopped, the beach strollers froze and watched, the noise at Rumheads quietened as all eyes turned to watch the sun meet the water. Gray and white clouds, the trailing remnants of the storm, lay low on the horizon and sank with the sun. Slowly they turned shades of orange and yellow and red, pale shades at first, then, suddenly, brilliant tones. For a few brief moments, the sky was a canvas and the sun splashed its awesome array of colors with bold strokes. Then the bright orange ball touched the water and within seconds was gone. The clouds became black and dissipated. A Cayman sunset.

With great fear and caution, Abby slowly maneuvered the jeep through the early-morning traffic in the shopping district. She was from Kentucky. She had never driven on the left side of the road for any substantial period of time. Mitch gave directions and watched the rearview mirror. The narrow streets and sidewalks were already crowded with tourists window-shopping for duty-free china, crystal, perfume, cameras and jewelry.

Mitch pointed to a hidden side street, and the jeep darted between two groups of tourists. He kissed her on the cheek. 'I'll meet you right here at five.'

'Be careful,' she said. 'I'll go to the bank, then stay on the beach near the condo.'

He slammed the door and disappeared between two small shops. The alley led to a wider street that led to Hogsty Bay. He ducked into a crowded T-shirt store filled with racks and rows of tourist shirts and straw hats and sunglasses. He selected a gaudy green and orange flowered shirt and a Panama hat. Two minutes later he darted from the store into the back seat of a passing taxi. 'Airport,' he said, 'And make it quick. Watch your tail. Someone may be following.'

The driver made no response, just eased past the bank buildings and out of town. Ten minutes later he stopped in front of the terminal.

'Anybody follow us?' Mitch asked, pulling money from his pocket.

'No, mon. Four dollars and ten cents.'

Mitch threw a five over the seat and walked quickly into the terminal. The Cayman Airways flight to Cayman Brac would leave at nine. At a gift shop Mitch bought a cup of coffee and hid between two rows of shelves filled with souvenirs. He watched the waiting area and saw no one. Of course, he had no idea what they looked like, but he saw no one sniffing around and searching for lost people. Perhaps they were following the jeep or combing the shopping district looking for him. Perhaps.

For seventy-five Cayman dollars he had reserved the last seat on the ten-passenger, three-engine Trislander. Abby had made the reservation by pay phone the night they arrived. At the last possible second, he jogged from the terminal onto the tarmac and climbed on board. The pilot slammed and locked the doors, and they taxied down the runway. No other planes were visible. A small hangar sat to the right.

The ten tourists admired the brilliant blue sea and said little during the twenty-minute flight. As they approached Cayman Brac, the pilot became the tour guide and made a wide circle around the small island. He paid special attention to the tall bluffs that fell into the sea on the east end. Without the bluffs he said the island would be as flat as Grand Cayman. He landed the plane softly on a narrow asphalt strip.

Next to the small white frame building with the word AIRPORT painted on all sides, a clean cut Caucasian waited and watched the passengers quickly disembark. He was Rick Acklin, special agent, and sweat dripped from his nose and glued his shirt to his back. He stepped slightly forward. 'Mitch,' he said almost to himself.

Mitch hesitated and then walked over.

'Car's out front,' Acklin said.

'Where's Tarrance?' Mitch looked around.

'He's waiting.'

'Does the car have air conditioning?'

'Afraid not. Sorry.'

The car was minus air, power anything and signal lights. It was a 1974 LTD, and Acklin explained as they followed the dusty road that there simply was not much of a selection of rental cars on Cayman Brac. And the U.S. government had rented the car because he and Tarrance had been unable to find a taxi. They were lucky to find a room, on such late notice.

The small neat homes were closer together, and sea appeared. They parked in the sand parking lot of an establishment called Brac Divers. An aging pier jutted into the water and anchored a hundred boats of all sizes. To the west along the beach a dozen thatched-roof cabins sat two feet above the sand and housed divers who came from around the world. Next to the pier was an open-air bar, nameless, but complete with a domino game and dartboard. Oak-and-brass fans hung from the ceiling through the rafters and rotated slowly and silently, cooling the domino players and the bartender.

Wayne Tarrance sat at a table by himself drinking a Coke and watching a dive crew load a thousand identical yellow tanks from the pier onto a boat. Even for a tourist, his dress was hysterical. Dark sunglasses with yellow frames, brown straw sandals, obviously brand-new, with black socks, a tight Hawaiian luau shirt with twenty loud colors and a pair of gold gym shorts that were very old and very short and covered little of the shiny, sickly white legs under the table. He waved his Coke at the two empty chairs.

'Nice shirt, Tarrance,' Mitch said in undisguised amusement.

'Thanks. You gotta real winner yourself.'

'Nice tan too.'

'Yeah, yeah, Gotta look the part, you know.'

The waiter hovered nearby and waited for them to speak. Acklin ordered a Coke. Mitch said he wanted a Coke with a slash of rum in it. All three became engrossed with the dive boat and the divers loading their bulky gear.

'What happened in Holly Springs?' Mitch finally asked.

'Sorry, we couldn't help it. They followed you out of Memphis and had two cars waiting in Holly Springs. We couldn't get near you.'

'Did you and your wife discuss the trip before you left?' asked Acklin.

'I think so. We probably mentioned it around the house a couple of times.'

Acklin seemed satisfied. 'They were certainly ready for you. A green Skylark followed you for about twenty miles, then got lost. We called it off then.'

Tarrance sipped his Coke and said, 'Late Saturday night the Lear left Memphis and flew nonstop to Grand Cayman. We think two or three of the goons were on board. The plane left early Sunday morning and returned to Memphis.'

'So they're here and they're following us?'

'Of course. They probably had one or two people on the plane with you and Abby. Might have been men, women or both. Could've been a black dude or an Oriental woman. Who knows? Remember, Mitch, they have plenty of money. There are two that we recognize. One was in Washington when you were there. A blond fellow, about forty, six-one, maybe six-two, with real short hair, almost a crew cut, and real strong, Nordic-looking features. He moves quickly. We saw him yesterday driving a red Escort he got from Coconut Car Rentals on the island.'

'I think I've seen him,' Mitch said.

'Where?' asked Acklin.

'In a bar in the Memphis airport the night I returned from Washington. I caught him watching me, and I thought at the time that I had seen him in Washington.'

'That's him. He's here.'

'Who's the other one?'

'Tony Verkler, or Two-Ton Tony as we call him. He's a con with an impressive record of convictions, most of it in Chicago. He's worked for Morolto for years. Weighs about three hundred pounds and does a great job of watching people because no one would ever suspect him.'

'He was at Rumheads last night,' Acklin added.

'Last night? We were there last night.'

With great ceremony, the dive boat pushed from the pier and

headed for open water. Beyond the pier, fishermen in their small cat-boats pulled their nets and sailors navigated their brightly colored catamarans away from land. After a gentle and dreamy start, the island was awake now. Half the boats tied to the pier had left or were in the process of leaving.

'So when did you boys get in town?' Mitch asked, sipping his drink, which was more rum than Coke.

'Sunday night,' Tarrance answered while watching the dive boat slowly disappear.

'Just out of curiosity, how many men do you have on the islands?'

'Four men, two women,' said Tarrance. Acklin became mute and deferred all conversation to his supervisor.

'And why exactly are you here?' Mitch asked.

'Oh, several reasons. Number one, we wanted to talk to you and nail down our little deal. Director Voyles is terribly anxious about reaching an agreement you can live with. Number two, we want to watch them to determine how many goons are here. We'll spend the week trying to identify these people. The island is small, and it's a good place to observe.'

'And number three, you wanted to work on your suntan?'

Acklin managed a slight giggle. Tarrance smiled and then frowned. 'No, not exactly. We're here for your protection.'

'My protection?'

'Yes. The last time I sat at this very table I was talking to Joe Hodge and Marty Kozinski. About nine months ago. The day before they were killed, to be exact.'

'And you think I'm about to be killed?'

'No. Not yet.'

Mitch motioned at the bartender for another drink. The domino game grew heated, and he watched the natives argue and drink beer.

'Look, boys, as we speak the goons, as you call them, are probably following my wife all over Grand Cayman. I'll be sort of nervous until I get back. Now, what about the deal?'

Tarrance left the sea and the dive boat and stared at Mitch. 'Two million's fine, and – '

'Of course it's fine, Tarrance. We agreed on it, did we not?'

'Relax, Mitch. We'll pay a million when you turn over all of your files. At that point, there's no turning back, as they say. You're in up to your neck.'

'Tarrance, I understand that. It was my suggestion, remember.'

'But that's the easy part. We really don't want your files, because they're all clean files. Good files. Legitimate files. We want the bad files, Mitch, the ones with indictments written all over them. And these files will be much harder to come by. But when you do so, we'll pay another half million. And the rest after the last trial.'

'And my brother?'

'We'll try.'

'Not good enough, Tarrance. I want a commitment.'

'We can't promise to deliver your brother. Hell, he's got at least seven more years.'

'But he's my brother, Tarrance. I don't care if he's a serial murderer sitting on death row waiting for his last meal. He's my brother, and if you want me, you have to release him.'

'I said we'll try, but we can't commit. There's no legal, formal, legitimate way to get him out, so we must try other means. What if he gets shot during the escape?'

'Just get him out, Tarrance.'

'We'll try.'

'You'll throw the power and resources of the FBI in assisting my brother in escaping from prison, right, Tarrance?'

'You have my word.'

Mitch sat back in his chair and took a long sip of his drink. Now the deal was final. He breathed easier and smiled in the direction of the magnificent Caribbean.

'So when do we get your files?' Tarrance asked.

'Thought you didn't want them. They're too clean, remember?'

'We want the files, Mitch because when we get the files then we've got you. You've proved yourself when you hand us your files, your license to practice law, so to speak.'

'Ten to fifteen days.'

'How many files?'

'Between forty and fifty. The small ones are an inch thick. The big ones wouldn't fit on this table. I can't use the copiers around the office, so we've had to make other arrangements.'

'Perhaps we could assist in the copying,' said Acklin.

'Perhaps not. Perhaps if I need your help, perhaps I'll ask for it.'

'How do you propose to get them to us?' Tarrance asked. Acklin withdrew again.

'Very simple, Wayne. When I've copied them all, and once I get the million where I want it, then I'll hand you a key to a certain little room in the Memphis area, and you can get them in your pickup.'

'I told you we'd deposit the money in a Swiss bank account,' Tarrance said.

'And I don't want it in a Swiss bank account, okay? I'll dictate the terms of the transfer, and it'll be done exactly as I say. It's my neck on the line from now on, boys, so I call the shots. Most of them, anyway.'

Tarrance smiled and grunted and stared at the pier. 'So you don't trust the Swiss?'

'Let's just say I have another bank in mind. I work for money launderers, remember, Wayne, so I've become an expert on hiding money in offshore accounts.'

'We'll see.'

'When do I see this notebook on the Moroltos?'

'After we get your files and pay our first installment. We'll brief you as much as we can, but for the most part you're on your own. You and I will need to meet a lot, and of course that'll be rather dangerous. May have to take a few bus rides.'

'Okay, but the next time I get the aisle seat.'

'Sure, sure. Anybody worth two million can surely pick his seat on a Greyhound.'

'I'll never live to enjoy it, Wayne. You know I won't.'

Three miles out of Georgetown, on the narrow and winding road to Bodden Town, Mitch saw him. The man was squatting behind an old Volkswagen Beetle with the hood up as if engine trouble had stopped him. The man was dressed like a native, without tourist clothes. He could easily pass for one of the Brits who worked for the government or the banks. He was well tanned. The man held a wrench of some sort and appeared to study it and watch the Mitsubishi jeep as it roared by on the left-hand side of the road. The man was the Nordic.

He was supposed to have gone unnoticed.

Mitch instinctively slowed to thirty miles per hour, to wait for him. Abby turned and watched the road. The narrow highway to Bodden Town clung to the shoreline for five miles, then forked, and the ocean disappeared. Within minutes the Nordic's green VW came racing around a slight bend. The McDeere jeep was much closer than the Nordic anticipated. Being seen, he abruptly slowed, then turned into the first white rock driveway on the ocean side.

Mitch gunned the jeep and sped to Bodden Town. West of the small settlement he turned south and less than a mile later found the ocean.

It was 10 A.M. and the parking lot of Abanks Dive Lodge was half full. The two morning dive boats had left thirty minutes earlier. The McDeeres walked quickly to the bar, where Henry was already shuffling beer and cigarettes to the domino players.

Barry Abanks leaned on a post supporting the thatched roof of the bar and watched as his two dive boats disappeared around the corner of the island. Each would make two dives, at places like Bonnie's Arch, Devil's Grotto, Eden Rock and Roger's Wreck Point, places he had dived and toured and guided through a thousand times. Some of the places he had discovered himself.

The McDeeres approached, and Mitch quietly introduced his wife to Mr. Abanks, who was not polite but not rude. They started for the small pier, where a deckhand was preparing a thirty-foot fishing boat. Abanks unloaded an indecipherable string of commands in the general direction of the young deckhand, who was either deaf or unafraid of his boss.

Mitch stood next to Abanks, the captain now, and pointed to the bar fifty yards away down the pier. 'Do you know all those people at the bar?' he asked.

Abanks frowned at Mitch.

'They tried to follow me here. Just curious,' Mitch said.

'The usual gang,' Abanks said. 'No stangers.'

'Have you noticed any strangers around this morning?'

'Look, this place attracts strange people. I keep no ledger of the strange ones and the normal ones.'

'Have you seen a fat American, red hair, at least three hundred pounds?'

Abanks shook his head. The deckhand eased the boat backward, away from the pier, then toward the horizon. Abby sat on a small padded bench and watched the dive lodge disappear. In a vinyl bag between her feet were two new sets of snorkeling fins and dive masks. It was ostensibly a snorkeling trip with maybe a little light fishing if they were biting. The great man himself had agreed to accompany them, but only after Mitch insisted and told him they needed to discuss personal matters. Private matters, regarding the death of his son.

From a screened balcony on the second floor of a Cayman Kai beach house, the Nordic watched the two snorkeled heads bob and disappear around the fishing boat. He handed the binoculars to Two-Ton Tony Verkler, who, quickly bored, handed them back. A striking blonde in a black one-piece with legs cut high, almost to the rib cage, stood behind the Nordic and took the binoculars. Of particular interest was the deckhand.

Tony spoke. 'I don't understand. If they were talking serious, why the boy? Why have another set of ears around?'

'Perhaps they're talking about snorkeling and fishing,' said the Nordic.

'I don't know,' said the blonde. 'It's unusual for Abanks to spend time on a fishing boat. He likes the divers. There must be a good reason for him to waste a day with two novice snorkelers. Something's up.'

'Who's the boy?' asked Tony.

'Just one of the gofers,' she said. 'He's got a dozen.'

'Can you talk to him later?' asked the Nordic.

'Yeah,' said Tony. 'Show him some skin, snort some candy. He'll talk.'

'I'll try,' she said.

'What's his name?' asked the Nordic.

'Keith Rook.'

Keith Rook maneuvered the boat alongside the pier at Rum Point. Mitch, Abby and Abanks climbed from the boat and headed for the beach. Keith was not invited to lunch. He stayed behind and lazily washed the deck.

The Shipwreck Bar sat inland a hundred yards under a heavy cover of rare shade trees. It was dark and damp with screened windows and squeaky ceiling fans. There was no reggae, dominoes, or dartboard. The noon crowd was quiet with each table engrossed in its own private talk.

The view from their table was out to sea, to the north. They ordered cheeseburgers and beer – island food.

'This bar is different,' Mitch observed quietly.

'Very much so,' said Abanks. 'And with good reason. It's a hangout for drug dealers who own many of the nice homes and condos around here. They fly in on their private jets, deposit their money in our many fine banks and spend a few days around here checking their real estate.'

'Nice neighborhood.'

'Very nice, really. They have millions and they keep to themselves.'

The waitress, a husky, well-mixed mulatto, dropped three bottles of Jamaican Red Stripe on the table without saying a word. Abanks leaned forward on his elbows with his head lowered, the customary manner of speaking in the Shipwreck Bar. 'So you think you can walk away?' he said.

Mitch and Abby leaned forward in unison, and all three heads met low in the center of the table, just over the beer. 'Not walk, but run. Run like hell, but I'll get away. And I'll need your help.'

Abanks thought about this for a moment and raised his head. He shrugged. 'But what am I to do?' He took the first sip of his Red Stripe.

Abby saw her first, and it would take a woman to spot another woman straining ever so elegantly to eavesdrop on their little conversation. Her back was to Abanks. She was a solid blonde partially hidden under cheap black rubber sunglasses that covered most of her face, and she had been watching the ocean and listening a bit too hard. When the three of them leaned over, she sat up straight and listened like hell. She was by herself at a table for two.

Abby dug her fingernails into her husband's leg, and their table became quiet. The blonde in black listened, then turned to her table and her drink.

Wayne Tarrance had improved his wardrobe by Friday of Cayman Week. Gone were the straw sandals and tight shorts and teenybop sunglasses. Gone were the sickly-pale legs. Now they were bright pink, burned beyond recognition. After three days in the tropical outback known as Cayman Brac, he and Acklin, acting on behalf of the U.S. government, had pounced on a rather cheap room on Grand Cayman, miles from Seven Mile Beach and not within walking distance of any remote portion of the sea. Here they had established a command post to monitor the comings and goings of the McDeeres and other interested people. Here, at the Coconut Motel, they had shared a small room with two single beds and cold showers. Wednesday morning, they had contacted the subject, McDeere, and requested a meeting as soon as possible. He said no. Said he was too busy. Said he and his wife were honeymooning and had no time for such a meeting. Maybe later, was all he said.

Then late Thursday, while Mitch and Abby were enjoying grilled grouper at the Lighthouse on the road to Bodden Town, Laney, Agent Laney, dressed in appropriate island garb and looking very much like an island Negro, stopped at their table and laid down the law. Tarrance insisted on a meeting.

Chickens had to be imported into the Cayman Islands, and not the best ones. Only medium grade chickens, to be consumed not by native islanders but by Americans away from home without this most basic staple. Colonel Sanders had the damnedest time teaching the island girls, though black or close to it, how to fry chicken. It was foreign to them.

And so it was that Special Agent Wayne Tarrance, of the Bronx, arranged a quick secret meeting at the Kentucky Fried Chicken franchise on the island of Grand Cayman. The only such franchise. He thought the place would be deserted. He was wrong.

A hundred hungry tourists from Georgia, Alabama, Texas and Mississippi packed the place and devoured extra crispy with cole slaw and creamed potatoes. It tasted better in Tupelo, but it would do.

Tarrance and Acklin sat in a booth in the crowded restaurant and nervously watched the front door. It was not too late to abort. There were just too many people. Finally, Mitch entered, by himself , and stood in the long line. He brought his little red box to their table and sat down. He did not say hello or anything. He began eating the three-piece dinner for which he paid $4.89, Cayman dollars. Imported chicken.

'Where have you been?' Tarrance asked.

Mitch attacked a thigh. 'On the island. It's stupid to meet here, Tarrance. Too many people.'

'We know what we're doing.'

'Yeah, like the Korean shoe store.'

'Cute. Why wouldn't you see us Wednesday?'

'I was busy Wednesday. I didn't want to see you Wednesday. Am I clean?'

'Of couse you're clean. Laney would've tackled you at the front door if you weren't clean.'

'This place makes me nervous, Tarrance.'

'Why did you go to Abanks?'

Mitch wiped his mouth and held the partially devoured thigh. A rather small thigh. 'He's got a boat. I wanted to fish and snorkel, so we cut a deal. Where were you, Tarrance? In a submarine trailing us around the island?'

'What did Abanks say?'

'Oh, he knows lots of words. Hello. Give me a beer. Who's following us? Buncha words.'

'They followed you, you know?'

'They! Which they? Your they or their they? I'm being followed so much I'm causing traffic jams.'

'The bad guys, Mitch. Those from Memphis and Chicago and New York. The ones who'll kill you tomorrow if you get real cute.'

'I'm touched. So they followed me. Where'd I take them? Snorkeling? Fishing? Come on, Tarrance. They follow me, you follow them, you follow me, they follow you. If I slam on brakes I get twenty noses up my ass. Why are we meeting here, Tarrance? This place is packed.'

Tarrance glanced around in frustration.

Mitch closed his chicken box. 'Look, Tarrance, I'm nervous and I've lost my appetite.'

'Relax. You were clean coming from the condo.'

'I'm always clean, Tarrance. I suppose Hodge and Kozinski were clean every time they moved. Clean at Abanks'. Clean on the dive boat. Clean at the funerals. This was not a good idea, Tarrance. I'm leaving.'

'Okay. When does your plane leave?'

'Why? You guys plan to follow? Will you follow me or them? What if they follow you? What if we all get real confused and I follow everybody?'

'Come on, Mitch.'

'Nine-forty in the morning. I'll try to save you a seat. You can have the window next to Two-Ton Tony.'

'When do we get your files?'

Mitch stood with his chicken box. 'In a week or so. Give me ten days, and, Tarrance, no more meetings in public. They kill lawyers, remember, not stupid FBI agents.'

# CHAPTER TWENTY-SIX

At eight Monday morning, Oliver Lambert and Nathan Locke were cleared through the concrete wall on the fifth floor and walked through the maze of small rooms and offices. DeVasher was waiting. He closed the door behind them and pointed to the chairs. His walk was not as quick. The night had been a long losing battle with the vodka. The eyes were red and the brain expanded with each breath.

'I talked with Lazarov yesterday in Las Vegas. I explained as best I could why you boys were so reluctant to fire your four lawyers, Lynch, Sorrell, Buntin and Myers. I gave him all your good reasons. He said he'd think about it, but in the meantime, make damned sure those four work on nothing but clean files. Take no chances and watch them closely.'

'He's really a nice guy, isn't he?' Oliver Lambert said.

'Oh yes. A real charmer. He said Mr. Morolto has asked about the firm once a week for six weeks now. Said they're all anxious.'

'What did you tell him?'

'Told him things are secure, for now. Leaks are plugged, for now. I don't think he believes me.'

'What about McDeere?' asked Locke.

'He had a wonderful week with his wife. Have you ever seen her in a string bikini? She wore one all week. Outstanding! We got some pictures, just for fun.'

'I didn't come here to look at pictures,' Locke snapped.

'You don't say. They spent an entire day with our little pal Abanks, just the three of them and a deckhand. They played in the water, did some fishing. And they did a lot of talking. About what, we don't know. Never could get close enough. But it makes me very suspicious, guys. Very suspicious.'

'I don't see why,' said Oliver Lambert. 'What can they talk about besides fishing and diving, and, or course Hodge and Kozinski? And so they talk about Hodge and Kozinski, what's the harm?'

'He never knew Hodge and Kozinski, Oliver,' said Locke. 'Why would he be so interested in their deaths?'

'Keep in mind,' said DeVasher, 'that Tarrance told him at their first meeting that the deaths were not accidental. So now he's Sherlock Holmes looking for clues.'

'He won't find any, will he, DeVasher?'

'Hell no. It was a perfect job. Oh sure, there are a few unanswered questions, but the Caymanian police damned sure can't answer them. Neither can our boy McDeere.'

'Then why are you worried?' asked Lambert.

'Because they're worried in Chicago, Ollie, and they pay me real good money to stay worried down here. And until the Fibbies leave us alone, everybody is worried, okay?'

'What else did he do?'

'The usual Cayman vacation. Sex, sun, rum, a little shopping and sightseeing. We had three people on the island, and they lost him a couple of times, but nothing serious, I hope. Like I've always said, you can't trail a man twenty-four hours a day, seven days a week, without getting caught. So we have to play it cool sometimes.'

'You think McDeere's talking?' asked Locke.

'I know he lies, Nat. He lied about the incident in the Korean shoe store a month ago. You guys didn't want to believe it, but I'm convinced he went into the store voluntarily because he wanted to talk with Tarrance. One of our guys made a mistake, got too close, so the little meeting broke up. That ain't McDeere's version, but that's what happened. Yeah, Nat, I think he's talking. Maybe he meets with Tarrance and tells him to go to hell. Maybe they're smoking dope together. I don't know.'

'But you have nothing concrete, DeVasher,' Ollie said.

The brain expanded and pressed mightily against the skull. It hurt too much to get mad. 'No, Ollie, nothing like Hodge and Kozinski, if that's what you mean. We had those boys on tape and knew they were about to talk. McDeere's a little different.'

'He's also a rookie,' said Nat. 'An eight-month lawyer who knows nothing. He's spent a thousand hours on sweat files and the only clients he's handled have been legitimate. Avery's been extremely careful about the files McDeere's touched. We've talked about it.'

'He has nothing to say, because he knows nothing,' added Ollie. 'Marty and Joe knew a helluva lot, but they'd been here for years. McDeere's a new recruit.'

DeVasher gently massaged his temples. 'So you've hired a real dumbass. Let's just suppose the FBI has a hunch who our biggest client is. Okay. Think along with me. And let's just suppose Hodge and Kozinski fed them enough to confirm the identity of this particular client. See where I'm going? And let's suppose the Fibbies have told McDeere all they know, along with a certain amount of embellishment. Suddenly, your ignorant rookie recruit is a very smart man. And a very dangerous one.'

'How do you prove this?'

'We step up surveillance, for starters. Put his wife under twenty-four-hour watch. I've already called Lazarov and requested more men. Told him we needed some fresh faces. I'm going to Chicago tomorrow to brief Lazarov, and maybe Mr. Morolto. Lazarov thinks Morolto has a lead on a mole within the Bureau, some guy who's close to Voyles and will sell information. But it's expensive, supposedly. They wanna assess things and decide where to go.'

'And you'll tell them McDeere's talking?' asked Locke.

'I'll tell them what I know and what I suspect. I'm afraid that if we sit back and wait for concrete, it might be too late. I'm sure Lazarov will wanna discuss plans to eliminate him.'

'Preliminary plans?' Ollie asked, with a touch of hope.

'We've passed the preliminary stage, Ollie.'

The Hourglass Tavern in New York City faces Forty-sixth Street, near its corner with Ninth Avenue. A small, dark hole-in-the-wall with twenty-two seats, it grew to fame with its expensive menu and fifty-nine-minute time limit on each meal. On the walls not far above the tables, hourglasses with white sand silently collect the seconds and minutes until the tavern's timekeeper – the waitress – finally makes her calculations and calls time. Frequented by the Broadway crowd, it is usually packed, with loyal fans waiting on the sidewalk.

Lou Lazarov liked the Hourglass because it was dark and private conversations were possible. Short conversations, under fifty-nine minutes. He liked it because it was not in Little Italy, and he was not Italian, and although he was owned by Sicilians, he did not have to eat their food. He liked it because he was born and spent the first forty years of his life in the theatre district. Then corporate headquarters was moved to Chicago, and he was transferred. But business required his presence in New York at least twice a week, and when the business included meeting a member of equal stature from another family, Lazarov always suggested the Hourglass. Tubertini and equal stature, and a little extra. Reluctantly, he agreed on the Hourglass.

Lazarov arrived first and did not wait for a table. He knew from experience the crowd thinned around 4 P.M., especially on Thursdays. He ordered a glass of red wine. The waitress tipped the hourglass above his head, and the race was on. He sat at a front table, facing the street, his back to the other tables. He was a heavy man of fifty-eight, with a thick chest and ponderous belly. He leaned hard on the red checkered tablecloth and watched the traffic on Forty-sixth.

Thankfully, Tubertini was prompt. Less than a fourth of the white sand was wasted on him. They shook hands politely, while Tubertini scornfully surveyed the tiny sliver of a restaurant. He flashed a plastic smile at Lazarov and glared at his seat in the window. His back would face the street, and this was extremely irritating. And dangerous. But his car was just outside with two of his men. He decided to be polite. He deftly maneuvered around the tiny table and sat down.

Tubertini was polished. He was thirty-seven, the son-in-law of old man Palumbo himself. Family. Married his only daughter. He was beautifully thin and tanned with his short black hair oiled to perfection and slicked back. He ordered red wine.

'How's my pal Joey Morolto?' he asked with a perfect brilliant smile.

'Fine. And Mr. Palumbo?'

'Very ill, and very ill-tempered. As usual.'

'Please give him my regards.'

'Certainly.'

The waitress approached and looked menacingly at the timepiece. 'Just wine,' said Tubertini. 'I won't be eating.'

Lazarov looked at the menu and handed it to her. 'Sautéed blackfish, with another glass of wine.'

Tubertini glanced at his men in the car. They appeared to be napping. 'So, what's wrong in Chicago?'

'Nothing's wrong. We just need a little information, that's all. We've heard, unconfirmed of course, that you have a very reliable man somewhere deep in the Bureau, somewhere close to Voyles.'

'And if we do?'

'We need some information from this man. We have a small unit in Memphis, and the Fibbies are trying like hell to infiltrate. We suspect one of our employees may be working with them, but we can't seem to catch him.'

'And if you caught him?'

'We'd slice out his liver and feed it to the rats.'

'Serious, huh?'

'Extremely serious. Something tells me the feds have targeted our little unit down there, and we've grown quite nervous.'

'Let's say his name is Alfred, and let's say he's very close to Voyles.'

'Okay. We need a very simple answer from Alfred. We need to know, yes or no, if our employee is working with the Fibbies.'

Tubertini watched Lazarov and sipped his wine. 'Alfred specializes in simple answers. He prefers the yes and no variety. We've used him twice, only when it's critical, and both times it was a question of "Are the feds coming here or there?" He's extremely cautious. I don't think he would provide too many details.'

'Is he accurate?'

'Deadly accurate.'

'Then he should be able to help us. If the answer is yes, we move accordingly. If no, the employee is off the hook and it's business as usual.'

'Alfred's very expensive.'

'I was afraid so. How much?'

'Well, he has sixteen years with the Bureau and is a career man. That's why he's so cautious. He has much to lose.'

'How much?'

'Half a million.'

'Damn!'

'Of course, we have to make a small profit on the transaction. After all, Alfred is ours.'

'A small profit?'

'Quite small, really. Most of it goes to Alfred. He talks to Voyles daily, you know. His office is two doors down.'

'All right. We'll pay.'

'Tubertini flashed a conquering smile and tasted his wine. 'I think you lied, Mr. Lazarov. You said it was a small unit in Memphis. That's not true, is it?'

'No.'

'What's the name of this unit?'

'The Bendini firm.'

'Old man Morolto's daughter married a Bendini.'

'That's it.'

'What's the employee's name?'

'Mitchell McDeere.'

'It might take two or three weeks. Meeting with Alfred is a major production.'

'Yes. Just be quick about it.'

# CHAPTER TWENTY-SEVEN

It was highly unusual for wives to appear at the quiet little fortress on Front Street. They were certainly welcome, they were told, but seldom invited. So Abby McDeere arrived through the front door, into the reception area uninvited and unannounced. It was imperative that she see her husband, she insisted. The receptionist phoned Nina on the second floor, and within seconds she appeared in a rush and warmly greeted her boss's wife. Mitch was in a meeting, she explained. He's always in a damned meeting, Abby replied. Get him out! They rushed to his office, where Abby closed the door and waited.

Mitch was observing another one of Avery's chaotic departures. Secretaries bumped into each other and packed briefcases while Avery yelled into the phone. Mitch sat on the sofa with a legal pad and watched. His partner was sheduled for two days on Grand Cayman. April 15 loomed on the calendar like a date with a firing squad, and the banks down there had certain records that had become critical. It was all work, Avery insisted. He talked about the trip for five days, dreading it, cursing it, but finding it completely unavoidable. He would take the Lear, and it was now waiting, said a secretary.

Probably waiting with a load of cash, thought Mitch.

Avery slammed the phone down and grabbed his coat. Nina walked through the door and glared at Mitch. 'Mr. McDeere, your wife is here. She says it's an emergency.'

The chaos became silent. He looked blankly at Avery. The secretaries froze. 'What is it?' he asked, standing.

'She's in your office,' Nina said.

'Mitch, I've gotta go,' Avery said. 'I'll call you tomorrow. I hope things are okay.'

'Sure.' He followed Nina down the stairs, saying nothing, to his office. Abby sat on his desk. He closed and locked the door. He watched her carefully.

'Mitch, I have to go home.'

'Why? What's happened?'

'My father just called at school. They found a tumor in one of Mother's lungs. They're operating tomorrow.'

He breathed deeply. 'I'm so sorry.' He did not touch her. She was not crying.

'I must go. I've taken a leave of absence at school.'

'For how long?' It was a nervous question.

She looked past him, to the Ego Wall. 'I don't know, Mitch. We need some time apart. I'm tired of a lot of things now, and I need time. I think it will be good for both of us.'

'Let's talk about it.'

'You're too busy to talk, Mitch. I've been trying to talk for six months, but you can't hear me.'

'How long will you be gone. Abby?'

'I don't know. I guess it depends on Mother. No, it depends on a lot of things.'

'You're scaring me, Abby.'

'I'll be back, I promise. I don't know when. Maybe a week. Maybe a month. I need to sort out some things.'

'A month?'

'I don't know, Mitch. I just need some time. And I need to be with Mother.'

'I hope she's okay. I mean that.'

'I know. I'm going home to pack a few things, and I'll leave in an hour or so.'

'All right. Be careful.'

'I love you, Mitch.'

He nodded and watched as she opened the door. There was no embrace.

On the fifth floor, a technician rewound the tape and pushed the emergency button direct to DeVasher's office. He appeared instantly and slapped the headphones over his extra-large cranium. He listened for a moment. 'Rewind,' he demanded. He was quiet for another moment.

'When did this happen?' he asked.

The technician looked at a panel of digital numbers. 'Two minutes fourteen seconds ago. In his office, second floor.'

'Damn, damn. She's leaving him, ain't she? No talk of separation or divorce before this?'

'No. You would've known about it. They've argued about his workaholic routine, and he hates her parents. But nothing like this.'

'Yeah, yeah. Check with Marcus and see if he's heard anything before. Check the tapes, in case we've missed something. Damn, damn, damn!'

Abby started for Kentucky, but did not make it. An hour west of

Nashville, she left Interstate 40, and turned north on Highway 13. She had noticed nothing behind her. She drove eighty at times, then fifty. Nothing. At the small town of Clarksville, near the Kentucky line, she abruptly turned east on Highway 112. An hour later she entered Nashville through a county highway, and the red Peugeot was lost in city traffic.

She parked it in the long-term section at Nashville Airport and caught a shuttle to the terminal. In a rest room on the first floor she changed into khaki walking shorts, Bass loafers and a navy knit pullover. It was a cool outfit, a little out of season, but she was headed for warmer weather. She pulled her shoulder-length hair into a ponytail and forced it under her collar. She changed sunglasses and stuffed the dress, heels and panty hose into a canvas gym bag.

Almost five hours after she left Memphis, she walked to the Delta boarding gate and presented her ticket. She asked for a window seat.

No Delta flight in the free world can bypass Atlanta, but fortunately she was not forced to change planes. She waited by her window and watched darkness fall on the busy airport. She was nervous, but tried not to think about it. She drank a glass of wine and read a *Newsweek*.

Two hours later she landed in Miami and left the plane. She walked rapidly through the airport, catching stares but ignoring them. They're just the usual everyday stares of admiration and lust, she told herself. Nothing more.

At the one and only Cayman Airways boarding gate, she produced her round-trip ticket and the required birth certificate and driver's license. Wonderful people, these Caymanians, but they won't allow you in their country unless you've already purchased a ticket to get out. Please come and spend your money, then leave. Please.

She sat in a corner of the crowded room and tried to read. A young father with a pretty wife and two babies kept staring at her legs, but no one else noticed her. The flight to Grand Cayman would leave in thirty minutes.

After a rough start, Avery gained momentum and spent seven hours at the Royal Bank of Montreal, Georgetown, Grand Cayman branch. When he left at 5 P.M., the complimentary conference room was filled with computer printouts and account summaries. He would finish tomorrow. He needed McDeere, but circumstances had worked to seriously curtail his travel plans. Avery was now exhausted and thirsty. And things were hot on the beach.

At Rumheads, he picked up a beer at the bar and worked his well-tanned body through the crowd to the patio, where he looked for a table. As he strode confidently past the domino game, Tammy Greenwood Hemphill, of Greenwood Services, nervously but non-chalantly entered the crowd and sat on a stool at the bar. She watched him. Her tan was store-bought, machine-inflicted, with some areas browner than others. But on the whole, it was an enviable tan for late March. The hair was now colored, not bleached, to a soft sandy blonde, and the make-up likewise had been tempered. The bikini was a state of the art, bright fluorescent orange that demanded attention. The large breasts hung wonderfully and stretched the strings and patches to their limit. The small patch across the rear was woefully incapable of covering anything. She was forty, but twenty sets of hungry eyes followed her to the bar, where she ordered a club soda and fired up a cigarette. She smoked it, and watched him.

He was a wolf. He looked good, and he knew it. He sipped his beer and slowly examined every female within fifty yards. He locked into one, a young blonde, and seemed ready to pounce when her man arrived and she sat in his lap. He sipped his beer and continued to survey.

Tammy ordered another club soda, with a twist of lime, and started for the patio. The wolf locked into the big breasts im-mediately and watched them bounce his way.

'Mind if I sit down?' she asked.

He half stood and reached for the chair. 'Please do.' It was a great moment for him. Of all the hungry wolves lusting around the bar and patio at Rumheads, she picked him. He'd had younger babes, but at this moment at this place, she was the hottest.

'I'm Avery Tolleson. From Memphis.'

'Nice to meet you. I'm Libby. Libby Lox from Birmingham.' Now she was Libby. She had a sister named Libby, a mother named Doris, and her name was Tammy. And she hoped to hell she could keep it all straight. Although she wore no rings, she had a husband whose legal name was Elvis, and he was supposed to be in Oklahoma City impersonating the King, and probably screwing teenage girls with LOVE ME TENDER T-shirts.

'What brings you here?' Avery asked.

'Just fun. Got in this morning. Staying at the Palms. You?'

'I'm a tax lawyer, and believe it or not, I'm here on business. I'm forced to come down several times a year. Real torture.'

'Where are you staying?'

He pointed. 'My firm owns those two condos over there. It's a nice little write-off.'

'Very pretty.'

The wolf did not hesitate. 'Would you like to see them?'

She giggled like a sophomore. 'Maybe later.'

He smiled at her. This would be easy. He loved the islands.

'What're you drinking?' he asked.

'Gin and tonic. Twist of lime.'

He left for the bar, and returned with the drinks. He moved his chair closer to her. Now their legs were touching. The breasts were resting comfortably on the table. He looked down between them.

'Are you alone?' Obvious question, but he had to ask it.

'Yeah. You?'

'Yeah. Do you have plans for dinner?'

'Not really.'

'Good. There's this great cookout there at the Palms beginning at six. The best seafood on the island. Good music. Rum punch. The works. No dress code.'

'I'm game.'

They moved closer together, and his hand was suddenly between her knees. His elbow nestled next to her left breast, and he smiled. She smiled. This was not altogether unpleasant, she thought, but there was business at hand.

The Barefoot Boys began to tune up, and the festival began. Beachcombers from all directions flocked to the Palms. Natives in white jackets and white shorts lined up folding tables and laid heavy cotton cloths over them. The smell of boiled shrimp and grilled amberjack and barbecued shark filled the beach. The lovebirds, Avery and Libby, walked hand in hand into the courtyard of the Palms and lined up for the buffet.

For three hours they dined and danced, drank and danced, and fell madly in heat over each other. Once he became drunk, she returned to straight club soda. Business was at hand. By ten, he was sloppy and she led him away from the dance floor, to the condo next door. He attacked her at the front door, and they kissed and groped for five minutes. He managed the key, and they were inside.

'One more drink,' she said, ever the party girl. He went to the bar and fixed her a gin and tonic. He was drinking scotch and water. They sat on the balcony outside the master bedroom and watched a half moon decorate the gentle sea.

She matched him drink for drink, he thought, and if she could handle another, then so could he. But nature was calling again, and he excused himself. The scotch and water sat on the wicker table between them, and she smiled at it. Much easier than she had prayed for. She took a small plastic packet from the orange strap between her legs and dumped two tablets of chloral hydrate into his drink. She sipped her gin and tonic.

'Drink it up, big boy,' she said when he returned. 'I'm ready for bed.'

He grabbed his whiskey and gulped it down. The taste buds had been numb for hours. He took another swallow, then began to relax. Another swallow. His head wobbled from shoulder to shoulder, and finally his chin hit his chest. The breathing became heavy.

'Sleep well, lover boy,' she said to herself.

With a man of a hundred eighty pounds, two shots of chloral hydrate would induce a dead sleep for ten hours. She took his glass and gauged what was left. Not much. Eight hours, to be safe. She rolled him out of the chair and dragged him to the bed, head first, then feet. Very gently, she pulled his yellow-and-blue surfer shorts down his legs and laid them on the floor. She stared for a long second then tucked the sheets and blankets around him. She kissed him good night.

On the dresser she found two key rings, eleven keys. Downstairs in the hall between the kitchen and the great room with a view of the beach, she found the mysterious locked door Mitch had found in November. He had paced off every room, upstairs and down, and determined this room to be at least fifteen by fifteen. It was suspicious because the door was metal, and because it was locked, and because a small STORAGE sign was affixed to it. It was the only labeled room in the condo. A week earlier in Unit B, he and Abby had found no such room.

One key ring held a key to a Mercedes, two keys to the Bendini Building, a house key, two apartment keys and a desk key. The keys on the other ring were unmarked and fairly generic. She tried it first, and the fourth key fit. She held her breath and opened the door. No electric shocks, no alarms, nothing. Mitch told her to open the door, wait five minutes and, if nothing happened, then turn on the light.

She waited ten minutes. Ten long and frightful minutes. Mitch had speculated that Unit A was used by the partners and trusted guests, and that Unit B was used by the associates and others who required constant surveillance. Thus, he hoped, Unit A would not be laden with wires and cameras and recorders and alarms. After ten minutes, she opened the door wide and turned on the light. She waited again, and heard nothing. The room was square, about fifteen by fifteen, with white walls, no carpet, and, as she counted, twelve fireproof legal-size file cabinets. Slowly, she walked over to one and pulled the top drawer. It was unlocked.

She turned off the light, closed the door and returned to the bedroom upstairs, where Avery was now comatose and snoring loudly. It was ten-thirty. She would work like crazy for eight hours and quit at six in the morning.

Near a desk in a corner, three large briefcases sat neatly in a row. She grabbed them, turned off the lights and left through the front door. The small parking lot was dark and empty with a gravel drive leading to the highway. A sidewalk ran next to the shrubbery in front of both units and stopped at a white board fence along the property line. A gate let to a slight grassy knoll, with the first building of the Palms just over it.

It was a short walk from the condos to the Palms, but the briefcases had grown much heavier when she reached Room 188. It was on the first floor, front side, with a view of the pool but not the beach. She was panting and sweating when she knocked on the door.

Abby yanked it open. She took the briefcases and placed them on the bed. 'Any problems?'

'Not yet. I think he's dead.' Tammy wiped her face with a towel and opened a can of Coke.

'Where is he?' Abby was all business, no smiles.

'In his bed. I figure we've got eight hours. Until six.'

'Did you get in the room?' Abby asked as she handed her a pair of shorts and a bulky cotton shirt.

'Yeah. There's a dozen big file cabinets, unlocked. A few cardboard boxes and other junk, but not much else.'

'A dozen?'

'Yeah, tall ones. All legal size. We'll be lucky to finish by six.'

It was a single motel room with a queen-size bed. The sofa, coffee table and bed were pushed to the wall, and a Canon Model 8580 copier with automatic feed and collator sat in the center with engines running. On lease from Island Office Supply, it came at the scalper's price of three hundred dollars for twenty-four hours, delivered. It was the newest and largest rental copier on the island, the salesman had explained, and he was not excited about parting with it for only a day. But Abby charmed him and began laying hundred-dollar bills on the counter. Two cases of copy paper, ten thousand sheets, sat next to the bed.

They opened the first briefcase and removed six thin files. 'Same type of files,' Tammy mumbled to herself. She unhitched the two-prong clasp on the inside of the file and removed the papers. 'Mitch says they're very particular about their files,' Tammy explained as she unstapled a ten-page document. 'He says lawyers have a sixth sense and can almost smell if a secretary or a clerk has been in a file. So you'll have to be careful. Work slowly. Copy one document, and when you restaple it, try to line up with the old stable holes. It's tedious. Copy only one document at a time, regardless of the number of pages. Then put it back together slowly and in order. Then staple your copy so everything stays in order.'

With the automatic feed, the ten-page document took eight seconds.

'Pretty fast,' Tammy said.

The first briefcase was finished in twenty minutes. Tammy handed the two key rings to Abby and picked up two new, empty, all-canvas Samsonite handbags. She left for the condo.

Abby followed her out the door, then locked it. She walked to the front of the Palms, to Tammy's rented Nissan Stanza. Dodging at oncoming traffic from the wrong side of the road, she drove along Seven Mile Beach and into Georgetown. Two blocks behind the stately Swiss Bank Building, on a narrow street lined with neat frame houses, she found the one owned by the only locksmith on the island of Grand Cayman. At least, he was the only one she'd been able to locate without assistance. He owned a green house with open windows and white trim around the shutters and the doors.

She parked in the street and walked through the sand to the tiny front porch, where the locksmith and his neighbors were drinking and listening to Radio Cayman. Solid-gold reggae. They quietened when she approached, and none of them stood. It was almost eleven. He had said that he would do the job in his shop out back, and that his fees were modest, and that he would like a fifth of Myers's Rum as a down payment before he started.

'Mr. Dantley, I'm sorry I'm late. I've brought you a little gift.' She held out the fifth of rum.

Mr. Dantley emerged from the darkness and took the rum. He inspected the bottle. 'Boys, a bottle of Myers's.'

Abby could not understand the chatter, but it was obvious the gang on the porch was terribly excited about the bottle of Myers's. Dantley handed it to them and led Abby behind his house to a small outbuilding full of tools and small machines and a hundred gadgets. A single yellow light bulb hung from the ceiling and attracted mosquitoes by the hundreds. She handed Dantley the eleven keys, and he carefully laid them on a bare section of a cluttered workbench. 'This will be easy,' he said without looking up.

Although he was drinking at eleven at night, Dantley appeared to be in control. Perhaps his system had built an immunity to rum. He

worked through a pair of thick goggles, drilling and carving each replica. After twenty minutes, he was finished. He handed Abby the
two original sets of keys and their copies.

'Thank you, Mr. Dantley. How much do I owe you?'

'They were quite easy,' he drawled. 'A dollar per key.'

She paid him quickly and left.

Tammy filled the two small suitcases with the contents of the top
drawer of the first file cabinet. Five drawers, twelve cabinets, sixty
trips to the copier and back. In eight hours. It could be done. There
were files, notebooks, computer printouts and more files. Mitch said
to copy it all. He was not exactly sure what he was looking for, so
copy it all.

She turned off the light and ran upstairs to check on lover boy. He
had not moved. The snoring was in slow motion.

The Samsonites weighed thirty pounds apiece, and her arms ached
when she reached Room 188. First trip out of sixty, she would not
make it. Abby had not returned from Georgetown, so Tammy unloaded the suitcases neatly on the bed. She took one drink from her
Coke and left with the empty bags. Back to the condo. Drawer two
was identical. She fitted the files in order into the suitcases and
strong-armed zippers. She was sweating and gasping for breath. Four
packs a day, she thought. She vowed to cut back to two. Maybe even
one pack. Up the stairs to check on him. He had not breathed since
her last trip.

The copier was clicking and humming when she returned from trip
two. Abby was finishing the second briefcase, about to start on the
third.

'Did you get the keys?' Tammy asked.

'Yeah, no problem. What's your man doing?'

'If the copier wasn't running, you could hear him snoring.'
Tammy unpacked into another neat stack on the bed. She wiped her
face with a wet towel and left for the condo.

Abby finished the third briefcase and started on the stacks from the
file cabinets. She quickly got the hang of the automatic feed, and after
thirty minutes she moved with the efficient grace of a seasoned copy-
room clerk. She fed copies and unstapled and restapled while the
machine clicked rapidly and spat the reproductions through the collator.

Tammy arrived from trip three out of breath and with sweat dripping from her nose. 'Third drawer,' she reported. 'He's still snoring.'
She unzipped the suitcases and made another neat pile on the bed.

She caught her breath, wiped her face and loaded the now copied contents of drawer one into the bags. For the rest of the night, she would be loaded coming and going.

At midnight, the Barefoot Boys sang their last song, and the Palms settled down for the night. The quiet hum of the copier could not be heard outside Room 188. The door was kept locked; the shades pulled tightly, and all lights extinguished except for a lamp near the bed. No one noticed the tired lady, dripping with sweat, lugging the same two suitcases to and from the room.

After midnight they did not speak. They were tired, too busy and scared, and there was nothing to report except lover boy's movements in bed, if any. And there was none, until around 1 A.M., when he subconsciously rolled onto his side, where he stayed for about twenty minutes, then returned to his back. Tammy checked on him with each visit and asked herself each time what she would do if his eyes suddenly opened and he attacked. She had a small tube of Mace in her shorts pocket, just in case a confrontation occurred and escape became necessary. Mitch had been vague on the details of such an escape. Just don't lead him back to the motel room, he said. Hit him with the Mace, then run like crazy and scream, 'Rape!'

But after twenty-five trips, she became convinced he was hours away from consciousness. And it was bad enough hiking like a pack mule to and from, but she also had to climb the stairs, fourteen of them, each trip to check on Casanova. So she went to check every other trip. Then one out of three.

By 2 A.M., halfway through the project, they had copied the contents from five of the file cabinets. They had made over four thousand copies, and the bed was covered with neat little stacks of materials. Their copies stood along the wall next to the sofa in seven even rows almost waist high.

They rested for fifteen minutes.

At five-thirty the first flicker of sunrise rose in the east, and they forgot about being tired. Abby quickened her movements around the copier and hoped it would not burn up. Tammy rubbed the cramps in her calves and walked quickly back to the condo. It was either trip number fifty-one or fifty-two. She had lost count. It would be her last trip for a while. He was waiting.

She opened the door and went straight to the storage room, as usual. She set the packed Samsonites on the floor, as usual. She quietly walked up the stairs, into the bedroom, and froze. Avery was sitting on the edge of the bed, facing the balcony. He heard her and turned slowly to face her. His eyes were swollen and glazed. He scowled at her.

Instinctively, she unbuttoned the khaki shorts and they fell to the floor. 'Hey, big boy,' she said, trying to breath normally and act like a party girl. She walked to the edge of the bed where he was sitting. 'You're up kinda early. Let's get some more sleep.'

His gaze returned to the window. He said nothing. She sat beside him and rubbed the inside of his thigh. She slid her hand up the inside of his leg, and he did not move.

'Are you awake?' she asked.

No response.

'Avery, talk to me, baby. Let's get some more sleep. It's still dark out there.'

He fell sideways, onto his pillow. He grunted. No attempt at speech. Just a grunt. Then he closed his eyes. She lifted his legs onto the bed and covered him again.

She sat by him for ten minutes, and when the snoring returned to its former intensity, she slid into the shorts and ran to the Palms.

'He woke up, Abby!' she reported in panic. 'He woke up, then passed out again.'

Abby stopped and stared. Both women looked at the bed, which was covered with uncopied documents.

'Okay. Take a quick shower,' Abby said coolly. 'Then go get in bed with him and wait. Lock the door to the storage room and call me when he wakes up and gets in the shower. I'll keep copying what's left, and we'll try to move it later, after he goes to work.'

'That's awfully risky.'

'It's all risky. Hurry.'

Five minutes later, Tammy/Doris/Libby with the bright orange string bikini made another trip – without the suitcases – to the condo. She locked the front door and the storage door and went to the bedroom. She removed the orange top and crawled under the covers.

The snoring kept her awake for fifteen minutes. Then she dozed. She sat up in bed to prevent sleep. She was scared, sitting there in bed with a nude man who could kill her if he knew. Her tired body relaxed, and sleep became unavoidable. She dozed again.

Lover boy broke from his coma at three minutes past nine. He moaned loudly and rolled to the edge of the bed. His eyelids were stuck together. They opened slowly, and the bright sun came piercing through. He moaned again. The head weighed a hundred pounds and rocked awkwardly from right to left, shifting the brain violently each time. He breathed deeply, and the fresh oxygen went screaming through his temples. His right hand caught his attention. He tried to raise it, but the nerve impulses would not penetrate the brain. Slowly it went up, and he squinted at it. He tried to focus with the right eye first, then the left. The clock.

He looked at the digital clock for thirty seconds before he could decipher the red numbers. Nine-oh-five. Damn! He was expected at the bank at nine. He moaned. The woman!

She had felt him move and heard his sounds, and she lay still with her eyes shut. She prayed he would not touch her. She felt him staring.

For this career rogue and bad boy, there had been many hangovers. But none like this. He looked at her face and tried to remember how good she had been. He could always remember that, if nothing else. Regardless of the size of the hangover, he could always remember the women. He watched her for a moment, then gave up.

'Damn!' he said as he stood and tried to walk. His feet were like lead boots and only reluctantly compiled with his wishes. He braced himself against the sliding door to the balcony.

The bathroom was twenty feet away, and he decided to go for it. The desk and dresser served as braces. One painful, clumsy step after another, and he finally made it. He hovered above the toilet and relieved himself.

She rolled to face the balcony, and when he finished she felt him sit on her side of the bed. He gently touched her shoulder. 'Libby, wake up.' He shook her, and she bolted stiff.

'Wake up, dear,' he said. A gentleman.

She gave him her best sleepy smile. The morning-after smile of fulfillment and commitment. The Scarlett O'Hara smile the morning after Rhett nailed her. 'You were great, big boy,' she cooed with her eyes closed.

In spite of the pain and nausea, in spite of the lead boots and bowling-ball head, he was proud of himself. The woman was impressed. Suddenly, he remembered that he was great last night.

'Look, Libby, we've overslept. I gotta go to work. I'm already late.'

'Not in the mood, huh?' she giggled. She prayed he wasn't in the mood.

'Naw, not now. How about tonight?'

'I'll be here, big boy.'

'Good. I gotta take a shower.'

'Wake me up when you get out.'

He stood and mumbled something, then locked the bathroom door. She slid across the bed to the phone and called Abby. After three rings, she answered.

'He's in the shower.'

'Are you okay?'

'Yeah. Fine. He couldn't do it if he had to.'

'What took so long?'

'He wouldn't wake up.'

'Is he suspicious?'

'No. He remembers nothing. I think he's in pain.'

'How long will you be there?'

'I'll kiss him goodbye when he gets out of the shower. Ten, maybe fifteen minutes.'

'Okay. Hurry.' Abby hung up, and Tammy slid to her side of the bed. In the attic above the kitchen, a recorder clicked, reset itself and was ready for the next call.

By ten-thirty, they were ready for the final assault on the condo. The contraband was divided into three equal parts. Three daring raids in open daylight. Tammy slid the shiny new keys into her blouse pocket and took off with the suitcases. She walked quickly, her eyes darting in all directions behind the sunglasses. The parking lot in front of the condos was still empty. Traffic was light on the highway.

The new key fit, and she was inside. The key to the storage door also fit, and she was inside. The key to the storage door also fit, and five minutes later she left the condo. The second and third trips were equally quick and uneventful. When she left the storage room for the last time, she studied it carefully. Everything was in order, just as she found it. She locked the condo and took the empty, well-worn Samsonites back to her room.

For an hour they lay beside each other on the bed and laughed at Avery and his hangover. It was over now, for the most part, and they had committed the perfect crime. And lover boy was a willing but ignorant participant. It had been easy, they decided.

The small mountain of evidence filled eleven and a half corrugated storage boxes. At two-thirty, a native with a straw hat and no shirt knocked on the door and announced he was from an outfit called Cayman Storage. Abby pointed at the boxes. With no place to go and no hurry to get there, he took the first box and ever so slowly carried it to his van. Like all the natives, he operated on Cayman time. No hurry, mon.

They followed him in the Stanza to a warehouse in Georgetown. Abby inspected the proposed storage room and paid cash for three months' rental.

# CHAPTER TWENTY-EIGHT

Wayne Tarrance sat on the back row of the 11:40 P.M. Greyhound from Louisville to Indianpolis to Chicago. Although he sat by himself, the bus was crowded. It was Friday night. The bus left Kentucky thirty minutes earlier, and by now he was convinced something had gone wrong. Thirty minutes, and not a word or signal from anyone. Maybe it was the wrong bus. Maybe McDeere had changed his mind. Maybe a lot of things. The rear seat was inches above the diesel engine, and Wayne Tarrance, of the Bronx, now knew why Greyhound Frequent Milers fought for the seats just behind the driver. His Louis L'Amour vibrated until he had a headache. Thirty minutes. Nothing.

The toilet flushed across the aisle, and the door flew open. The odor filtered out, and Tarrance looked away, to the south-bound traffic. From nowhere, she slid into the aisle seat and cleared her throat. Tarrance jerked to his right, and there she was. He'd seen her before, somewhere.

'Are you Mr. Tarrance?' She wore jeans, white cotton sneakers and a heavy green rag sweater. She hid behind dark glasses.

'Yeah. And you?'

She grabbed his hand and shook it firmly. 'Abby McDeere.'

'I was expecting your husband.'

'I know. He decided not to come, and so here I am.'

'Well, uh, I sort of wanted to talk to him.'

'Yes, but he sent me. Just think of me as his agent.'

Tarrance laid his paperback under the seat and watched the highway. 'Where is he?'

'Why is that important, Mr. Tarrance? He sent me to talk business, and you're here to talk business. So let's talk.'

'Okay. Keep your voice down, and if anybody comes down the aisle grab my hand and stop talking. Act like we're married or something. Okay? Now, Mr. Voyles – do you know who he is?'

'I know everything, Mr. Tarrance.'

'Good. Mr. Voyles is about to stroke out because we haven't got Mitch's files yet. The good files. You understand why they're important, don't you?'

'Very much so.'

'So we want the files.'

624

'And we want a million dollars.'

'Yes, that's the deal. But we get the files first.'

'No. That's not the deal. The deal, Mr. Tarrance, is that we get the million dollars exactly where we want it, then we hand over the files.'

'You don't trust us?'

'That's correct. We don't trust you, Voyles or anyone else. The money is to be deposited by wire transfer to a certain numbered account in a bank in Freeport, Bahamas. We will immediately be notified, and the money will then be wired by us to another bank. Once we have it where we want it, the files are yours.'

'Where are the files?'

'In a mini-storage in Memphis. There are fifty-one files in all, all boxed up real neat and proper like. You'll be impressed. we do good work.'

'We? Have you seen the files?'

'Of course. Helped box them up. There are these surprises in box number eight.'

'Okay. What?'

'Mitch was able to copy three of Avery Tolleson's files, and they appear to be questionable. Two deal with a company called Dunn Lane, Ltd., which we know to be a Mafia-controlled corporation chartered in the Caymans. It was established with ten million laundered dollars in 1986. The files deal with two construction projects financed by the corporation. You'll find it fascinating reading.'

'How do you know it was chartered in the Caymans? And how do you know about the ten million? Surely that's not in the files.'

'No, it's not. We have other records.'

Tarrance thought about the other records for six miles. It was obvious he wouldn't see them until the McDeeres had the first million. He let it pass.

'I'm not sure we can wire the money as you wish without first getting the files.' It was a rather weak bluff. She read it perfectly and smiled.

'Do we have to play games, Mr. Tarrance? Why don't you just give us the money and quit sparring.'

A foreign student of some sort, probably an Arab, sauntered down the aisle and into the rest room. Tarrance froze and stared at the window. Abby patted his arm like a real girlfriend. The flushing sounded like a short waterfall.

'How soon can this happen?' Tarrance asked. She was not touching him anymore.

'The files are ready. How soon can you round up a million bucks?'

'Tomorrow.'

Abby looked out the window and talked from the left corner of her mouth. 'Today's Friday. Next Tuesday, at ten A.M. Eastern time, Bahamas time, you transfer by wire the million dollars from your account at the Chemical Bank in Manhattan to a numbered account at the Ontario Bank in Freeport. It's a clean, legitimate wire transfer – take about fifteen seconds.'

Tarrance frowned and listened hard. 'What if we don't have an account at the Chemical Bank in Manhattan?'

You don't now, but you will Monday. I'm sure you've got someone in Washington who can handle a simple wire transfer.'

'I'm sure we do.'

'Good.'

'But why the Chemical Bank?'

'Mitch's orders, Mr. Tarrance. Trust him, he knows what he's doing.'

'I see he's done his homework.'

'He always does his homework. And there's something you need to always remember. He's much smarter than you are.'

Tarrance snorted and faked a light chuckle. They rode in silence for a mile or two, each thinking of the next question and answer.

'Okay,' Tarrance said, almost to himself. 'And when do we get the files?'

'When the money's safe in Freeport, we'll be notified. Wednesday morning before ten-thirty, you'll receive at your Memphis office a Federal Express package with a note and the key to the mini-storage.'

'So I can tell Mr. Voyles we'll have the files by Wednesday afternoon?'

She shrugged and said nothing. Tarrance felt stupid for asking the question. Quickly, he thought of a good one.

'We'll need the account number in Freeport.'

'It's written down. I'll give it to you when the bus stops.'

The particulars were now complete. He reached under the seat and retrieved his book. He flipped pages and pretended to read. 'Just sit here a minute,' he said.

'Any questions?' she asked.

'Yeah. Can we talk about these other records you mentioned?'

'Sure.'

'Where are they?'

'Good question. The way the deal was explained to me, we would first get the next installment, a half million, I believe, in return for enough evidence to allow you to obtain the indictments. These other records are part of the next installment.'

Tarrance flipped a page. 'You mean you've already obtained the, uh, dirty files?'

'We have most of what we need. Yes, we have a bunch of dirty files.'

'Where are they?'

She smiled softly and patted his arm. 'I assure you they're not in the mini-storage with the clean files.'

'But you have possession of them?'

'Sort of, Would you like to see a couple?'

He closed the book and breathed deeply. He looked at her. 'Certainly.'

'I thought so. Mitch says we'll give you ten inches of documents on Dunn Lane, Ltd. – copies of bank records, corporate charters, minutes, bylaws, officers, stockholders, wire transfer records, letters from Nathan Locke to Joey Morolto, working papers, a hundred other juicy morsels that'll make you lose sleep. Wonderful stuff. Mitch says you can probably get thirty indictments just from the Dunn Lane records.'

Tarrance hung on every word, and believed her. 'When can I see it?' he asked quietly but so eagerly.

'When Ray is out of prison. It's part of the deal, remember?'

'Aw yes. Ray.'

'Aw yes. He gets over the wall, Mr. Tarrance, or you can forget the Bendini firm. Mitch and I will take our paltry million and disappear into the night.'

'I'm working on it.'

'Better work hard.' It was more than a threat, and he knew it. He opened the book again and stared at it.

Abby pulled a Bendini, Lambert & Locke business card from her pocket and dropped in on the book. On the back she had written the account number: 477DL-19584, Ontario Bank, Freeport.

'I'm going back to my seat near the front, away from the engine. Are we clear about next Tuesday?'

'No problems, mon. Are you getting off in Indianapolis?'

'Yes.'

'Where are you going?'

'To my parents' home in Kentucky. Mitch and I are separated.' She was gone.

Tammy stood in one of a dozen long, hot lines at Miami customs. She wore shorts, sandals, halter top, sunglasses and a straw hat and looked just like the other thousand weary tourists returning from the sun-drenched beaches of the Caribbean. In front of her were two ill-tempered newlyweds carrying bags of duty-free liquor and perfume and obviously in the middle of a serious disagreement. Behind her were two brand-new Hartman leather suitcases filled with enough documents and records to indict forty lawyers. Her employer, also a lawyer, had suggested she purchase luggage with little wheels on the bottom so they could be pulled through the Miami International Airport. She also had a small overnight bag with a few clothes and a toothbrush, to look legitimate.

About every ten minutes, the young couple moved forward six inches, and Tammy followed with her baggage. An hour after she had entered the line, she made it to the checkpoint.

'No declarations!' the agent snapped in broken English.

'No!' she snapped back.

He nodded at the big leather bags. 'What's in there?'

'Papers.'

'Papers?'

'Papers.'

'What kind of papers?'

Toilet paper, she thought. I spend my vacations traveling the Caribbean collecting toilet paper. 'Legal documents, crap like that. I'm a lawyer.'

'Yeah, yeah.' He unzipped the overnight bag and glanced in. 'Okay. Next!'

She carefully pulled the bags, just so. They were inclined to tip over. A bellboy grabbed them and loaded all three pieces onto a two-wheeler. 'Delta Flight 282, to Nashville. Gate 44, Concourse B,' she said as she handed him a five dollar bill.

Tammy and all three bags arrived in Nashville at midnight Saturday. She loaded them into her Rabbit and left the airport. In the suburb of Brentwood, she parked in her designated parking place and, one at a time, pulled the Hartmans into a one-bedroom apartment.

Except for a rented foldaway sofa, there was no furniture. She unpacked the suitcases in the bedroom and began the tedious process of arranging the evidence. Mitch wanted a list of each document, each blank record, each corporation. He wanted it just so. He said one day he would pass through in a great hurry, and he wanted it all organized.

For two hours she took inventory. She sat on the floor and made careful notes. After three one-day trips to Grand Cayman, the room was beginning to fill. Monday she would leave again.

She felt like she'd slept three hours in the past two weeks. But it was urgent, he said. A matter of life and death.

Tarry Ross, alias Alfred, sat in the darkest corner of the lounge of the Washington Phoenix Inn. The meeting would be terribly brief. He drank coffee and waited on his guest.

He waited and vowed to wait only five more minutes. The cup shook when he tried to sip it. Coffee splashed on the table. He looked at the table and tried desperately not to look around. He waited.

His guest arrived from nowhere and sat with his back to the wall. His name was Vinnie Cozzo, a thug from New York. From the Palumbo family.

Vinnie noticed the shaking cup and the spilled coffee. 'Relax, Alfred. This place is dark enough.'

'What do you want?' Alfred hissed.

'I wanna drink.'

'No time for drinks. I'm leaving.'

'Settle down, Alfred. Relax, pal. There ain't three people in here.'

'What do you want?' he hissed again.

'Just a little information.'

'It'll cost you.'

'It always does.' A waiter ventured by, and Vinnie ordered Chivas and water.

'How's my pal Denton Voyles?' Vinnie asked.

'Kiss my ass, Cozzo. I'm leaving. I'm walking outta here.'

'Okay, pal. Relax. I just need some info.'

'Make it quick.' Alfred scanned the lounge. His cup was empty, most of it on the table.

The Chivas arrived, and Vinnie took a good drink. 'Gotta little situation down in Memphis. Some of the boys're sorta worried about it. Ever hear of the Bendini firm?'

Instinctively, Alfred shook his head in the negative. Always say no, at first. Then, after careful digging, return with a nice little report and say yes. Yes, he'd heard of the Bendini firm and their prized client. Operation Laundromat. Voyles himself had named it and was so proud of his creativity.

Vinnie took another good drink. 'Well there's a guy down there named McDeere, Mitchell McDeere, who works for this Bendini firm, and we suspect he's also playing grab-ass with your people. Know what I mean? We think he's selling info on Bendini to the feds. Just need to know if it's true. That's all.'

Alfred listened with a straight face, although it was not easy. He knew McDeere's blood type and his favorite restaurant in Memphis. He knew that McDeere had talked to Tarrance half a dozen times now and that tomorrow, Tuesday, McDeere would become a millionaire. Piece of cake.

'I'll see what I can do. Let's talk money.'

Vinnie lit a Salem Light. 'Well, Alfred, it's a serious matter. I ain't gonna lie. Two hundred thousand cash.'

Alfred dropped the cup. He pulled a handkerchief from his rear pocket and furiously rubbed his glasses. 'Two hundred? Cash?'

'That's what I said. What'd we pay you last time?'

'Seventy-five.'

'See what I mean. It's pretty damn serious, Alfred. Can you do it?'

'Yes.'

'When?'

'Give me two weeks.'

# CHAPTER TWENTY-NINE

A week before April 15, the workaholics at Bendini, Lambert & Locke reached maximum stress and ran at full throttle on nothing but adrenaline. And fear. Fear of missing a deduction or a write-off or some extra depreciation that would cost a rich client an extra million or so. Fear of picking up the phone and calling the client and informing him that the return was now finished and, sorry to say, an extra eight hundred thousand was due. Fear of not finishing by the fifteenth, and being forced to file extensions and incurring penalties and interest. The parking lot was full by 6 A.M. The secretaries worked twelve hours a day. Tempers were short. Talk was scarce and hurried.

With no wife to go home to, Mitch worked around the clock. Sonny Capps had cursed and berated Avery because he owed $450,000. On earned income of twelve million. Avery had cursed Mitch, and together they plowed through the Capps files again, digging and cursing. Mitch created two very questionable write-offs that lowered it to $320,000. Capps said he was considering a new tax firm. One in Washington.

With six days to go, Capps demanded a meeting with Avery in Houston. The Lear was available, and Avery left at midnight. Mitch drove him to the airport, receiving instructions along the way.

Shortly after 1:30 A.M., he returned to the office. Three Mercedes, a BMW and a Jaguar were scattered through the parking lot. The security guard opened the rear door, and Mitch rode the elevator to the fourth floor. As usual, Avery locked his office door. The partners' doors were always locked. At the end of the hall, a voice could be heard. Victor Milligan, head of tax, sat at his desk and said ugly things to his computer. The other offices were dark and locked.

Mitch held his breath and stuck his key into Avery's door. The knob turned, and he was inside. He switched on all the lights and went to the small conference table where he and his partner had spent the day and most of the night. Files were stacked like bricks around the chairs. Papers thrown here and there. IRS reg. books were piled on top of each other.

Mitch sat at the table and continued his research for Capps. According to the FBI notebook, Capps was a legitimate businessman who had used the firm for at least eight years. The Fibbies weren't interested in Sonny Capps.

After an hour, the talking stopped and Milligan closed and locked the door. He took the stairs without saying goodnight. Mitch quickly checked each office on the fourth floor, then the third. All empty. It was almost 3 A.M.

Next to the bookshelves on one wall of Avery's office, four solid oak file cabinets sat undisturbed. Mitch had noticed them for months but had never seen them used. The active files were kept in three metal cabinets next to the window. Secretaries dug through these, usually while Avery yelled at them. He locked the door behind him and walked to the oak cabinets. Locked of course. He had narrowed it down to two small keys, each less than an inch long. The first one fit the first cabinet, and he opened it.

From Tammy's inventory of the contraband in Nashville, he had memorized many of the names of the Cayman companies operating with dirty money that was now clean. He thumbed through the files in the top drawer, and the names jumped at him. Dunn Lane Ltd., Eastpointe Ltd., Virgin Bay Ltd., Inland Contractors Ltd., Gulf-South Ltd. He found more familiar names in the second and third drawers. The files were filled with loan documents from Cayman banks, wire-transfer records, warranty deeds, leases, mortgage deeds and a thousand other papers. He was particularly interested in Dunn Lane and Gulf-South. Tammy had recorded a significant number of documents for these two companies.

He picked out a Gulf-South file full of wire-transfer records and loan documents from the Royal Bank of Montreal. He walked to a copier in the center of the fourth floor and turned it on. While it warmed, he casually glanced around. The place was dead. He looked along the ceilings. No cameras. He had checked it many times before. The ACCESS NUMBER light flashed, and he punched in the file number for Mrs. Lettie Plunk. Her tax return was sitting on his desk on the second floor, and it could spare a few copies. He laid the contents on the automatic feed, and three minutes later the file was copied. One hundred twenty-eight copies, charged to Lettie Plunk. Back to the file cabinet. Back to the copier with another stack of Gulf-South evidence. He punched in the access number for the file of Greenmark Partners, a real estate development company in Bartlett, Tennessee. Legitimate folks. The tax return was sitting on his desk and could spare a few copies. Ninety-one, to be exact.

Mitch had eighteen tax returns sitting in his office waiting to be signed and filed. With six days to go, he had finished his deadline work. All eighteen received automatic billings for copies of Gulf-South and Dunn Lane evidence. He had scribbled their access numbers on a sheet of notepaper, and it sat on the table next to the copier.

After using the eighteen numbers, he accessed with three numbers borrowed from Lamar's files and three numbers borrowed from the Capps files.

A wire ran from the copier through a hole in the wall and down the inside of a closet, where it connected with wires from three other copiers on the fourth floor. The wire, larger now, ran down through the ceiling and along a baseboard to the billing room on the third floor, where a computer recorded and billed every copy made within the firm. An innocuous-looking little gray wire ran from the computer up a wall and through the ceiling to the fourth floor, and then up to the fifth, where another computer recorded the access code, the number of copies and the location of the machine making each copy.

At 5 P.M., April 15, Bendini, Lambert & Locke shut down. By six, the parking lot was empty, and the expensive automobiles reassembled two miles away behind a venerable seafood establishment called Anderton's. A small banquet room was reserved for the annual April 15 blowout. Every associate and active partner was present, along with eleven retired partners. The retirees were tanned and well rested, the actives were haggard and frayed. But they were all in a festive spirit, ready to get plastered. The stringent rules of clean living and moderation would be forgotten this night. Another firm rule prohibited any lawyer or secretary from working on April 16.

Platters of cold boiled shrimps and raw oysters sat on tables along the walls. A huge wooden barrel filled with ice and cold Moosehead greeted them. Ten cases stood behind the barrel. Roosevelt popped tops as quickly as possible. Late in the night, he would get drunk with the rest of them, and Oliver Lambert would call a taxi to haul him home to Jessie Frances. It was a ritual.

Roosevelt's cousin, Little Bobby Blue Baker, sat at a baby grand and sang sadly as the lawyers filed in. For now, he was the entertainment. Later he would not be needed.

Mitch ignored the food and took an icy green bottle to a table near the piano. Lamar followed with two pounds of shrimp. They watched their colleagues shake off coats and ties and attack the Moosehead.

'Get 'em all finished?' Lamar asked, devouring the shrimp.

'Yeah. I finished mine yesterday. Avery and I worked on Sonny Capps's until five P.M. It's finished.'

'How much?'

'Quarter of a mill.'

'Ouch.' Lamar turned up the bottle and drained half of it. 'He's never paid that much, has he?'

'No, and he's furious. I don't understand the guy. He cleared twelve million from all sorts of ventures, and he's mad as hell because he had to pay two percent in taxes.'

'How's Avery?'

'Somewhat worried. Capps made him fly to Houston last week, and it did not go well. He left on the Lear at midnight. Told me later Capps was waiting at his office at four in the morning, furious over his tax mess. Blamed it all on Avery. Said he might change firms.'

'I think he says that all the time. You need a beer?'

Lamar left and returned with four Mooseheads. 'How's Abby's mom?'

Mitch borrowed a shrimp and peeled it. 'She's okay, for now. They removed a lung.'

'And how's Abby?' Lamar was watching his friend, and not eating.

Mitch started another beer. 'She's fine.'

'Look, Mitch, our kids go to St. Andrew's. It's no secret Abby took a leave of absence. She's been gone for two weeks. We know it, and we're concerned.'

'Things will work out. She wants to spend a little time away. It's no big deal, really.'

'Come on, Mitch. It's a big deal when your wife leaves home without saying when she'll return. At least that's what she told the headmaster at school.'

'That's true. She doesn't know when she'll come back. Probably a month or so. She's had a hard time coping with the hours at the office.'

The lawyers were all present and accounted for, so Roosevelt shut the door. The room became noisier. Bobby Blue took requests.

'Have you thought about slowing down?' Lamar asked.

'No, not really. Why should I?'

'Look, Mitch, I'm your friend, right? I'm worried about you. You can't make a million bucks the first year.'

Oh yeah, he thought. I made a million bucks last week. In ten seconds the little account in Freeport jumped from ten thousand to a million ten thousand. And fifteen minutes later, the account was closed and the money was resting safely in a bank in Switzerland. Aw, the wonder of wire transfer. And because of the million bucks, this would be the first and only April 15 party of his short, but distinguished legal career. And his good friend who is so concerned about his marriage will most likely be in jail before long. Along with everyone else in the room, except for Roosevelt. Hell, Tarrance might get so excited he'll indict Roosevelt and Jessie Frances just for the fun of it.

Then the trials. 'I, Mitchell, Y. McDeere, do solemnly swear to tell the truth, the whole truth and nothing but the truth. So help me God.' And he'd sit in the witness chair and point the finger at his good friend Lamar Quin. And Kay and the kids would be sitting in the front row for jury appeal. Crying softly.

He finished the second beer and started the third. 'I know, Lamar, but I have no plans to slow down. Abby will adjust. Things'll be fine.'

'If you say so. Kay wants you over tomorrow for a big steak. We'll cook on the grill and eat on the patio. How about it?'

'Yes, on one condition. No discussion about Abby. She went home to see her mother, and she'll be back. Okay?'

'Fine. Sure.'

Avery sat across the table with a plate of shrimp. He began peeling them.

'We were just discussing Capps.' Lamar said.

'That's not a pleasant subject,' Avery replied. Mitch watched the shrimp intently until there was a little pile of about six freshly peeled. He grabbed them across the table and shoved the handful into his mouth.

Avery glared at him with tired, sad eyes. Red eyes. He struggled for something appropriate, then began eating the unpeeled shrimp. 'I wish the heads were still on them,' he said between bites. 'Much better with the heads.'

Mitch raked across two handfuls and began crunching. 'I like the tails myself. Always been a tail man.'

Lamar stopped eating and gawked at them. 'You must be kidding.'

'Nope,' said Avery. 'When I was a kid in El Paso, we used to go out with our nets and scoop up a bunch of fresh shrimp. We'd eat 'em on the spot, while they were still wiggling.' Chomp, chomp. 'The heads are the best part because of all the brain juices.'

'Shrimp, in El Paso?'

'Yeah, Rio Grande's full of them.'

Lamar left for another round of beer. The wear, tear, stress and fatigue mixed quickly with the alcohol and the room became rowdier. Bobby Blue was playing Steppenwolf. Even Nathan Locke was smiling and talking loudly. Just one of the boys. Roosevelt added five cases to the barrel of ice.

At ten, the singing started. Wally Hudson, minus the bow tie, stood on a chair by the piano and led the howling chorus through a riotous medley of Australian drinking songs. The restaurant was closed now, so who cared. Kendall Mahan was next. He had played rugby at Cornell and had an amazing repertoire of raunchy beer songs. Fifty untalented and drunk voices sang happily along with him.

Mitch excused himself and went to the rest room. A busboy unlocked the rear door, and he was in the parking lot. The singing was pleasant at this distance. He started for his car, but instead walked to a window. He stood in the dark, next to the corner of the building, and watched and listened. Kendall was now on the piano, leading his choir through an obscene refrain.

Joyous voices, of rich and happy people. He studied them one at a time, around the tables. Their faces were red. Their eyes were glowing. They were his friends – family men with wives and children – all caught up in this terrible conspiracy.

Last year Joe Hodge and Marty Kozinski were singing with the rest of them.

Last year he was a hotshot Harvard man with job offers in every pocket.

Now he was a millionaire, and would soon have a price on his head.

Funny what a year can do.

Sing on, brothers.

Mitch turned and walked away.


Around midnight, the taxis lined up on Madison, and the richest lawyers in town were carried and dragged into the back seats. Of course, Oliver Lambert was the soberest of the lot, and he directed the evacuation. Fifteen taxis in all, with drunk lawyers lying everywhere.

At the same time, across town on Front Street, two identical navy blue-and-yellow Ford vans with DUSTBUSTER painted brightly on the sides pulled up to the gate. Dutch Hendrix opened it and waved them through. They backed up to the rear door, and eight women with matching shirts began unloading vacuum cleaners and buckets filled with spray bottles. They unloaded brooms and mops and rolls of paper towels. They chattered quietly among themselves as they went through the building. As directed from above, the technicians cleaned one floor at a time, beginning with the fourth. The guards walked the floors and watched them carefully.

The women ignored them and buzzed about their business of emptying garbage cans, polishing furniture, vacuuming and scrubbing bathrooms. The new girl was slower than the others. She noticed things. She pulled on desk drawers and file cabinets when the guards weren't looking. She paid attention.

It was her third night on the job, and she was learning her way around. She'd found the Tolleson office on the fourth floor the first night, and smiled to herself.

She wore dirty jeans and ragged tennis shoes. The blue DUST-BUSTERS shirt was extra large, to hide the figure and make her appear plump, like the other technicians. The patch above the pocket read DORIS. Doris, the cleaning technician.

When the crew was half finished with the second floor, a guard told Doris and two others, Susie and Charlotte, to follow him. He inserted a key in the elevator panel, and it stopped in the basement. He unlocked a heavy metal door, and they walked into a large room divided into a dozen cubicles. Each small desk was cluttered, and dominated by a large computer. There were terminals everywhere. Black file cabinets lined the walls. No windows.

'The supplies are in there,' the guard said, pointing to a closet. They pulled out a vacuum cleaner and spray bottles and went to work.

'Don't touch the desks,' he said.

# CHAPTER THIRTY

Mitch tied the laces of his Nike Air Cushion jogging shoes and sat on the sofa waiting by the phone. Hearsay, depressed after two weeks without the woman around, sat next to him, and tried to doze. At exactly ten-thirty, it rang. It was Abby.

There were no mushy 'sweethearts' and 'babes' and 'honeys.' The dialogue was cool and forced.

'How's your mother?' he asked.

'Doing much better. She's up and around, but very sore. Her spirits are good.'

'That's good to hear. And your dad?'

'The same. Always busy. How's my dog?'

'Lonesome and depressed. I think he's cracking up.'

'I miss him. How's work?'

'We survived April 15 without disaster. Everyone's in a better mood. Half the partners left for vacation on the sixteenth, so the place is a lot quieter.'

'I guess you've cut back to sixteen hours a day?'

He hesitated, and let it sink in. No sense starting a fight. 'When are you coming home?'

'I don't know. Mom will need me for a couple more weeks. I'm afraid Dad's not much help. They've got a maid and all, but Mom needs me now.' She paused, as if something heavy was coming. 'I called St Andrew's today and told them I wouldn't be back this semester.'

He took it in stride. 'There are two months left in this semester. You're not coming back for two months?'

'At least two months, Mitch. I just need some time, that's all.'

'Time for what?'

'Let's not start it again, okay? I'm not in the mood to argue.'

'Fine. Fine. Fine. What are you in the mood for?'

She ignored this, and there was a long pause. 'How many miles are you jogging?'

A couple. I've been walking to the track, then running about eight laps.'

'Be careful at the track. It's awfully dark.'

'Thanks.'

Another long pause. 'I need to go,' she said. 'Mom's ready for bed.'

'Will you call tomorrow night?'

'Yes. Same time.'

She hung up without a 'goodbye' or 'I love you' or anything. Just hung up.

Mitch pulled on his white athletic socks and tucked in his white long-sleeved T-shirt. He locked the kitchen door and trotted down the dark street. West Junior High School was six blocks to the east of East Meadowbrook. Behind the red brick classrooms and gymnasium was the baseball field, and farther away at the end of a dark driveway was the football field. A cinder track circled the field, and was a favorite of local joggers.

But not at 11 P.M., especially with no moon. The track was deserted, and that was fine with Mitch. The spring air was light and cool, and he finished the first mile in eight minutes. He began walking a lap. As he passed the aluminum bleachers on the home side, he saw someone from the corner of his eye. He kept walking.

'Psssssst.'

Mitch stopped. 'Yeah. Who is it?'

A hoarse, scratchy voice replied, 'Joey Morolto.'

Mitch started for the bleachers. 'Very funny, Tarrance. Am I clean?'

'Sure you're clean. Laney's sitting up there in a school bus with a flashlight. He flashed green when you passed, and if you see something red flash, get back to the track and make like Carl Lewis.'

They walked to the top of the bleachers and into the unlocked press box. They sat on stools in the dark and watched the school. The buses were parked in perfect order along the driveway.

'Is this private enough for you?' Mitch asked.

'It'll do. Who's the girl?'

'I know you prefer to meet in daylight, preferably where a crowd has gathered, say like a fast-food joint or a Korean shoe store. But I like these places better.'

'Great. Who's the girl?'

'Pretty clever, huh?'

'Good idea. Who is she?'

'An employee of mine.'

'Where'd you find her?'

'What difference does it make? Why are you always asking questions that are irrelevant?'

'Irrelevant? I get a call today from some woman I've never met, tells me she needs to talk to me about a little matter at the Bendini Building, says we gotta change phones, instructs me to go to a certain pay phone outside a certain grocery store and be there at a certain time, and she'll call exactly at one-thirty. And I go there, and she calls at exactly one-thirty. Keep in mind, I've got three men within a hundred feet of the phone watching everybody that moves. And she tells me to be here at exactly ten forty-five tonight, to have the place sealed off, and that you'll come trotting by.'

'Worked, didn't it?'

'Yeah, so far. But who is she? I mean, now you got someone else involved, and that really worries me, McDeere. Who is she and how much does she know?'

'Trust me, Tarrance. She's my employee and she knows everything. In fact, if you knew what she knows you'd be serving indictments right now instead of sitting here bitching about her.'

Tarrance breathed deeply and though about it. 'Okay, so tell me what she knows.'

'She knows that in the last three years the Morolto gang and its accomplices have taken over eight hundred million bucks in cash out of this country and deposited it in various banks in the Caribbean. She knows which banks, which accounts, the dates, a bunch of stuff. She knows that the Moroltos control at least three hundred and fifty companies chartered in the Caymans, and that these companies regularly send clean money back into the country. She knows the dates and amounts of the wire transfers. She knows of at least forty U.S. corporations owned by Cayman corporations owned by the Moroltos. She knows a helluva lot, Tarrance. She's a very knowledgeable woman, don't you think?'

Tarrance could not speak. He stared fiercely into the darkness up the driveway.

Mitch found it enjoyable. 'She knows how they take their dirty cash, trade it up to one-hundred-dollar bills and sneak it out of the country.'

'How?'

'The firm Lear, of course. But they also mule it. They've got a small army of mules, usually their minimum wage thugs and their girlfriends, but also students and other free-lancers, and they'll give them ninety-eight hundred in cash and buy them a ticket to the Caymans or the Bahamas. No declarations are required for amounts under ten thousand, you understand. And the mules will fly down like regular tourists with pockets full of cash and take the money to their banks. Doesn't sound like much money, but you get three hundred people making twenty trips a year, and that's some serious cash walking out of the country. It's also called smurfing, you know.'

Tarrance nodded slightly, as if he knew.

'A lot of folks wanna be smurfers when they can get free vacations and spending money. Then they've got their super mules. These are the trusted Morolto people who take a million bucks in cash, wrap it up real neat in newspaper so the airport machines won't see it, put it in big briefcases and walk it onto the planes like everybody else. They wear coats and ties and look like Wall Streeters. Or they wear sandals and straw hats and mule it in carry-on bags. You guys catch them occasionally, about one percent of the time, I believe, and when that happens the super mules go to jail. But they never talk, do they, Tarrance? And every now and then a smurfer will start thinking about all this money in his briefcase and how easy it would be just to keep flying and enjoy all the money himself. And he'll disappear. But the Mob never forgets, and it may take a year or two, but they'll find him somewhere. The money'll be gone, of course, but then so will he. The Mob never forgets, does it, Tarrance? Just like they won't forget about me.'

Tarrance listened until it was obvious he needed to say something. 'You got your million bucks.'

'Appreciate it. I'm almost ready for the next installment.'

'Almost?'

'Yeah, me and the girl have a couple more jobs to pull. We're trying to get a few more records out of Front Street.'

'How many documents do you have?'

'Over ten thousand.'

The lower jaw collapsed and the mouth fell open. He stared at Mitch. 'Damn! Where'd they come from?'

'Another one of your questions.'

'Ten thousand documents,' said Tarrance.

'At least ten thousand. Bank records, wire transfer records, corporate charters, corporate loan documents, internal memos, correspondence between all sorts of people. A lot of good stuff, Tarrance.'

'Your wife mentioned a company called Dunn Lane, Ltd. We've reviewed the files you've already given us. Pretty good material. What else do you know about it?'

'A lot. Chartered in 1986 with ten million, which was transferred into the corporation from a numbered account in Banco de México, the same ten million that arrived in Grand Cayman in cash on a certain Lear jet registered to a quiet little law firm in Memphis, except that it was originally fourteen million but after payoffs to Cayman customs and Cayman bankers it was reduced to ten million. When the company was chartered, the registered agent was a guy named Diego Sánchez, who happens to be a VP with Banco de México. The president was a delightful soul named Nathan Locke, the secretary was our old pal Royce McKnight and the treasurer of this cozy little corporation was a guy named Al Rubinstein. I'm sure you know him. I don't.'

'He's a Morolto operative.'

'Surprise, surprise. Want more?'

'Keep talking.'

After the seed money of ten million was invested into this venture, another ninety million in cash was deposited over the next three years. Very profitable enterprise. The company began buying all sorts of things in the U.S. – cotton farms in Texas, apartment complexes in Dayton, jewelry stores in Beverly Hills, hotels in St. Petersburg and Tampa. Most of the transactions were by wire transfer from four or five different banks in the Caymans. It's a basic money laundering operation.'

'And you've got all this documented?'

'Stupid question, Wayne. If I didn't have the documents, how would I know about it? I only work on clean files, remember?'

'How much longer will it take you?'

'Couple of weeks. Me and my employee are still snooping around Front Street. And it doesn't look good. It'll be very difficult to get files out of there.'

'Where'd the ten thousand documents come from?'

Mitch ignored the question. He jumped to his feet and started for the door. 'Abby and I want to live in Albuquerque. It's a big town, sort of out of the way. Start working on it.'

'Don't jump the gun. There's a lot of work to do.'

'I said two weeks, Tarrance. I'll be ready to deliver in two weeks, and that means I'll have to disappear.'

'Not so fast. I need to see a few of these documents.'

'You have a short memory, Tarrance. My lovely wife promised a big stack of Dunn Lane documents just as soon as Ray goes over the wall.'

Tarrance looked across the dark field. 'I'll see what I can do.'

Mitch walked to him and pointed a finger in his face. 'Listen to me, Tarrance, and listen closely. I don't think we're getting through. Today is April 17. Two weeks from today is May 1, and on May 1 I will deliver to you, as promised over ten thousand very incriminating and highly admissable documents that will seriously cripple one of the largest organized crime families in the world. And, eventually, it will cost me my life. But I promised to do it. And you've promised to get my brother out of prison. You have a week, until April 24. If not, I'll disappear. And so will your case, and career.'

'What's he gonna do when he gets out?'

'You and your stupid questions. He'll run like hell, that's what he'll do. He's got a brother with a million dollars who's an expert in money laundering and electronic banking. He'll be out of the country within twelve hours, and he'll go find the million bucks.'

'The Bahamas.'

'Bahamas. You're an idiot, Tarrance. That money spent less than ten minutes in the Bahamas. You can't trust those corrupt fools down there.

'Mr. Voyles doesn't like deadlines. He gets real upset.'

'Tell Mr. Voyles to kiss my ass. Tell him to get the next half million, because I'm almost ready. Tell him to get my brother out or the deal's off. Tell him whatever you want, Tarrance, but Ray goes over the wall in a week or I'm gone.'

Mitch slammed the door and started down the bleachers. Tarrance followed. 'When do we talk again?' he yelled.

Mitch jumped the fence and was on the track. 'My employee will call you. Just do as she says.'

# CHAPTER THIRTY-ONE

Nathan Locke's annual three-day post-April 15 vacation in Vail had been canceled. By DeVasher, on order from Lazarov. Locke and Oliver Lambert sat in the office on the fifth floor and listened. DeVasher was reporting the bits and pieces and trying unsuccessfully to put the puzzle together.

'His wife leaves. Says she's gotta go home to her mother, who's got lung cancer. And that she's tired of a bunch of his crap. We've detected a little trouble here and there over the months. She bitched a little about his hours and all, but nothing this serious. So she goes home to Mommy. Says she don't know when she's coming back. Mommy's sick, right? Removed a lung, right? But we can't find a hospital that's heard of Maxine Sutherland. We've checked every hospital in Kentucky, Indiana and Tennessee. Seems odd, doesn't it, fellas?'

'Come on, DeVasher,' Lambert said. 'My wife had surgery four years ago, and we flew to the Mayo Clinic. I know of no law requiring one to have surgery within a hundred miles of home. That's absurd. And these are society people. Maybe she checked in under another name to keep quiet. Happens all the time.'

Locke nodded and agreed. 'How much has he talked to her?'

'She calls about once a day. They've had some good talks, about this and that. The dog. Her mom. The office. She told him last night she ain't coming back for at least two months.'

'Has she ever indicated which hospital?' asked Locke.

'Never. She's been real careful. Doesn't talk much about the surgery. Mommy is supposedly home now. If she ever left.'

'What're you getting at, DeVasher?' asked Lambert.

'Shut up and I'll finish. Just suppose it's all a ruse to get her outta town. To get her away from us. From what's coming down. Follow?'

'You're assuming he's working with them?' asked Locke.

'I get paid for making those assumptions, Nat. I'm assuming he knows the phones are bugged, and that's why they're so careful on the phone. I'm assuming he got her outta town to protect her.'

'Pretty shaky,' said Lambert. 'Pretty shaky.'

DeVasher paced behind his desk. He glared at Ollie and let it pass. 'About ten days ago, somebody makes a bunch of unusual copies on the fourth floor. Strange because it was three in the morning. According to our records, when the copies were made only two lawyers were

644

here. McDeere and Scott Kimble. Neither of whom had any business on the fourth floor. Twenty-four access numbers were used. Three belong to Lamar Quin's files. Three belong to Sonny Capps. The other eighteen belong to McDeere's files. None belong to Kimble. Victor Milligan left his office around two-thirty, and McDeere was working in Avery's office. He had taken him to the airport. Avery says he locked his office, but he could have forgotten. Either he forgot or McDeere's got a key. I pressed Avery on this, and he feels almost certain he locked it. But it was midnight and he was dead tired and in a hurry. Could've forgotten, right? But he did not authorize McDeere to go back to his office and work. No big deal, really, because they had spent the entire day in there working on the Capps return. The copier was number eleven, which happens to be the closest one to Avery's office. I think it's safe to assume McDeere made the copies.'

'How many?'

'Two thousand and twelve.'

'Which files?'

'The eighteen were all tax clients. Now, I'm sure he'd explain it all by saying he had finished the returns and was merely copying everything. Sounds pretty legitimate, right? Except the secretaries always make the copies, and what the hell was he doing on the fourth floor at three A.M. running two thousand copies? And this was the morning of April 7. How many of your boys finish their April 15 work and run all the copies a week early.

He stopped pacing and watched them. They were thinking. He had them. 'And here's the kicker. Five days later his secretary entered the same eighteen access numbers on her copier on the second floor. She ran about three hundred copies, which, I ain't no lawyer, but I figure to be more in line. Don't you think?'

They both nodded, but said nothing. They were lawyers trained to argue five sides of every issue. But they said nothing. DeVasher smiled wickedly and returned to his pacing. 'Now, we caught him making two thousand copies that cannot be explained. So the big question is: what was he copying? If he was using wrong access numbers to run the machine, what the hell was he copying? I don't know. All of the offices were locked, except, of course, Avery's. So I asked Avery. He's got a row of metal cabinets where he keeps the real files. He keeps 'em locked, but he and McDeere and the secretaries have been rummaging through those files all day. Could've forgot to lock 'em when he ran to meet the plane. Big deal. Why would McDeere copy legitimate files? He wouldn't. Like everybody else on the fourth floor, Avery's got those four wooden cabinets with the secret stuff. No one touches them, right? Firm rules. Not even other partners. Locked up tighter than my files. So McDeere can't get in without a key. Avery showed me his keys. Told me he hadn't touched those cabinets in two days, before the seventh. Avery has gone through those files, and everything seems to be in order. He can't tell if they've been tampered with. But can you look at one of your files and tell if it's been copied? No, you can't. Neither can I. So I pulled the files this morning, and I'm sending them to Chicago. They're gonna check 'em for fingerprints. Take about a week.'

'He couldn't copy those files,' Lambert said.

'What else would he copy, Ollie? I mean, everything's locked on the fourth floor and the third floor. Everything, except Avery's office. And assuming he and Tarrance are whispering in each other's ears, what would he want from Avery's office? Nothing but the secret files.'

'Now you're assuming he's got keys,' Locke said.

'Yes. I'm assuming he's made a set of Avery's keys.'

Ollie snorted and gave an exasperated laugh. 'This is incredible. I don't believe it.'

Black Eyes glared at DeVasher with a nasty smile. 'How would he get a copy of the keys?'

'Good question, and one that I can't answer. Avery showed me his keys. Two rings, eleven keys. He keeps 'em with him at all times. Firm rule, right? Like a good little lawyer's supposed to do. When he's awake, the keys are in his pocket. When he's asleep away from home, the keys are under the mattress.'

'Where's he traveled in the last month?' Black Eyes asked.

'Forget the trip to see Capps in Houston last week. Too recent. Before that, he went to Grand Cayman for two days on April 1.'

'I remember,' said Ollie, listening intently.

'Good for you, Ollie. I asked him what he did both nights, and he said nothing but work. Sat at a bar one night, but that's it. Swears he slept by himself both nights.' DeVasher pushed a button on a portable tape recorder. 'But he's lying. This call was made at nine fifteen, April 2, from the phone in the master bedroom of Unit A.' The tape began:

'He's in the shower.' First female voice.

'Are you okay?' Second female voice.

'Yeah. Fine. He couldn't do it if he had to.'

'What took so long?'

'He wouldn't wake up.'

'Is he suspicious?'

'No. He remembers nothing. I think he's in pain.'

'How long will you be there?'

'I'll kiss him goodbye when he gets out of the shower. Ten, maybe fifteen minutes.'

'Okay. Hurry.'

DeVasher punched another button and continued pacing. 'I have no idea who they are, and I haven't confronted Avery. Yet he worries me. His wife has filed for divorce, and he's lost control. Chases women all the time. This is a pretty serious breach of security, and I suspect Lazarov will go through the roof.'

'She talked like it was a bad hangover,' Locke said.

'Evidently.'

'You think she copied the keys?' Ollie asked.

DeVasher shrugged and sat in his worn leather chair. The cockiness vanished. 'It's possible, but I doubt it. I've thought about it for hours. Assuming it was some woman he picked up in a bar, and they got drunk, then it was probably late when they went to bed. How would she make copies of the keys in the middle of the night on that tiny island? I just don't think so.'

'But she had an accomplice,' Locke insisted.

'Yeah, and I can't figure that out. Maybe they were trying to steal his wallet and something went wrong. He carries a couple of thousand in cash, and if he got drunk, who knows what he told them. Maybe she planned to lift the money at the last second and haul ass. She didn't do it. I don't know.'

'No more assumptions?' Ollie asked.

'Not now. I love to make them, but it goes too far to assume these women took the keys, somehow managed to copy them in the middle of the night on the island, without his knowledge, and then the first one crawled back in the bed with him. And that somehow all of this is related to McDeere and his use of the copier on the fourth floor. It's just too much.'

'I agree,' said Ollie.

'What about the storage room?' asked Black Eyes.

'I've thought about that, Nat. In fact, I've lost sleep thinking about it. If she was interested in the records in the storage room, there must be some connection with McDeere, or someone else poking around. And I can't make that connection. Let's say she found the room and the records, what could she do with them in the middle of the night with Avery asleep upstairs?'

'She could read them.'

'Yeah, there's only a million. Keep in mind, now, she must have been drinking along with Avery, or he would've been suspicious. So she's spent the night drinking and screwing. She waits until he goes to sleep, then suddenly she has this urge to go downstairs and read bank records. It don't work, boys.'

'She could work for the FBI,' Ollie said proudly.

'No, she couldn't.'

'Why?'

'It's simple, Ollie. The FBI wouldn't do it because the search would be illegal and the records would be inadmissible. And there's a much better reason.'

'What?'

'If she was a Fibbie, she wouldn't have used the phone. No professional would've made that call. I think she was a pickpocket.'

The pickpocket theory was explained to Lazarov, who poked a hundred holes but could devise nothing better. He ordered changes in all the locks on the third and fourth floors, and the basement, and both condos on Grand Cayman. He ordered a search for all the locksmiths on the island – there couldn't be many, he said – to determine if any had reproduced keys the night of April 1 or the early morning of April 2. Bribe them, he told DeVasher. They'll talk for a little money. He ordered a fingerprint examination of the files from Avery's office. DeVasher proudly explained he had already started this. McDeere's prints were on file with the state bar association.

He also ordered a sixty-day suspension of Avery Tolleson. DeVasher suggested this might alert McDeere to something unusual. Fine, said DeVasher, tell Tolleson to check into the hospital with chest pains. Two months off – doctor's orders. Tell Tolleson to clean up his act. Lock up his office. Assign McDeere to Victor Milligan.

'You said you had a good plan to eliminate McDeere,' DeVasher said.

Lazarov grinned and picked his nose. 'Yeah. I think we'll use the plane. We'll send him down to the islands on a little business trip, and there will be this mysterious explosion.'

'Waste two pilots?' asked DeVasher.

'Yeah. It needs to look good.'

'Don't do it anywhere around the Caymans. That'll be too coincidental.'

'Okay, but it needs to happen over water. Less debris. We'll use a big device, so they won't find much.'

'That plane's expensive.'

'Yeah. I'll run it by Joey first.'

'You're the boss. Let me know if we can help down there.'

'Sure. Start thinking about it.'

'What about your man in Washington?' DeVasher asked.

'I'm waiting. I called New York this morning, and they're checking into it. We should know in a week.'

'That would make it easy.'

'Yeah. If the answer is yes, we need to eliminate him within twenty-four hours.'

'I'll start planning.'

The office was quiet for a Saturday morning. A handful of partners and a dozen associates loitered about in khakis and polos. There were no secretaries. Mitch checked his mail and dictated correspondence. After two hours he left. It was time to visit Ray.

For five hours, he drove east on Interstate 40. Drove like an idiot. He drove forty-five, then eighty-five. He darted into every rest stop and weigh station. He made sudden exits from the left lane. He stopped at an underpass and waited and watched. He never saw them. Not once did he notice a suspicious car or truck or van. He even watched a few eighteen-wheelers. Nothing. They simply were not back there. He would have caught them.

His care package of books and cigarettes was cleared through the guard station, and he was pointed to stall number nine. Minutes later, Ray sat through the thick screen.

'Where have you been?' he said with a hint of irritation. 'You're the only person in the entire world who visits me, and this is only the second time in four months.'

'I know. It's tax season, and I've been swamped. I'll do better. I've written, though.'

'Yeah, once a week I get two paragraphs. 'Hi, Ray. How's the bunk? How's the food? How are the walls? How's the Greek or Italian? I'm fine. Abby's great. Dog's sick. Gotta run. I'll come visit soon. Love, Mitch.' You write some rich letters, little brother. I really treasure them.'

'Yours aren't much better.'

'What have I got to say? The guards are selling dope. A friend got stabbed thirty-one times. I saw a kid get raped. Come on, Mitch, who wants to hear it?'

'I'll do better.'

'How's Mom?'

'I don't know. I haven't been back since Christmas.'

'I asked you to check on her, Mitch. I'm worried about her. If that goon is beating her, I want it stopped. If I could get out of here, I'd stop it myself.'

'You will.' It was a statement, not a question. Mitch placed a finger over his lips and nodded slowly. Ray leaned forward on his elbows and stared intently.

Mitch spoke softly. '*Español. Hable despacio.*' Spanish. Speak slowly. Ray smiled slightly. '*¿Cuándo?*' When?

'*La semana próxima.*' Next week.

'*¿Qué día?*' What day?

Mitch thought for a second. '*Martes o miércoles.*' Tuesday or Wednesday.

'*¿Que tiempo?*' What time?

Mitch smiled and shrugged, and looked around.

'How's Abby?' Ray asked.

'She's been in Kentucky for a couple of weeks. Her mother's sick.' He stared at Ray and softly mouthed the words 'Trust me.'

'What's wrong with her?'

'They removed a lung. Cancer. She's smoked heavy all her life. You should quit.'

'I will if I ever get out of here.'

Mitch smiled and nodded slowly. 'You've got at least seven more years.'

'Yeah, and escape is impossible. They try it occasionally, but they're either shot or captured.'

'James Earl Ray went over the wall, didn't he?' Mitch nodded slowly as he asked the question. Ray smiled and watched his brother's eyes.

'But they caught him. They bring in a bunch of mountain boys with bloodhounds, and it gets pretty nasty. I don't think anyone's ever survived the mountains after they got over the wall.'

'Let's talk about something else,' Mitch said.

'Good idea.'

Two guards stood by a window behind the row of visitors' booths. They were enjoying a stack of dirty pictures someone took with a Polaroid and tried to sneak through the guard station. They giggled among themselves and ignored the visitors. On the prisoners' side, a single guard with a stick walked benignly back and forth, half asleep.

'When can I expect little nieces and nephews?' Ray asked.

'Maybe in a few years. Abby wants one of each, and she would start now if I would. I'm not ready.'

The guard walked behind Ray, but did not look. They stared at each other, trying to read each other's eyes.

'*¿Adónde voy?*' Ray asked quickly. Where am I going?

'Perdido Beach Hilton. We went to the Cayman Islands last month, Abby and I. Had a beautiful vacation.'

650

'Never heard of the place. Where is it?'

'In the Caribbean, below Cuba.'

'*¿Que es mi nombre?*' What is my name?

Lee Stevens. Did some snorkeling. The water is warm and gorgeous. The firm owns two condos right on Seven Mile Beach. All I paid for was the airfare. It was great.'

'Get me a book. I'd like to read about it. '*¿Pasaporte?*'

Mitch nodded with a smile. The guard walked behind Ray and stopped. They talked of old times in Kentucky.

At dusk he parked the BMW on the dark side of a suburban mall in Nashville. He left the keys in the ignition and locked the door. He had a spare in his pocket. A busy crowd of Easter shoppers moved en masse through the Sears doors. He joined them. Inside he ducked into the men's clothing department and studied socks and underwear while watching the door. Nobody suspicious. He left Sears and walked quickly through the crowd down the mall. A black cotton sweater in the window of a men's store caught his attention. He found one inside, tried it on and decided to wear it out of there, he liked it so much. As the clerk laid his change on the counter, he scanned the yellow pages for the number of a cab. Back into the mall, he rode the escalator to the first floor, where he found a pay phone. The cab would be there in ten minutes.

It was dark now, the cool early dark of spring in the South. He watched the mall entrance from inside a singles bar. He was certain he had not been followed through the mall. He walked casually to the cab. 'Brentwood,' he said to the driver, and disappeared into the back seat.

Brentwood was twenty minutes away. 'Savannah Creek Apartments,' he said. The cab searched through the sprawling complex and found number 480E. He threw a twenty over the seat and slammed the door. Behind an outside stairwell he found the door to 480E. It was locked.

'Who is it?' a nervous female voice asked from within. He heard the voice and felt weak.

'Barry Abanks,' he said.

Abby pulled the door open and attacked. They kissed violently as he lifted her, walked inside and slammed the door with his foot. His hands were wild. In less than two seconds, he pulled her sweater over her head, unsnapped her bra and slid the rather loose fitting skirt to her knees. They continued kissing. With one eye, he glanced apprehensively at the cheap, flimsy rented fold-a-bed that was waiting.

Either that or the floor. He laid her gently on it and took off his clothes.

The bed was too short, and it squeaked. The mattress was two inches of foam rubber wrapped in a sheet. The metal braces underneath jutted upward and were dangerous.

But the McDeeres did not notice.

When it was good and dark, and the crowd of shoppers at the mall thinned for a moment, a shiny black Chevrolet Silverado pickup pulled behind the BMW and stopped. A small man with a neat haircut and sideburns jumped out, looked around and stuck a pointed screwdriver into the door lock of the BMW. Months later when he was sentenced, he would tell the judge that he had stolen over three hundred cars and pickups in eight states, and that he could break into a car and start the engine faster than the judge could with the keys. Said his average time was twenty-eight seconds. The judge was not impressed.

Occasionally, on a very lucky day, an idiot would leave the keys in the car, and the average time was reduced dramatically. A scout had found this car with the keys. He smiled and turned them. The Silverado raced away, followed by the BMW.

The Nordic jumped from the van and watched. It was too fast. He was too late. The pickup just pulled up, blocked his vision for an instant, then wham! the BMW was gone. Stolen! Before his very eyes. He kicked the van. Now, how would he explain this!

He crawled back into the van, and waited for McDeere.

After an hour on the couch, the pain of loneliness had been forgotten. They walked through the small apartment holding hands and kissing. In the bedroom, Mitch had his first viewing of what had become known among the three as the Bendini Papers. He had seen Tammy's notes and summaries, but not the actual documents. The room was like a chessboard with rows of neat stacks of papers. On two of the walls, Tammy had tacked sheets of white poster board, then covered them with the notes and lists and flowcharts.

One day soon he would spend hours in the room, studying the papers and preparing his case. But not tonight. In a few minutes, he would leave her and return to the mall.

She led him back to the couch.

# CHAPTER THIRTY-TWO

The hall on the tenth floor, Madison Wing, of the Baptist Hospital was empty except for an orderly and a male nurse writing on his clipboard. Visiting hours had ended at nine, and it was ten-thirty. He eased down the hall, spoke to the orderly, was ignored by the nurse and knocked on the door.

'Come in,' a strong voice said.

He pushed the heavy door open and stood by the bed.

'Hello, Mitch,' Avery said. 'Can you believe this?'

'What happened?'

'I woke up at six this morning with stomach cramps, I thought. I took a shower and felt a sharp pain right here, on my shoulder. My breathing got heavy, and I started sweating. I thought no, not me. Hell, I'm forty-four, in great shape, work out all the time, eat pretty good, drink a little too much, maybe, but not me. I called my doctor, and he said to meet him here at the hospital. He thinks it was a slight heart attack. Nothing serious, he hopes, but they're running tests for the next few days.'

'A heart attack.'

'That's what he said.'

'I'm not surprised, Avery. It's a wonder any lawyer in that firm lives past fifty.'

'Capps did it to me, Mitch. Sonny Capps. This is his heart attack. He called Friday and said he'd found a new tax firm in Washington. Wants all his records. That's my biggest client. I billed him almost four hundred thousand last year, about what he paid in taxes. He's not mad about the attorney's fees, but he's furious about the taxes. It doesn't make sense, Mitch.'

'He's not worth dying for.' Mitch looked for an IV, but did not see one. There were no tubes or wires. He sat in the only chair and laid his feet on the bed.

'Jean filed for divorce, you know.'

'I heard. That's no surprise, is it?'

'Surprised she didn't do it last year. I've offered her a small fortune as a settlement. I hope she takes it. I don't need a nasty divorce.'

Who does? thought Mitch. 'What did Lambert say?'

'It was kind of fun, really. In nineteen years I've never seen him

653

lose his cool, but he lost it. He told me I was drinking too much, chasing women and who knows what else. Said I had embarrassed the firm. Suggested I see a psychiatrist.'

Avery spoke slowly, deliberately, and at times with a raspy, weak voice. It seemed phony. A sentence later he would forget about it and return to his normal voice. He lay perfectly still like a corpse, with the sheets tucked neatly around him. His color was good.

'I think you need a psychiatrist. Maybe two.'

'Thanks. I need a month in the sun. Doc said he would discharge me in three or four days, and that I couldn't work for two months. Sixty days, Mitch. Said I cannot, under any circumstances, go near the office for sixty days.'

'What a blessing. I think I'll have a slight heart attack.'

'At your pace, it's guaranteed.'

'What are you, a doctor now?'

'No. Just scared. You get a scare like this, and you start thinking about things. Today is the first time in my life I've ever thought about dying. And if you don't think about death, you don't appreciate life.'

'This is getting pretty heavy.'

'Yeah, I know. How's Abby?'

'Okay. I guess. I haven't seen her in a while.'

'You'd better go see her and bring her home. And get her happy. Sixty hours a week is plenty, Mitch. You'll ruin your marriage and kill yourself if you work more. She wants babies, then get them. I wish I had done things differently.'

'Damn, Avery. When's the funeral? You're forty-four, and you had a slight heart attack. You're not exactly a vegetable.'

The male nurse glided in and glared at Mitch. 'Visiting hours are over, sir. You need to leave.'

Mitch jumped to his feet. 'Yeah, sure.' He slapped Avery's feet and walked out. 'See you in a couple of days.'

'Thanks for coming. Tell Abby I said hello.'

The elevator was empty. Mitch pushed the button to the sixteenth floor and seconds later got off. He ran two flights of stairs to the eighteenth, caught his breath and opened the door. Down the hall, away from the elevators, Rick Acklin watched and whispered into a dead telephone receiver. He nodded at Mitch, who walked toward him. Acklin pointed, and Mitch stepped into a small area used as a waiting room by worried relatives. It was dark and empty, with two rows of folding chairs and a television that did not work. A Coke machine provided the only light. Tarrance sat next to it and flipped through an old magazine. He wore a sweat suit, headband, navy socks and white canvas sneakers. Tarrance the jogger.

Mitch sat next to him, facing the hall.

'You're clean. They followed you from the office to the parking lot, then left. Acklin's in the hall. Laney's around somewhere. Relax.'

'I like the headband.'

'Thanks.'

'I see you got the message.'

'Obviously. Real clever, McDeere. I'm sitting at my desk this afternoon, minding my own business, trying to work on something other than the Bendini case. I've got others, you know. And my secretary comes in and says there's a woman on the phone who wants to talk about a man named Marty Kozinski. I jump from my chair, grab the phone, and of course it's your girl. She says it's urgent, as always. So I say okay, let's talk. No, she don't play it. She makes me drop everything I'm doing, run over to the Peabody, go to the lounge – what's the name of it? Mallards – and have a seat. So I'm sitting there, thinking about how stupid this is because our phones are clean. Dammit, Mitch, I know our phones are clean. We can talk on our phones! I'm drinking coffee and the bartender walks over and asks if my name is Kozinski. Kozinski who? I ask. Just for fun. Since we're having a ball, right? Marty Kozinski, he says with a puzzled look on his face. I say, yeah, that's me. I felt stupid, Mitch. And he says I have a call. I walk over to the bar, and it's your girl. Tolleson's had a heart attack or something. And you'll be here around eleven. Real clever.'

'Worked, didn't it?'

'Yeah, and it would work just as easily if she would talk to me on my phone in my office.'

'I like it better my way. It's safer. Besides, it gets you out of the office.'

'Damned right, it does. Me and three others.'

'Look, Tarrance, we'll do it my way, okay? It's my neck on the line, not yours.'

'Yeah, yeah. What the hell are you driving?'

'A rented Celebrity. Nice, huh?'

'What happened to the little black lawyer's car?'

'It had an insect problem. Full of bugs. I parked it at a mall Saturday night in Nashville and left the keys in it. Someone borrowed it. I love to sing, but I have a terrible voice. Ever since I could drive I've done my singing in the car, alone. But with the bugs and all, I was too embarrassed to sing. I just got tired of it.'

Tarrance could not resist a smile. 'That's pretty good, McDeere, Pretty good.'

'You should've seen Oliver Lambert this morning when I walked in and laid the police report on his desk. He stuttered and stammered and told me how sorry he was. I acted like I was real sad. Insurance will cover it, so old Oliver says they'll get me another one. Then he says they'll go get me a rental car for the meantime. I told him I already had one. Got it in Nashville Saturday night. He didn't like this, because he knew it was insect free. He calls the BMW dealer himself, while I'm standing there to check on a new one for me. He asked me what color I wanted. I said I was tired of black and wanted a burgundy one with tan interior. I drove to the BMW place yesterday and looked around. I didn't see a burgundy of any model. He told the guy on the phone what I wanted, and then he tells him they don't have it. How about black, or navy, or gray, or red or white? No, no, no, I want a burgundy one. They'll have to order it, he reports. Fine, I said. He hung up the phone and asked me if I was sure I couldn't use another color. Burgundy, I said. He wanted to argue, but realized it would seem foolish. So, for the first time in ten months, I can sing in my car.'

'But a Celebrity. For a hotshot tax lawyer. That's got to hurt.'

'I can deal with it.'

Tarrance was still smiling, obviously impressed. 'I wonder what the boys in the chop shop will do when they strip it down and find all those bugs.'

'Probably sell it to a pawnshop as stereo equipment. How much was it worth?'

'Our boys said it was the best. Ten, fifteen thousand. I don't know. That's funny.'

Two nurses walked by talking loudly. They turned a corner, and the hall was quiet. Acklin pretended to place another phone call.

'How's Tolleson?' Tarrance asked.

'Superb. I hope my heart attack is as easy as his. He'll be here for a few days, then off for two months. Nothing serious.'

'Can you get in his office?'

'Why should I? I've already copied everything in it.'

Tarrance leaned closer and waited for more.

'No, I cannot get in his office. They've changed the locks on the third and fourth floors. And the basement.'

'How do you know this?'

'The girl, Tarrance. In the last week, she's been in every office in the building, including the basement. She's checked every door, pulled on every drawer, looked in every closet. She's read mail, looked at files and rummaged through the garbage. There's not much garbage, really. The building has ten paper shredders in it. Four in the basement. Did you know that?'

Tarrance listened intently and did not move a muscle. 'How did she – '

'Don't ask, Tarrance, because I won't tell you.'

'She works there! She's a secretary or something. She's helping you from the inside.'

Mitch shook his head in frustration. 'Brilliant, Tarrance. She called you twice today. Once at about two-fifteen and then about an hour later. Now, how would a secretary make two calls to the FBI an hour apart?'

'Maybe she didn't work today. Maybe she called from home.'

'You're wrong, Tarrance, and quit guessing. Don't waste time worrying about her. She works for me, and together we'll deliver the goods to you.'

'What's in the basement?'

'One big room with twelve cubicles, twelve busy desks and a thousand file cabinets. Electronically wired file cabinets. I think it's the operations center for their money-laundering activities. On the walls of the cubicles, she noticed names and phone numbers of dozens of banks in the Caribbean. There's not much information lying around down there. They're very careful. There's a smaller room off to the side, heavily locked, and full of computers larger than refrigerators.'

'Sounds like the place.'

'It is, but forget it. There's no way to get the stuff out without alerting them. Impossible. I know of only one way to bring the goods out.'

'Okay.'

'A search warrant.'

'Forget it. No probable cause.'

'Listen to me, Tarrance. This is how it's gonna be, okay. I can't give you all the documents you want. But I can give you all you need. I have in my possession over ten thousand documents, and although I have not reviewed all of them, I've seen enough to know that if you had them, you could show them to a judge and get a search warrant for Front Street. You can take the records I have now and obtain indictments for maybe half the firm. But the same documents will get your search warrant and, consequently, a truckload of indictments. There's no other way to do it.'

Tarrance walked to the hall and looked around. Empty. He stretched his legs and walked to the Coke machine. He leaned on it and looked through the small window to the east. 'Why only half the firm?'

'Initially, only half. Plus a number of retired partners. Scattered through my documents are various names of partners who've set up the bogus Cayman companies with Morolto money. Those indictments will be easy. Once you have all the records, your conspiracy theory will fall in place and you can indict everyone.'

'Where did you get the documents?'

'I got lucky. Very lucky. I sort of figured the firm had more sense than to keep the Cayman bank records in this country. I had a hunch the records might be in the Caymans. Fortunately, I was right. We copied the documents in the Caymans.'

'We?'

'The girl. And a friend.'

'Where are the records now?'

'You and your questions, Tarrance. They're in my possession. That's all you need to know.'

'I want those documents from the basement.'

'Listen to me, Tarrance. Pay attention. The documents in the basement are not coming out until you go in with a search warrant. It is impossible, do you hear?'

'Who are the guys in the basement?'

'Don't know. I've been there ten months and never seen them. I don't know where they park or how they get in and out. They're invisible. I figure the partners and the boys in the basement do the dirty work.'

'What kind of equipment is down there?'

'Two copiers, four shredders, high-speed printers and all those computers. State of the art.'

Tarrance walked to the window, obviously deep in thought. 'That makes sense. Makes a lot of sense. I've always wondered how the firm, with all those secretaries and clerks and paralegals, could maintain such secrecy about Morolto.'

'It's easy. The secretaries and clerks and paralegals know nothing about it. They're kept busy with the real clients. The partners and senior associates sit in their big offices and dream up exotic ways to launder money, and the basement crew does the grunt work. It's a great set-up.'

'So there are plenty of legitimate clients?'

'Hundreds. They're talented lawyers with an amazing clientele. It's a great cover.'

'And now you're telling me, McDeere, that you've got the documents now to support the indictments and search warrants? You've got them – they're in your possession?'

'That's what I said.'

'In this country?'

'Yes, Tarrance, the documents are in this country. Very close to here, actually.'

Tarrance was fidgety now. He rocked from one foot to the other and cracked his knuckles. He was breathing quickly. 'What else can you get out of Front Street?'

'Nothing. It's too dangerous. They've changed the locks, and that sort of worries me. I mean, why would they change the locks on the third and fourth floors and not on the first and second? I made some copies on the fourth two weeks ago, and I don't think it was a good idea. I'm getting bad vibes. No more records from Front Street.'

'What about the girl.'

'She no longer has access.'

Tarrance chewed his fingernails, rocking back and forth. Still staring at the window. 'I want the records, McDeere, and I want them real soon. Like tomorrow.'

'When does Ray get his walking papers?'

'Today's Monday. I think it's set up for tomorrow night. You wouldn't believe the cussing I've taken from Voyles. He's had to pull every string in the book. You think I'm kidding? He called in both senators from Tennessee, and they personally flew to Nashville to visit the governor. Oh, I've been cussed, McDeere. All because of your brother.'

'He appreciates it.'

'What's he gonna do when he gets out?'

'I'll take care of that. You just get him out.'

'No guarantees. If he gets hurt, it ain't our fault.'

Mitch stood and looked at his watch. 'Gotta run. I'm sure someone's out there waiting for me.'

'When do we meet again?'

'She'll call. Just do as she says.'

'Oh, come on, Mitch! Not that routine again. She can talk to me on my phone. I swear! We keep our lines clean. Please, not that again.'

'What's your mother's name, Tarrance?'

'What? Doris.'

'Doris?'

'Yeah, Doris.'

'Small world. We can't use Doris. Whom did you take to your senior prom?'

'Uh, I don't think I went.'

'I'm not surprised. Who was your first date, if you had one?'

'Mary Alice Brenner. She was hot too. She wanted me.'

'I'm sure. My girl's name is Mary Alice. The next time Mary Alice calls, you do exactly as she says, okay?'

'I can't wait.'

'Do me a favor, Tarrance. I think Tolleson's faking, and I've got a weird feeling his fake heart attack is somehow related to me. Get your boys to snoop around here and check out his alleged heart attack.'

'Sure. We have little else to do.'

# CHAPTER THIRTY-THREE

Tuesday morning the office buzzed with concern for Avery Tolleson. He was doing fine. Running tests. No permanent damage. Overworked. Stressed out. Capps did it. Divorce did it. Leave of absence.

Nina brought a stack of letters to be signed. 'Mr. Lambert would like to see you, if you're not too busy. He just called.'

'Fine. I'm supposed to meet Frank Mulholland at ten. Do you know that?'

'Of course I know that. I'm the secretary. I know everything. Your office or his?'

Mitch looked at his appointment book and pretended to search. Mulholland's office. In the Cotton Exchange Building.

'His,' he said with a frown.

'You met there last time, didn't you? Didn't they teach you about turf in law school? Never, I repeat, never meet two times in a row on the adversary's turf. It's unprofessional. It's uncool. Shows weakness.'

'How can you ever forgive me?'

'Wait till I tell the other girls. They all think you're so cute and macho. When I tell them you're a wimp, they'll be shocked.'

'They need to be shocked, with a cattle prod.'

'How's Abby's mother?'

'Much better. I'm going up this weekend.'

She picked up two files. 'Lambert's waiting.'

Oliver Lambert pointed at the stiff sofa and offered coffee. He sat perfectly erect in a wing chair and held his cup like a British aristocrat. 'I'm worried about Avery,' he said.

'I saw him last night,' Mitch said. 'Doctor's forcing a two-month retirement.'

'Yes, that's why you're here. I want you to work with Victor Milligan for the next two months. He'll get most of Avery's files, so it's familiar territory.'

'That's fine. Victor and I are good friends.'

'You'll learn a lot from him. A genius at taxation. Reads two books a day.'

Great, thought Mitch. He should average ten a day in prison. 'Yes, he's a very smart man. He's helped me out of a jam or two.'

'Good. I think you'll get along fine. Try and see him sometime this morning. Now, Avery had some unfinished business in the Caymans. He goes there a lot, as you know, to meet with certain bankers. In fact, he was scheduled to leave tomorrow for a couple of days. He told me this morning you're familiar with the clients and the accounts, so we need you to go.'

The Lear, the loot, the condo, the storage room, the accounts. A thousand thoughts flashed in his mind. It did not add up. 'The Caymans? Tomorrow?'

'Yes, it's quite urgent. Three of his clients are in dire need of summaries of their accounts and other legal work. I wanted Milligan to go, but he's due in Denver in the morning. Avery said you could handle it.'

'Sure I can handle it.'

'Fine. The Lear will take you. You'll leave around noon and return by commercial flight late Friday. Any problems?'

Yes, many problems. Ray was leaving prison. Tarrance was demanding the contraband. A half million bucks had to be collected. And he was scheduled to disappear anytime.

'No problems.'

He walked to his office and locked the door. He kicked off his shoes, lay on the floor and closed his eyes.

The elevator stopped on the seventh floor, and Mitch bolted up the stairs to the ninth. Tammy opened the door and locked it behind him. He walked to the window.

'Were you watching?' he asked.

'Of course. The guard by your parking lot stood on the sidewalk and watched you walk here.'

'Wonderful. Even Dutch follows me.'

He turned and inspected her. 'You look tired.'

'Tired? I'm dead. In the past three weeks I've been a janitor, a secretary, a lawyer, a banker, a whore, a courier and a private investigator. I've flown to Grand Cayman nine times, bought nine sets of new luggage and hauled back a ton of stolen documents. I've driven to Nashville four times and flown ten. I've read so many bank records and legal crap I'm half blind. And when it's bedtime, I put on my little Dustbusters shirt and play maid for six hours. I've got so many names, I've written them on my hand so I won't get confused.'

'I've got another for you.'

'This doesn't surprise me. What?'

'Mary Alice. From now on, when you talk to Tarrance, you're Mary Alice.'

'Let me write that down. I don't like him. He's very rude on the phone.'

'I've got great news for you.'

'I can't wait.'

'You can quit Dustbusters.'

'I think I'll lie down and cry. 'Why?'

'It's hopeless.'

'I told you that a week ago. Houdini couldn't get files out of there, copy them, and sneak them back in without getting caught.'

'Did you talk to Abanks?' Mitch asked.

'Yes.'

'Did he get the money?'

'Yes. It was wired Friday.'

'Is he ready?'

'Said he was.'

'Good. What about the forger?'

'I'm meeting with him this afternoon.'

'Who is he?'

'An ex-con. He and Lomax were old pals. Eddie said he was the best documents man in the country.'

'He'd better be. How much?'

'Five thousand. Cash, of course. New IDs, passports, driver's licenses and visas.'

'How long will it take him?'

'I don't know. When do you need it?'

Mitch sat on the edge of the rented desk. He breathed deeply and tried to think. To calculate. 'As soon as possible. I thought I had a week, but now I don't know. Just get it as soon as possible. Can you drive to Nashville tonight?'

'Oh yes. I'd love to. I haven't been there in two days.'

'I want a Sony camcorder with a tripod set up in the bedroom. Buy a case of tapes. and I want you to stay there, by the phone, for the next few days. Review the Bendini Papers again. Work on your summaries.'

'You mean I have to stay there?'

'Yeah. Why?'

'I've ruptured two disks sleeping on that couch.'

'You rented it.'

'What about the passports?'

'What's the guy's name?'

'Doc somebody. I've got his number.'

'Give it to me. Tell him I'll call in a day or so. How much money do you have?'

'I'm glad you asked. I started with fifty thousand, right? I've spent ten thousand on airfare, hotels, luggage and rental cars. And I'm still spending. Now you want a video camera. And fake IDs. I'd hate to lose money on this deal.'

Mitch started for the door. 'How about another fifty thousand?'

'I'll take it.'

He winked at her and closed the door, wondering if he would ever see her again.

The cell was eight by eight, with a toilet in a corner and a set of bunk beds. The top bunk was uninhabited and had been for a year. Ray lay on the bottom bunk with wires running from his ears. He spoke to himself in a very foreign language. Turkish. At that moment on that floor, it was safe to bet he was the only soul listening to Berlitz jabber in Turkish. There was quiet talk up and down the hall, but most lights were out. Eleven o'clock, Tuesday night.

The guard walked silently to his cell. 'McDeere,' he said softly, secretly, through the bars. Ray sat on the edge of the bed, under the bunk above, and stared at him. He removed the wires.

'Warden wants to see you.'

Sure, he thought, the warden's sitting at his desk at 11 P.M. waiting on me. 'Where are we going?' It was an anxious question.

'Put your shoes on and come on.'

Ray glanced around the cell and took a quick inventory of his worldly possessions. In eight years he had accumulated a black-and-white television, a large cassette player, two cardboard boxes full of tapes and several dozen books. He made three dollars a day working in the prison laundry, but after cigarettes there had been little to spend on tangibles. These were his only assets. Eight years.

The guard fitted a heavy key in the door and slid it open a few inches. He turned off the light. 'Just follow me, and no cute stuff. I don't know who you are, mister, but you got some heavy-duty friends.'

Other keys fit other doors, and they were outside under the basketball hoop. 'Stay behind me,' the guard said.

Ray's eyes darted around the dark compound. The wall loomed like a mountain in the distance, beyond the courtyard and walking area where he had paced a thousand miles and smoked a ton of cigarettes. It was sixteen feet tall in the daylight, but looked much larger at night. The guard towers were fifty yards apart and well lit. And heavily armed.

The guard was casual and unconcerned. Of course, he had a uniform and a gun. He moved confidently between two cinder block buildings, telling Ray to follow and be cool. Ray tried to be cool. They stopped at the corner of a building, and the guard gazed at the wall, eighty feet away. Floodlights made a routine sweep of the courtyard, and they backed into the darkness.

Why are we hiding? Ray asked himself. Are those guys up there with the guns on our side? He would like to know before he made any dramatic moves.

The guard pointed to the exact spot on the wall where James Earl Ray and his gang went over. A rather famous spot, studied and admired by most of the inmates at Brushy Mountain. Most of the white ones anyway. 'In about fifteen minutes, they'll throw a ladder up there. The wire has already been cut on top. You'll find a heavy rope on the other side.'

'Mind if I ask a few questions?'

'Make it quick.'

'What about all these lights?'

'They'll be diverted. You'll have total darkness.'

'And those guns up there?'

'Don't worry. They'll look the other way.'

'Dammit! Are you sure?'

'Look, man, I've seen some inside jobs before, but this takes the cake. Warden Lattemer himself planned this one. He's right up there.' The guard pointed to the nearest tower.

'The warden?'

'Yep. Just so nothing'll go wrong.'

'Who's throwing up the ladder?'

'Coupla guards.'

Ray wiped his forehead with his sleeve and breathed deeply. His mouth was dry and his knees were weak.

The guard whispered, 'There'll be a dude waiting for you. His name is Bud. White dude. He'll find you on the other side, and just do what he says.'

The floodlights swept through again, then died. 'Get ready,' the guard said. Darkness settled in, followed by a dreadful silence. The wall was now black. From the nearest tower, a whistle blew two short signals. Ray knelt and watched.

From behind the next building, he could see the silhouettes running to the wall. They grabbed at something in the grass, then hoisted it.

'Run, dude,' the guard said. 'Run!'

Ray sprinted with his head low. The homemade ladder was in place. The guards grabbed his arms and threw him to the first step.

the ladder bounced as he scurried up the two-by-fours. The top of the wall was two-feet wide. A generous opening had been cut in the coiled barbed wire. He slid through without touching it. The rope was right where it was supposed to be, and he eased down the outside of the wall. Eight feet from pay dirt, he turned loose and jumped. he squatted and looked around. Still dark. The floodlights were on hold.

The clearing stopped a hundred feet away, and the dense woods began. 'Over here,' the voice said calmly. Ray started for it. Bud was waiting in the first cluster of black bushes.

'Hurry. Follow me.'

Ray followed him until the wall was out of sight. They stopped in a small clearing next to a dirt trail. He stuck out a hand. 'I'm Bud Riley. Kinda fun, ain't it?'

'Unbelievable. Ray McDeere.'

Bud was a stocky man with a black beard and a black beret. He wore combat boots, jeans and, a camouflage jacket. No gun was in sight. He offered Ray a cigarette.

'Who are you with?' Ray asked.

'Nobody. I just do a little free-lance work for the warden. They usually call me when somebody goes over the wall. Course, this is a little different. Usually I bring my dogs. I thought we'd wait here for a minute until the sirens go off, so you can hear. Wouldn't be right if you didn't get to hear 'em. I mean, they're sorta in your honor.'

'That's okay. I've heard them before.'

'Yeah, but it's different out here when they go off. It's a beautiful sound.'

'Look, Bud, I – '

'Just listen, Ray. We got plenty of time. They won't chase you, much.'

'Much?'

'Yeah, they gotta make a big scene, wake ever'body up, just like a real escape. But they ain't coming after you. I don't know what kinda pull you got, but it's something.'

The sirens began screaming, and Ray jumped. Lights flashed across the black sky, and the faint voices of the tower guards were audible.

'See what I mean?'

'Let's go,' Ray said, and began walking.

'My truck's just up the road a piece. I brought you some clothes. Warden gave me your sizes. Hope you like them.'

Bud was out of breath when they reached the truck. Ray quickly changed into the olive Duckheads and navy cotton work shirt. 'Very nice, Bud,' he said.

'Just throw them prison clothes in the bushes.'

They drove the winding mountain trail for two miles, then turned onto blacktop. Bud listened to Conway Twitty and said nothing.

'Where are we going, Bud?' Ray finally asked.

'Well, the warden said he didn't care and really didn't want to know. Said it was up to you. I'd suggest we get to a big town where there's a bus station. After that, you're on your own.'

'How far will you drive me?'

'I got all night, Ray. You name the town.'

'I'd like to get some miles behind us before I start hanging around a bus station. How about Knoxville?'

'Knoxville it is. Where are you going from there?'

'I don't know. I need to get out of the country.'

'With your friends, that should be no problem. Be careful, though. By tomorrow, your picture will be hanging in every sheriff's office in ten states.'

Three cars with blue lights came blazing over the hill in front of them. Ray ducked onto the floorboard.

'Relax, Ray. They can't see you.'

He watched them disappear through the rear window. 'What about roadblocks?'

'Look, Ray. Ain't gonna be no roadblocks, okay? Trust me.' Bud stuck a hand in a pocket and threw a wad of cash on the seat. 'Five hundred bucks. Hand-delivered by the warden. You got some stout friends, buddy.'

# CHAPTER THIRTY-FOUR

Wednesday morning. Tarry Ross climbed the stairs to the fourth floor of the Phoenix Inn. He paused on the landing outside the hall door and caught his breath. Sweat beaded across his eyebrows. He removed the dark sunglasses and wiped his face with the sleeve of his overcoat. Nausea hit below the belt, and he leaned on the stair rail. He dropped his empty briefcase on the concrete and sat on the bottom step. His hands shook like severe palsy, and he wanted to cry. He clutched his stomach and tried not to vomit.

The nausea passed, and he breathed again. Be brave, man, be brave. There's two hundred thousand waiting down the hall. If you got guts, you can go in there and get it. You can walk out with it, but you must have courage. He breathed deeper, and his hands settled down. Guts, man, guts.

The weak knees wobbled, but he made it to the door. Down the hall, past the rooms. Eighth door on the right. He held his breath, and knocked.

Seconds passed. He watched the dark hall through the dark glasses and could see nothing. 'Yeah,' a voice inside said, inches away.

'It's Alfred.' Ridiculous name, he thought. Where'd it come from?

The door cracked, and a face appeared behind the little chain. The door closed, then opened wide. Alfred walked in.

'Good morning, Alfred,' Vinnie Cozzo said warmly. 'Would you like coffee?'

'I didn't come here for coffee,' Alfred snapped. He placed the briefcase on the bed and stared at Cozzo.

'You're always so nervous, Alfred. Why don't you relax. There's no way you can get caught.'

'Shut up, Cozzo. Where's the money?'

Vinnie pointed to a leather handbag. He stopped smiling. 'Talk to me, Alfred.'

The nausea hit again, but he kept his feet. He stared at them. His heart beat like pistons. 'Okay, your man, McDeere, has been paid a million bucks already. Another million is on the way. He's delivered one load of Bendini documents and claims to have ten thousand more.' A sharp pain hit his groin, and he sat on the edge of the bed. He removed his glasses.

'Keep talking,' Cozzo demanded.

McDeere's talked to our people many times in the last six months. He'll testify at the trials, then hit the road as a protected witness. He and his wife.'

'Where are the other documents?'

'Dammit, I don't know. He won't tell. But they're ready to be delivered. I want my money, Cozzo.'

Vinnie threw the handbag on the bed. Alfred opened it and the briefcase. He attacked the stack of bills, his hands shaking violently.

'Two hundred thousand?' he asked desperately.

Vinnie smiled. 'That was the deal, Alfred. I got another job for you in a couple of weeks.'

'No way, Cozzo. I can't take any more of this.' He slammed the briefcase shut and ran to the door. He stopped and tried to calm himself. 'What will you do with McDeere?' he asked, staring at the door.

'What do you think, Alfred.'

He bit his lip, clenched the briefcase and walked from the room. Vinnie smiled and locked the door. He pulled a card from his pocket and placed a call to the Chicago home of Mr. Lou Lazarov.

Tarry Ross walked in panic down the hall. He could see little from behind the glasses. Seven doors down, almost to the elevator, a huge hand reached from the darkness and pulled him into a room. The hand slapped him hard, and another fist landed in his stomach. Another fist to the nose. He was on the floor, dazed and bleeding. The briefcase was emptied on the bed.

He was thrown into a chair, and the lights came on. Three FBI agents, his comrades, glared at him. Director Voyles walked up to him, shaking his head in disbelief. The agent with the huge efficient hands stood nearby, within striking distance. Another agent was counting money.

Voyles leaned into his face. 'You're a traitor, Ross. The lowest form of scum. I can't believe it.'

Ross bit his lip and began sobbing.

'Who is it?' Voyles asked intently.

The crying was louder. No answer.

Voyles swung wildly and slapped Ross's left temple. He shrieked in pain. 'Who is it, Ross? Talk to me.'

'Vinnie Cozzo,' he blurted between sobs.

'I know it's Cozzo! Dammit! I know that! But what did you tell him?'

Tears ran from his eyes and blood poured from his nose. His body shook and gyrated pitifully. No answer.

Voyles slapped him again, and again. 'Tell me, you little son of a bitch. Tell me what Cozzo wants.' He slapped him again.

Ross doubled over and dropped his head on his knees. The crying softened.

'Two hundred thousand dollars,' an agent said.

Voyles dropped to one knee and almost whispered to Ross. 'Is it McDeere, Ross? Please, oh please, tell me it's not McDeere. Tell me, Tarry, tell me it's not McDeere.'

Tarry stuck his elbows on his knees and stared at the floor. The blood dripped neatly into one little puddle on the carpet. Gut check, Tarry. You don't get to keep your money. You're on the way to jail. You're a disgrace, Tarry. You're a slimy little scuzzball of a chicken, and it's over. What could possible be gained by keeping secrets? Gut check, Tarry.

Voyles was pleading softly. Sinners, won't you come? 'Please say it ain't McDeere. Tarry, please tell me it ain't.'

Tarry sat straight and wiped his eyes with his fingers. He breathed deeply. Cleared his throat. He bit his lip, looked squarely at Voyles and nodded.

DeVasher had no time for the elevator. He ran down the stairs to the fourth floor, to the corner, a power one, and barged into Locke's office. Half the partners were there. Locke, Lambert, Milligan, McKnight, Dunbar, Denton, Lawson, Banahan, Kruger, Welch and Shottz. The other half had been summoned.

A quiet panic filled the room. DeVasher sat at the head of the conference table, and they gathered around.

'Okay, boys. It's not time to haul ass and head for Brazil. Not yet, anyway. We confirmed this morning that he has talked extensively to the Fibbies, that they have paid him a million cash, that they have promised another million, that he has certain documents that are believed to be fatal. This came straight from the FBI. Lazarov and a small army are flying into Memphis as we speak. It appears as though the damage has not been done. Yet. According to our source – a very high ranking Fibbie – McDeere has over ten thousand documents in his possession, and he is ready to deliver. But he has only delivered a few so far. We think. Evidently, we have caught this thing in time. If we can prevent further damage, we should be okay. I say this, even though they have some documents. Obviously, they don't have much or they would've been here with search warrants.'

DeVasher was onstage. He enjoyed this immensely. He spoke with a patronizing smile and looked at each of the worried faces. 'Now, where is McDeere?'

Milligan spoke. 'In his office. I just talked to him. He suspects nothing.'

'Wonderful. He's scheduled to leave in three hours for Grand Cayman. Correct, Lambert?'

'That's correct. Around noon.'

'Boys, the plane will never make it. The pilot will land in New Orleans for an errand, then he'll take off for the island. About thirty minutes over the Gulf, the little blip will disappear from radar, forever. Debris will scatter over a thirty-square-mile area, and no bodies will ever be found. It's sad, but necessary.'

'The Lear?' asked Denton.

'Yes, son, the Lear. We'll buy you another toy.'

'We're assuming a lot, DeVasher,' Locke said. 'We're assuming the documents already in their possession are harmless. Four days ago you thought McDeere had copied some of Avery's secret files. What gives?'

'They studied the files in Chicago. Yeah, they're full of incriminating evidence, but not enough to move with. They couldn't get the first conviction. You guys know the damning materials are on the island. And, of course, in the basement. No one can penetrate the basement. We checked the files in the condo. Everything looked in order.'

Locke was not satisfied. 'Then where did ten thousand come from?'

'You're assuming he has ten thousand. I rather doubt it. Keep in mind, he's trying to collect another one million bucks before he takes off. He's probably lying to them and snooping around for more documents. If he had ten thousand, why wouldn't the Fibbies have them by now?'

'Then what's to fear?' asked Lambert.

'The fear is the unknown, Ollie. We don't know what he's got, except that he's got a million bucks. He's no dummy, and he just might stumble across something if left alone. We cannot allow that to happen. Lazarov, you see, said to blow his ass outta the air. Quote unquote.'

'There's no way a rookie associate could find and copy that many incriminating records,' Kruger said boldly, and looked around the group for approval. Several nodded at him with intense frowns.

'Why is Lazarov coming?' asked Dunbar, the real estate man. He said 'Lazarov' as if Charles Manson was coming to dinner.

'That's a stupid question,' DeVasher snapped, and looked around for the idiot. 'First, we've got to take care of McDeere and hope the damage is minimal. Then we'll take a long look at this unit and make whatever changes are necessary.'

Locke stood and glared at Oliver Lambert. 'Make sure McDeere's on that plane.'

Tarrance, Acklin and Laney sat in stunned silence and listened to the speaker phone on the desk. It was Voyles in Washington, explaining exactly what had happened. He would leave for Memphis within the hour. He was almost desperate.

'You gotta bring him in, Tarrance. And quick. Cozzo doesn't know that we know about Tarry Ross, but Ross told him McDeere was on the verge of delivering the records. They could take him out at any time. You've got to get him. Now! Do you know where he is?'

'He's at the office,' Tarrance said.

'Okay. Fine. Bring him in. I'll be there in two hours. I wanna talk to him. Goodbye.'

Tarrance punched the phone, then dialed the number.

'Who are you calling?' Acklin asked.

'Bendini, Lambert & Locke. Attorneys-at-law.'

'Are you crazy, Wayne?' Laney asked.

'Just listen.'

The receptionist answered the phone. 'Mitch McDeere, please,' Tarrance said.

'One moment, please.' she said. Then the secretary: 'Mr. McDeere's office.'

'I need to speak to Mitchell McDeere.'

'I'm sorry, sir. he's in a meeting.'

'Listen, young lady, this is Judge Henry Hugo, and he was supposed to be in my courtroom fifteen minutes ago. We're waiting for him. It's an emergency.'

'Well, I see nothing on his calendar for this morning.'

'Do you schedule his appointments?'

'Well, yes, sir.'

'Then it's your fault. Now get him on the phone.'

Nina ran across the hall and into his office. 'Mitch, there's a Judge Hugo on the phone. Says you're supposed to be in court right now. You'd better talk to him.'

Mitch jumped to his feet and grabbed the phone. He was pale. 'Yes,' he said.

'Mr. McDeere,' Tarrance said. 'Judge Hugo. You're late for my court. Get over here.'

'Yes, Judge.' He grabbed his coat and briefcase and frowned at Nina.

'I'm sorry,' she said. 'It's not on your calendar.'

Mitch raced down the hall, down the stairs, past the receptionist and out the front door. He ran north on Front Street to Union and darted through the lobby of the Cotton Exchange Building. On Union, he turned east and ran toward the Mid-America Mall.

The sight of a well-dressed young man with a briefcase running like a scared dog may be a common sight in some cities, but not in Memphis. People noticed.

He hid behind a fruit stand and caught his breath. He saw no one running behind him. He ate an apple. If it came to a footrace, he hoped Two-Ton Tony was chasing him.

He had never been particularly impressed with Wayne Tarrance. The Korean shoe store was a fiasco. The chicken place on Grand Cayman was equally dumb. His notebook on the Moroltos would bore a Cub Scout. But his idea about a May-day code, a 'don't ask questions just run for your life' alert, was a brilliant idea. For a month, Mitch knew if Judge Hugo called, he had to hit the door on a dead run. Something bad had gone wrong, and the boys on the fifth floor were moving in. Where was Abby? he thought.

A few pedestrians walked in pairs along Union. He wanted a crowded sidewalk, but there was none. He stared at the corner of Front and Union and saw nothing suspicious. Two blocks east, he casually entered the lobby of the Peabody and looked for a phone. On the mezzanine overlooking the lobby, he found a neglected one in a short hallway near the men's room. He dialed the Memphis office of the Federal Bureau of Investigation.

'Wayne Tarrance, please. It's an emergency. This is Mitch McDeere.'

Tarrance was on the phone in seconds. 'Mitch, where are you?'

'Okay, Tarrance, what's going on?'

'Where are you?'

'I'm out of the building, Judge Hugo. I'm safe for now. What's happened?'

'Mitch, you've gotta come in.'

'I don't have to do a damned thing, Tarrance. And I won't until you talk to me.'

'Well, we've, uh, we've had a slight problem. There's been a small leak. You need – '

'Leak, Tarrance? Did you say leak? There's no such thing as a small leak. Talk to me, Tarrance, before I hang up this phone and disappear. You're tracing this call, aren't you, Tarrance? I'm hanging up.'

'No! Listen, Mitch. They know. They know we've been talking, and they know abut the money and the files.'

There was a long pause. 'A small leak, Tarrance. Sounds like the dam burst. Tell me about this leak, and quick.'

'God this hurts. Mitch, I want you to know how much this hurts. Voyles is devastated. One of our senior men sold the information. We caught him this morning at a hotel in Washington. They paid him two hundred thousand for the story on you. We're in shock, Mitch.'

'Oh, I'm touched. I'm truly concerned over your shock and pain, Tarrance. I guess now you want me to run down there to your office so we can all sit around and console each other.'

'Voyles will be there by noon, Mitch. He's flying in with his top people. He wants to meet with you. We'll get you out of town.'

'Right. You want me to rush into your arms for protection. You're all idiots. And I'm a fool for trusting you. Are you tracing this call, Tarrance?'

'No!'

'You're lying. I'm hanging up, Tarrance. Sit tight and I'll call you in thirty minutes from another phone.'

'No! Mitch, listen. You're dead if you don't come in.'

'Goodbye, Wayne. Sit by the phone.'

Mitch dropped the receiver and looked around. He walked to a marble column and peeked at the lobby below. The ducks were swimming around the fountain. The bar was deserted. A table was surrounded with rich old ladies sipping their tea and gossiping. A solitary guest was registering.

Suddenly, the Nordic stepped from behind a potted tree and stared at him. 'Up there!' he yelled across the lobby to an accomplice. They watched him intently and glanced at the stairway under him. The bartender looked up at Mitch, then at the Nordic and his friend. The old ladies stared in silence.

'Call the police!' Mitch yelled as he backed away from the railing. Both men sprang across the lobby and hit the stairs. Mitch waited five seconds, and returned to the railing. The bartender had not moved. The ladies were frozen.

There were heavy noises on the stairs. Mitch sat on the railing, dropping his briefcase, swung his legs over, paused, then jumped twenty feet onto the carpet of the lobby. He fell like a rock, but landed squarely on both feet. Pain shot through his ankles and hips. The football knee buckled, but did not collapse.

Behind him, next to the elevators, was a small haberdashery with windows full of ties and Ralph Lauren's latest. He limped into it. A kid of no more than nineteen waited eagerly behind the counter. There were no customers. An outside door opened onto Union.

'Is that door locked?' Mitch asked calmly.

'Yes, sir.'

'You wanna make a thousand dollars cash? Nothing illegal.' Mitch quickly peeled off ten hundred-dollar bills and threw them on the counter.

'Uh, sure. I guess.'

'Nothing illegal, okay? I swear. I wouldn't get you in trouble. Unlock that door, and when two men come running in here in about twenty seconds, tell them I ran through that door and jumped in a cab.'

The kid smiled even brighter and raked up the money. 'Sure. No problem.'

'Where's the dressing room?'

'Yes, sir, over there next to the closet.'

'Unlock the door,' Mitch said as he slid into the dressing room and sat down. He rubbed his knees and ankles.

The clerk was straightening ties when the Nordic and his partner ran through the door from the lobby. 'Good morning,' he said cheerfully.

'Did you see a man running through here, medium build, dark gray suit, red tie?'

'Yes, sir. He just ran through there, through that door, and jumped in a cab.'

'A cab! Damn!' The door opened and closed, and the store was silent. The kid walked to a shoe rack near the closet. 'They're gone, sir.'

Mitch was rubbing his knees. 'Good. Go to the door and watch for two minutes. Let me know if you see them.'

Two minutes later, he was back. 'They're gone.'

Mitch kept his seat and smiled at the door. 'Great. I want one of those kelly green sports coats, forty-four long, and a pair of white buckskins, ten D. Bring them here, would you? And keep watching.'

'Yes, sir.' He whistled around the store as he collected the coat and shoes, then slid them under the door. Mitch yanked off his tie and changed quickly. He sat down.

'How much do I owe you?' Mitch asked from the room.

'Well, let's see. How about five hundred?'

'Fine. Call me a cab, and let me know when it's outside.'


Tarrance walked three miles around his desk, The call was traced to the Peabody, but Laney arrived too late. He was back now, sitting nervously with Acklin. Forty minutes after the first call, the secretary's voice blasted through the intercom. 'Mr. Tarrance. It's McDeere.'

Tarrance lunged at the phone. 'Where are you?'

'In town. But not for long.'

'Look, Mitch, you won't last two days on your own. They'll fly in enough thugs to start another war. You've got to let us help you.'

'I don't know, Tarrance. For some strange reason I just don't trust you boys right now. I can't imagine why. Just a bad feeling.'

'Please, Mitch. Don't make this mistake.'

'I guess you want me to believe you boys can protect me for the rest of my life. Sorta funny, isn't it, Tarrance? I cut a deal with the FBI, and I almost get gunned in my own office. That's real protection.'

Tarrance breathed deeply into the phone. There was a long pause. 'What about the documents? We've paid you a million for them.'

'You're cracking up, Tarrance. You paid me a million for my clean files. You got them, and I got the million. Of course, that was just part of the deal. Protection was also part of it.'

'Give us the damned files, Mitch. They're hidden somewhere close to us, you told me that. Take off if you want to, but leave the files.'

'Won't work, Tarrance. Right now I can disappear, and the Moroltos may or may not come after me. If you don't get the files, you don't get the indictments. If the Moroltos don't get indicted, maybe, if I'm lucky, one day they'll just forget about me. I gave them a real scare, but no permanent damage. Hell, they may even hire me back one of these days.'

'You don't really believe that. They'll chase you until they find you. If we don't get the records, we'll be chasing too. It's that simple, Mitch.'

'Then I'll put my money on the Moroltos. If you guys find me first, there'll be a leak. Just a small one.'

'You're outta your mind, Mitch. If you think you can take your million and ride into the sunset, you're a fool. They'll have goons on camels riding the deserts looking for you. Don't do it, Mitch.'

'Goodbye, Wayne. Ray sends his regards.'

The line was dead. Tarrance grabbed the phone and threw it against the wall.

Mitch glanced at the clock on the airport wall. He punched in another call. Tammy answered.

'Hello, sweetheart. Hate to wake you.'

'Don't worry, the couch kept me awake. What's up?'

'Major trouble. Get a pencil and listen very carefully. I don't have a second to waste. I'm running, and they're right behind me.'

'Fire away.'

'First, call Abby at her parents'. Tell her to drop everything and get out of town. She doesn't have time to kiss her mother goodbye or pack any clothes. Tell her to drop the phone, get in her car and drive away. And don't look back. She takes Interstate 55 to Huntingdon, West Virginia, and goes to the airport. She flies from Huntingdon to Mobile. In Mobile, she rents a car and drives east on Interstate 10 to Gulf Shores, then east on Highway 182 to Perdido Beach. She checks in at the Perdido Beach Hilton under the name of Rachel James. And she waits. Got that?'

'Yeah.'

'Second. I need you to get on a plane and fly to Memphis. I called Doc, and the passports, etc., are not ready. I cussed him, but to no avail. He promised to work all night and have them ready in the morning. I will not be here in the morning, but you will. Get the documents.'

'Yes, sir.'

'Third. Get on a plane and get back to the apartment in Nashville. Sit by the phone. Do not, under any circumstances leave the phone.'

'Got it.'

'Fourth. Call Abanks.'

'Okay. What are your travel plans?'

I'm coming to Nashville, but I'm not sure when I'll be there. I gotta go. Listen, Tammy, tell Abby she could be dead within the hour if she doesn't run. So run, dammit, run!'

'Okay, boss.'

He walked quickly to Gate 22 and boarded the 10:04 Delta flight to Cincinnati. He clutched a magazine full of one way tickets, all bought with MasterCard. One to Tulsa on American Flight 233, leaving at 10:14, and purchased in the name of Mitch McDeere; one to Chicago on Northwest Flight 861, leaving at 10:15, and purchased in the name of Mitchell McDeere; one to Dallas on United Flight 562, leaving at 10:30, and purchased in the name of Mitchell McDeere; and one to Atlanta on Delta Flight 790, leaving at 11:10, and purchased in the name of Mitchell McDeere.

The ticket to Cincinnati had been bought with cash, in the name of Sam Fortune.

Lazarov entered the power office on the fourth floor and every head bowed. DeVasher faced him like a scared, whipped child. The partners studied their shoelaces and held their bowels.

'We can't find him,' DeVasher said.

Lazarov was not one to scream and cuss. He took great pride in being cool under pressure. 'You mean he just got up and walked out of here?' he asked coolly.

There was no answer. None was needed.

'All right, DeVasher, this is the plan. Send every man you've got to the airport. Check with every airline. Where's his car?'

'In the parking lot.'

'That's great. He left here on foot. He walked out of your little fortress on foot. Joey'll love this. Check with every rental car company. Now, how many honorable partners do we have here.'

'Sixteen present.'

'Divide them up in pairs and send them to the airports in Miami, New Orleans, Houston, Atlanta, Chicago, L.A., San Francisco and New York. Roam the concourses of these airports. Live in these airports. Eat in these airports. Watch the international flights in these airports. We'll send reinforcements tomorrow. You honorable esquires know him well, so go find him. It's a long shot, but what have we got to lose? It'll keep you counselors busy. And I hate to tell you boys, but these hours are not billable. Now, where's his wife?'

'Danesboro, Kentucky. At her parents'.'

'Go get her. Don't hurt her, just bring her in.'

'Do we start shredding?' DeVasher asked.

'We'll wait twenty-four hours. Send someone to Grand Cayman and destroy those records. Now hurry, DeVasher.'

The power office emptied.

Voyles stomped around Tarrance's desk and barked commands. A dozen lieutenants scribbled as he yelled. 'Cover the airport. Check every airline. Notify every office in every major city. Contact customs. Do we have a picture of him?'

'We can't find one, sir.'

'Find one, and find it quick. It needs to be in every FBI and customs office by tonight. He's on the run. Son of a bitch!'

# CHAPTER THIRTY-FIVE

The bus left Birmingham shortly before 2 P.M., Wednesday. Ray sat in the rear and studied every person who climbed in and found a seat. He looked sporty. He had taken a cab to a mall in Birmingham and in thirty minutes had purchased a new pair of faded Levis, a plaid short-sleeved gold shirt and a pair of red-and-white Reeboks. He had also eaten a pizza and received a severe Marine-style haircut. He wore aviator sunshades and an Auburn cap.

A short, fat, dark-skinned lady sat next to him.

He smiled at her. '*¿De dónde es usted?*' he asked. Where are you from?

Her face broke into unrestrained delight. A wide smile revealed few teeth. '*México,*' she said proudly. '*¿Habla español?*' she asked eagerly.

'*Sí.*'

For two long hours, they jabbered in Spanish as the bus rolled along to Montgomery. She had to repeat occasionally, but he surprised himself. He was eight years out of practice and a little rusty.

Behind the bus, Special Agent Jenkins and Jones followed in a Dodge Aries. Jenkins drove while Jones slept. The trip had become boring ten minutes out of Knoxville. Just routine surveillance they were told. If you lose him, no big deal. But try not to lose him.

The flight from Huntington to Atlanta was two hours away, and Abby sat in a secluded corner of a dark lounge watching. Just watching. In the chair next to her was a carry-on bag. Contrary to her urgent instructions, she had packed a toothbrush, make-up and a few clothes. She had also written a note to her parents, giving a brief story about how she had to run to Memphis, needed to see Mitch, everything's fine, don't worry, hugs and kisses, love, Abby. She ignored the coffee and watched the arriving and departing.

She did not know if he was dead or alive. Tammy said he was scared, but very much in control. As always. She said he was flying to Nashville, and she, Tammy, was flying to Memphis. Confusing, but she was certain he knew what he was doing. Get to Perdido Beach and wait.

Abby had never heard of Perdido Beach. And she was certain he'd never been there either.

The lounge was nerve-racking. Every ten minutes a drunk businessman would venture over and throw something suggestive at her. Get lost, she said a dozen times.

After two hours, they boarded. Abby was stuck in the aisle seat. She buckled her belt and relaxed. And then she saw her.

She was a striking blonde with high cheekbones and a firm jaw that was almost unfeminine, yet strong and attractive. Abby had seen the partial face before. Partial, because the eyes were covered, as before. She looked at Abby and glanced away as she passed and went to her seat somewhere in the rear.

The Shipwreck Bar! The blonde in the Shipwreck Bar. The blonde who was eavesdropping on her and Mitch and Abanks. They had found her. And if they had found her, where was her husband? What had they done to him? She thought of the two-hour drive from Danesboro to Huntington, through the winding mountain roads. She had driven like a maniac. They could not have followed her.

They taxied from the terminal and minutes later lifted off for Atlanta.

For a second time in three weeks, Abby watched dusk from the inside of a 727 at the airport in Atlanta. She and the blonde. They were on the ground for thirty minutes and then left for Mobile.

From Cincinnati, Mitch flew to Nashville. He arrived at 6 P.M., Wednesday, long after the banks had closed. He found a U-Haul truck rental place in the phone book and flagged a cab.

He rented one of the smaller models, a sixteen-footer. He paid cash, but was forced to use his driver's license and a credit card for a deposit. If DeVasher could track him to a U-Haul place in Nashville, so be it. He bought twenty cardboard packing boxes and left for the apartment.

He had not eaten since Tuesday night, but he was in luck. Tammy had left a bag of microwave popcorn and two beers. He ate like a pig. At eight, he made his first call to the Perdido Beach Hilton. He asked for Lee Stevens. He had not arrived, she said. He stretched out on the den floor and thought of a hundred things that could happen to Abby. She could be dead in Kentucky and he wouldn't know. He couldn't call.

The couch had not been folded, and the cheap sheets hung off the end and fell to the floor. Tammy was not much for housework. He looked at the small, temporary bed and thought of Abby. Only five nights ago, they had tried to kill each other on the bed. Hopefully, she was on the plane. Alone.

In the bedroom, he sat on the unopened Sony box and marveled at the roomful of documents. Across the carpet she had built perfect columns of paper, all painstakingly divided into Cayman banks and Cayman companies. On top of each stack was a yellow legal pad, with the company name followed by pages of dates and entries. And names!

Even Tarrance could follow the paper trail. A grand jury would eat it up. The U.S. Attorney would call press conferences. And the trial juries would convict, and convict and convict.


Special Agent Jenkins yawned into the telephone receiver and punched the numbers to the Memphis office. He had not slept in twenty-four hours. Jones was snoring in the car.

'FBI,' a male voice said.

'Yeah, who's there?' Jenkins asked. Just a routine check in.

'Acklin.'

'Hey, Rick. This is Jenkins. We've – '

'Jenkins! Where have you been? Hold on!'

Jenkins quit yawning and looked around the bus terminal. An angry voice yelled into the earpiece.

'Jenkins! Where are you?' It was Wayne Tarrance.

'We're at the bus station in Mobile. We've lost him.'

'You what? How could you lose him?'

Jenkins was suddenly alert and leaning into the phone.

'Wait a minute, Wayne. Our instructions were to follow him for eight hours to see where he went. Routine, you said.'

'I can't believe you lost him.'

'Wayne, we weren't told to follow him for the rest of his life. Eight hours, Wayne. We've followed for twenty hours, and he's disappeared. What's the big deal?'

'Why haven't you called in before now?'

'We called in twice. In Birmingham and Montgomery. Line was busy both times. What's going on, Wayne?'

'Just a minute.'

Jenkins grabbed the phone tighter and waited. Another voice: 'Hello Jenkins?'

'Yes.'

'Director Voyles here. What the hell happened?'

Jenkins held his breath and looked wildly around the terminal. 'Sir, we lost him. We followed him for twenty hours, and when he got off the bus here in Mobile, we lost him in the crowd.'

'That's great, son. How long ago?'

'Twenty minutes.'

'All right, listen. We desperately need to find him. His brother has taken our money and disappeared. Call the locals there in Mobile. Tell them who you are, and that an escaped murderer is on the loose in town. They've probably got Ray McDeere's name and picture stuck to the walls. His mother lives in Panama City Beach, so alert every local between there and Mobile. I'm sending in our troops.'

'Okay. I'm sorry, sir. We weren't told to trail him forever.'

'We'll discuss it later.'

At ten Mitch called the Perdido Beach Hilton for the second time. He asked for Rachel James. No arrival. He asked for Lee Stevens. One moment, she said. Mitch sat on the floor and waited intently. The line to the room was ringing. After a dozen rings, someone picked up.

'Yeah.' It was quick.

'Lee?' Mitch asked.

A pause. 'Yeah.'

'This is Mitch. Congratulations.'

Ray fell on the bed and closed his eyes. 'It was so easy, Mitch. How'd you do it?'

'I'll tell you when we have time. Right now, there are a bunch of folks trying to kill me. And Abby. We're on the run.'

'Who, Mitch?'

'It would take ten hours to tell the first chapter. We'll do it later. Write this number down. 615-889-4380.'

'That's not Memphis.'

'No, it's Nashville. I'm in an apartment that's serving as mission control. Memorize that number. If I'm not here, the phone will be answered by a girl named Tammy.'

'Tammy?'

'It's a long story. Just do as I say. Sometime tonight, Abby will check in there under the name of Rachel James. She'll be in a rented car.'

'She's coming here!'

'Just listen, Ray. The cannibals are chasing us, but we're a step ahead of them.'

'Ahead of who?'

'The Mafia. And the FBI.'

'Is that all?'

'Probably. Now listen to me. There is a slight chance Abby is being followed. You've got to find her, watch her and make damned sure no one is behind her.'

'And if they are?'

'Call me, and we'll talk about it.'

'No problem.'

'Don't use the phone except to call this number. And we can't talk much.'

'I've got a bunch of questions, little brother.'

'And I've got the answers, but not now. Take care of my wife and call me when she gets there.'

'Will do. And, Mitch, thanks.'

'*Adios.*'

An hour later she turned off Highway 182 onto the winding driveway to the Hilton. She parked the four door Cutlass with Alabama tags and walked nervously under the sprawling veranda to the front doors. She stopped for a second, looked behind her at the driveway and went inside.

Two minutes later, a yellow cab from Mobile stopped under the veranda, behind the shuttle vans. Ray watched the cab. A woman was in the back seat leaning forward and talking to the driver. They waited a minute. She pulled money from her purse and paid him. She got out and waited until the cab drove away. The woman was a blonde, and that was the first thing he noticed. Very shapely, with tight black corduroy pants. And black sunglasses, which seemed odd to him because it was pushing midnight. She walked suspiciously to the front doors, waited a minute, then went in. He watched her carefully. He moved towards the lobby.

The blonde approached the only clerk behind the registration desk. 'A single room, please.' he heard her say.

The clerk slid a registration form across the counter. The blonde wrote her name and asked, 'That lady who just checked in before me, what's her name? I think she's an old friend.'

The clerk flipped through the registration cards. 'Rachel James.'

'Yeah, that's her. Where's she from?'

'It's a Memphis address,' the clerk said.

'What's her room number? I'd like to say hello.'

'I can't give room numbers,' the clerk said.

The blonde quickly pulled two twenties from her purse and slid them across the counter. 'I just want to say hello.'

The clerk took the money. 'Room 622.'

The woman paid in cash. 'Where are the phones?'

'Around the corner,' the clerk said. Ray slid around the corner and found four pay phones. He grabbed a middle one and began talking to himself.

The blonde took a phone on the end and turned her back to him. She spoke softly. He could hear only pieces.

' . . . checked in . . . Room 622 . . . Mobile . . . some help . . . I can't . . . an hour? . . . yes . . . hurry . . . '

She hung up, and he talked louder into his dead phone.

Ten minutes later, there was a knock at the door. The blonde jumped from the bed, grabbed her .45 and stuck it in the corduroys under the shirt. She ignored the safety chain and cracked the door.

It burst open and knocked her against the wall. Ray lunged at her, grabbed the gun, and pinned her to the floor. With her face in the carpet, he stuck the barrel of the .45 in her ear. 'If you make a sound, I'll kill you!'

She stopped struggling and closed her eyes. No response.

'Who are you?' Ray demanded. He pushed the barrel deeper into her ear. Again, no response.

'Not a move, not a sound. Okay? I'd love to blow your head off.'

He relaxed, still sitting on her back, and ripped open her flight bag. He dumped its contents on the floor and found a paid of clean tennis socks. 'Open your mouth,' he demanded.

She did not move. The barrel returned to her ear, and she slowly opened her mouth. Ray crammed the socks in between her teeth, then blindfolded her with the silk nightshirt. He bound her feet and hands with panty hose, then ripped the bedsheets into long strips. The woman did not move. When he finished the binding and gagging, she resembled a mummy. He slid her under the bed.

The purse contained six hundred dollars in cash and a wallet with an Illinois driver's license. Karen Adair from Chicago. Date of birth: March 4, 1962. He took the wallet and gun.


The phone rang at 1 A.M., and Mitch was not asleep. He was in bank records up to his waist. Fascinating bank records. Highly incriminating.

'Hello,' he answered cautiously.

'Is this mission control?' The voice was in the vicinity of a loud jukebox.

'Where are you, Ray?'

'A joint called the FloraBama lounge. Right on the state line.'

'Where's Abby?'

'She's in the car. She's fine.'

Mitch breathed easier and grinned into the phone. He listened.

'We had to leave the hotel. A woman followed Abby in – same

woman you saw in some bar in the Caymans. Abby is trying to explain everything. The woman followed her all day and showed up at the hotel. I took care of her, and we disappeared.'

'You took care of her?'

'Yeah, she wouldn't talk, but she's out of the way for a short time.'

'Abby's fine?'

'Yeah. We're both dead tired. Exactly what do you have in mind?'

'You're about three hours away from Panama City Beach. I know you're dead tired, but you need to get away from there. Get to Panama City Beach, ditch the car and get two rooms at the Holiday Inn. Call me when you check in.'

'I hope you know what you're doing.'

'Trust me, Ray.'

'I do, but I'm beginning to wish I was back in prison.'

'You can't go back, Ray. We either disappear or we're dead.'

# CHAPTER THIRTY-SIX

The cab stopped at a red light in downtown Nashville, and Mitch hopped out on stiff and aching legs. He limped through the busy intersection dodging the morning traffic.

The Southeastern Bank Building was a thirty-story glass cylinder, designed along the same lines as a tennis-ball can. The tint was dark, almost black. It stood prominently away from the street corner amidst a maze of sidewalks and fountains and manicured greenery.

Mitch entered the revolving doors with a swarm of employees rushing to work. In the marble-laden atrium he found the directory and rode the escalators to the third floor. He opened a heavy glass door and walked into a large circular office. A striking woman of forty or so watched him from behind the glass desk. She offered no smile.

'Mr. Mason Laycock, please,' he said.

She pointed. 'Have a seat.'

Mr. Laycock wasted no time. He appeared from around a corner and was as sour as his secretary. 'May I help you?' he asked through his nose.

Mitch stood. 'Yes, I need to wire a little money.'

'Yes. Do you have an account at Southeastern?'

'Yes.'

'And your name?'

'It's a numbered account.' In other words, you don't get a name, Mr Laycock. You don't need a name.

'Very well. Follow me.' His office had no windows, no view. A row of keyboards and monitors sat on the credenza behind his glass desk. Mitch sat down.

'The account number, please.'

It came from memory. '214–31–35.'

Laycock pecked at his keyboard and watched a monitor. 'That's a Code Three account, opened by a T. Hemphill, with access only by her and a certain male meeting the following physical requirements: approximately six feet tall, one seventy-five to one eighty-five, blue eyes, brown hair, about twenty-five or twenty-six years old. You fit that description, sir.' Laycock studied the screen. 'And the last four digits of your Social Security number are?'

'8585.'

'Very well. You are accessed. Now what can I do for you?'

'I want to wire in some funds from a bank in Grand Cayman.'

Laycock frowned and took a pencil from his pocket. 'Which bank in Grand Cayman?'

'Royal Bank of Montreal.'

'What type of account?'

'It's a numbered account.'

'I presume you have the number?'

'499DFH2122.'

Laycock wrote the number and stood. 'I'll be just a moment.' He left the room.

Ten minutes passed. Mitch tapped his bruised feet and looked at the monitors across the desk.

Laycock returned with his supervisor, Mr Nokes, a vice president or something. Nokes introduced himself from behind the desk. Both men appeared nervous. They stared downward at Mitch.

Nokes did the talking. He held a small sheet of computer paper. 'Sir, that is a restricted account. You must have certain information before we can start the wire.'

Mitch nodded confidently.

'The dates and amounts of the last three deposits, sir?' They watched him intensely, knowing he would fail.

Again it came from memory. No notes. 'February third of this year, six and a half million. December fourteenth, last year, nine point two million. And October eight, last year, eleven million.'

Laycock and Nokes gaped at the small printout. Nokes managed a tiny professional smile. 'Very well. You are cleared to the Pen number.'

Laycock stood ready with his pencil.

'Sir, what is your Pen number?' Nokes asked.

Mitch smiled and recrossed his damaged legs. '72083.'

'And the terms of the wire?'

'Ten million dollars wired immediately into this bank, account 214–31–35. I'll wait.'

'It's not necessary to wait, sir.'

'I'll wait. When the wire is complete, I've got a few more for you.'

'We'll be a moment. Would you like some coffee?'

'No. Thanks. Do you have a newspaper?'

'Certainly,' Laycock said. 'On the table there.'

They scurried from the office, and Mitch's pulse began its descent. He opened the Nashville *Tennessean* and scanned three sections before he found a brief paragraph about the escape at Brushy Mountain. No picture. Few details. They were safe at the Holiday Inn on the Miracle Strip in Panama City Beach, Florida.

Their trail was clear, so far. He thought. He hoped.

Laycock returned alone. He was friendly now. A real back-slapper. 'Wire's complete. The money is here. Now what can we do for you?'

'I want to wire it out. Most of it, anyway.'

'How many transfers?'

'Three.'

'Give me the first one.'

'A million dollars to the Coast National Bank in Pensacola, to a numbered account, accessible to only one person, a white female, approximately fifty years of age. I will provide her with the Pen number.'

'Is this an existing account?'

'No. I want you to open it with the wire.'

'Very well. The second transfer?'

'One million dollars to the Dane County Bank in Danesboro, Kentucky, to any account in the name of Harold or Maxine Sutherland, or both. It's a small bank, but it has a correspondent relationship with United Kentucky in Louisville.'

'Very well. The third transfer?'

'Seven million to the Deutschbank in Zurich. Account number 772–03BL–600. The remainder of the money stays here.'

'This will take about an hour,' Laycock said as he wrote.

'I'll call you in an hour to confirm.'

'Very well.'

'Thank you, Mr. Laycock.'

Each step was painful, but the pain was not felt. He moved in a controlled jog down the escalators and out of the building.

On the top floor of the Royal Bank of Montreal, Grand Cayman branch, a secretary from Wire Transfers slid a computer printout under the very pointed and proper nose of Randolph Osgood. She had circled an unusual transfer of ten million. Unusual because the money in this account did not normally return to the United States and unusual because it went to a bank they had never dealt with. Osgood studied the printout and called Memphis. Mr. Tolleson was on leave of absence, the secretary informed him. Then Nathan Locke? he asked. Mr. Locke is out of town. Victor Milligan? Mr. Milligan is away also.

Osgood placed the printout in the pile of things to do tomorrow.

Along the Emerald Coast of Florida and Alabama, from the outskirts of Mobile east through Pensacola, Fort Walton Beach, Destin and

Panama City, the warm spring night had been peaceful. Only one violent crime along the coast. A young woman was robbed, beaten and raped in her room at the Perdido Beach Hilton. Her boyfriend, a tall blond headed man with strong Nordic features, had found her bound and gagged in her room. His name was Rimmer, Aaron Rimmer, and he was from Memphis.

The real excitement of the night was a massive manhunt in the Mobile area for the escaped murderer, Ray McDeere. He had been seen arriving at the bus station after dark. His mug shot was on the front page of the morning paper, and before ten, three witnesses had come forth and reported sightings. His movements were traced across Mobile Bay to Foley, Alabama, then to Gulf Shores.

Since the Hilton is only ten miles from Gulf Shores along Highway 182, and since the only known escaped murderer was in the vicinity when the only violent crime occurred, the conclusion was quick and inescapable. The hotel's night clerk made a probable ID of Ray McDeere, and the records reflected that he checked in around nine-thirty as a Mr. Lee Stevens. And he paid cash. Later, the victim checked in and was attacked. The victim also identified Mr. Ray McDeere.

The night clerk remembered that the victim asked about a Rachel James, who checked in five minutes before the victim and paid cash. Rachel James vanished sometime during the night without bothering to check out. Likewise Ray McDeere, alias Lee Stevens. A parking-lot attendant made a probable ID of McDeere and said he got in a white four-door Cutlass with a woman between midnight and one. Said she was driving and appeared to be in a hurry. Said they went east on 182.

Calling from his room on the sixth floor of the Hilton, Aaron Rimmer anonymously told a Baldwin Country sheriff's deputy to check the car rental companies in Mobile. Check them for an Abby McDeere. That's your white Cutlass, he told them.

From Mobile to Miami, the search began for the Cutlass rented from Avis by Abby McDeere. The sheriff's investigator promised to keep the victim's boyfriend, Aaron Rimmer, posted on all developments.

Mr. Rimmer would wait at the Hilton. He shared a room with Tony Verkler. Next door was his boss, DeVasher. Fourteen of his friends sat in their rooms on the seventh floor and waited.

It took seventeen trips from the apartment to the U-Haul, but by noon the Bendini Papers were ready for shipment. Mitch rested his swollen legs. He sat on the couch and wrote instructions to Tammy. He detailed the transactions at the bank and told her to wait a week before contacting his mother. She would soon be a millionaire.

He set the telephone in his lap and prepared himself for an unpleasant task. He called the Dane County Bank and asked for Hugh Sutherland. It was an emergency, he said.

'Hello,' his father-in-law answered angrily.

'Mr. Sutherland, this is Mitch. Have you – '

'Where's my daughter. Is she okay?'

'Yes. She's fine. She's with me. We'll be leaving the country for a few days. Maybe weeks. Maybe months.'

'I see,' he replied slowly. 'And where might you be going?'

'Not sure. We'll just knock around for a while.'

'Is something wrong, Mitch?'

'Yes, sir. Something is very wrong, but I can't explain now. Maybe one of these days. Watch the newspapers closely. You'll see a major story out of Memphis within two weeks.'

'Are you in danger?'

'Sort of. Have you received any unusual wire transfers this morning?'

'As a matter of fact we have. Somebody parked a million bucks here about an hour ago.'

'That somebody was me, and the money is yours.'

There was a very long pause. 'Mitch, I think I deserve an explanation.'

'Yes, sir, you do. But I can't give you one. If we make it safely out of the country, you'll be notified in a week or so. Enjoy the money. Gotta run.'

Mitch waited a minute and called Room 1028 at the Holiday Inn, Panama City Beach.

'Hello.' It was Abby.

'Hi, babe. How are you?'

'Terrible, Mitch. Ray's picture is on the cover of every newspaper down here. At first it was the escape and the fact that someone saw him in Mobile. Now the TV news is claiming he is the prime suspect in a rape last night.'

'What! Where!'

'At the Perdido Beach Hilton. Ray caught that blonde following me into the hotel. He jumped her in her room and tied her up. Nothing serious. He took her gun and her money, and now she's claiming she was beaten and raped by Ray McDeere. Every cop in Florida is looking for the car I rented last night in Mobile.'

'Where's the car?'

'We left it about a mile west of here at a big condo development. I'm so scared, Mitch.'

'Where's Ray?'

'He's lying on the beach trying to sunburn his face. The picture in the paper is an old one He's got long hair and looks real pale. It's not a good picture. Now he's got a crew cut and he's trying to turn pink. I think it will help.

'Are both rooms in your name?'

'Rachel James.'

'Listen, Abby. Forget Rachel and Lee and Ray and Abby. Wait until almost dark, then leave the rooms. Just walk away. About half a mile east is a small motel called the Blue Tide. You and Ray enjoy a little walk on the beach until you find it. You go to the desk and get two rooms next to each other. Pay in cash. Tell them your name is Jackie Nagel. Got that? Jackie Nagel. Use that name, because when I get there I'll ask for it.'

'What if they don't have two rooms next to each other?'

'Okay, if anything goes wrong, two doors down is another dump called the Seaside. Check in there. Same name. I'm leaving here now, say one o'clock, and I should be there in ten hours.'

'What if they find the car?'

'They'll find it, and they'll throw a blanket over Panama City Beach. You've got to be careful. After dark, try to sneak into a drugstore and buy some hair dye. Cut your hair extremely short and dye it blond.'

'Blond!'

'Or red. I don't give a damn. But change it. Tell Ray not to leave his room. Do not take any chances.'

'He's got a gun, Mitch.'

'Tell him I said not to use it. There will be a thousand cops around there, probably tonight. He can't win a gunfight.'

'I love you, Mitch. I'm so scared.'

'It's okay to be scared, babe. Just keep thinking. They don't know where you are, and they can't catch you if you move. I'll be there by midnight.'

Lamar Quin, Wally Hudson and Kendall Mahan sat in the conference room on the third floor and contemplated their next move. As senior associates, they knew about the fifth floor and the basement, about Mr. Lazarov and Mr Morolto, about Hodge and Kozinski. They knew that when one joined the firm, one did not leave.

They told their stories about the Day. They compared it to the day they learned the sad truth about Santa Claus. A sad and frightening day, when Nathan Locke talked to them in his office and told them about their biggest client. And then he introduced them to DeVasher. They were employees of the Morolto family, and they were expected to work hard, spend their handsome paychecks and remain very quiet about it. All three did. There had been thoughts of leaving, but never serious plans. They were family men. In time, it sort of went away. There were so many clean clients to work for. So much hard, legitimate work.

The partners handled most of the dirty work, but growing seniority had brought increasing involvement in the conspiracy. They would never be caught, the partners assured them. They were too smart. They had too much money. It was a perfect cover. Of particular concern at the conference table was the fact that the partners had skipped town. There was not a single partner in Memphis. Even Avery Tolleson had disappeared. He had walked out of the hospital.

They talked about Mitch. He was out there somewhere, scared and running for his life. If DeVasher caught him, he was dead and they would bury him like Hodge and Kozinski. But if the feds caught him, they got the records, and they got the firm, which, of course, included the three of them.

What if, they speculated, no one caught him? What if he made it, just vanished? Along with his documents, of course. What if he and Abby were now somewhere on a beach, drinking rum and counting their money? They liked this thought and talked about it for a while.

Finally they decided to wait until tomorrow. If Mitch was gunned down somewhere, they would stay in Memphis. If he was never found, they would stay in Memphis. If the feds caught him, they would hit the road, Jack.

Run, Mitch, run!

The rooms at the Blue Tide Motel were narrow and tacky. The carpet was twenty years old and badly worn. The bedspreads had cigarette burns. But luxury was unimportant.

After dark Thursday, Ray stood behind Abby with a pair of scissors and snipped delicately around her ears. Two towels under the chair were covered with her dark hair. She watched him carefully in the mirror next to the antique color television and was free with her instructions. It was a boyish cut, well above the ears, with bangs. He stepped back and admired his work.

'Not bad,' he said.

She smiled and brushed hair from her arms. 'I guess I need to color it now,' she said sadly. She walked to the tiny bathroom and closed the door.

She emerged an hour later as a blonde. A yellowish blonde. Ray was asleep on the bedspread. She knelt on the dirty carpet and scooped up the hair.

She picked it from the floor and filled a plastic garbage bag. The empty dye bottle and the applicator were thrown in with the hair, and she tied the bag. There was a knock at the door.

Abby froze, and listened. The curtains were pulled tightly. She slapped Ray's feet. Another knock. Ray jumped from the bed and grabbed the gun.

'Who is it?' she whispered loudly at the window.

'Sam Fortune,' he whispered back.

Ray unlocked the door, and Mitch stepped in. He grabbed Abby and bear-hugged Ray. The door was locked, the lights turned off, and they sat on the bed in the darkness. He held Abby tightly. With so much to say, the three said nothing.

A tiny, weak ray of light from the outside filtered under the curtains and, as minutes passed, gradually lit the dresser and television. No one spoke. There were no sounds from the Blue Tide. The parking lot was virtually empty.

'I can almost explain why I'm here,' Ray finally said, 'but I'm not sure why you're here.'

'We've got to forget why we're here,' Mitch said, 'and concentrate on leaving here. All together. All safe.'

'Abby's told me everything.' Ray said.

'I don't know everything,' she said. 'I don't know who's chasing us.'

'I'm assuming they're all out there,' Mitch said. 'DeVasher and his gang are nearby. Pensacola, I would guess. It's the nearest airport of any size. Tarrance is somewhere along the coast directing his boys in their all-out search for Ray McDeere, the rapist. And his accomplice, Abby McDeere.'

'What happens next?' Abby asked.

'They'll find the car, if they haven't already done so. That will pinpoint Panama City Beach. The paper said the search extended from Mobile to Miami, so now they're spread out. When they find the car, they zero in here. Now, there's a thousand cheap motels just like this one along the Strip. For twelve miles, nothing but motels, condos and T-shirt shops. That's a lot of people, a lot of tourists with shorts and sandals, and tomorrow we'll be tourists too, shorts, sandals, the whole bit. I figure even if they have a hundred men after us, we've got two or three days.'

'Once they decide we're here, what happens?' she asked.

'You and Ray could have simply abandoned the car and taken off in another one. They can't be certain we're on the Strip, but they'll start looking here. But they're not the Gestapo. They can't crash a door and search without probable cause.'

'DeVasher can,' Ray said.

'Yeah, but there's a million doors around here. They'll set up road-blocks and watch every store and restaurant. They'll talk to every hotel clerk, show them Ray's mug shot. They'll swarm like ants for a few days, and with luck, they'll miss us.'

'What are you driving, Mitch?' Ray asked.

'A U-Haul.'

'I don't understand why we don't get in the U-Haul, right now, and haul ass. I mean the car is sitting a mile down the road, just wait-ing to be found, and we know they're coming. I say we haul it.'

'Listen, Ray. They might be setting roadblocks right now. Trust me. Did I get you out of prison? Come on.'

A siren went screaming past on the strip. They froze, and listened to it fade away.

'Okay, gang,' Mitch said, 'we're moving out. I don't like this place. The parking lot is empty and too close to the highway. I've parked the U-Haul three doors down at the elegant Sea Gull's Rest Motel. I've got two lovely rooms there. The roaches are much smaller. We're taking a quiet stroll on the beach. Then we get to un-pack the truck. Sound exciting?'

# CHAPTER THIRTY-SEVEN

Joey Morolto and his squad of storm troopers landed at the Pensacola airport in a chartered DC-9 before sunrise Friday. Lazarov waited with two limos and eight rented vans. He briefed Joey on the past twenty-four hours as the convoy left Pensacola and traveled east on Highway 98. After an hour of briefing, they arrived at a twelve-floor condo called the Sandpiper, in the middle of the Strip at Destin. An hour from Panama City Beach. The penthouse on the top floor had been procured by Lazarov for only four thousand dollars a week. Off-season rates. The remainder of the twelfth floor and all of the eleventh had been leased, for the goons.

Mr. Morolto snapped orders like an agitated drill sergeant. A command post was set up in the great room of the penthouse, overlooking the calm emerald water. Nothing suited him. He wanted breakfast, and Lazarov sent two vans to a Delchamps supermarket nearby. He wanted McDeere, and Lazarov asked him to be patient.

By daybreak, the troops had settled into their condos. They waited.

Three miles away along the beach, and within view of the Sandpiper, F. Denton Voyles and Wayne Tarrance sat on the balcony of an eighth-floor room at the Sandestin Hilton. They drank coffee, watched the sun rise gently on the horizon and talked strategy. The night had not gone well. The car had not been found. No sign of Mitch. With sixty FBI agents and hundreds of locals scouring the coast, they should have at least found the car. With each passing hour, the McDeeres were farther away.

In a file by a coffee table inside were the warrants. For Ray McDeere, the warrant read: escape, unlawful flight, robbery and rape. Abby's sin was merely being an accomplice. The charges for Mitch required more creativity. Obstruction of justice and a nebulous racketeering charge. And of course the old standby, mail fraud. Tarrance was not sure where the mail fraud fit, but he worked for the FBI and had never seen a case that did not include mail fraud.

The warrants were issued and ready and had been fully discussed with dozens of reporters from newspapers and television stations throughout the Southeast. Trained to maintain a stone face and loathe the press, Tarrance was having a delightful time with the reporters.

Publicity was needed. Publicity was critical. The authorities must find the McDeeres before the Mob did.

Rick Acklin ran through the room to the balcony. 'They've found the car!'

Tarrance and Voyles jumped to their feet. 'Where?'

'Panama City Beach. In the parking lot of a high rise.'

'Call our men in, every one of them!' Voyles yelled. 'Stop searching everywhere. I want every agent in Panama City Beach. We'll turn the place inside out. Get all the locals you can. Tell them to set up roadblocks on every highway and gravel road in and out of here. Dust the car for prints. What's the town look like?'

'Similar to Destin. A twelve mile strip along the beach with hotels, motels, condos, the works,' Acklin answered.

'Start our men door to door at the hotels. Is her composite ready?'

'Should be,' Acklin said.

'Get her composite, Mitch's composite, Ray's composite and Ray's mug shot in the hands of every agent and cop. I want people walking up and down the Strip waving those damn composites.'

'Yes, sir.'

'How far away is Panama City Beach?'

'About fifty minutes due east.'

'Get my car.'

The phone woke Aaron Rimmer in his room at the Perdido Beach Hilton. It was the investigator with the Baldwin County Sheriff's Department. They found the car, Mr. Rimmer, he said, in Panama City Beach. Just a few minutes ago. About a mile from the Holiday Inn. On Highway 98. Sorry again about the girl, he said. Hope she's doing better, he said.

Mr Rimmer said thanks, and immediately called Lazarov at the Sandpiper. Ten minutes later, he and his roommate, Tony, and DeVasher and fourteen others were speeding east. Panama City Beach was three hours away.

In Destin, Lazarov mobilized the storm troopers. They moved out quickly, piled into the vans and headed east. The blitzkrieg had begun.

It took only a matter of minutes for the U-Haul to become a hot item. The assistant manager of the rental company in Nashville was a guy named Billy Weaver. He opened the office early Friday morning, fixed his coffee, and scanned the paper. On the bottom half of the front page, Billy read with interest the story about Ray McDeere and the search along the coast. And then Abby was mentioned. Then the escapee's brother, Mitch McDeere, was mentioned. The name rang a bell.

Billy opened a drawer and flipped through the records of outstanding rentals. Sure enough, a man named McDeere had rented a sixteen-footer late Wednesday night. M. Y. McDeere, said the signature, but the driver's license read Mitchell Y. From Memphis.

Being a patriot and honest taxpayer, Billy called his cousin at Metro Police. The cousin called the Nashville FBI office, and fifteen minutes later, the U-Haul was a hot item.

Tarrance took the call on the radio while Acklin drove. Voyles was in the back seat. A U-Haul? Why would he need a U-Haul? He left Memphis without his car, clothes, shoes or toothbrush. He left the dog unfed. He took nothing with him, so why the U-Haul?

The Bendini records, of course. Either he left Nashville with the records in the truck or he was in the truck en route to get them. But why Nashville?

Mitch was up with the sun. He took one long, lustful look at his wife with the cute blond hair and forgot about sex. It could wait. He let her sleep. He walked around the stack of boxes in the small room and went to the bathroom. He showered quickly and slipped on a gray sweat suit he'd bought at a Wal-Mart in Montgomery. He eased along the beach for a half mile until he found a convenience store. He bought a sackful of Cokes, pastries and chips, sunglasses, caps and three newspapers.

Ray was waiting by the U-Haul when he returned. They spread the papers on Ray's bed. It was worse than they expected. Mobile, Pensacola and Montgomery had front-page stories with composites of Ray and Mitch, along with the mug shot again. Abby's composite had not been released, according to the Pensacola paper.

As composites go, they were close here and there and badly off in other areas. But it was hard to be objective. Hell, Mitch was staring at his own composite and trying to give an unbiased opinion about how close it was. The stories were full of all sorts of wild statements from one Wayne Tarrance, special agent, FBI. Tarrance said Mitchell McDeere had been spotted in the Gulf Shores–Pensacola area; that he and Ray both were known to be heavily armed and extremely dangerous; that they had vowed not to be taken alive; that reward money was being gathered; that if anyone saw a man who faintly resembled either of the McDeere brothers, please call the local police.

They ate pastries and decided the composites were not close. The mug shot was even comical. They eased next door and woke Abby. They began unpacking the Bendini Papers and assembling the video camera.

At nine, Mitch called Tammy, collect. She had the new IDs and passports. He instructed her to Federal Express them to Sam Fortune, front desk, Sea Gull's Rest Motel, 16694 Highway 98, West Panama City Beach, Florida. She read to him the front-page story about himself and his small gang. No composites.

He told her to ship the passports, then leave Nashville. Drive four hours to Knoxville, check into a big motel and call him at Room 39, Sea Gull's Rest. He gave her the number.

Two FBI agents knocked on the door of the old ragged trailer at 486 San Luis. Mr. Ainsworth came to the door in his underwear. They flashed their badges.

'So whatta you want with me?' he growled.

An agent handed him the morning paper. 'Do you know those two men?'

He studied the paper. 'I guess they're my wife's boys. Never met them.'

'And your wife's name is?'

'Ida Ainsworth.'

'Where is she?'

Mr. Ainsworth was scanning the paper. 'At work. At the Waffle Hut. Say they're around here, huh?'

'Yes, sir. You haven't seen them?'

'Hell no. But I'll get my gun.'

'Has your wife seen them?'

'Not to my knowledge.'

'Thanks, Mr Ainsworth. We've got orders to set up watch here in the street, but we won't bother you.'

'Good. These boys are crazy. I've always said that.'

A mile away, another pair of agents parked discreetly next to a Waffle Hut and set up watch.

By noon, all highways and county roads into the coast around Panama City Beach were blocked. Along the Strip, cops stopped traffic every four miles. They walked from one T-shirt shop to the next, handing out composites. They posted them on the bulletin boards in Shoney's, Pizza Hut, Taco Bell and a dozen more fast-food places. They told the cashiers and waitresses to keep their eyes open for the McDeeres. Very dangerous people.

Lazarov and his men camped at the Best Western, two miles west of the Sea Gull's Rest. He rented a large conference room and set up command. Four of his troops were dispatched to raid a T-shirt shop, and they returned with all sorts of tourist clothes and straw hats and caps. He rented two Ford Escorts and equipped them with police scanners. They patrolled the Strip and listened to the endless squawking. They immediately caught the search for the U-Haul and joined in. DeVasher strategically spread the rented vans along the Strip. They sat innocently in large parking lots and waited with their radios.

Around two, Lazarov received an emergency call from an employee on the fifth floor of the Bendini Building. Two things. First, an employee snooping around the Caymans had found an old locksmith who, after being paid, recalled making eleven keys around midnight of April 1. Eleven keys, on two rings. Said the woman, a very attractive American, a brunette with nice legs, had paid cash and was in a hurry. Said the keys had been easy, except for the Mercedes key. He wasn't sure about that one. Second, a banker from Grand Cayman called. Thursday at 9.33 A.M. ten million dollars had been wired from the Royal Bank of Montreal to the Southeastern Bank in Nashville.

Between four and four-thirty, the police scanners went wild. The squawking was non-stop. A clerk at the Holiday Inn made a probable ID of Abby, as the woman who paid cash for two rooms at 4:17 A.M., Thursday. She paid for three nights, but had not been seen since the rooms were cleaned around one on Thursday. Evidently, neither room had been slept in Thursday night. She had not checked out, and the rooms were paid for through noon Saturday. The clerk saw no sign of a male accomplice. The Holiday Inn was swamped with cops and FBI agents and Morolto thugs for an hour. Tarrance himself interrogated the clerk.

They were there! Somewhere in Panama City Beach. Ray and Abby were confirmed. It was suspected Mitch was with them, but it was unconfirmed. Until 4:58, Friday afternoon.

The bombshell. A county deputy pulled into a cheap motel and noticed the gray-and-white hood of a truck. He walked between two buildings and smiled at the small U-Haul truck hidden neatly between a row of two-story rooms and a large garbage Dumpster. He wrote down all the numbers on the truck and called it in.

It hit! In five minutes the motel was surrounded. The owner charged from the front office and demanded and explanation. He looked at the composites and shook his head. Five FBI badges flapped in his face, and he became cooperative.

Accompanied by a dozen agents, he took the keys and went door to door. Forty-eight doors.

Only seven were occupied. The owner explained as he unlocked doors that it was a slow time of the year at the Beachcomber Inn. All of the smaller hotels struggle until Memorial Day, he explained.

Even the Sea Gull's Rest, four miles to the west, was struggling.

Andy Patrick received his first felony conviction at the age of nineteen and served four months for bad checks. Branded as a felon, he found honest work impossible, and for the next twenty years worked unsuccessfully as a small-time criminal. He drifted across the country shoplifting, writing bad checks and breaking into houses here and there. A small, frail nonviolent man, he was severely beaten by a fat, arrogant county deputy in Texas when he was twenty-seven. He lost an eye and lost all respect for the law.

Six months earlier, he landed in Panama City Beach and found an honest job paying four bucks an hour working the night shift at the front and only desk of the Sea Gull's Rest Motel. Around nine, Friday night, he was watching TV when a fat, arrogant county deputy swaggered through the door.

'Got a manhunt going on,' he announced, and laid copies of the composites and mug shot on the dirty counter. 'Looking for these folks. We think they're around here.'

Andy studied the composites. The one of Mitchell Y. McDeere looked pretty familiar. The wheels in his small-time felonious brain began to churn.

With his one good eye, he looked at the fat, arrogant county deputy and said, 'Ain't seen them. But I'll keep an eye out.'

'They're dangerous,' the deputy said.

You're the dangerous one, Andy thought.

'Post these up on the wall there,' the deputy instructed.

Do you own this damned place? Andy thought. 'I'm sorry, but I'm not authorized to post anything on the walls.'

The deputy froze, cocked his head sideways and glared at Andy through thick sunglasses. 'Listen, Peewee, I authorized it.'

'I'm sorry, sir, but I can't post anything on the walls unless my boss tells me to.'

'And where is your boss?'

'I don't know. Probably in a bar somewhere.'

The deputy carefully picked up the composites, walked behind the counter and tacked them on the bulletin board. When he finished, he glared down at Andy and said, 'I'll come back in a coupla hours. If you remove these, I'll arrest you for obstruction of justice.'

Andy did not flinch. 'Won't stick. They got me for that one time in Kansas, so I know all about it.'

The deputy's fat cheeks turned red and he gritted his teeth. 'You're a little smart-ass, aren't you?'

'Yes, sir.'

'You take these down and I promise you you'll go to jail for something.'

'I've been there before, and it ain't no big deal.'

Red lights and sirens screamed by on the Strip a few feet away, and the deputy turned and watched the excitement. He mumbled something and swaggered out the door. Andy threw the composites in the garbage. He watched the squad cars dodge each other on the Strip for a few minutes, then walked through the parking lot to the rear building. He knocked on the door of Room 38.

He waited and knocked again.

'Who is it?' a woman asked.

'The manager,' Andy replied, proud of his title. The door opened, and the man who favored the composite of Mitchell Y. McDeere slid out.

'Yes, sir,' he said. 'What's going on?'

He was nervous, Andy could tell. 'Cops just came by, know what I mean?'

'What do they want?' he asked innocently.

Your ass, Andy thought. 'Just asking questions and showing pictures. I looked at the pictures, you know.'

'Uh-huh,' he said.

'Pretty good pictures,' Andy said.

Mr. McDeere stared at Andy real hard.

Andy said, 'Cop said one of them escaped from prison. Know what I mean. I been in prison, and I think everybody ought to escape. You know?'

Mr. McDeere smiled, a rather nervous smile. 'What's your name?' he asked.

'Andy.'

'I've got a deal for you, Andy. I'll give you a thousand bucks now, and tomorrow, if you're still unable to recognize anybody, I've give you another thousand bucks. Same for the next day.'

A wonderful deal, thought Andy, but if he could afford a thousand bucks a day, certainly he could afford five thousand a day. It was the opportunity of his career.

'Nope,' Andy said firmly. 'Five thousand a day.'

Mr. McDeere never hesitated. 'It's a deal. Let me get the money.' He went into the room and returned with a stack of bills.

'Five thousand a day, Andy, that's our deal?'

Andy took the money and glanced around. He would count it later. 'I guess you want me to keep the maids away?' Andy asked.

'Great idea. That would be nice.'

'Another five thousand,' Andy said.

Mr. McDeere sort of hesitated. 'Okay, I've got another deal. Tomorrow morning, a Fed Ex package will arrive at the desk for Sam Fortune. You bring it to me, and keep the maids away, and I'll give you another five thousand.'

'Won't work. I do the night shift.'

'Okay, Andy. What if you worked all weekend, around the clock, kept the maids away and delivered my package? Can you do that?'

'Sure. My boss is a drunk. He'd love for me to work all weekend.'

'How much money, Andy?'

Go for it, Andy thought. 'Another twenty thousand.'

Mr. McDeere smiled. 'You got it.'

Andy grinned and stuck the money in his pocket. He walked away without saying a word, and Mitch retreated to Room 38.

'Who was it?' Ray snapped.

Mitch smiled as he glanced between the blinds and the windows.

'I knew we would have to have a lucky break to pull this off. And I think we just found it.'

# CHAPTER THIRTY-EIGHT

Mr. Morolto wore a black suit and a red tie and sat at the head of the plastic-coated executive conference table in the Dunes Room of the Best Western on the Strip. The twenty chairs around the table were packed with his best and brightest men. Around the four walls stood more of his trusted troops. Though they were thick-necked killers who did their deeds efficiently and without remorse, they looked like clowns in their colorful shirts and wild shorts and amazing potpourri of straw hats. He would have smiled at their silliness, but the urgency of the moment prevented smiling. He was listening.

On his immediate right was Lou Lazarov, and on his immediate left was DeVasher, and every ear in the small room listened as the two played tag team back and forth across the table.

'They're here. I know they're here,' DeVasher said dramatically, slapping both palms on the table with each syllable. The man had rhythm.

Lazarov's turn: 'I agree. They're here. Two came in a car, one came in a truck. We've found both vehicles abandoned, covered with fingerprints. Yes, they're here.'

DeVasher: 'Buy why Panama City Beach? It makes no sense.'

Lazarov: 'For one, he's been here before. Came here Christmas, remember? He's familiar with this place, so he figures with all these cheap motels on the beach it's a great place to hide for a while. Not a bad idea, really. But he's had some bad luck. For a man on the run, he's carrying too much baggage, like a brother who everybody wants. And a wife. And a truckload of documents, we presume. Typical schoolboy mentality. If I gotta run, I'm taking everybody who loves me. Then his brother rapes a girl, they think, and suddenly every cop in Alabama and Florida is looking for them. Some pretty bad luck, really.'

'What about his mother?' Mr. Morolto asked.

Lazarov and DeVasher nodded at the great man and acknowledged this very intelligent question.

Lazarov: 'No, purely coincidental. She's a very simple woman who serves waffles and knows nothing. We've watched her since we got here.'

DeVasher: 'I agree. There's been no contact.'

Morolto nodded intelligently and lit a cigarette.

703

Lazarov: 'So if they're here, and we know they're here, then the feds and the cops also know they're here. We've got sixty people here, and they got hundreds. Odds are on them.'

'You're sure they're all three together?' Mr. Morolto asked.

DeVasher: 'Absolutely. We know the woman and the convict checked in the same night at Perdido, that they left and three hours later she checked in here at the Holiday Inn and paid cash for two rooms and that she rented the car and his fingerprints were on it. No doubt. We know Mitch rented a U-Haul Wednesday in Nashville, that he wired ten million bucks of our money into a bank in Nashville Thursday morning and then evidently hauled ass. The U-Haul was found here four hours ago. Yes, sir, they are together.'

Lazarov: 'If he left Nashville immediately after the money was wired, he would have arrived here around dark. The U-Haul was found empty, so they had to unload it somewhere around here, then hide it. That was probably sometime late last night, Thursday. Now, you gotta figure they need to sleep sometime. I figure they stayed here last night with plans of moving on today. But they woke up this morning and their faces were in the paper, cops running around bumping into each other, and suddenly the roads were blocked. So they're trapped here.'

DeVasher: 'To get out, they've got to borrow, rent or steal a car. No rental records anywhere around here. She rented a car in Mobile in her name. Mitch rented a U-Haul in Nashville in his name. Real proper ID. So you gotta figure they ain't that damned smart after all.'

Lazarov: 'Evidently they don't have fake IDs. If they rented a car around here for the escape, the rental records would be in the real name. No such records exist.'

Mr. Morolto waved his hand in frustration. 'All right, all right. So they're here. You guys are the geniuses. I'm so proud of you. Now what?'

DeVasher's turn: 'The Fibbies are in the way. They're in control of the search, and we can't do nothing but sit and watch.'

Lazarov: 'I've called Memphis. Every senior associate in the firm is on the way down here. They know McDeere and his wife real well, so we'll put them on the beach and in restaurants and hotels. Maybe they'll see something.'

DeVasher: 'I figure they're in one of the little motels. They can give fake names, pay in cash and nobody'll be suspicious. Fewer people too. Less likelihood of being seen. They checked in at the Holiday Inn but didn't stay long. I bet they moved on down the Strip.'

Lazarov: 'First, we'll get rid of the feds and the cops. They don't know it yet, but they're about to move their show on down the road. Then, early in the morning, we start door to door at the small motels. Most of the dumps have less than fifty rooms. I figure two of our men can search one in thirty minutes. I know it'll be slow, but we can't just sit here. Maybe when the cops pull out, the McDeeres will breathe a little and make a mistake.'

'You mean you want our men to start searching hotel rooms?' Mr. Morolto asked.

DeVasher: 'There's no way we can hit every door, but we gotta try.'

Mr. Morolto stood and glanced around the room. 'So what about the water?' he asked in the direction of Lazarov and DeVasher.

They stared at each other, thoroughly confused by the question.

'The water!' Mr. Morolto screamed. 'What about the water?'

All eyes shot desperately around the table and quickly landed upon Lazarov. 'I'm sorry, sir, I'm confused.'

Mr. Morolto leaned into Lazarov's face. 'What about the water, Lou? We're on a beach, right? There's land and highways and railroads and airports on one side, and there's water and boats on the other. Now, if the roads are blocked and the airports and railroads are out of the question, where do you think they might go? It seems obvious to me they would try to find a boat and ease out in the dark. Makes sense, don't it, boys?'

Every head in the room nodded quickly. DeVasher spoke first. 'Makes a hell of a lot of sense to me.'

'Wonderful,' said Mr. Morolto. 'Then where are our boats?'

Lazarov jumped from his seat, turned to the wall and began barking orders at his lieutenants. 'Go down to the docks! Rent every fishing boat you can find for tonight and all day tomorrow. Pay them whatever they want. Don't answer any questions, just pay 'em the money. Get our men on those boats and start patrolling as soon as possible. Stay within a mile of the shore.'

Shortly before eleven, Friday night, Aaron Rimmer stood at the checkout counter at an all-night Texaco in Tallahassee and paid for a root beer and twelve gallons of gas. He needed change for the call. Outside next to the car wash, he flipped through the blue pages and called the Tallahassee Police Department. It was an emergency. He explained himself, and the dispatcher connected him with a shift captain.

'Listen!' Rimmer yelled urgently, 'I'm here at this Texaco, and five

minutes ago I saw these convicts everybody is looking for! I know it
was them!'

'Which convicts?' asked the captain.

'The McDeeres. Two men and a woman. I left Panama City Beach
not two hours ago, and I saw their pictures in the paper. Then I
stopped here and filled up, and I saw them.'

Rimmer gave his location and waited thirty seconds for the first
patrol car to arrive with blue lights flashing. It was quickly followed
by a second, third and fourth. They loaded Rimmer in a front seat
and raced him to the South Precinct. The captain and a small crowd
waited anxiously. Rimmer was escorted like a celebrity into the captain's office, where the three composites and mug shot were waiting
on the desk.

'That's them!' he shouted. 'I just saw them, not ten minutes ago.
They were in a green Ford pickup with Tennessee plates, and it was
pulling a long double-axle U-Haul trailer.'

'Exactly where were you?' asked the captain. The cops hung on
every word.

'I was pumping gas, pump number four, regular unleaded, and
they eased into the parking lot, real suspicious like. They parked
away from the pumps, and the woman got out and went inside.' He
picked up Abby's composite and studied it. 'Yep. That's her. No
doubt. Her hair's a lot shorter, but it's dark. She came right back out,
didn't buy a thing. She seemed nervous and in a hurry to get back to
the truck. I was finished pumping, so I walked inside. Right when I
opened the door, they drove within two feet of me. I saw all three of
them.'

'Who was driving?' asked the captain. Rimmer stared at Ray's
mug shot. 'Not him. The other one.' He pointed at Mitch's composite.

'Could I see your driver's license,' a sergeant said.

Rimmer carried three sets of identification. He handed the sergeant an Illinois driver's license with his picture and the name Frank
Temple.

'Which direction were they headed?' the captain asked.

'East.'

At the same moment, about four miles away, Tony Verkler hung
up the pay phone, smiled to himself and returned to the Burger King.

The captain was on the phone. The sergeant was copying information from Rimmer/Temple's driver's license and a dozen cops
chatted excitedly when a patrolman rushed into the office. 'Just got a
call! Another sighting, at a Burger King east of town. Same info! All

three of them in a green Ford pickup pulling a U-Haul. Guy wouldn't leave a name, but said he saw their pictures in the paper. Said they pulled through the carry-out window, bought three sacks of food and took off.'

'Its' gotta be them!' the captain said with a huge smile.

The Bay County sheriff sipped thick black coffee from a Styrofoam cup and rested his black boots on the executive conference table in the Caribbean Room at the Holiday Inn. FBI agents were in and out, fixing coffee, whispering and updating each other on the latest. His hero, the big man himself, Director F. Denton Voyles, sat across the table and studied a street map with three of his underlings. Imagine, Denton Voyles in Bay County. The room was a beehive of police activity. Florida state troopers filtered in and out. Radios and telephones rang and squawked on a makeshift command post in a corner. Sheriffs' deputies and city policemen from three counties loitered about, thrilled with the chase and suspense and presence of all those FBI agents. And Voyles.

A deputy burst through the door with a wild-eyed glow of sheer excitement. 'Just got a call from Tallahassee! They've got two positive IDs in the last fifteen minutes! All three of them in a green Ford pickup with Tennessee tags!'

Voyles dropped his street map and walked over to the deputy. 'Where were the sightings?' The room was silent, except for the radios.

'First one was at a Texaco Quick Shop. Second one was four miles away at a Burger King. They drove through the drive-in window. Both witnesses were positive and gave identical IDs.'

Voyles turned to the sheriff. 'Sheriff, call Tallahassee and confirm. How far away is it?'

The black boots hit the floor. 'Hour and a half. Straight down Interstate 10.'

Voyles pointed at Tarrance, and they stepped into a small room used as the bar. The quiet roar returned to mission control.

'If the sightings are real,' Voyles said quietly in Tarrance's face, 'we're wasting our time here.'

'Yes, sir. They sound legitimate. A single sighting could be a fluke or a prank, but two that close together sound awfully legitimate.'

'How the hell did they get out of here?'

'It's gotta be that woman, Chief. She's been helping him for a month. I don't know who she is, or where he found her, but she's on the outside watching us and feeding him whatever he needs.'

'Do you think she's with them?'

'Doubt it. She's probably just following closely, away from the action, and taking directions from him.'

'He's brilliant, Wayne. He's been planning this for months.'

'Evidently.'

'You mentioned the Bahamas once.'

'Yes, sir. The million bucks we paid him was wired to a bank in Freeport. He later told me it didn't stay there long.'

'You think maybe, he's headed there?'

'Who knows. Obviously he has to get out of the country. I talked to the warden today. He told me Ray McDeere can speak five or six languages fluently. They could be going anywhere.'

'I think we should pull out,' Voyles said.

'Let's get the roadblocks set up around Tallahassee. They won't last long if we've got a good description of the vehicle. We should have them by morning.'

'I want every cop in central Florida on the highways in an hour. Roadblocks everywhere. Every Ford pickup is automatically searched, okay? Our men will wait here until daybreak, then we'll pull up stakes.'

'Yes, sir,' Tarrance answered with a weary grin.

Word of the Tallahassee sightings spread instantly along the Emerald Coast. Panama City Beach relaxed. The McDeeres were gone. For reasons unknown only to them, their flight had moved inland. Sighted and positively identified, not once but twice, they were now somewhere else speeding desperately toward the inevitable confrontation on the side of a dark highway.

The cops along the coast went home. A few roadblocks remained through the night in Bay County and Gulf County, the predawn hours of Saturday were almost normal. Both ends of the Strip remained blocked, with cops making cursory exams of drivers' licenses. The roads north of town were free and clear. The search had moved east.

On the outskirts of Ocala, Florida near Silver Springs on Highway 40, Tony Verkler lumbered from a 7-Eleven and stuck a quarter in a pay phone. He called the Ocala Police Department with the urgent report that he had just seen those three convicts everybody was looking for up around Panama City Beach. The McDeeres! Said he saw their pictures in the paper the day before when he was driving through Pensacola, and now he had just seen them. The dispatcher informed him all patrolmen were on the scene of a bad accident and asked if he would mind driving over to the police station so they could file a report. Tony said he was in a hurry, but since it was somewhat important, he would be there in a minute.

When he arrived, the chief of police was waiting in a T-shirt and blue jeans. His eyes were swollen and red, and his hair was not in place. He led Tony into his office and thanked him for coming by. He took notes as Tony explained how he was pumping gas in front of the 7-Eleven, and a green Ford pickup with a U-Haul trailer behind it pulled up next to the store and a woman got out and used the phone. Tony was in the process, he explained, of driving from Mobile to Miami and had driven through the manhunt up around Panama City. He had seen the newspapers and had been listening to his radio and knew all about the three McDeeres. Anyway, he went in and paid for the gas and thought that he had seen the woman somewhere before. Then he remembered the papers. He walked over to a magazine rack in the front window and got a good look at the men. No doubt in his mind. She hung up, got back in the truck between the men, and they left. Green Ford with Tennessee plates.

The chief thanked him and called the Marion County Sheriff's Department. Tony said goodbye and returned to his car, where Aaron Rimmer was asleep in the back seat.

They headed north, in the direction of Panama City Beach.

# CHAPTER THIRTY-NINE

Saturday, 7 A.M. Andy Patrick looked east and west along the Strip, then walked quickly across the parking lot to Room 39. He knocked gently.

After a delay, she asked, 'Who is it?'

'The manager,' he answered. The door opened, and the man who resembled the composite of Mitchell Y. McDeere slid out. His hair was now very short and gold-colored. Andy stared at his hair.

'Good morning, Andy,' he said politely while glancing around the parking lot.

'Good morning. I was kinda wondering if you folks were still here.'

Mr. McDeere nodded and continued to look around the parking lot.

'I mean, according to the television this morning, you folks traveled halfway across Florida last night.'

'Yeah, we're watching it. They're playing games, aren't they, Andy?'

Andy kicked at a rock on the sidewalk. 'Television said there were three positive identifications last night. At three different places. Kinda strange, I thought. I was here all night, working and being on the lookout and all, and I didn't see you leave. Before sunrise I sneaked across the highway to a coffee shop, just over there, and as usual, there were cops in there. I sat close to them. According to them, the search has been called off around here. They said the FBI moved out right after the last sighting came in, around four this morning. Most of the other cops left too. They're gonna keep the Strip blocked until noon and call if off. Rumor has it you've got help from the outside, and you're trying to get to the Bahamas.'

Mr. McDeere listened closely as he watched the parking lot. 'What else did they say?'

'They kept talking about a U-Haul truck full of stolen goods, and how they found the truck, and it was empty, and how nobody can figure out how you loaded the stolen goods into a trailer and sneaked outta town right under their noses. They're very impressed, all right. Of course, I didn't say nothing, but I figured it was the same U-Haul you drove in here Thursday night.'

Mr. McDeere was deep in thought and did not say anything. He didn't appear to be nervous. Andy studied his face carefully.

'You don't seem too pleased,' Andy said. 'I mean, the cops are leaving and calling off the search. That's good, ain't it?'

'Andy, can I tell you something?'

'Sure.'

'It's more dangerous now than before.'

Andy thought about this for a long minute, then said, 'How's that?'

'The cops just wanted to arrest me, Andy. But there are some people who want to kill me. Professional killers, Andy. Many of them. And they're still here.'

Andy narrowed his good eye and stared at McDeere. Professional killers! Around here? On the Strip? Andy took a step backward. He wanted to ask exactly who they were and why they were chasing him, but he knew he wouldn't get much of an answer. He saw an opportunity. 'Why don't you escape?'

'Escape? How could we escape?'

Andy kicked another rock and nodded in the direction of a 1971 Pontiac Bonneville parked behind the office. 'Well, you could use my car. You could get in the trunk, all three of you, and I could drive you outta town. You don't appear to be broke, so you could catch a plane and be gone. Just like that.'

'And how much would that cost?'

Andy studied his feet and scratched his ear. The guy was probably a doper, he thought, and the boxes were probably full of cocaine and cash. And the Colombians were probably after him. 'That'd be pretty expensive, you know. I mean, right now, at five thousand a day, I'm just an innocent hotel clerk who's not very observant. Not part of nothing, you understand. But if I drive you outta here, then I become an accomplice, subject to indictment and jail and all that other crap I've been through, you know. So it'd be pretty expensive.'

'How much, Andy?'

'A hundred thousand.'

Mr. McDeere did not flinch or react; he just kept a straight face and glanced across the beach to the ocean. Andy knew immediately it was not out of the question.

'Let me think about it, Andy. For right now, you keep your eyes open. Now that the cops are gone, the killers will move in. This could be a very dangerous day, Andy, and I need your help. If you see anyone suspicious around here, call us quick. We're not leaving these rooms, okay?'

Andy returned to the front desk. Any fool would jump in the trunk and haul ass. It was the boxes, the stolen goods. That's why they wouldn't leave.

The McDeeres enjoyed a light breakfast of stale pastries and warm soft drinks. Ray was dying for a cold beer, but another trip to the convenience store was too risky. They ate quickly and watched the early-morning news. Occasionally a station along the coast would flash their composites on the screen. It scared them at first, but they got used to it.

A few minutes after 9 A.M., Saturday, Mitch turned off the television and resumed his spot on the floor among the boxes. He picked up a stack of documents and nodded at Abby, the camera operator. The deposition continued.

Lazarov waited until the maids were on duty, then scattered his troops along the Strip. They worked in pairs, knocking on doors, peeking in windows and sliding through dark hallways. Most of the small places had two or three maids who knew every room and every guest. The procedure was simple, and most of the time it worked. A goon would find a maid, hand her a hundred-dollar bill, and show her the composites. If she resisted, he would continue giving her money until she became cooperative. If she was unable to make the ID, he would ask if she had noticed a U-Haul truck, or a room full of boxes, or two men and a woman acting suspicious or scared, or anything unusual. If the maid was no help, he would ask which rooms were occupied, then go knock on the doors.

Start with the maids, Lazarov had instructed them. Enter from the beach side. Stay away from the front desks. Pretend to be cops. And, if you hit pay dirt, kill them instantly and get to a phone.

DeVasher placed four of the rented vans along the Strip near the highway. Lamar Quin, Kendall Mahan, Wally Hudson and Jack Aldrich posed as drivers and watched every vehicle that passed. They had arrived in the middle of the night on a private plane with ten other senior associates of Bendini, Lambert & Locke. In the souvenir shops and cafés, the former friends and colleagues of Mitch McDeere milled about with the tourists and secretly hoped they would not see him. The partners had been called home from airports around the country, and by midmorning they were walking the beach and inspecting pools and hotel lobbies. Nathan Locke stayed behind with Mr. Morolto, but the rest of the partners disguised themselves with golf caps and sunglasses and took orders from General DeVasher. Only Avery Tolleson was missing. Since walking out of the hospital, he had not been heard from. Including the thirty-three lawyers, Mr. Morolto had almost a hundred men participating in his private little manhunt.

At the Blue Tide Motel, a janitor took a hundred-dollar bill, looked at the composites and said he thought he might have seen the woman and one of the men check into two rooms early Thursday evening. He stared at Abby's sketch and became convinced it was her. He took some money and went to the office to check the registration records. He returned with the information that the woman had checked in as Jackie Nagel and paid cash for two rooms for Thursday, Friday and Saturday. He took some more money, and the two gunmen followed him to the rooms. He knocked on both doors. No answer. He unlocked them and allowed his new friends to inspect them. The rooms had not been used Friday night. One of the troops called Lazarov, and five minutes later DeVasher was poking around the rooms looking for clues. He found none, but the search was immediately constricted to a four-mile stretch of beach between the Blue Tide and the Beachcomber, where the U-Haul was found.

The vans moved the troops closer. The partners and senior associates secured the beach and restaurants. And the gunmen knocked on doors.

Andy signed the Federal Express ticket at 10:35 and inspected the package for Sam Fortune. It had been shipped by Doris Greenwood, whose address was listed as 4040 Poplar Avenue, Memphis, Tennessee. No phone number. He was certain it was valuable and for a moment contemplated another quick profit. But its delivery had already been contracted for. He gazed along both ends of the Strip and left the office with the package.

After years of dodging and hiding, Andy had subconsciously trained himself to walk quickly in the shadows, near the corners, never in the open. As he turned the corner to cross the parking lot, he saw two men knocking on the door to Room 21. The room happened to be vacant, and he was immediately suspicious of the two. They wore odd-fitting matching white shorts that fell almost to their knees, although it was difficult to tell exactly where the shorts stopped and the snow-white legs began. One wore dark socks with battered loafers. The other wore cheap sandals and walked in obvious pain. White Panama hats adorned their beefy heads.

After six months on the Strip, Andy could spot a fake tourist. The one beating on the door hit it again, and when he did Andy saw the bulge of a large handgun stuck in the back of his shorts.

He quickly retraced his quiet footsteps and returned to the office. He called Room 39 and asked for Sam Fortune.

'This is Sam.'

'Sam, this is Andy at the desk. Don't look out, but there are two very suspicious men knocking on doors across the parking lot.'

'Are they cops?'

'I don't think so. They didn't check in here.'

'Where are the maids?' Sam asked.

'They don't come in till eleven on Saturday.'

'Good. We're turning off the lights. Watch them and call when they leave.'

From a dark window in a closet, Andy watched the men go from door to door, knocking and waiting, occasionally getting one to open. Eleven of the forty-two rooms were occupied. No response at 38 and 39. They returned to the beach and disappeared. Professional killers! At his motel.

Across the Strip, in the parking lot of a miniature golf course, Andy saw two identical fake tourists talking to a man in a white van. They pointed here and there and seemed to be arguing.

He called Sam. 'Listen, Sam, they're gone. But this place is crawling with these people.'

'How many?'

'I can see two more across the Strip. You folks better run for it.'

'Relax, Andy. They won't see us if we stay in here.'

'But you can't stay forever. My boss'll catch on before much longer.'

'We're leaving soon, Andy. What about the package?'

'It's here.'

'Good. I need to see it. Say, Andy, what about food? Could you ease across the street and get something hot?'

Andy was a manager, not a porter. But for five thousand a day the Sea Gull's Rest could provide a little room service. 'Sure. Be there in a minute.'

Wayne Tarrance grabbed the phone and fell across the single bed in his Ramada Inn room in Orlando. He was exhausted, furious, baffled and sick of F. Denton Voyles. It was 1:30 P.M., Saturday. He called Memphis. The secretary had nothing to report, except Mary Alice called and wanted to talk to him. They had traced the call to a pay phone in Atlanta. Mary Alice said she would call again at 2 P.M. to see if Wayne – she called him Wayne – had checked in. Tarrance gave his room number and hung up. Mary Alice. In Atlanta. McDeere in Tallahassee, then Ocala. Then no McDeere. No green Ford pickup with Tennessee plates and trailer. He had vanished again.

The phone rang once. Tarrance slowly lifted the receiver. 'Mary Alice,' he said softly.

'Wayne baby! How'd you guess?'

'Where is he?'

'Who?' Tammy giggled.

'McDeere. Where is he?'

'Well, Wayne, you boys were close for a while, but then you chased a wild rabbit. Now you're not even close, baby. Sorry to tell you.'

'We've got three positive IDs in the past fourteen hours.'

'Better check them out, Wayne. Mitch told me a few minutes ago he's never been to Tallahassee. Never heard of Ocala. Never driven a green Ford pickup. Never pulled a U-Haul trailer. You boys bit hard, Wayne. Hook, line and sinker.'

Tarrance pinched the bridge of his nose and breathed into the phone.

'So how's Orlando?' she asked. 'Gonna see Disney World while you're in town?'

'Where the hell is he!'

'Wayne, Wayne, relax, baby. You'll get the documents.'

Tarrance sat up. 'Okay, when?'

'Well, we could be greedy and insist on the rest of our money. I'm at a pay phone, Wayne, so don't bother to trace it, okay? But we're not greedy. You'll get the records within twenty-four hours. If all goes well.'

'Where are the records?'

'I'll have to call you back, baby. If you stay at this number, I'll call you every four hours until Mitch tells me where the documents are. But, Wayne, if you leave this number, I might lose you, baby. So stay put.'

'I'll be here. Is he still in the country?'

'I think not. I'm sure he's in Mexico by now. His brother speaks the language you know?'

'I know.' Tarrance stretched out on the bed and said to hell with it. Mexico could have them, as long as he got the records.

'Stay where you are, baby. Take a nap. You gotta be tired. I'll call around five or six.'

Tarrance laid the phone on the nightstand, and took a nap.

The dragnet lost its steam Saturday afternoon when the Panama City Beach police received the fourth complaint from motel owners. The cops were dispatched to the Breakers Motel, where an irate owner told of armed men harassing the guests. More cops were sent to the

Strip, and before long they were searching the motels for gunmen who were searching for the McDeeres. The Emerald Coast was on the brink of war.

Weary and hot, DeVasher's men were forced to work alone. They spread themselves even thinner along the beach and stopped the door-to-door work. They lounged in plastic chairs around the pools, watching the tourists come and go. They lay on the beach, dodging the sun, hiding behind dark shades, watching the tourists come and go.

As dusk approached, the army of goons and thugs and gunmen, and lawyers, slipped into the darkness and waited. If the McDeeres were going to move, they would do it at night. A silent army waited for them.

DeVasher's thick forearms rested uncomfortably on a balcony railing outside his Best Western room. He watched the empty beach below as the sun slowly disappeared on the horizon. Aaron Rimmer walked through the sliding glass door and stopped behind DeVasher. 'We found Tolleson,' Rimmer said.

DeVasher did not move. 'Where?'

'Hiding in his girlfriend's apartment in Memphis.'

'Was he alone?'

'Yeah. They iced him. Made it look like a robbery.'

In Room 39, Ray inspected for the hundredth time the new passports, visas, drivers' licenses and birth certificates. The passport photos for Mitch and Abby were current, with plenty of dark hair. After the escape, time would take care of the blondness. Ray's photo was a slightly altered Harvard Law School mug shot of Mitch, with the long hair, stubble and rough academic looks. The eyes, nose and cheekbones were similar, after careful analysis, but nothing else. The documents were in the name of Lee Stevens, Rachel James and Sam Fortune, all with addresses in Murfreesboro, Tennessee. Doc did good work, and Ray smiled as he studied each one.

Abby packed the Sony vide camera into its box. The tripod was folded and leaned against the wall. Fourteen video cassette tapes with stick-on-labels were stacked neatly on the television.

After sixteen hours, the video deposition was over. Starting with the first tape, Mitch had faced the camera, raised his right hand and sworn to tell the truth. He stood next to the dresser with documents covering the floor around him. Using Tammy's notes, summaries and flowcharts, he methodically walked through the bank records first. He identified over two hundred and fifty secret accounts in eleven Cayman banks. Some had names, but most were just numbered. Using copies of computer printouts, he constructed the histories of the accounts. Cash deposits, wire transfers and withdrawals. At the bottom of each document used in his deposition, he wrote with a black marked the initials MM and then the exhibit number: MM1, MM2, MM3 and so on. After Exhibit MM1485, he had identified nine hundred million dollars hiding in Cayman banks.

After the bank records, he painstakingly pieced together the structure of the empire. In twenty years, more than four hundred Cayman corporations had been chartered by the Moroltos and their incredibly rich and incredibly corrupt attorneys. Many of the corporations owned all or pieces of each other and used the banks as registered agents and permanent addresses. Mitch learned quickly that he had only a fraction of the records and speculated, on camera, that most documents were hidden in the basement in Memphis. He also explained, for the benefit of the jury, that it would take a small army of IRS investigators a year or so to piece together the Morolto corporate puzzle. He slowly explained each exhibit, marked it carefully and filed it away. Abby operated the camera. Ray watched the parking lot and studied the fake passports.

Mitch testified for six hours on various methods used by the Moroltos and their attorneys to turn dirty money into clean. Easily the most favored method was to fly in a load of dirty cash on a Bendini plane, usually with two or three lawyers on board to legitimate the trip. With dope pouring in by land, air and sea, U.S. customs cares little about what's leaving the country. It was a perfect setup. The planes left dirty and came back clean. Once the money landed on Grand Cayman, a lawyer on board handled the required payoffs to Cayman customs and to the appropriate banker. On some loads, up to twenty-five percent went for bribes.

Once deposited, usually in unnamed, numbered accounts, the money became almost impossible to trace. But many of the bank transactions coincided nicely with significant corporate events. The money was usually deposited into one of a dozen numbered holding accounts. Or 'super accounts,' as Mitch called them. He gave the jury these account numbers, and the names of the banks. Then, as the new corporations were chartered, the money was transferred from the super accounts to the corporate accounts, often in the same bank. Once the dirty money was owned by a legitimate Cayman corporation, the laundering began. The simplest and most common method was for the company to purchase real estate and other clean assets in the United States. The transactions were handled by the creative attorneys at Bendini, Lambert & Locke, and all money moved by wire transfer. Often, the Cayman corporation would purchase another Cayman corporation that happened to own a Panama corporation that owned a holding company in Denmark. The Danes would purchase a ball-bearing factory in Toledo and wire in the purchase money from a subsidiary bank in Munich. And the dirty money was now clean.

After marking Exhibit MM4292, Mitch quit the deposition. Sixteen hours of testimony was enough. Tarrance and his buddies could show the tapes to a grand jury and indict at least thirty lawyers from the Bendini firm. He could show the tapes to a federal magistrate and get his search warrants.

Mitch had held to his end of the bargain. Although he would not be around to testify in person, he had been paid only a million dollars and was about to deliver more than was expected. He was physically and emotionally drained, and sat on the edge of the bed with the lights off. Abby sat in a chair with her eyes closed.

Ray peeked through the blinds. 'We need a cold beer,' he said.

'Forget it,' Mitch snapped.

Ray turned and stared at him. 'Relax, little brother. It's dark, and the store is just a short walk down the beach. I can take care of myself.'

'Forget it, Ray. There is no need to take chances. We're leaving in a few hours, and if all goes well, you'll have the rest of your life to drink beer.'

Ray was not listening. He pulled a baseball cap firmly over his forehead, stuck some cash in his pockets and reached for the gun.

'Ray, please, at least forget the gun,' Mitch pleaded.

Ray stuck the gun under his shirt and eased out the door. He walked quickly in the sand behind the small motels and shops, hiding in the shadows and craving a cold beer. He stopped behind the convenience store, looked quickly around and was certain no one was watching, then walked to the front door. The beer cooler was in the rear.

In the parking lot next to the Strip, Lamar Quin hid under a large straw hat and made small talk with some teenagers from Indiana. He saw Ray enter the store and thought he might recognize something. There was a casualness about the man's stride that looked vaguely familiar. Lamar moved to the front window and glanced in the direction of the beer cooler. The man's eyes were covered with sunglasses, but the nose and cheekbones were certainly familiar. Lamar eased inside the small store and picked up a sack of potato chips. He waited at the checkout counter and came face to face with the man, who was not Mitchell McDeere but greatly resembled him.

It was Ray. It had to be. The face was sunburned, and the hair was too short to be stylish. The eyes were covered. Same height. Same weight. Same walk.

'How's it going?' Lamar said to the man.

'Fine. You?' the voice was similar.

Lamar paid for his chips and returned to the parking lot. He calmly dropped the bag in a garbage can next to a phone booth and quickly walked next door to a souvenir shop to continue his search for the McDeeres.

# CHAPTER FORTY

Darkness brought a cool breeze to the beach along the Strip. The sun disappeared quickly, and there was no moon to replace it. A distant ceiling of harmless dark clouds covered the sky, and the water was black.

Darkness brought fishermen to the Dan Russell Pier in the center of the Strip. They gathered in groups of three and four along the concrete structure and stared silently as their lines ran into the black water twenty feet below. They leaned motionless on the railing, occasionally spitting or talking to a friend. They enjoyed the breeze and the quietness and the still water much more than they enjoyed the occasional fish that ventured by and hit a hook. They were vacationers from the North who spent the same week each year at the same motel and came to the pier each night in the darkness to fish and marvel at the sea. Between them sat buckets full of bait and small coolers full of beer.

From time to time throughout the night, a nonfisherman or a pair of lovebirds would venture onto the pier and walk a hundred yards to the end of it. They would gaze at the black, gentle water for a few minutes, then turn and admire the glow of a million flickering lights along the Strip. They would watch the inert, huddled fishermen leaning on their elbows. The fishermen did not notice them.

The fishermen did not notice Aaron Rimmer as he casually walked behind them around eleven. He smoked a cigarette at the end of the pier and tossed the butt into the ocean. He gazed along the beach and thought of the thousands of motel rooms and condos.

The Dan Russell Pier was the westernmost of the three at Panama City Beach. It was the newest, the longest and the only one built with nothing but concrete. The other two were older and wooden. In the center there was a small brick building containing a tackle shop, a snack bar and rest rooms. Only the rest rooms were open at night.

It was probably a half mile east of the Sea Gull's Rest. At eleven-thirty, Abby left Room 39, eased by the dirty pool and began walking east along the beach. She wore shorts, a white straw hat and a windbreaker with the collar turned up around her ears. She walked slowly, with her hands thrust deep in the pockets like an experienced, contemplative beachcomber. Five minutes later, Mitch left the room, eased by the dirty pool and followed her footsteps. He gazed at the ocean as he walked. Two joggers approached, splashing in the water and talking between breaths. On a string around his neck and tucked under his black cotton shirt was a whistle, just in case. In all four pockets he had crammed sixty thousand in cash. He looked at the ocean and nervously watched Abby ahead of him. When he was two hundred yards down the beach, Ray left Room 39 for the last time. He locked it and kept a key. Wrapped around his waist was a forty-foot piece of black nylon rope. The gun was stuck under it. A bulky windbreaker covered it all nicely. Andy had charged another two thousand for the clothing and items.

Ray eased by the pool and onto the beach. He watched Mitch and could barely see Abby. The beach was deserted.

It was almost midnight, Saturday, and most of the fishermen had left the pier for another night. Abby saw three in a small cluster near the rest rooms. She eased past them and nonchalantly strolled to the end of the pier, where she leaned on the concrete railing and stared at the vast blackness of the Gulf. Red buoy lights were scattered as far as she could see. Blue and white channel lights formed a neat line to the east. A blinking yellow light on some vessel inched away on the horizon. She was alone at the end of the pier.

Mitch hid in a beach chair under a folded umbrella near the entrance to the pier. He could not see her, but had a good view of the ocean. Fifty feet away, Ray sat in the darkness on a brick ledge. His feet dangled in the sand. They waited. They checked their watches.

At precisely midnight, Abby nervously unzipped her windbreaker and untied a heavy flashlight. She glanced at the water below and gripped it fiercely. She shoved it into her stomach, shielded it with the windbreaker, aimed at the sea and pushed the switch three times. On and off. On and off. On and off. The green bulb flashed three times. She held it tightly and stared at the ocean.

No response. She waited an eternity and two minutes later flashed again. Three times. No response. She breathed deeply and spoke to herself. 'Be calm, Abby, be calm. He's out there somewhere.' She flashed three more times. Then waited. No response.

Mitch sat on the edge of the beach chair and anxiously surveyed the sea. From the corner of an eye, he saw a figure walking, almost running from the west. It jumped onto the steps of the pier. It was the Nordic. Mitch bolted across the beach after him.

Aaron Rimmer walked behind the fishermen, around the small building, and watched the woman in the white hat at the end of the pier. She was bent over clutching something. It flashed again, three times. He walked silently up to her.

'Abby.'

She jerked around and tried to scream. Rimmer lunged at her and shoved her into the railing. From the darkness, Mitch dived head first into the Nordic's legs, and all three went down hard onto the slick concrete. Mitch felt the gun at the Nordic's back. He swung wildly with a forearm and missed. Rimmer whirled and landed a wicked smash to Mitch's left eye. Abby kicked and crawled away. Mitch was blind and dazed. Rimmer stood quickly and reached for the gun, but never found it. Ray charged like a battering ram and sent the Nordic crashing into the railing. He landed four bulletlike jabs to the eyes and nose, each one drawing blood. Skills learned in prison. The Nordic fell to all fours, and Ray snapped his head with four powerful kicks. He groaned pitifully and fell, face first.

Ray removed the gun and handed it to Mitch, who was standing now and trying to focus with his good eye. Abby watched the pier. No one.

'Start flashing,' Ray said as he unwound the rope from his waist. Abby faced the water, shielded the flashlight, found the switch and began flashing like crazy.

'What're you gonna do?' Mitch whispered, watching Ray and the rope.

'Two choices. We can either blow his brains out or drown him.'

'Oh my god!' Abby said as she flashed.

'Don't fire the gun,' Mitch whispered.

'Thank you,' Ray said. He grabbed a short section of rope, twisted it tightly around the Nordic's neck and pulled. Mitch turned his back and stepped between the body and Abby. She did not try to watch. 'I'm sorry. We have no choice.' Ray mumbled almost to himself.

There was no resistance, no movement from the unconscious man. After three minutes, Ray exhaled loudly and announced, 'He's dead.' He tied the other end of the rope to a post, slid the body under the railing and lowered it quietly into the water.

'I'm going down first,' Ray said as he crawled through the railing and eased down the rope. Eight feet under the deck of the pier, an iron cross brace was attached to two of the thick concrete columns that disappeared into the water. It made a nice hideout. Abby was next. Ray grabbed her legs as she clutched the rope and eased downward. Mitch, with his one eye, lost his equilibrium and almost went for a swim.

But they made it. They sat on the cross brace, ten feet above the cold, dark water. Ten feet above the fish and the barnacles and the body of the Nordic. Ray cut the rope so the corpse could fall to the bottom properly before it made its ascent in a day or two.

They sat like three owls on a limb, watching the buoy lights and channel lights and waiting for the messiah to come walking across the water. The only sounds were the soft splashing of the waves below and the steady clicking of the flashlight.

And then voices from the deck above. Nervous, anxious, panicked voices, searching for someone. Then they were gone.

'Well, little brother, what do we do now?' Ray whispered.

'Plan B,' Mitch said.

'And what's that?'

'Start swimming.'

'Very funny,' Abby said, clicking away.

An hour passed. The iron brace, though perfectly located, was not comfortable.

'Have you noticed those two boats out there?' Ray asked quietly.

The boats were small, about a mile offshore, and for the past hour had been cruising slowly and suspiciously back and forth in sight of the beach. 'I think they're fishing boats,' Mitch said.

'Who fishes at one o'clock in the morning?' Ray asked.

The three of them thought about his. There was no explanation.

Abby saw it first, and hoped and prayed it was not the body now floating toward them. 'Over there,' she said, pointing fifty yards out to sea. It was a black object, resting on the water and moving slowly in their direction. They watched intently. Then the sound, like that of a sewing machine.

'Keep flashing,' Mitch said. It grew closer.

It was a man in a small boat.

'Abanks!' Mitch whispered loudly. The humming noise died.

'Abanks!' he said again.

'Where the hell are you?' came the reply.

'Over here. Under the pier. Hurry, dammit!'

The hum grew louder, and Abanks parked an eight-foot rubber raft under the pier. They swung from the brace and landed in one joyous pile. They quietly hugged each other, then hugged Abanks. He revved up the five-horsepower electric trolling motor and headed for the open water.

'Where's the boat?' Mitch asked.

'About a mile out,' answered Abanks.

'What happened to your green light?'

Abanks pointed to a flashlight next to the motor. 'Battery went dead.'

The boat was a forty-foot schooner that Abanks had found in

Jamaica for only two hundred thousand. A friend waited by the ladder and helped them aboard. His name was George, just George, and he spoke English with a quick accent. Abanks said he could be trusted.

'There's whiskey if you like. In the cabinet,' Abanks said. Ray found the whiskey. Abby found a blanket and lay down on a small couch. Mitch stood on the deck and admired his new boat. When Abanks and George had the raft aboard, Mitch said, 'Let's get out of here. Can we leave now?'

'As you wish,' George snapped properly.

Mitch gazed at the lights along the beach and said farewell. he went below and poured a cup of scotch.

Wayne Tarrance slept across the bed in his clothes. He had not moved since the last call, six hours earlier. The phone rang beside him. After four rings, he found it.

'Hello.' His voice was slow and scratchy.

'Wayne baby. Did I wake you?'

'Of course.'

'You can have the documents now. Room 39, Sea Gull's Rest Motel, Highway 98, Panama City Beach. The desk clerk is a guy named Andy, and he'll let you in the room. Be careful with them. Our friend has them all marked real nice and precise, and he's got sixteen hours of videotape. So be gentle.'

'I have a question,' Tarrance said.

'Sure, big boy. Anything.'

'Where did he find you? This would've been impossible without you.'

'Gee, thanks, Wayne. He found me in Memphis. We got to be friends, and he offered me a bunch of money.'

'How much?'

'Why is that important, Wayne?' I'll never have to work again. Gotta run, baby. It's been real fun.'

'Where is he?'

'As we speak, he's on a plane to South America. But please don't waste your time trying to catch him. Wayne, baby, I love you, but you couldn't even catch him in Memphis. Bye now.' She was gone.

# CHAPTER FORTY-ONE

Dawn. Sunday. The forty-foot schooner sped south with full sails under a clear sky. Abby was in a deep sleep in the master suite. Ray was in a scotch-induced coma on a couch. Abanks was somewhere below catching a nap.

Mitch sat on the deck sipping cold coffee and listening to George expound on the basics of sailing. He was in his late fifties, with long, gray, bleached hair and dark, sun-cured skin. He was small and wiry, much like Abanks. He was Australian by birth, but twenty-eight years earlier had fled his country after the largest bank heist in its history. He and his partner split eleven million in cash and silver and went their separate ways. His partner was now dead, he had heard.

George was not his real name, but he'd used it for twenty-eight years and forgotten the real one. He discovered the Caribbean in the late sixties, and after seeing its thousands of small, primitive English-speaking islands, decided he'd found home. He put his money in banks in the Bahamas, Belize, Panama and, of course, Grand Cayman. He built a small compound on a deserted stretch of beach on Little Cayman and had spent the past twenty-one years touring the Caribbean in his thirty-foot schooner. During the summer and early fall, he stayed close to home. But from October to June, he lived on his boat and hopped from island to island. He'd been to three hundred of them in the Caribbean. He once spent two years just in the Bahamas.

'There are thousands of islands,' he explained. 'And they'll never find you if you move a lot.'

'Are they still looking for you?' Mitch asked.

'I don't know. I can't call and ask, you know. But I doubt it.'

'Where's the safest place to hide?'

'On this boat. It's a nice little yacht, and once you learn to sail it, it'll be your home. Find you a little island somewhere, perhaps Little Cayman or Brac – they're both still primitive – and build a house. Do as I've done. And spend most of your time on this boat.'

'When do you stop worrying about being chased?'

'Oh, I still think about it, you know. But I don't worry about it. How much did you get away with?'

'Eight million, give or take,' Mitch said.

'That's nice. You've got the money to do as you please, so forget

725

about them. Just tour the islands for the rest of your life. There are worse things, you know.'

For days they sailed towards Cuba, then around it in the direction of Jamaica. They watched George and listened to his lectures. After twenty years of sailing through the Caribbean, he was a man of great knowledge and patience. Ray, the linguist, listened to and memorized words like spinnaker, mast, bow, stern, aft, tiller, halyard winches, masthead fittings, shrouds, lifelines, stanchions, sheet winch, bow pulpit, coamings, transom, clew outhaul, genoa sheets, mainsail, jib, jibstays, jib sheets, cam cleats and boom vangs. George lectured on heeling, luffing, running, blanketing, backwinding, heading up, trimming and pointing. Ray absorbed the language of sailing; Mitch studied the technique.

Abby stayed in the cabin, saying little and smiling only when necessary. Life on the boat was not something she dreamed about. She missed her house and wondered what would happen to it. Maybe Mr. Rice would cut the grass and pull the weeds. She missed the shady streets and neat lawns and the small gangs of children riding bicycles. She thought of her dog, and prayed that Mr. Rice would adopt it. She worried about her parents – their safety and their fear. When would she see them again? It would be years, she decided, and she could live with that if she knew they were safe.

Her thoughts could not escape the present. The future was inconceivable.

During the second day of the rest of her life, she began writing letters; letters to her parents, Kay Quin, Mr. Rice and a few friends. The letters would never be mailed, she knew, but it helped to put the words on paper.

Mitch watched her carefully, but left her alone. He had nothing to say, really. Maybe in a few days they could talk.

By the end of the fourth day, Wednesday, Grand Cayman was in sight. They circled it slowly once and anchored a mile from shore. After dark, Barry Abanks said goodbye. The McDeeres simply thanked him, and he eased away in the rubber raft. He would land three miles from Bodden Town at another dive lodge, then call one of his dive captains to come get him. He would know if anyone suspicious had been around. Abanks expected no trouble.

George's compound on Little Cayman consisted of a small main house of white-painted wood and two smaller outbuildings. It was inland a quarter of a mile, on a tiny bay. The nearest house could not be seen. A native woman lived in the smallest building and maintained the place. Her name was Fay.

The McDeeres settled in the main house and tried to begin the process of starting over. Ray, the escapee, roamed the beaches for hours and kept to himself. He was euphoric, but could not show it. He and George took the boat out several hours each day and drank scotch while exploring the islands. They usually returned drunk.

Abby spent the first days in a small room upstairs overlooking the bay. She wrote more letters and began a diary. She slept alone.

Twice a week, Fay drove the Volkswagen bus into town for supplies and mail. She returned one day with a package from Barry Abanks. George delivered it to Mitch. Inside the package was a parcel sent to Abanks from Doris Greenwood in Miami. Mitch ripped open the thick legal-sized envelopes and found three newspapers, two from Atlanta and one from Miami.

The headlines told of the mass indicting of the Bendini law firm in Memphis. Fifty-one present and former members of the firm were indicted, along with thirty-one alleged members of the Morolto crime family in Chicago. More indictments were coming, promised the U.S. Attorney. Just the tip of the iceberg. Director F. Denton Voyles allowed himself to be quoted as saying it was a major blow to organized crime in America. It should be a dire warning, he said, to legitimate professionals and businessmen who are tempted to handle dirty money.

Mitch folded the newspapers and went for a long walk on the beach. Under a cluster of palms, he found some shade and sat down. The Atlanta paper listed the names of every Bendini lawyer indicted. He read them slowly. There was no joy in seeing the names. He almost felt sorry for Nathan Locke. Almost. Wally Hudson, Kendall Mahan, Jack Aldrich and, finally, Lamar Quin. He could see their faces. He knew their wives and their children. Mitch gazed across the brilliant ocean and thought about Lamar and Kay Quin. He loved them, and he hated them. They had helped seduce him into the firm, and they were not without blame. But they were his friends. What a waste! Maybe Lamar would only serve a couple of years and then be paroled. Maybe Kay and the kids could survive. Maybe.

'I love you, Mitch.' Abby was standing behind him. She held a plastic pitcher and two cups.

He smiled at her and waved to the sand next to him. 'What's in the pitcher?'

'Rum punch. Fay mixed it for us.'

'Is it strong?'

She sat next to him on the sand. 'It's mostly rum. I told Fay we needed to get drunk, and she agreed.'

He held her tightly and sipped the rum punch. They watched a small fishing boat inch through the sparkling water.

'Are you scared, Mitch?'

'Terrified.'

'Me too. This is crazy.'

'But we made it, Abby. We're alive. We're safe. We're together.'

'But what about tomorrow? And the next day?'

'I don't know, Abby. Things could be worse, you know. My name could be in the paper there with the other freshly indicted defendants. Or we could be dead. There are worse things than sailing around the Caribbean with eight million bucks in the bank.'

'Do you think my parents are safe?'

'I think so. What would Morolto have to gain by harming your parents? They're safe, Abby.'

She refilled the cups with rum punch and kissed him on the cheek. 'I'll be okay Mitch. As long as we're together. I can handle anything.'

'Abby,' Mitch said slowly, staring at the water, 'I have a confession to make.'

'I'm listening.'

'The truth is I never wanted to be a lawyer anyway.'

'Oh, really.'

'Naw. Secretly I've always wanted to be a sailor.'

'Is that so. Have you ever made love on the beach?'

Mitch hesitated for a slight second. 'Uh, no.'

'Then drink up, sailor. Let's get drunk and make a baby.'